TWENTY YEARS AFTER

ALEXANDRE DUMAS
1802–1870

TWENTY YEARS AFTER

ALEXANDRE DUMAS

With an Introduction by

R. BRIMLEY JOHNSON

COLLINS
LONDON AND GLASGOW

First published, 1845
This edition, 1953
Latest reprint, 1964

The D'ARTAGNAN ROMANCES should be read in the following order: *The Three Musketeers, Twenty Years After, The Vicomte de Bragelonne, Louise de la Vallière, The Man in the Iron Mask.*

PRINTED IN GREAT BRITAIN BY
COLLINS CLEAR-TYPE PRESS

ALEXANDRE DUMAS

ALEXANDRE DUMAS (known as Dumas Père) was born on July 24, 1802 at Villers-Cotterets, a small town about forty-five miles north-east of Paris. His father, General Dumas, was a mulatto, the natural son of Antoine Alexandre Davy de la Pailleterie, a nobleman who had settled in St. Domingo, and of a black slave girl, named Marie-Céssette Dumas. General Dumas had a distinguished career during the wars of the French Republic and under Bonaparte. At the time of his son's birth, General Dumas was living in retirement at Villers-Cotterets where in the year 1792 he had married Marie Élisabeth Labouret. He died in 1806, leaving his widow and small son in straitened circumstances.

However, for Alexandre Dumas the years of childhood and adolescence were carefree enough; his education was scanty. At sixteen he became a clerk with a local solicitor, and in 1823, determined to make his way in life, he went to Paris. He succeeded in obtaining a post on the secretarial staff of the Duc d'Orléans (the future King Louis Philippe) at a yearly salary of 1200 francs.

Soon Dumas established contact with young men of the literary world. He read avidly—especially history and the works of great writers—frequented the theatre and soon he himself began to write for the stage.

After a number of false starts and two minor successes his romantic play *Henry III et sa Cour* was accepted by the Théâtre-Français and given its first performance in 1829. It established his fame, literally, over night and brought him the friendship of Victor Hugo, Vigny, and other writers and poets. The Duc d'Orléans gave him the sinecure of a librarian at 1200 francs a year.

Already, then, Dumas found himself up against a problem which was to trouble him all his life and was later to assume gigantic proportions—he could not adapt expenditure to revenue. It was a problem deeply rooted in traits of his character, *e.g.* in his extravagant tastes, his vanity, his lack of common sense, his generosity. Another inexhaustible source of trouble throughout his life was his unending amorous entanglements. During the first weeks in Paris (1823) he formed a liaison with a young woman, Marie Lebay, by whom he had a son in 1824 whom he fully acknowledged in 1831. In 1831 also he had another child—

a daughter—by another mistress. His marriage (1840) to the actress Ida Ferrier was of short duration.

After *Henry III.* Dumas wrote further plays in rapid succession, among them *Antony*, a modern romantic drama, the success of which even surpassed the success of *Henry III.* In 1830 he participated in a somewhat comic opera fashion in the July revolution, and again in 1832, having only just recovered from the cholera, took part in a rising against Louis Philippe, his former protector. In 1844 appeared *The Three Musketeers*, the first and perhaps the most famous of Dumas' historical romances which, in three distinct cycles, cover almost three centuries of French history. In 1844 also he produced *The Count of Monte Cristo*, the romantic adventure story of the prisoner of *Château d'If*. Dumas' industry was prodigious. For nearly forty years, during which he lived as full a life as any man could ever wish to live, he poured out books, plays, and articles in an uninterrupted stream. He was frequently accused during his life-time of having employed (and exploited) others to write the books which brought him fame and fortune. The truth is that he employed collaborators who supplied and arranged material and submitted ideas for plots.

At the height of his success Dumas' prosperity and extravagance of living knew no bounds. He built himself a fantastic castle which he called "Monte Cristo" (it was later sold piecemeal by order of his creditors), financed theatres and lavished hospitality on friends and strangers alike. In 1851 he went to live in Brussels where he worked on his *Mémoires*. Back in Paris he launched into some newspaper ventures which kept him in the public limelight but ultimately failed. Years of wandering followed. He went to Russia (1858), travelling in the style of a potentate, and soon after his return he set out for Sicily where he joined Garibaldi, in whose cause he worked enthusiastically for four years.

The last years of his life Dumas spent in an atmosphere of ever-increasing financial chaos, of loneliness, domestic difficulties, and failing health. He died at his son's house in Dieppe on December 5, 1870.   H. d. R.

INTRODUCTION

CARDINAL MAZARIN, whatever his faults and his limitations, was not the least of the four Ministers who "were responsible for the great transformation of France, for her internal prosperity, and for the amazing increase in her prestige as a European power during the ensuing century".

Sully, indeed, developed Henry IV. into the true type of benevolent despot, who would promote prosperity by patriotic finance and generous expenditure on social reform: Colbert stirred Louis XIV. to measures of active and personal rule, which created a new era for industry and manufacture. But Richelieu, and his pupil Mazarin, were almost exclusively concerned with European complications. They regarded internal policy as a department in foreign affairs; and were possessed by the single idea of raising France to a prominent position among the nations, without regard either to misery at home or honour abroad. It was the age of the diplomats; and, in diplomacy, both were supreme.

Though history supports Dumas in declaring Richelieu a finer and greater personality, it may be doubted whether he could have concluded the Thirty Years' War so favourably to France; and, without doubt, the Italian chose abler men, civil and military, to carry out "high politics", and wisely gave them a freer hand.

The contrast in Dumas is more emphatic, because his personal cunning and small-mindedness were more marked in the petty and cruel intrigues by which the Court-party taxed and bullied the people to support its wars; and again, Dumas seldom even alludes to international events.

Among private men, in their civil or domestic life, no period of French history reveals such deplorable conditions as that of the *fronde*. The *frondeurs* had no programme of reform, no motive but self-interest, no able or honest leaders, and no cohesion. No movement has ever caused so much bloodshed and misery, for such frivolous rivalries in private ambition; none, certainly, was ever less representative of the people or less concerned for their welfare. The word *fronde* was originally applied to children who "threw stones and ran away on the appearance of the police"; only to throw more stones directly the law turned its back.

7

Such, in fact, were the "veteran" Broussel, the intriguing coadjutor Bishop, and that old disturber of the peace Madame de Chevreuse. The *Parlement* was not a parliament, and its irresponsible self-importance was freely used by discontented Princes of the Blood and other adventurous quasi-aristocrats of the order which Richelieu had set himself so deliberately to degrade, by opening its ranks to the highest bidder.

The struggle, in fact, was a last flicker of the old fight between Kings and Peers, by which all nations have taken their first step from political childhood; though with incurable absence of principle none of the *frondeurs* dare ever avow hostility to the throne.

There is a saying of some truth that "the French killed their king two hundred years too late", and to realise how little reality stood behind the Beggar of St. Eustache and his street barricades, English readers must look on this riot "that became a revolution", as no more than a caricature of our own Civil War. While we were "removing" Charles I., the "reds" of Paris went home again, on the release of Broussel!

It should be observed that the idealist, Athos, mistook the *frondeurs* for genuine sons of Liberty, and read into their bloodthirsty defiance of Mazarin a generous vision of freedom, prosperity, and peace; but when despatched by an exiled Queen to the comforting of a royal martyr, we see him stirred to a passionate loyalty that has all the selfless fire of religious faith. In England, where the people's voice *could*, in fact, be heard, and a Constitution was in its birth-throes, he did not think of even examining their cause.

The novelist, of course, must transform history into romance; and romance will always be with the fallen, or threatened, king. That was generally Shakespeare's way, always Scott's; and it is Scott with whom we at least must associate or compare Dumas. Both writers acquired copious information about the periods they describe; both seized, by dramatic instinct, upon scenes and persons that could be best worked into the tale; neither, perhaps, very highly esteemed the scholar's equipment or observed strict accuracy towards a stubborn fact.

But their delight in the past is infectious. They bring to life for us these breathless, picturesque days, in which man was born to adventure as the sparks fly upward; when, despite Richelieu's edict against duelling, the sharp sword instantly followed the angry word; when heroes had "thews of iron, a wrist of steel".

Dumas is far more theatrical than Scott; and does not, indeed, attempt serious characterisation or aim at being true to life. His is the old, heroic romance of medieval supermen, with the Homeric gesture. We are not meant to judge d'Artagnan's wit or the muscles of Porthos by comparison with the possible. The startling coincidences and surprising encounters of the plot; its breathless rapidity of movement, and the frequent smiting of ten strong men by one long arm are no better than traveller's tales to make fools gape; if, indeed, any be fools enough to think them true.

That, however, was not the aim of Dumas, who had certainly no intention to deceive. The romance of action has always thrived on impossibilities, through which the impetuous rush of words and deeds should carry the hero to our heart. Such were beyond the will, if not the imagination of Scott, but they constitute the genius of Dumas. For, in characteristically French fashion, he did for France what the author of *Waverley* achieved for Great Britain. And, in some ways, he is the easier of the two to read. Romance, or drama, confronts us at the first page; he seldom delays the narrative by descriptive passages or reflection; and the initial difficulty of foreign names and allusions is more apparent than real. The true historical romance is no less fictitious in essence than any other novel. The hero and his exploits are for the most part created by the imagination, and the emotion is purely personal. The real characters introduced from history, the actual events or scenes described, are but costume and scenery for the setting of a human tale. We can enjoy *Twenty Years After*, and applaud its unceasing vitality, without a thought of what really happened in those "brave days". It is interesting, no doubt, to compare the picture with history; but not essential to our pleasure or our understanding. We associate it much more closely with *The Three Musketeers* than with "Mazarin" and the minority of Louis XIV. in the years 1643–61. Nor should the critic complain; for those are blind indeed who do not "count Scott and Dumas among the makers of good literature"; and literature is not life, however much it should resemble, and may illuminate, mankind.

In Dumas, too, detailed analysis is almost silenced before "the swiftness of work combined with vast diligence . . . the intensity, and the animated movement, the clear daylight, and the inspired delight with which he invented and wrote his stories. It is not composition, it is the author actually present in each of his personages, doing their deeds and speaking their thoughts . . . all is great; material, effect, characters, execution."

D'Artagnan's "portrait" was first sketched for us "at a dash". "A Don Quixote of eighteen; a Don Quixote without his corselet, without his coat of mail, without his cuistres; a Don Quixote clothed in a woollen doublet . . . face long and brown; high

cheek-bones . . . the maxillary muscles highly developed . . . the
eye open and intelligent, the nose hooked but finely chiselled."

And in the end, said the Gascon: "Give me your apartment on
the first floor; now that I am a captain of the musketeers I must
make an appearance; nevertheless, reserve my old room on the
fifth storey for me; *one never knows what may happen.*" That is the
secret of Romance—"one never knows".

R. BRIMLEY JOHNSON

CONTENTS

THE GHOST OF CARDINAL RICHELIEU

In a room of the Cardinal's Palace of Paris, since known as the Royal Palace, or, to retain the French title, the Palais Royal, there sat a man in deep thought, his head resting on his hands. He leaned over a table, the corners of which were of silver gilt, and which was covered with letters and papers. Behind him was an enormous fireplace, red with fire. Large masses of wood blazed and crackled on the gilded andirons, and the flames shone upon the superb habiliments of the solitary inhabitant of the chamber, while, in front, his figure was illumined by a candelabrum filled with wax candles.

Gazing on that pale brow furrowed with thought, on that red simar—the gorgeous robe of office—and on the rich laces, one accustomed to the court of France in former days might have fancied, in the solitude of the apartment, combined with the silence of the antechambers, and the measured tread of the guards, that the shade of Cardinal Richelieu still lingered in his accustomed haunt.

But such an one would have been mistaken. It was, alas! only the ghost of former greatness. France enfeebled, the royal authority mocked at, the nobles returning to their former turbulence and insolence, the enemy within the frontiers—all bore witness that Richelieu was no longer there.

But what proved more convincingly than all these things that the red robe was not that of the old Cardinal was the solitude which, as we have said, was like a phantom's rather than a living being's. No courtiers thronged the corridors. The courts were crowded with guards. From the streets below, a spirit of bitter mockery arose and penetrated through the very windows of the chamber, which was shaken by the murmurs of a whole city leagued against the minister. The sound, too, of incessant firing was heard in the distance—happily without object or result further than to show the guards, the Swiss troops, and the military surrounding the Palais Royal that the people also had arms.

This ghost of Richelieu was Mazarin—Mazarin, alone, and feeling that he was weak.

" 'Foreigner!' " he muttered. " 'Italian!' That is the reproach they cast upon me. With the same watchword they assassinated, hanged, and destroyed Concini, and with the same watchword— if I were weak enough to yield to them—they would destroy me, although they have nothing to complain of, except now and then a tax or two. Fools! who know not their real enemies. They do not see that it is not the Italian who speaks bad French, but those who can make fine speeches to them in the purest Parisian accent, who are their real enemies. Yes, yes," continued the minister, "these murmurs prove to me that the lot of favourites is precarious. But if they know that, they ought also to know that I am no common favourite. The Earl of Essex, it is true, wore a splendid ring, encircled with diamonds, given to him by his royal mistress, whilst I have only a plain ring with a cipher and a date. But this ring has been blessed in the chapel of the Palais Royal. Therefore they will never ruin me, as they would like. Let them shout, 'Down with Mazarin!' as they will—it will still be my work to set them by the ears, for to-day my partisans shall shout in the streets, 'Long live the Prince de Condé!' while on the following day my followers shall be shouting in every corner of Paris, 'Long live the Parliament!'"

At the word, a smile of intense hatred swept over the face of the Cardinal.

"The parliament," he mused—"we shall soon see how to dispose of the parliament. We have Orléans and Montargis. Oh! I will give it time enough; but those who have begun with crying, 'Down with Mazarin!' will finish by crying, 'Down with all those gentry', every one in his turn. Richelieu, whom they hated when he was living, and of whom they are always talking now that he is dead, was even less popular than I am. He was frequently driven from power, and still more frequently feared that he should be. The queen will never discard me; and if I am obliged to yield to the populace, she will yield with me. If I fly, she will fly; and then we shall see how these rebels will get on without either king or queen.

"Oh! if I were not a foreigner! If only I were a Frenchman! If I were even merely a gentleman!"

The position of the Cardinal was, in truth, critical, and several recent events had added to his difficulties. The people were actually in revolt; for Mazarin had imposed the most crushing taxation, and the land was in a state bordering upon bankruptcy. The Advocate-General Talon had graphically described the condition of the French people in a single phrase—"They have nothing that they can call theirs except their souls."

Their bodies had been claimed for the army and navy, both of which had been very successful, especially in the Spanish war; but victories do not yield food, and the people were beginning to feel the pinch of hunger.

Nor was this all. The upper classes had risen against the rapacious minister, who had favoured his own family in the most insolent manner. Mazarin, too, had defied public opinion to the extent of selling no less than ten new judgeships, and at a very high price.

In Paris, political affairs had become very agitated. On the seventh of January of the year in which this tale commences, between seven and eight hundred tradesmen had assembled in Paris to resist a new tax upon house property. Ten of their number had been deputed to lay their grievance before the Duke of Orléans, who, as was customary with him, was seeking popularity. He promised them to use his influence with the queen, and dismissed them with the ordinary expression of princes, "We will see what we can do."

A couple of days after, the judges of the Court of Requests, who resented the appointment of the ten extra judges, had waited upon the Cardinal, and had spoken with so much fearlessness and determination that the Cardinal was astonished. However, he dismissed them royally, using the same formula as that expressed by the Duke of Orléans, "We will see what we can do."

In order to *see*, a council of state was assembled, and d'Emery, the minister of finance, was ordered to attend.

This d'Emery was greatly detested by the people. He was the son of a banker at Lyons named Particelli, one of those clever Italians who overran France in the seventeenth century. Particelli having become a bankrupt, his son abandoned his Italian name for a French one—d'Emery. Cardinal Richelieu had discovered young d'Emery to be a wonderful financier, and presented him to Louis XIII., with a view to his appointment in the ministry of finance.

"I am glad to hear you speak well of this stranger," said the king, "and that he is clever. I was quite afraid that you would have wanted the appointment for that clever scoundrel, Particelli."

"Sire, make yourself quite easy," replied the Cardinal, "the Particelli of whom you speak was hanged."

"So much the better," answered the king. "It is not for nothing that I am called Louis the Just." And he signed the nomination of M. d'Emery.

D'Emery never once let go his hold on the finance office, and after the death of Louis XIII., he obtained, under Mazarin, who, as an Italian himself, patronised Italians, the position of minister of finance.

This was the minister called upon to appease the angry Paris tradesfolk, and the still angrier judges. He appeared before the council pale and trembling, and explained his condition by the statement that his son had been nearly assassinated the day previous, almost within the shadow of the royal walls. He did not add that the mob had hissed him on account of his wife's vulgar display. This luxurious creature had been nobody in particular before her marriage. She was the daughter of one Nicholas de Camus, who had reached Paris with the proverbial ducat in his pocket, and had become secretary of state. In the process he had acquired such wealth as to enable him to divide nine millions of francs amongst his children, whilst keeping forty millions to himself.

The fact was, that d'Emery's son had run a great chance of being suffocated; one of the rioters having proposed to squeeze him until he gave up all the gold he had swallowed. Nothing therefore was settled that day, as d'Emery's head was not steady enough for business after such an occurrence.

Other disturbances had followed this outrage.

Matthew Mole, chief president of the parliament, and esteemed equal in courage to Condé and de Beaufort, had been insulted and threatened. The queen, in going to mass at Notre Dame, as she always did on Saturdays, was followed by more than two hundred women, requesting justice. The poor creatures had no bad intentions. They wished only to be allowed to fall on their knees before their sovereign, and that they might move her to compassion; but they were prevented by the royal guard, and the queen proceeded on her way, haughtily disdainful of their entreaties.

At length parliament was convoked—the authority of the king was to be upheld.

One day, the king, Louis XIV., then ten years of age, went in state, under pretext of returning thanks for his recovery from the smallpox, to Notre Dame. He took the opportunity of calling out his guard, the Swiss troops, and the Musketeers, and he had them arranged round the Palais Royal, on the quays, and on the Pont Neuf. After mass, the young monarch drove to the parliament house, where, upon the throne, he hastily confirmed not only the edicts which he had already passed, but issued new ones; each one, according to Cardinal de Retz, more ruinous than the others—a proceeding which drew forth a strong remonstrance from the Chief-President Mole—while President Blancmesnil and Councillor Broussel raised their voices in indignation against fresh taxes.

The king returned amidst the silence of a vast multitude to the

Palais Royal. All minds were uneasy—most were foreboding—many of the people using threatening language.

At first, indeed, they were doubtful whether the king's visit to the parliament had been in order to lighten or to increase their burdens; but scarcely was it known that the taxes were even to be increased, than cries of "Down with Mazarin!" "Long live Broussel!" "Long live Blancmesnil!" resounded through the city. All attempts to disperse the groups now collected in the streets, or to silence their exclamations, were vain. Orders had just been given to the royal guard, and to the Swiss Guards, not only to stand firm, but to send out patrols to the streets of Saint Denis and Saint Martin, where the people thronged, and where they were the most vociferous, when the Mayor of Paris was announced at the Palais Royal.

He was at once shown in: he came to say that if these offensive precautions were not discontinued, in two hours Paris would be under arms.

Deliberations were being held, when a lieutenant in the Guards, named Comminges, made his appearance, with his clothes all torn, his face streaming with blood. The queen, on seeing him, uttered a cry of surprise, and asked him what was going on.

As the mayor had foreseen, the sight of the Guards had exasperated the mob. The tocsin was sounded. Comminges had arrested one of the leaders, and had ordered him to be hanged near the cross of Du Trahoir; but, in attempting to execute this command, the soldiers were attacked in the market-place with stones and pikes: the delinquents all escaped to the Rue des Lombards, and rushed into a house. They broke open the doors, and searched the dwelling, but in vain. Comminges, wounded by a stone which had struck him on the forehead, had left a picket in the street, and returned to the Palais Royal, followed by a menacing crowd, to tell his story.

This account confirmed that of the mayor. The authorities were not in a condition to contend with a serious riot. Mazarin endeavoured to circulate among the people a report that troops had only been stationed on the quays, and on the Pont Neuf, on account of the ceremony of the day, and that they would soon withdraw. In fact, about four o'clock they were all concentrated about the Palais Royal, the courts and ground floors of which were filled with Musketeers and Swiss Guards, and there awaited the event of all this disturbance.

Such was the state of affairs at the very moment when we introduced our readers into the study of Cardinal Mazarin—once that of Cardinal Richelieu. We have seen in what state of mind he listened to the murmurs from below, which even reached him in his seclusion, and to the guns, the firing of which resounded in that room. All at once he raised his head : his brow slightly contracted, like that of a man who has formed a resolution; he fixed his eyes upon an enormous clock which was about to strike ten, and taking up a whistle, of silver gilt, which was placed on the table near him, he whistled twice.

A door hidden in the tapestry opened noiselessly, and a man dressed in black stood behind the chair on which Mazarin sat.

"Bernouin," said the Cardinal, not turning round, for, having whistled, he knew that it was his valet-de-chambre who was behind him, "what musketeers are there in the palace?"

"The Black Musketeers, my lord."

"What company?"

"Treville's company."

"Is there any officer belonging to this company in the ante-chamber?"

"Lieutenant d'Artagnan."

"A man on whom we can depend, I hope."

"Yes, my lord."

"Give me a uniform of one of these musketeers, and help me to dress."

The valet went out as silently as he came in, and reappeared in a few minutes, bringing with him the dress required.

The Cardinal, in deep thought, and in silence, began to take off the robes of state which he had assumed in order to be present at the sitting of parliament, and to attire himself in the military coat, which he wore with a decidedly easy grace, owing to his former campaigns in Italy. When he was completely dressed, he said :

"Bring Monsieur d'Artagnan hither."

The valet went out of the room, this time by the centre door, but still as silently as before; one might have fancied him an apparition.

When he was left alone, the Cardinal looked at himself in the glass with a feeling of self-satisfaction. Still young—for he was scarcely forty-six years of age—he possessed great elegance of form, and was above the middle height; his complexion was brilliant and beautiful; his glance full of expression; his nose, though large, was well proportioned; his forehead broad and majestic; his hair, of a chestnut colour, was rather frizzed; his beard, which was darker than his hair, was turned carefully with a curling-iron, which greatly improved it. After a short time the Cardinal arranged his shoulder-belt, then looked with great complacency at his hands, which were very beautiful, and of which he took the greatest care; and throwing on one side the large kid gloves which he tried on at first, as belonging to the uniform, he put on others of silk only. At this instant the door opened.

"Monsieur d'Artagnan," said the valet-de-chambre.

An officer, as he spoke, entered the apartment. He was a man between thirty-nine and forty years of age, of a small but well-proportioned figure; thin, with an intellectual and animated physiognomy; his beard black, and his hair turning grey, as often happens when people have found this life either too gay or too sad, more especially when they happen to be of a dark complexion.

D'Artagnan slowly advanced into the apartment. How perfectly he remembered his former entrance into that very room. Seeing, however, no one there except a musketeer of his own troop, he fixed his eyes upon the supposed soldier, in whose dress, nevertheless, he recognised, at the first glance, the Cardinal.

The lieutenant then stood in a dignified but respectful posture; such as became a man of good birth, who had in the course of his life been frequently in the society of the highest nobles.

The Cardinal looked at him with a glance, cunning rather than serious; yet he examined his countenance with attention, and after a momentary silence, he said:

"You are Monsieur d'Artagnan?"

"I am that individual," replied the officer.

Mazarin gazed once more at a countenance full of intelligence, the play of which had been nevertheless subdued by age and experience; and d'Artagnan received the penetrating glance like one who had formerly sustained many a searching look, very different, indeed, from those which were inquiringly directed towards him at that instant.

"Sir," resumed the Cardinal, "you are to come with me, or rather I am to go with you."

"I am at your commands, my lord," answered d'Artagnan.

"I wish to visit in person the outposts which surround the Palais Royal; do you think that there is any danger in so doing?"

"Danger, my lord!" exclaimed d'Artagnan, with a look of astonishment; "what danger?"

"I am told that there is a general insurrection."

"The uniform of the King's Musketeers carries a certain respect with it; and even if that were not the case, I would engage, with four of my men, to put to flight a hundred of these clowns."

"Did you witness the injuries sustained by Comminges?"

"Monsieur de Comminges is in the Guards, and not in the Musketeers——"

"Which means, I suppose, that the Musketeers are better soldiers than the Guards." The Cardinal smiled as he spoke.

"Every one likes his own uniform the best, my lord."

"Myself excepted?" and again Mazarin smiled; "for you perceive that I have left off mine, and put on yours."

"Lord bless us! this is modesty, indeed," cried d'Artagnan. "Had I such a uniform as your Eminence possesses, I protest I should be mighty content; and I would take an oath never to wear any other costume——"

"Yes, but for to-night's adventure, I don't suppose my dress would have been a very safe one. Give me my felt hat, Bernouin." The valet instantly brought to his master a regimental hat with a wide brim. The Cardinal put it on in a soldierly style.

"Your horses are already saddled in their stables, are they not?" he said, turning to d'Artagnan.

"Yes, my lord."

"Well, let us set out."

"How many men does your Eminence wish to escort you?"

"You say that with four men you will undertake to disperse a hundred low fellows; as it may happen that we shall have to encounter two hundred, take eight——"

"As many as my lord desires."

"I shall follow you. This way—light us downstairs, Bernouin."

The valet held a light; the Cardinal took a key from his bureau, and, opening the door of a secret stair, descended into the court of the Palais Royal.

2

A NIGHT PATROL

TEN minutes afterwards Mazarin and his party were traversing the Rue des Bons Enfants, behind the theatre built by Richelieu expressly for the play of *Mirame*, and in which Mazarin—a greater lover of music than of literature—had introduced into France the first opera that was ever acted in that country.

The aspect of the town denoted the greatest agitation. Numerous groups paraded the streets; and, whatever d'Artagnan might think of it, it was obvious that the citizens had, for the night, laid aside their usual forbearance, in order to assume a warlike aspect. From time to time noises came from the direction of the public markets. The report of firearms was heard near the Rue Saint

Denis, and now and again church bells began to ring indiscriminately, and at the caprice of the populace.

D'Artagnan, meantime, pursued his way with the indifference of a man upon whom such acts of folly made no impression. When one of these groups blocked up the middle of the road, he pushed on his horse without giving a note of warning; and, as if those assembled, whether rebels or not, knew the kind of man they had to deal with, they gave way, and allowed the patrol to pass on. The Cardinal envied his composure, which he ascribed to the habit of encountering danger. On approaching an outpost near the Barrière des Sergens, the sentinel cried out, "Who's there?" and d'Artagnan answered—having first asked the word of the Cardinal—"Louis and Rocroy." After which he inquired if Lieutenant Comminges were not the commanding officer at the outpost. The soldier replied by pointing out to him an officer who was conversing, on foot, with his hand upon the neck of a horse on which the individual to whom he was talking sat. Here was the officer whom d'Artagnan was seeking.

"Here is Monsieur Comminges," said d'Artagnan, returning to the Cardinal. The Cardinal directed his horse towards them, while d'Artagnan discreetly retired. It was, however, evident that the Cardinal was recognised by both Comminges and the other officer on horseback.

"Bravo, Guitant," cried the Cardinal to the horseman; "I see plainly, that in spite of your sixty-four years, you are still the same man, active and zealous. What were you saying to the young man?"

"My lord," replied Guitant, "I was remarking that we live in strange times, and that to-day's events are very like those in the days of the Ligue, of which I heard so much in my youth. Are you aware that the mob have even suggested throwing up barricades in the Rue Saint Denis and the Rue Saint Antoine?"

"And what was Comminges saying to you in reply, dear Guitant?"

"My lord," said Comminges, "I answered that to compose a Ligue, only one ingredient was wanting—in my opinion an essential one—a Duc de Guise. Besides, no one ever does the same thing twice over."

"No, but they mean to make a Fronde, as they call it," said Guitant.

"And what is a Fronde?" inquired the Cardinal.

"It is the name which the discontented give to their party, my lord."

"And what is the origin of this name?"

"It seems that some days since, Councillor Backaumont remarked at the palace that rebels and agitators reminded him of schoolboys slinging stones from the moats round Paris—young urchins who run off the moment the constable appears, only to return to their mischief the instant that his back is turned. So they have picked up the word, and the insurrectionists are called 'Frondeurs'; and yesterday every article sold was 'à la Fronde'; bread 'à la Fronde', hats 'à la Fronde', to say nothing of gloves, pocket handkerchiefs, and fans—but listen——"

At that moment a window opened, and a man started singing—

> A breeze from the Fronde
> Blew to-day;
> I think that it blows
> Against Mazarin.

"Insolent rascal!" cried Guitant.

"My lord," said Comminges, who, smarting from his wounds, wished for revenge, and longed to give back blow for blow, "shall I fire off a ball to punish that jester, and to warn him not to sing so much out of tune in future?"

And, as he spoke, he put his hand on the holster of his horse's saddle-bow.

"No, no!" exclaimed Mazarin. "*Diavola*! my dear friend, you are going to spoil everything—everything is going on famously. I understand the French as well as if I had made them myself from first to last. They sing—let them pay the piper. During the Ligue, about which Guitant was speaking just now, the people sang nothing except the Mass, so everything went to destruction. Come, Guitant, come along, and let's see if they keep watch at the Quinze-Vingts as at the Barrière des Sergens."

And waving his hand to Comminges, he rejoined d'Artagnan, who instantly put himself at the head of his troop, followed by the Cardinal, Guitant, and the rest of the escort.

"Just so," muttered Comminges, looking after Mazarin. "True, I forgot—provided he can get money out of the people, that is all he wants."

The street of Saint Honoré, when the Cardinal and his party passed through it, was crowded by an assemblage, who, standing in groups, discussed the edicts of that memorable day—they pitied the young king, who was unconsciously ruining his country, and threw all the odium of his proceedings on Mazarin. Addresses to the Duke of Orléans and to Condé were suggested. Blancmesnil and Broussel seemed in the highest favour.

D'Artagnan passed through the very midst of this discontented multitude, just as if his horse and he had been made of steel. Mazarin and Guitant conversed in a low tone. The musketeers, who had already discovered who Mazarin was, followed in strict silence. In the street of Saint Thomas-du-Louvre, they stopped at that barrier which was distinguished by the name of Quinze-Vingts. Here Guitant spoke to one of the subalterns, and asked him how matters went on.

"Ah, captain!" said the officer, "everything is quiet hereabouts —if I did not know that something is going on in yonder house!"

And he pointed to a magnificent hotel, situated on the very spot whereon the Vaudeville now stands.

"In that hotel?—it is the Hôtel Rambouillet," cried Guitant.

"I really don't know what hotel it is—all I do know is that I observed some suspicious-looking people go in the——"

"Nonsense!" exclaimed Guitant, bursting out laughing. "Why, they are poets."

"Come, Guitant, speak, if you please, respectfully of these gentlemen," said Mazarin; "don't you know that I was in my youth a poet? I wrote verses in the style of Beuserade——"

"You, my lord?"

"Yes, I—shall I repeat to you some of the verses?"

"Just as you please, my lord. I do not understand Italian."

"Yes, but you understand French"; and Mazarin laid his hand upon Guitant's shoulder. "My good, my brave Guitant, whatsoever command I may give you in that language—in French— whatever I may order you to do, will you not do it?"

"Without doubt, my lord. I have already answered that question in the affirmative; but that command must come from the queen herself."

"Yes! ah, yes!" Mazarin bit his lips as he spoke. "I know your devotion to her majesty."

"I have been a captain in the Queen's Guards for twenty years," was the reply.

D'Artagnan, in the meantime, had taken the head of his detachment without a word, and with that ready and profound obedience which characterises an old soldier.

He led the way towards the hut of Saint Roche. The Rue Richelieu and the Rue Villedot were then, owing to their vicinity to the ramparts, less frequented than any others in that direction, for the town was thinly populated thereabouts. He therefore chose these streets to pass through in preference to those more crowded.

"Who is in command here?" asked Mazarin.

"Villequier," said Guitant.

"*Diavola*! Speak to him yourself, for ever since you were deputed by me to arrest the Duc de Beaufort, this officer and I have been on bad terms. He laid claim to that honour as captain of the Royal Guards."

Guitant accordingly rode forward, and desired the sentinel to call Monsieur de Villequier.

"Ah! so you are here!" cried the officer, in that ill-natured tone which was habitual with him; "what the devil are you doing here?"

"I am come to ask if there is anything fresh happening in this part of the town?"

"What do you mean? People cry out, 'Long live the king! down with Mazarin'—that's nothing new—no, we've been used to those acclamations for some time."

"And you join in the chorus," replied Guitant, laughing.

"Faith, I've half a mind to do it. In my opinion the people are right: and cheerfully would I give up five years of my pay—which I am never paid, by the way—to make the king five years older."

"Indeed! And pray what is to come to pass assuming the king were five years older than he is?"

"Why, as soon as ever the king comes of age, he will issue his commands himself, and 'tis far pleasanter to obey the grandson of Henry IV. than the grandson of Peter Mazarin. S'death! I would die willingly for the king; but supposing I happened to be killed on account of Mazarin, as your nephew was near being to-day, there could be nothing in Paradise—so well off as I have been in this world—that could console me for being a martyr."

"Well, well, Monsieur de Villequier," here Mazarin interposed, "I shall take care that the king hears of your loyalty. Come, gentlemen," he addressed the troop, "let us return."

"Stop," exclaimed Villequier; "so, Mazarin is here! so much the better. I have been waiting a long time to tell him what I think of him. I'm obliged to you, Guitant, for the opportunity."

And turning on his heel, he went off to his post, whistling a tune, then popular among the party called the "Fronde".

Mazarin, however, returned, in a pensive mood, towards the Palais Royal. All that he had heard from these three different men, Comminges, Guitant, and Villequier, confirmed him in his conviction that in case of serious tumults there would be no one on his side except the queen: and then, Anne of Austria had so often deserted her friends, that her support seemed rather precarious. During the whole of this nocturnal ride, and the whole time that he was endeavouring to understand the various characters of Comminges, Guitant, and Villequier, Mazarin was, in truth, studying more especially one man. This man—who had remained immovable when menaced by the mob—not a muscle of whose face was altered either by Mazarin's witticisms, or by the jests of the multitude—seemed to the Cardinal a peculiar being, who, having participated in past events similar to those which were now occurring, was calculated to cope with those which were on the eve of taking place.

Besides, the name of d'Artagnan was not altogether unknown to Mazarin, who, although he had not arrived in France before the year 1634, or 1635, that is to say, about eight or nine years after the events which we have related in *The Three Musketeers*, fancied that he had heard d'Artagnan's name mentioned as a man who, in some half-forgotten affair, had made himself conspicuous as a model of courage, address, and loyalty.

This idea took such strong possession of the Cardinal's mind, that he resolved to know all about d'Artagnan immediately; of course he could not inquire from d'Artagnan himself who he was, and what had been his career; he remarked, however, in the course of conversation, that the lieutenant of musketeers spoke with a Gascon accent. Now the Italians and the Gascons are too much alike, and know each other too well, ever to trust to what any one of them may say of himself; so, on reaching the walls which surrounded the Palais Royal, the Cardinal knocked at the little door, and after thanking d'Artagnan, and requesting him to wait in the court of the Palais Royal, he made a sign to Guitant to follow him in.

"My dear Guitant," said the Cardinal, leaning, as they walked through the gardens, on his friend's arm, "you told me just now that you had been twenty years in the queen's service."

"Yes, it is true; I have," returned Guitant.

"Now, my dear Guitant, I have often observed that in addition to your courage, which is indisputable, and to your fidelity, which is invincible, you possess an admirable memory."

"You have found that out, have you, my lord? Deuce take it—all the worse for me!"

"And why so?"

"One of the chief qualities in a courtier is to know when to forget."

"But you are not a courtier, Guitant. You are a brave soldier, one of the few remaining veterans of the days of Henry IV.—alas! how few exist still——!"

"Plague on it, my lord—have you brought me here to get my horoscope out of me?"

"No," returned Mazarin, smiling; "I only brought you here

to ask you if you have taken any particular notice of our Lieutenant of Musketeers?"

"Monsieur d'Artagnan? I do not care to notice him particularly; he's an old acquaintance. He's a Gascon. De Treville knows him, and esteems him greatly, and de Treville, as you know, is one of the queen's greatest friends. As a soldier the man ranks well: he did his duty, and even more than his duty, at the siege of Rochelle—as well as Suze and Perpignan."

"But you know, Guitant, we poor ministers often want men with other qualities besides courage; we want men of talent. Pray was not Monsieur d'Artagnan, in the time of the Cardinal, mixed up in some intrigue from which he came out, according to report, rather cleverly?"

"My lord, as to the report you allude to"—Guitant saw that the Cardinal wished him to speak out—"I know nothing but what the public knows. I never meddle in intrigues; and if I occasionally become a confidant in the intrigues of others, I am sure your Eminence will approve of my keeping them secret."

Mazarin shook his head.

"Ah!" he said; "some ministers are very fortunate, and find out all that they wish to know."

"My lord," replied Guitant, "such ministers do not weigh men in the same balance; they get their information on war from the warriors; on intrigues, from the politician. Consult some politician of the period of which you speak, and if you pay well for it, you will certainly get to know what you want."

Mazarin, with a grimace which he always made when spoken to about money—"People must be paid—one can't do otherwise," he said.

"Does my lord seriously wish me to name any one who was mixed up in the cabals of that day?"

"By Jupiter!" rejoined Mazarin impatiently, "it's about an hour ago since I asked you a question about d'Artagnan, thick-headed as you are."

"There is one man for whom I can answer, if he will speak out."

"That's my concern; I must make him speak."

"Ah! my lord, 'tis not easy to make people say what they don't wish to say."

"Pooh! patience, we're coming to it at last. Well, this man. Who is he?"

"The Comte de Rochefort."

"The Comte de Rochefort!"

"Unfortunately he has disappeared these four or five years, and I don't know where he is."

"*I* know, Guitant," said Mazarin.

"Well, then, how is it that your Eminence complained just now of want of information on some points?"

"You think," resumed Mazarin, "that Rochefort——"

"He was Cardinal Richelieu's creature, my lord. I warn you, however, his services will be expensive. The Cardinal was lavish to his underlings."

"Yes, yes, Guitant," said Mazarin; "Richelieu was a great man, a very great man, but he had that defect. Thanks, Guitant; I shall benefit by your advice this very evening."

Here they separated, and bidding adieu to Guitant in the court of the Palais Royal, Mazarin approached an officer who was walking up and down within that enclosure.

It was d'Artagnan, who was awaiting him.

"Come hither," said Mazarin, in his softest voice, "I have an order to give you."

D'Artagnan bent low, and following the Cardinal up the private staircase, soon found himself in the study whence he had first set out.

The Cardinal seated himself before his bureau, and taking a sheet of paper, wrote some lines upon it, whilst d'Artagnan remained standing, imperturbable, and without showing either impatience or curiosity. He was like a military automaton acting (or, rather, obeying the will of others) upon springs.

The Cardinal folded and sealed the letter.

"Monsieur d'Artagnan," he said, "you are to take this despatch to the Bastille, and to bring back here the person whom it concerns. You must take a carriage and an escort, and guard the prisoner carefully."

D'Artagnan took the letter, touched his hat with his hand, turned round upon his heel, like a drill-sergeant, and, a moment afterwards, was heard in his dry and monotonous tone, commanding. "Four men and an escort, a carriage and a horse." Five minutes afterwards the wheels of the carriage and the horses' shoes were heard resounding on the pavement of the courtyard.

3

TWO OLD ENEMIES

D'ARTAGNAN reached the Bastille just as it was striking half-past eight. His visit was announced to the governor, who, on hearing that he came from the Cardinal, went to meet him, and received him at top of the great flight of steps outside the door. The governor of the Bastille was Monsieur du Tremblay, the brother of the famous Capuchin Joseph, that fearful favourite of Richelieu's who went by the name of the Grey Cardinal.

During the period that the Duc de Bassompierre passed in the Bastille—where he remained for twelve whole years—when his companions, in their dreams of liberty, said to each other, "As for me, I shall go out of prison at such a time," and another, at such and such a time, the duke used to answer, "As for me, gentlemen, I shall leave only when Monsieur du Tremblay leaves"; meaning that at the death of the Cardinal, du Tremblay would certainly lose his place at the Bastille, and then de Bassompierre would regain his at court.

His prediction was nearly being fulfilled, but in a far different way from what de Bassompierre supposed; for, after the death of Richelieu, everything went on, contrary to expectation, in the same way as before; and de Bassompierre had little chance of leaving his prison.

Monsieur du Tremblay received d'Artagnan with extreme politeness, and invited him to sit down with him to supper, of which he was himself about to partake.

"I should be delighted to do so," was the reply; "but if I am not much mistaken, the words, 'In haste,' are written on the envelope of the letter which I brought."

"You are right," said du Tremblay. "Hallo, major, tell them to order number 256 to come downstairs."

The unhappy wretch who entered into the Bastille ceased, as he crossed the threshold, to be a man, and became a number.

D'Artagnan shuddered at the noise of the keys; he therefore remained on horseback, having no inclination to dismount, and sat looking at the bars, at the thick strong windows, and the immense walls which he had hitherto only seen from the other side of the moat, and by which he had, for twenty years, been awestruck.

A bell sounded.

"I must leave you," said du Tremblay; "I am sent for to sign the release of the prisoner. I shall be happy to meet you again, sir."

"May the devil have me if I return thy wish!" murmured d'Artagnan, smiling as he pronounced the imprecation; "I declare I feel quite ill, after only being five minutes in the court-yard. Go to—go to! I would rather die upon straw, than hoard up five hundred a year by being governor of the Bastille."

He had scarcely finished this soliloquy before the prisoner arrived. On seeing him d'Artagnan could hardly suppress an exclamation of surprise. The prisoner, however, did not seem to recognise the musketeer.

"Gentlemen," said d'Artagnan, addressing the four musketeers, "I am ordered to exercise the greatest possible care in guarding the prisoner; and, since there are no locks to the carriage, I shall sit beside him. Monsieur de Lillebonne, lead my horse by the bridle, if you please." As he spoke, he dismounted, gave the bridle of his horse to the musketeer, and placing himself by the side of the prisoner, said, in a voice perfectly composed, "To the Palais Royal, at a full trot."

The carriage drove on, and d'Artagnan, availing himself of the darkness in the archway under which they were passing, threw himself into the arms of the prisoner.

"Rochefort!" he exclaimed: "you—is it you; you, indeed? I am not mistaken?"

"D'Artagnan!" cried Rochefort.

"Ah! my poor friend!" resumed d'Artagnan, "not having seen you for four or five years, I concluded that you were dead."

"I'faith," said Rochefort, "there's no great difference, I think, between a dead man, and one who has been buried alive; now I have been buried alive, or very nearly so."

"And for what crime are you imprisoned in the Bastille?"

"Do you wish me to tell you the truth?"

"Yes."

"Well, then, I don't know."

"Have you any suspicion of me, Rochefort?"

"No! on the honour of a gentleman; but I cannot be imprisoned for the reason alleged—it is impossible."

"What reason?" asked d'Artagnan.

"For stealing."

"For stealing! you—Rochefort—you are laughing at me. It is impossible that it could have been that, my dear Rochefort, which was alleged against you; it is a mere pretext; but you will, perhaps, soon know on what account you have been in prison."

"Ah, indeed! I forgot to ask you—where are you taking me?"

"To the Cardinal."

"What does he require of me?"

"I do not know. I did not even know that you were the person whom I was sent to fetch."

"Impossible! You—a favourite of the minister!"

"A favourite! no, indeed!" cried d'Artagnan. "Ah, my poor friend! I am just as poor a man as when I saw you at Meung, twenty-two years ago, you know; alas!" and he concluded his speech with a deep sigh.

"Nevertheless, you come as one in authority."

"Because I happened to be in the antechamber when the Cardinal called me, just by chance. I am still a lieutenant in the musketeers, and have been so these twenty years."

"Then no misfortune has happened to you?"

"And what misfortune could happen to me? To quote some Latin verses which I have forgotten, or rather, never knew well, 'the thunderbolt never falls on the valley'; and I am a valley, dear Rochefort, and one of the lowest that can be."

"Then Mazarin is still Mazarin?"

"The same as ever, my friend; it is said that he is married to the queen."

"Married?"

"If not her husband, he is undoubtedly her lover."

"You surprise me; to resist Buckingham, and yield to Mazarin."

"Just like the women," said d'Artagnan coolly.

"Like women—but not like queens."

"Egad! queens are the weakest of their sex, when we come to such matters as these."

The count then made several careful inquiries after his friends. The Duc de Beaufort, was he still in prison? To this d'Artagnan answered in the affirmative.

"And," said the prisoner, "what talk is there of war with Spain?"

"With Spain—no," answered d'Artagnan; "but with Paris."

"What do you mean?" cried Rochefort.

"Do you hear the guns, pray? The citizens are amusing themselves in the meantime."

"And you—do you really think that anything could be done with these *bourgeois*?"

"Yes, they might do well, if they had any leader to unite them in one body."

"How miserable not to be free!"

"Don't be downcast. Since Mazarin has sent for you, it is

because he wants you. I congratulate you! Many a long year has passed since any one has wanted to employ me; so you see in what a situation I am."

"Make your complaints known; that's my advice."

"Listen, Rochefort; let's make a compact. We are friends, are we not?"

"Egad! I bear the traces of our friendship—three cuts from your sword."

"Well, if you should be restored to favour, don't forget me."

"On the honour of a Rochefort; but you must do the like for me."

"There's my hand; I promise."

"Therefore, whenever you find an opportunity of saying something in my behalf——"

"I shall say it; and you?"

"I shall do the same."

"Apropos, are we to speak about your friends as well,—Athos, Porthos, and Aramis? or have you forgotten them?"

"Almost!"

"What's become of them?"

"I don't know; we separated, as you know. They are alive, and that's all I can say about them. From time to time I hear of them indirectly, but in what part of the world they are, I really do not know. No, on my honour, I have not a friend in the world but you, Rochefort."

"And the illustrious—what's the name of the lad whom I made a sergeant in Piedmont's regiment?"

"Planchet!"

"The illustrious Planchet. What's become of him?"

"I shouldn't wonder if he is not at the head of the mob at this very moment. He married a woman who keeps a confectioner's shop in the Rue des Lombards; for he's a man that was always fond of sweetmeats; he's now a citizen of Paris. You'll see that that dear fellow will be a sheriff before I shall be a captain."

"Come, d'Artagnan, a little courage. It is when one is lowest on the wheel of fortune that the wheel turns round and raises us. This evening your destiny begins to change."

"Amen!" exclaimed d'Artagnan, stopping the carriage.

He got out, and remounted his steed, not wishing to arrive at the gate of the Palais Royal in the same carriage with the prisoner.

In a few minutes the party entered the courtyard, and d'Artagnan led the prisoner up the great staircase, and across the corridor and antechamber.

As they stopped at the door of the Cardinal's study, d'Artagnan was about to be announced, when Rochefort slapped him on the shoulder.

"D'Artagnan, let me confess to you what I've been thinking about during the whole of my drive, as I looked out upon the parties of citizens who perpetually crossed our path, and looked at you and your four men, with their torches."

"Speak out," answered d'Artagnan.

"I had only to cry out 'Help!' for you and your companions to be cut to pieces, and then I should have been free."

"Why didn't you do it?" asked the lieutenant.

"Come, then!" cried Rochefort. "We swore friendship! Ah! Had any one but you been there—I don't say——"

D'Artagnan bowed.

But the impatient voice of Mazarin summoned Rochefort to the room where the Cardinal awaited him. "Tell Monsieur d'Artagnan to wait outside—I don't require him yet," said the Cardinal.

Rochefort, rendered suspicious and cautious by these words, entered the apartment, where he found Mazarin seated at the table, dressed in his ordinary garb, and as one of the prelates of the Church, his costume being similar to that of the abbés in that day, excepting that his scarf and stockings were violet.

As the door was closed, Rochefort cast a glance towards Mazarin, which was answered by one, equally furtive, from the minister.

The minister was unchanged; still dressed with sedulous care, his hair well arranged and well curled, his person perfumed, he looked, owing to his extreme taste in dress, only half his age. But Rochefort, who had passed five years in prison, had become old in the lapse of years; the dark locks of this estimable friend of the deceased Cardinal Richelieu were now white; the heavy bronze of his complexion had been succeeded by a deep paleness, which betokened debility. As he gazed at him, Mazarin shook his head slightly, as much as to say, "This is a man who does not appear to me fit for much."

After a pause, which appeared an age to Rochefort, Mazarin, however, took from a bundle of papers a letter, and showing it to the count, he said:

"I find here a letter in which you sue for liberty, Monsieur de Rochefort. You are in prison, then?"

Rochefort trembled in every limb at this question. "But I thought," he said, "that your Eminence knew that circumstance better than any one——"

"I? Oh no! There's a mass of prisoners in the Bastille who were sent there in the time of Cardinal Richelieu. I don't even know their names."

"Yes, but in regard to myself, my lord, it cannot be so, for I was removed from the Châtelet to the Bastille owing to an order from your Eminence."

"You think you were."

"I am certain of it."

"Ah, yes! I think I remember it. Did you not once refuse to undertake a journey to Brussels for the queen?"

"Ah! ah!" exclaimed Rochefort. "There is the true reason! Idiot as I am, though I have been trying to find it out for five years, I never found it out."

"But I do not say that it was the cause of your imprisonment. I merely ask you, did you not refuse to go to Brussels for the queen, whilst you had consented to go there to do some service for the late Cardinal?"

"That is the very reason that I declined to go back again to Brussels. I was there at a fearful moment. I was sent there to intercept a correspondence between Chalais and the archduke, and even then, when I was discovered, I was nearly torn to pieces. How then could I return to Brussels?"

"Well, then, since the best motives are liable to misconstruction, the queen saw in your refusal nothing but a refusal—a distinct refusal; she had also much to complain of you during the lifetime of the Cardinal—yes—her majesty the queen——"

Rochefort smiled contemptuously.

"Since I was a faithful servant, my lord, to Cardinal Richelieu during his life, it stands to reason that now, after his death, I should serve you well, in defiance of the whole world."

"With regard to myself, Monsieur de Rochefort," replied Mazarin, "I am not like Richelieu, all-powerful. I am but a minister, who wants no servants, being myself nothing but a servant of the queen's. Now, the queen is of a sensitive nature; hearing of your refusal to obey her, she looked upon it as a declaration of war; and as she considers you a man of superior talent, and therefore dangerous, she desired me to make sure of you—that is the reason of your being shut up in the Bastille—but your release can be arranged. You are one of the men who can comprehend certain matters: and have understood them, and can act with energy——"

"Such was Cardinal Richelieu's opinion, my lord."

"The Cardinal," interrupted Mazarin, "was a great politician, and there was his vast superiority over me. I am a straightforward, simple man; that's my great disadvantage. I am of a frankness of character quite French."

Rochefort bit his lip in order not to smile.

"Now to the point. I want friends. I want faithful servants. When I say I want, I mean the queen wants them. I do nothing without her commands; pray, understand that—not like Cardinal Richelieu, who went on just as he pleased—so I shall never be a great man, as he was; but, to compensate for that, I shall be a good man, Monsieur de Rochefort, and I hope to prove it to you."

Rochefort knew well the tones of that soft voice, in which there was something of a gentle lisp, like the hissing of a viper.

"I am disposed to believe your Eminence," he replied; "but have the kindness not to forget that I have been five years in the Bastille, and that no way of viewing things is so false as through the grating of a prison."

"Ah, Monsieur de Rochefort! have I not told you already that I had nothing to do with that! The queen—cannot you make allowances for the pettishness of a queen and a princess? But that has passed away as suddenly as it came, and is forgotten."

"I can easily suppose, sir, that her majesty has forgotten it amid the fêtes and the courtiers of the Palais Royal, but I, who have passed those years in the Bastille——"

"Ah! *mon Dieu*! my dear Monsieur de Rochefort! do you absolutely think that the Palais Royal is the abode of gaiety? No. We have had great annoyances there. As for me, I play my game fair and above board, as I always do. Let us arrive at some conclusion. Are you one of us, Monsieur de Rochefort?"

"I am very desirous of being so, my lord; but I am totally in the dark about everything. In the Bastille one talks politics only with soldiers and gaolers, and you have no idea, my lord, how little that kind of people really know of the state of affairs; I am of Monsieur de Bassompierre's party. Is he still one of the seventeen peers of France?"

"He is dead, sir;—'tis a great loss. His devotion to the queen was great; and men of loyalty are scarce."

"I think so, indeed," said Rochefort; "and when you find any of them you send them off to the Bastille. However, there are plenty of them in the world, but you don't look in the right direction for them, my lord."

"Indeed! explain to me. Ah! my dear Monsieur de Rochefort, how much you must have learned during your intimacy with the late Cardinal! Ah! he was a great man!"

"Will your Eminence be angry if I read you a lesson?"

"I! never! you know you may say anything to me. I try to be beloved, and not to be feared."

"Well, I myself, on the wall of my cell, scratched with a nail, a proverb, which says, 'Like master, like servant.' "

"Pray, what does that mean?"

"It means that Cardinal Richelieu was able to find trusty servants—dozens and dozens of them."

"He! the point aimed at by every poignard! Richelieu, who passed his life in warding off blows which were for ever aimed at him!"

"But he *did* ward them off," said de Rochefort, "and the reason was, that though he had bitter enemies he possessed also true friends. I have known persons," he continued—for he thought he might avail himself of the opportunity of speaking of d'Artagnan— "who, by their sagacity and address, have deceived the penetration of Cardinal Richelieu; who, by their valour, have got the better of his guards and his spies; persons without money, without support, without credit, yet who have preserved to the crowned head its crown, and made the Cardinal sue for pardon."

"Ah," cried Mazarin, with his wonted grace, "could I but find such men!"

"My lord, there has stood for six years at your very door a man such as I describe, and during those six years he has been unappreciated and unemployed by you."

"Who is it?"

"It is Monsieur d'Artagnan, a Gascon, who has done all this, saved his queen, and made Cardinal Richelieu confess, that in point of talent, address, and political skill, he was to him only a tyro."

"Tell me how it all happened."

"No, my lord, the secret is not mine; it is a secret which concerns the queen. In what he did this man had three colleagues, three brave men, such men as you were wishing for just now."

"And were these four men attached to each other, true in heart, really united?"

"As if they had been one man, as if their four hearts had pulsated in one breast."

"You arouse my curiosity, dear Rochefort; pray tell me the whole story."

"That is impossible; but I will tell you a true story, my lord."

"Pray do so—I delight in stories," cried the Cardinal.

"Listen then," returned Rochefort, as he spoke endeavouring to read in that subtle countenance, the Cardinal's motive. "Once upon a time there lived a queen—a powerful monarch—who reigned over one of the greatest kingdoms of the universe; and a minister; and this minister wished much to injure the queen, whom once he had loved too well. Do not try, my lord, you cannot guess who it is; all this happened long before you came into the country where this queen reigned. There came to the court an ambassador so brave, so magnificent, so elegant, that every woman lost her heart to him; and the queen had even the indiscretion to give him certain ornaments so rare, that they could never be replaced by any like them.

"As these ornaments belonged to the king, the minister persuaded his majesty to insist upon the queen's appearing in them as part of her jewels, at a ball which was soon to take place. There is no occasion to tell you, my lord, that the minister knew for a fact that these ornaments had been sent after the ambassador, who was far away beyond the sea. This illustrious queen had fallen as low as the least of her subjects—fallen from her high estate."

"Indeed!"

"Well, my lord, four men determined to save her. These four men were not princes, neither were they dukes, neither were they men in power, they were not even rich men. They were four honest soldiers, each with a good heart, a good arm, and a sword at the service of those who wanted it. They set out. The minister knew of their departure, and had placed people on the road to prevent them ever reaching their destination. Three of them were overwhelmed and disabled by numerous assailants; one of them alone arrived at the port, having either killed or wounded those who wished to stop him. He crossed the sea and brought back the set of ornaments to the great queen who was able to wear them on her shoulder on the appointed day, and this very nearly ruined the minister. What think you of that trait, my lord?"

"It is splendid," said Mazarin.

"Well, I know ten such men."

"And was Monsieur d'Artagnan one of these four men?" asked the Cardinal.

"It was he who carried out the enterprise."

"And who were the others?"

"I leave it to Monsieur d'Artagnan to name them, my lord."

"You suspect me, Monsieur de Rochefort; I want him, and you, and all to aid me."

"Begin by telling me why, my lord; for after five or six years of imprisonment, it is natural to feel some curiosity as to one's destination."

"You, my dear Monsieur de Rochefort, shall have the post of

confidence; you shall go to Vincennes, where Monsieur de Beaufort is confined; you will guard him well for me."

"My lord," replied Rochefort, "to go out of the Bastille in order to go into Vincennes is only to change one's prison."

"Say at once that you are on the side of Monsieur de Beaufort—that will be the most sincere line of conduct," said Mazarin.

"My lord, I have been so long shut up, that I am only of one party—I am for fresh air. Employ me in any other way; employ me even actively—but let it be on the high-roads."

"My dear Monsieur de Rochefort," Mazarin replied in a tone of raillery, "you think yourself still a young man—your spirit is still juvenile, but your strength fails you. Believe me, you ought now to take rest. Hallo, there, some one!"

"You settle then, nothing about me, my lord?"

"On the contrary, I have come to a decision about you."

Bernouin came into the room.

"Call an officer of justice," he said, "and stay close to me," he added in a low tone.

The officer entered—Mazarin wrote a few words, which he gave to this man—then he bowed.

"*Adieu*, Monsieur de Rochefort," he said.

Rochefort bent low.

"I see, my lord, that I am to be taken back to the Bastille."

"You are sagacious."

"I shall return thither, my lord, but you are wrong not to employ me."

"You? the friend of my greatest foes? don't imagine that you are the only person that can serve me, Monsieur de Rochefort. I shall find many as able men as you are."

"I hope you may, my lord," replied de Rochefort.

He was then reconducted by the little staircase, instead of passing through the antechamber where d'Artagnan was waiting. In the courtyard the carriage and the four musketeers were ready, but he looked around in vain for his friend.

"Ah!" he muttered to himself, "things are altered indeed;" yet he jumped into the carriage with the alacrity of a man of five-and-twenty.

4

ANNE OF AUSTRIA, THE QUEEN-MOTHER

MAZARIN, when left alone with Bernouin, was for some minutes lost in thought. He had gained much information, but not enough.

"My lord, have you any orders?" asked Bernouin.

"Yes, yes," replied Mazarin. "Light me; I am going to the queen."

Bernouin took up a candlestick, and led the way.

There was a secret passage between the Cardinal's apartments and those of the queen; and through this corridor Mazarin passed whenever he wished to visit Anne of Austria.

In the bedroom in which this passage ended Bernouin encountered Madame de Beauvais, like himself entrusted with the secret of these subterranean love affairs: and Madame de Beauvais undertook to prepare Anne of Austria, who was in her oratory with the young king, Louis XIV., to receive the Cardinal.

Anne, reclining in a large easy-chair, her head supported by her hand, her elbow resting on a table near her, was looking at her son, who was turning over the leaves of a book filled with pictures of battles. This celebrated woman fully understood the art of being dull with dignity. It was her custom to pass hours either in her oratory, or in her room, without either reading or praying.

When Madame de Beauvais appeared at the door, and announced the Cardinal, the child, who had been engrossed in the pages of Quintus Curtius, enlivened as they were by engravings of Alexander's feats of arms, frowned, and looked at his mother.

"Why," he said, "does he come in without asking first for an audience?"

Anne coloured slightly.

"The prime minister," she said, "is compelled, in these unsettled times, to inform the queen of all that is happening from time to time, without exciting the curiosity or remarks of the court."

"But Richelieu never entered in this manner," said the pertinacious boy.

"How can you remember what Cardinal Richelieu did? You were too young to know that."

"I do not remember what he did; but I have asked, and I have been told all about it."

At this very moment Mazarin entered. The king rose immediately, took his book, closed it, and went to place it on the table, near which he continued standing, in order that Mazarin might be obliged to stand also.

Mazarin contemplated these proceedings with a thoughtful glance. They explained what had occurred that evening.

He bowed respectfully to the king, who gave him a somewhat cavalier reception, but a look from his mother reproved him for the hatred which, from his infancy, Louis XIV. had entertained towards Mazarin, and he tried to receive with a smile the minister's homage.

"It is time that the king should retire to rest," said the queen, speaking to Madame de Beauvais—for Anne was surprised at this early visit from Mazarin, who scarcely ever came into her apartments until every one had withdrawn for the night.

The queen had many times already told her son that he ought to go to bed; and, several times, Louis had coaxingly insisted on staying where he was; but now he made no reply, but turned white, and bit his lips with anger.

In a few minutes La Porte came into the room. The child went directly to him without kissing his mother.

"Well, Louis," said Anne, "why do you not kiss me?"

"I thought you were angry with me, madam; you sent me away."

"I do not send you away: but you have had the smallpox, and I am afraid that sitting up late may fatigue you."

"You had no fears of my being tired when you ordered me to go to the palace to-day to pass the odious decrees, which have raised up murmurs among the people."

"Sire!" interposed La Porte, in order to turn the subject—"to whom does your majesty wish me to give the candle?"

"To any one, La Porte," the child said; and then added, in a loud voice, "to any one but Mancini."

Now Mancini was a nephew of Mazarin, and was as much detested by Louis as the Cardinal himself, although placed near his person by the minister.

And the king went out of the room, without either embracing his mother, or even bowing to the Cardinal.

"Good," said Mazarin. "I am glad to see that his majesty is brought up with a hatred of dissimulation."

The queen, however, asked, with some impatience, what important business had brought the Cardinal there that evening.

Mazarin sank into a chair, with the deepest melancholy depicted on his countenance.

"It is likely," he replied, "that we shall soon be compelled to separate, unless you love me well enough to follow me into Italy."

"Why," cried the queen; "how is that?"

"Because, as they say in the opera of Thisbe—'The whole world conspires to break our bonds.'"

"You jest, sir!" answered the queen, endeavouring to assume something of her former dignity.

"Alas! I do not, madam," rejoined Mazarin. "Mark well what I say. The whole world conspires to break our bonds. Now as you are one of the whole world, I mean to say that you also desert me."

"Cardinal!"

"Heavens! did I not see you the other day smile on the Duke of Orléans? or rather at what he said?"

"And what was he saying?"

"He said this, madam. 'Mazarin is a stumbling-block. Send him away, and all will go well.'"

"What do you wish me to do?"

"Oh, madam—you are the queen!"

"Queen, forsooth! when I am at the mercy of every scribbler in the Palais Royal, who covers waste paper with nonsense, or of every country squire in the kingdom."

"Nevertheless, you have still the power of banishing from your presence those whom you do not like!"

"That is to say, whom *you* do not like," returned the queen.

"I!—persons whom *I* do not like!"

"Yes, indeed. Who dismissed Madame de Chevreuse?"

"A woman of intrigue; who tried to keep up against me the spirit of cabal which she had raised against Richelieu."

"Then who sent away Madame de Hautefort?"

"A prude, who told you every night as she undressed you, that it was a sin to love a priest; just as if one were a priest, because one happens to be a cardinal."

"Who ordered Monsieur de Beaufort to be arrested?"

"An incendiary; the burden of whose song was his intention to assassinate me. My enemies, madam, ought to be yours, and your friends my friends."

"My friends, sir!" The queen shook her head. "Alas! I have none. In vain do I look about me for friends. I have no influence over any one. Monsieur, the Duke of Orléans, is led by his favourite to-day, Choisy; to-morrow it will be La Rivière, or some one else. The prince is led by Madame de Longueville, who is, in her turn, led by the Prince de Marsillac, her lover. Monsieur de Conti is under the influence of the deputy, who is the slave of Madame de Guemenée."

"Do you know Monsieur de Rochefort?" said Mazarin.

"One of my bitterest enemies—the faithful friend of Cardinal Richelieu."

"I know that, and we sent him to the Bastille," said Mazarin.

"Is he free?" asked the queen.

"No; still there—but I only speak of him in order that I may mention the name of another man. Do you know Monsieur d'Artagnan?" he added, looking steadfastly at the queen.

Anne of Austria received the blow with a beating heart.

"Has the Gascon been indiscreet?" she murmured; then said aloud:

"D'Artagnan! stop an instant; that name is certainly familiar to me. D'Artagnan! there was a musketeer who was in love with one of my women, poor young creature! she was poisoned on my account."

"That's all you know about him?" asked Mazarin.

The queen looked at him, surprised.

"You seem, sir," she remarked, "to be making me undergo a regular interrogation."

"Which you answer according to your own will," replied Mazarin.

"Tell me your wishes, and I will comply with them."

The queen spoke with some impatience.

"Well then, madam, not a day passes in which I do not suffer affronts from your princes and your lordly servants; every one of that automata do not perceive that I hold the spring which makes them move, nor do they see that beneath my quiet demeanour there is the scoff of an injured and irritated man, who has sworn to himself to master them one of these days. We have arrested Monsieur de Beaufort, but he is the least dangerous among them. There is the Prince de Condé——"

"The hero of Rocroy! do you think of *him*?"

"Yes, madam, often and often; but *pazienza*, as we say in Italy. Next, after Monsieur de Condé, comes the Duke of Orléans."

"What are you saying? The first prince of the blood—the king's uncle!"

"No! not the first prince of the blood, not the king's uncle, but the base conspirator, the soul of every cabal, who pretends to lead the brave people who are weak enough to believe in the honour of a prince of the blood—not the prince nearest to the throne, not the king's uncle, I repeat, but the murderer of Chalais, of Montmorency, and of Cinq-Mars, who is playing now the same game that he played long ago, and who fancies he shall gain an advantage; instead of having an opponent who frowns, he has one before him, face to face, who smiles. But he is mistaken. I shall not leave so near the queen that source of discord with which the dead cardinal so often caused the anger of the king to boil over."

Anne blushed, and buried her head in her hands.

"What am I to do?" she said, bowed down beneath the voice of her tyrant.

"Endeavour to remember the names of those devoted servants who crossed the Channel, in spite of Cardinal Richelieu—marking the roads along which they passed by their blood—to bring back to your majesty certain jewels given by you to his Grace of Buckingham."

Anne arose, full of majesty, and, as if touched by a spring, started up, and looking at the Cardinal with the haughty dignity which, in the days of her youth, had made her so powerful, "You insult me, sir," she said.

"I wish," continued Mazarin, finishing as it were, the speech which this sudden movement of the queen had cut short; "I wish, in fact, that you should now do for your husband what you formerly did for your lover."

"Again, that accusation?" cried the queen; "I thought that calumny was stifled or extinct. You have spared me till now; but since you speak of it, once and for all I tell you——"

"Madam, what I wish is, to know all," said Mazarin, astounded by this returning courage.

"I will tell you all," replied Anne. "Listen: there were, in truth, at that epoch, four devoted hearts, four loyal spirits, four faithful swords who saved more than my life—my honour——"

"Ah! you confess it," exclaimed Mazarin.

"Is it only the guilty whose honour is at the sport of others, sir; and cannot women be ruined by appearances? However, I swear I was not guilty; I swear it by——"

The queen looked around her for some sacred object by which she could swear; and taking out of a cupboard, hidden in the tapestry, a small coffer of rosewood, set in silver, and laying it on the altar—

"I swear," she said, "by these sacred relics that Buckingham was not my lover."

"What relics are those by which you swear?" asked Mazarin, smiling. "I am incredulous."

The queen untied from around her throat a small golden key which hung there, and gave it to the Cardinal.

"Open," she said, "sir, and see for yourself."

Mazarin opened the coffer; a knife, covered with rust, and two letters, one of which was blood-stained, alone met his gaze.

"What are these things?" he asked.

"What are these things?" replied Anne, with hauteur, and extending towards the open coffer an arm, despite the lapse of years, still beautiful. "These two letters are the only letters that I ever wrote to him. That knife is the knife with which Felton stabbed him. Read the letters, and see if I have lied, or spoken the truth."

But Mazarin, notwithstanding this permission, instead of reading the letters, took the knife which the dying Buckingham had snatched out of the wound, and sent by La Porte to the queen. The blade was red, for the blood had become rust; after a careful examination, during which the queen became as white as the cloth which covered the altar on which she was leaning, he put it back into the coffer with an involuntary shudder.

"It is well, madam; I believe your oath."

"No, no, read," exclaimed the queen indignantly; "read, I command you, for I am resolved that everything shall be finished to-night, and never will I allude to this subject again. Do you think," she said, with a sickly smile, "that I shall be inclined to re-open this coffer to answer any future accusations?"

Mazarin, overcome by this determination, read the letters. In one the queen asked for the return of the ornaments. This letter had been conveyed by d'Artagnan, and had arrived in time. The other was that which La Porte had placed in the hands of the Duke of Buckingham, warning him that he was about to be assassinated; this had arrived too late.

"It is well, madam," said Mazarin; "nothing can be said against this testimony."

"Sir," replied the queen, closing the coffer, and leaning her hand upon it, "if there is anything to be said, it is that I have always been ungrateful to the brave men who saved me—that I have given nothing to that gallant officer, d'Artagnan, you were speaking of just now, but my hand to kiss, and this diamond."

As she spoke she extended her beautiful hand to the Cardinal, and showed him a superb diamond which sparkled on her finger.

"It appears," she resumed, "that he sold it—he sold it in order to save me on another occasion—to be able to send a messenger to the duke to warn him of his danger—— He sold it to Monsieur des Essarts, on whose finger I remarked it. I bought it from him, but it belongs to d'Artagnan. Give it back to him, sir; and since you have such a man in your service, make him useful."

"And now," added the queen, her voice broken by her emotion, "have you any other question to ask me?"

"Nothing"—the Cardinal spoke in the most conciliatory manner—"except to beg of you to forgive my unworthy suspicions. I love you so tenderly that I cannot help being jealous—even of the past."

A smile, which was indefinable, passed over the lips of the queen.

"If you have no further interrogations to make, leave me, I beseech you," she said. "I wish, after such a scene, to be alone."

Mazarin bent low before her.

"I shall retire, madam; have I your permission to return?"

"Yes, to-morrow."

The Cardinal took the queen's hand, and pressed it, with an air of gallantry, to his lips.

Scarcely had he left her than the queen went into her son's room, and inquired from La Porte if the king was in bed. La Porte pointed to the child, who was asleep.

Anne ascended the steps aside of the bed, and kissed softly the placid forehead of her son; then she retired as silently as she came, merely saying to La Porte:

"Try, my dear La Porte, to make the king more considerate to Monsieur le Cardinal, to whom both he and I are under such great obligations."

5

THE GASCON AND THE ITALIAN

IN the meantime the Cardinal returned to his own room; and after asking Bernouin, who stood at the door, whether anything had happened during his absence, and being answered in the negative, he desired that he might be left alone.

When he was alone, he opened the door of the corridor, and then that of the antechamber. There d'Artagnan was asleep upon a bench.

The Cardinal went up to him, and touched his shoulder. D'Artagnan started, awakened himself, and, as he awoke, stood up exactly like a soldier under arms.

"Monsieur d'Artagnan," said the Cardinal, sitting down on a *fauteuil*, "you have always seemed to me to be a brave and an honourable man."

"Possibly," thought d'Artagnan; "but he has taken a long time to let me know his thoughts;" nevertheless he bent very low to the ground in gratitude for Mazarin's compliment.

"Monsieur d'Artagnan," continued Mazarin, "you have performed many exploits in the last reign."

"Your Eminence is too good to remember that. It is true I fought with tolerable success."

"I don't speak of your warlike exploits, monsieur," said Mazarin; "although they gained you much reputation, they were surpassed by others."

D'Artagnan pretended astonishment.

"Well, you do not answer?" resumed Mazarin.

"I am waiting, my lord, till you tell me of what exploits you speak."

"I speak of certain adventures. I speak of the adventure referring to the queen—of the ornaments, of the journey you made with three of your friends."

"Ha, ho-o!" thought the Gascon; "is this a snare or not? Let me be on my guard."

And he assumed a look of simplicity which Mendori or Bellerose, two of the first actors of the day, might have envied him.

"Bravo," cried Mazarin; "they told me that you were the man I wanted. Come, let us see what you will do for me!"

"Everything that your Eminence may please to command me," was the reply.

"You will do for me what you have done for the queen?"

"Certainly," d'Artagnan said to himself, "he wishes to make me speak out. He's not more cunning than Richelieu was! Devil take him!" then he said aloud:

"The queen, my lord! I don't comprehend."

"You don't comprehend that I want you and your three friends to be of service to me?"

"What friends, my lord?"

"Your three friends—the friends of former days."

"Of former days, my lord! In former days I had not only three friends, I had fifty—at twenty, one calls every one one's friend."

"Well, sir," returned Mazarin, "prudence is a fine thing, but to-day you might be sorry for having been too prudent."

"My lord, Pythagoras made his disciples keep silence for five years, that they might learn to hold their tongues."

"But you have been silent for twenty years, sir. Speak, now, for the queen herself releases you from your promise."

"The queen!"

"Yes, the queen! And as a proof of what I say she commanded me to show you this diamond, which she thinks you know."

And so saying, Mazarin extended his hand to the officer, who sighed as he recognised the ring which had been given to him by the queen on the night of the ball at the Hotel de Ville.

"'Tis true. I well remember that diamond."

"You see, then, that I speak to you in the queen's name. Answer me, and not as if you were on the stage—your interests are concerned in your doing so. Where are your friends?"

"I know not, my lord. We have separated this long time; all three have left the service."

"Where can you find them, then?"

"Wherever they are, that's my business."

"Well, now what are your conditions if I employ you?"

"Money, my lord; as much money as what you wish me to undertake will require."

"The devil he does! Money! and a large sum!" said Mazarin. "Pray are you aware that the king has little money now at his command?"

"Do then as I did, my lord. Sell the crown diamonds. Trust me, don't let us try to do things cheaply. Great undertakings are badly done with small means."

"Well," returned Mazarin. "we will satisfy you."

"Richelieu," thought d'Artagnan, "would have given me five hundred pistoles in advance."

"You will then be at my service?" asked Mazarin.

"And what are we to do?"

"Make your mind easy; when the time for action arrives, you shall be in full possession of what I require from you; wait till that time appears, and find out your friends."

"My lord, possibly they are not in Paris. I must, perhaps, make a long journey to find them out. Travelling is dear, and I am only a poor lieutenant in the musketeers; besides, I have been in the service for twenty-two years, and have accumulated nothing but debts."

Mazarin remained for some moments in serious thought, as if he combated with himself; then going to a large cupboard closed with a triple lock, he took from it a bag of silver, and weighed it twice in his hands before he gave it to d'Artagnan.

"Take this," he said, with a sigh, "'tis for your journey."

D'Artagnan bowed, and plunged the bag into the depth of an immense pocket.

"Well, then, all is settled; you are to set off," said the Cardinal.

"Yes, my lord."

"Apropos, what are the names of your friends?"

"The Count de la Fère, formerly styled Athos; Monsieur du

Valon, whom we used to call Porthos; the Chevalier d'Herblay—now the Abbé d'Herblay—whom we used to call Aramis——"

The Cardinal smiled.

"Younger sons," he said, "who enlisted in the musketeers under feigned names in order not to lower their family names. Long rapiers, but light purses, you know."

"If, God willing, these rapiers should be devoted to the service of your Eminence," said d'Artagnan, "I shall venture to express a wish—which is, that, in its turn, the purse of your Eminence may become light, and theirs heavy—for with these three men, your Eminence may rouse all Europe, if you like."

"These Gascons," said the Cardinal, laughing, "almost beat the Italians in effrontery."

"—At all events," answered d'Artagnan, with a smile equal to the Cardinal's, "they beat them when they draw their swords."

He then withdrew, and as he passed into the courtyard he stopped near a lamp, and dived eagerly into the bag of money.

"Crown pieces only, silver pieces! I suspected it. Ah, Mazarin! Mazarin! thou hast no confidence in me! so much the worse for thee—harm may come of it!"

The Cardinal, however, congratulated himself upon his success.

"A hundred pistoles! a hundred pistoles! for a hundred pistoles I have discovered a secret for which Richelieu would have paid a thousand crowns: without reckoning the value of that jewel"—he cast a complacent look at the ring, which he had kept, instead of restoring it to d'Artagnan—"which is worth, at least, ten thousand francs."

He returned to his room, and, after depositing the ring in a casket filled with brilliants of every kind—for the Cardinal was a connoisseur in precious stones—he called to Bernouin to undress him, regardless of the noises, or of the firing of guns which continued to resound through Paris, although it was now nearly midnight.

Meanwhile d'Artagnan proceeded towards the Rue Tiquetonne, where he lived, at the Hôtel de la Chevrette.

6

D'ARTAGNAN IN HIS FORTIETH YEAR

ALAS! since we bade farewell to d'Artagnan in No. 12 Rue des Fossoyeurs, many years have elapsed, and many things have happened. D'Artagnan had not failed in his career, but circumstances had been adverse to him. So long as he was surrounded by his friends, he retained his youth and the poetry of his character. His nature was of that fine, and ingenuous order, which assimilates itself easily to the dispositions of others. Athos imparted to him his greatness of soul; Porthos, his enthusiasm; Aramis, his elegance. Had d'Artagnan continued his intimacy with these three men, he would have become a superior character. Athos was the first to leave him, in order that he might retire to a small patrimony which he had inherited near Blois. Porthos, the second, to marry an attorney's wife; and lastly, Aramis, the third, to take orders, and become an abbé. From that day d'Artagnan felt lonely and powerless, without courage to pursue a career in which he could only distinguish himself on condition that each of his three companions should endow him with one of the gifts which each had received from heaven.

Notwithstanding his commission in the musketeers, d'Artagnan felt entirely solitary. For a time the delightful remembrance of Madame Bonancieux left on his character a certain poetic tinge, perishable, and, like all other recollections in this world, these impressions were, by degrees, effaced. A garrison life is fatal even to the most aristocratic organisations; and, imperceptibly, d'Artagnan, always in the camp, always on horseback, always in garrison, became (I know not how in the present age one would express it) a complete trooper. His early refinement of character was not only not lost, but was even greater than before; but it was now applied to the little, instead of to the great things of life—to the material condition of the soldier—comprised under the heads of a good lodging, a good table, a good hostess. These important advantages d'Artagnan found to his own taste in the Rue Tiquetonne, at the sign of the Roe, where a pretty Flemish woman, named Madeleine, presided.

In the evening, after his conversation with Mazarin, he returned to his lodgings, absorbed in reflection. His mind was full of the fine diamond, which he had once called his own, and which he had seen on the Cardinal's finger that night.

"Should that diamond ever fall into my hands again," was his reflection, "I should turn it at once into money; I should buy, with the proceeds, certain lands around my father's château, which is a pretty place—well enough—but with no land to it at all, except a garden about the size of the Cemetery des Innocents: and I should wait in all my glory, till some rich heiress, attracted by my good looks, chose to marry me. Then I should like to have three sons; I should make the first a nobleman, like Athos; the second a good soldier, like Porthos; the third an excellent abbé, like Aramis. Faith! that would be a much better life than I lead now; but Monsieur Mazarin is mean, and won't dispossess himself of my diamond in my favour."

On entering the Rue Tiquetonne he heard a tremendous noise, and found a dense crowd near the house.

"Oh! oh!" said he, "is the hotel on fire?" On nearing the hotel of the Roe, he found, however, that it was in front of the next house that the mob was assembled. The people were shouting, and running about with torches. By the light of one of these torches, d'Artagnan perceived men in uniform.

He asked what the matter was.

He was told that twenty citizens, headed by one man, had attacked a carriage, which was escorted by a troop of the Cardinal's bodyguard; but a reinforcement having come up, the assailants had been put to flight, and the leader had taken refuge in the hotel, next to his lodgings; the house was now being searched.

In his youth, d'Artagnan had often headed the *bourgeoisie* against the military, but he was cured of all those hot-headed propensities; besides, he had the Cardinal's hundred pistoles in his pocket: so he went into the hotel without saying a word; he found Madeleine alarmed for his safety, and anxious to tell him all the events of the evening, but he cut her short by ordering her to put his supper in his room, and to give him with it a bottle of good Burgundy.

He took his key and his candle, and went upstairs to his bed-room. He had been contented, for the convenience of the house, to lodge on the fourth storey; and truth obliges us even to confess that his chamber was just above the gutter and below the roof. His first care on entering it was to lock up in an old bureau with a new lock, his bag of money, and then as soon as supper was ready, he sent away the waiter who brought it up, and sat down to table.

Not to reflect on what had passed, as one might fancy. No— d'Artagnan considered that things are never well done when they are not reserved to their proper time. He was hungry; he supped, he went to bed. Neither was he one of those who think that the silence of the night brings good counsel with it. In the night he slept, but in the morning, calm and refreshed, he was inspired with the clearest views of everything. It was long since he had had any reason for his morning's inspiration, but he had always slept through the night. He awoke at daybreak, and made a turn round his room.

"In '43," he said, "just before the death of the late Cardinal, I received a letter from Athos. Where was I then? Let me see. Oh! at the siege of Besançon! I was in the trenches. He told me—let me think—what was it? That he was living on a small estate—but where? I was just reading the name of the place when the wind blew my letter away—I suppose to the Spaniards; there's no use in thinking any more about Athos. Let me see,—with regard to Porthos, I received a letter from him, too. He invited me to a hunting party on his property in the month of September, 1646. Unluckily, as I was then in Béarn, on account of my father's death, the missive followed me there. I had left Béarn when it arrived, and I never received it until the month of April, 1647; and as the invitation was for September, 1646, I couldn't accept it. Let me look for this letter, it must be with my title-deeds."

D'Artagnan opened an old casket which stood in a corner of the room, and which was full of parchments, referring to an estate, during a period of two hundred years lost to his family. He uttered an exclamation of delight, for the large handwriting of Porthos was discernible, and beneath it some lines traced by his worthy wife.

D'Artagnan eagerly searched for the date of this letter; it was dated from the Château du Valon.

Porthos had forgotten that any other address was necessary; in his pride he fancied that every one must know the Château du Valon.

"Devil take the vain fellow," said d'Artagnan. "However, I had better seek him first, since he can't want for money. Athos must have become an imbecile by this time from drinking. Aramis must be absorbed in his devotional exercises."

He cast his eyes again on the letter. There was a postscript.

"I write by the same courier to our worthy friend Aramis in his convent."

"In his convent! what convent? There are about two hundred in Paris, and three thousand in France; and then, perhaps, on entering the convent he has changed his name. Ah! if I were but learned in theology, I should recollect what it was he used to dispute about with the Curate of Montdidier and the Superior of the Jesuits, when we were at Crevecour: I should know what doctrine he leans to, and I should glean from that what saint he has adopted as his patron.

"Well, suppose I go back to the Cardinal and ask him for a passport into all the convents one can find; even into the nunneries? It would be a curious idea, and maybe I should find my friend under the name of Achilles. But, no! I should lose myself in the Cardinal's opinion. Great people only thank you for doing for them what's impossible; what's possible, they say, they can do themselves, and they are right."

So he was perfectly ignorant either where to find Aramis any more than Porthos, and the matter was becoming of great perplexity, when he fancied he heard a pane of glass break in his room window. He thought directly of his bag, and rushed from the inner room where he was sleeping. He was not mistaken; as he entered his bedroom, a man was getting in by the window.

"Ah! you scoundrel!" cried d'Artagnan, taking the man for a thief, and seizing his sword.

"Sir," cried the man. "In the name of heaven put your sword back into the sheath, and don't kill me unheard. I'm no thief, but an honest citizen, well off in the world, with a house of my own. My name is—ah! but surely you are Monsieur d'Artagnan?"

"And thou—Planchet!" cried the lieutenant.

"At your service, sir," said Planchet, transported with joy; "and I'm still capable of serving you."

"Perhaps so," replied d'Artagnan. "But why the deuce dost thou run about the tops of houses at seven o'clock of the morning in the month of January?"

"Sir," said Planchet, "you must know; but, perhaps, you ought not to know——"

"Tell me what," returned d'Artagnan, "but first put a napkin against the window, and draw the curtains."

"Sir," said the prudent Planchet, "in particular, are you on good terms with Monsieur de Rochefort?"

"Perfectly; one of my dearest friends."

"Ah! so much the better!"

"But what has de Rochefort to do with the manner you have of invading my room?"

"Ah, sir! I must tell you that Monsieur de Rochefort is——"

Planchet hesitated.

"Egad, I know where he is," said d'Artagnan. "He's in the Bastille!"

"That is to say, he was there," replied Planchet. "But in returning thither last night, when fortunately you did not accompany him, as his carriage was crossing the Rue de la Ferronnerie, his guards insulted the people, who began to abuse them. The prisoner thought this a good opportunity for escape; he called out his name, and cried for help. I was there. I heard the name of Rochefort. I remembered him well. I said in a loud voice that he was a prisoner, a friend of the Duc de Beaufort, who called for help. The people were infuriated; they stopped the horses, overpowered the escort, whilst I opened the doors of the carriage, and Monsieur de Rochefort jumped out and was lost amidst the crowd. At this moment a patrol passed by. I was compelled to beat a retreat towards the Rue Tiquetonne; I was pursued, and took refuge in a house next to this, where I have been concealed till this morning on the top of the house, between two mattresses. I ventured to run along the gutters, and——"

"Well," interrupted d'Artagnan, "I am delighted that de Rochefort is free; but as for thee, if thou shouldst fall into the hands of the king's servants, they will hang thee without doubt. Nevertheless, I promise thee thou shalt be hidden here, though I risk by concealing thee neither more nor less than my lieutenancy, if it was found out that I gave a rebel an asylum."

"Ah! sir, you know well I would risk my life for you."

"Thou canst add that thou hast risked it, Planchet. I have not forgotten all I owe thee. Sit down there, and eat in security. I see thee cast expressive glances at the remains of my supper."

"Yes, sir; for all I've had since yesterday was a slice of bread and butter with preserve on it. Although I don't despise sweet things in proper time and place, yet I found that supper rather light."

"Poor fellow!" said d'Artagnan. "Well, come; set to."

"Ah, sir! you are going to save my life a second time," cried Planchet.

And he seated himself at the table, and ate as he did in the merry days of the Rue de Fossoyeurs, whilst d'Artagnan walked to and fro, and pondered as to how he could make use of Planchet under present circumstances. While he turned this over in his mind, Planchet did his best to make up for lost time at the table.

At last he uttered a sigh of satisfaction, and paused, as if he had partially appeased his hunger.

"Come," said d'Artagnan, who thought that it was now a convenient time to begin his interrogations, "dost thou know where Athos is?"

"No, sir," said Planchet.

"The devil thou dost not! Dost know where Porthos is?"

"No—not at all."

"And Aramis?"

"Not in the least."

"The devil! the devil! the devil!"

"But, sir," said Planchet, with a look of surprise, "I know where Bazin is."

"Where is he?"

"At Notre Dame."

"What has he to do at Notre Dame?"

"He is beadle."

"Bazin beadle at Notre Dame! He must know where his master is!"

"Without doubt he must."

D'Artagnan thought for a moment, then took his sword, and put on his cloak ready to go out.

"Sir," said Planchet, in great distress, "do you abandon me thus to my fate! Think, if I am found out here, the people of the house, who have not seen me enter it, must take me for a thief."

"True," said d'Artagnan. "Let's see. Canst thou speak any patois?"

"I can do something better than that, sir, I can speak Flemish."

"Where on earth didst thou learn it?"

"In Artois, where I fought for two years. Listen, sir. Goeden morgen, mynheer, ith ben begeeray le weeten de ge sond heets omstand."

"Which means?"

"Good-day, sir! I am anxious to know the state of your health."

"He calls that knowing a language! but, never mind, that will do capitally."

D'Artagnan opened the door, and called out to a waiter to desire Madeleine to come upstairs.

When that lady made her appearance, she expressed much astonishment at seeing Planchet.

"My dear landlady," said d'Artagnan, "I beg to introduce you to your brother, who has arrived from Flanders, and whom I am going to take into my service."

"My brother?"

"Wish your sister good-morning, Master Peter."

"Wilkom, suster," said Planchet.

"Goeden day, broder," replied the astonished landlady.

"This is the case," said d'Artagnan: "this is your brother, Madeleine; you don't know him, perhaps, but I know him; he has arrived from Amsterdam. You must dress him up during my absence. When I return, which will be in about an hour, you must offer him to me as a servant, and, upon your recommendation, though he doesn't speak a word of French, I take him into my service. You understand?"

"That is to say, I guess your wishes; and that is all that's necessary," said Madeleine.

"You are a precious creature, my dear hostess, and I'm obliged
to you."

The next moment d'Artagnan was on his way to Notre Dame.

7

THE DIFFERENT EFFECTS WHICH HALF A PISTOLE MAY PRODUCE UPON A BEADLE AND A CHOIR-BOY

D'ARTAGNAN went over the Pont Neuf, congratulating himself
upon having found Planchet again; for at that time an intelligent
servant was essential to him; nor was he sorry that through
Planchet, and the situation which he held in the Rue des Lombards, a connection with the *bourgeoisie* might be commenced, at
that critical period when that class were preparing for war with
the court party. It was like having a spy in the enemy's camp. In
this frame of mind, grateful for the accidental meeting with
Planchet, pleased with himself, d'Artagnan reached Notre Dame.
He ran up the steps, entered the church, and addressing a verger
who was sweeping the chapel, asked him if he knew Monsieur
Bazin.

"Monsieur Bazin, the beadle," said the verger. "Yes; there he
is, attending mass, in the chapel of the Virgin."

D'Artagnan nearly jumped for joy—he had despaired of finding
Bazin; but now, he thought, since he held one of the threads, he
should be pretty sure to reach the other end of the clue.

He knelt down just opposite to the chapel, in order not to lose
sight of his man; and as he had almost forgotten his prayers, and
had omitted to take a book with him, he made use of his time in
observing Bazin.

Bazin wore his dress, it may be observed, with equal dignity and
saintly propriety. It was not hard to understand that he had gained
the summit of his ambition, and that the silver-mounted wand
which he brandished was, in his eyes, as honourable a distinction
as the marshal's baton, which Condé threw, or did not throw, into
the enemy's line of battle at Fribourg. His person had undergone
a change, analogous to the change in his dress; his figure was
rounded, and, as it were, canonised. The striking points of his face
were effaced; he had still a nose; but his cheeks, fattened out, each
took a portion of it into themselves; his chin was joined to his

throat; his eyes were swollen up with the puffiness of his cheeks; his hair, cut straight in holy guise, covered his forehead as far as his eyebrows.

The officiating priest was just finishing the mass, whilst d'Artagnan was gazing at Bazin; he pronounced the words of the holy sacrament, and retired, giving the benediction, which was received by the kneeling communicants, to the astonishment of d'Artagnan, who recognised in the priest the Coadjutor himself, the famous Jean François Goneli, who at that time, having a presentiment of the part he was to play, was beginning to court popularity by alms-giving. It was to this end that he performed from time to time some of those early masses which the common people generally alone attended.

D'Artagnan knelt as well as the others, received his share of the benediction, and made the sign of the cross; but when Bazin passed in his turn, with his eyes raised to heaven, and walking, in all humility, the very last, d'Artagnan pulled him by the hem of his garment.

Bazin looked down and started as if had he seen a serpent.

"Monsieur d'Artagnan!" he cried; "Vade retra, Satanas!"

"So, my dear Bazin," said the officer, laughing, "this is the way you receive an old friend."

"Sir," replied Bazin, "the true friends of a Christian are those who aid him in working out his salvation; not those who hinder him in so doing."

"I fail to understand you, Bazin; nor can I see how I can be a stumbling-block in the way of your salvation," said d'Artagnan.

"You forget, sir, that you very nearly ruined for ever that of my master; and that it was owing to you that he was very nearly being damned eternally for remaining a musketeer, whilst his true vocation was for the church."

"My dear Bazin, you ought to know," said d'Artagnan, "from the place in which you find me, that I am much changed in everything. Age produces sound sense, and, as I doubt not but that your master is on the road to salvation, I want you to tell me where he is, that he may help me to mine."

"Rather say—to take him back with you into the world. Fortunately, I don't know where he is."

"How?" cried d'Artagnan; "you don't know where Aramis is?"

"Formerly," replied Bazin, "Aramis was his name of perdition. By Aramis is meant Simara, which is the name of a demon. Happily for him, he has ceased to bear that name."

D'Artagnan saw clearly that he should get nothing out of this man, who was evidently telling a falsehood in his pretended ignorance of the abode of Aramis, but whose falsehoods were bold and decided.

"Well, Bazin," said d'Artagnan, "since you do not know where your master lives, let us speak of it no more; let us part good friends. Accept this half pistole to drink to my health."

"I do not drink, sir," answered Bazin, pushing away with dignity the officer's hand; "'tis good only for the laity."

"Incorruptible!" murmured d'Artagnan; "I am unlucky;" and whilst he was deep in thought, Bazin retreated towards the sacristy, where he was only, as he thought, secure by shutting the door and closing himself in.

D'Artagnan was still lost in thought, when some one touched him on the shoulder. He turned, and uttered an exclamation of surprise.

"You here, Rochefort?" he said in a low tone.

"Hush!" replied Rochefort. "Do you know that I am at liberty?"

"I knew it from the fountain-head—from Planchet. And what brought you here?"

"I came to thank God for my happy deliverance," said Rochefort.

"And nothing more? I suppose that is not all."

"To take my orders from the Coadjutor, and to see if we cannot somewhat plague Mazarin."

"A bad plan; you'll be again caged in the Bastille."

"Oh, as to that, I shall take care, I assure you. The air, the fresh free air, is so good; besides"—and Rochefort drew a deep breath as he spoke—"I am going into the country to make a tour."

"Stop," cried d'Artagnan; "I, too, am going."

"And if I may, without impertinence, ask—where are you going?"

"To seek my friends. To find out Athos, Porthos, and Aramis."

"And when do you start?"

"I am now on my road."

"Good luck to you."

"And to you—a good journey."

"Perhaps we shall meet on our road. Adieu! till we meet again! Apropos, should Mazarin speak to you about me, tell him that I have requested you to acquaint him that in a short time he will see whether I am, as he says, too old for action."

And Rochefort went away with one of those Satanic smiles which used formerly to make d'Artagnan shudder, but d'Artagnan could now see it without anguish, and smiling in his turn, with an expression of melancholy, which the recollections called up by that smile could, perhaps, alone give to his countenance, he said:

"Begone, demon, do what thou wilt! it matters little to me. There is not a second Constance in the world."

On his return into the cathedral, d'Artagnan saw Bazin, who was conversing with the sacristan. Bazin was making with his spare, little, short arms ridiculous gestures. D'Artagnan perceived that he was enforcing prudence with respect to himself.

D'Artagnan slipped out of the cathedral, and placed himself in ambuscade at the corner of the Rue des Canettes; it was impossible that Bazin could go out of the cathedral without his seeing him.

In five minutes Bazin made his appearance, looking in every direction to see if he were observed, but he saw no one. Tranquillised by appearances, he ventured to walk through the Rue Notre Dame. Then d'Artagnan rushed out of his hiding-place, and arrived in time to see Bazin turn down the Rue de la Juiverie, and enter, in the Rue de la Calandre, a quiet-looking house; ard this d'Artagnan felt no doubt was the habitation of the worthy beadle. Afraid of making any inquiries at this house, d'Artagnan entered a small tavern at the corner of the street, and asked for a cup of hypocras. This beverage required a good half-hour to prepare it, and d'Artagnan had time, therefore, to watch Bazin unsuspected.

He perceived in the tavern a pert boy between thirteen and fifteen years of age, whom he fancied he had seen not twenty minutes before, under the guise of a chorister. He questioned him; and as the boy had no interest in deceiving, d'Artagnan learned that he exercised from six o'clock in the morning till nine the office of chorister, and from nine o'clock till midnight that of a waiter in the tavern.

Whilst he was talking to this lad, a horse was brought to the door of Bazin's house. It was saddled and bridled. Almost immediately Bazin came downstairs.

"Look!" said the boy, "there's our beadle, who is going a journey."

"And where is he going?" asked d'Artagnan.

"Forsooth, I don't know."

"Half a pistole if you can find out," said d'Artagnan.

"For me?" cried the boy, his eyes sparkling with joy, "if I can find out where Bazin is going? 'Tis not difficult. You are not joking—are you?"

"No, on the honour of an officer; there is the half pistole;" and he showed him the seductive coin, but did not give it him.

"I shall ask him."

"Just the very way not to know. Wait till he is set out, and then, marry, come up—ask, and find out. The half pistole is ready;" and he returned it again into his pocket.

"I understand," said the boy, with that jeering smile which marks especially the "gamin de Paris." "Well, we must wait."

They had not long to wait. Five minutes afterwards Bazin set off on a full trot, urging on his horse by the blows of a paraphine, which he was in the habit of using instead of a riding-whip.

Scarcely had he turned the corner of the Rue de la Juiverie, than the boy rushed after him like a bloodhound on full scent.

Before five minutes had elapsed he returned.

"Well!" said d'Artagnan.

"Well!" answered the boy; "it is done."

"Where is he gone?"

"The half pistole is for me?"

"Doubtless; answer me."

"I want to see it. Give it me, that I may see that it is not false."

"There it is."

The boy put the piece of money into his pocket.

"And now, where is he gone?" inquired d'Artagnan.

"He is gone to Noisy."

"How dost thou know?"

"Ah, faith! there was no great ingenuity necessary. I knew the horse he rode; it belongs to the butcher who lets it out now and then to Bazin. Now, I thought as much that the butcher would not let his horse out like that without knowing where it went to. And he answered, 'that Monsieur Bazin went to Noisy. 'Tis his custom. He goes two or three times a week.'"

"Dost thou know Noisy well?"

"I think so, truly; my nurse lives there."

"Is there a convent at Noisy?"

"Isn't there, a grand one—a convent of Jesuits."

"What's thy name?"

"Friquet."

D'Artagnan wrote down the boy's name in his tablets.

"Please, sir," said the boy, "do you think I can get any more half pistoles any way?"

"Perhaps," replied d'Artagnan.

And, having got out all he wanted, he paid for the hypocras, which he did not drink, and went quickly back to the Rue Tique-tonne.

8

D'ARTAGNAN DISCOVERS THAT HIS FRIEND ARAMIS WAS RIDING BEHIND HIM

THE plan adopted by d'Artagnan was soon perfected. He did not wish to reach Noisy in the daytime, for fear of being recognised: he had therefore plenty of time before him, for Noisy is only three or four leagues from Paris, on the road to Meaux.

He began his day by breakfasting very substantially—a bad beginning when one wishes to employ the head, but an excellent precaution when one wants to work the body; and about two o'clock he had his two horses saddled, and followed by Planchet, he quitted Paris by the Barrière de la Villette.

At about a league and a half from the city, d'Artagnan, finding that in his impatience he had set out too soon, stopped to give the horses breathing time. The inn was full of disreputable-looking people, who appeared as if they were on the point of commencing some nightly expedition. A man, wrapped in a cloak, came to the door; but seeing a stranger, he beckoned to his companions, and two men who were drinking in the inn went out to speak to him.

D'Artagnan, on his part, went up to the landlady, extolled her wine, which was a horrible production from the country of Montreuil, and heard from her that there were only two houses of importance in the village; one of these belonged to the Archbishop of Paris, and was at that time the abode of his niece, the Duchess de Longueville; the other was a convent of Jesuits, and was the property—a by no means unusual circumstance—of these worthy fathers.

At four o'clock d'Artagnan recommenced his journey. He proceeded slowly, and in a deep reverie. Planchet was also lost in thought, but the subject of their reflections was not the same.

One word which their landlady had pronounced had given a particular turn to d'Artagnan's deliberations—this was the name of Madame de Longueville.

That name was, indeed, one to inspire imagination, and to produce thought. Madame de Longueville was one of the highest ladies in the realm; she was also one of the greatest beauties at the court. She had formerly been suspected of an intimacy of too tender a nature with Coligny—who, for her sake, had been killed in a duel, in the Place Royale, by the Duc de Guise. She was now connected by a bond of a political nature with the Prince de Marsillac, the eldest son of the old Duc de Rochefoucauld, whom she was trying to inspire with an enmity towards the Duc de Condé, her brother-in-law, whom she now hated mortally.

D'Artagnan thought of all these matters. He remembered how, at the Louvre, he had often seen, as she passed by him in the full radiance of her dazzling charms, the beautiful Madame de Longueville. He thought of Aramis, who, without possessing any greater advantages than he had, had formerly been the lover of Madame de Chevreux, who had been in another court than Madame de Longueville was in that day; and he wondered why it was that there should be in the world people who succeed in every wish—some in ambition, others in love—whilst others, either from chance or from ill-luck, or from some natural defect or impediment, remain only halfway on the road towards the goal of their hopes and expectations.

He was confessing to himself that he belonged to the latter class of persons, when Planchet approached, and said:

"I will lay a wager, your honour, that you and I are thinking of the same thing."

"I doubt it, Planchet," replied d'Artagnan—"but what are you thinking of?"

"I am thinking, sir, of those desperate-looking men who were drinking in the inn where we rested."

"Always cautious, Planchet."

"'Tis instinct, your honour."

"Well, what does your instinct tell you now?"

"Sir, it told me that those people were assembled there for no good purpose; and I was reflecting on what my instinct had told me, in the darkest corner of the stable, when a man, wrapped in a cloak, and followed by two other men, came in."

"Ah!"

"One of these men said, 'He must certainly be at Noisy, or be coming there this evening, for I have seen his servant.'"

"'Art thou certain?' said the man in the cloak.

"'Yes, my prince.'"

"My prince!" interrupted d'Artagnan.

"Yes, 'my prince'—but listen. 'If he is here'—this is what the other man said—'let's see decidedly what to do with him.'

"'What to do with him?' answered the prince.

"'Yes, he's not a man to allow himself to be taken anyhow—he'll defend himself.'

"'Well—we must try to take him alive. Have you cords to bind him with, and a gag to stop his mouth?'

" 'We have.'

" 'Remember that he will most likely be disguised as a horseman.'

" 'Yes, yes, my lord—don't be uneasy.'

" 'Besides, I shall be present.'

" 'You will assure us that justice——'

" 'Yes, yes—I answer for all that,' the prince replied.

" 'Well, then, we'll do our best.' Having said that, they left the stable."

"Well—what matters all that to us?" said d'Artagnan; "this is one of those attempts that happen every day."

"Are you sure that we are not its objects?"

"We—why?"

"Just remember what they said;" and Planchet recapitulated what he had just stated.

"Alas! my dear Planchet," said d'Artagnan, sighing, "we are unfortunately no longer in those times in which princes would care to assassinate me. Those were good old days: never fear— these people owe us no grudge."

"Is your honour sure?"

"I can answer for it they do not."

"Well—we won't speak of it any more, then;" and Planchet took his place behind d'Artagnan with that sublime confidence which he had always had in his master, and which fifteen years of separation had not destroyed.

They had travelled onwards about half a mile, when Planchet came close up to d'Artagnan.

"Stop, sir; look yonder," he whispered; "don't you see, in the darkness, something pass by, like shadows? I fancy I hear horses' feet."

"Impossible!" returned d'Artagnan. "The ground is soaked in rain; yet I fancy, as thou sayest, that I see something."

At this moment the neighing of a horse struck upon his ear— coming through darkness and space.

"There are men somewhere about; but that's of no consequence to us," said d'Artagnan; "let us ride forward."

At about half-past eight o'clock they reached the first houses in Noisy; every one had retired, and not a light was to be seen in the village. The obscurity was broken only now and then by the dark lines of the roofs of houses. Here and there a dog barked behind a door, or an affrighted cat fled precipitately from the midst of the pavement, to take refuge behind a heap of faggots, from which retreat her eyes shone like carbuncles. These seemed to be the only living creatures that inhabited the village.

Towards the middle of the town, commanding the principal open space, rose a dark mass, separated from the rest by two lanes, and overshadowed in the front by enormous lime-trees. D'Artagnan looked attentively at the building.

"This," he said to Planchet, "must be the archbishop's château, the abode of the fair Madame de Longueville; but the convent, where is that?"

"The convent, your honour, is at the end of the village; I know it well."

"Well, then, Planchet, gallop up to it, whilst I tighten my horse's girth, and come back and tell me if there is a light in any of the Jesuits' windows."

In about five minutes Planchet returned.

"Sir," he said, "there is one window of the convent lighted up."

"Hem! If I were a 'Frondeur,'" said d'Artagnan, "I should knock here, and should be sure of a good supper. If I were a monk, I should knock yonder, and should have a good supper there, too; whereas 'tis very possible that, between the castle and the convent, we shall sleep on hard beds, suffering from hunger and thirst."

"Yes," added Planchet, "like the famous ass of Buridan. Shall I knock?"

"Hush!" answered d'Artagnan; "the light in the window is extinguished."

"Do you hear nothing?" whispered Planchet.

"What is that noise?"

There came a sound like a whirlwind, and at the same time two troops of horsemen, each composed of ten men, sallied forth from each of the lanes which encompassed the house, and surrounded d'Artagnan and Planchet.

"Heyday!" cried d'Artagnan, drawing his sword, and taking refuge behind his horse; "are you not mistaken? is it us you wish to attack—us?"

"There he is! we have him now," said the horsemen, rushing on d'Artagnan with naked swords.

"Don't let him escape," said a loud voice.

"No, my lord; be assured, he shall not."

D'Artagnan thought it was now time for him to join in the conversation.

"Hallo, gentlemen!" he called out in his Gascon accent, "What do you want—what is your demand?"

"Thou wilt soon know," shouted a chorus of horsemen.

"Stop, stop!" cried he whom they had addressed as "my lord"; "'tis not his voice."

"Ah! just so, gentlemen! pray do people get into passions at random at Noisy? Take care, for I warn you that the first man that comes within the length of my sword—and my sword is long— I kill him."

The chief of the party now approached.

"What are you doing here?" he asked, in a lofty tone, and as one accustomed to command.

"And you—what are *you* doing here?" replied d'Artagnan.

"Be civil, or I shall beat you; for although one may not choose to proclaim oneself, one insists on respect suitable to one's rank."

"You don't choose to discover yourself, because you are the leader of an ambuscade," returned d'Artagnan; "but with regard to myself, who am travelling quietly with my own servant, I have not the same reasons as you have to conceal my name!"

"Enough! enough! what is your name?"

"I shall tell you my name in order that you may know where to find me, my lord, or my prince, as it may suit you best to be called," said our friend, who did not choose to seem to yield to a threat. "Do you know Monsieur d'Artagnan?"

"Lieutenant in the king's regiment of musketeers?" said the voice; "you are Monsieur d'Artagnan?"

"I am."

"Then you are come here to defend him?"

"Him? whom? Him?"

"Him whom we are seeking."

"It appears," said d'Artagnan, "that whilst I thought I was coming to Noisy, I have entered, without suspecting it, into the kingdom of mysteries."

"Come," replied the same lofty tone, "answer. Are you waiting for him beneath these windows? Did you come to Noisy to defend him?"

"I am waiting for no one," replied d'Artagnan, who was beginning to be angry.

"Well, well," rejoined the leader, "there's no doubt 'tis a Gascon who is speaking, and therefore not the man we are looking for. We shall meet again, Monsieur d'Artagnan; let us go onwards, gentlemen."

And the troop, angry and complaining, disappeared in the darkness, and took the road to Paris. D'Artagnan and Planchet remained for some moments still on the defensive; then, as the noise of the horsemen became more and more distant, they sheathed their swords.

"Thou seest, simpleton," said d'Artagnan to Planchet, "that they wished us no harm."

"But to whom, then?"

"I'faith! I neither know, nor care. What I care for now, is to make my way into the Jesuits' convent; so, to horse, and let us knock at their door. Happen what will—devil take them—they won't eat us."

And he mounted his horse. Planchet had just done the same, when an unexpected weight fell upon the back of his horse, which sank down.

"Hey! your honour!" he cried, "I've a man behind me."

D'Artagnan turned round, and saw, plainly, two human forms upon Planchet's horse.

"'Tis then the devil that pursues us!" he cried, drawing his sword, and preparing to attack the new foe.

"No, no, dear d'Artagnan," said the figure, "'tis not the devil, 'tis Aramis; gallop fast, Planchet, and when you come to the end of the village, go to the left."

And Planchet, carrying Aramis on the crupper, set off full gallop, followed by d'Artagnan, who began to think he was dreaming some incoherent and fantastic dream.

9

THE ABBÉ D'HERBLAY

AT the end of the village Planchet turned to the left, in obedience to the orders of Aramis, and stopped underneath the window which had a light in it. Aramis alighted, and rapped three times with his hands. Immediately the window was opened, and a ladder of rope was let down from it.

"My friend," said Aramis, "if you like to ascend, I shall be delighted to receive you."

"Pass on before me, I beg of you."

"As the late Cardinal used to say to the late king—only to show you the way, sire." And Aramis ascended the ladder quickly, and gained the window in an instant.

D'Artagnan followed, but less nimbly, showing plainly that this mode of ascent was not one to which he was accustomed.

"Sir," said Planchet, when he saw d'Artagnan at the top of the ladder, "this way is easy for Monsieur Aramis, and even for you; in case of necessity I might also climb up, but the horses cannot mount the ladder."

"Lead them to yonder shed, my friend," said Aramis, pointing to a building on the plain, "there you will find hay and straw for them; then come back here, and knock thrice, and we will give you out some provisions. Make yourself easy, my good fellow, no one dies of hunger here."

And Aramis, drawing in the ladder, closed the window. D'Artagnan then looked around him attentively.

Never was there an apartment at the same time more warlike and more elegant. At each corner there were trophies, presenting to the view swords of all sorts, and four great pictures representing in their ordinary military costume the Cardinal de Lorraine, the Cardinal de Richelieu, the Cardinal de la Valette, and the Archbishop of Bordeaux. Outwardly nothing in the room showed that it was the habitation of an abbé. The hangings were of damask, the carpets came from Alençon, and the bed, more especially, had more the look of a fine lady's couch, with trimmings of fine lace, and embroidered counterpane, than of a man who had made a vow that he would endeavour to gain heaven by fasting and mortification.

Whilst d'Artagnan was engaged in contemplation, the door opened, and Bazin entered; on perceiving the musketeer he uttered an exclamation which was almost a cry of despair.

"My dear Bazin," said d'Artagnan, "I am delighted to see with what wonderful composure you tell a lie even in a church!"

"Sir," replied Bazin, "I have been taught by the good Jesuit fathers, that it is permitted to tell a falsehood when it is told in a good cause."

"So far so well," said Aramis; "we are dying of hunger. Serve up the best supper you can, and especially bring some good wine."

Bazin bowed low, and left the room.

"Now we are alone, dear Aramis," said d'Artagnan, "tell me how the devil did you manage to light upon the back of Planchet's horse?"

"Eh! faith!" answered Aramis, "as you see, from heaven."

"From heaven!" replied d'Artagnan, shaking his head; "you have no more appearance of coming from thence than you have of going there."

"My friend," said Aramis, with a quaint look on his face which d'Artagnan had never observed whilst he was in the musketeers, "if I did not come from heaven, at least I was leaving paradise, which is almost the same."

"Here, then, is a puzzle for the learned," observed d'Artagnan; "until now they have never been able to agree as to the situation of paradise: some place it on Mount Ararat, others between the Tigris and the Euphrates; it seems that they have been looking very far off for it, while it was actually very near. Paradise is at Noisy le See, upon the site of the archbishop's château. People do not go out from it by the door, but by the window; one doesn't descend here by the marble steps of a peristyle, but by the branches of a lime-tree; and the angel with a flaming sword who guards this elysium, seems to have changed his celestial name of Gabriel into that of the more terrestrial one of the Prince de Marsillac."

Aramis burst out into a fit of laughter.

"You were always a merry companion, my dear d'Artagnan," he said, "and your witty Gascon fancy has not deserted you. Yes, there is a deal in what you say; nevertheless, do not believe that it is Madame de Longueville with whom I am in love."

"A plague on't! I shall not do so. After having been so long in love with Madame de Chevreuse, you would not lay your heart at the feet of her mortal enemy!"

"Yes," returned Aramis, with an absent air, "yes, that poor duchess! I once loved her greatly, and, to do her justice, she was very useful to us. Eventually she was obliged to leave France. He was a relentless enemy, that remorseless Cardinal," continued Aramis, glancing at the portrait of the old minister. "He had even given orders to arrest her, and would have had her beheaded, had she not escaped with her waiting-maid—poor Kitty! The duchess escaped in man's clothes, and a couplet was made upon her"— and Aramis hummed a few lines of a well-known song of the day.

"Bravo!" cried d'Artagnan, "you sing charmingly, dear Aramis. I do not perceive that singing masses has altered your voice."

"My dear d'Artagnan," replied Aramis, "you understand, when I was a musketeer I mounted guard as seldom as I could; now, when I am an abbé, I say as few masses as I can. But to return to our duchess."

"Which? the Duchesse de Chevreuse or the Duchesse de Longueville?"

"Have I not told you already that there is nothing between me and the Duchesse de Longueville? little flirtations, perhaps, and that's all. No, I spoke of the Duchesse de Chevreuse; did you see her after her return from Brussels, after the king's death?"

"Yes, she is still beautiful."

"Yes," said Aramis, "I saw her also at that time. I gave her good advice, by which she did not profit. I ventured to tell her that Mazarin was the lover of Anne of Austria. She wouldn't believe me, saying, that she knew Anne of Austria, who was too proud to love such a worthless coxcomb. She since plunged into the cabal headed by the Duke of Beaufort; and the 'coxcomb' arrested de Beaufort, and banished Madame de Chevreuse."

"You know," resumed d'Artagnan, "that she has had leave to return to France?"

"Yes, she has come back, and is going to commit some new folly or another; she is much changed."

"In that respect unlike you, my dear Aramis, for you are still the same; you have still your beautiful dark hair, still your elegant figure, still your feminine hands, which are admirably suited to a prelate."

"Yes," replied Aramis, "I am extremely careful of my appearance. Do you know that I am growing old; I am nearly thirty-seven."

"Mind, Aramis"—d'Artagnan smiled as he spoke—"since we are together again, let us agree on one point, what age shall we be in future?"

"How?"

"Formerly, I was your junior by two or three years, and, if I am not mistaken, I am more than forty years old."

"Indeed! Then 'tis I who am mistaken, for you have always been a good chronologist. By your reckoning I must be forty-three at least. The devil I am! Don't let it out at the Hôtel Rambouillet, it would be my ruin," replied the abbé.

"Don't be afraid, I shall not," said d'Artagnan.

"And now let us go to supper," said Aramis, seeing that Bazin had returned and prepared the table.

The two friends sat down, and Aramis began to carve fowls, partridges, and hams with admirable skill.

"The deuce!" cried d'Artagnan; "do you live in this style always?"

"Yes, pretty well. The Coadjutor has given me dispensations from fasting on the *jours maigres*, on account of my health; then I have engaged as my cook, the cook who lived with Lafol-lome—you know whom I mean?—the friend of the Cardinal, and the famous epicure whose grace after dinner used to be—'Good Lord, do me the favour to make me digest what I have eaten.'"

"Nevertheless, he died of indigestion, in spite of his grace," said d'Artagnan.

"What can you expect?" replied Aramis, in a tone of resignation; "a man must fulfil his destiny."

"If it be not an indelicate question," resumed d'Artagnan; "are you grown rich?"

"Oh, heaven! no. I make about twelve thousand francs a year, without counting a little benefice which the prince gave me."

"And how do you make your twelve thousand francs?—by your poems?"

"No, I've given up poetry, except now and then to write a drinking song, some gay sonnet, or some innocent epigram; I make sermons, my friend."

"How! sermons? Do you preach them?"

"No; I sell them to those of my cloth who wish to become great orators."

"Ah, indeed! and you have not been tempted by the hopes of reputation yourself?"

"I should, my dear d'Artagnan, have been so, but fate said 'No.' When I am in the pulpit, if by chance a pretty woman looks at me, I look at her again; if she smiles, I smile also. Then I speak at random; instead of preaching about the torments of hell, I talk of the joys of paradise. An event took place in the Church of Saint Louis au Marais. A gentleman laughed in my face. I stopped short to tell him that he was a fool; the congregation went out to get stones to stone me with; but whilst they were away, I found means to conciliate the priests who were present, so that my foe was pelted instead of me. 'Tis true that he came the next morning to my house, thinking that he had to do with an abbé—like all other abbés."

"And what was the end of the affair?"

"We met in the Place Royale—Egad you know about it."

"Was I not your second?" cried d'Artagnan.

"You were—you know how I settled that matter!"

"Was he killed?"

"I don't know. But, at all events, I gave him absolution *in articulo mortis.* 'Tis enough to kill the body, without killing the soul."

A long silence ensued after this disclosure. Aramis was the first to break it.

"What are you thinking about, d'Artagnan?" he began.

"I was thinking, my good friend, that when you were a musketeer you turned your thoughts incessantly to the Church, and now that you are an abbé you are perpetually longing to be a musketeer."

"'Tis true," said Aramis; "man, as you know, is a strange animal, made up of contradictions. Since I became an abbé I dream of nothing but battles. I practise shooting all day long, with an excellent master whom we have here."

"How! here?"

"Yes, in this convent—we have always a 'master-at-arms' in a convent of Jesuits."

"Then you would have killed the Prince de Marsillac if he had attacked you singly?"

"Certainly," replied Aramis, "with the greatest of ease."

"Well, dear Aramis, you ask me why I have been searching for you. I sought you, in order to offer you a way of killing Monsieur de Marsillac whenever you please—prince though he may be. Are you ambitious?"

"As ambitious as Alexander."

"Well, my friend, I bring you the means of being rich, powerful, and free, if you wish. Have you, my dear Aramis, thought sometimes of those happy days of our youth that we passed laughing, and drinking, and fighting each other for play?"

"Certainly; and more than once regretted them. It was a happy time."

"Well, these happy days may return; I am commissioned to find my companions, and I began by you—who were the very soul of our society."

Aramis bowed more from respect than pleasure at the compliment.

"To meddle in politics," he exclaimed, in a languid voice, leaning back in his easy-chair. "Ah! dear d'Artagnan! see how regularly I live— and how agreeable it is here. We have experienced the ingratitude of 'the great,' as you know."

"'Tis true," replied d'Artagnan. "Yet the great sometimes repent of their ingratitude."

"In that case, it would be quite another thing. Come! let's be merciful to every sinner; besides, you are right in another respect, which is, in thinking that if we were to interfere with politics there could not be a better time than this."

"How can you know that? You would never interest yourself in politics?"

"Ah! without caring about them myself, I live among those who are much occupied in them. Poet as I am, I am intimate with Sarazin, who is devoted to the Prince de Conti, and with Monsieur de Bois-Robert, who, since the death of Cardinal Richelieu, is of all or any party, so that political discussions have not altogether been uninteresting to me."

"I have no doubt of it," said d'Artagnan.

"Now, my dear friend, don't look upon all I tell you as simply the statement of a monk—but of a man who resembles an echo—repeating that which he hears. I understand that Mazarin is, at this very moment, extremely uneasy as to the state of affairs; that his orders are not respected like those of our former bugbear, the deceased Cardinal, whose portrait you see here;—for whatever may be thought of him, it must be allowed that Richelieu was a great man."

"I shall not contradict you there," said d'Artagnan.

"My first impressions were favourable to the minister; but, as I am very ignorant of those sort of things, and as the humility which I profess induces me not to rest on my own judgment, but to ask the opinion of others, I have inquired—Eh?—my friend——"

Aramis paused.

"Well?—what?" asked d'Artagnan.

"Well—I must mortify myself. I must confess that I was mistaken: Monsieur de Mazarin is not a man of genius, as I thought: he is a man of no origin—once a servant of Cardinal Bentivoglio, and he got on by intrigue. He is an upstart, a man of no name, who will only be the tool of a party in France. He will amass wealth, he will injure the king's revenue, and pay to himself that which Richelieu paid to others. He is neither a gentleman in manner nor in feeling, but a sort of buffoon, a punchinello, a pantaloon. Do you know him?—I do not?"

"Hem!" said d'Artagnan, "there is some truth in what you say,—but you speak of him, not of his party, nor of his resources."

"It is true—the queen is for him."

"Something in his favour."

"But he will never have the king."

"A mere child."

"A child who will be of age in four years. Then he has neither the parliament nor the people with him—they represent the wealth of the country; nor the nobles, nor the princes—who are the military power of France; but perhaps I am wrong in speaking thus to you, who have evidently a leaning to Mazarin."

"I!" cried d'Artagnan, "not in the least."

"You spoke of a mission."

"Did I?—I was wrong then—no, I said what you say—there is a crisis at hand. Well! let's fly the feather before the wind, let us join with that side to which the wind will carry it, and resume our adventurous life. We were once four valiant knights—four hearts fondly united; let us unite again, not our hearts, which have never been severed, but our courage and our fortunes. Here's a good opportunity for getting somewhat better than a diamond."

"You are right, d'Artagnan; I held a similar project, but, as I have not your fruitful and vigorous imagination, the idea was suggested to me. Every one nowadays wants auxiliaries; propositions have been made to me, and I confess to you truthfully, that the Coadjutor has made me speak out."

"The Prince de Conti! the Cardinal's enemy?"

"No!—the king's friend."

"But the king is with Mazarin."

"He is, but unwillingly—in appearance, not in heart; and that is exactly the snare that the king's enemies prepare for a poor child."

"Ah! but this is, indeed, civil war which you propose to me, dear Aramis."

"War for the king."

"Yet the king will be at the head of the army on Mazarin's side."

"But his heart will be in the army commanded by the Duc de Beaufort."

"Monsieur de Beaufort? He is at Vincennes."

"Did I name Monsieur de Beaufort?" said Aramis.

"Monsieur de Beaufort or some one else. The prince, perhaps. But Monsieur de Conti is going to be made a Cardinal."

"Are there not warlike Cardinals?" said Aramis.

"Do you see any great advantage in adhering to this party?" asked d'Artagnan.

"I foresee in it the aid of powerful princes."

"With the hate of the government."

"Counteracted by parliament and insurrections."

"That may be done, if they can separate the king from his mother."

"That is possible," said Aramis.

"Never!" cried d'Artagnan. "You, Aramis, know Anne of Austria better than I do. Do you think she will ever forget that her son is her safeguard, her shield, the pledge for her dignity, for her fortune, for her life? Should she forsake Mazarin she must join her son, and go over to the prince's side; but you know better than I do that there are certain reasons why she can never abandon Mazarin."

"Perhaps you are right," said Aramis thoughtfully; "therefore I shall not pledge myself."

"To them, or to us, do you mean, Aramis?"

"To no one."

"I am a priest," resumed Aramis. "What have I to do with politics? I am not obliged to read any breviary. I have a little circle of holy abbés and pretty women; everything goes on smoothly; so certainly, dear friend, I shall not interfere with politics."

"Well, listen, my dear Aramis," said d'Artagnan; "your philosophy convinces me, on my honour. I don't know what devil of an insect stung me, and made me ambitious. I have a post by which I live; at the death of Monsieur de Treville, who is old, I may be a captain, which is a very good position for a poor Gascon. Instead of running after adventures, I shall accept an invitation from Porthos; I shall go and shoot on his estate. You know he has estates,—Porthos?"

"Yes, indeed. Ten leagues of wood, marsh land, and valleys; he is lord of the hill and the plain, and is now carrying on a suit for his feudal rights against the bishop of Noyon!"

"Good," thought d'Artagnan. "That's what I wanted to know. Porthos is in Picardy!"

Then aloud—

"And he has taken his ancient name of Valon?"

"To which he adds that of Bracieux—an estate which has been a barony, by my truth."

"So that Porthos will be a baron."

"I don't doubt it. The 'Baroness Porthos' will be particularly charming."

And the two friends laughed.

"So," d'Artagnan resumed, "you will not become a partisan of Mazarin's."

"Nor you of the Prince de Condé?"

"No, lovers belong to no party, but remain friends; let us be neither Cardinalists nor Frondists."

"*Adieu*, then." And d'Artagnan poured out a glass of wine.

"To old times," he said.

"Yes," answered Aramis. "Unhappily those times are passed."

"Nonsense! They will return," said d'Artagnan. "At all events, if you want me, remember the Rue Tiquetonne, Hôtel de la Chevrette."

"And I shall be at the convent of Jesuits, from six in the morning to eight at night; come by the door. From eight in the evening until six in the morning come in by the window. Go then, my friend," he added, "follow your career; Fortune smiles on you; do not let her fly from you. As for me, I remain in my humility and my indolence. *Adieu*!"

"Thus 'tis quite decided," said d'Artagnan, "that what I have to offer you is not to your taste?"

"On the contrary, it would be so were I like any other man," rejoined Aramis; "but, I repeat, I am made up of contradictions. What I hate to-day, I adore to-morrow, and vice versa. You see that I cannot, like you for instance, settle on any fixed plan."

"Thou liest, subtle one," said d'Artagnan to himself. "Thou

alone, on the contrary, knowest how to choose thy object, and to
gain it stealthily."

The friends embraced. They descended into the plain by the
ladder. Planchet met them close by the shed. D'Artagnan jumped
on his saddle, then the old companions in arms once more shook
hands. D'Artagnan and Planchet spurred on their horses and took
the road to Paris.

But after he had gone about two hundred steps, d'Artagnan
stopped short, alighted, threw the bridle of his horse over the arm
of Planchet, and took the pistols from his saddle-bow and fastened
them to his girdle.

"What's the matter?" asked Planchet.

"This is the matter; be he ever so cunning, he shall never say
that I was his dupe. Stand here, don't stir, turn your back to the
road and wait for me."

Having thus spoken, d'Artagnan cleared the ditch by the roadside, and crossed the plain so as to wind round the village. He had
observed between the house that Madame de Longueville inhabited and the convent of Jesuits, an open space surrounded by
a hedge.

The moon had now risen, and he could see well enough to
retrace his road.

He reached the hedge, and hid himself behind it; in passing by
the house where the scene which we have related took place, he
remarked that the window was again lighted up, and he was sure
that Aramis had not yet returned to his own apartment, and that
when he did return there, it would not be alone.

In truth, in a few minutes he heard steps approaching, and low
whispers.

Close to the hedge the steps stopped.

D'Artagnan knelt down near the thickest part of the hedge.

Two men—to the astonishment of d'Artagnan—appeared
shortly: soon, however, his surprise vanished, for he heard the
murmurs of a soft, harmonious voice; one of these two men was a
woman disguised as a cavalier.

"Be not afraid, dear Réné," said the soft voice, "the same thing
shall never happen again. I have discovered a kind of subterranean passage which lies under the street, and we shall only
have to raise one of the marble slabs before the door to open you
an entrance and an outlet."

"Oh!" answered another voice, which d'Artagnan soon recognised as that of Aramis. "I swear to you, princess, that your
reputation does not depend on precautions, and that I would risk
my life rather than——"

"Yes, yes! I know you are brave and venturesome as any man in the world, but you do not belong to me alone; you belong to all our party. Be prudent! be careful!"

"I always obey, madam, when I am commanded by so gentle a voice."

He kissed her hand tenderly.

"Ah!" exclaimed the owner of the soft voice.

"What's the matter?" said Aramis.

"Do you not see that the wind has blown off my hat?"

Aramis rushed after the fugitive hat. D'Artagnan took advantage of the circumstance to find a place in the hedge not so thick, where his glance could penetrate to the supposed cavalier. At that instant, the moon, inquisitive, perhaps, like d'Artagnan, came from behind a cloud, and by the light d'Artagnan recognised the large blue eyes, the golden hair, and the classic head of the Duchesse de Longueville.

Aramis returned, laughing; one hat on his head, and the other in his hand; and he and his companion resumed their walk towards the convent.

"Good!" said d'Artagnan, getting up and brushing his knees; "now I have you; you are a Frondeur, and the lover of Madame de Longueville."

10

M. PORTHOS DU VALON DE BRACIEUX DE PIERREFONDS

THANKS to the information Aramis had given him, d'Artagnan, who knew already that Porthos called himself du Valon, was now aware that he styled himself, from his estate, de Bracieux; and that he was, on account of his estate, engaged in a lawsuit with the bishop of Noyon.

At eight o'clock in the evening, he and Planchet again left the hotel of Chevrette, quitting Paris by the Porte Saint Denis.

Their route lay through Daumartin—and then, taking one of two roads that branched off—to Compiègne, when it was necessary to inquire the situation of the estate of Bracieux.

They travelled always at night; and having learned at Villars-Cotterets that Porthos was at the property which he had lately bought, called Pierrefonds, they set out, taking the road which leads from Villars-Cotterets to Compiègne.

It was a beautiful morning; and in this early springtime the birds sang on the trees, and the sunbeams shone through the misty glades, like curtains of golden gauze.

In other parts of the forest the light could scarcely penetrate through the foliage; and the stems of two old oak-trees—the refuge of the squirrel, startled by the travellers—were in deep shadow.

There came up from all nature in the dawn of day a perfume of herbs, flowers, and leaves, which delighted the heart. D'Artagnan, tired of the closeness of Paris, thought that when a man had three names of his different estates joined one to another, he ought to be very happy in such a paradise; then he shook his head, saying, "If I were Porthos, and d'Artagnan came to make to me such a proposition as I am going to offer him, I know what I should say to it."

As to Planchet, he thought of nothing.

At the extremity of the wood d'Artagnan perceived the road which had been described to him; and at the end of the road he saw the towers of an immense feudal castle.

"Oh, oh!" he said, "I fancied this castle belonged to the ancient branch of Orléans. Can Porthos have negotiated for it with the Duc de Longueville?"

"Faith!" exclaimed Planchet, "here's land in fine condition; if it belongs to Monsieur Porthos, I shall wish him joy."

"Zounds!" cried d'Artagnan, "don't call him Porthos, nor even Valon: call him de Bracieux or de Pierrefonds; thou wilt damage my mission otherwise."

As he approached the castle, which had first attracted his eye, d'Artagnan was convinced that it could not be there that his friend dwelt: the towers, though solid, as if built yesterday, were open and broken. One might have fancied that some giant had cloven them with blows from a hatchet.

On arriving at the extremity of the castle, d'Artagnan found himself overlooking a beautiful valley, in which, near a charming little lake, stood several scattered houses, which, humble in their aspect, and covered, some with tiles and others with thatch, seemed to acknowledge as their sovereign lord a pretty château, built about the beginning of the reign of Henry the Great, and surmounted by some stately weathercocks. D'Artagnan felt now no doubt of this being the dwelling of Porthos.

The road led straight up to this château, which, compared to its ancestor on the hill, was exactly what a fop of the coterie of the Duc d'Enghien would have been beside a knight in steel armour in the time of Charles VI. D'Artagnan spurred his horse on and pursued his road, followed by Planchet at an equal pace.

In a few minutes d'Artagnan reached the end of an alley regularly planted with fine poplars, and terminating in an iron gate, the points and crossed bars of which were gilded. In the midst of this avenue was a personage dressed in green, and with as much gilding about him as the iron gate, riding on a tall horse. On his right hand and his left were two footmen, with the seams of their dresses laced. A considerable number of peasants were assembled, and rendered homage to their lord.

"Ah!" said d'Artagnan to himself, "can this be the Seigneur du Valon de Bracieux de Pierrefonds? Well-a-day! how he is wrinkled since he has given up the name of Porthos!"

"This cannot be Monsieur Porthos," observed Planchet, replying, as it were, to his master's thoughts. "Monsieur Porthos was six feet high; this man is scarcely five."

"Nevertheless," said d'Artagnan, "the people are bowing extremely low to this person."

As he spoke he rode towards the tall horse—to the man of importance and his valets. As he approached he seemed to recognise the features of this individual.

"Jesu!" cried Planchet, "can it be he?"

At this exclamation the horseman turned slowly, and with a lofty air; and the two travellers could see, displayed in all their brilliancy, the large eyes, the vermilion visage, and the eloquent smile of Mousqueton.

It was, indeed, Mousqueton—Mousqueton, as fat as a pig, rolling about with rude health, puffed out with good living, who, recognising d'Artagnan, and acting very differently from the hypocrite Bazin, slipped off his horse and approached the officer with his hat off: so that the homage of the assembled crowd was turned towards this new sun, which eclipsed the former luminary.

"Monsieur d'Artagnan! Monsieur d'Artagnan!" cried Mousqueton, his fat cheeks swelling out, and his whole frame perspiring with delight. "Monsieur d'Artagnan! oh! what joy for my lord and master du Valon de Bracieux de Pierrefonds!"

"Thou good Mousqueton! where is thy master?"

"You are on his domains, sir."

"But how handsome thou art—how fat! how thou hast prospered and grown stout!" and d'Artagnan could not restrain his astonishment at the change which good fortune had produced upon the once famished one.

"Ah, yes, thank God, I am pretty well," said Mousqueton.

"But dost thou say nothing to thy friend Planchet?"

"How? my friend Planchet? Planchet, art thou there?" cried Mousqueton, with open arms and eyes full of tears.

"My very self," replied Planchet; "but I wanted first to see if thou wert grown proud."

"Proud towards so old a friend? never, Planchet! thou would'st not have thought thus hadst thou known Mousqueton well."

"So far so well," answered Planchet, alighting, and extending his arms to Mousqueton, and the two servants embraced with an emotion which was touching to those present, and made them suppose that Planchet was a great lord in disguise, so greatly did they estimate the position of Mousqueton.

"And now, sir," resumed Mousqueton, when he had rid himself of Planchet, who had vainly endeavoured to join his hands behind his friend's back, "now, sir, allow me to leave you, for I could not allow my master to hear of your arrival from any one but myself; he would never forgive me for not having preceded you."

"My dear friend, then," said d'Artagnan, carefully avoiding to utter either the former name borne by Porthos, or his new one, "has not forgotten me?"

"Forgotten! he!" cried Mousqueton; "there's not a day, sir, that we don't expect to hear that you were made marshal, either instead of Monsieur de Gassion or of Monsieur de Bassompierre."

On d'Artagnan's lips there played one of those rare and melancholy smiles which seemed to come from the depth of his heart; the last trace of youth and happiness which had survived disappointment.

"And you—fellows," resumed Mousqueton, "remain near Monsieur le Comte d'Artagnan, and pay him all the attention in your power, whilst I go to prepare my lord for his visit."

And mounting his horse, Mousqueton rode off down the avenue, on the grass, in an easy gallop.

"Ah! there!—there's something promising," said d'Artagnan. "No mysteries, no cloak to hide oneself in—no cunning policy here; people laugh outright, they weep for joy here. I see nothing but happy faces; in short, it seems to me that Nature herself wears a holiday suit, and that the trees, instead of leaves and flowers, are covered with red and green ribbons, as on gala days."

"As for me," said Planchet, "I seem to smell from this place even a most enjoyable smell of roast meat, and to see the scullions in a row by the hedge, hailing our approach. Ah! sir, what a cook must Monsieur Pierrefonds have, when he was so fond of eating and drinking, even whilst he was only called Monsieur Porthos!"

"Say no more!" cried d'Artagnan. "If the reality corresponds with appearances, I'm lost; for a man so well off will never change his happy condition;—and I shall fail with him, as I have already done with Aramis."

II

HOW D'ARTAGNAN, DURING HIS VISIT TO PORTHOS, SEES THAT WEALTH IS NOT PRODUCTIVE OF HAPPINESS

D'ARTAGNAN passed through the iron gate, and arrived in front of the château. He alighted,—as he saw a species of giant on the steps. Let us do justice to d'Artagnan; that, independent of all selfish wishes, his heart palpitated with joy when he saw that tall form and martial demeanour, which recalled to him a good and brave man.

He ran to Porthos and threw himself into his arms; the whole body of servants, arranged in a circle at a respectful distance, looked on with humble curiosity. Mousqueton, at the head of them, wiped his eyes. Porthos put his arm in that of his friend.

"Ah! how delightful to see you again, dear friend," he cried, in a voice which was now changed from a baritone into a bass; "you've not then forgotten me?"

"Forgotten you, oh! dear du Valon, does one forget the happiest days of one's youth—one's dearest friends—the dangers we have shared together? on the contrary, there is not an hour that we have passed together that is not present to my memory."

"Yes, yes," said Porthos, trying to give to his moustache a curl which it had lost in his retirement.

"Yes, we did some fine things in our time, and we gave that poor Cardinal some thread to unravel."

And he heaved a sigh.

"Under any circumstance," he resumed, "you are welcome, my dear friend; you will help me to recover my spirits; to-morrow we will hunt the hare on my plain, which is a superb tract of land, or we'll pursue the deer in my woods, which are magnificent. I have four harriers, which are considered the swiftest in our county, and a pack of hounds which are unequalled for twenty leagues round."

And Porthos heaved another sigh.

"But first," interposed d'Artagnan, "you must present me to Madame du Valon."

A third sigh from Porthos.

"I lost Madame du Valon two years ago," he said, "and you find me still in affliction on that account. That was the reason why I left my Château du Valon, near Corbeil, and came to my estate, Bracieux. Poor Madame du Valon! her temper was uncertain, but she came at last to accustom herself to my ways and to understand my little wishes."

"So, you are free now—and rich?"

"Alas!" replied Porthos, "I am a widower, and have forty thousand francs a year. Let us go to breakfast."

"I shall be glad to do so; the morning air has given me an appetite."

"Yes," said Porthos, "my air is excellent."

They entered the château; there was nothing but gilding, high and low; the cornices were gilt, the mouldings were gilt, the legs and arms of the chairs were gilt. A table, ready set out, awaited them.

"You see," said Porthos, "this is my usual style."

"Devil take me!" answered d'Artagnan, "I wish you joy of it. The king has nothing like this."

"No," answered Porthos; "I hear it said that he is very badly fed by the Cardinal, Monsieur de Mazarin. Taste this cutlet, my dear d'Artagnan; 'tis from one of my sheep."

"You have very tender mutton, and I congratulate you upon it," said d'Artagnan.

"Yes, the sheep are fed in my meadows, which are excellent pasture."

"Give me another cutlet."

"No, taste this hare, which I had killed yesterday in one of my warrens."

"Zounds! what a flavour!" cried d'Artagnan; "ah! they are fed on thyme only, your hares."

"And what do you think of my wine?" asked Porthos, "it is pleasant, isn't it?"

"Capital."

"It's simply a wine of the country—nothing more."

"Really."

"Yes, a small declivity to the south, yonder, on my hill, gives me twenty hogsheads."

"Quite a vineyard, eh?"

Porthos sighed for the fifth time—d'Artagnan had counted his sighs. He was curious to solve the problem.

"Well, now," he said, "it seems, my dear friend, that something vexes you; you are not well, perhaps? That health, which——"

"Excellent, my dear friend; better than ever. I could kill an ox with a blow of my fist."

"Well, then, family affairs, perhaps?"

"Family! I have, happily, only myself in the world to care for."

"But what makes you sigh?"

"My dear fellow," replied Porthos; "to be frank with you, I am not happy."

"You are not happy, Porthos? You, who have a château, meadows, hills, woods—you who have forty thousand francs a year—you not happy."

"My dear friend, all those things I have, but I am alone in the midst of them."

"Surrounded, I suppose, only by peasantry, with whom you could not associate."

Porthos changed colour, and drank off a large glass of wine.

"No; but just think, there are paltry country squires who have all some title or another, and pretend to go back as far as Charlemagne, or at least to Hugh Capet. When I first came here, being the last comer, it was to me to make the first advances. I made them, but, you know, my dear friend, Madame du Valon——"

Porthos, in pronouncing these words, seemed to gulp down something.

"Madame du Valon was of doubtful gentility. She had in her first marriage (I don't think, d'Artagnan, I am telling you anything new) married a lawyer; they thought that 'nauseous'; you can understand that's a word bad enough to make one kill thirty thousand men. I have killed two, which has made people hold their tongues, but has not made me their friend. So that I have no society—I live alone: I am sick of it—my mind preys on itself."

D'Artagnan smiled. He now saw where the breastplate was weak, and prepared the blow.

"But now," he said, "that you are a widower, your wife's connections cannot injure you."

"Yes, but understand me; not being of a race of historic fame, like the de Coucy's, who were content to be plain sirs, or the Rohans, who didn't wish to be dukes, all these people, who are all either viscounts or counts, go before me in all the church ceremonies, and I can say nothing to them. Ah! if I were merely a——"

"A baron, don't you mean?" cried d'Artagnan, completing his friend's sentence.

"Ah!" cried Porthos; "would I were but a baron!"

"Well, my friend, I am come to give you this very title, which you desire so much."

Porthos gave a jump which quite shook the room, two or three bottles fell and were broken. Mousqueton ran thither, hearing the noise.

Porthos motioned to Mousqueton to pick up the bottles.

"I am glad to see," said d'Artagnan, "that you have still that honest lad with you."

"He's my steward," replied Porthos; "he will never leave me. Go away now, Mouston."

"So he's called Mouston," thought d'Artagnan; "'tis too long a word to pronounce, Mousqueton."

"Well," he said aloud, "let us resume our conversation later— your people may suspect something—there may be spies about. You can suppose, Porthos, what I have to say relates to important matters."

"Devil take them, let us walk in the park," answered Porthos, "for the sake of digestion."

"Egad," said d'Artagnan, "the park is like everything else, and there are as many fish in your pond as rabbits in your warren; you're a happy man, my friend, since you have retained your love of the chase, and acquired that of fishing."

"My friend," replied Porthos, "I leave fishing to Mousqueton —it is a vulgar pleasure; but oftentimes I shoot, that is to say, when I am dull, and I sit on one of those marble seats, have my gun brought to me, my favourite dog, and I shoot rabbits."

"Really, how very amusing!"

"Yes," replied Porthos with a sigh; "it *is* very amusing!"

D'Artagnan now no longer counted the sighs.

"However, what had you to say to me," he resumed, "let us return to that subject."

"With pleasure," replied d'Artagnan; "I must, however, first frankly tell you that you must change your mode of living."

"How?"

"Go into harness again, gird on your sword, run after adventures, and leave, as in old times, a little of your fat on the roadside."

"Ah! dash it!" said Porthos.

"I see you are spoiled, dear friend, you are fat, your arm has no longer that movement of which the late Cardinal's guards had so many proofs."

"Ah! my fist is strong enough, I swear," cried Porthos, extending a hand like a shoulder of mutton.

"So much the better."

"Are we then to go to war?"

"By my troth, yes."

"Against whom?"

"Are you a politician, my friend?"

"Not in the least."

"Are you for Mazarin, or for the princes?"

"I am for myself."

"That is to say you are for us. Well, I tell you that I come to you from the Cardinal."

This speech was heard by Porthos in the same sense as if it had still been in the year 1640, and related to Richelieu.

"Ho! ho! what are the wishes of his Eminence?"

"He wishes for you to enter his service. Rochefort has spoken of you—and since, the queen—and, to inspire us with confidence, she has even placed in Mazarin's hands that famous diamond— you know about it—that I had sold to Monsieur des Essarts, and of which I don't know how she regained possession."

"But it seems to me," said Porthos, "that she would have done much better to give it back to you."

"So I think," replied d'Artagnan: "but kings and queens are strange beings, and have curious fancies; nevertheless, since it is they who have riches and honours, one is devoted to them."

"Yes, one is devoted to them," repeated Porthos; "and you, to whom are you devoted, now?"

"To the king, the queen, and to the Cardinal; moreover, I have answered for your devotion also; for notwithstanding your forty thousand francs a year, and, perhaps, even for the very reason that you have forty thousand francs a year, it seems to me that a little coronet would look well on your carriage, eh?"

"Yes, indeed," said Porthos.

"Well, my dear friend, win it—it is at the point of our swords. We shall not interfere with each other—your object is a title; mine, money. If I can get enough to rebuild Artagnan, which my ancestors impoverished by the Crusades, allowed to fall into ruins, and to buy thirty acres of land about it, it is all I wish. I shall retire, and die tranquilly there."

"For my part," said Porthos, "I wish to be made a baron."

"You shall be one."

"And have you not seen any of our other friends?"

"Yes; I have seen Aramis."

"And what does he wish? To be a bishop?"

"Aramis," answered d'Artagnan, who had no wish to deceive Porthos, "Aramis, fancy! has become a monk and a Jesuit, and lives like a bear. My offers could not rouse him."

"So much the worse! He was a clever man—and Athos?"

"I have not yet seen him. Do you know where I shall find him?"

"Near Blois. He is called Bragelonne. Only imagine, my dear friend. Athos, who was of as high birth as an emperor, and who inherits one estate which gives him the title of Comte, what is he to do with all those dignities—Comte de la Fère, Comte de Bragelonne?"

"And has he no children with all these titles?"

"Ah!" said Porthos, "I have heard that he had adopted a young man who greatly resembles him."

"What, Athos? Our Athos, who was as virtuous as Scipio? Have you seen him?"

"No."

"Well, I shall see him to-morrow, and tell him about you; but I am afraid, between ourselves, that his liking for wine has aged and debased him."

"Yes, he used to drink a good deal," replied Porthos.

"And then he was older than any of us," added d'Artagnan.

"A few years only. His gravity made him appear older."

"Well, then, if we can get Athos, all will be well. If we cannot we shall have to do without him. We two are worth a dozen."

"Yes," said Porthos, smiling at the remembrance to his former exploits; "but we four, altogether, would be equal to thirty-six; more especially as you say the work will not be easy. Will it last long?"

"By'r lady—two or three years, perhaps."

"So much the better," cried Porthos. "You have no idea, my friend, how my bones ache since I came here. Sometimes, on a Sunday, I take a ride in the fields, and on the property of my neighbours, in order to pick up some nice little quarrel, which I am really in want of, but nothing happens. Either they respect or they fear me, which is most likely; but they let me trample down the clover with my dogs, insult and obstruct every one, and I come back still more weary and low-spirited—that's all. At any rate, tell me—there's more chance of fighting at Paris, is there not?"

"In that respect, my dear friend, it's delightful. No more edicts, no more of the Cardinal's guards, no more De Jussac's, nor other bloodhounds. I'Gad! beneath a lamp, in an inn, anywhere, they ask, 'Are you one of the Fronde?' They unsheathe, and that's all that is said. The Duke de Guise killed Monsieur de Coligny in the Place Royale, and nothing was said of it."

"Ah, things go on well, then," said Porthos.

"Besides which, in a short time," continued d'Artagnan, "we shall have set battles, cannonades, conflagrations, in great variety."

"Well, then, I decide."

"I have your word, then?"

"Yes, 'tis given. I shall fight heart and soul for Mazarin; but——"

"But!"

"But he must make me a baron."

"Zounds!" said d'Artagnan, "that's settled already. I answer for your barony."

On this promise being given, Porthos, who had never doubted his friend's assurance, turned back with him towards the castle.

12

IN WHICH IT IS SHOWN THAT THOUGH PORTHOS WAS
DISCONTENTED WITH HIS CONDITION, MOUSQUETON
WAS PERFECTLY SATISFIED

As he returned to the château, and while Porthos was dreaming of his barony, d'Artagnan thought of the miseries of poor human nature, always dissatisfied with what it has, always desirous of what it has not.

In the position of Porthos, d'Artagnan would have been completely happy; and, to make Porthos contented, there was short—what?—five letters to put before his three names, and a little coronet to paint upon the panels of his carriage!

"I shall pass all my life," thought d'Artagnan, "in seeking for a man who is really contented with his lot."

Whilst making this reflection, chance seemed, as it were, to give him the lie direct. When Porthos had left him, he saw Mousqueton approaching. The face of the steward, despite one slight shade of care, light as a summer cloud, seemed one of perfect felicity.

"Here is what I am looking for," thought d'Artagnan; "but alas! the poor fellow does not know the purpose for which I am here."

He then made a sign for Mousqueton to come to him.

"Sir," said the servant, "I have a favour to ask you."

"Speak out, my friend."

"I do not care to do so. Perhaps you will think, sir, that prosperity has spoiled me?"

"Art thou happy, friend?" asked d'Artagnan.

"Yes, I think so; and yet, sir, you may make me even happier than I am."

"Well, speak, if it depends on me."

"Oh, sir! it depends on you only."

"I listen: I am waiting to hear."

"Sir, the favour I have to ask of you is, not to call me 'Mousqueton,' but 'Mouston.' Since I have had the honour of being my lord's steward, I have taken the last name as more dignified, and calculated to make my inferiors respect me. You, sir, know how necessary subordination is in an establishment of servants."

D'Artagnan smiled. Porthos lengthened out his names—Mousqueton shortened his.

"Well, my dear Mouston," he said, "rest satisfied. I will call thee Mouston; and if it will make thee happy I will not address you as a lackey any longer."

"Oh," cried Mousqueton, colouring with joy; "if you do me, sir, such an honour, I shall be grateful all my life—'tis too much to ask."

D'Artagnan was secretly touched with remorse. He did not regret inducing Porthos to enter into schemes in which his life and fortune would be in jeopardy—for Porthos, the title of baron was his object and reward. But poor Mousqueton, whose only wish was to be called Mouston—was it not cruel to snatch him from the delightful state of peace and contentment in which he was?

He was thinking on these matters when Porthos summoned him to dinner.

Whilst dessert was on the table the steward came in to consult his master upon the proceedings of the next day, and also with regard to the shooting party which had been proposed.

"Tell me, Mouston," said Porthos—"are my arms in good condition?"

"Your arms, my lord—what arms?"

"Zounds!—my weapons."

"What weapons?"

"My military weapons."

"Yes, my lord—I think so."

"Make sure of it; and if they want it, have them rubbed up. Which is my best cavalry horse?"

"Vulcan."

"And the best hack?"

"Bayard."

"What horse wouldst thou choose for thyself?"

"I like Rustand, my lord; a good animal, whose pace suits me."

"Strong, think'st thou?"

"Half Norman, half Mecklenburger—will go day and night."

"That will do for us. See to those horses. Clean up, or get some one else to clean my arms. Then take pistols with thee, and a hunting-knive."

"Are we then going to travel, my lord?" asked Mousqueton, somewhat uneasy.

"Something better still, Mouston."

"An expedition, sir?" asked the steward, whose roses began to change into lilies.

"We are to return to the service, Mouston," replied Porthos, still trying to restore his moustache to the military curl that it had lost.

"Into the service—the king's service?" Mousqueton trembled; even his fat smooth cheeks shook as he spoke, and he looked at d'Artagnan with an air of reproach; he staggered, and his voice was almost choked.

"Yes and no. We shall serve in a campaign, search for all sorts of adventures; in short, return to our former life."

These last words fell on Mousqueton like a thunderbolt. It was these former days which made the present so delightful; and the blow was so great that he rushed out, overcome, and forgot to shut the door.

The two friends remained alone to speak of the future, and to build castles in the air. The good wine which Mousqueton had placed before them gave to d'Artagnan a perspective shining with quadruples and pistoles, and showed to Porthos a blue ribbon and a ducal mantle; they were, in fact, asleep on the table when the servants came to beg them to go to bed.

Mousqueton was, however, a little consoled by d'Artagnan, who the next day told him that in all probability war would always be carried on in the heart of Paris, and within reach of the Château du Valon, which was near Corbeil; of Bracieux, which was near Melun; and of Pierrefonds, which was between Compiègne and Villars-Cotterets.

"But—formerly—it appears," began Mousqueton timidly.

"Oh," said d'Artagnan, "we don't now make war as we did formerly. To-day it's a sort of diplomatic arrangement; ask Planchet."

Mousqueton inquired, therefore, the state of the case of his old friend, who confirmed the statement of d'Artagnan. "But," he added, "in this war prisoners stand a chance of being hung."

"Oh, do they?" said Mousqueton; "I think I should like the siege of Rochelle better than this war then!"

Porthos, meantime, asked d'Artagnan to instruct him how to proceed on his journey.

"Four days," replied his friend, "are necessary to reach Blois; one day to rest there; three or four days to return to Paris. Set out, therefore, in a week, with your suite, and go to the Hôtel de la Chevrette, Rue Tiquetonne, and wait for me there."

"That's agreed," said Porthos.

"As to myself, I shall go round to see Athos; for though I don't rely so much upon his aid, one must, with one's friends, observe all due politeness," said d'Artagnan.

The friends then took leave of each other on the very border of the estate of Pierrefonds, to which Porthos escorted his friend.

"At least," thought d'Artagnan, as he took the road to Villars-Cotterets, "at least I shall not be alone in my undertaking. That devil, Porthos, is a man of immense strength; still, if Athos joins us, well—we shall be three of us to laugh at Aramis—that vain fellow, with his good luck."

At Villars-Cotterets he wrote to the Cardinal:—

"MY LORD,

"I have already one man to offer to your Eminence, and he is well worth twenty men. I am just journeying to Blois. The Comte de la Fère inhabits the castle of Bragelonne, in the suburbs of that city."

And thereupon he took the road to Blois, chatting as he rode with Planchet, whose company was a great relief to him during this journey.

13

TWO ANGELIC FACES

THEY had a long ride before them, but the horses upon which d'Artagnan and Planchet rode had been refreshed in the well-supplied stables of the Lord of Bracieux; the master and servant rode side by side, conversing as they went, for d'Artagnan had, by degrees, thrown off the master, and Planchet had entirely ceased to assume the manners of a servant. He had been raised by circumstances to the rank of a confidant to his master. It was many years since d'Artagnan had opened his heart to any one; it happened, however, that these two men, on meeting again, assimilated perfectly. Planchet was, in truth, no vulgar companion in these new adventures; he was a man of good sense. Without seeking danger, he never shrank from an attack; he was a soldier in every sense, and arms ennoble a man; and it was on the firm footing of friendship that d'Artagnan and Planchet arrived in the neighbourhood of Blois.

Going along, d'Artagnan shook his head, and said:

"I know that going to Athos is useless; but I owe this step to my old friend, a man who had in him materials for the most noble and generous of characters."

"Oh, Monsieur Athos was a noble gentleman," said Planchet, "was he not? Scattering money about him as Heaven scatters hail. Do you remember, sir, that duel with the Englishman in the enclosure Des Carmes? Ah! how lofty, how magnificent Monsieur Athos was that day, when he said to his antagonist, 'You have insisted on knowing my name, sir; so much the worse for you, since I shall be obliged to kill you.' I was near him, those were his exact words. And I saw the glance of his eye when he stabbed his foe, as he said he would, and his adversary fell without saying, Oh! Ah, monsieur, he was a noble gentleman—Monsieur Athos."

"Yes, true as gospel," said d'Artagnan, "but one single fault has swallowed up all these fine qualities."

"I remember well," said Planchet; "he was fond of drinking. In truth he drank, but not as other men did. One seemed, as he raised the wine to his lips, to hear him say, 'Come, juice of the grape, and chase away my sorrows.' And how he used to break the stem of a glass, or the neck of a bottle! There was no one like him for that."

"And now," replied d'Artagnan, "behold the sad spectacle that awaits us. This noble gentleman, with his lofty glance, this handsome cavalier, so brilliant in feats of arms, that every one was surprised that he held in his hand a sword only instead of a baton of command! Alas! we shall find him changed into a bent-down old man, with red nose, and eyes that water; we shall find him extended on some lawn, whence he will look at us with a languid eye, and, perhaps, not recognise us. God knows, Planchet, that I should flee from such a sad sight, if I did not wish to show my respect for the illustrious shadow of what was once the Comte de la Fère, whom we loved so much."

Planchet shook his head and held his peace.

"And then," resumed d'Artagnan, "to this decrepitude is probably added poverty; for he must have neglected the little that he had, and the dirty scoundrel, Grimaud, more taciturn than ever, and still more drunken than his master—stay, Planchet, all this breaks my heart to think of."

"I fancy myself there, and that I see him staggering and hear him muttering," said Planchet, in a piteous tone, "but at all events, we shall soon know the real state of things, for I think those lofty walls, reddened by the setting sun, are those of Blois."

"Probably; and yon steeples, pointed and sculptured, that we catch a glimpse of yonder, are like what I have heard described of Chambord."

Just then, one of those heavy wagons, drawn by bullocks, which carry the wood cut in the fine forests of the country to the ports of the Loire, came out of a by-road full of ruts, and turned into that which the two horsemen were following. A man carrying a long switch with a spike at the end of it, with which he urged on the beasts, was walking with the team.

"Ho! friend," cried Planchet.

"What's your pleasure, gentlemen?" replied the peasant, with a purity of accent peculiar to the people of that district, and which might well have put to shame the polished dwellers near the Sorbonne and the Rue de l'Université.

"We are seeking the house of Monsieur de la Fère," said d'Artagnan.

The peasant took off his hat on hearing this revered name.

"Gentlemen," he said, "the wood that I am carting is his; I cut it in his copse, and I am taking it to the château."

D'Artagnan determined not to question this man; he did not wish to hear from another what he had himself said to Planchet.

"The château," he said to himself; "what château? Ah, I understand: Athos is not a man to be thwarted; he has obliged his peasantry, as Porthos has done his, to call him 'my lord,' and to call his paltry place a château. He had a heavy hand—that dear Athos—after drinking."

D'Artagnan, after asking the man the right way, continued his route, agitated, in spite of himself, at the thought of seeing once more that singular man whom he had so truly loved, and who had contributed so much by his advice and example to his education as a gentleman. He slackened the pace of his horse, and went on, his head drooping, thinking deeply.

Soon as the road turned, the Château de la Vallière appeared in view, then, a quarter of a mile farther, a white house, encircled in sycamores, was visible at the farther end of a group of trees, which spring had powdered with a snow of flowers.

On beholding this house, d'Artagnan, calm as he was in general, felt a deep agitation troubling his heart—so powerful during the whole course of his life were the remembrances of his youth. He proceeded, nevertheless, and came opposite to an iron gate, ornamented in the taste which marked the works of that period.

Through the gate were seen kitchen-gardens, carefully attended to, a spacious courtyard, in which were several horses held by valets in various liveries, and a carriage drawn by two horses of the district.

"We are mistaken," said d'Artagnan; "this cannot be the house of Athos. Good heavens! suppose he is dead, and that this property now belongs to some one who bears his name. Alight, Planchet, and inquire, for I confess my heart fails me."

Planchet alighted.

"Thou must add," said d'Artagnan, "that a gentleman who is passing by wishes to have the honour of paying his respects to the Comte de la Fère, and if thou art satisfied with what thou hearest, then announce my name!"

Planchet obeyed these instructions. An old servant opened the door and took in the message which d'Artagnan had ordered Planchet to deliver, in case that his servant was satisfied that this was the Comte de la Fère whom they sought.

Whilst Planchet was standing on the steps before the house he heard a voice say:

"Well, where is this gentleman, and why do they not bring him here?"

This voice—the sound of which reached d'Artagnan—re-awakened in his heart a thousand sentiments, a thousand recollections that he had forgotten. He hastily sprang from his horse, while Planchet, with a smile on his lips, was advancing towards the master of the house.

"But I know him—I know the lad yonder," said Athos, appearing on the threshold.

"Oh, yes—Monsieur le Comte, you know me, and I know you. I am Planchet—Planchet, whom you know well." But the honest servant could say no more, so much was he overcome by this unexpected interview.

"What, Planchet, is Monsieur d'Artagnan here?"

"Here I am, my friend, dear Athos!" cried d'Artagnan, in a faltering voice, and almost staggering from excitement.

At these words a visible emotion was expressed on the beautiful countenance and calm features of Athos. He rushed towards d'Artagnan, with his eyes fixed upon him, and clasped him in his arms. D'Artagnan, equally moved, pressed him also closely to him, while tears stood in his eyes. Athos then took him by the hand and led him into the drawing-room, where there were several people. Every one rose.

"I have the honour to present to you," he said, "Monsieur le Chevalier d'Artagnan, lieutenant of his Majesty's musketeers, a devoted friend, and one of the most excellent and brave gentlemen that I have ever known."

D'Artagnan received the compliments of those who were present in his own way; and whilst the conversation became general, he looked long and earnestly at Athos.

Strange! Athos was scarcely aged at all! His fine eyes, no longer surrounded by that dark line which nights of dissipation draw round them, seemed larger and more liquid than before. His face, a little elongated, had gained in calm dignity what it had lost in feverish excitement. His hand, always wonderfully beautiful and strong, was set off by a ruffle of lace, like certain hands by Titian and Vandyck. He was less stiff than formerly. His long dark hair, scattered here and there with grey locks, fell elegantly over his shoulders with a wavy curl; his voice was still youthful, as if at only twenty-five years old; and his magnificent teeth, which he had preserved white and sound, gave an indescribable charm to his smile.

Meanwhile, the guests, observing that the two friends were longing to be alone, prepared to depart, when a noise of dogs barking resounded through the courtyard, and many persons said, at the same moment:

"Ah! 'tis Raoul who has arrived home."

Athos, as the name of Raoul was pronounced, looked inquiringly at d'Artagnan, in order to see if any curiosity was depicted on his face. But d'Artagnan was still in confusion, and turned round almost mechanically, when a fine youth of fifteen years of age, dressed simply, but in perfect taste, entered the room, raising, as he came, his hat, adorned with a long plume of red feathers.

Nevertheless, d'Artagnan was struck by the appearance of this new personage. It seemed to explain to him the change in Athos; a resemblance between the boy and the man explained the mystery of this regenerated existence. He remained listening and gazing.

"Here you are, home again, Raoul," said the Comte.

"Yes, sir," replied the youth with deep respect, "and I have performed the commissions you gave me."

"But what's the matter, Raoul?" said Athos. "You are pale and agitated."

"Sir," answered the young man; "it is on account of an accident which has happened to our little neighbour."

"To Mademoiselle de la Vallière?" asked Athos quickly.

"What is it?" asked some of the persons present.

"She was walking with her nurse Madeline, in the place where the woodmen cut the wood, when, passing on horseback, I stopped. She saw me also, and in trying to jump from the end of a pile of wood on which she had mounted, the poor child fell, and lay still, unable to rise again. She has, I fear, sprained her ankle."

"Oh, heavens!" cried Athos. "And her mother, Madame de Saint-Remy, has she been informed of it?"

"No, sir; Madame de Saint-Remy is at Blois, with the Duchess of Orléans. I am afraid that what was first done was unskilful and useless. I am come, sir, to ask your advice."

"Send directly to Blois, Raoul; or rather take your horse, and ride there yourself."

Raoul bowed.

"But where is Louisa?" asked the Comte.

"I have brought her here, sir, and I have deposited her in the charge of Charlotte, who, till better advice comes, has put the foot into iced water."

The guests now all took leave of Athos, excepting the old Duke de Barbé, who, as an old friend of the family of La Vallière, went to see little Louisa, and offered to take her to Blois in his carriage.

"You are right, sir," said Athos. "She will be better with her mother. As for you, Raoul, I am sure that you are to blame; some giddiness or folly on your part."

"No, sir, I assure you," murmured Raoul, "it is not."

"Oh, no, no, I declare it is not!" cried the young girl, while Raoul turned pale at the idea of his being, perhaps, the cause of her disaster.

"Nevertheless, Raoul, you must go to Blois, and you must make your excuses and mine to Madame de Saint-Remy."

The youth looked pleased. He again took in his strong arms the little girl, whose pretty golden head and smiling face rested on his shoulder, and placed her gently in the carriage; then, jumping on his horse with the elegance and agility of a first-rate esquire, after bowing to Athos and d'Artagnan, he went off close by the door of the carriage, in the inside of which his eyes were incessantly fixed.

14

AT THE CASTLE OF BRAGELONNE

D'ARTAGNAN had remained during all this scene with a bewildered look. He had found things so completely different from what he had anticipated that he was almost stupid with astonishment.

Athos, who had been observing him, and guessing his thoughts, took his arm, and led him into the garden.

"Whilst supper is being prepared," he said, smiling, "you will not, my friend, be sorry to have the mystery which so puzzles you cleared up."

"True, Monsieur le Comte," replied d'Artagnan, who felt that by degrees Athos was resuming that great influence which he had formerly exercised over him.

Athos smiled.

"First and foremost, dear d'Artagnan, in this place, we have no such title as Count. When I call you 'chevalier,' it is in presenting you to my guests, that they may know who you are. But to you, d'Artagnan, I am, I hope, still dear Athos, your comrade, your friend. Do you intend to be ceremonious because you are less attached to me than you were?"

"Oh! God forbid!"

"Then let us be as we used to be; let us be open to each other. You are astonished at what you see here?"

"Extremely."

"But above all things, I am a marvel to you?"

"Yes, that is so."

"I am still young, am I not? Should you not have known me again, in spite of my eight-and-forty years of age?"

"On the contrary, I do not think you the same person at all."

"Ah, I understand," cried Athos, with a slight blush. "Everything, d'Artagnan, even folly, has its limit."

"Then your means, it appears, are improved; you have a capital house, you own, I presume? You have a park, horses, servants."

Athos smiled.

"Yes; I inherited this little property when I quitted the army, as I told you. The park is twenty acres—twenty, comprising kitchen gardens and a meadow. I have two horses—I don't count my servant's short-tailed nag. My sporting dogs consist of two pointers, two harriers, and two setters. But then all this extravagance is not for myself," added Athos, laughing.

"Yes, I see, for our youthful friend, Raoul," replied d'Artagnan.

"In that you are correct; this youth is an orphan, deserted by his mother, who left him in the house of a poor country priest. I have brought him up. It is he who has caused the change you see in me: I was dried up like a miserable tree, isolated, attached to nothing on earth; it was only a deep affection which could make me take root again, and bind me to life. This child has caused me to recover what I had lost. I had no longer any desire to live for myself. I have lived for him. I have corrected the vices that I had. I have assumed the virtues that I had not. Precept is much, example is more. I may be mistaken, but I believe that Raoul will be as accomplished a gentleman as our degenerate age could display."

The remembrance of Lady de Winter recurred to d'Artagnan.

"And you are happy?" he said to his friend.

"As happy as it is allowed to one of God's creatures to be on this earth; but express all your thoughts, d'Artagnan, for you have not yet done so."

"You are too bad, Athos; one can hide nothing from you," answered d'Artagnan. "I wished to ask you if you ever feel any emotions resembling——"

"Remorse! I finish your phrase—yes and no. I do not feel remorse, because that woman, I believe, deserved her punishment. I do not feel remorse, because, had we permitted her to live, she would have persisted in her work of destruction. But I do not mean, my friend, that we were right in what we did. Perhaps all blood that is shed demands an expiation. Hers has been accomplished; it remains, possibly, for us to accomplish ours."

"I have sometimes thought as you do, Athos."

"She had a son, that unhappy woman?"

"Yes."

"Have you heard of him?"

"Never."

"He must be about twenty-three years of age," said Athos, in a low tone. "I often think of that young man, d'Artagnan."

"Strange! for I had forgotten him," said the lieutenant.

Athos smiled—the smile was melancholy.

"And Lord de Winter—do you know anything about him?"

"I know that he is in high favour with Charles I."

"The fortunes of that monarch are now at a low ebb. He shed

the blood of Strafford: that confirms what I said just now—blood
will have blood: and the queen?"

"Henrietta of England is at the Louvre?"

"Yes, and I hear in great poverty. Her daughter, during the
bitterest cold, was obliged, for want of fire, to remain in bed. Why
did she not ask from any one of us a home instead of from Mazarin?
She should have wanted for nothing."

"Have you ever seen the Queen of England?" inquired
d'Artagnan.

"No, but my mother saw her, when she was little. Did I ever
tell you that my mother was maid of honour to Marie de Medici?"

"Never. You do not talk of such things, Athos."

"Oh yes, I did," replied Athos; "but only on suitable occasions."

"Porthos was not as reserved," replied d'Artagnan, with a smile.

"Every one according to his nature, my dear d'Artagnan.
Porthos has excellent qualities, in spite of his vanity. Have you
seen him?"

"I left him only five days ago," said d'Artagnan.

And then, with all the vivacity of his Gascon humour, he
described the splendours of Porthos in his château of Pierrefonds;
not forgetting, whilst slightly caricaturing his friend, to launch a
few arrows in the direction of the worthy Mouston.

"I often wonder," replied Athos, smiling with that gaiety which
recalled former days, "that we formed, by chance, a society of
men, still so closely bound together, notwithstanding a separation
of twenty years. Friendship strikes its roots deep in honest hearts,
d'Artagnan; it is only the worthless that deny the existence of
friendship. They are incapable of feeling its power. And Aramis?"

"I have seen him likewise," said d'Artagnan, "but he appears
cold."

"Ah! you have seen Aramis?" replied Athos, fixing his searching eyes upon d'Artagnan. "Why, as the poets say, this is a real
pilgrimage to the temple of friendship you are making."

"Something like it," said d'Artagnan, a little embarrassed.

"Aramis, you know," continued Athos, "is naturally cold: and
then he is always entangled in some intrigue with women."

"I fancy he is at this moment engaged in a very complicated
one."

Athos made no reply.

"He is not at all curious," thought d'Artagnan.

Athos not only made no reply, but he changed the conversation.

"You see," said he, causing d'Artagnan to observe that they
had returned to the château in an hour's walk, "we have nearly
made the tour of my dominions."

"Everything is charming," replied d'Artagnan; "and above all, everything savours of the gentleman."

At that moment the steps of a horse were heard.

"There is Raoul returned," said Athos; "we shall learn how it fares with the poor little girl."

In fact, the young man appeared at the gate, and entered the court, covered with dust. Springing from his horse, which he placed in the care of a sort of groom, he saluted the count and d'Artagnan with respectful politeness.

"This gentleman," said Athos, placing his hand upon the shoulder of d'Artagnan, "is the Chevalier d'Artagnan, of whom you have heard me speak so often, Raoul."

"Sir," said the young man, bowing again and more profoundly, "the count has mentioned your name whenever he wished to cite the example of a noble and intrepid gentleman."

This little compliment did not fail to touch d'Artagnan. He stretched out his hand to Raoul, saying:

"My young friend, all the praises bestowed on me must revert to the count, who trained me in all things; and it is not his fault if his pupil has not profited by his instructions. But he will be more successful in you, I am sure. I like your bearing, Raoul; and your politeness has given me great pleasure."

This interchange of good feeling rather than of compliments delighted Athos more than he could express. He looked at d'Artagnan with gratitude, and then bestowed upon Raoul one of those strange smiles of which children are so proud when they can catch them.

"Now," said d'Artagnan to himself, whom this silent play of countenance had not escaped; "now I am certain!"

"Well!" said Athos, "I hope the accident has had no ill consequences?"

"They don't yet know, sir, on account of the swelling; but the doctor is afraid that some muscle may be injured."

At this moment a nicely dressed page-boy came to announce supper.

Athos led his guest into a dining-room of moderate size, the windows of which opened on one side on a garden—on the other on a hothouse, full of beautiful flowers.

D'Artagnan glanced at the dinner-service. The plate was magnificent, old, and belonging to the family. D'Artagnan stopped to look at a sideboard, on which was a superb ewer of silver.

"That is splendid workmanship," he exclaimed.

"Yes, a chef-d'œuvre of the great Florentine sculptor, Benvenuto Cellini," replied Athos.

"What battle does it represent?"

"That of Marignan, where one of my forefathers is offering his sword to Francis the First, who had broken his. It was then that my ancestor, Emguerrand de la Fère, was made a knight of the Order of St. Michael; besides which the king, fifteen years afterwards, gave him this ewer, and a sword which you may have seen formerly in my house, also this beautiful specimen of workmanship. Men were giants in those times," said Athos; "now we are pigmies in comparison. Let us sit down to supper. Call Charles," he added, addressing the boy who waited.

"My good Charles, I particularly recommend to your care Planchet, the lacquey of Monsieur d'Artagnan. He likes good wine, and you have the key of the cellar. He has slept a long time on a hard bed, so he won't object to a soft one—take care of him, I beg of you." Charles bowed and retired.

"You think of everything," said d'Artagnan; "and I thank you for Planchet, my dear Athos."

Raoul started on hearing this name, and looked at his adopted father to be quite sure that it was he whom the lieutenant thus addressed.

"That name sounds strange to you," said Athos, smiling; "it was my 'nom de guerre,' when Monsieur d'Artagnan, two other gallant friends, and myself performed some feats of arms at the siege of La Rochelle, under the deceased Cardinal and Monsieur de Bassompierre. My friend is still so kind as to address me by that old and dear appellation, which makes my heart glad when I hear it."

"'Tis an illustrious name," said the lieutenant, "and had one day triumphal honours paid to it."

"What do you mean, sir?" inquired Raoul.

"You have not forgotten Saint Gervais, Athos, and the napkin which was converted into a banner;" and he then related to Raoul the story of the bastion, and Raoul thought he was listening to one of those deeds of arms belonging to days of chivalry, and recounted by Tasso and Ariosto.

"D'Artagnan does not tell you, Raoul," said Athos, in his turn, "that he was reckoned one of the finest swordsmen of his time— a knuckle of iron, a wrist of steel, a sure eye, and a glance of fire —that's what his adversaries met with from him. He was eighteen, only three years older than you are, Raoul, when I saw him at this work—pitted against well-tried men."

"And was Monsieur d'Artagnan the conqueror?" said the young man, with glistening eyes.

"I killed one man, I believe," replied d'Artagnan, with a look

of inquiry directed to Athos; "another I disarmed, or wounded.
I don't remember which——"

"Wounded," said Athos; "oh! you were strong."

The young man would willingly have prolonged this conversation, but Athos pointed out to him that his guest needed repose. D'Artagnan would fain have declared that he was not fatigued; but Athos insisted on his retiring to his chamber, conducted thither by Raoul.

15

ATHOS'S DIPLOMACY

D'ARTAGNAN went to bed, not to sleep, but to think over all that he had heard that night. As he was good-hearted, and had once had for Athos a liking, which had grown into a sincere friendship, he was delighted at thus meeting a man of high intelligence and of great moral strength, instead of a weak and debased drunkard. He admitted, without annoyance, the continued superiority of Athos over himself, devoid as he was of that jealousy which might have saddened a less generous disposition: he was delighted also that the high qualities of Athos appeared to promise favourably for his mission. Nevertheless, it seemed to him that Athos was not, in all respects, sincere and frank. Who was the youth whom he had adopted, and who bore so great a resemblance to him? What could explain Athos's having re-entered the world, and the extreme sobriety which he had observed at table? The absence of Grimaud, whose name had never once been uttered by Athos, gave d'Artagnan a feeling of uneasiness. It was evident either that he no longer possessed the confidence of his friend, or that Athos was bound by some invisible chain, or that he had been forewarned of the lieutenant's visit.

He could not help thinking of M. Rochefort, whom he had seen in Notre Dame;—could de Rochefort have preceded him to Athos? Again, the moderate fortune which Athos possessed, concealed, as it was, so skilfully, seemed to show a regard for appearances, and to betray a latent ambition, which might be easily aroused. The clear and vigorous intellect of Athos would render him more open to conviction than a less able man would be. He would enter into the schemes of the Cardinal with the more ardour, because his natural activity would be doubled by a dose of necessity.

Resolving to seek an explanation on all these points on the following day, d'Artagnan, in spite of his fatigue, prepared for an attack, and determined that it should take place after breakfast. He determined to cultivate the goodwill of the youth Raoul, and, either whilst fencing with him, or in shooting, to extract from his simplicity some information which would connect the Athos of old times with the Athos of the present. But d'Artagnan, at the same time, being a man of extreme caution, was quite aware what injury he should do himself, if, by any indiscretion or awkwardness, he should betray his manœuvring to the experienced eye of Athos. Besides, whilst d'Artagnan was quite disposed to adopt a subtle course against the cunning of Aramis, or the vanity of Porthos, he was ashamed to equivocate with Athos, the true-hearted, open Athos. It seemed to him that if Porthos and Aramis deemed him superior to them in the arts of diplomacy, they would like him all the better for it, but that Athos, on the contrary, would despise him.

"Ah! why is not Grimaud, the taciturn Grimaud, here?" thought d'Artagnan; "there are things which his silence would have shown me—his silence was eloquence!"

There was now perfect quietude in the house. D'Artagnan had heard the doors shut, and the shutters barred; then the dogs became, in their turn, silent. At last a nightingale, lost in a thicket of shrubs, had dropped off in the midst of its most melodious cadences, and fallen asleep. Not a single sound was heard in the castle, except that of a footstep, up and down in the chamber above—as he supposed, the bedroom of Athos.

"He is walking about, and thinking," thought d'Artagnan, "but of what? It is not possible to know; anything else might be guessed, but not that."

At length, apparently, Athos went to bed, for the noise ceased.

Silence, and fatigue together, overcame d'Artagnan, and sleep overtook him also. He was not, however, a sound sleeper. Scarcely had dawn gilded his window-curtains, than he sprang from his bed, and opened the windows. Somebody, he perceived, was in the courtyard, but moving stealthily. True to his custom of never passing anything over that it was within his power to know, d'Artagnan looked out of the window, and perceived the close red coat and brown hair of Raoul.

The young man was opening the door of the stable. He then, with noiseless haste, took out the horse that he had ridden on the previous evening, saddled and bridled it, and led the animal into the alley to the right of the kitchen-garden, opened a side-door which conducted him to a bridle-road, shut it after him, and d'Artagnan saw him pass by like a dart, bending, as he went, beneath pendant flowery branches of the maple-trees and acacias. The road, as d'Artagnan had observed, was that to Blois.

"So!" thought the Gascon, "here's a young blade who has already his love affair, who doesn't at all agree with Athos in his hatred to the fair sex. He's not going to hunt, for he has neither dogs nor arms; he's not going on a message, for he goes secretly. Why does he go in secret? Is he afraid of me, or of his father? for I am sure that Athos is his father. By Jove! I shall know about that soon, for I shall speak out to Athos."

Day was now advanced: all the noises that had ceased the night before were reawakened, one after the other. The birds in the branches, the dog in his kennel, the sheep in the field, the boats which were moored in the Loire, even, seemed to be animated, and, leaving the shore, to abandon themselves to the current of the stream. The Gascon gave a last twist to his moustache, a last turn to his hair, brushed, from habit, the brim of his hat with the sleeve of his doublet, and went downstairs. Scarcely had he descended the last step of the threshold than he saw Athos, bent down towards the ground, as if he were reaching for a crown-piece in the dust.

"Good-morning, my dear host," cried d'Artagnan.

"Good-day to you; I trust you have slept well?"

"Excellently well, Athos; but what are you looking for? you are, perhaps, a tulip fancier?"

"My dear friend, if I were, you should not laugh at me for being so. In the country, people change; one gets to like, without knowing it, all those beautiful objects that God causes to spring from the bottom of the earth, and which are despised in cities. I was looking anxiously for some iris roots which I planted here, close to this reservoir, and which some one has trampled upon this morning. These servants are the most careless people in the world: in bringing the horse out of the water, they've allowed him to walk over the border."

D'Artagnan smiled.

"Ah! you think so, do you?"

And he took his friend along the alley, where a number of tracks, like those which had trampled down the flower-beds, were visible.

"Here are the horse's hoofs again, it seems, Athos," he said carelessly.

"Yes, indeed; the impression is recent."

"Quite so," replied the lieutenant.

"Who went out this morning?" Athos asked uneasily. "Has any horse got loose from the stable?"

"Not likely," answered the Gascon; "these marks are regular."

"Where is Raoul?" asked Athos; "how is it that I have not seen him?"

"Hush!" exclaimed d'Artagnan, putting his finger on his lips; and he related what he had seen, watching Athos all the while.

"Ah! he's gone to Blois; the poor boy——"

"For what purpose?"

"Ah! to inquire after little La Vallière; she has sprained her foot, you know."

"You think he is?"

"I am sure of it," answered Athos; "don't you see that Raoul is in love?"

"Indeed! with whom? with a child of seven years old?"

"Dear friend, at Raoul's age the heart is so ardent that it must expand towards some object or another, fancied or real; well, his love is half one—half the other. She is the prettiest little creature in the world, with flaxen hair, blue eyes—at once saucy and languishing."

"But what say you to Raoul's fancy?"

"Nothing; I laugh at Raoul; but this first desire of his heart is imperious. I remember, just at his age, how in love I was with a Grecian statue, which our good king, then Henry IV., gave my father, insomuch that I was stricken with grief when they told me that the story of Pygmalion was simply a fable."

"'Tis want of occupation; you do not make Raoul work, so he takes his own way of employing himself."

"Exactly so: therefore I think of sending him away from this place."

"There would be much wisdom in that."

"No doubt of it; but his heart will be broken. So long as three or four years ago, he used to adorn and adore his little idol, whom he will some day fall in love with in good earnest, if he remains here. The parents of little La Vallière have for a long time perceived, and been amused at it; but now they begin to look grave concerning it."

"Nonsense! however, Raoul must be diverted from this fancy; send him away and you will make a man of him."

"I think I shall send him to Paris."

"So!" thought d'Artagnan; and it seemed to him that the moment for action had arrived.

"Suppose," he said, "we chalk out a career for this young man. I want to consult you about something."

"Do so."

"Do you think it is time to enter into the service?"

"But are you not still in the service? you—d'Artagnan?"

"I mean into active service. Our former life—has it still no attractions for you? should you not be happy to begin anew in my society, and in that of Porthos, the exploits of our youth?"

"Do you propose to me to do so, d'Artagnan?"

"Decidedly and honestly."

"On whose side?" asked Athos, fixing his clear benevolent glance on the countenance of the Gascon.

"Ah! devil take it, you speak in earnest——"

"And must have a definite answer. Listen, d'Artagnan. There is but one person, or rather one cause, to whom a man like me can be useful—that of the king."

"Exactly," answered the musketeer.

"Yes, but let us understand each other," returned Athos seriously. "If by the cause of the king you mean that of Cardinal Mazarin, we do *not* understand each other."

"I don't say, exactly," answered the Gascon, confused.

"Come, d'Artagnan, do not let us equivocate; your hesitation, your evasion, tell me at once on whose side you are; for that party no one dares openly to recruit, and when people recruit for it, it is with a downcast head and low voice."

"Ah! my dear Athos!"

"You know that I am not alluding to you; you are the pearl of brave and bold men. I speak of that spiteful and intriguing Italian —of the pedant who has attempted to put on his own head a crown which he stole from under a pillow, of the scoundrel who calls his party the party of the king, who wants to send the princes of the blood to prison, not daring to kill them, as our great Cardinal— our Cardinal did—of the miser who weighs his gold pieces, and keeps the clipped ones for fear, though he is rich, of losing them at play next morning, of the impudent fellow who insults the queen, as they say, so much the worse for her, and who is going, in three months, to make war upon us, in order that he may retain his pensions. Is that the master whom you propose to me? Thanks, d'Artagnan."

"You are more impetuous than you were," replied d'Artagnan. "Age has warmed, not chilled, your blood. Who told you that that was the master I proposed to you? Devil take it," he muttered to himself, "let me not betray my secrets to a man not inclined to receive them well."

"Well, then," said Athos, "what are your schemes? what do you propose?"

"Zounds! nothing can be more natural; you live on your estate, happy in your golden mediocrity. Porthos has, perhaps, sixty thousand francs income. Aramis has always fifty duchesses who are quarrelling for the priest, as they quarrelled formerly for the musketeer; but I—what have I in the world? I have worn my cuirass for these twenty years, kept down in this inferior rank, without going forward or backward, without living. In fact, I am dead. Well! when there is some idea of being resuscitated—you say he's a scoundrel—an impudent fellow—a miser—a bad master! By Jove! I'm of your opinion; but find me a better one, or give me the means of living."

Athos was, for a few minutes, thoughtful.

"Good! d'Artagnan is for Mazarin," he said to himself.

From that moment he became very guarded.

And on his side d'Artagnan was more cautious also.

"You spoke of Porthos," Athos resumed; "have you persuaded him to seek his fortune? but he has wealth, I believe, already?"

"Doubtless he has; but such is man, that satisfaction to him is unknown."

"What does Porthos wish for?"

"To be a baron."

"Ah! true! I forgot," said Athos, laughing.

"'Tis true!" thought the Gascon, "where has he heard it? Does he correspond with Aramis? Ah! if I knew that he did, I should know all."

The conversation was interrupted by the entrance of Raoul.

"Is our little neighbour worse?" asked Athos, seeing a troubled look on the face of the youth.

"Ah, sir!" replied Raoul, "her fall is a very serious one; and without any apparent injury, the physician fears that she will be lame for life."

"That is terrible," said Athos.

"And what makes me wretched, sir, is that I am the cause of this misfortune."

"There's but one remedy, dear Raoul—that is, to marry her as a compensation," remarked d'Artagnan.

"Ah, sir!" answered Raoul, "you joke about a real misfortune; that is cruel, indeed."

The good understanding between the two friends was not in the least altered by the morning's skirmish. They breakfasted with a good appetite, looking now and then at poor Raoul, who, with moist eyes and a full heart, scarcely ate at all.

After breakfast two letters arrived for Athos, who read them with deep attention; whilst d'Artagnan could not restrain himself from jumping up several times, on seeing him read these epistles, in one of which, having a very strong sight, he perceived the fine writing of Aramis. The other was in a feminine hand, long and crossed.

"Come," said d'Artagnan to Raoul—seeing that Athos wished to be alone—"come, let us take a turn in the fencing-gallery, that will amuse you."

And they went into a low room, where there were foils, gloves, masks, breast-plates, and all the accessories for a fencing match.

In a quarter of an hour Athos joined them; and, at the same moment, Charles brought in a letter for d'Artagnan, which a messenger had just desired might be instantly delivered.

It was now the turn of Athos to take a sly look.

D'Artagnan read the letter with apparent calmness, and said, shaking his head:

"See, dear friend, what the army is; my faith, you are, indeed, right not to return to it. Monsieur de Tréville is ill—so my company can't do without me; there! my leave is at an end!"

"Do you go back to Paris?" asked Athos quietly.

"Egad! yes; but why don't you come there also?"

Athos coloured a little, and answered:

"Should I go, I shall be delighted to see you there."

"Hallo, Planchet!" cried the Gascon from the door, "we must set out at once; give the horses some hay."

Then turning to Athos:

"I seem to miss something here. I am really sorry to leave without having seen Grimaud."

"Grimaud!" replied Athos. "I'm surprised you have never asked after him. I have lent him to a friend——"

"Who will understand the signs he makes," returned d'Artagnan.

"I hope so."

The friends embraced cordially; d'Artagnan pressed Raoul's hand.

"Will you not come with me?" he said; "I shall pass by Blois."

Raoul turned towards Athos, who showed him by a secret sign that he did not wish him to go.

"*Adieu*, then, to both, my good friends," said d'Artagnan; "may God preserve you! as we used to say when we parted from each other in the late Cardinal's time."

Athos waved his hand, Raoul bowed, and d'Artagnan and Planchet set out.

The count followed them with his eyes—his hands resting on the shoulders of the youth, whose height was almost equal to his own; but, as soon as they were out of sight, he said:

"Raoul—to-night we set out for Paris."

"How!" cried the young man, turning pale.

"You may go and offer your adieux and mine to Madame de Saint-Remy. I shall wait for you here till seven."

The young man bent low, with an expression of sorrow and gratitude mingled, and retired.

As to d'Artagnan, scarcely, on his side, was he out of sight, than he drew from his pocket a letter, which he read over again.

"Return immediately to Paris.—T. M."

"The epistle is laconic," said d'Artagnan; "and if there had not been a postscript, probably I should not have understood it; but, happily, there is a postscript."

Then he read the postscript, which made him forget the abruptness of the letter.

"P.S. Go to the king's treasurer at Blois; tell him your name, show him this letter, and you will receive two hundred pistoles."

"Assuredly," said d'Artagnan; "I like this piece of prose, and the Cardinal writes better than I thought. Come, Planchet, let us pay a visit to the king's treasurer, and then set off."

"Towards Paris, your honour?"

"Towards Paris."

And they set off at full speed.

16

MONSIEUR DE BEAUFORT

WE must now relate the circumstances which had hastened the return of d'Artagnan to Paris:—

One evening when Mazarin went to visit the queen, in passing the guard-chamber he heard the sound of loud talking. Wishing to know on what subject the soldiers were conversing, he approached, with his wonted stealthy and catlike step, pushed the door open slightly, and put his head close to the chink.

There was a dispute among the guards.

"I tell you," one of them was saying, "that if Coysel predicted that, 'tis as good as true; I know nothing about it, but I've heard say that he's not only an astrologer, but a magician."

"Deuce take it, friend, if he's one of thy friends, thou wilt ruin him in saying so."

"Why?"

"Because he may be tried for it."

"Ah, absurd! they don't burn sorcerers nowadays."

"No? 'Tis not a long time since the late Cardinal burnt Urban Grandier though."

"My friend, Urban Grandier wasn't a sorcerer; he was a learned man. He didn't predict the future; he knew the past—often a much worse thing."

Mazarin nodded an assent; but wishing to know what the prediction was about which they disputed, he remained in the same place.

"I don't say," resumed the guard, "that Coysel is not a sorcerer; but I say that if his prophecy gets wind, it's a sure way to prevent its coming true."

"How so?"

"Why, in this way—if Coysel says, loud enough for the Cardinal to hear him, on such or such a day such a prisoner will escape, 'tis plain that the Cardinal will take measures of precaution, and that the prisoner will not escape."

"Good Lord!" said another guard, who inclined lazily on a bench, but who had not lost a word of the conversation, "do you think that men can escape their destiny? If it is written yonder, in heaven, that the Duc de Beaufort is to escape, he will escape; and all the precautions of the Cardinal will not hinder it."

Mazarin started. He was an Italian, and therefore superstitious. He walked straight into the midst of the guards, who, on seeing him, were silent.

"What were you saying?" he asked, with his flattering manner, "that Monsieur de Beaufort had escaped—did you not?"

"Oh, no, my lord!" said the incredulous soldier. "He's well guarded now; we said, only, that he might escape."

"Who said so?"

"Repeat your story, Saint Laurent," replied the man, addressing the originator of the tale.

"My lord," said the guard, "I have simply mentioned the prophecy that I heard from a man named Coysel, who believes that be he ever so closely guarded, the Duc de Beaufort will escape before Whitsuntide."

"Coysel is a madman!" returned the Cardinal.

"No," replied the soldier, tenacious in his credulity; "he has foretold many things which have come to pass—for instance, that the queen would have a son; that Monsieur de Coligny would be killed in a duel with the Duc de Guise; and finally, that the Coadjutor would be made Cardinal. Well! the queen has not only one son, but two; then Monsieur de Coligny was killed, and——"

"Yes," said Mazarin; "but the Coadjutor is not yet made a Cardinal!"

"No, my lord—but he will be," answered the guard.

Mazarin made a grimace, as if he meant to say—"But he does not yet wear the coloured cap;" then he added:

"So, my friend, it's your opinion that Monsieur de Beaufort will escape?"

"That's my idea, my lord; and if your Eminence were to offer to make me at this moment governor of the castle of Vincennes, I should decline it. After Whitsuntide it would be a different thing."

There is nothing so convincing as a firm conviction. It has an effect upon the most incredulous; and, far from being incredulous, Mazarin was superstitious. He went away thoughtful and anxious and returned to his own room, where he summoned Bernouin, and desired him to fetch there the next morning the special guard whom he had placed near Monsieur de Beaufort, and to awaken him whenever he should arrive on the following morning.

The guard had, in fact, touched the Cardinal in his tenderest part. During the whole five years in which the Duc de Beaufort had been in prison, not a day had passed in which the Cardinal had not felt a secret dread of his escape. It was not possible, as he knew well, to confine for the whole of his life the grandson of Henry IV., especially when this young prince was scarcely thirty years of age. But, however and whensoever he did escape, what hatred he would cherish against him, the cause of his long imprisonment; who had taken him, rich, brave, glorious, beloved by women, feared by men, to cast off from his life its happiest years; for it is not life, it is merely existence, in prison. Meantime, Mazarin redoubled the surveillance over the duke. But, like the miser in the fable, he could not sleep near his treasure. Many times he awoke in the night, suddenly, dreaming that he had been robbed of Monsieur de Beaufort. Then he inquired about him, and had the vexation of hearing that the prisoner played, drank, sang—but that whilst playing, drinking, singing, he often stopped short, to vow that Mazarin should pay dear for all the amusements which he had forced him to enter into at Vincennes.

So much did this one idea haunt the Cardinal, even in his sleep, that when, at seven in the morning, Bernouin came and aroused him, his first words were:—"Well—what's the matter? Has Monsieur de Beaufort escaped from Vincennes?"

"I do not think so, my lord," said Bernouin; "but you will hear about him, for La Ramée is here, and awaits your Eminence's commands."

"Tell him to come in," said Mazarin, arranging his pillows, so that he might receive him sitting, in bed.

The officer entered—a big, stout man, with a good physiognomy. His air of perfect serenity made Mazarin uneasy.

"Approach, sir," said the Cardinal.

The officer obeyed.

"Do you know what they are saying here?"

"No, your Eminence."

"Well, they say that Monsieur de Beaufort is going to escape from Vincennes, if he has not done so already."

The officer's face expressed complete stupefaction. He opened at once his great eyes and his little mouth to inhale better the joke that his Eminence deigned to address him, and ended by a burst of laughter, so violent, that his limbs shook in his hilarity as they would have done in a fever.

"Escape! my lord—escape! Your Eminence is not then aware where Monsieur de Beaufort is confined?"

"Yes, I am, sir; in the keep at Vincennes."

"Yes, sir; in a room, the walls of which are seven feet thick, with grated windows, each bar being as thick as my arm."

"Sir," replied Mazarin, "with perseverance one may penetrate through a wall; with a watch-spring one may saw through iron bars."

"Then my lord has not been informed that there are eight guards about him; four in his chamber, four in the antechamber—and they never leave him."

"But he leaves the room to play at tennis at the Mall?"

"Sir, those amusements are allowed; but if your Eminence wishes it, we will discontinue the permission."

"No, no," cried Mazarin, fearing that should his prisoner ever leave his prison he would be the more exasperated against him, if he thus debarred his amusements,—he then asked with whom he played.

"My lord—either with the officers of the guard, with the other prisoners, or with me."

"Hum!" said the Cardinal, beginning to feel more comfortable.

"You mean to say then, my dear Monsieur la Ramée——"

"That unless Monsieur de Beaufort can contrive to metamorphose himself into a little bird, I answer for him."

"Take care—you assert a great deal," said Mazarin. "M. de Beaufort told the guards who took him to Vincennes that he had often thought what he should do in case he were put into prison, and that he had found out forty ways of escaping."

"My lord—if among these forty there had been one good way, he would have been out long ago."

"Come, come; not such a fool as I fancied!" thought Mazarin. "But when you leave him, for instance?"

"Oh! when I leave him! I have, in my stead, a bold fellow who aspires to be his majesty's special guard. I promise you, he keeps a good watch over the prisoner. During the three weeks that he has been with me, I have only had to reproach him with one thing—being too severe with the prisoners."

"And who is this Cerberus?"

"A certain Monsieur Grimaud, my lord."

"And what was he before he went to Vincennes?"

"He was in the country, as I was told by the person who recommended him."

"And who recommended this man to you?"

"The steward of the Duc de Grammont."

"He is not a gossip, I hope?"

"Lord-a-mercy, my lord! I thought for a long time that he was dumb; he answers only by signs. It seems his former master accustomed him to that. The fact is, I fancy he got into some trouble in the country from his stupidity, and that he wouldn't be sorry in the royal livery to find impunity."

"Well, dear Monsieur la Ramée," said the Cardinal, "let him prove a firm and faithful keeper, and we will close our eyes upon his rural misdeeds, and put on his back a uniform to make him respectable, and in the pockets of that uniform some pistoles to drink to the king's health."

Mazarin was large in the promises—quite different to the virtuous Grimaud, so much eulogised by La Ramée: for he said nothing, and did much.

It was now nine o'clock. The Cardinal, therefore, got up, perfumed himself, dressed, and went to the queen to acquaint her as to the cause of his detention. The queen, who was scarcely more afraid of Monsieur de Beaufort than she was of the Cardinal himself, and who was almost as superstitious as he was, made him repeat word for word all La Ramée's praises of his deputy. Then, when the Cardinal had ended:

"Alas! sir! why have we not a Grimaud near every prince?"

"Patience!" replied Mazarin, with a meaning smile; "that may happen one day; but in the meantime——"

"Well! in the meantime?"

"I shall take precautions."

Upon which he wrote to d'Artagnan to hasten his return.

17

HOW M. DE BEAUFORT AMUSED HIMSELF IN THE PRISON OF VINCENNES

THE prisoner, who gave such uneasiness to the Cardinal, and whose means of escape disturbed the repose of the whole court, was wholly unconscious of the terrors which he inspired in the Palais Royal.

He had found himself so strictly guarded, that he soon saw the fruitlessness of any attempt at escape. His vengeance, therefore, consisted in uttering curses on the head of Mazarin; he even tried to make some verses on him, but soon gave up the attempt. For Monsieur de Beaufort had not only not received from Heaven the gift of versifying, but he had even the greatest possible difficulty in expressing himself in prose.

The duke was the grandson of Henri Quatre and of Gabrielle d'Estrees—as good-natured, as brave, as proud, and, above all, as Gascon as his ancestor, but less educated. After having been for some time, after the death of Louis XIII., the favourite, the confidant, the first man, in fact, at the court, he had been compelled to yield his place to Mazarin, and to become the second in influence and favour; and, eventually, as he was stupid enough to be vexed at this change of position, the queen had had him arrested, and sent to Vincennes, in charge of Guitant, who made his appearance in these pages in the beginning of this history, and whom we shall see again. Be it understood, that when we say the queen, we mean Mazarin.

During the five years of his seclusion, which would have improved and matured the intellect of any other man, M. de Beaufort, had he not affected to brave the Cardinal, to despise princes, and to walk alone, without adherents or followers, would either have regained his liberty, or made partisans. But these considerations never occurred to the duke, and every day the Cardinal received fresh accounts of him, which were as unpleasant as possible to the minister.

After having failed in poetry, Monsieur de Beaufort tried drawing. He drew portraits with a piece of coal, of the Cardinal; and as his talents did not enable him to produce a very good likeness, he wrote under the picture, that there might be no doubt of the original—"Portrait of the Illustrious Coxcomb Mazarin."

Monsieur de Chavigny, the governor of Vincennes, waited upon the duke, to request that he would amuse himself in some other way, or, that, at all events, if he drew likenesses, he would not put mottoes to them. The next day the prisoner's room was full of pictures and of mottoes. Monsieur de Beaufort, in common with many other prisoners, was bent upon doing things which were prohibited; and the only resource which the governor had was, one day when the duke was playing at tennis, to efface all these drawings, consisting chiefly of profiles. M. de Beaufort did not venture to draw the Cardinal's fat face.

The duke thanked Monsieur de Chavigny for having, as he said, cleaned his drawing paper for him; he then divided the walls of his room into compartments, and dedicated each of these compartments to some incident in Mazarin's life. In one was depicted the "Illustrious Coxcomb" receiving a shower of blows from Cardinal Bentivoglio, whose servant he once was; another the "Illustrious Mazarin," acting the part of Ignatius Loyola in a comedy of that name; a third, the "Illustrious Mazarin" stealing the portfolio of prime minister from Monsieur de Chavigny, who had expected to have it; a fourth, the "Illustrious Coxcomb Mazarin" refusing to give La Porte, the young king's valet, clean sheets; and saying that it was quite enough for the king of France to have sheets every three months.

The governor, of course, thought fit to threaten his prisoner that if he did not give up sketching such pictures, he should be obliged to deprive him of all means of amusing himself in that manner. To this Monsieur de Beaufort replied, that since every opportunity of distinguishing himself in arms was taken from him, he wished to make himself celebrated in the fine arts; since he could not be a Bayard, he would become a Raphael, or a Michaelangelo. Nevertheless, one day when Monsieur de Beaufort was walking in the grounds, his fire was put out; his coal was taken away, and all means of drawing completely destroyed.

The duke swore, fell into a rage, shouted, and declared that they wished to starve him to death, as they had starved the Maréchal Ornano, and the Grand Prior of Vendôme; but he refused to promise that he would not make any more sketches, and remained without any fire in the room all the winter.

His next act was to purchase a dog from one of his keepers. With this animal, which he called Pistache, he was often shut up for hours alone, superintending, as every one supposed, its education.

At last, when Pistache was sufficiently well trained, Monsieur de Beaufort invited the governor and officers of Vincennes to attend a representation which he was going to have in his apartment.

The party assembled; the room was lighted with wax-lights, and the prisoner, with a bit of plaster he had taken out of the wall of his room, had traced a long white line, representing a cord, on the floor. Pistache, on a signal from his master, placed himself on this line, raised himself on his hind paws, and holding in his front paws a wand with which clothes used to be beaten, he began to dance upon the line with as many contortions as a rope-dancer. Having been several times up and down it, he gave the wand back to his master, and began, without hesitation, to perform the same revolutions over again.

The intelligent creature was received with loud applause.

The first part of the entertainment being finished, Pistache was desired to say what o'clock it was; he was shown Monsieur de Chavigny's watch; it was then half-past six. The dog raised and dropped his paw six times; the seventh he let it remain upraised. Nothing could be better done; a sundial could not have shown the hour with greater precision.

Then the question was put to him who was the best gaoler in all the prisons in France?

The dog performed three evolutions round the circle, and laid himself, with great respect, at the feet of Monsieur de Chavigny, who at first seemed inclined to like the joke, and laughed loud; but a frown soon succeeded, and he bit his lips with vexation.

Then the duke put to Pistache this difficult question: who was the most expert thief in the world?

Pistache went again the round of the circle, but stopped at no one; and, at last, went to the door, and began to scratch and bark.

"See, gentlemen," said the duke, "this wonderful animal, not finding here what is asked for, seeks it out of doors; you shall, however, have his answer. Pistache, my friend, come here. Is not the greatest thief in the field, Monsieur La Camus, who entered Paris with twenty francs in his pocket, and who now possesses six millions?"

The dog shook his head.

"Then is it not," resumed the duke, "the Superintendent Emery, who gave his son, when he was married, three hundred thousand francs and a house, compared to which the Tuileries are a heap of ruins and the Louvre a paltry building?"

The dog again shook his head, as if to say "no."

"Then," said the prisoner, "let's think who it can be. Can it be, can it possibly be, the illustrious coxcomb, Mazarin de Piscina, hey?"

Pistache made violent signs that it was, by raising and lowering his head eight or ten times successively.

"Gentlemen, you see," said the duke to those assembled, who dared not even smile, "that it is the 'illustrious coxcomb' who is the most expert thief in the world; at least, according to Pistache. Let us go on to another of his exercises."

"Gentlemen!"—there was a profound silence in the room when the duke again addressed them—"do you not remember that the Duc de Guise taught all the dogs in Paris to jump for Mademoiselle de Pons, whom he styled 'the fairest of the fair'? Pistache is going to show you how superior he is to all other dogs. Monsieur de Chavigny, be so good as to lend me your cane. Now Pistache, my dear, jump the height of this cane for Madame de Montbazon."

The dog found no difficulty in it, and jumped joyfully for Madame de Montbazon.

"But," interposed M. de Chavigny, "it seems to me that Pistache is only doing what other dogs have done when they jumped for Mademoiselle de Pons."

"Stay," said the duke; "Pistache, jump for the queen." And he raised the cane six inches higher.

The dog sprang, and in spite of the height, jumped lightly over it.

"And now," said the duke, raising it still six inches higher, "jump for the king."

The dog obeyed, and jumped successfully over the cane.

"Now, then," said the duke, and as he spoke, lowered the cane almost level with the ground; "Pistache, my friend, jump for the illustrious Cardinal, Mazarin de Piscina."

The dog turned his back to the cane.

"What," asked the duke, "what do you mean?" and he gave him the cane again, first making a semicircle from the head to the tail of Pistache. "Jump then, Pistache." But Pistache, as at first, turned round on his legs, and stood with his back to the cane.

Monsieur de Beaufort made the experiment a third time: but this time the dog rushed furiously on the cane and broke it with his teeth.

Monsieur de Beaufort took the pieces out of his mouth and presented them with great courtesy to Monsieur de Chavigny, saying that for that evening the entertainment was ended, but in three months it should be repeated, when Pistache would have learned some new tricks.

Three days afterwards Pistache was poisoned.

Then the duke said openly that his dog had been killed by a

drug with which they meant to poison him; and one day after dinner, he went to bed, calling out that he had pains in the stomach, and that Mazarin had poisoned him.

This fresh impertinence reached the ears of the Cardinal, and alarmed him much. The prison at Vincennes was considered very unhealthy, and Madame de Rambouillet had said that the room in which the Maréchal Ornano and the Grand Prior de Vendôme had died was worth its weight in arsenic—a jest which had great success. So the prisoner was henceforth to eat nothing that was not previously tasted, and La Ramée was, in consequence, placed near him as taster.

Every kind of indignity was heaped upon the duke by the governor, in return for the insults of the innocent Pistache. De Chavigny, who, according to report, was a son of Richelieu's, understood tyranny. He took from the duke all the steel knives and silver forks, and replaced them with silver knives and wooden forks, pretending that, as he had been informed that the duke was to pass the remainder of his life at Vincennes, he was afraid of his prisoner's attempting suicide. A fortnight afterwards the duke, going to the tennis court, found two rows of trees about the size of his little finger planted by the roadside; he inquired what they were for, and was told that they were to shade him from the sun on some future day. One morning the gardener went to him and told him, as if to please him, that he was going to plant a bed of asparagus for his use. Now, as every one knows, asparagus takes four years in arriving at perfection, this civility completely enraged Monsieur de Beaufort.

At last his patience was exhausted. He assembled his keepers and, notwithstanding his well-known difficulty of utterance, addressed them as follows:—

"Gentlemen! will you permit a grandson of Henry IV. to be overwhelmed with insults and ignominy? Odds fish! as my grand-father used to say, I once reigned in Paris; do you know that? The queen at that time liked me, and called me the most honest man in the kingdom. Gentlemen and citizens, set me free; I shall go to the Louvre and strangle Mazarin. You shall be my body-guard. I will make you all captains, with good pensions! Odds fish!—on—march forward!"

But, eloquent as he might be, the eloquence of the grandson of Henry IV. did not turn those hearts of stone; not one man stirred, so Monsieur de Beaufort was obliged to be satisfied with calling them rascals, and cruel foes.

Sometimes, when Monsieur de Chavigny paid him a visit, the duke used to ask him what he should think if he saw an army of

Parisians, all fully armed, appear at Vincennes to deliver him from prison.

"My lord," answered de Chavigny, with a low bow, "I have on the ramparts twenty pieces of artillery, and in my casemates thirty thousand guns. I should cannonade the troops as well as I could."

"Yes—but after you had fired off your thirty thousand guns, they would take the prison; the prison being taken, I should be obliged to let them hang you—for which I should be very unhappy, assuredly."

And, in his turn, the duke bowed low to Monsieur de Chavigny.

"For myself, on the other hand, my lord," returned the governor, "the first rebel that should pass the threshold of my postern doors, I should be obliged to kill you with my own hand, since you were confided peculiarly to my care, and as I am obliged to give you up—dead or alive."

And again he bowed low, almost to the ground.

These bitter and sweet pleasantries lasted ten minutes, or sometimes longer; but always finished thus:

Monsieur de Chavigny, turning towards the door, used to call out:

"Hallo! La Ramée!"

La Ramée entered the room.

"La Ramée, I recommend Monsieur le Duc to you, particularly; treat him as a man of his rank and family ought to be treated; therefore never leave him alone an instant."

La Ramée became therefore the duke's dinner guest, by compulsion, his eternal keeper, the shadow of his person; but La Ramée, gay, frank, convivial, fond of play, a great hand at tennis, had one defect in the duke's eyes—he was incorruptible.

One may be a jailer or a keeper, and at the same time a good father and husband. La Ramée adored his wife and children, whom now he could only catch a glimpse of from the top of the wall, when, in order to please him, they used to walk on the opposite side of the moat. 'Twas too brief an enjoyment, and La Ramée felt that the gaiety of heart which he had regarded as the cause of that health (of which it was, perhaps, rather the result) would not long survive such a mode of life.

He accepted, therefore, with delight, an offer made to him by his friend the steward of the Duc de Grammont, to give him a substitute: he also mentioned it to Monsieur de Chavigny, who promised that he would not oppose it in any way—that is, if he approved of the person proposed.

We consider it as useless to draw a physical or moral portrait of Grimaud: if, as we hope, our readers have not wholly forgotten our previous effort, they must have preserved a clear idea of that estimable individual, who is wholly unchanged, except that he is twenty years older, an advance in life that has made him only more silent; although, since the alteration that had been working in himself, Athos had given Grimaud permission to speak.

But at this period Grimaud had for twelve or fifteen years preserved an habitual silence, and a habit of fifteen or twenty years' duration becomes a second nature.

18

GRIMAUD BEGINS HIS NEW WORK

GRIMAUD therefore entered the prison of Vincennes under the most favourable auspices. Now Monsieur de Chavigny prided himself on his infallible penetration; for that which almost proved that he was the son of Richelieu was his everlasting pretension; he examined attentively the countenance of the applicant for place, and fancied that the contracted eyebrows, thin lips, hooked nose, and prominent cheeks of Grimaud, were good signs. He addressed about twelve words to him; Grimaud answered in four.

"There's a promising fellow, and I have found out his merits," said Monsieur de Chavigny. "Go," he added, "and make yourself agreeable to Monsieur la Ramée, and tell him that you suit me in every respect."

Grimaud had every quality which could attract a man on duty who wishes to have a deputy. So, after a thousand questions which met with only a word in reply, La Ramée, fascinated by this sobriety in speech, rubbed his hands, and engaged Grimaud.

"My orders?" inquired Grimaud.

"They are these: never to leave the prisoner alone; to keep away from him every sharp or piercing instrument; and to prevent his conversing any length of time with the keepers."

"Those are all?" asked Grimaud.

"At present," replied La Ramée.

"Good," answered Grimaud; and he went right to the prisoner.

The duke was in the act of combing his beard, which he had allowed to grow as well as his hair, in order to reproach Mazarin with his wretched appearance and condition. But having, some days previously, seen from the top of the donjon, Madame de Montbazon pass in her carriage, and still holding an affection for that beautiful woman, he did not wish to be to her what he wished to be to Mazarin; and in the hope of seeing her again, had asked for a leaden comb, which was allowed him. The comb was to be a leaden one, because his beard, like that of most fair people, was rather red; he therefore dyed it when he combed it out.

As Grimaud came in he saw this comb on the tea table; he took it up, and, as he took it, he made a low bow.

The duke looked at this strange figure with surprise. The figure put the comb in its pocket.

"Ho!—eh! what's that?" cried the duke, "and who is this creature?"

Grimaud did not answer, but bowed a second time.

"Art thou dumb?" cried the duke.

Grimaud signalled that he was not.

"What art thou, then? Answer! I command thee!" said the duke.

"A keeper," replied Grimaud.

"A keeper!" reiterated the duke; "there was nothing wanting in my collection except this gallows-bird. Hallo! La Ramée!—some one!"

La Ramée ran in haste to obey the call.

"Who is this wretch who takes my comb and puts it in his pocket?" asked the duke.

"One of your guards, your highness; a man full of talent and merit, whom you will like, as I and Monsieur de Chavigny do, I am sure."

"Why does he abstract my comb?"

"Why do you take my lord's comb?" asked La Ramée.

Grimaud drew the comb out of his pocket, and passing his fingers over the largest teeth, pronounced this one word—"Piercing."

"True," said La Ramée.

"What does the clown say?" asked the duke.

"That the king has forbidden your lordship to have any piercing instrument."

"Are you mad, La Ramée?—you yourself gave me this comb."

"I was very wrong, my lord; for in giving it to you I acted contrary to my orders." The duke looked furiously at Grimaud.

"I perceive that that creature will become odious to me," he muttered.

Grimaud, nevertheless, was resolved, for certain reasons, not at once to come to a full rupture with the prisoner; he wanted to inspire, not a sudden repugnance, but a good, and sound, and steady hatred; he retired, therefore, and gave place to four guards who, having breakfasted, could attend on the prisoner.

A fresh practical joke had now occurred to the duke. He had asked for craw-fish for his breakfast on the following morning: he intended to pass the day in making a small gallows, and hang one of the finest of these fish in the centre of his room—the red colour evidently conveying an allusion to the Cardinal—so that he might have the pleasure of hanging Mazarin in effigy, without being accused of having hung anything except a craw-fish.

The day was employed in preparing for the execution. Every one grows childish in prison; but the character of Monsieur de Beaufort was particularly disposed to become so. In the course of his morning's walk he collected two or three small branches from a tree, and found a small piece of broken glass, a discovery which pleased him greatly. When he came home he formed his handkerchief into a loop.

Nothing of this escaped Grimaud, but La Ramée looked on with the curiosity of a father who thinks that he may perhaps get an idea of a new toy for his children; the guards regarded it all with indifference. When everything was ready—the gallows hung in the middle of the room—the loop made—and when the duke had cast a look upon the plate of craw-fish, in order to select the best from among them, he looked round for his piece of glass—it had disappeared.

"Who has taken my piece of glass?" asked the duke, frowning.

Grimaud made a sign to denote that he had done so.

"How! thou, again! Why didst thou take it?"

"Yes—why?" remarked La Ramée.

Grimaud, who held the piece of glass in his hand, said:

"Sharp."

"True, my lord!" exclaimed La Ramée. "Ah! deuce take it! we have got a precious lad."

"Monsieur Keeper!" said the duke, "for your sake, I beg of you, never come within the reach of my fist!"

"Hush! hush!" cried La Ramée, "give me your gibbet, my lord, I will shape it out for you with my knife."

And he took the gibbet and shaped it out as neatly as possible.

"That's it," said the duke; "now make me a little hole in the floor whilst I go and fetch the culprit."

La Ramée knelt down and made a hole in the floor; meanwhile the duke hung the craw-fish up by a thread. Then he placed the gibbet in the middle of the room, bursting with laughter.

La Ramée laughed also, and the guards laughed in chorus; Grimaud, however, did not even smile. He approached La Ramée and showing him the craw-fish, hung up by the thread.

"Cardinal!" he said.

"Hung by his highness the Duc de Beaufort!" cried the prisoner, laughing violently, "and by Master Jacques Chryostom La Ramée, the king's commissioner."

La Ramée uttered a cry of horror, and rushed towards the gibbet, which he smashed at once, and threw the pieces out of the window. He was about to throw the craw-fish out also, when Grimaud snatched it from his hands.

"Good to eat!" he said; and he placed it in his pocket.

This scene so enchanted the duke that, at the moment, he forgave Grimaud for his part in it; but, on reflection, he hated him more and more, being convinced that he had some bad motive for his conduct.

The prisoner happened to notice among the guards one man, with very good features; and he favoured this man the more as Grimaud became the more and more odious to him. One morning he took this man on one side and had succeeded in speaking to him, when Grimaud entered, saw what was going on, approached the duke respectfully, but took the guard by the arm.

"Go away," he said.

The guard obeyed.

"You are unbearable," cried the duke; "I shall beat you."

Grimaud bowed.

"I shall break every bone in your body," cried the duke.

Grimaud bowed, and stepped back.

"Monsieur Spy," cried the duke, more and more enraged, "I shall strangle you with my own hands."

And he extended his hands towards Grimaud, who merely thrust the guard out, and shut the door behind him. At the same time he felt the duke's arms on his shoulders, like two iron claws; but instead of either calling out or defending himself, he placed his forefinger on his lips, and said in a low tone:

"Hush!"—smiling as he uttered the word.

A gesture, a smile, and a word from Grimaud, all at once, were so unusual, that his highness stopped short, amazed.

Grimaud took advantage of that instant to draw from his vest a charming little note, with an aristocratic seal, and presented it to the duke without a word.

The duke, more and more bewildered, let Grimaud loose, and took the note.

"From Madame de Montbazon!" he said.

Grimaud nodded assent.

The duke tore open the note, passed his hands over his eyes, for he was dazzled and confused, and read:

"My Lord Duke,—

"You may entirely confide in the brave man who will give you this note; he has consented to enter into the service of your keeper, and to shut himself up at Vincennes with you, in order to prepare and assist your escape, which we are contriving. The moment of your deliverance is at hand; have patience and courage, and remember that, in spite of time and absence, all your friends continue to cherish for you the sentiments that they have professed.

"Yours sincerely, and most affectionately,

"Marie De Montbazon.

"*P.S.*—I sign my full name, for I should be vain if I could suppose that after five years of absence you would remember my initials."

The duke became perfectly giddy. What for five years he had been wanting—a faithful servant—a friend—a helping hand—seemed to have fallen from heaven just when he least expected it.

"Oh, dearest Marie! she thinks of me, then, after five years of separation! Heavens! there is constancy!" Then turning to Grimaud, he said:

"And thou, my brave fellow, dost thou consent then to aid me?"

Grimaud signified his assent.

"What then shall we do? how proceed?"

"It is now eleven," answered Grimaud. "Let my lord at two o'clock ask leave to make up a game at tennis with La Ramée, and let him send two or three balls beyond the ramparts."

"And then?"

"Your highness will approach the walls and call out to a man who works in the moat to send them back again."

"I understand," said the duke.

Grimaud made a sign that he was going away.

"Ah!" cried the duke, "will you not accept a present from me?"

"I wish my lord would make me one promise."

"What? speak!"

"'Tis this—when we escape together, that I shall go everywhere, and be always first; for if my lord should be overtaken and caught, there's every chance of his being brought back to prison, whereas, if I'm caught, the least that can befall me—is to be hung."

"True; on my honour as a gentleman, it shall be as thou dost suggest."

"Now," resumed Grimaud, "I've only one thing more to ask, that your highness will continue to detest me."

"Very well," said the duke.

At this moment La Ramée, after the interview which we have described with the Cardinal, entered the room. The duke had thrown himself—as he was wont to do in moments of dullness and vexation—on his bed. La Ramée cast an inquiring look around him.

"Well, my lord," said La Ramée, with a rude laugh; "you still set yourself against this poor fellow?"

"So 'tis you, La Ramée; in faith 'tis time you came back again. I threw myself on the bed, and turned my nose to the wall that I mightn't break my promise and strangle Grimaud. I feel dull."

"Then let us have a match in the tennis court," exclaimed La Ramée.

"If you wish it."

"I am at your service, my lord."

"I protest, my dear La Ramée," said the duke, "that you are a charming person, and that I would stay for ever at Vincennes, to have the pleasure of your society."

"My lord," replied La Ramée, "I think if it depended on the Cardinal, your wishes would be fulfilled."

"How?"

"He sent for me to-day; in fact, my lord, you are his nightmare." The duke smiled bitterly.

"Ah, La Ramée! if you would but accept my offers! I would make your fortune."

"How? you would no sooner be out of prison than your goods would be confiscated."

"I shall no sooner be out of prison than I shall be master of Paris."

"Pshaw! pshaw! I cannot hear such things said; I see my lord, that it will be my duty to fetch Grimaud."

"Well, then, let us go and have a game at tennis, La Ramée."

"My lord—I beg your highness's pardon—but I must beg for half an hour's leave of absence."

"Why?"

"Because Monseigneur Mazarin is a prouder man than your highness, though not of such high birth; he forgot to ask me to breakfast."

"Well, shall I send for some breakfast here?"

"No, my lord; I must tell you that the confectioner who lived opposite the Castle—Father Marteau, as they called him——"

"Well?"

"Well, he sold his business a week ago to a confectioner from Paris—an invalid, ordered country air for his health."

"Well, what is that to do with me?"

"Why, my lord! this man, when he saw me stop before his shop, where he has a display of things which would make your mouth water, asked me to get him the custom of the prisoners in the donjon. 'I bought,' says he, 'the business of my predecessor, on the strength of his assurance that he supplied the Castle; whereas, on my honour, Monsieur de Chavigny, though I've been here a week, has not ordered so much as a tartlet.' So, my lord, I am going to try his pastry; and, as I am fasting, you understand, I would, with your highness's leave——" And La Ramée bent low.

"Go, then, La Ramée," said the duke; "but remember, I only allow you half an hour."

"May I promise your custom to the successor of Father Marteau, my lord?"

"Yes—if he does not put mushrooms in his pies—thou knowest that mushrooms from the wood of Vincennes are fatal to my family."

La Ramée went out, but in five minutes one of the officers of the guard entered, in compliance with the strict orders of the Cardinal, that the prisoner should never be left one moment.

But, during these five minutes, the duke had had time to read over again the note from Madame de Montbazon, which proved to the prisoner that his friends were concerting plans for his deliverance; but in what way he fathomed not.

But his confidence in Grimaud, whose petty persecutions he now perceived were simply a subterfuge, increased, and he conceived the highest opinion of his intellect, and resolved to trust entirely to his guidance.

19

WHAT THE PIES OF FATHER MARTEAU'S SUCCESSOR CONTAINED

HALF an hour later La Ramée returned joyous and happy, like most men who have eaten, and more especially drunk, to their hearts' content. The pastry was excellent, and the wine delicious.

The weather was fine, and the game at tennis took place in the open air.

At two o'clock the tennis balls began, according to Grimaud's directions, to take the direction of the moat, much to the delight of La Ramée, who marked fifteen whenever the duke sent a ball into the moat; and very soon balls were wanting, so many had gone over. La Ramée then proposed to send some one to pick them up. But the duke rejoined that it would be losing time; and going near the rampart himself, and looking over, he saw a man working in one of the numerous little gardens cleared out by the peasants on the opposite side of the moat.

"Hey, friend!" cried the duke.

The man raised his head, and the duke was about to utter a cry of surprise. The peasant, the gardener, was Rochefort, whom he believed to be in the Bastille.

"Well, who's up there?" said the man.

"Be so kind as to send us back our balls," said the duke.

The gardener nodded, and began to throw up the balls, which were picked up by La Ramée and the guard. One, however, fell at the duke's feet; and seeing that it was intended for him, he put it into his pocket.

La Ramée was in ecstasies at having beaten a prince of the blood.

The duke went indoors, and retired to bed, where he spent, indeed, the greater part of every day, as they had taken his books away. La Ramée carried off all his clothes, in order to be certain that the duke would not stir. However, the duke contrived to hide the ball under his bolster, and as soon as the door was closed, he tore off the cover of the ball, and found underneath it the following letter:

"MY LORD,—

"Your friends watch over you, and the hour of your deliverance is at hand. Ask to-morrow to have a pie made by the new confectioner opposite the castle, and who is no other than Noirmont, your former 'maître d'hôtel.' Do not open the pie till you are alone. I trust you will be satisfied with its contents.

> "Your highness's most devoted servant,
>> "In the Bastille, as elsewhere,
>>> "DE ROCHEFORT."

The duke, who had latterly been permitted a fire, burned the letter, but kept the ball, and went to bed, hiding the ball under his bolster. La Ramée entered: he smiled kindly on the prisoner, for he was an excellent man who had taken a great liking for the captive prince. He endeavoured to cheer him up in his solitude.

"Ah, my friend!" cried the duke, "you are so good; if I could but go, as you do, and eat pastry and drink Burgundy at the house of Father Marteau's successor!"

"'Tis true, my lord," answered La Ramée, "that his pastry is famous, and his wine magnificent."

"Good," thought the duke; "it seems that one of Master La Ramée's seven deadly sins is gluttony."

Then aloud:

"Well, my dear La Ramée! the day after to-morrow is a holiday."

"Yes, my lord, Pentecost."

"Will you give me a lesson the day after to-morrow?"

"In what?"

"In gastronomy."

"Willingly, my lord."

"But between ourselves. The guards shall go to sup in the canteen of Monsieur de Chavigny—we'll have a supper here, under your direction."

"Hum!" said La Ramée.

The duke watched the countenance of La Ramée, with an anxious glance.

"Well," he asked, "that will do? Will it not?"

"Yes, my lord, on one condition."

"What?"

"That Grimaud should wait on us at table."

Nothing could be more agreeable to the duke; however, he had presence of mind enough to exclaim:

"Send your Grimaud to the devil! he'll spoil our feast. I see you distrust me."

"My lord, the day after to-morrow is Pentecost."

"Well! what of that?"

"I have already told you what that magician has predicted."

"And what was it?"

"That the day of Pentecost would not pass without your highness being out of Vincennes."

"You believe in sorcerers, then, you fool!"

"I—I care for them, that——" and he snapped his fingers; "but it is my Lord Giulio who cares for them—as an Italian, he is superstitious."

The duke shrugged his shoulders.

"Well, then," with a well-acted good-humour, "I allow of Grimaud, but no one else—you must arrange it all. Order whatever you like for supper—the only thing I specify is one of those pies; and tell the confectioner that I will promise him my custom if he excels this time in his pies—not only now, but when I leave my prison."

"Then you think you will leave it?" said La Ramée.

"The devil!" replied the prince; "surely at the death of Mazarin. I am fifteen years younger than he is. At Vincennes, 'tis true, one lives faster——"

"My lord," replied La Ramée, "my lord——"

"Or one dies sooner, so it comes to the same thing."

La Ramée was going out. He stopped, however, at the door for an instant.

"Whom does your highness wish me to send to you?"

"Any one, but not Grimaud."

"The officer of the guard, then? with his chessboard?"

"Yes."

Five minutes afterwards the officer entered, and the duke seemed to be engaged in the sublime combinations of chess.

It was midnight before he went to sleep that evening, and he awoke at daybreak. Wild dreams had disturbed his repose. He dreamed that he had been gifted with wings—he wished to fly away. For a time these wings had supported him; but, when he had gained a certain height, this new aid had failed him. His wings were broken, and he seemed to sink into a bottomless abyss, whence he awoke, bathed in perspiration, and as much overcome as if he had really fallen. He went to sleep again, and another vision appeared. He was in a subterranean passage, by which he was to leave Vincennes. Grimaud was walking before him with a lantern. By degrees the passage narrowed, yet the duke continued his course. At last it became so narrow that the fugitive tried in vain to advance. The sides of the walls seemed to close in, and to press against him. He made fruitless efforts to proceed; it was impossible. Nevertheless, he still saw Grimaud, with his lantern in front, advancing. He wished to call out to him, but could not utter

r

a word. Then, at the other extremity, he heard the footsteps of those who were pursuing him. These steps came on—they came fast. He was discovered—all hopes of flight were gone. Still the walls seemed to be closing on him; they appeared to be in concert with his enemies. At last he heard the voice of La Ramée. La Ramée took his hand, and laughed aloud. He was captured again, and conducted to the low and vaulted chamber, in which Ornano Puylaurens, and his uncle had died. Their graves were there, rising above the ground, and a third was also there—yawning to receive a corpse.

The duke was obliged to make as many efforts to awaken as he had done to go to sleep; and La Ramée found him so pale and fatigued, that he inquired whether he was ill.

"Is anything the matter with your highness?" he asked.

"'Tis thy fault, thou simpleton," answered the duke. "With your idle nonsense yesterday, about escaping, you worried me so, that I dreamed that I was attempting an escape, and broke my neck in doing so."

La Ramée laughed.

"Come," he said, "'tis a warning from heaven. Never commit such an imprudence as to try to escape, except in your dreams. Listen! your supper is ordered."

"Ah! and what is it to be? Monsieur, my major-domo, will there be a pie?"

"I think so indeed; as high as a turret."

"You told him it was for me?"

"Yes; and he said he would do his best to please your highness."

"Good!" exclaimed the duke with glee.

"Devil take it, my lord! what a gourmand you are becoming. I haven't seen you with such a cheerful face these five years."

At this moment Grimaud entered, and whispered to La Ramée that he had something to say to him.

The duke instantly recovered his composure.

"I forbade that man to come here," he said.

"'Tis my fault," replied La Ramée; "but he must stay here whilst I go to see Monsieur de Chavigny, who has some orders to give me."

And La Ramée went out. Grimaud looked after him, and when the door was closed, he drew from his pocket a pencil and a sheet of paper.

"Write, my lord," he said.

"And what?"

Grimaud dictated.

"All is ready for to-morrow evening. Keep watch from seven

till nine o'clock. Have two riding-horses quite ready. We shall descend by the first window in the gallery."

"What next?"

"Sign your name, my lord."

The duke signed.

"Now, my lord, give me, if you have not lost it, the ball which contained the letter."

The duke took it from under his pillow and gave it to Grimaud. Grimaud gave a grim smile.

"Now," said the duke, "tell me what this famous raised pie is to contain."

"Two poignards, a knotted rope, and a *poire d'angoisse*." *

"Yes, I understand;—we shall take to ourselves the poignards and the rope," replied the duke.

"And make La Ramée eat the pear," answered Grimaud.

"My dear Grimaud, thou speakest seldom, but when thou dost thou speakest golden words."

20

THE COMTE AND THE DUCHESSE

ABOUT the same time that these plans of escape were being formed by the Duc de Beaufort and Grimaud, the Comte de la Fère and the Vicomte de Bragelonne were entering Paris by the Rue du Faubourg Saint Marcel.

They stopped at the sign of the Fox, in the Rue de Vieux Colombier, a tavern known for many years by Athos, and asked for two bedrooms.

"You must dress yourself, Raoul," said Athos. "I am going to present you to some one. I want you to look well, so arrange your dress with care."

"I hope, sir," replied the youth, smiling, "that you have no idea of a marriage for me; you know my engagement to Louise?"

Athos, in his turn, smiled also.

"No, don't be fearful—although it is to a lady that I am going to present you—and I am anxious that you should love her——"

"What age is she?" inquired the Vicomte de Bragelonne.

* The *poire d'angoisse* was an improved gag, shaped like a pear, which, being thrust into the mouth, by the aid of a spring, dilated so as to distend the jaws to their utmost extent.

"My dear Raoul, learn once for all, that that is a question which is never asked. When you can find out a woman's age by her face it is needless to ask it; when you cannot do so it is indiscreet."

"Is she beautiful?"

"During sixteen years she was deemed not only the prettiest but the most graceful woman in France."

This reply reassured the vicomte. A woman who had been a reigning beauty for sixteen years could not be the subject of any scheme for him. He retired to his toilet. When he reappeared, Athos received him with the same paternal smile as that which he had often bestowed on d'Artagnan; but a more profound tenderness for Raoul was now visibly impressed upon his face.

Athos cast a glance at his feet, hands, and hair—those three marks of rank. The youth's dark hair was neatly parted, and hung in curls, forming a sort of dark frame round his face—such was the fashion of the day. Gloves of grey kid, matching the hat, displayed the form of a slender and elegant hand; whilst his boots, similar in colour to the hat and gloves, confined the feet, small as those of a child of ten years old.

"Come," thought Athos, "if she is not proud of him, she will be difficult to please."

It was three o'clock in the afternoon. The two travellers proceeded to the Rue St. Dominique, and stopped at the door of a magnificent hotel, surmounted with the arms of de Luynes.

"'Tis here," said Athos.

He entered the hotel, and ascended the front steps, and addressing a footman who waited there in grand livery, asked if the Duchesse de Chevreuse was in, and if so, would she receive the Comte de la Fère?

The servant returned with a message to say that though the duchess had not the honour of knowing Monsieur de la Fère, she would receive him. He was accordingly announced.

Madame de Chevreuse, whose name appears so often in our story, *The Three Musketeers*, without her actually having appeared in any scene, was still a most beautiful woman. Although about forty-four or forty-five years old, she scarcely seemed thirty-eight. She still possessed rich fair hair; her large, animated, intelligent eyes, so often opened by intrigue, so often closed by the blindness of love. She had still her nymphlike form, so that when her back was turned she seemed to be still the girl who had jumped with Anne of Austria over the moat of the Tuileries in 1563. In all other respects she was the same mad creature who threw over her amours such an air of originality as to make them almost a proverb in her family.

She was in a little boudoir looking upon a garden, and hung with blue damask, adorned by red flowers, with a foliage of gold; and reclined upon a sofa, her head supported on the rich tapestry which covered it. She held a book in her hand, and her arm was resting upon a cushion.

At the footman's announcement she raised herself a little and looked up, with some curiosity.

Athos appeared.

He was dressed in violet-coloured velvet, trimmed with the same colour. His shoulder-knots were of burnished silver; his cloak had no gold nor embroidery on it, and a simple plume of violet feathers adorned his hat; his boots were of black leather; and at his girdle hung that sword with a magnificent hilt that Porthos had so often admired in the Rue Feronnière. Splendid lace formed the falling collar of his shirt, and lace fell also over the tops of his boots.

In his whole person he bore such an impress of high condition, that Madame de Chevreuse half rose from her seat when she saw him, and made him a sign to sit down near her. He obeyed, the servant disappeared, and the door was shut.

There was a momentary pause, during which these two persons looked at each other attentively.

The duchess was the first to break the silence.

"Well, sir! I am waiting to hear what you wish to say to me—with impatience."

"And I, madame," replied Athos, "am looking with admiration."

"Sir," said Madame de Chevreuse, "you must excuse me, but I long to know to whom I am talking. You belong to the court, doubtless, yet I have never seen you at court. Have you been in the Bastille by any mischance?"

"No, madame, I have not; but perhaps I am on the road to it."

"Ah! then tell me who you are, and be quick about it," replied the duchess, with the gaiety which made her so charming, "for I am sufficiently in bad odour there already, without compromising myself still more."

"Who I am, madame? My name has been mentioned to you—the Comte de la Fère—you do not know that name. I once bore another, which you knew; but you have certainly forgotten it."

"Tell it me, sir."

"Formerly," said the count, "I was known as Athos."

Madame de Chevreuse looked astonished. The name was not altogether forgotten, but mixed up and confused with some old recollections.

"Stop," she said.

And she placed her hands on her brow, as if to force the fugitive ideas it contained to be concentrated for a moment.

"Shall I help you, madame?" asked Athos.

"Yes, please, do," said the duchesse.

"This Athos was associated with three young musketeers, named Porthos, d'Artagnan, and——"

He stopped short.

"And Aramis," said the duchesse quickly.

"And Aramis; you have not forgotten that name."

"No," she said: "poor Aramis; a charming man, elegant, discreet, and a writer of poetry verses. I am afraid he has turned out ill," she added.

"He has; he is an abbé."

"Ah, that is indeed unfortunate!" exclaimed the duchesse, toying carelessly with her fan. "Indeed, sir, I thank you; you have recalled one of the most agreeable recollections of my youth."

"Will you allow me, then, to recall another to you?"

"Anything relating to him?"

"Yes and no. Aramis was intimate with a young needlewoman from Tours, a cousin of his, named Marie Michon."

"Ah, I knew her!" cried the duchesse. "It was to her he wrote from the siege of Rochelle, to warn her of a plot against the Duke of Buckingham."

"Exactly so; will you allow me to speak to you of her?"

"If," replied the duchesse, with a meaning look, "you do not say too much against her."

Thus cautioned, Athos proceeded with his narrative. He recalled the incidents of a journey in disguise made long years ago into Spain by Marie Michon, the supposed needlewoman of Tours, but who was in reality the beautiful, wayward, once-powerful Duchesse de Chevreuse. The recital amazed the duchesse, for it revealed the Comte de la Fère as the father, the duchesse as the mother of the Vicomte de Bragelonne, who was in waiting in the next room. Her surprise soon gave way to joy, and she eagerly requested to see Raoul.

"I bring him to you, madame," said Athos, withdrawing his hand, "hoping that, in your turn, you will do something for him; till now I have watched over his education, and I have made him, I hope, an accomplished gentleman; but I am now obliged to return to the dangerous and wandering life of party faction. To-morrow I plunge into an adventurous affair in which I may be killed. Then it will devolve on you to push him on in that world where he is called on to occupy a place."

"Rest assured," cried the duchesse, "I shall do the best I can. I have but little influence now, but all that I have shall be his. As to his title and fortune——"

"As to that, madame, I have made over to him the estate of Bragelonne, my inheritance, which will give him ten thousand francs a year, and the title of vicomte;—and now I will call him."

Athos moved towards the door; the duchesse held him back.

"Is he handsome?" she asked.

Athos smiled.

"He resembles his mother," he said.

And he opened the door, and desired the young man to come in.

The duchesse could not forbear uttering a cry of joy on seeing so handsome a young cavalier, who surpassed all that her pride had been able to conceive.

"Vicomte, come here," said Athos; "the duchesse permits you to kiss her hand."

The youth approached with his charming smile, his head bare, and, kneeling down, kissed the hand of the Duchesse de Chevreuse.

"Sir," he said to Athos, "was it not in compassion to my timidity that you told me that this lady was the Duchesse de Chevreuse, and is she not the queen?"

"No," said the duchesse, extending her hand to him; "no, unhappily, I am not the queen, for, if I were, I should do for you at once all that you desire: but let us see; whatever I may be," she added, her eyes glistening with pleasure, "let us see what profession you wish to follow?"

Athos, standing, looked at them both with indescribable joy.

"Madame," answered the youth in his sweet voice, "it seems to me that there is only one career for a gentleman—that of the army. I have been brought up by Monsieur le Comte with the intention, I believe, of becoming a soldier; and he gave me reason to hope that, at Paris, he would present me to some one who would recommend me to the favour of the prince."

"Yes, I understand it well. Personally I am on bad terms with him, on account of the quarrels between Madame de Montbazon, my mother-in-law, and Madame de Longueville. But the Prince de Marsillac! yes, indeed, that's the best thing. The Prince de Marsillac, my old friend—he will recommend our young friend to Madame de Longueville, who will give him a letter to her brother, the prince, who loves her too tenderly not to do what she wishes immediately."

"Well, that will do charmingly," said the count; "but may I beg that the greatest haste may be made, for I have reasons for wishing the vicomte not to stay longer than to-morrow night in Paris?"

"Do you wish it known that you are interested about him, Monsieur le Comte?"

"Better for him, in future, that he should be supposed never to have seen me."

"Oh, sir!" cried Raoul.

"You know, Bragelonne," said Athos, "I never act without reflection."

"Well, comte, I am going at once," interrupted the duchesse, "to send for the Prince de Marsillac, who is, happily, in Paris just now. What are you going to do this evening?"

"We intend to visit the Abbé Scarron, for whom I have a letter of introduction, and at whose house I expect to meet some of my friends."

"'Tis well; I shall go there also, for a few minutes," said the duchesse; "do not quit his *salon* until you have seen me."

Athos bowed, and was leaving the room.

"Well, Monsieur le Comte," said the duchesse, laughing, "do old friends part so unceremoniously?"

"Ah," murmured Athos, kissing her hand, "had I but known sooner how charming a creature Marie Michon was!"

And he left the room with a sigh.

21

THE ABBÉ SCARRON

In the Rue des Tournelles, there was once a house, which, though belonging to neither a great lord nor a rich man, was nevertheless known to all the sedan-chairmen and footmen in Paris. There was neither dining, nor playing at cards, nor dancing in that house. Yet, it was the resort of all the great world, and all Paris went there. It was the abode of little Scarron.

There, in the home of that witty abbé, there was incessant laughter; there all the news of the day had their source, and were so quickly transformed, contorted, and converted, some into epigrams, some into falsehoods, that every one was anxious to pass an hour with little Scarron, listening to what he said, and reporting it to others.

The diminutive Abbé Scarron, who, however, was only an abbé because he owned an abbey, and not because he was in orders, had formerly been one of the gayest prebendaries of the town of Maur; but he had become lame; every means had been in vain employed to restore the use of his limbs. He had been subjected to a severe discipline; at length he sent away all his doctors, declaring that he preferred the disease to the treatment, and came to Paris, where the fame of his wit had preceded him. There he had a chair made on a new plan; and one day, visiting Anne of Austria in this chair, she asked him, charmed as she was with his wit, if he did not desire a title.

"Yes, your majesty, there is a title which I covet much," replied Scarron.

"And what is that?"

"That of being *your* invalid," answered Scarron.

So he was called The Queen's Invalid, with a pension of fifteen hundred francs.

From that lucky moment Scarron led a happy life, spending both income and principal. One day, however, an emissary of the Cardinal's gave him to understand that he was wrong in receiving the Coadjutor so often.

"And why?" asked Scarron; "is he not a man of good birth?"

"Certainly."

"Agreeable?"

"Undeniably."

"Witty?"

"He has, unluckily, too much wit."

"Well, then, why do you wish me to give up seeing such a man?"

"Because he is an enemy."

"Of whom?"

"Of the Cardinal."

"How?" answered Scarron; "I continue to receive Monsieur Gilles Despreaux, who does not think well of me, and you wish me to give up seeing the Coadjutor, because he thinks ill of another man."

Now, the very morning of which we speak, was that of his quarter-day's payment, and Scarron, as usual, had sent his servant to fetch his money at the pension-office, but he had returned, and said that the Department had no more money to give Monsieur Scarron.

It was a Thursday, the abbé's day of reception; people attended in crowds. The Cardinal's refusal to pay the pension was known about the town in less than half an hour, and he was vigorously abused.

Athos made two visits to Paris; at seven o'clock he and Raoul directed their steps to the Rue des Tournelles; it was stopped up by porters, horses, and footmen. Athos forced his way through and entered, followed by the young man. The first person that attracted his attention was Aramis, planted near a great chair on castors, very large, covered with a canopy of tapestry, under which there moved, enveloped in a quilt of brocade, a little face, rather young, rather merry, but somewhat pale,—whilst its eyes never ceased to express a sentiment at once lively, intellectual, and amiable. This was the Abbé Scarron, always laughing, joking, complimenting,—yet suffering—and scratching himself with a little switch.

Around this kind of rolling tent pressed a crowd of ladies and gentlemen. The room was neatly and comfortably furnished. Large vallancies of silk, embroidered with flowers of gay colours, which were rather faded, fell from the wide windows; the fitting-up of the room was simple, but in good taste. Two men servants, well trained, attended on the company. On perceiving Athos, Aramis advanced towards him, took him by the hand, and presented him to Scarron. Raoul remained silent, for he was not prepared for the dignity of the "bel esprit."

After some minutes the door opened, and a footman announced Mademoiselle Paulet.

Athos touched the shoulder of the vicomte.

"Look at this lady, Raoul, she is an historic personage; it was to visit her that the 'Bearnhais' was going, when he was assassinated."

Every one thronged round Mademoiselle Paulet, for she was always much in fashion. She was a tall woman, with a wavy and slender figure, and a forest of golden curls, such as Raphael was fond of, and as Titian has painted all his Magdalens with. This fawn-coloured hair—or, perhaps, the sort of ascendancy which she had over other women—gave her the name of "La Lionne."

Mademoiselle Paulet took her accustomed seat; but before sitting down, she cast, in all her queenlike grandeur, a look round the room—and her eyes became fixed on Raoul.

Athos smiled.

"Mademoiselle Paulet has observed you, vicomte; go and bow to her; don't try to appear anything but what you are—a true country youth—on no account speak to her of Henry IV."

"When shall we two talk together?" Athos then said to Aramis.

"Presently—there are not a sufficient number of people here yet—we shall be noticed."

At that moment the door opened, and the Coadjutor entered.

At this name every one looked round, for it was already a name very celebrated. Athos did the same. His knowledge of the Abbé de Gondy was only by report.

He saw a little dark man, ill-made and awkward with his hands in everything—except when drawing a sword and firing a pistol, and with something haughty and contemptuous in his face.

Scarron turned round towards him, and came to meet him in his chair.

"Well," said the Coadjutor, on seeing him, "you are in disgrace, then, abbé?"

This was the orthodox phrase. It had been said that evening a hundred times—and Scarron was at his hundredth *bon mot* on the subject—he was very near stopping short, but one despairing effort saved him.

"Monsieur, the Cardinal Mazarin has been so kind as to think of me," he said.

"But how can you continue to receive us?" asked the Coadjutor; "if your income is reduced, I shall be obliged to make you a canon of Notre Dame."

"Oh, no," cried Scarron, "I should compromise you too much."

"Perhaps you have resources of which we are ignorant?"

"I shall borrow from the queen."

"But her majesty has no property," interposed Aramis.

At this moment the door opened, and Madame de Chevreuse was announced. Every one rose. Scarron turned his chair towards the door; Raoul flushed; Athos made a sign to Aramis, who went to hide himself in the enclosure of a window.

In the midst of all the compliments that awaited her on her entrance, the duchesse seemed to be looking for some one: at last she found out Raoul, and her eyes glistened; she saw Athos, and became grave; she saw Aramis in the seclusion of the window, and gave a start of surprise behind her fan.

"Apropos," she said, as if to drive away thoughts that pursued her in spite of herself, "how is poor Voiture; do you know, Scarron?"

"What! is Monsieur Voiture ill?" inquired a gentleman who had spoken to Athos in the Rue St. Honoré; "what is the matter with him?"

"He was acting—but forgot to take the precaution to have clean linen brought to change," said the Coadjutor, "so he took cold, and is not going to live."

"Is he then so ill, dear Voiture?" asked Aramis, half hidden by the window curtain.

"He die!" cried Mademoiselle Paulet bitterly: "he! why he is surrounded by sultanas, like a Turk. Madame de Saintot has hastened to him with broth; La Renaudet warms his sheets; the Marquise de Rambouillet sends him his gruel."

"You don't like him, my dear Parthenie," suggested Scarron.

"What an injustice, my dear invalid! I hate him so little, that I should be delighted to order masses for the repose of his soul."

"You are not called 'Lionne' for nothing," observed Madame de Chevreuse, "you bite most cruelly."

"You are ungenerous to a great poet, so it seems to me," Raoul ventured to say.

"A great poet! he! come, one may easily see, vicomte, that you are lately from the provinces, and have never seen him. A great poet! he is scarcely five feet high."

"Bravo! bravo!" cried a tall man with a fierce moustache and a long rapier, "bravo, fair Paulet; it is high time to put little Voiture in his right place. For my part I always thought his poetry execrable, and I think I know something about poetry."

"Who is this officer," inquired Raoul of Athos, "who is speaking?"

"Monsieur de Scudéry, the author of *Delia*, and of *Le Grand Cyrus*, which were composed partly by him, and partly by his sister, who is now speaking to that pretty person yonder, near Monsieur Scarron."

Raoul turned, and saw two new faces just arrived. One was perfectly charming, delicate, pensive, shaded by beautiful dark hair, with eyes soft as velvet, like those lovely flowers—the heartsease, under which shine the golden petals. The other, of mature age, seemed to have the former one under her charge, and was cold, dry, and yellow—the true type of a duenna or a devotee.

Raoul resolved not to quit the room without having spoken to the beautiful girl with the soft eyes, who by a strange fancy—although she bore no resemblance—reminded him of his poor little Louise, whom he had left in the Château de la Vallière, and whom, in the midst of all the party, he had never one moment forgotten. Meantime Aramis had drawn near to the Coadjutor, who, smiling all the while, had contrived to whisper some words to him quietly. Raoul, following the advice of Athos, went towards them. Athos had now joined the other two, and they were in deep consultation as the youth approached them.

"'Tis a rouleau by Monsieur Voiture that Monsieur l'Abbé is repeating to me," said Athos, in a loud voice, "and I confess I think it incomparable."

Raoul stayed only a few minutes near them, and then mingled in the group around Madame de Chevreuse.

"Well, then," asked Athos, in a low tone, as soon as the three friends were unobserved, "to-morrow?"

"Yes, to-morrow," said Aramis quickly, "at six o'clock."

"Where?"

"At St. Maude."

"Who told you?"

"The Count de Rochefort."

Some one drew nigh.

"And then philosophic ideas are wholly wanting in Voiture's works—but I am of the same opinion as the Coadjutor—he is a poet, a true poet." Aramis spoke so as to be heard by everybody.

"And I too," murmured the young lady with the velvet eyes; "I have the misfortune also to admire his poetry extremely."

"Monsieur Scarron, do me the honour," said Raoul, blushing, "to tell me the name of that young lady whose opinion seems so different to that of the others of the company generally."

"Ah! my young vicomte," replied Scarron, "I suppose you wish to propose to her an alliance, offensive and defensive."

Raoul blushed again.

"You wish to know that young lady's name. She is called the fair Indian."

"Excuse me, sir," replied Raoul, blushing still more deeply, "I know no more than I did before. Alas! I am from the country."

"Which means that you know very little about the nonsense which flows here, down our streets. So much the better, young man! so much the better! Don't try to understand it—you will only lose your time."

"You forgive me, then, sir," said Raoul; "and you will deign to tell me who is the person that you call the young Indian?"

"Certainly; one of the most charming persons that lives— Mademoiselle Frances d'Aubigné."

"Does she belong to the family of the celebrated Agrippus, the friend of Henri Quatre?"

"His granddaughter. She comes from Martinique, so I call her the beautiful Indian."

Raoul looked satisfied, and his eyes met those of the young lady, who smiled.

The company went on speaking of the poet Voiture.

"Monsieur," said Mademoiselle d'Aubigné to Scarron, as if she wished to join in the conversation he was engaged in with Raoul, "do you not admire Monsieur Voiture's friends? See how they pluck him to pieces, even whilst they praise him; one takes away from him all claim to good sense, another runs off with his poetry, another with his originality, another with his humour, another with his independence of character, another—but, good heavens! how will they leave him? as Mademoiselle de Scudéry remarks."

Scarron and Raoul laughed. The fair Indian, astonished at the sensation her observations produced, looked down and resumed her air of naïveté.

Athos—still within the enclosure of the window—watched this scene with a disdainful smile on his lips.

"Tell the Count de la Fère to come to me," said Madame de Chevreuse, "I want to speak to him."

"And I," said the Coadjutor, "want it to be thought that I do *not* speak to him. I admire, I love him—for I know many of his good qualities—but I shall not speak to him until the day after to-morrow."

"And what then?" asked Madame de Chevreuse.

"You shall know to-morrow evening," answered the Coadjutor, laughing.

Athos then drew near her.

"Monsieur le Comte," said the duchesse, handing him a letter, "here is what I promised you; our young friend will be extremely well received."

"Madame, he is very happy in owing any obligation to you."

Madame de Chevreuse rose to depart.

"Vicomte," said Athos to Raoul, "follow the duchesse; beg her to do you the favour to take your arm in going downstairs, and thank her as you descend."

The fair Indian approached Scarron.

"You are leaving already," he said.

"One of the last, as you see; if you hear anything of Monsieur Voiture, be so kind as to send me word to-morrow."

"Oh!" said Scarron, "he may die now."

"Why?" asked the young girl with soft eyes.

"Certainly—his panegyric has been uttered."

They parted, laughing; she turning back to gaze at the poor paralytic man with interest, he looking after her with eyes of love.

So the invalid retired soon afterwards, and went into his sleeping-room; and one by one the lights in the *salon* of La Rue des Tournelles were extinguished.

22

ST. DENIS

The day was beginning to break when Athos arose and dressed himself. It was plain, by the paleness still greater than usual, and by those traces which loss of sleep leaves on the face, that he must have passed a painfully sleepless night. Contrary to the custom of a man so firm and decided, there was this morning in his personal appearance something slow and irresolute. He was evidently occupying himself in preparations for the departure of Raoul; after employing nearly an hour in these cares, he opened the door of the room in which the vicomte slept, and entered.

The sun, already high, penetrated into the room through the window, the curtains of which Raoul had neglected to close on the previous evening. He was still asleep, his head gracefully reposing on his arm.

Athos approached and hung over the youth in an attitude full of tender melancholy; he looked long on this young man, whose smiling mouth, and half-closed eyes, bespoke soft dreams and light slumbers, as if his guardian angel watched over him with solicitude and affection. By degrees Athos gave himself up to the charms of his reverie in the proximity of youth, so pure, so fresh. His own youth seemed to reappear, bringing with it all those soft remembrances, which are like perfumes more than thoughts. Between the past and the present there was an abyss. But imagination has the flight of an angel of light, and travels over the seas where we have been almost shipwrecked,—the darkness in which our associations are lost—the precipice, whence our happiness has been hurled and swallowed up. He remembered that all the first part of his life had been embittered by a woman, and he thought with alarm of the influence which love might possess over so fine, and, at the same time, so vigorous an organisation as that of Raoul.

In recalling all that he had suffered, he foresaw all that Raoul would suffer; and the expression of the deep and tender compassion which throbbed in his heart was pictured in the moistened eye with which he gazed on the young man.

At this moment Raoul awoke, with a fresh look on his face; his eyes were fixed on those of Athos, and he, perhaps, comprehended all that passed in the mind of the man who had been awaiting his awakening as a lover awaits the awakening of his mistress, for his glance, in return, had all the tenderness of infinite love.

"You are there, sir," he said respectfully.

"Yes, Raoul," replied the count.

"And you did not disturb me?"

"I wished to leave you still to enjoy some moments of sleep, my child; you must be fatigued by our long day yesterday."

"Oh, sir! how good you are!"

Athos smiled.

"How are you?" he said.

"Perfectly well; quite rested, sir."

"You are still growing," Athos continued, with that charming and paternal interest felt by a grown man for a youth.

"Oh, sir! I beg your pardon," exclaimed Raoul, ashamed of so much attention; "in an instant, I shall be dressed."

Athos then called Olivain.

"Everything, Monsieur le Count," said Olivain to Athos, "has been done according to your directions; the horses are waiting."

"And I was asleep!" cried Raoul; "whilst you, sir, you had the kindness to attend to all these details. Truly, sir, you overweight me with benefits!"

"Therefore you do love me, a little, I hope," replied Athos feelingly.

"Oh, sir! God knows that I love, I revere you."

"See that nothing is forgotten!" said Athos, appearing to look about him that he might hide his emotion.

"No, indeed, sir," answered Raoul.

The servant then approached Athos, and said hesitatingly:

"Monsieur le Vicomte has no sword."

"'Tis well," said Athos, "I will take care of that."

They went downstairs; Raoul looking every now and then at the count to see if the moment of farewell was at hand, but Athos was silent. When they reached the steps, Raoul saw three horses.

"Oh, sir! then you are going with me?"

"I shall conduct you part of the way," said Athos.

They set out, passing over the Pont Neuf; they pursued their way along the quay then called L'Abreuvoir Pepin, and went along by the walls of the Grand Châtelet. They proceeded to the Rue St. Denis.

After passing through the Porte Saint Denis, Athos looked at Raoul's horse, and said:

"Take care, Raoul! That is what I do not like to see. See! your horse is tired already, he froths at the mouth, whilst mine looks as if he had only just left the stable. You hold the bit too tight, and so make his mouth hard; so that you will not be able to make him manœuvre quickly, which is a great defect in a rider. The safety of a cavalier often depends on the prompt obedience of his horse. In a week, remember, you will no longer be performing your manœuvres, as a practice, but on a field of battle."

Then, suddenly, in order not to give too sad an importance to this observation:—

"See, Raoul!" he resumed; "what a fine plain for partridge shooting! I have remarked also another thing," said Athos, "which is, that in firing off your pistol, you hold your arm too much stretched out. This tension lessens the accuracy of the aim. So, in twelve times you thrice missed the mark."

"Which you, sir, hit twelve times," answered Raoul, smiling.

"Because I bent my arm, and resting my hand on my elbow—so—do you understand what I mean?"

"Yes, sir. I fired since in that manner, and was completely successful."

"What a cold wind!" resumed Athos. "A wintry blast. Apropos, if you fire—and you will do so, for you are recommended to a young general who has a liking for powder—remember in single combat (which often takes place in the cavalry) never to fire the first shot. He who fires the first shot rarely hits his man, for he fires with the apprehension of being disarmed before an armed foe; then, whilst he fires, make your horse rear; that manœuvre has saved my life many times."

"I shall do so, if only in love for——"

"Eh!" cried Athos, "are not those poachers whom they have arrested yonder? They are. Then another important thing, Raoul; should you be wounded in a battle, and fall from your horse—if you have any strength left, disentangle yourself from the line that your regiment has formed; otherwise, it may be driven back, and you will be trampled to death by the horses. In any case, if you should be wounded, write to me the very instant, or make some one write to me. We are judges of wounds, we old soldiers," Athos added, smiling.

"Thank you, sir," answered the young man, much moved.

They arrived that very moment at the gate of the town, guarded by two sentinels.

"Here comes a young gentleman," said one of the guard, "who seems as if he were going to join the army."

"How do you find that out?" inquired Athos.

"By his appearance, sir, and his age; he is the second to-day."

"Has a young man, such as I am, gone through this morning, then?" asked Raoul.

"Faith, yes, with a haughty presence and fine equipage; such as a son of a noble house would have."

"He was to be my companion on the journey, sir," cried Raoul. "Alas! he cannot make me forget what I shall have lost!"

Thus talking, they traversed the streets, full of people on account of the fête, and arrived opposite the old cathedral where the first mass was going on.

"Let us dismount, Raoul," said Athos. "Olivain, take care of our horses, and give me my sword."

The two gentlemen then went into the church. Athos gave Raoul some of the holy water. A love as tender as that of a lover for his mistress dwells without doubt in some paternal hearts for a son.

"Come, Raoul," he said.

A verger opened the iron grating which guarded the royal tombs, and stood on the topmost step, whilst Athos and Raoul descended. The depths of the sepulchral descent were dimly lighted by a silver lamp, on the lowest step; and just below this lamp there was laid, wrapped in a large mantle of violet velvet worked with fleurs-de-lis of gold, a catafalque resting upon trestles of oak.

The young man, prepared for this scene by the state of his own feelings, which were mournful, and by the majesty of the cathedral which he had passed through, had descended in a slow and solemn manner, and stood with his head uncovered before these mortal remains of the last king, who was not to be placed by the side of his forefathers until his successor should take his place there; and who appeared to abide on that spot, that he might thus address human pride, so sure to be exalted by the glories of a throne: "Dust of the earth! I await thee!"

There was a profound silence.

Then Athos raised his hand, and pointing to the coffin,—

"This temporary sepulchre is," he said, "that of a man of small and feeble mind; yet whose reign was full of great events: because, over this king watched the spirit of another man, even as this lamp keeps vigil over this coffin, and illumines it. He whose intellect was thus supreme, was the actual sovereign; the other, nothing but a phantom to whom he gave a soul; and yet, so powerful is majesty amongst us, this man has not even the honour of a tomb even at the feet of him in whose service his life was worn away. Remember, Raoul, this! If Richelieu made the king, by comparison, small, he made royalty great. The palace of the Louvre contains two things—the king, who must die—and royalty, which dieth not. The minister, so feared, so hated by his master, has descended into the tomb, drawing after him the king—whom he would not leave alone on earth, lest he should destroy what he had done. So blind were his contemporaries that they regarded the Cardinal's death as a deliverance; and even I opposed the designs of the great man who held the destinies of France in his hands. Raoul, learn how to distinguish the king from royalty; the king is but a man; royalty is the gift of God. Whenever you hesitate as to whom you ought to serve, abandon the exterior, the material appearance, for the invisible principle: for the invisible principle is everything. Raoul, I seem to read your future destiny as through a cloud. It will be brighter, I think, than ours has been. Different in your fate to us—you will have a king without a minister, whom you may serve, love, respect. Should the king prove a tyrant, for power begets tyranny, serve, love, respect royalty, that Divine right, that celestial spark which makes this dust still powerful and holy, so that we—gentlemen, nevertheless, of rank and condition—are as nothing in comparison with that cold corpse extended here."

"I shall adore God, sir," said Raoul. "I shall respect royalty, I shall serve the king, and I shall, if death be my lot, hope to die for God, for royalty, and for the king. Have I, sir, comprehended your instructions?"

Athos smiled.

"Yours is a noble nature," he said; "here is your sword."

Raoul bent his knee to the ground.

"It was worn by my father, a loyal gentleman. I have worn it in my turn, and it has never been disgraced when the hilt was in my hand, and the sheath at my side. Should your hand still be too weak to use this sword, Raoul, so much the better. You will have more time to learn to draw it only when it should be used."

"Sir," replied Raoul, placing the sword to his lips as he received it from the count, "I owe everything to you, and yet this sword is the most precious gift you have made me. I shall wear it, I swear to you, as a grateful man should do."

"'Tis well—arise, vicomte, embrace me."

Raoul threw himself with deep emotion into the count's arms.

"*Adieu*," faltered the count, who felt his heart die away within him; "*adieu*, and think of me."

"Oh! for ever and ever!" cried the youth; "oh! I swear to you, sir, should any harm happen to me, your name shall be the last that I shall utter—the remembrance of you, my last thought."

Athos hastened upstairs to conceal his emotion, and regained, with hurried steps, the porch where Olivain was waiting with the horses.

"Olivain," said Athos, showing the servant Raoul's shoulder-belt; "tighten the buckle of this sword, which falls a little too low. You will accompany Monsieur le Vicomte till Grimaud has rejoined you. You know, Raoul, Grimaud is an old and zealous servant, he will follow you.

"Yes, sir," answered Raoul.

"Now to horse, that I may see you depart."

Raoul obeyed.

"Good-bye, Raoul," said the count; "good-bye, my dear boy!"

"Good-bye, sir—good-bye—my beloved protector!"

Athos waved his hand; he dared not trust himself to speak, and Raoul went away, head uncovered. Athos remained motionless, looking after him until he turned the corner of the street. He then threw his bridle into the hands of a peasant who was standing by, reascended the steps slowly, entered the church, knelt down in the most obscure corner, and prayed.

23

ONE OF M. DE BEAUFORT'S FORTY METHODS OF ESCAPE

TIME, however, passed away with the prisoner as well as with those who occupied themselves with his escape, only it did not pass away quite so quickly. Unlike some men, who eagerly undertake a perilous adventure, and grow cold as the moment of execution approaches, the Duc de Beaufort, whose reckless courage was proverbial, and who had been chained down to inaction for five years, seemed to urge time forward, and to pant for the hour of action. There was in his escape alone, apart from the future projects which he cherished, a foretaste of vengeance which made his heart dilate.

M. de Beaufort, who had such a complete knowledge of the interior of the Palais Royal, pictured to himself, even in his prison, the commotion which was about to be excited when the cry resounded, from the cabinet of the cardinal to the chamber of the queen, "M. de Beaufort has escaped!" While saying all this to himself, M. de Beaufort smiled gently, and already fancied himself breathing the free air of the plains and the forests, grasping a horse between his legs, and exclaiming, with a loud voice, "I am free!"

True, on waking from such day-dreams, he found himself between his four walls; saw La Ramée at ten paces' distance from him, twirling his thumbs as usual, and in the antechamber his eight guards, laughing and drinking.

The only thing that relieved him in this odious picture—so great is the instability of the human mind—was the stolid face of Grimaud, that face for which he had at first conceived such a hatred, and which had since become his only hope.

It is unnecessary to say that all this was the play of the prisoner's excited imagination. Grimaud was still the same; he had, therefore, retained the confidence of La Ramée, his superior, who now would trust to him more willingly than to himself, for we have said that La Ramée felt at his heart a certain weak partiality for M. de Beaufort.

Thus it was that the good La Ramée made quite a little festival of this *tête-à-tête* supper with his prisoner. La Ramée had but one fault—he was a gourmand. He had found the pies good, and the wine excellent. Now the successor of Father Marteau had promised him a pie of pheasants, instead of a pie of chickens, and some Chambertin instead of Macon. All this, set off by the presence of this excellent prince, who was so good at bottom, who invented such droll tricks against M. de Chavigny, and such capital jokes against Mazarin, caused the approaching Whitsuntide to be one of the four great festivals of the year to the worthy La Ramée.

La Ramée, therefore, longed for six o'clock in the evening as impatiently as the duke. Since the morning he had been engaged in all the preparations, and trusting to no one but himself, had paid a visit to Father Marteau's successor. The latter had surpassed himself; he showed him a real monster pie, ornamented on the outside with the arms of M. de Beaufort. The pie was, as yet, empty, but near it were pheasants and partridges, larded so closely as to look like pincushions. The water came into the mouth of La Ramée, and he returned to the chamber of the duke rubbing his hands. To complete his happiness, Monsieur de Chavigny, relying entirely upon La Ramée, was gone a short journey, and had gone that very morning, which made La Ramée sub-governor of the castle.

As for Grimaud, he seemed more surly than ever. In the morning, Monsieur de Beaufort made a party at tennis with La Ramée; a sign from Grimaud gave him to understand that he must pay attention to everything. Grimaud, walking before, traced the way they were to take in the evening. The game was played in what was called the enclosure of the little court of the castle. It was a solitary place, where no sentinels were posted, except when Monsieur de Beaufort played there, and the walls were so high that such a precaution seemed quite unnecessary.

There were three doors to be opened before arriving at this enclosure. Each of these was opened with a different key.

On arriving at the enclosure, Grimaud went mechanically to seat himself near a loop-hole, with his legs hanging outside the wall. It was evident, therefore, that the rope ladder was to be suspended from this place. This manœuvre, well understood by the Duc de Beaufort, was, of course, quite unintelligible to La Ramée.

The game began. This time, M. de Beaufort was in good form, and sent the balls wherever he liked. La Ramée was completely beaten.

Four of the guards, who were placed over the prisoner, assisted in picking up the tennis balls. When the game was over, the duke, laughing at La Ramée for his bad play, offered these men two louis-d'or to go and drink his health, with their four other comrades.

The guards asked permission of La Ramée, who gave it to them, but not till the evening, however—until then he had business, and the prisoner was not to be left alone.

Six o'clock came, and, although they were not to sit down to table until seven o'clock, dinner was ready and served up. Upon a sideboard appeared the colossal pie with the duke's arms on it, and, seemingly, cooked to a turn, as far as one could judge by the golden colour which illumined the crust.

The rest of the dinner was to come.

Every one was impatient; La Ramée to sit down to table—the guards to go and drink—the duke to escape.

Grimaud alone was calm as ever. One might have fancied that Athos had educated him with a forethought of this great event.

There were moments when, looking at Grimaud, the duke asked himself if he was not dreaming, and if that marble figure was really at his service, and would become animate when the moment arrived for action.

La Ramée sent away the guards, desiring them to drink to the duke's health, and, as soon as they were gone, he locked all the doors, put the keys in his pocket, and showed the table to the prince with an air which meant——

"Whenever my lord pleases."

The prince looked at Grimaud—Grimaud looked at the clock—it was hardly a quarter past six. The escape was fixed to take place at seven o'clock. They had, therefore, three-quarters of an hour to wait.

The duke, in order to delay a quarter of an hour, pretended to be reading something that interested him, and said he wished they would permit him to finish his chapter. La Ramée went up to him and scanned over his shoulder to see what book it was that had so singular an influence over the prisoner as to make him put off his dinner.

It was *Cæsar's Commentaries*, which La Ramée had lent him, contrary to the orders of the governor; and La Ramée resolved never again to disobey those injunctions.

Meantime he uncorked the bottles, and went to smell if the pie was good.

At half-past six the duke arose, and said very gravely:

"Certainly, Cæsar was the greatest man of ancient times."

"You think so, my lord?" answered La Ramée.

"Yes."

"Well, as for me, I prefer Hannibal."

"And why, pray, Master La Ramée?" asked the duke.

"Because he left no Commentaries," replied La Ramée, with a coarse laugh.

The duke made no reply, but sitting down at the table, made a sign that La Ramée should also seat himself opposite to him. There is nothing so expressive as the face of an epicure who finds himself before a well-spread table: so La Ramée, when receiving his plate of soup from Grimaud, presented a type of perfect bliss.

The duke smiled.

"Zounds!" he said; "I don't suppose there is a happier man at this moment in the kingdom than you are!"

"You are right, my lord duke," answered the officer; "I don't know a pleasanter sight than a well-covered table; and when, added to that, he who does the honours is the grandson of Henry the Great, you will, my lord duke, easily comprehend that the honour one receives doubles the pleasure one enjoys."

The duke bowed in his turn, and an imperceptible smile appeared on the face of Grimaud, who kept behind La Ramée.

"My dear La Ramée," said the duke, "you're the only man who can so gracefully turn a compliment."

"No, my lord duke," replied La Ramée, in the fullness of his heart; "I say what I think—there is no compliment in what I say to you——"

"That you are devoted to me?" asked the duke.

"To own the truth, I should be inconsolable if you were to leave Vincennes."

"A droll way of showing your affliction." The duke meant to say "affection."

"But, my lord," returned La Ramée, "what would you do if

you got out? Every folly you committed would entangle you with the court, and they would put you into the Bastille, instead of Vincennes. Now, Monsieur de Chavigny is not amiable, I allow; but Monsieur du Tremblay is much worse."

"Indeed!" said the duke, who from time to time looked at the clock, the fingers of which seemed to move with a sickening slowness; "but what could you expect from the brother of a Capuchin monk, brought up in the school of Cardinal Richelieu?"

"Ah, my lord, it is a great happiness that the queen, who always wished you well, had a fancy to send you here, where there's a promenade and a tennis-court, good air, and a good table."

"In short," answered the duke, "if I comprehend you, La Ramée, I am ungrateful for having ever thought of leaving this place?"

"Oh! my lord duke, 'tis the height of ingratitude; but your highness has not seriously thought of it?"

"Yes," returned the duke; "I must confess I do sometimes think of it."

"Still by one of your forty methods, your highness?"

"Yes—yes, indeed."

"My lord," said La Ramée, "now we are quite at our ease, and enjoying ourselves, pray tell me one of these forty ways invented by your highness."

"Willingly," answered the duke; "hand me the pie!"

"I am listening," said La Ramée, leaning back in his armchair, and raising his glass of Madeira to his lips, and winking his eye that he might see the sun through the rich liquid that he was about to taste.

The duke glanced at the clock. In ten minutes it would strike seven.

Grimaud placed the pie before the duke, who took a knife with a silver blade to raise the upper crust; but La Ramée, who was afraid of any harm happening to this fine work of art, passed his knife, which had an iron blade, to the duke.

"Thank you, La Ramée," said the prisoner.

"Well, my lord! this famous invention of yours?"

"Must I tell you," replied the duke, "on what I most reckon, and what I determine to try first?"

"Yes, that one! my lord."

"Well—I should hope, in the first instance, to have as a keeper an honest man, like you."

"And you have one, my lord—well?"

"Having then a keeper like La Ramée, I should next try to

have introduced to me by some friend a man who would be devoted to me, and who would assist me in my flight."

"Come, come," said La Ramée, "not a bad idea."

"Isn't it? For instance, the former serving man of some brave gentleman, an enemy himself to Mazarin, as every gentleman ought to be."

"Hush—don't let us speak of politics, my lord!"

"Then my keeper will begin to trust this man, and to depend upon him; and then I shall obtain news from those without the prison walls."

"Ah, yes! but how can the news be brought to you?"

"Nothing easier—in a game of tennis. I send a ball into the moat; a man is there who picks it up; the ball contains a letter."

"The devil it does! The devil it does!" said La Ramée, scratching his head; "you are wrong to tell me that, my lord. I shall watch the men who pick up balls."

The duke smiled.

"But," said La Ramée, "that is only one manner of corresponding."

"In my opinion a very good one."

"But not a sure one."

"Pardon me. For instance, I say to my friends, 'Be on a certain day, on a certain hour, at the other side of the moat, with two horses.' "

"Well, what then?"—La Ramée began to be uneasy—"unless the horses have wings to mount up to the ramparts and to come and fetch you."

"That's not needed. I have," replied the duke, "a way of descending from the ramparts."

"What?"

"A rope ladder."

"Yes—but," answered La Ramée, trying to laugh, "a rope ladder can't be sent round a ball, like a letter."

"No; but it can come in another way—in a pie, for instance," replied the duke. "The guards are away. Grimaud is here alone; and Grimaud is the man whom a friend has sent to second me in everything. The moment for my escape is fixed—seven o'clock. Well—at a few minutes to seven——"

"At a few minutes to seven?" cried La Ramée, with cold sweat on his brow.

"At a few minutes to seven," returned the duke (suiting the action to the words), "I raise the crust of the pie. I find in it two poignards, a ladder of ropes, and a gag. I point one of the poignards at La Ramée's breast, and I say to him, 'My friend, I am sorry for it; but if thou movest, if you utterest a cry, thou art a dead man!'"

The duke, in pronouncing these words, suited, as we have before said, the action to the words. He was standing near the officer, and he directed the point of the poignard in such a manner, close to La Ramée's heart, that there could be no doubt in the mind of that individual as to his determination. Meanwhile, Grimaud, still mute as ever, drew from the pie the other sword, the rope-ladder, and the gag.

La Ramée followed all these objects with his eyes; his alarm every moment increasing.

"Oh, my lord!" he cried, with an expression of prostration in his face; "you surely would not kill me!"

"No; not if thou dost not oppose my flight."

"But, my lord, if you escape, I am a ruined man."

"I shall compensate thee for the loss of thy place."

"You are determined to leave the château?"

"By heaven and earth! This evening I shall be free."

"And if I defend myself, or call, or cry out?"

"I shall kill thee; on the honour of a gentleman, I shall."

At this moment the clock struck.

"Seven o'clock!" said Grimaud, who had not spoken a word.

La Ramée made one movement in order to satisfy his conscience. The duke frowned; the officer felt the point of the poignard, which, having penetrated through his clothes, was close to his heart.

"Let us despatch," said the duke.

"My lord—one last favour."

"What? speak—make haste.⁵⁹

"Bind my arms, my lord, fast."

"Why bind thee?"

"That I may not be condemned as your accomplice."

"Your hands?" asked Grimaud.

"Not before me, behind me."

"But with what?" asked the duke.

"With your belt, my lord," replied La Ramée.

The duke undid his belt and gave it to Grimaud, who bound La Ramée in such a way as to satisfy him.

"Your feet also," said Grimaud.

La Ramée stretched out his legs, Grimaud took a napkin, tore it into strips, and tied La Ramée's feet together.

"Now, my lord," said the poor man, "let me have the *poire d'angoisse*. I ask for it; without it I should be tried in a court of justice because I did not cry out. Thrust it into my mouth, my lord, thrust it in."

Grimaud prepared to comply with this request, when the officer made a sign as if he had something to say.

"Well," said the duke.

"Now, my lord, do not forget if any harm happens to me, on your account, that I have a wife and four children."

"Rest assured—put in the gag, Grimaud."

In a second La Ramée was gagged, and laid prostrate. Two or three chairs were thrown down, as if there had been a struggle. Grimaud then took from the pocket of the officer all the keys it contained, and first opened the door of the room in which they were, then closed it, and double locked it, and both he and the duke proceeded rapidly down the gallery, which led to the little enclosure. At last they came to the tennis-court. It was completely deserted. No sentinels—no one at the windows.

The duke ran out on to the rampart, and perceived, on the other side of the ditch, three cavaliers with two riding horses. The duke exchanged a signal with them. It was well for him that they were there.

Grimaud, meantime, got ready the means of escape.

This was not, however, a rope-ladder, but a ball of silk cord, with a narrow board, which was to pass between the legs and to unwind itself by the weight of the person who sat astride upon the board.

"Go!" said the duke.

"The first, my lord?" inquired Grimaud.

"Certainly. If I am caught, I risk nothing but being taken back to prison. If they catch thee, thou wilt be hung."

"True," replied Grimaud.

And, instantly, Grimaud, sitting upon the board, as if on horseback, commenced his perilous descent.

The duke followed him with his eyes with involuntary terror. He had gone down about three-quarters of the length of the wall, when the cord broke. Grimaud fell—precipitated into the moat.

The duke uttered a cry, but Grimaud did not utter a single moan. He must have been fearfully hurt, for he did not move from the place where he fell.

Immediately, one of the men who were waiting, slipped down into the moat, tied under Grimaud's shoulders the end of a rope, and the other two, who held the other end, drew Grimaud to them.

"Come down, my lord," said the man in the moat. "There are only fifteen feet more from the top down here, and the grass is soft."

The duke had already started. His task was the more difficult, as he had no board to support him. He was obliged to let himself down by his hands, and from a height of fifty feet. But, as we have said, he was active, strong, and full of presence of mind. In less than five minutes he arrived at the end of the cord. He was then only fifteen feet from the ground, as the gentleman beneath had told him. He let go the rope, and fell upon his feet, without receiving any injury.

He instantly began to climb up the slope of the moat, on the top of which he met de Rochefort. The other two gentlemen were unknown to him. Grimaud, in a swoon, was tied on to a horse.

"Gentlemen," said the duke, "I shall thank you later; now we have not a moment to lose. On, then! on! those who love me, follow me!"

And he sprang on his horse, and set off on full gallop, drawing in the fresh air, and crying out, with an expression of face which it would be impossible to describe:

"Free! free! free!"

24

D'ARTAGNAN ARRIVES AT THE RIGHT MOMENT

At Blois, d'Artagnan received the money paid to him by Mazarin for any future services he might render the Cardinal.

From Blois to Paris was a journey of four days for ordinary travellers, but d'Artagnan arrived on the third day at the Barrière Saint Denis. In turning the corner of the Rue Montmarre, in order to reach the Rue Tiquetonne and the Hôtel de la Chevrette, where he had requested Porthos to meet him, he saw at one of the windows of the hotel, his friend Porthos, dressed in a sky-blue waistcoat, embroidered with silver, and gaping, till he showed all down his throat; whilst the people passing by admiringly gazed at this gentleman, so handsome and so rich, who seemed so weary of his riches and his greatness.

Porthos, seeing d'Artagnan, hastened to receive him at the entrance to the hotel.

"Ah! my dear friend!" he cried, "what bad stabling for my horses here!"

"Indeed!" said d'Artagnan; "I am most unhappy to hear it, on account of those fine animals."

"And I also—I was also wretchedly off," he answered, moving backwards and forwards as he spoke—"and had it not been for the hostess," he added, with an air of self-complacency, "who is very agreeable, and understands a joke, I should have got a lodging somewhere else."

"Yes, I see," said d'Artagnan, "the air of La Rue Tiquetonne is not like that of Pierrefonds; but console yourself, I shall soon conduct you to one much better."

Then, taking Porthos aside:

"My dear du Valon," he said, "here you are in full dress most fortunately, for I shall take you directly to the Cardinal's."

"Gracious me!—really!" cried Porthos, opening his great, wondering eyes.

"Yes, my friend."

"A presentation?—indeed!"

"Does that distress you?"

"No; but it agitates me."

"Oh! don't be alarmed; you have not to deal with the other Cardinal; and this one will not oppress you by his dignity."

" 'Tis the same thing—you understand me, d'Artagnan—a court."

"There's no court now. Alas!"

"The queen!"

"I was nearly saying, there's no longer a queen. The queen! Be assured we shall not see her."

"But you, my friend; are you not going to change your dress?"

"No, I shall go as I am. This travelling dress will show the Cardinal my haste to obey his commands."

They set out on Vulcan and Bayard, followed by Mousqueton on Phœbus, and arrived at the Palais Royal at about a quarter to seven. The streets were crowded, for it was the day of Pentecost—and the crowd looked in wonder at our two cavaliers; one as fresh as if he had come out of a bandbox, the other so covered with dust that he looked as if he had come from a field of battle.

Mousqueton also attracted attention; and as the romance of Don Quixote was then the fashion, they said that he was Sancho, who, after having lost one master, had found two.

On reaching the palace, d'Artagnan sent in to his Eminence the letter in which he had been ordered to return without delay. He was soon ordered to enter into the presence of the Cardinal.

"Courage!" he said to Porthos, as they proceeded. "Do not be intimidated. Believe me, the eye of the eagle is closed for ever. We have only the vulture to deal with. Hold yourself up as stiff as on

the day of the bastion of Saint Gervais; and do not bend too low
to this Italian: that might give him a poor idea of us."

"Good!" answered Porthos. "Good!"

Mazarin was in his study, working at a list of pensions and
benefices, of which he was attempting to reduce the number. He
saw d'Artagnan and Porthos enter with pleasure, yet exhibited no
joy in his countenance.

"Ah! you, is it? Monsieur le Lieutenant, you have been very
prompt. 'Tis well. Welcome."

"Thanks, my lord. Here I am at your Eminence's service, as
well as Monsieur du Valon, one of my old friends, who used to
conceal his nobility under the name of Porthos."

"A magnificent cavalier," remarked Mazarin.

Porthos bowed to the Cardinal.

Porthos turned his head to the right and to the left, and drew
himself up with a movement full of dignity.

"The best swordsman in the kingdom, my lord," said
d'Artagnan.

Porthos bowed to his friend.

Mazarin was as fond of fine soldiers, as, in later times, Frederick
of Prussia used to be. He admired the strong hands, the broad
shoulders, and steady eye of Porthos. He seemed to see before him
the salvation of his administration, and of the kingdom, sculptured
in flesh and bone. He remembered that the old association of
musketeers was composed of but four persons.

"And your other friends?" he asked.

Porthos opened his mouth, thinking it a good opportunity to
put in a word in his turn; d'Artagnan checked him by a glance
from the corner of his eye.

"They are prevented at this moment, but will join us later."

Mazarin coughed a little.

"And this gentleman being disengaged, takes to the service
willingly?" he asked.

"Yes, my lord, and from complete devotion to the cause, for
Monsieur du Valon is rich."

"Fifty thousand francs a year," said Porthos.

These were the first words he had spoken.

"From pure zeal," resumed Mazarin, with a meaning smile;
"from pure zeal and devotion?"

"My lord has, perhaps, no faith in that word," said d'Artagnan.

"Have you, Monsieur le Gascon?" asked Mazarin, supporting
his elbows on his desk, and his chin on his hands.

"I," replied the Gascon, "I believe in devotion as a word at
one's baptism, for instance, which naturally comes before one's

proper name; every one is naturally more or less devout, certainly; but there should be, at the end of one's devotion, something to gain."

"Your friend, therefore, what does he wish for as the reward of his devotion?"

D'Artagnan was about to explain that the end and aim of the zeal of Porthos, was, that one of his estates should be erected into a barony, when a great noise was heard in the ante-chamber; at the same time the door of the study was thrown open, and a man, covered with dust, rushed into it, exclaiming:

"My lord the Cardinal! my lord the Cardinal!"

Mazarin thought that some one was going to assassinate him, and he drew back, pushing his chair on the castors. D'Artagnan and Porthos moved so as to place themselves between the person entering and the Cardinal.

"Well, sir," exclaimed Mazarin, "what's the matter? and why do you rush in here as if you were just going into a market-place?"

"My lord," replied the messenger, "I wish to speak to your Eminence in secret. My name is du Poins, captain in the guards, on duty at the donjon of Vincennes."

Mazarin, remarking from the paleness and agitation of the messenger that he had something of importance to say, made a sign that d'Artagnan and Porthos should retire.

When they were alone:

"What I have to say is, my lord, that the Duc de Beaufort has contrived to escape from the Château of Vincennes."

Mazarin uttered a cry, and became paler than he who brought this news. He fell, almost fainting, back in his chair.

"Escaped? Monsieur de Beaufort escaped?"

"My lord, I saw him run off from the top of the terrace."

"And you did not fire upon him?"

"He was beyond reach of my gun."

"Monsieur de Chavigny—where was he?"

"Absent."

"And La Ramée?"

"He was found locked up in the prisoner's room, a gag in his mouth, and a poignard near him."

"But the man who was under him?"

"Was an accomplice of the duke's, and escaped with him."

Mazarin groaned.

"My lord," said d'Artagnan, advancing towards the Cardinal, "it seems to me that your Eminence is losing precious time. It may still be possible to recapture the prisoner. France is large; the nearest frontier is sixty leagues from here."

"And who is to pursue him?" cried Mazarin.

"I! Egad! if my lord orders me to pursue the devil, I would do so, and seize him by the horns, and bring him back again."

"And I, too," said Porthos.

"Go, then; take what guards you want, and pursue him."

"You command us, my lord, to do so?"

"And I sign my orders," said Mazarin, taking a piece of paper, and writing some lines: "Monsieur du Valon, your barony is on the back of the Duc de Beaufort's horse; all you have to do is to overtake it. As for you, my dear lieutenant, I promise you nothing; but if you bring him back to me, dead or alive, you shall ask all you wish."

"To horse, Porthos!" said d'Artagnan, taking his friend by the hand.

"Here I am," replied Porthos, with his sublime composure.

They descended the great staircase, taking with them all the guards that they found on their road, and crying out, "To horse! To horse!" and they spurred on their horses, which set off along the Rue St. Honoré with the speed of a whirlwind.

"Well, baron! I promised you some good exercise!" said the Gascon.

"Yes, my captain."

As they went, the citizens, awakened, left their doors, and the fierce dogs followed the cavaliers, barking. At the corner of the Cimetière Saint Jean, d'Artagnan upset a man: it was too slight an occurrence to delay people so eager to get on. The troop continued its course as if their steeds were winged.

Alas! there are no unimportant events in this world! and, we shall see, that this apparently slight one was near endangering the monarchy.

25

ON THE HIGH ROAD

THE musketeers rode the whole length of the Faubourg St. Antoine, and the road to Vincennes, and soon found themselves out of the town, then in a forest, and then in sight of a village.

From the top of an acclivity d'Artagnan perceived a group of people collected on the other side of the moat, in front of that part of the donjon which looks towards Saint Maur. He rode on, convinced that he should in that direction gain intelligence of the fugitive; and he gained from the people that composed that group, that the duke had been pursued without success; that his party consisted of four able men, and one wounded, and that they were two hours and a quarter in advance of their pursuers.

"Only four!" cried d'Artagnan, looking at Porthos: "baron, only four of them!"

Porthos smiled.

"And only two hours and a quarter before us, and we so well mounted, Porthos!"

Porthos sighed, and thought of all that was awaiting his poor horses.

The troop then continued their course with their wonted ardour; but some of them could no longer sustain this rapidity; three of them stopped after an hour's run, and one fell down.

D'Artagnan, who never turned his head, did not perceive it. Porthos told him of it in his calm manner.

"If we can only keep two," said d'Artagnan, "it will be enough, since the duke's troop are only four in number."

And he spurred his horse on.

At the end of another two hours the horses had gone twelve leagues without stopping; their legs began to tremble; and the foam that they shed whitened the doublets of their riders.

"Let us stop here an instant to give these miserable creatures breathing time," said Porthos.

"Let us rather kill them! yes, kill them!" cried d'Artagnan; "I see new tracks; 'tis not a quarter of an hour since they passed this place."

In fact, the road was trodden by horses' feet, visible even in the approaching gloom of evening.

They set out; after a run of two leagues, Mousqueton's horse sank.

"Gracious me!" said Porthos, "there's Phœbus ruined."

"The Cardinal will pay you a hundred pistoles."

"I'm above that."

"Let us set out again at a full gallop."

"Yes, if we can."

But, at last, the lieutenant's horse refused to go on; he could not breathe; one last spur, instead of making him advance, caused him to fall.

"The devil!" exclaimed Porthos, "there's Vulcan foundered."

"Zounds!" cried d'Artagnan, "we must then stop! Give me your horse, Porthos! What the devil are you doing?"

"By Jove, I am falling, or rather Bayard is falling," replied Porthos.

All three then called out, "All's over."

"Silence!" said d'Artagnan.

"What is it?"

"I hear a horse, 'tis on before; it is at a hundred steps from hence, and in advance of us."

There was, in truth, the neighing of a horse heard.

"Sir," said Mousqueton, "at a hundred steps from us there's a hunting seat."

"Mousqueton, my pistols."

"They are in my hand, sir."

"Porthos, keep yours in your saddle bags."

"I have them."

"Now, we require horses for the king's service."

"For the king's service," repeated Porthos.

"Then not a word, and to work!"

They went on, through the night, silent as phantoms; they saw a light shine in the midst of some trees.

"There is the house, Porthos," said the Gascon; "let me do what I please, and you do what I do."

They glided from tree to tree, till they arrived at twenty steps from the house unperceived, and saw, by means of a lanthorn suspended under a hut, four fine horses. A groom was rubbing them down; near them were saddles and bridles.

"I want to buy those horses," said d'Artagnan, approaching the groom.

"These horses are not to be sold," was the reply.

"I take them, then," said the lieutenant.

And he took hold of one within his reach: his two companions did the same thing.

"Sir," cried the groom, "they have just been six leagues, and have only been unharnessed about half an hour."

"Half an hour's rest is enough," replied the Gascon.

The groom called aloud for help. A steward appeared, just as d'Artagnan and his companions were preparing to mount. The steward wished to expostulate.

"My dear friend," cried the lieutenant, "if you say a word I will blow out your brains."

"But, sir," answered the steward, "do you know that these horses belong to Monsieur de Montbazon?"

"So much the better; they must be good animals, then."

"Sir, I shall call for assistance."

"And I also; I've ten guards behind me; don't you hear them gallop; and I'm one of the king's musketeers; come, Porthos, come, Mouston."

They mounted the horses as quickly as possible.

"Here! here!" cried the steward; "the house servants with the carbines."

"On! on!" cried d'Artagnan! "there'll be firing! on!"

They all set off, swift as the winds.

"Here!" cried the steward, "here!" whilst the groom ran to a neighbouring building.

"Take care of your horses," shouted d'Artagnan.

"Fire!" replied the steward.

A gleam, like a flash of lightning, illuminated the road, and, with the flash, was heard the whistling of balls, which were fired in the air.

"They fire like grooms," said Porthos; "in the time of the Cardinal, people fired better than that; do you remember the road to Crevecœur, Mousqueton?"

"Ah, sir! my left side still pains me."

"Are you sure we are on the right track, lieutenant?"

"Egad, didn't you hear—these horses belong to Monsieur de Montbazon: well, Monsieur de Montbazon is the husband of Madame de Montbazon——"

"And——"

"And Madame de Montbazon is the mistress of the Duc de Beaufort."

"Ah, I see," replied Porthos; "she has ordered relays of horses."

"Exactly so."

"And we are pursuing the duke with the very horses he has just left?"

"My dear Porthos, you are really a man of superior understanding," said d'Artagnan.

"Pooh!" said Porthos, "I am what I am."

They rode on for an hour, till their horses were covered with foam.

"Zounds! what is yonder?" cried d'Artagnan.

"You are very lucky, if you see anything in such a night as this," said Porthos.

"Something bright."

"I, too," cried Mousqueton, "see something."

"Yes, a dead horse," said d'Artagnan, pulling up his horse, which shied: "it seems that they also are broken-winded as well as ourselves."

"I seem to hear the noise of a troop of horsemen," exclaimed Porthos, leaning over his horse's mane.

"Impossible!"

"They appear to be numerous."

"Then, 'tis something else."

"Another horse!" said Porthos.

"Dead?"

"No: dying."

"Saddled?"

"Yes, saddled and bridled."

"Then 'tis the fugitives."

"Courage, they cannot escape us!"

"But, if they are numerous," observed Mousqueton, "'tis not we who have them, but they who have us."

"Not so!" cried d'Artagnan, "they'll suppose us to be stronger than themselves, as we're in pursuit, they'll be afraid, and disperse."

"Certainly," remarked Porthos.

"Ah! do you see?" cried the lieutenant.

"The lights again! this time I too saw them," said Porthos.

"On! on! forward! forward!" cried d'Artagnan, in his stentorian voice, "we shall laugh over all this in five minutes."

And they darted on afresh. The horses, excited by pain and emulation, raced over the dark road, in the midst of which was now seen a moving mass, more dense and obscure than the rest of the horizon.

26

THE COLLISION

THEY rode on in this way for some minutes. Suddenly, two dark forms seemed to separate from the mass, advanced, grew in size and, as they grew larger and larger, assumed the appearance of two horsemen.

"Oh, oh!" cried d'Artagnan, "they're coming towards us."

"So much the worse for them," said Porthos.

"Who goes there?" cried a voice.

The three horsemen answered not, stopped not, and all that was heard was the noise of swords, drawn from the scabbards, and of the cocking of the pistols, with which the two phantoms were armed.

"Arm to the teeth," said d'Artagnan.

Porthos understood him, and he and the lieutenant each one took from his left hand a pistol, and armed himself each in his turn.

"Who goes there?" was demanded a second time. "Not a step farther, or you're dead men!"

"Stuff!" cried Porthos, almost choked with dust. "Stuff and nonsense! we have seen plenty of dead men in our time."

Hearing these words, the two shadows blockaded the road, and by the light of the stars might be seen the shining of their arms.

"Back!" cried d'Artagnan; "or you are dead!"

Two shots were the reply to this threat; but the assailants attacked their foes with such velocity, that in a moment they were upon them; a third pistol-shot was heard, aimed by d'Artagnan; and one of his assailants fell. As to Porthos he assaulted his with such violence, that although his sword was thrust aside, the enemy was thrown off his horse, and fell about ten steps from it.

"Finish! Mouston—finish the work!" cried Porthos. And he darted on, beside his friend, who had already begun a fresh pursuit.

"Well?" said Porthos.

"I've broken his head," cried d'Artagnan. "And you——"

"I've only thrown him down; but hark!"

Another shot of a carbine was heard. It was Mousqueton, who was obeying his master's command.

"On! on!" cried d'Artagnan; "all is well! we have the first throw."

"Ha! ha!" laughed Porthos, "behold, other players appear."

And in fact, two other cavaliers made their appearance detached, as it seemed, from the principal group; they again disputed the road.

This time the lieutenant did not wait for the opposite party to speak.

"Stand aside," he cried; "stand off the road."

"What do you want?" asked a voice.

"The duke!" Porthos and d'Artagnan roared out both at once.

A burst of laughter was the answer, but finished with a groan. D'Artagnan had, with his sword, cut the poor wretch in two who had laughed.

At the same time Porthos and his adversary fired on each other, and d'Artagnan turned to him:

"Bravo!—you've killed him, I think."

"No, wounded his horse."

"But what ails my horse?"

"What ails your horse is, that he's falling down," replied Porthos.

In truth, the lieutenant's horse stumbled, and fell on his knees; then a rattling in his throat was heard, and he lay down to die. This caused d'Artagnan to swear.

"Does your honour want a horse?" asked Mousqueton.

"Zounds! want one?" cried the Gascon.

"Here's one, sir——"

"How on earth hast thou two horses?" asked d'Artagnan, jumping on one of them.

"Their masters are dead! I thought they would be useful, so I took them."

Meantime Porthos had reloaded his pistols.

"Be on the alert!" cried d'Artagnan. "Here are two other cavaliers."

As he spoke two horsemen came up at full speed.

"Ho! your honour," cried Mousqueton, "the man you upset is rising up."

"Why didn't thou serve him as thou didst the first man?" said Porthos.

"I held the horses, my hands were full, your honour."

A shot was fired that moment—Mousqueton shrieked with pain.

"Ah, sir! I'm hit in the other side! exactly in the other! This hurt is just the fellow of that I had on the road to Amiens."

Porthos turned round like a lion—plunged on the dismounted cavalier, who tried to draw his sword; but, before it was out of the scabbard, Porthos, with the hilt of his, had hit him such a terrible blow on the head, that he fell like an ox beneath the butcher's knife.

Mousqueton, groaning, slipped down from his horse—his wound not allowing him to sit in his saddle.

On perceiving the cavaliers, d'Artagnan had stopped and charged his pistol afresh; besides, his horse, he found, had a carbine on the bow of the saddle.

"Well!" exclaimed Porthos calmly. "Shall we wait, or shall we charge?"

"Let us charge them," answered the Gascon.

"Charge!" cried Porthos.

They spurred on their horses; the other cavaliers were only twenty steps from them.

"For the king!" cried d'Artagnan.

"The king has no authority here!" answered a deep voice, which seemed to proceed from a cloud—so enveloped was the cavalier in a whirlwind of dust.

"'Tis well; we will see if the king's name is not a passport everywhere," replied the Gascon.

"See!" answered the voice.

Two shots were fired at once; one by d'Artagnan, the other by the adversary of Porthos. D'Artagnan's ball took off his enemy's hat. The ball fired by Porthos's foe went through the throat of his horse, which fell, groaning.

"Ah! this," cried the voice, the tone of which was at once piercing and jeering—"this! 'tis nothing but a butchery of horses, and not a combat between men. To the sword, sir!—the sword!"

And he jumped off his horse.

"To our swords!—be it so!" replied d'Artagnan—"that will suit me."

D'Artagnan, in two steps, was engaged with his foe, whom, according to his custom, he attacked impetuously; but he met this time with a skill and a strength of arm which made him pause. Twice he was obliged to step back; his adversary stirred not one inch. D'Artagnan returned, and again attacked him.

Twice or thrice, blows were struck on both sides without effect; sparks were emitted from the swords, like water spouting out.

Then d'Artagnan thought it was time to try one of his favourite feints in fencing. He brought it to bear; skilfully executed it with the rapidity of lightning; and struck the blow with a force which he fancied would prove irresistible.

The blow was parried.

"Sdeath!" he cried, with his Gascon accent.

At this exclamation his adversary bounded back, and, bending his bare head, tried to distinguish in the gloom the features of the lieutenant.

As to d'Artagnan, afraid of some feint, he still stood on the defensive.

"Have a care," cried Porthos to his opponent; "I've still two pistols charged."

"The more reason you should fire the first," cried his foe.

Porthos fired; a flash threw a gleam of light over the field of battle.

As the light shone on them, a cry was heard from the other two combatants.

"Athos!" exclaimed d'Artagnan.

"D'Artagnan!" ejaculated Athos.

Athos raised his sword—d'Artagnan lowered his.

"Aramis!" cried Athos—"don't fire!"

"Ha! ha! is it you, Aramis?" said Porthos.

And he threw away his pistol.

Aramis put his back into his saddle bags, and sheathed his sword.

"My son!" exclaimed Athos, extending his hand to d'Artagnan.

This was the name which he gave him in former days—in their moments of tender intimacy.

"Athos!" cried d'Artagnan, wringing his hands. "So you defend him! And I, who have sworn to take him dead or alive, I am dishonoured—Ah!"

"Kill me!" replied Athos, showing his breast, "if your honour requires my death."

"Oh! woe's me! woe's me!" cried the lieutenant; "there's only one man in the world who could stay my hand; by a fatality that very man comes across my path. What shall I say to the Cardinal?"

"You can tell him, sir," answered a voice, which was a voice of high command in that battlefield, "that he sent against me the only two men capable of getting the better of four men;—of fighting man to man, without discomfiture against the Count de la Fère and the Chevalier d'Herblay, and of surrendering only to fifty men!"

"The prince!" exclaimed at the same moment Athos and Aramis, uncovering as they spoke; "the Duc de Beaufort!" whilst d'Artagnan and Porthos stepped backwards.

"Fifty cavaliers!" cried the Gascon.

"Look round you, gentlemen, if you doubt the facts," said the duke.

The two friends looked to the right—to the left; they were surrounded by a troop of horsemen.

"Hearing the noise of the fight," resumed the duke, "I fancied you had about twenty men with you, so I came back with those around me, tired of always running away, and wishing to draw my sword for my own cause; but you are only two."

"Yes, my lord; but, as you have said, two equal to twenty," said Athos.

"Come, gentlemen, your swords," said the duke.

"Our swords!" cried d'Artagnan, raising his head and regaining his self-possession—"Never!"

"Never," added Porthos.

Some of the men moved towards them.

"One moment, your highness," whispered Athos; and he said something in a low tone.

"As you will," replied the duke. "I am too much indebted to you to refuse your request. Gentlemen," he said to his escort, "withdraw. Monsieur d'Artagnan, Monsieur du Valon, you are at liberty."

The order was obeyed; d'Artagnan and Porthos then found themselves in the centre of a large circle.

"Now d'Herblay," said Athos, "dismount and come here."

Aramis dismounted, and went to Porthos; while Athos approached d'Artagnan. All the four were together.

"Friends!" said Athos; "do you regret that you have not shed our blood?"

"No," replied d'Artagnan; "I regret to see that we, hitherto united, are opposed to each other. Ah! nothing will ever succeed with us now!"

"Oh! heaven! No, all is over!" said Porthos.

"Well—be on our side now," resumed Aramis.

"Peace, d'Herblay!" cried Athos; "such proposals are not to be made to gentlemen such as these. 'Tis a matter of conscience with them, as with us."

"Meanwhile, here we are enemies!" said Porthos. "Grammercy! who would ever have thought it?"

D'Artagnan only sighed.

Athos looked at them both, and took their hands in his.

"Friends!" he said, "this is a serious business, and my heart bleeds as if you had pierced it through and through. Yes, we are severed; there is the great—the sad truth! but we have not as yet declared war; perhaps we shall have to make certain conditions, therefore a solemn conference is indispensable."

"For my own part, I demand it," said Aramis.

"I accept it," interposed d'Artagnan proudly.

Porthos bowed, in assent.

"Let us choose a place of rendezvous," continued Athos; "and, in a last interview, arrange our mutual position, and the conduct we are to maintain towards each other."

"Good!" the other three exclaimed.

"Well, then, the place?"

"Will the Place Royale suit you?" asked d'Artagnan.

"In Paris?"

"Yes."

Athos and Aramis looked at each other.

"The Place Royale—be it so!" said Athos.

"When?"

"To-morrow evening, if you please."

"At what hour?"

"At ten in the evening if that suits you—we shall have returned."

"Good."

"There," continued Athos, "either peace or war will be decided—our honour, at all events, will be secured."

"Alas!" murmured d'Artagnan, "our honour as soldiers is lost for ever! Now, Porthos; now we must hence, to bear back our shame to the Cardinal."

"And tell him," cried a voice, "that I am not too old to be still a man of action."

D'Artagnan recognised the voice of de Rochefort.

"Can I do anything for you, gentlemen?" asked the duke.

"Be witness that we have done what we have done."

"That shall be done, be assured. Adieu! we shall meet soon, I trust, in Paris, where you shall have your revenge."

The duke, as he spoke, kissed his hand, spurred his horse into a gallop, and disappeared, followed by his troop, who were soon lost in distance and darkness.

D'Artagnan and Porthos were now alone with a man who held their two horses; they thought it was Mousqueton, and went up to him.

"What do I see?" cried the lieutenant. "Grimaud, is it thou?"

Grimaud motioned that he was not mistaken.

"And whose horses are these?" cried d'Artagnan.

"Who has given them to us?" asked Porthos.

"The Count de la Fère."

"Athos! Athos!" muttered d'Artagnan, "you think of every one; you are indeed a noble man! Where art thou bound to, Grimaud?"

"To join the Vicomte de Bragelonne in Flanders, your honour."

They were taking the road towards Paris, when groans, which seemed to proceed from a ditch, attracted their attention.

"What is that?" asked d'Artagnan.

"It is I, Mousqueton," said a mournful voice, while a sort of shadow arose out of the side of the road.

Porthos ran to him. "Art thou dangerously wounded, my dear Mouston?" he said.

"No, sir, but I am severely wounded."

"What is to be done?" said d'Artagnan; "we must return to Paris."

"I will see to Mousqueton," said Grimaud; and he gave his arm to his old comrade, whose eyes were filled with tears, and Grimaud could not tell whether the tears were caused by his wounds, or by the pleasure of seeing him again.

D'Artagnan and Porthos went on, meantime, to Paris. They were passed by a courier, covered with dust, the bearer of a letter from the duke to the Cardinal, giving testimony to the valour of d'Artagnan and Porthos.

Mazarin had passed a very bad night, when this letter was brought to him, announcing that the duke was free, and that he should henceforth raise up a mortal strife against him.

"What consoles me," said the Cardinal, after perusing the letter, "is, that at least, in this chase, d'Artagnan has done me one good turn; he has destroyed Broussel. This Gascon is a precious fellow; even his mishaps are beneficial."

The Cardinal referred to that man whom d'Artagnan upset at the corner of the Cimetière Saint Jean, in Paris, and who was no other than the Councillor Broussel.

27

THE FOUR OLD FRIENDS PREPARE TO MEET

"WELL," said Porthos, seated in the courtyard of the Hôtel de la Chevrette, to d'Artagnan, who with a long and melancholy face had returned from the Palais Royal, "did he receive you ungraciously, my dear friend?"

"I'faith, yes! a hideous brute that Cardinal—what are you eating there, Porthos?"

"I am dipping a biscuit into a glass of Spanish wine. Do the same."

"You are right. Gimblon, a glass of wine!"

"Well! how has all gone off?"

"Zounds! you know there's only one way of saying things; so I went in and I said: 'My lord, we were not the strongest party.'

"'Yes, I know that,' he said, 'but give me the particulars.'

"You know, Porthos, I could not give him the particulars without naming our friends—to name them would be to commit them to ruin, so I merely said they were fifty and we were two.

"'There was firing, nevertheless, I heard,' he said; 'and your swords, they saw the light of day, I presume?'

"'That is, the night, my lord,' I answered.

"'Ah!'" cried the Cardinal; 'I thought you were a Gascon, my friend.'

"'I am only a Gascon,' said I, 'when I succeed.' So the answer pleased, and he laughed."

"Well, not so bad a reception as I thought," remarked Porthos.

"No, no, but 'tis the manner in which he spoke. Gimblon, another bottle—'tis almost incredible what a quantity of wine these biscuits will hold."

"Hem—didn't he mention me?" inquired Porthos.

"Ah! yes, indeed!" cried d'Artagnan, who was afraid of disheartening his friend by telling him that the Cardinal had not breathed a word about him; "yes, surely! he said——"

"He said?" resumed Porthos.

"Stop, I want to recall his exact words. He said, 'As to your friend, tell him that he may sleep in peace.'"

"Good, very good," said Porthos; "that means as clear as daylight that he still intends making me a baron."

At this moment nine o'clock struck. D'Artagnan started.

"Ah, yes," said Porthos; "there is nine o'clock. We have a rendezvous, you recollect, at the Place Royale."

"Ah! stop! hold your peace, Porthos—don't remind me of it; 'tis that which has upset me so much since yesterday. I shall not go."

"Why," asked Porthos.

"Why, suppose this appointment is but a ruse, that there's something hidden beneath it?"

D'Artagnan did not believe Athos to be capable of a deception, but he sought an excuse for not going to the rendezvous.

"We must go," said the superb lord of Bracieux, "lest they should say we were afraid. We, who have faced fifty foes on the high-road, can well meet two in the Place Royale."

"Yes, yes, but they took part with the princes without apprising us of it—perhaps the duke may try to catch us in his turn."

"Nonsense! He had us in his power, and let us go. Besides, we can be on our guard—let us take arms, and let Planchet go with us with his carbine."

"Planchet is a Frondeur," answered d'Artagnan.

"Deuce take these civil wars! one can no more reckon on one's friends than on one's footmen," said Porthos; "ah, if Mousqueton were here! there's one who will never desert me!"

"So long as you are rich! ah! my friend! 'tis not civil war that disunites us! It is that we are, each of us, twenty years older; it is that the honest emotions of youth have given place to the suggestions of interest—to the whispers of greed—to the counsels of selfishness. Yes, you are right—let us go, Porthos! but let us go well armed—were we not to go they would say we were afraid. Hollo! Planchet, here! saddle our horses—take your carbine."

"Whom are we going to attack, sir?"

"No one, a mere matter of precaution," answered the Gascon.

"You know, sir, that they wished to murder that good Councillor Broussel, the friend of the people?"

"Really, did they?" said d'Artagnan.

"Yes, but he has been avenged. He was carried home in the arms of the people. His house has been filled ever since. He has received visits from the Coadjutor, from Madame de Longueville, and the Prince de Conti—Madame de Chevreuse and Madame de Vendôme have left their names at his door."

"How did you hear this?" inquired d'Artagnan.

"From a good source, sir—I heard it from Friquet."

"From Friquet? I know that name——"

"A son of Monsieur de Broussel's servant, and one that I promise you, in a revolt, will not cast away his share to the dogs."

"Is he not a chorister at Notre Dame?" asked d'Artagnan.

"Yes, that's he, patronised by Bazin."

"Ah, yes, I know."

"What is this boy to you?" asked Porthos.

"Gad!" replied d'Artagnan; "he has already given me good information, and he may do the same again."

Whilst all this was going on, Athos and Aramis were entering Paris by the Faubourg St. Antoine. They had taken some refreshment on the road, and hastened on that they might not fail at the rendezvous. Bazin was their only attendant, for Grimaud had stayed behind to take care of Mousqueton. As they were passing onwards, Athos proposed that they should lay aside their arms and military costume, and assume a dress suited to the city.

"Oh, no, dear count!" cried Aramis, "is it not a warlike encounter that we are entering upon?"

"What do you mean, Aramis?"

"That the Place Royale is the termination to the main road to Vendômois, and nothing else."

"How, our friends——"

"Are become our most dangerous enemies, Athos; let us be on our guard."

"Oh! my dear d'Herblay!"

"Who knows but that d'Artagnan has betrayed us to the Cardinal? who can say whether Mazarin may not take advantage of this rendezvous and arrest us?"

Athos folded his arms, and his noble head fell drooping on his breast.

"What do you expect, Athos?" pursued Aramis; "such are men, and, remember, they are not always twenty years of age; let us take precautions, Athos!"

"But suppose they come unarmed? what a disgrace to us."

"Oh, never fear! besides, if they do, we can make an excuse; we come straight from a journey, and are insurgents, also."

"An excuse for us! to meet d'Artagnan with a false excuse! to have to make a false excuse to Porthos! Oh, Aramis!" continued Athos, shaking his head, "upon my soul, you make me the most miserable of men; you disenchant a heart not wholly dead to friendship. Go in whatsoever guise you will, as for me I shall go disarmed."

"No, for I will not allow you to do so. 'Tis not one man, 'tis not Athos only, 'tis not the Count de la Fère, whom you will ruin by this weakness, but the whole party to which you belong, and who depend upon you."

"Be it so, then," replied Athos sorrowfully.

And they went on in mournful silence.

Scarcely had they reached by the Rue de la Mule—the iron gate of the Place Royale—than they perceived three cavaliers, d'Artagnan, Porthos, and Planchet, the two former wrapped up in their military cloaks, under which their swords were hidden, and Planchet, his musket by his side. They were waiting at the entrance of the Rue St. Catherine, and their horses were fastened to the rings of the arcade. Athos, therefore, commanded Bazin to fasten up his horse and that of Aramis in the same manner.

They then advanced, two and two, and saluted each other politely.

"Now, where will it be agreeable to you that we hold our conference?" inquired Aramis, perceiving that people were stopping to look at them, supposing that they were going to engage in one of those far-famed duels still extant in the memory of the Parisians —and especially the inhabitants of the Place Royale.

"The gate is shut," said Aramis, "but if these gentlemen like a cool retreat, under the trees, and a perfect seclusion, I will get the key from the Hôtel de Rohan, and we shall be well situated."

D'Artagnan darted a look into the obscurity of the place. Porthos ventured to put his head between the railings, to try if his glance could penetrate the gloom.

"If you prefer any other place," said Athos, in his persuasive voice, "choose for yourselves."

"This place, if Monsieur d'Herblay can procure the key, is the best that we can have," was the answer.

Aramis went off at once, begging Athos not to stay within reach of d'Artagnan and Porthos; a piece of advice which was received with a contemptuous smile.

Aramis returned soon with a man from the Hôtel de Rohan, who said:

"You swear, sir, that it is not so?"

"Stop," and Aramis gave him a piece of gold.

"Ah! your honour will not swear," said the *concierge*, shaking his head.

"Well, one can never say what may happen; at present these gentlemen are our friends."

"Yes, assuredly," added Athos, "and the other two——"

"You hear that?" said d'Artagnan to Porthos; "he won't swear."

"No?"

"No; then we must be cautious."

Athos did not lose sight of these two speakers. Aramis opened the gate, and faced round in order that d'Artagnan and Porthos might enter. In passing through the gate, the hilt of the lieutenant's sword was caught in the grating, and he was obliged to pull off his cloak; in doing so he showed the butt-end of his pistols, and a ray of the moon was reflected on the shining metal.

"Do you see?" whispered Aramis to Athos, touching his shoulder with one hand, and pointing with the other to the arms which the Gascon wore under his belt.

"Alas, I do!" replied Athos, with a deep sigh.

He entered third, and Aramis, who shut the gate after him, last. The two serving-men waited without, but, as if they likewise mistrusted each other, kept their respective distances.

28

THE PLACE ROYALE

THEY proceeded silently to the centre of the Place; but as at this very moment the moon had just emerged from behind a cloud, it was considered that they might be observed if they remained on that spot, and they regained the shade of the lime-trees.

There were benches here and there—the four gentlemen stopped near them; at a signal from Athos, Porthos and d'Artagnan sat down, the two others stood in front of them.

After a few minutes of silent embarrassment, Athos spoke.

"Gentlemen," he said, "our presence here is a proof of our former friendship; not one of us has failed at this rendezvous; not one has, therefore, to reproach himself."

"Hear me, count," replied d'Artagnan; "instead of paying compliments, let us explain our conduct to each other, like men of right and honest hearts."

"I desire nothing more; have you any cause of anger against me or Monsieur d'Herblay? If so, speak out," answered Athos.

"I have," replied d'Artagnan. "When I saw you at your château at Bragelonne, I made certain proposals to you, which you perfectly understood; instead of answering me as a friend, you played with me as a child: the friendship, therefore, that you boast of was not broken yesterday by the shock of our swords, but by your dissimulation at your castle."

"D'Artagnan!" said Athos reproachfully.

"You asked for candour—there it is. You ask what I have against you—I tell you. And I have the same sincerity to show you, if you wish, Monsieur d'Herblay; I acted in a similar way to you, and you also deceived me; I reproach you with nothing, however; 'tis only because Monsieur de la Fère has spoken of friendship that I question your conduct."

"And what do you find in it to blame?" asked Aramis haughtily.

The blood mounted instantly to the temples of d'Artagnan, who rose, and replied:

"I consider it the conduct of a pupil of Loyola."

On seeing d'Artagnan rise, Porthos rose also; these four men were, therefore, all standing at the same time, with a menacing aspect towards each other.

Upon hearing d'Artagnan's reply, Aramis seemed about to draw his sword, when Athos prevented him.

"D'Artagnan," he said, "you come here to-night, still infuriated by our yesterday's adventure. I believed that your heart was sufficiently noble to enable a friendship of twenty years to be stronger than an affront of a quarter of an hour. Come, do you really think you have anything to say against me? say it then; if I am to blame, I will avow my fault."

The grave and harmonious tones of that beloved voice had still over d'Artagnan its former influence, whilst that of Aramis, which had become sharp and piercing in his moments of ill-humour, irritated him. He answered therefore:

"I think, Monsieur le Comte, that you had something to communicate to me at your château of Bragelonne, and that gentleman"—he pointed to Aramis—"had also something to tell me, when I was in his convent. At that time I was not concerned in the adventure during which you barricaded the road that I was going; however, because I was prudent, you must not think me a fool. If I had wished to widen the breach between those whom Monsieur d'Herblay chooses to receive with a rope-ladder, and those whom he receives with a wooden ladder, it was in my power to do so."

"Have a care, d'Artagnan," cried Aramis, pale with anger, and seeing that the lieutenant had watched him with Madame de Longueville.

"I never interfere in that which concerns me not, but I hate hypocrites, and, among that number, I place musketeers who are abbés, and abbés who are musketeers; and," he added, turning to Porthos, "here's a gentleman who is of the same opinion as myself."

Porthos, who had not yet spoken, answered merely by a word and a gesture.

He said "yes," and he put his hand on his sword. Aramis started back, and drew his. D'Artagnan bent forward, ready either to attack, or to stand on his defence.

All were intensely excited.

Then Athos extended his hand with the air of supreme command which characterised him alone, drew out his sword and the scabbard at the same time, broke the blade in the sheath on his knee, and threw the pieces on the ground. Then turning to Aramis:

"Aramis," he said, "break your sword in two."

Aramis hesitated.

"It must be done," said Athos; then in a lower and more gentle voice, he added, "I wish it."

Then Aramis, paler than before, but subdued by these words, broke the flexible blade with his hands, and then, folding his arms, stood trembling with rage.

These proceedings made d'Artagnan and Porthos draw back. D'Artagnan did not draw his sword; Porthos returned his to the sheath.

"Never!" exclaimed Athos, raising his right hand to heaven. "Never! I swear before God, who seeth us, and who in the darkness of this night heareth us, never shall my sword cross yours, never my eye cast a glance of anger, nor my heart a throb of hatred, to you. We lived together, we loved, we hated together; we shed, we mingled our blood together, and, too probably, I may still add, that there may be yet a bond between us closer even than that of friendship—perhaps there may be the bond of crime; for we four, we once did condemn, judge, and slay a human being whom we had not any right to cut off from this world, although apparently fitter for hell than for this life. D'Artagnan, I have always loved you as my son; Porthos, we slept six years side by side; Aramis is your brother as well as mine, and Aramis has once loved you, as I love you now, and as I have ever loved you. What can Cardinal Mazarin be to us, who compelled such a man as Richelieu to act as we pleased? What is such or such a prince to us, who have fixed the crown on the queen's head. D'Artagnan, I ask your pardon for having yesterday crossed swords with you; Aramis does the same to Porthos; now hate me if you can; but, for my own part, I shall ever, even if you do hate me, retain esteem and friendship for you; repeat my words, Aramis, and then, if you desire it, and if they desire it, let us separate for ever from our old friends."

There was a solemn, though momentary, silence, which was broken by Aramis.

"I swear," he said with a calm brow, and kindly glance, but in a voice still trembling with recent emotion, "I swear that I no longer bear animosity to those who were once my friends. I regret that I ever crossed swords with you, Porthos: I swear not only that it shall never again be pointed at your breast, but that from the bottom of my heart there will never in future be the slightest hostile sentiment; now, Athos, come."

Athos was about to retire.

"Oh! no! no! no! do not go away!" cried d'Artagnan, impelled by one of those irresistible impulses which showed the ardour of his nature, and the clear uprightness of his character: "I swear that I would shed the last drop of my blood, and the last fragment of my limbs, to preserve the friendship of such a man as you, Athos—

of such a man as you, Aramis." And he threw himself into the arms of Athos.

"My son!" exclaimed Athos, pressing him to his heart.

"And as for me!" said Porthos, "I swear nothing, but I'm choked—forsooth! If I were obliged to fight against you, I think I should allow myself to be pierced through and through—for I never loved any one but you in the world;" and honest Porthos burst into tears as he embraced Athos.

"My friends," said Athos, "this is what I expected from such hearts as yours—yes—I have said it, and I now repeat it! our destinies are irrevocably united, although we pursue different roads. I respect your convictions; and while we fight for opposite sides, let us remain firm friends. Ministers, princes, kings, will pass away like a torrent; civil war, like a flame; but we,—we shall remain; I have a presentiment that we shall."

"Yes," replied d'Artagnan, "let us still be musketeers, and let us retain as our colours that famous napkin of the Bastion Saint Gervais—on which the great Cardinal had three fleurs-de-lis embroidered."

"Be it so," cried Aramis. "Cardinalists or Frondeurs, what matters—whenever we meet again let it be as devoted friends and merry companions."

"And should," added Athos, "we meet in battle, at the words—'Place Royale!'—let us put our swords into our left hands, and shake hands with the right—even in the very thick of the carnage."

"You speak nobly," said Porthos.

"And are the first of men!" added d'Artagnan. "You excel us all!"

Athos smiled with ineffable pleasure.

"'Tis then all settled—gentlemen, your hands—are we not good Christians?"

"Egad!" said d'Artagnan, "by Heaven—yes."

"We should be so on this occasion, if only to be faithful to our oath," said Aramis.

"Ah, I'm ready to do what you will," cried Porthos—"to swear by Mahomet;—devil take me if I've ever been so happy as at this moment!"

And he wiped his still moistened eyes.

"Has not one of you a cross?" inquired Athos.

Aramis smiled, and drew from his vest a cross of diamonds, which was hung round his neck by a string of pearls. "Here is one," he said.

"Well," resumed Athos, "swear by this cross, which, in spite of its material, is still a cross; swear to be united in spite of every-thing, and for ever, and may this oath bind us to each other—and even, also our descendants! Does this oath satisfy you?"

"Yes!" said they all with one accord.

"Ah! traitor!" muttered d'Artagnan to himself, leaning towards Aramis, and whispering in his ear, "you have sworn us upon the crucifix of a Frondeuse."

29

THE FERRY ON THE OISE

WE hope our readers have not quite forgotten the young traveller whom we left on his road to Flanders.

In losing sight of his guardian, whom he had quitted, gazing after him in front of the royal Basilica, Raoul spurred on his horse, in order not only to escape from his own melancholy reflections, but also to hide from Olivain the emotion which his face might betray.

An hour's rapid progress, however, was sufficient to disperse the gloomy fancies which had clouded the young man's bright anticipations; and the hitherto unknown pleasure of freedom, a pleasure which has its sweetness even for those who have never suffered from dependence, seemed to gild for Raoul, not only both heaven and earth, but more particularly that distant horizon of life which we call the future.

And yet he found out, after several attempts at conversation with Olivain, that many long days passed thus would be very dull; and the count's agreeable voice, his gentle and persuasive eloquence, recurred to his mind, at the various towns through which they passed, and about which he had no one any longer to give him those interesting details which he would have drawn from Athos, the most amusing and best informed of guides. Another recollection contributed also to sadden Raoul: on their arrival at Sonores, he perceived, hidden between a screen of poplars, a little château, which so vividly recalled that of La Vallière to his mind, that he halted for some minutes to gaze at it, and had resumed his journey with a sigh, too abstracted even to reply to Olivain's respectful inquiry about the cause of this fixed attention. The aspect of external objects is often a mysterious guide communicating with the fibres of memory, which, in spite of us, will arouse them at times; this thread, like that of Ariadne, when once unravelled, will conduct one through a labyrinth of thought, in which one loses oneself in endeavouring to follow that phantom of the past which is called recollection.

Now the sight of this château had taken Raoul back fifty leagues westward, and had caused him to review his life from the moment when he had taken leave of little Louise to that in which he had seen her for the first time; and every branch of oak, every weather-cock seen on a roof of slates, reminded him, that instead of returning to the friends of his childhood, every instant removed him farther from them, and that perhaps he had even left them for ever.

With a beating heart and burning head, he desired Olivain to lead on the horses to a little inn, which he observed by the wayside within gun-shot range, a little in advance of the place they had reached.

As for himself, he dismounted, and remained under a beautiful group of chestnuts in flower, among which were murmuring multitudes of bees, and bade Olivain send the host to him with writing-paper and ink, to be placed on a table which he found there, conveniently ready for writing. Olivain obeyed and continued his road, while Raoul remained sitting with his elbow leaning on the table, from time to time gently taking the flowers from his head, which fell upon him like snow, and his eyes fixed vaguely on the pretty landscape before him, studded with green fields and groups of trees.

Raoul had been there about ten minutes, during five out of which he was lost in reverie, when there appeared within the circle comprised in his wandering gaze a rubicund figure, who, with a napkin round his body, another under his arm, and a white cap upon his head, approached him, holding paper, pen, and ink, in his hand.

"Ah! ah!" said this figure, "every gentleman seems to have the same fancy, for, not a quarter of an hour ago, a young man, well-mounted like you, as tall as you, and about your age, halted before this clump of trees, and had this table and this chair brought here, and dined here, with an old gentleman who seemed to be his tutor, upon a pie, of which they haven't left a mouthful, and a bottle of Mâcon wine, of which they haven't left a drop; but fortunately we have still got some of the same wine, and some of the same pies left, and if your worship will only give your orders——"

"No, friend," replied Raoul, "I am obliged to you, but at this moment I want nothing but the things for which I have asked;— only I shall be very glad if the ink prove black and the pen good;

upon these conditions, I will pay for the pen the price of the bottle,
and for the ink the price of the pie."

"Very well, sir," said the host, "I'll give the pie and the bottle
of wine to your servant, and in this way you will have the pen and
ink into the bargain."

"Do as you please," said Raoul, who was beginning his
apprenticeship with that particular class of society, who, when
there were robbers on the high-roads, were associated with them,
and who, since highwaymen no longer exist, have advantageously
supplied their place.

The host, his mind quite at ease about the bill, placed pen, ink,
and paper upon the table. By a lucky chance the pen was tolerably
good, and Raoul began to write. The host remained standing in
front of him, looking with a kind of involuntary admiration at his
handsome face, combining both gravity and sweetness of expression. Beauty has always been, and always will be, all-absorbing.

"He's not a guest like the other one here just now," observed the
host to Olivain, who had rejoined his master to see if he wanted
anything, "and our young master has no appetite."

"My master had appetite enough three days ago; but what can
one do? he lost it the day before yesterday."

And Olivain and the host took their way together towards the
inn. Olivain, according to the custom of grooms contented with
their places, related to the tavern-keeper all that he thought he
could say about the young gentleman; and Raoul wrote on thus:—

"Sir,—After a four hours' march I stop to write to you, for I
miss you every moment, and I am always on the point of turning
my head as if to reply when you speak to me. I was so bewildered
by your departure, and so overcome with grief at our separation,
that I but very feebly expressed all the affection and the gratitude
that I feel towards you. You will pardon me, sir, for your heart is
of such a generous nature, that you can well understand all that
passed in mine. I entreat you to write to me, for you form a part
of my existence, and if I may be permitted to tell you so, I also
feel anxious. It seemed to me as if you were preparing for some
dangerous undertaking, about which I did not dare to question
you, since you had told me nothing. I have, therefore, as you see,
great need to hear from you. Now that you are no longer with me,
I am afraid every moment of erring. You sustained me powerfully,
sir, and I protest to you that to-day I feel most lonely. Will you
have the goodness, sir, should you receive news from Blois, to
send me a few lines about my little friend, Mademoiselle de la
Vallière, about whose health, when we left, some anxiety was felt?

You can understand, honoured and dear guardian, how precious and indispensable to me is the remembrance of the time that I have passed with you. I hope that you will sometimes, too, think of me, and if at certain hours you should miss me, if you should experience any regret at my absence, I shall be overwhelmed with joy at the thought that you have appreciated my affection and my devotion for yourself, and that I have been able to prove them to you whilst I had the happiness of living with you."

After completing this letter, Raoul felt more composed; he looked around him to see that he was not observed, whilst he impressed a kiss upon the paper, a mute and touching caress, which the heart of Athos might well divine on opening the letter.

During this time Olivain had finished his bottle and eaten his pie; the horses also were refreshed. Raoul motioned the host to approach, threw a crown down on the table, mounted his horse, and posted his letter at Senlis. The rest that had been thus afforded to men and horses enabled them to proceed on their way without stopping. At Verbérie, Raoul desired Olivain to make some inquiry about the young man who was preceding them; he had been observed to pass only three-quarters of an hour previously, but he was well mounted, as the landlord had already said, and rode at a rapid pace.

"Let us try to overtake this gentleman," said Raoul to Olivain; "like ourselves, he is on his way to join the army, and may prove agreeable company."

It was about four o'clock in the afternoon when Raoul arrived at Compiègne; there he dined heartily, and again inquired about the young gentleman who was in advance of them. He had stopped, like Raoul, at the hotel of the Bell and Bottle, the best at Compiègne, and had started again on his journey, saying that he should sleep at Noyon.

"Well, let us sleep at Noyon," said Raoul.

"Sir," replied Olivain respectfully, "allow me to remark, that we have already much fatigued the horses this morning. I think it would be well to sleep here, and to start again very early to-morrow. Eighteen leagues is sufficient for the first stage."

"The Count de la Fère wished me to hasten on," replied Raoul, "that I might rejoin the prince on the morning of the fourth day; let us push on, then, to Noyon, it will be a stage similar to those that we travelled from Blois to Paris. We shall arrive at eight o'clock. The horses will have a long night's rest, and at five o'clock to-morrow morning we can be again on the road."

Olivain dared not offer any opposition to this determination; but he followed his master grumbling.

"Go on, go on," said he, between his teeth, "expend your ardour the first day; to-morrow, instead of journeying twenty miles, you will do ten; the day after to-morrow, five, and in three days you will be in bed. There you must rest; all these young people are such braggarts."

It is easy to see that Olivain had not been taught in the same school as Planchet and Grimaud. Raoul really felt tired; but he was desirous of testing his strength, and, brought up in the principles of Athos, and certain of having heard him speak a thousand times of stages of twenty-five leagues, he did not wish to fall short of his model. D'Artagnan, that man of iron, who seemed to be made of nerve and muscle only, had struck him with admiration. Therefore, in spite of all Olivain's objections, he continued to urge on his steed more and more, and following a pleasant little path, leading to a ferry, and which he had been assured shortened the journey by the distance of one league, he came to the summit of a hill, and perceived the river flowing before him. A little troop of men on horseback were waiting on the edge of the stream, ready to embark. Raoul did not doubt that this was the gentleman and his escort; he called out to him, but he was too distant to be heard; then, in spite of the weariness of his beast, he made it gallop; but the rising ground soon deprived him of the sight of the travellers, and when he had again attained a new height, the ferry-boat had left the shore, and was making for the opposite bank. Raoul, seeing that he could not arrive in time to cross the ferry with the travellers, halted to wait for Olivain. At this moment a cry was heard which seemed to come from the river. Raoul turned towards the side whence the cry had sounded, and shaded his eyes from the glare of the setting sun with his hand.

"Olivain!" he exclaimed, "what do I see below there?"

A second cry, more piercing than the first, now sounded.

"Oh, sir!" cried Olivain, "the rope which holds the ferry-boat has broken, and the boat is drifting away. But what do I see in the water? something struggling."

"Oh! yes," exclaimed Raoul, fixing his glance on one point in the stream, splendidly illumined by the setting sun, "a horse, a rider!"

"They are sinking!" cried Olivain, in his turn.

It was true, and Raoul was convinced that some accident had happened, and that a man was drowning; he gave his horse its head, struck his spurs into its sides, and the animal, urged on by pain, and feeling that he had space open before him, bounded over a kind of paling which enclosed the landing-place, and fell into the river, scattering to a distance waves of white froth.

"Ah, sir!" cried Olivain, "what are you doing? Good God!"

Raoul was guiding his horse towards the unhappy man in danger. This was, in fact, a custom familiar to him. Having been brought up on the banks of the Loire, he might have been said to have been cradled on its waves; a hundred times he had crossed it on horseback, a thousand times he had swum across. Athos, foreseeing the time when he should make a soldier of the viscount, had inured him to all these kinds of undertakings.

"Oh, heavens!" continued Olivain, in despair, "what would the count say if he only saw you?"

"The count would do exactly as I do," replied Raoul, urging his horse vigorously forward.

"But I—but I," cried Olivain, pale and disconsolate, rushing about on the shore, "how shall I cross?"

"Leap, coward," cried Raoul, swimming on; then addressing the traveller, who was struggling twenty yards in advance of him, "Courage, sir," said he, "courage, we are coming to your aid."

Olivain advanced, retired, then made his horse rear—turned it, and then, struck to the core by shame, leapt, as Raoul had done, only repeating:

"I am a dead man!"

In the meantime the ferry-boat floated away, carried down by the stream; and the cries of those whom it contained resounded more and more. A man with grey hair had thrown himself from the boat into the river, and was swimming vigorously towards the person who was drowning; but being obliged to go against the current, he advanced but slowly. Raoul continued his way, and was rapidly gaining the shore; but the horse and its rider, of whom he did not lose sight, were evidently sinking. The nostrils of the horse were no longer above water, and the rider, who had lost the reins in struggling, fell with his head back and his arms extended. One moment longer, and all had disappeared.

"Courage," cried Raoul, "courage."

"Too late!" murmured the young man, "too late!"

The water passed over his head, and stifled his voice in his mouth.

Raoul sprang from his horse, to which he left the charge of its own preservation, and in three or four strokes was at the gentleman's side; he seized the horse by the curb, and raised its head above water. The animal then breathed more freely, and, as if he comprehended that they had come to his aid, redoubled his efforts. Raoul at the same time seized one of the young man's hands, and placed it on the mane, at which it grasped with the tenacity of a drowning man. Thus, sure that the rider would not release his hold, Raoul now only directed his attention to the horse, which he guided to the opposite bank, helping it through the water, and encouraging it with words.

All at once the horse stumbled against a ridge, and then placed its foot on the sand.

"Saved!" exclaimed the man with grey hair, who sprang on the shore.

"Saved," mechanically repeated the young gentleman, releasing the mane, and gliding from the saddle into Raoul's arms; Raoul was but ten yards from the shore; he bore the fainting man there, and laying him down on the grass, unfastened the buttons of his collar, and unhooked his doublet. A moment later the grey-headed man was beside him. Olivain managed in his turn to land, after crossing himself repeatedly, and those in the boat guided themselves as well as they were able towards the bank, with the aid of a hook which happened to be in the boat.

Thanks to the attention of Raoul, and the man who accompanied the young gentleman, the colour gradually returned to the pale cheeks of the young man, who opened two eyes at first bewildered, but who soon fixed his glance upon the person who had saved him.

"Ah, sir," he exclaimed, "it was you I wanted; without you I was a dead man—thrice dead."

"But one recovers, sir, as you see," replied Raoul, "and we shall but have had a bath."

"Oh! sir, what gratitude I feel," cried the man with grey hair.

"Ah, there you are, my good d'Arminges, I have given you a great fright, have I not? but it is your own fault; you were my tutor, why did you not teach me to swim better?"

"Oh, Monsieur le Count!" replied the old man, "had any misfortune happened to you, I should never have dared to have shown myself to the marshal again."

"But how did the accident happen?" asked Raoul.

"Oh, sir, in the most natural manner possible," replied he whom they had addressed as the count. "We were about a third of the way across the river when the cord of the ferry-boat broke. Alarmed by the cries and the gestures of the boatmen, my horse sprang into the water. I swim badly, and dared not throw myself into the water. Instead of aiding the movements of my horse, I paralysed them; and I was just about to drown myself, with the best grace in the world, when you arrived just in time to save me from certain death; therefore, sir, if you will agree, henceforth we are friends always, and for ever."

"Sir," replied Raoul, bowing, "I am entirely at your service, I assure you."

"I am called the Count de Guiche," continued the young man; "my father is the Maréchal de Grammont; and now that you know who I am, do me the honour to inform me who you are."

"I am the Viscount de Bragelonne," answered Raoul, blushing at being unable to name his father, as the Count de Guiche had done.

"Viscount, your countenance, your goodness, and your courage incline me towards you; my gratitude is already due to you—shake hands;—I request your friendship."

"Sir," said Raoul, returning the count's pressure of the hand, "I like you already from my heart; pray regard me as a devoted friend, I beseech you."

"And now, where are you going, viscount?" inquired de Guiche.

"To the army, under the prince, count."

"And I too," exclaimed the young man, in a transport of joy.—"Oh, so much the better; we shall fire off our first pistol shots together."

"It is well—be friends," said the tutor; "young as you both are, you were perhaps born under the same star, and were destined to meet. And now," continued he, "you must change your clothes; your servants, to whom I gave directions the moment they had left the ferry-boat, ought to be already at the inn. Linen and wine are both being warmed—come."

The young men had no objection to make to this proposition; on the contrary, they thought it an excellent one. They mounted again at once, whilst looks of admiration passed between them. They were indeed two elegant horsemen, with figures slight and upright, two noble faces, with open foreheads, bright and proud looks, loyal and intelligent smiles.

De Guiche might have been about eighteen years of age; but he was scarcely taller than Raoul, who was only fifteen.

They held out their hands to each other by a spontaneous movement, and, putting their horses in motion, rode side by side to the hostelry, the one feeling good and smiling for recovering the life he had so nearly lost; the other, thanking Heaven for having allowed him already to live long enough to do something that would be agreeable to his protector.

As for Olivain, he was the only person whom this noble action of his master did not entirely satisfy; he wrung the sleeves and flaps

of his coat, thinking that a halt at Compiègne would not only have
saved him the risk from which he had just escaped, but likewise
the fluxions of the chest and the rheumatisms which would
naturally be the result.

30

SKIRMISHING

THE sojourn at Noyon was short, and every one slept soundly.
Raoul had desired to be awakened if Grimaud arrived; but
Grimaud did not arrive. Doubtless, too, the horses, on their parts,
appreciated the eight hours of repose, and the abundant stabling
which was supplied to them. The Count de Guiche was awakened
at five o'clock in the morning by Raoul, who came to wish him
good-day. They breakfasted in haste, and at six o'clock had
already gone ten miles.

The young count's conversation was most interesting to Raoul;
therefore he listened eagerly, whilst the count talked. Brought up
in Paris, where Raoul had been but once, at the court, which
Raoul had never seen, his follies as page, two duels, which he had
already found the means of engaging, in spite of the edicts against
them, and more especially in spite of his tutor's vigilance—these
things excited the utmost curiosity in Raoul. Raoul had only been
at Monsieur Scarron's house; he named to de Guiche the people
whom he had seen there. De Guiche knew everybody—Madame
de Muillan, Mademoiselle d'Aubigné, Mademoiselle de Scudéry,
Mademoiselle Paulet, Madame de Chevreuse. He criticised everybody humorously. Raoul trembled lest he should laugh among the
rest at Madame de Chevreuse, for whom he entertained deep and
genuine sympathy, but either instinctively, or from affection for
the Duchesse de Chevreuse, he said everything possible in her
favour. His praises increased Raoul's friendship for him twofold.
Then came the question of gallantry and love affairs. Under this
head also, Bragelonne had much more to hear than to tell. He
listened attentively, and fancied that he discovered through three
or four rather frivolous adventures, that the count, like himself,
had a secret to hide in the depths of his heart.

De Guiche, as we have said before, had been educated at the
court, and the intrigues of this court were known to him. It was the
same court of which Raoul had so often heard the Count de la
Fère speak, except that its aspect had much changed since the

period when Athos had himself witnessed it; therefore everything which the Count de Guiche related was new to his travelling companion. The young count, witty and caustic, passed all the world in review; the queen herself was not spared, and Cardinal Mazarin came in for his share of ridicule.

The day passed away as rapidly as an hour. The count's tutor, a man of the world, and an accomplished and profound scholar, as his pupil described him, often recalled the deep erudition, the witty and caustic satire, of Athos to Raoul; but, as regarded grace, delicacy, and nobility of external appearance, no one in these points was to be compared to the Count de la Fère.

The horses, which were better cared for than on the previous day, stopped at Arras at four o'clock in the evening. They were approaching the seat of war; and as bands of Spaniards sometimes took advantage of the night to make expeditions even as far as the neighbourhood of Arras, they determined to remain in this town until the next day. The French army held all between Pont-à-Mare as far as Valenciennes, falling back upon Douai. The prince was said to be in person in Béthune.

The enemy's army extended from Cassel to Courtray; and as there was no species of violence or pillage which it did not commit, the poor people on the frontier quitted their isolated dwellings, and fled for refuge into the strong cities which held out a shelter to them. Arras was encumbered with fugitives. An approaching battle was much spoken of, the prince having manœuvred until that moment, only in order to await a reinforcement, which had just reached him.

The young men congratulated themselves on having arrived so opportunely. The evening was employed in discussing the war; the grooms polished the arms; the young men loaded the pistols in case of a skirmish, and they awoke in despair, having both dreamt that they had arrived too late to participate in the battle. In the morning it was rumoured that Prince Condé had evacuated Béthune and fallen back upon Carvin, leaving, however, a strong garrison in the former city.

But as there was nothing positive in this report, the young men decided to continue their way towards Béthune, free, on the road, to diverge to the right, and to march to Carvin if necessary.

The count's tutor was well acquainted with the country; he consequently proposed to take a cross road, which lay between that of Lens and that of Béthune. They obtained information at Ablain, and a statement of their route was left for Grimaud.

About seven o'clock in the morning they started. De Guiche, who was young and impulsive, said to Raoul, "Here we are, three masters and three servants. Our valets are well armed, and yours seems to be tough enough."

"I have never seen him put to the test," replied Raoul, "but he is a Breton, which counts for something."

"Yes, yes," resumed de Guiche; "I am sure he can fire a musket when required. On my side, I have two very able men, who have been in action with my father. We, therefore, represent six fighting-men; if we should meet a small troop of enemies, equal, or even superior in number to our own, shall we charge them, Raoul?"

"Certainly, sir," replied the viscount.

"Holloa! young people—stop there!" said the tutor, joining in the conversation. "Zounds! You are laying your plans nicely! And what becomes of me and my instructions? You seem to forget the order I received to conduct you safe and sound to his highness the prince! Once with the army, you may be killed at your good pleasure; but, until that time, I warn you, that in my capacity of general of the army, I shall order a retreat, and turn my back on the first red-coat I see."

De Guiche and Raoul glanced at each other, smiling.

They arrived at Ablain without accident. There they inquired, and learned that the prince had in reality quitted Béthune, and placed himself between Cambria and La Venthie. Therefore, leaving directions at every place for Grimaud, they took a cross-road, which conducted the little troop upon the bank of a small stream flowing into the Lys. The country was beautiful, intersected by valleys as green as the emerald. Every here and there they passed little copses crossing the path which they were following. In anticipation of some ambuscade in each of these little woods, the tutor placed his two servants at the head of the band, thus forming the advance guard. Himself and the two young men represented the body of the army, whilst Olivain, with his rifle ready to fire, and his eye on the watch, protected the rear.

They had observed for some time before them on the horizon a rather dense wood; and when they had arrived at a distance of a hundred yards from it, Monsieur d'Arminges took his usual precautions, and sent on in advance the count's two grooms. The servants had just disappeared under the trees, followed by the tutor, and the young men were laughing and talking about a hundred yards off. Olivain was at the same distance in the rear, when suddenly there resounded five or six musket-shots. The tutor cried halt; the young men obeyed, pulling up their steeds, and at the same moment the two valets were seen returning at a gallop.

The young men, impatient to learn the cause of the firing, spurred on towards the servants. The tutor followed them.

"Were you stopped?" inquired the two youths.

"No," replied the servants, "it is even probable that we have not been seen; the shots were fired about a hundred steps in front of us, almost in the thickest part of the wood, and we returned to ask your advice."

"My advice," said Monsieur d'Arminges, "and, if needs be, my will is, that we beat a retreat. There may be an ambuscade concealed in this wood."

"Did you see anything there?" asked the count.

"I thought I saw," said one of the servants, "some horsemen dressed in yellow, creeping along the side of the stream."

"That's it," said the tutor. "We have fallen in with a party of Spaniards. Come back, gentlemen—back."

The two youths looked at each other, and at this moment a pistol-shot and several cries for help were heard. Another glance between the young men convinced them both that neither had any wish to go back, and as the tutor had already turned his horse's head, they both spurred on forward, Raoul crying, "Follow me, Olivain;" and Count de Guiche, "Follow, Urban and Blanchet." And before the tutor could recover his surprise, they had both disappeared into the forest. When they spurred their steeds, they he'd their pistols ready also. Five minutes after, they arrived at the place whence the noise had proceeded; therefore, restraining their horses, they advanced cautiously.

"Hush," said de Guiche; "these are cavaliers."

"Yes, three on horseback, and three who have dismounted."

"Can you see what they are doing?"

"Yes, they appear to be searching a wounded or dead man."

"It is some dastardly assassination," said de Guiche.

"They are soldiers, though," resumed Raoul.

"Yes, skirmishers; that is to say, highway robbers."

"At them!" cried Raoul. "At them!" echoed de Guiche.

"Oh! sirs, sirs; in the name of Heaven!" cried the tutor.

But he was not listened to, and his cries only served to arouse the attention of the Spaniards.

The men on horseback at once rushed at the two youths, leaving the three others to complete the plunder of the two travellers; for, on approaching nearer, instead of one extended figure, the young men discovered two. De Guiche fired the first shot at ten paces, and missed his man; and the Spaniard, who had advanced to meet Raoul, aimed in his turn, and Raoul felt a pain in his left arm, similar to that of a blow from a whip. He let off his fire, at but four paces. Struck in the breast, and extending his arms, the Spaniard fell back on the croup of his horse, which, turning round, carried him off.

Raoul, at this moment, perceived the muzzle of a gun pointed at him, and remembering the recommendation of Athos, he, with the rapidity of lightning, made his horse rear as the shot was fired. His horse bounded to one side, losing its footing, and fell, entangling Raoul's leg under its body. The Spaniard sprang forward, and seized the gun by its muzzle, in order to strike Raoul on the head by the butt-end. In the position in which Raoul lay, unhappily, he could neither draw his sword from the scabbard, nor his pistols from their holsters. The butt-end of the musket hovered over his head, and he could scarcely restrain himself from closing his eyes, when, with a bound, de Guiche reached the Spaniard, and placed a pistol at his throat. "Yield!" he cried, "or you are a dead man." The gun fell from the soldier's hands, who yielded at the instant.

De Guiche summoned one of the grooms, and delivering the prisoner into his charge, with orders to shoot him through the head if he attempted to escape, he leaped from his horse and approached Raoul.

"Faith, sir," said Raoul, smiling, although his pallor somewhat betrayed the excitement consequent on a first affair—"you are in a great hurry to pay your debts, and have not been long under any obligation to me. Without your aid," continued he, repeating the count's words, "I should have been a dead man—thrice dead."

"My antagonist took flight," replied de Guiche, "and left me at liberty to come to your aid. But you are seriously wounded? you are covered with blood!"

"I believe," said Raoul, "that I have something like a scratch on the arm. If you will assist me to drag myself from under my horse, I hope nothing need prevent us continuing our journey."

Monsieur d'Arminges and Olivain had already dismounted, and were attempting to raise the horse, which struggled in terror. At last Raoul succeeded in drawing his foot from the stirrup, and his leg from under the animal, and in a second he was on his feet again.

"Any bones broken?" asked de Guiche.

"Faith, no, thank Heaven!" replied Raoul; "but what has become of the poor fellows whom these scoundrels were murdering?"

"I fear we arrived too late. They had killed them and taken flight, carrying off their booty. My two servants are examining the bodies."

"Let us go and see whether they are quite dead, or if they can be recovered," suggested Raoul. "Olivain, we have got possession of two horses, but I have lost my own; take the best of the two for yourself, and give me yours."

And they drew near to the spot where the victims lay.

31

THE MONK

Two men lay stretched out on the ground; one bathed in his blood, and motionless, with his face towards the sky; he was dead. The other leaned against the tree, supported there by the two valets, and was praying fervently, with clasped hands and eyes raised to heaven. He had received a ball in his thigh, which had broken the upper part of it. The young men first approached the dead man.

"He is a priest," said Bragelonne, "he has worn the tonsure. Oh, the villains! to lift their hands against a minister of God."

"Come here, sir," said Urban, an old soldier who had served under the cardinal-duke in most of his campaigns. "Come here, nothing can be done for him; whilst we may perhaps be able to save this one."

The wounded man smiled sadly. "Save me! oh, no," said he; "but help me to die, you can."

"Are you a priest?" asked Raoul.

"No, sir."

"I ask, as your unfortunate companion appeared to me to belong to the Church."

"He is the curate of Béthune, sir, and was carrying the holy vessels belonging to his church, and the treasures of the chapter, to a safe place, the prince having abandoned our town yesterday; and as it was known that bands of the enemy were prowling about the country, no one dared to accompany the good man, so I offered to do so."

"And, sir," continued the wounded man, "I suffer much, and would like, if possible, to be taken to some house."

"Where you can be relieved?" asked de Guiche.

"No, where I can confess myself."

"But perhaps you are not so dangerously wounded as you suppose," said Raoul.

"Sir," replied the wounded man, "believe me there is no time to lose; the ball has broken the thigh-bone, and entered the intestines."

"Are you a surgeon?" asked de Guiche.

"No, but I know a little about wounds, and mine is mortal. Try, therefore, either to convey me to some place where I may see a priest, or take the trouble to send one to me here. It is my soul that must be saved; as for my body, that is lost."

"Good God! good God!" added the wounded man, in an accent of terror which made the young men shudder; "you will not allow me to die without receiving absolution? that would be indeed terrible!"

"Calm yourself, sir," replied de Guiche. "I swear to you that you shall receive the consolation that you ask. Only tell us where we shall find a house at which we can demand aid, and a village from which we can fetch a priest."

"Thank you, and God will reward you! About half a mile from this, on the same road, there is an inn; and about a mile farther on, after leaving the inn, you will reach the village of Greney. There you will find the curé; or if he is not at home, go to the convent of St. Augustine, which is the last house on the right in the village, and bring me one of the brothers. Monk or priest, it matters not, provided he has received from our holy church the power of absolving *in articulo mortis*!"

"Monsieur d'Arminges," said de Guiche, "remain beside this unfortunate man, and see that he is removed as gently as possible. The vicomte and myself will go and find a priest."

"Go, sir," replied the tutor; "but in Heaven's name, do not expose yourself to any danger!"

"Do not fear. Besides, we are safe to-day; you know the axiom —*Non bis in idem*."

"Courage, sir," said Raoul to the wounded man. "We are going to carry out your wishes."

"May Heaven prosper you!" replied the dying man, with an accent of gratitude impossible to describe.

The two young men galloped off in the direction mentioned to them, and ten minutes after reached the inn. Raoul, without dismounting, called to the host, and announced that a dying man was about to be brought to his house, and begged him in the meantime to prepare everything necessary for relieving the pain. He desired him also, should he know in the neighbourhood any doctor, surgeon, or operator, to fetch him, taking on himself the payment of the messenger. Raoul had already proceeded for more than a mile, and had begun to descry the first houses of the village, the red tiled roofs of which stood out strongly from the green trees which surrounded them, when, coming towards them, mounted on a mule, they perceived a monk, whose large hat and grey worsted dress made him appear to them an Augustine brother. Chance for once had seemed to favour them in sending what they were in search of. He was a man about twenty-two or twenty-three years old, but who appeared to be aged by his ascetic exercises. His complexion was pale, not of that deadly pallor which is a beauty, but of a bilious, yellow hue; his light colourless hair was short, and scarcely extended beyond the circle formed by the hat round his head, and his light blue eyes seemed entirely destitute of any expression.

"Sir," said Raoul, with his habitual politeness, "are you an ecclesiastic?"

"Why do you ask me that?" replied the stranger, with a coolness which was barely civil.

"Because we want to know," said de Guiche haughtily.

The stranger touched his mule with his heel, and continued his way.

In a second de Guiche had sprung in front of him and barred his passage. "Answer, sir," exclaimed he; "you have been asked politely, and every question is worth an answer."

"I suppose I am free to say who I am, or not, to any kind of people who choose to take a fancy to ask me?"

It was with difficulty that de Guiche restrained the intense desire he had of breaking the monk's head.

"In the first place," he said, making an effort to control himself, "we are not people who may be treated with incivility; my friend there is the Vicomte de Bragelonne, and I am the Count de Guiche. Nor is it from a matter of caprice that we asked you the question: for there is a wounded and dying man who demands the succour of the Church. If you be a priest, I conjure you in the name of humanity to follow me to aid this man; if you be not, it is a different matter, and I warn you, in the name of courtesy, of which you appear so entirely ignorant, that I shall punish you for your insolence."

The pale face of the monk became so livid, and his smile was so strange, that Raoul, whose eyes were still fixed upon him, felt as if this smile had struck to his heart like some insult.

"He is some Spanish or Flemish spy," said he, putting his hand to his pistols. A glance, threatening and as transient as lightning, replied to Raoul.

"Well, sir," said de Guiche, "are you going to reply?"

"I am a priest," said the young man.

7

"Then, father," said Raoul, forcing himself to give a respect to his speech which did not come from his heart, "if you are a priest, then you have an opportunity, as my friend has told you, of exercising your vocation. At the next inn you will find a wounded man, who has asked the assistance of a minister of God, attended to by our servants."

"I will go," said the monk.

And he touched his mule.

"If you do not go, sir," said de Guiche, "remember that we have two horses quite able to catch your mule, and the power of having you seized wherever you may be; and then I swear your trial will be short; one can always find a tree and a rope."

The monk's eye again flashed, but that was all; he merely repeated his phrase, "I will go,"—and he went.

"Let us follow him," said de Guiche; "it will be the more sure plan."

"I was about to propose doing so," answered Bragelonne.

In the space of a few minutes the monk turned round to ascertain whether he was followed or not.

"You see," said Raoul, "we have acted wisely."

"What a horrible face that monk has," said de Guiche.

"Horrible!" replied Raoul, "especially in expression."

"Yes, yes," said de Guiche, "a peculiar face; but these monks are subject to such degrading practices; the fasts make them pale; the blows of the discipline make them hypocrites; and their eyes become inflamed in weeping for the good things of this life which we enjoy, and which they have lost."

"Well," said Raoul, "the poor man will get his priest; but by Heaven, the penitent appears to have a better conscience than the confessor. I own that I am accustomed to see priests of a very different appearance."

"Ah!" exclaimed de Guiche, "you must understand that this is one of those wandering brothers, who go begging on the high road, until some day a benefice falls down from heaven for them; they are mostly foreigners—Scotch, Irish, or Danish."

"What a misfortune for that poor wounded fellow to die under the hands of such a friar!"

"Pshaw!" said de Guiche. "Absolution comes not from him who administers it, but from God. However, let me tell you that I would rather die unshriven than have anything to say to such a confessor. You are of my opinion, are you not, viscount? and I saw you playing with the pommel of your sword, as if you had a great inclination to break his head."

"Yes, count, it is a strange thing, and one which might astonish you; but I feel an indescribable horror at the sight of that man. Have you ever seen a snake rise up in your path?"

"Never," answered de Guiche.

"Well, it has happened to me to do so in our Blaisois forests, and I remember that the first time I encountered one with its eyes fixed upon me, curled up, swinging its head, and pointing its tongue, that I remained fixed, pale, and as if fascinated, until the moment when the Count de la Fère——"

"Your father?" inquired de Guiche.

"No, my guardian," replied Raoul, colouring.

"Very well——"

"Until the moment when the Count de la Fère," resumed Raoul, "said, 'Come, Bragelonne, draw your sword;' then only I rushed upon the reptile, and cut it in two; just at the moment when it was rising on its tail and hissing ere it sprang upon me. Well, I felt exactly the same sensation at the sight of that man when he said, 'Why do you ask me that?' and looked at me."

"Then you are sorry that you did not cut your serpent in two pieces?"

"Faith, yes, almost," said Raoul.

They had now arrived in sight of the little inn, and could see on the opposite side the procession bearing the dying man, and guided by Monsieur d'Arminges. The youths hurried on.

"There is the wounded man," said de Guiche, passing close to the Augustine brother. "Be good enough to hurry yourself a little, sir monk."

As for Raoul, he avoided the monk the whole width of the road, and passed him, turning his head away in disgust.

The young men rode up to the wounded man to announce that they were followed by the monk. He raised himself to glance in the direction which they pointed out, saw the monk, and fell back upon the litter, his face being lightened up with joy.

"And now," said the youths, "we have done all we can for you; and as we are in haste to join the prince's army we must continue our journey. You will excuse us, sir, but we are told that a battle is expected, and we do not wish to arrive the day after it."

"Go, good gentlemen," said the sick man; "and may you both be blessed for your piety. God protect you and all dear to you!"

"Sir," said de Guiche to his tutor, "we will precede you, and you can rejoin us on the road to Cambrin."

The host was at his door, and everything was prepared—bed, bandages, and lint.

"Everything," said he to Raoul, "shall be done as you wish; but will you not stop to have your wound dressed?"

"Oh, my wound—mine—it is nothing," replied the viscount; "it will be time to think upon it when we next halt; only have the goodness, should you see a horseman pass who should make inquiries from you about a young man mounted on a chestnut horse, and followed by a servant, to tell him, in fact, that you have seen me, but that I have continued my journey, and intend to dine at Mazingarbe, and to stop at Cambrin. This horseman is my attendant."

"Would it not be safer and more sure that I should ask him his name, and tell him yours?" demanded the host.

"There is no harm in over-precaution. I am the Viscount de Bragelonne, and his name is Grimaud."

At this moment the wounded man passed on one side, and the monk on the other, the latter dismounting from his mule and requesting that it should be taken to the stables without being unharnessed.

"Come, count," said Raoul, who seemed instinctively to dislike the vicinity of the monk; "come, it feels nauseous here," and the two young men spurred on.

The litter, borne by the two servants, now entered the house. The host and his wife were standing on the steps of the staircase, whilst the unhappy man seemed to suffer dreadful pain, and yet only to be anxious to know if he was followed by the monk. At the sight of this pale, bleeding man, the wife grasped her husband's arm.

"Well, what ails you?" said the latter; "are you going to be ill?"

"No, but look," replied the hostess, pointing to the wounded man; "I ask you if you recognise him?"

"That man—wait a bit."

"Ah! I see that you know him," exclaimed the wife; "for you have become pale in your turn."

"In truth," cried the host, "misfortune has come upon this house; it is the executioner of Béthune!"

"The former executioner of Béthune!" murmured the young monk, shrinking back, and showing on his countenance the feeling of repugnance which his penitent inspired.

Monsieur d'Arminges, who was at the door, perceived his hesitation.

"Holy father," said he, "whether he is now or has been an executioner, this unfortunate being is no less a man. Render to him, then, the last service he will ask from you, and your work will be the more meritorious."

The monk made no reply, but silently wended his way to the

room where the two valets had deposited the dying man on a bed. D'Arminges and Olivain, and the two grooms, then mounted their horses, and all four started off at a quick trot to rejoin Raoul and his companion. Just as the tutor and his escort disappeared in their turn, a new traveller stepped on to the threshold of the inn.

"What does your worship want?" demanded the host, pale and trembling from the discovery he had just made.

The traveller made a sign as if he wished to drink, pointed to his horse, and gesticulated like a man rubbing something.

"Ah! hang it," said the host to himself, "this man seems dumb. And where will your worship drink?"

"There," answered the traveller, pointing to a table.

"I was mistaken," said the host; "he's not quite dumb. And what else does your worship wish for?"

"To know if you have seen a young man pass, fifteen years of age, mounted on a chestnut horse, and followed by a groom."

"The Viscount de Bragelonne?"

"Exactly."

"Then you are Monsieur Grimaud?"

The traveller made a sign of assent.

"Well, then," said the host, "that young gentleman was here a quarter of an hour ago; he will dine at Mazingarbe, and sleep at Cambrin."

"How far from Mazingarbe?"

"Two miles and a half."

"Thank you."

Grimaud was drinking his wine silently, and had just placed his glass on the table to be filled a second time, when a fearful scream resounded from the room occupied by the monk and the dying man. Grimaud sprang up,—

"What is that?" said he; "whence that cry?"

"From the dying man's room," replied the host.

"What dying man?"

"The former executioner of Béthune, who has just been brought in here assassinated by the Spaniards, and who is now being shriven by an Augustine friar."

"The old executioner of Béthune?" muttered Grimaud; "a man between fifty-five and sixty, tall, strong, swarthy, black hair and beard."

"That is he—do you know him?" asked the host.

"I have seen him once," replied Grimaud, a cloud darkening his countenance at the picture called up by his recollections.

At this instant a second cry, less piercing than the first, but followed by prolonged groaning, was heard.

"We must see what it is," said Grimaud.

If Grimaud was slow in speaking, we know that he was quick in action; he sprang to the door and shook it violently, but it was fastened on the other side.

"Open the door," cried the host, "open it instantly, good father!" No reply.

"Open it, or I will burst in the panel," said Grimaud.

The same silence, and then, ere the host could oppose his design, Grimaud seized on some pincers which he perceived lying in a corner, and had forced the bolt. The room was inundated with blood, streaming through the mattresses upon which lay the wounded man speechless—the monk had disappeared.

"The priest!" cried the host; "where is the priest?"

Grimaud sprang to an open window which looked into the courtyard.

"He has escaped by this means," exclaimed he.

"Do you think so?" said the host bewildered; "boy, see if the mule belonging to the monk is still in the stable."

"There's no mule," replied the person to whom this question was addressed.

The host held up his hand, and looked around him suspiciously, whilst Grimaud knit his brows and approached the wounded man, whose worn, hard features awoke in his mind such awful recollections of the past.

"There can be no longer any doubt but that it is himself," said he.

"Does he still live?" asked the innkeeper.

Making no reply, Grimaud opened the poor man's jacket to feel if the heart beat, whilst the host approached in his turn; but in a moment they both fell back, the host uttering a cry of horror, and Grimaud becoming pallid. The blade of a dagger was buried up to the hilt in the left side of the executioner.

"Run—run for help!" cried Grimaud, "and I will remain beside him here."

The host rushed out in a state of bewilderment; the wife had fled at the exclamation uttered by her husband.

32

THE ABSOLUTION

THIS is what had passed. We have seen that it was not voluntarily, but much against his inclination, that the monk attended the wounded man, who had been recommended to him in such a singular manner. Perhaps he might have endeavoured to fly if he had seen any possibility of succeeding, but the menaces of the two gentlemen, their attendants, who had remained after them, and who, doubtless, had received their instructions, and to tell the whole truth, reflection itself had prevailed upon the monk to play to the end, without allowing too much ill-will to appear, his part of a confessor; and when once in the chamber, he approached the pallet of the wounded man.

The executioner examined, with that rapid glance peculiar to those who are dying, and who, consequently have no time to spare, the countenance of him who was about to be his consoler.

He made a movement of surprise, and said, "You are very young, father."

"Those who wear my robe have no age," coldly responded the monk.

"Alas! speak more gently to me, father," said the wounded man; "I want much a friend in my last moments."

"Are you suffering severely?" demanded the monk.

"Yes; but in soul more than in body."

"We will save your soul," replied the young man; "but are you really the executioner of Béthune, as these people said?"

"That is to say," replied the wounded man with great quickness, doubtless fearing lest the name of executioner should deprive him of the last benefits of religion which he required, "I was the executioner, but am so no longer. I gave up the office fifteen years ago. I still attend the executions officially, but no longer strike the blow myself. Oh, no!"

"You feel great repugnance to your office, do you not?"

The executioner heaved a deep sigh.

"As long as I struck in the name of the law and of justice, my occupation did not prevent me from sleeping tranquilly enough, sheltered as I was by justice and the law; but from that terrible night on which I served as an instrument for private vengeance, and on which I lifted the sword, with hatred, over one of Heaven's creatures—from that day——"

The executioner stopped, shaking his head, with a look of despair.

"Speak!" said the monk, who had seated himself at the foot of the bed, and who began to take an interest in a recital which commenced in so strange a fashion.

"Ah!" exclaimed the dying man, with all the force of a secret sorrow long repressed, and at last unburdened, "ah! how I have endeavoured to stifle my remorse by twenty years of good works. I have struggled to conquer that ferocity natural to those who shed blood; on every opportunity I have exposed my own life to save the lives of those who were in danger; and I have preserved many lives in exchange for those I have taken away. And that is not all: the property I have acquired by my profession I have distributed among the poor; I have been assiduous in church going; and the people who avoided me have become accustomed to the sight of me. All have forgiven, some have even loved me; but I believe that God has not pardoned me; for the recollection of this execution never leaves me for one single instant, and methinks the spectre of that woman rises before me every night."

"A woman! So you assassinated a woman?" exclaimed the monk.

"And you also!" cried the executioner. "You make use of that word which is incessantly ringing in my ear—'assassinated.' So then I assassinated her, and not executed her! So then I am an assassin and not an instrument of the law!"

And he closed his eyes, uttering a groan.

The monk, no doubt, feared he would die without saying more, for he exclaimed earnestly, "Go on, go on; I know nothing yet. When you have finished your recital, Heaven and I will judge."

"Oh, father," continued the executioner, without opening his eyes, as if he dreaded, if he did, to see again some frightful object, "it is at night, and when I cross some river, that this terror which I cannot overcome is redoubled. It appears then that my hand becomes heavy, as if my cutlass weighed it down, that the water becomes the colour of blood, and that all the voices of nature—the moaning of the trees, the murmuring of the winds, the dashing of the waves—unite to form a weeping, despairing, terrible voice, which cries to me, 'Let the justice of Heaven be done!'"

"Delirious," said the monk, shaking his head.

The executioner reopened his eyes, endeavoured to turn towards the young man, and seized his arm.

"Delirious!" repeated he; "delirious, say you? Oh, no; for it was by night that I cast her body into the river, for the words which my remorse repeats—those words are the words which I pronounced in the pride of my heart. After having become the instrument of human justice, I thought to become that of the justice of Heaven."

"But let us hear how it all happened. Speak," said the monk.

"It was night. A man came to seek me, and showed me an order. I followed him. Four other gentlemen awaited me. They took me with them, masked. I secretly determined to refuse, should the purpose for which they required me appear to me to be unjust. We proceeded for about five or six leagues, gloomy and silent, almost without exchanging a word. At last, through the window of a small cottage, they showed me a woman leaning on a table. and said, 'There is the woman whom you must execute.' "

"Horror!" said the monk; "and you obeyed them?"

"My father, that woman was a monster. It was said she had poisoned her second husband, and had attempted to assassinate her brother-in-law, who was one of these men. She had just poisoned a young woman, who was her rival; and it was said that before she left England, she had caused the king's favourite to be stabbed."

"Buckingham?" exclaimed the monk.

"Yes, Buckingham."

"She was an Englishwoman, then?"

"No, she was a Frenchwoman, but she had married in England."

The monk became paler. He wiped his brow, and went and bolted the door.

The executioner thought he had abandoned him, and sank back groaning on his bed.

"No, no; here I am," cried the monk, returning eagerly to the bedside. "Go on. Who were these men?"

"One was a foreigner—an Englishman, I believe. The four others were Frenchmen, and wore the uniform of musketeers."

"But their names—their names?" cried the monk vehemently.

"I do not know their names; but the Englishman was called, 'My lord.' "

"And was the woman handsome?"

"Young and handsome. Yes, particularly beautiful. I see her still, when on her knees at my feet she prayed, with her head thrown back. I have never since been able to understand how I could strike off that head, so beautiful, though so pale."

The monk appeared agitated by extraordinary emotion. All his limbs trembled. It was plain he wanted to put a question, but durst not.

At length after a violent effort, "The name of that woman?" gasped he.

"I do not know it, as I have told you. She had been twice married, it appeared—once in France and once in England."

"And you say she was young?"

"Twenty-five years old."

"Beautiful?"

"Exceedingly."

"Fair?"

"Yes."

"With long hair reaching to her shoulders—was it not so?"

"Yes."

"With eyes of admirable expression?"

"When she chose. Oh, yes, it was so."

"And a voice of singular sweetness?"

"How do *you* know all this?"

And the executioner raised himself upon his elbow, and fixed his terrified eyes upon the monk, whose face had become livid.

"And you killed her?" said the monk. "You acted as an instrument to those cowardly wretches who did not dare to kill her themselves? You had no pity on her youth, her beauty, or her weakness? You killed that woman?"

"Alas! I have told you, father, that that woman, under that heavenly envelope, concealed an infernal spirit; and when I saw her—when I remembered all the evil she had done to me myself——"

"To you? And what had she done to you? Tell me."

"She had seduced and ruined my brother, who was a priest. She ran away with him from a convent."

"With your brother."

"Yes; my brother had been her first lover. She was the cause of the death of my brother. Oh, father, father, do not look at me in that manner! Oh, I am, then, guilty! Oh, you will not pardon me!"

The monk composed his countenance.

"Yes, yes," said he, "I will pardon you, if you tell me all."

"Oh!" exclaimed the executioner, "all! all!"

"Then answer me. If she led your brother astray—you said that she led him astray?"

"Yes."

"If she caused his death—you said that she caused his death?"

"Yes," repeated the executioner.

"Then you must know her maiden name."

"Oh, my God! my God!" cried the executioner, "I feel as if I were dying. Absolution, father! The absolution!"

"Tell me her name!" exclaimed the monk, "and I will give it to you."

"She was named—my God, have pity on me!" murmured the executioner, as he fell back on the bed, pale, shuddering, and like a man at the point of death.

"Her name!" repeated the monk, bending down over him, as if to tear the name away in case he would not tell it,—"her name! Speak, or no absolution!"

The dying man appeared to collect all his strength.

The monk's eyes sparkled.

"Anne de Breuil," murmured the wounded man.

"Anne de Breuil!" cried the monk, stretching himself to his full height and raising his hands to heaven, "Anne de Breuil! You really said Anne de Breuil, did you not?"

"Yes, yes, that was the name. And now give me absolution, for I am dying."

"I absolve you?" said the priest, with a laugh that made the dying man's hair stand erect on his head,—"I absolve you? I am not a priest!"

"You are not a priest!" exclaimed the executioner; "and who are you, then?"

"You wretch, I will soon tell you."

"Ah, my God!"

"I am John Francis de Winter."

"I do not know you!" cried the executioner.

"Wait a moment, and you shall know me; I am John Francis de Winter," repeated he, "and that woman——"

"And that woman?"

"Was my mother!"

The executioner then uttered a cry, the terrible cry that was first heard.

"Pardon me, oh, pardon me," murmured he, "if not in the name of God, at least in your own name. If not as a priest, at any rate as a son."

"Pardon you!" exclaimed the false priest; "pardon you! God may do so, perhaps; but I never—never!"

"For pity's sake!" said the executioner, stretching forth his hand towards him.

"No pity for him who had no pity. Die impenitent—die in despair—die, and be damned."

And drawing a dagger from beneath his frock, and burying it in his breast,—

"There," said he, "there is my absolution!"

Then was heard that second cry, feebler than the first, and

followed by a prolonged groan. The monk, without withdrawing the dagger from the wound, ran to the window, opened it, jumped down upon a flowerbed, glided into the stable, took his mule out by a back door, hastened to the first clump of trees, where he threw off his monk's frock, drew from his valise a complete horseman's dress, clothed himself in it, gained the first posting-house on foot, procured a horse, and in that manner rode post in the direction of Paris.

33

GRIMAUD OPENS HIS MOUTH

GRIMAUD was left alone with the executioner, who in a few moments opened his eyes.

"Help, help," he murmured; "oh, God! have I not a single friend in the world who will aid me either to live or to die?"

"Take courage," said Grimaud; "they have gone for assistance."

"Who are you?" asked the wounded man, fixing his half-opened eyes on Grimaud.

"An old acquaintance," replied Grimaud.

"You?" and the wounded man sought to recall the features of the person who was before him.

"Under what circumstances did we meet?" he asked again.

"One night, twenty years ago, my master fetched you from Béthune, and conducted you to Armentières."

"I know you well, now," said the executioner; "you are one of the four servants."

"Yes."

"Where do you come from now?"

"I was passing by on the road, and drew up at this inn to rest my horse. They were relating to me how the executioner of Béthune was here, and wounded, when you uttered two piercing cries. At the first we ran to the door, and at the second forced it open."

"And the monk?" exclaimed the executioner; "did you see the monk?"

"What monk?"

"The monk that was shut in with me."

"No, he was no longer here; he appears to have fled by that window. Was it he who struck you?"

"Yes," said the executioner.

Grimaud moved, as if to leave the room.

"What are you going to do?" asked the wounded man.

"We must find him."

"Do not attempt it; he has revenged himself, and has done well. Now I may hope that God will forgive me, since my crime has been expiated."

"Explain yourself," said Grimaud.

"—The woman, whom you and your masters commanded me to kill——"

"Milady?"

"Yes, milady; it is true you called her thus."

"Well, what has the monk to do with milady?"

"He is her son."

Grimaud trembled, and stared at the dying man in a dull and vacant manner.

"Her son!" repeated he.

"Yes, her son."

"But does he know this secret, then?"

"I mistook him for a monk, and revealed it to him in confession."

"Unhappy man," cried Grimaud, whose face was covered with sweat, at the bare idea of the evil results which such a revelation might cause—"unhappy man, you named no one, I hope?"

"I pronounced no name, for I knew none, except his mother's, as a young girl, and it was by this name that he recognised her; but he knows that his uncle was among her judges."

Thus speaking, he fell back exhausted. Grimaud, wishing to relieve him, advanced his hand towards the hilt of the dagger.

"Touch me not!" said the executioner; "if this dagger is withdrawn, I shall die."

Grimaud remained with his hand extended; then, striking his forehead, he exclaimed, "Oh! if this man should ever discover the names of the others, my master is lost."

"Haste! haste to him, and warn him," cried the dying man, "if he still lives; warn his friends too. My death, believe me, will not be the end of this terrible adventure."

"Where was the monk going?" asked Grimaud.

"Towards Paris."

"Who stopped him?"

"Two young gentlemen who were on their way to join the army, and the name of one, of whom I heard his companion mention, was the Vicomte de Bragelonne."

"And it was this young man who brought the monk to you.

Then it was the will of God that it should be so, and this it is which is so awful," continued Grimaud; "and yet that woman deserved her fate; do you not think so?"

"On one's death-bed the crimes of others appear very small in comparison with one's own," said the executioner, and he fell back exhausted, and closed his eyes.

At this moment the host re-entered the room, followed not only by a doctor, but by many other persons, whom curiosity had attracted to the spot. The doctor approached the dying man, who seemed to have fainted.

"We must first extract the steel from the side," said he, shaking his head in a significant manner.

The warning which the wounded man had just uttered recurred to Grimaud, who turned away his head. The weapon, as we have already stated, was plunged into the body to the hilt, and as the surgeon, taking it by the end, drew it from the wound, the dying man opened his eyes, and fixed them in a manner truly dreadful. When, at last, the blade had been entirely withdrawn, a red froth issued from the mouth of the dying man, and a stream of blood rushed from the wound, when he at length drew breath; then, fixing his eyes on Grimaud with singular expression, he uttered the last death rattle and expired.

Then Grimaud, raising the dagger from the pool of blood which was gliding along the room—to the horror of all present—made a sign to the host to follow him, paid him with a generosity worthy of his master, and again mounted his horse. Grimaud's first intentions had been to return to Paris, but he remembered the anxiety which his prolonged absence might occasion to Raoul, and, reflecting that there were now only two miles between Raoul and himself, that a quarter of an hour's riding would unite them, and that the going, returning, and explanation would not occupy an hour, he put spurs to his horse, and, ten minutes after, had reached the inn of Mazingarbe.

Raoul was seated at table with the Count de Guiche and his tutor, when all at once the door opened, and Grimaud presented himself, travel-stained and dirty, still covered with the blood of the unfortunate executioner.

"Grimaud, my good Grimaud!" exclaimed Raoul, "here you are at last! Excuse me, sirs, this is a friend. How did you leave the count?" continued he; "does he regret me a little? Have you seen him since I left him? Answer, for I have many things to tell you, too; indeed, the last three days some odd adventures have happened,—but, what has occurred?—how pale you are!—and blood, too! what is this?"

"It is the blood of the unfortunate man whom you left at the inn, and who died in my arms."

"In your arms?—that man! But know you who he was?"

"I know that he was the old headsman of Béthune."

"You knew him? and he is dead?"

"Yes."

"Well, sir," said d'Arminges, "it is the common lot, and even an executioner is not exempted from it. I had a bad opinion of him the moment I saw his wound, and, since he asked for a monk, you know it was his own opinion too that death must ensue."

At the mention of the monk Grimaud turned pale.

"Come, come," continued d'Arminges, "to dinner;" for, like most men of his age and generation, he did not allow any sentiment to interfere with a good dinner.

"You are right, sir," said Raoul. "Come, Grimaud, order some dinner for yourself, and when you have rested a little, we can talk."

"No, sir, no," said Grimaud; "I cannot stay a moment; I must start for Paris again at once."

"How now? you start for Paris? Explain yourself! do you intend to disobey me for a change?"

"I dare not explain myself, and must disobey, unless you wish me to leave his honour, the count, to be killed!"

"Grimaud, my friend," said the viscount, "will you leave me thus, in such anxiety? Speak, speak in Heaven's name!"

"I can tell you but one thing, sir, for the secret you wish to know is not my own. You met this monk, did you not."

"Yes."

"You conducted him to the wounded man, and you had time to observe him, and perhaps you would know him again were you to meet him?"

"Yes! yes!" exclaimed both the young men.

"Very well! if ever you meet him again, wherever it may be, whether on the high road, or in the street, or in a church, anywhere that he or you may be, put your foot on his neck and crush him without pity, without mercy, as you would crush a viper, a snake, an asp; destroy him, and leave him not till he is dead; the lives of five men are not safe, in my opinion, as long as he lives!"

And without another word, Grimaud, profiting by the astonishment and terror into which he had thrown his auditors, rushed from the room. Five minutes later the gallop of a horse was heard on the road—it was Grimaud on his way to Paris. When once in the saddle, Grimaud reflected upon two things; the first that, at the pace he was going, his horse would not carry him ten miles;

and secondly, that he had no money. But Grimaud's imagination
was more prolific than his speech; and, therefore, at the first halt
he sold his steed, and with the money obtained from the pur-
chaser he took post-horses.

34

THE EVE OF BATTLE

RAOUL was aroused from his melancholy reflections by the host,
who rushed into the room, crying, "The Spaniards! the
Spaniards!"

This cry was sufficient to drive every previous thought from the
mind. The young men made some inquiries, and found that the
enemy was really advancing by Houdain and Béthune. While
M. d'Arminges was giving orders to bring the horses round, the
two young men ran up to the highest windows in the house, which
commanded a view of the surrounding country, and actually
beheld a numerous force of infantry and cavalry, just making their
appearance from the direction of Marsin and of Lens. This time
it was not a straggling body of partisans; it was a whole army.
There was, therefore, nothing to be done but to follow the prudent
advice of M. d'Arminges, and beat a retreat. The young men ran
down again. M. d'Arminges was already on horseback. Olivain
was holding the horses, and the count's lackeys were carefully
guarding the Spanish prisoner.

The little troop took the road to Cambrin, at a trot, where it
was thought they would find the prince; but he had not been
there since the preceding evening, and had retired to La Bassée,
false intelligence having led him to believe that the enemy meant
to cross the Lys at Estaire. In fact, the prince, being deceived by
this information, had evacuated Béthune and concentrated all his
forces between Vieille Chapelle and La Venthie; and he himself,
having been reconnoitring the whole line with the Maréchal de
Grammont, had just returned, and sat down questioning the
officers around him as to the information he had ordered each of
them to collect. But no one had positive news; the enemy's army
had disappeared forty-eight hours previously, and seemed to have
vanished.

Now, an enemy's army is never so near, and consequently so
formidable, as when it has completely disappeared. So the prince,

contrary to his usual habit, was sullen and anxious, when an officer on duty entered, and announced to Maréchal de Grammont that some one requested to speak to him. The Duc de Grammont took permission from the look of the prince, and went out. The prince followed him with his eyes, and his looks remained fixed upon the door, no one daring to speak to him for fear of disturbing his reflections.

Suddenly a dull sound was heard. The prince started up, stretching his hand towards the side whence the noise came. This noise was a familiar one to him; it was the report of cannon.

Every one rose as he had done. At that moment the door opened.

"Monseigneur," said de Grammont, all radiant with joy, "will your highness permit my son, the Count de Guiche, and his travelling companion, the Vicomte. de Bragelonne, to come and give you news of the enemy we were seeking, and whom they have found?"

"What!" said the prince warmly. "Will I permit them? Not only will I permit them, but desire them to do so. Let them come in."

The marshal brought the two young men forward, and they found themselves face to face with the prince.

"Speak, gentlemen," said the prince, bowing to them, "speak, at once; we will afterwards exchange the usual compliments. That which is most pressing now is to know where the enemy is and what he is doing."

It naturally devolved on the Count de Guiche to speak; not only was he the elder of the two, but he was also introduced to the prince by his father. Besides, he had long known the prince, while Raoul now saw him for the first time. He therefore recounted to the prince everything they had seen at the inn at Mazingarbe.

In the meantime Raoul was studying this young general, already so famous by his battles of Rocroy, Fribourg, and Nordlingen. Louis de Bourbon, Prince de Condé, was a young man of not more than twenty-six or twenty-seven, with an eagle eye—*agl' vichi grifani*, as Dante says—a hooked nose, and long hair flowing in curls down his back, of medium height, but well-built; having all the qualities of a great warrior; that is to say, a quick sight, a rapid decision, and undaunted courage—all which did not prevent his being, at the same time, a man of elegance and wit; so much so that, besides the revolution he made in war, by the improvements which he introduced into it, he had also caused a revolution at Paris among the young courtiers, of whom he was the natural leader.

From the first words of the Count de Guiche, and from the

direction whence the sound of the cannon was heard, the prince thoroughly understood everything. The enemy must have passed the Lys at Saint-Venant, and was marching on Lens, with the intention, doubtless, of taking possession of that town and cutting the French army off from France. The cannon which they heard from time to time dominating the others were the large guns of the town, which were replying to the artillery of the Spaniards and Flemish.

But of what force was this body of men? Was it a corps destined to effect a simple diversion? Was it the whole army? This was the prince's last question, to which it was impossible for de Guiche to reply. Now, as this was most important, it was also that to which the prince would have desired an exact, positive, and precise reply.

Raoul, surmounting the natural timidity he felt, in spite of himself, to approach the prince, addressed him saying, "Will monseigneur permit me to hazard a few words on the subject, which may relieve him from his embarrassment?"

The prince turned sharply towards him, and, enveloping the young man from head to foot with a glance, he smiled at seeing his counsellor was a youth of less than sixteen.

"Without doubt, sir; speak," said he, softening his usually sharp, clear voice, as if he had been addressing a woman.

"Monseigneur," replied Raoul, blushing, "might question the Spanish prisoner."

"Have you made a Spanish prisoner, then?" cried the prince.

"Yes, monseigneur."

"Ah, that's true," said de Guiche; "I had forgotten it."

"That's natural enough," said Raoul, smiling, "as you took him yourself, count."

The old marshal turned towards the viscount, grateful for the praise thus bestowed on his son; while the prince cried out:

"The young man is right; bring in the prisoner."

In the meantime the prince took de Guiche aside and questioned him how this prisoner had been made, at the same time inquiring who this young man was.

"Sir," said the prince, turning to Raoul, "I hear that you bring a letter from my sister, Madame de Longueville; but I find that you prefer recommending yourself by giving me good advice."

"Monseigneur," said Raoul, colouring, "I did not wish to interrupt your highness in such an important conversation as that you were engaged in with the count; but here is the letter."

"Very well," said the prince, "give it to me by and by. Here is the prisoner; let us attend to more pressing business."

In fact, they were bringing in the prisoner. He was one of those *condottieri* of whom some remained even at that period, selling their blood to any one who would purchase it, and grown old in brigandage and plunder. Since he had been taken prisoner, he had not uttered one single word, so that those who had captured him could not themselves tell to what nation he belonged.

The prince looked at him with an air of unspeakable distrust.

"Of what country are you?" he demanded.

The prisoner answered in some strange language.

"Ah, it seems that he is a Spaniard. Do you speak Spanish, Grammont?"

"Faith, very little, monseigneur!"

"And I not at all," said the prince, laughing. "Gentlemen," added he, turning towards those around him, "is there any one among you who speaks Spanish, and can serve me as an interpreter?"

"I can, monseigneur," said Raoul.

"Ah! you speak Spanish?"

"Sufficiently, I believe, to execute your highness's orders on this occasion."

The prisoner during this colloquy had remained impassible, and as if he had not understood a word that had been said.

"Monseigneur has asked you of what nation you are," said the young man, in very pure Castilian.

"*Ich bin ein Deutscher!*" replied the prisoner.

"What the devil does he say?" demanded the prince, "and what fresh gibberish is that?"

"He says he is a German, monseigneur; and yet I doubt it, for his accent is false, and his pronunciation defective."

"Do you speak German also, then?" asked the prince.

"Yes, monseigneur," replied Raoul.

"Sufficiently to question him in that language?"

"Yes, monseigneur."

"Interrogate him, then."

Raoul commenced the interrogatory; but facts supported his opinion. The prisoner did not understand, or feigned not to understand, what Raoul said to him. Raoul, on his side, but ill understood his replies, delivered in a mixture of German and Alsatian.

In the midst, however, of all the prisoner's efforts to elude a regular interrogatory, Raoul caught the accent natural to the man.

"*Non siete Spagnuolo*," said he, "*non siete Tedesco, siete Italiano.*"

The prisoner was confused, and bit his lips.

"Ah, that's the thing, I can see!" said the prince; "and as he is an Italian, I will continue the interrogatory myself. Thank you, vicomte," continued he; "you shall be henceforth my interpreter."

But the prisoner was not more disposed to reply in Italian than in any other language. His principal effort was to elude the questions put to him. Thus he knew nothing—neither the number of the enemy, the name of the general who commanded them, nor the object of their march.

"That is well," said the prince, who understood the cause of this ignorance. "This man has been captured whilst assassinating and plundering. He might have purchased his life by speaking; but he will not speak, so take him away, and shoot him!"

The prisoner grew pale, the two soldiers who had led him in took him by the arms, and conducted him towards the door, whilst the prince, turning towards de Grammont, appeared to have forgotten the order he had given.

Having reached the threshold, the prisoner stopped; the soldiers, who considered only their orders, wished to force him along.

"One moment," said the prisoner, in French; "I am willing to speak, monseigneur."

"Aha!" said the prince, laughing, "I knew well enough we should come to that at last. I have a wonderful secret for unlocking tongues. Young men, take advantage of this lesson when you come to have a command."

"But," said the prisoner, "it is on condition that your highness will swear that my life shall be safe."

"On the word of a gentleman," said the prince.

"Then put your questions, monseigneur."

"Where did the army pass the Lys?"

"Between Saint-Venant and Aire."

"By whom is it commanded?"

"By the Count de Fuonsaldagna, by General Beck, and by the archduke in person."

"Of how many men is it composed?"

"Of eighteen thousand men and thirty-six field pieces."

"And its march?"

"On Lens."

"There, do you see, gentlemen?" said the prince, turning with an air of triumph toward the Maréchal de Grammont and the other officers.

"Yes, monseigneur," replied the marshal; "you have divined all that the human mind could divine."

"Recall Le Plessis, Bellièvre, Villequier, and d'Erlac," said the prince; "recall all the troops that are on this side of the Lys, and let them hold themselves in readiness to march to-night. To-morrow, in all probability we shall attack the enemy."

"But, monseigneur," said the Maréchal de Grammont, "consider that, in uniting all our disposable forces, we shall not be able to muster more than thirteen thousand men."

"Marshal," replied the prince, with that wonderful look characteristic of him, "all great battles are gained with small armies."

Then turning toward the prisoner, he said:

"Take this man and guard him carefully. His life depends on his communication: should it be true, he shall be liberated; if false, have him shot."

The prisoner was led off.

"Count de Guiche," resumed the prince, "you have not seen your father for some time; remain with him. Monsieur," continued he, turning to Raoul, "if you are not too much fatigued, follow me."

"To the end of the world, monseigneur!" cried Raoul, experiencing for this young general, who appeared to him so worthy of his renown, an enthusiasm to which he had been a stranger.

The prince smiled. He despised flatterers, but loved enthusiasm.

"Come, monsieur," said he, "you have proved good in council, to-morrow we shall see how you are in action."

"And I, monseigneur," said de Grammont, "what shall I do?"

"Remain to receive the troops. I will either return to fetch them myself, or I will send you a courier for you to bring them to me. Twenty of my best mounted guards are all I want for my escort."

"That's very few!" said the maréchal.

"Quite enough," said the prince. "Have you a good horse, Monsieur de Bragelonne?"

"Mine was killed this morning, monsiegneur, and I am riding provisionally that of my lackey."

"Ask for, and choose for yourself in my stables, the one you like best. No false shame; take the horse you really prefer. You will, perhaps, want a good one this evening—certainly to-morrow."

Raoul did not require to be told twice. He knew that with superiors, particularly when these superiors are princes, politeness consists in obeying without delay, and without reasoning. He descended to the stables, chose an Andalusian horse of an Isabelle colour, and saddled and bridled it himself, for Athos had recommended him in moments of danger not to trust these important cares to anybody, and he rejoined the prince, who at that moment was mounting his horse.

"Now, sir," said he to Raoul, "will you give me the letter of which you are the bearer?"

Raoul held out the letter to the prince.

"Keep near to me, sir," continued the latter.

The prince put spurs to his horse, hooked his bridle to the pommel of his saddle, as he was accustomed to do when he wished to have his hands free, opened Madame de Longueville's letter, and set off at a hand-gallop towards Lens, accompanied by Raoul, and followed by his little escort; whilst the messengers, who were to recall the troops, departed at speed in an opposite direction. The prince read as he rode.

"Sir," said he an instant after, "they speak most favourably of you. I have only one thing to tell you, which is that, from the little that I have heard and seen, I think still more highly of you than they have spoken."

Raoul bowed.

In the meantime, at every step that brought them nearer to Lens, the firing of cannon grew louder. The prince's eyes were directed, with the intenseness of a bird of prey, on the point whence this sound came. It might have been imagined that he had the power of piercing through the screen of trees which were before him, and which bounded the horizon.

From time to time his nostrils dilated as if he was anxious to inhale the smell of powder, and he breathed hard like his horse.

At last the sound of the cannon was so near that it was evident they were not more than a league from the battlefield. In fact, at a turn of the road they could see the little village of Aunay.

The peasants were in great confusion; the report of the cruelty of the Spaniards had spread abroad and excited general consternation; the women had already fled in the direction of Vitry; some few men only remained.

At sight of the prince they ran up; one of them recognised him.

"Ah, monseigneur," said he, "are you come to drive away all those beggarly Spaniards and those brigands of Lorraine?"

"Yes," said the prince, "if you will act as my guide."

"Most willingly, monseigneur. Where does your highness wish me to conduct you?"

"To some elevated spot, whence I may see Lens and its neighbourhood."

"In that case, I am your man."

"Can I trust you? Are you a good Frenchman?"

"I am an old soldier of Rocroy, monseigneur."

"Here," said the prince, giving him his purse, "this is for Rocroy. Now, do you wish to have a horse, or do you prefer going on foot?"

"On foot, monseigneur, on foot. I have always served in the

infantry. Besides, I expect to lead your highness through paths where you will be obliged to dismount."

"Come, then," said the prince, "let us not lose any time."

The peasant set off, running before the prince's horse. Then, about a hundred yards from the village, he took a narrow path hidden in the bottom of a pretty valley; for about half a league they proceeded thus, under the cover of the trees, the artillery sounding so near that at each report they might have expected to hear the whistling of the balls. At last they came to a path that branched off from the direct road to climb up the side of the mountain. The peasant took this path, requesting the prince to follow him. He dismounted, and ordering one of his aides-de-camp and Raoul to do the same, and the others to remain there and keep a good lookout, he began to climb the path.

In ten minutes they reached the ruins of an old château; these ruins crowned the summit of a hill, from which they could command a view of the surrounding country. Barely a league away they could perceive Lens, at bay; and before Lens, all the enemy's army.

At a single glance the prince embraced the whole extent of country spread before his eyes, from Lens even to Vimy. In an instant the whole plan of the battle, which on the next day was to save France a second time from invasion, displayed itself before his mind. He took a pencil, tore a leaf from his tablets, and wrote:—

"My dear Marshal,—

"In one hour Lens will be in the enemy' hands. Come and rejoin me; bring the whole army with you. I shall be at Vendin, to place the men in position. To-morrow we shall retake Lens and whip the enemy."

Then, turning to Raoul—

"Go, sir," said he, "at full speed, and put this letter into M. de Grammont's hands."

Raoul bowed, took the paper, ran down the mountain, threw himself on his horse, and set off full gallop. In a quarter of an hour he was with the maréchal. Part of the troops were already there; they expected the rest instantly.

The Maréchal de Grammont placed himself at the head of all the disposable infantry and cavalry, and took the road to Vendin, leaving the Duc de Châtillon to bring up the others as soon as they should arrive. The artillery was all ready, and instantly set forward.

It was seven o'clock in the evening when the maréchal arrived at the rendezvous. The prince was there before him. As he had foreseen, Lens had fallen into the hands of the enemy soon after Raoul's departure. This event was announced by the cessation of the cannonade.

As darkness came on, the troops arrived successively. Strict orders were given that not a drum should be beaten or a trumpet sounded.

By nine o'clock night had set in, and yet a last glow of twilight illumined the plain. The march commenced in perfect silence, the prince leading the column.

On arriving at the side of Aunay the army came in sight of Lens; two or three houses were in flames, and the dismal murmur indicating the agony of a city taken by assault reached the ears of the soldiers.

The prince assigned every one his post. The Maréchal de Grammont was to hold the extreme left, leaning upon Méricourt; the Duc de Châtillon headed the centre; the prince, on the right, was in front of Aunay.

The order of battle in the morning was to be the same as that of the positions taken in the evening. Every one on awaking would find himself upon the ground on which he was to manœuvre. The movements were executed in the most profound silence, and with the utmost precision. At ten o'clock every one was in his position; at half-past ten the prince went the rounds of the posts, and gave his orders for the next day.

Three things were recommended above all to the leaders, who were to watch that the soldiers observed them scrupulously. The first was, that the different corps should closely observe the march of the rest, in order that the cavalry and infantry might be upon the same line, and that each might guard its intervals.

The second was, not to charge but at the common step.

The third, to be sure to allow the enemy to fire first.

The prince gave the Count de Guiche to his father, and kept Bragelonne himself; but the two young men asked permission to pass the night together, which was granted.

A tent was pitched for them near the Maréchal's. Although the day had been fatiguing, neither of them felt any inclination to sleep.

Besides, the eve of battle is a serious and imposing thing, even to old soldiers, and much more so to young men who are about to view this terrible spectacle for the first time.

On the eve of battle, you think of a thousand things that have hitherto been forgotten. On the eve of battle, common acquaintances become friends, friends become brothers.

It is needless to say that if there be any more tender sentiment at the bottom of the heart, that sentiment then naturally reaches its highest degree of tensity.

We may easily believe that some such feeling was experienced by each of the young men; for in a short time they both sat down at the end of the tent and began writing on their knees. The letters were long, the four pages were one after another filled with closely written and delicate manuscripts. Occasionally they looked up and smiled. They understood each other, without a word being said. These two exquisite and delicate organisations were so constructed as to sympathise without speaking.

When the letters were finished they enclosed them in double envelopes, that no one might read the address without tearing open the first envelope; then they exchanged the letters.

"If any misfortune should befall me"—said Bragelonne.

"If I should be killed"—said de Guiche.

"Do not distress yourself about that," they both said.

Then, having kissed each other like brothers, they wrapped themselves in their cloaks, and slept the fresh and graceful sleep of birds, flowers, and children.

35

A DINNER IN THE OLD STYLE

THE second interview between the former musketeers had not been so pompous and stiff as the first. Athos, with his superior understanding, wisely deemed that the table would be the most speedy and complete point of reunion, and at the moment when his friends, doubtful of his deportment and his sobriety, dared scarcely speak of some of their former good dinners, he was the first to propose that they should all assemble round some well-spread table, and abandon themselves unreservedly to their own natural character and manners, a freedom which had formerly contributed so much to the good understanding between them as to give them the name of the inseparables. For various reasons this was an agreeable proposition to them all, and it was therefore agreed that each should leave a very exact address, and that upon the request of any of the associates, a meeting should be convened at a famous eating-house in the Rue de la Monnaie, of the sign of the Hermitage; the first rendezvous was fixed for the following Wednesday, at eight o'clock in the evening.

On that day, in fact, the four friends arrived punctually at the hour arranged, each from his own abode. Porthos had been trying a new horse; d'Artagnan came from being on guard at the Louvre; Aramis had been to visit one of his parishioners; and Athos, whose domicile was established in the Rue Guénégaud, found himself close at hand. They were therefore somewhat surprised to meet altogether at the door of the Hermitage; Athos starting out from the Pont Neuf, Porthos by the Rue du Roule, d'Artagnan by the Rue des Fossées St. Germain l'Auxerrois, and Aramis by the Rue de Bethisy.

The first words exchanged between the four friends, on account of the ceremony which each of them mingled with their demonstration, were somewhat forced, and even the repast began with a kind of stiffness. Athos perceived this embarrassment, and by way of supplying a prompt remedy, called for four bottles of champagne.

At this order, given in Athos's habitually calm manner, the face of the Gascon relaxed, and Porthos's brow was smooth. Aramis was astonished. He knew that Athos not only seldom drank, but that more, he had a kind of repugnance to wine. This astonishment was doubled when Aramis saw Athos fill a glass, and drink with his former enthusiasm. His companions followed his example, and in an instant the four bottles were empty, and this excellent specific succeeded in dissipating even the slightest cloud which might have rested on their spirits. Now the four friends began to speak loudly, scarcely waiting till one had finished for another to begin, and to assume each his favourite attitude at the table. Soon —strange fact—Aramis unfastened two buttons of his doublet, seeing which, Porthos unhooked his entirely.

Battles, long journeys, blows given and received, sufficed for the first subject of conversation; which then turned upon the silent struggles sustained against him who was now called the great Cardinal.

"Faith," said Aramis, laughing, "we have praised the dead enough, let us revile the living a little. I should like to say something spiteful of Mazarin; is it allowable?"

"Go on—go on," replied d'Artagnan, laughing heartily, "relate your story, and I will applaud if it is a good one."

"A great prince," said Aramis, "with whom Mazarin sought an alliance, was invited by him to send him a list of the conditions on which he would do him the honour to negotiate with him. The prince, who had a great repugnance to treat with such an ill-bred fellow, made his list, though unwillingly, and sent it. In this list there were three conditions which displeased Mazarin, and he offered the prince ten thousand crowns to cancel them."

"Ah, ah, ah!" exclaimed the three friends, "not a bad bargain; and there was no fear of being taken at his word; what did the prince then?"

"The prince immediately sent fifty thousand francs to Mazarin, begging him never to write to him again, and offered twenty thousand francs more, on condition that he would never speak to him."

"What did Mazarin do?"

"He stormed?" suggested Athos.

"He beat the messenger?" cried Porthos.

"He accepted the money?" said d'Artagnan.

"You guessed it," answered Aramis; and they all laughed so heartily, that the host appeared in order to inquire whether the gentlemen wanted anything; he thought they were fighting.

At last their hilarity was calmed, and—

"Faith!" exclaimed d'Artagnan to his two friends, "you may well wish ill to Mazarin; for I assure you, on his side, he wishes you no good."

"Pooh! really?" said Athos. "If I thought that the fellow knew me by my name, I would be rebaptized, for fear I should be thought to know him."

"He knows you more by your actions than by your name; he is quite aware that there are two gentlemen who have greatly aided the escape of Monsieur de Beaufort, and he has instigated an active search for them, I can answer for it."

"By whom?"

"By me; and this morning he sent for me to ask me if I had obtained any information."

"And what did you reply?"

"That I had not as yet; but that I was to dine to-day with two gentlemen, who would be able to give me some."

"You told him that?" said Porthos, his broad smile spreading over his honest face, "bravo! and you do not fear, Athos?"

"No," replied Athos; "it is not the search of Mazarin that I fear."

"Now," said Aramis, "tell me what you do fear."

"Nothing for the present, at least, in good earnest."

"And with regard to the past?" asked Porthos.

"Oh! the past is another thing," said Athos, sighing; "the past and the future."

"Are you afraid for young Raoul?" asked Aramis.

"Well," said d'Artagnan, "one is seldom killed in a first engagement."

"Nor in the second," said Aramis.

"Nor in the third," returned Porthos; "and even when one is killed, one rises again, the proof of which is, that here we are!"

"No," said Athos, "it is not Raoul about whom I am anxious, for I trust he will conduct himself like a gentleman; and if he is killed—well—he will die bravely; but hold—should such a misfortune happen—well——" Athos passed his hand across his brow.

"Well?" asked Aramis.

"Well, I shall look upon it as an expiation."

"Oh! ah!" said d'Artagnan; "I know what you mean."

"And I, too," added Aramis; "but you must not think of that, Athos; what is past is past."

"I don't understand," said Porthos.

"The affair at Armentières," murmured d'Artagnan.

"The affair at Armentières?"

"Milady."

"Oh, yes!" said Porthos; "true, I had forgotten it."

Athos looked at him intently.

"You have forgotten it, Porthos?" he echoed.

"Faith! yes, it is so long ago," answered Porthos.

"This thing does not, then, weigh on your conscience?"

"Faith, no."

"And you, d'Artagnan?"

"I—I own that when my mind recalls that terrible event, I remember nothing but the stiffened corpse of that poor Madame Bonancieux. Yes, yes," murmured he, "I have often felt regret for the victim, but never any remorse for the assassin."

Athos shook his head doubtfully.

"Consider," said Aramis, "if you admit divine justice and its participation in the things of this world, that woman was punished by the will of heaven. We are but the instruments—that is all."

"But as to free will?"

"How acts the judge? He has a free will, and he condemns fearlessly. What does the executioner? he is master of his arm, and yet he strikes without hesitation."

"The executioner!" muttered Athos, as if arrested by some recollection.

"I know that it is terrible," said d'Artagnan; "but when I reflect that we have killed English, Rochellais, Spaniards, nay, even French, who never did us any other harm but to aim at and to miss us, whose only fault was to cross swords with us, and not to be able to ward us off quick enough—I can, on my honour, find an excuse for my share of the judgment on that woman."

"As for me," said Porthos, "now that you have reminded me of it, Athos, I have the scene again before me, as if I was there! Milady was there, as it were in your place."—Athos changed colour.—"I—I was where d'Artagnan stands. I wore a short sword which cut like a Damascus—you remember it, Aramis, for you——"

"And you, Aramis?"

"Well, I think of it sometimes," said Aramis. "And I swear to you all three, that had the executioner of Béthune—was he not of Béthune?—yes, egad! of Béthune!—not been there, I would have cut off the head of that infamous being without remembering who I am, and even remembering it. She was a bad woman."

"And then," resumed Aramis, with the tone of philosophical indifference which he had assumed since he belonged to the Church, and in which there was more scepticism than confidence in God, "what is the use of thinking of it? At the last hour we must confess this action, and God knows better than we can whether it is a crime, a fault, or a meritorious action. I repent of it? Egad! no. By my honour, and by the holy cross, I only regret it because she was a woman."

"The most satisfactory part of the matter," said d'Artagnan, "is that there remains no trace of it."

"She had a son," observed Athos.

"Oh! yes; I know that," said d'Artagnan, "and you mentioned it to me; but who can tell what has become of him? If the serpent be dead, why not its brood? Do you think that his uncle de Winter would have brought up that young viper? De Winter probably condemned the son as he had done the mother."

"Then," said Athos, "woe to de Winter, for the child had done no harm."

"May the devil take me if the child be not dead," said Porthos. "There is so much fog in that detestable country—at least so d'Artagnan declares."

Just as this conclusion arrived at by Porthos was about probably to bring back hilarity to the faces now more or less clouded, footsteps were heard on the stairs, and a knock was given at the door.

"Come in," cried Athos.

"Please your honours," said the host, "a person in a great haste wishes to speak to one of you."

"To which of us?" asked all the four friends.

"To him who is called the Count de la Fère."

"It is I," said Athos; "and what is the name of the person?"

"Grimaud."

"Ah!" exclaimed Athos, turning pale. "Returned already. What has happened, then, to Raoul?"

"Let him enter," cried d'Artagnan, "let him come up."

But Grimaud had already mounted the staircase, and was waiting on the last step; so springing into the room, he motioned the host to leave it. The door being closed, the four friends waited in expectation. Grimaud's agitation, his pallor, the sweat which covered his face, the dust which soiled his clothes, all indicated that he was the messenger of some important and terrible news.

"Your honours," said he, "milady had a child; that child has become a man; the tigress had a little one, the tiger has roused himself; he is ready to spring upon you—beware!"

Athos glanced around at his friends with a melancholy smile. Porthos turned to look at his sword which was hung up against the wall: Aramis seized his knife; d'Artagnan rose.

"What do you mean, Grimaud?" he exclaimed.

"That milady's son has left England; that he is in France on his road to Paris, if he be not here already."

"The deuce he is!" said Porthos. "Are you sure of it?"

"Certain!" replied Grimaud.

This announcement was received in silence. Grimaud was so breathless, so exhausted, that he had fallen back upon a chair. Athos filled a glass with wine, and gave it to him.

"Well, and after all," said d'Artagnan, "supposing that he lives, that he comes to Paris, we have seen many other such. Let him come."

"Yes," echoed Porthos, stroking his sword, suspended to the wall, "we can wait for him, let him come."

"Moreover, he is but a child," said Aramis.

Grimaud rose.

"A child!" he exclaimed. "Do you know what he has done—this child? Disguised as a monk, he discovered the whole history in confession from the executioner of Béthune, and having confessed him, after having learnt everything from him, he gave him absolution by planting this dagger into his heart. See, it is still red and wet, for it is not thirty hours ago since it was taken from the wound."

And Grimaud threw the dagger on the table.

D'Artagnan, Porthos, and Aramis rose, and in one spontaneous motion rushed to their swords. Athos alone remained seated, calm and thoughtful.

"And you say he is dressed as a monk, Grimaud?"

"Yes, as an Augustine monk."

"What sized man is he?"

"About my height, the host said; thin, pale, with light-blue eyes, and light hair."

"And he did not see Raoul?" asked Athos.

"Yes, on the contrary, they met, and it was the viscount himself who conducted him to the bed of the dying man."

Athos rose, in his turn, without speaking—went and unhooked his sword.

"Heigh, sir," said d'Artagnan, forcing a laugh; "do you know we look very much like silly women! How is it that we, four men, who have faced armies without flinching, begin to tremble at the sight of a child!"

"Yes," said Athos, "but this child comes in the name of Heaven."

And they left the hotel in haste.

36

THE LETTER OF KING CHARLES THE FIRST

THE reader must now accompany us across the Seine, and follow us to the gate of the Carmelite Convent in the Rue St. Jacques. It is eleven o'clock in the morning, and the pious sisters have just finished saying a mass for the success of the armies of King Charles I. Leaving the church, a woman and a young girl dressed in black, the one as a widow and the other also in mourning, have re-entered their cell. The elder lady kneels on a *prie-dieu* of painted wood, and at a short distance from her stands the young girl, leaning against a chair, weeping. The woman must have been handsome, but the traces of sorrow have aged her. The young girl is lovely, and her tears only embellish her; the lady appears to be about forty years of age, the girl about fourteen.

"Oh, God!" prayed the kneeling suppliant, "protect my husband, guard my son, and take my wretched life instead!"

"Oh, God!" murmured the girl, "leave me my mother!"

"Your mother can be of no use to you in this world, Henrietta," said the lady, turning round. "Your mother has no longer either throne or husband, nor son, nor money, nor friends—the whole world, my poor child, has abandoned your mother!" And she fell back, weeping, into her daughter's arms.

"Courage, take courage, my dear mother!"

"Ah! 'tis an unfortunate year for kings," replied the mother. "And no one thinks of us in this country, for each must think of his own affairs. As long as your brother was with me he kept me up; but he is gone, and can no longer send us news of himself, either to me or to your father. I have pledged my jewels, sold all your clothes and my own to pay his servants, who refused to accompany him unless I made this sacrifice. We are now reduced to live at the expense of these daughters of Heaven; we are the poor succoured by God."

"But why not address yourself to your sister the queen?" asked the girl.

"Alas! the queen, my sister, is no longer queen, my child. Another reigns in her name. One day you will be able to understand how this is."

"Well, then, to the king, your nephew; shall I speak to him? You know how much he loves me, my mother."

"Alas! my nephew is not yet king, and you know La Porte has told us twenty times that he himself is in need of almost everything."

"Then let us pray to Heaven," said the girl.

The two women who thus knelt together in prayer were the daughter and granddaughter of Henry IV., the wife and daughter of Charles I.

They had just completed their prayers, when a nun softly tapped at the door of the cell.

"Enter, my sister," said the queen.

"I trust your majesty will pardon this intrusion on her meditations, but a nobleman has arrived from England, and waits in the parlour, requesting the honour of presenting a letter to your majesty."

"Oh! a letter! a letter from the king, perhaps. News from your father, do you hear, Henrietta.—And the name of this nobleman?"

"Lord de Winter."

"Lord de Winter!" exclaimed the queen, "the friend of my husband. Oh, let him come in!"

And the queen advanced to meet the messenger, whose hand she seized affectionately, whilst he knelt down, and presented a letter to her contained in a gold case.

"Ah! my lord," said the queen, "you bring us three things which we have not seen for a long time. Gold, a devoted friend, and a letter from the king, our husband and master."

De Winter bowed again, unable to reply from excess of emotion.

On their side the mother and daughter retired into the embrasure of a window to read eagerly the following letter:

"DEAR WIFE,—We have now reached the moment of decision. I have concentrated here at Naseby camp all the resources which Heaven has left me; and I write to you in haste from thence. Here

I await the army of my rebellious subjects, and I am about to fight for the last time against them. If victorious, I shall continue the struggle; if vanquished, I am completely lost. In the latter case (alas! in our position, one must provide for everything), I shall try to gain the coast of France. But can they, will they receive an unhappy king, who will bring such a sad story into a country already agitated by civil discord? Your wisdom and your affection must serve me as guides. The bearer of this letter will tell you, madam, what I dare not trust to the risk of miscarrying. He will explain to you the course which I expect you to adopt. I charge him also with my blessing for my children, and with the sentiments of my heart for yourself, dear wife."

The letter bore the signature, not of "Charles, King," but of "Charles—still King."

"And let him be king no longer," cried the queen. "Let him be conquered, exiled, proscribed, provided he still lives. Alas! in these days the throne is too dangerous a place for me to wish him to keep it! But, my lord, tell me," she continued, "hide nothing from me—what is, in truth, the king's position? Is it as hopeless as he thinks?"

"Alas! madame, more hopeless even than he thinks. His majesty has so good a heart, that he cannot understand hatred;—is so loyal, that he does not suspect treason! England is disturbed by a spirit of excitement, which, I greatly fear, blood alone can extinguish."

"But Lord Montrose," replied the queen. "I have heard of his great and rapid successes, of battles won. I heard that he was marching to the frontier to join the king."

"Yes, madame; but on the frontier he was met by Leslie. He had tried victory by means of superhuman undertakings. Now victory has abandoned him. Montrose, beaten at Philiphaugh, was obliged to disperse the remains of his army, and to fly disguised as a servant. He is at Bergen, in Norway."

"Heaven preserve him!" said the queen. "It is at least a consolation to know that some who have so often risked their lives for us are in safety. And now, my lord, that I see how hopeless the position of the king is, tell me with what you are charged on the part of my royal husband."

"Well, then, your majesty," said de Winter, "the king desires you to try and discover the dispositions of the king and queen towards him."

"Alas! you know, the king is but still a child, and the queen is a woman weak enough too. Monsieur Mazarin is everything here."

"Does he desire to play the part in France that Cromwell plays in England?"

"Oh, no! He is a subtle and cunning Italian, who, though he may dream of crime, dares never commit it; and unlike Cromwell, who disposes of both houses, Mazarin has had the queen to support him in his struggle with the parliament."

"—More reason, then, that he should protect a king pursued by his parliament."

The queen shook her head mournfully.

"If I judge for myself, my lord," she said, "the Cardinal will not do anything, and will even, perhaps, act against us. The presence of my daughter and myself in France is already irksome to him; much more so would be that of the king. My lord," added Henrietta, with a sad smile, "it is sad, and almost shameful, to be obliged to say that we have passed the winter in the Louvre without money, without linen—almost without bread, and often not rising from bed because we wanted fire."

"Horrible!" cried de Winter; "the daughter of Henry IV., and the wife of King Charles! Wherefore did you not apply then, madame, to the first person you saw from us?"

"Such is the hospitality shown to a queen by the minister, from whom a king would demand it."

"But I heard that a marriage between the Prince of Wales and Mademoiselle d'Orléans was spoken of," said de Winter.

"Yes, for an instant I hoped it was so. The young people felt a mutual esteem; but the queen, who at first sanctioned their affection, changed her mind, and Monsieur the Duc d'Orléans, who had encouraged the familiarity between them, has forbidden his daughter to think any longer about the union. Oh, my lord!" continued the queen, without restraining her tears, "it is better to fight as the king has done, and to die, as perhaps he will, than to live begging as I have."

"Courage, madame! courage! Do not despair! The interests of the French crown, endangered this moment, are to discourage civil rebellion in a nation so near to it. Mazarin, as a statesman, will understand the necessity of doing so."

"But are you sure," said the queen doubtfully, "that you have not been forestalled?"

"By whom?"

"By the Joyces, the Prinns, the Cromwells."

"By a tailor, by a coachmaker, by a brewer! Ah! I hope, madame, that the Cardinal will not enter into negotiations with them!"

"Ah! what wishes he himself?" asked the queen.

"Solely the honour of the king—of the queen."

"Well, let us hope that he will do something for the sake of their honour," said the queen. "A true friend's eloquence is so powerful, my lord, that you have reassured me. Give me your hand, and let us go to the minister; and yet," she added, "suppose he refuse, and that the king loses the battle!"

"His majesty will then take refuge in Holland, where I hear that his royal highness the Prince of Wales is."

"And can his majesty count upon many such subjects as yourself for his flight?"

"Alas! no, madame," answered de Winter; "but the case is provided for, and I am come to France to seek allies."

"Allies!" said the queen, shaking her head.

"Madame!" replied de Winter, "provided I can find some old friends of former times, I can answer for everything."

"Come, then, my lord," said the queen, with the painful doubt that is felt by those who have suffered much; "come, and may Heaven hear you."

The queen entered her carriage, and de Winter on horseback, followed by two servants, rode by its side.

37

CROMWELL'S LETTER

AT the moment Queen Henrietta quitted the convent to go to the Palais Royal, a young man dismounted at the gate of this royal abode, and announced to the guards that he had something of consequence to communicate to Cardinal Mazarin. Although the Cardinal was often tormented by fear, he was more often in need of counsel and information, and he was therefore sufficiently accessible. The difficulty of being admitted was not to be found at the first door, and even the second was passed easily enough; but at the third door, besides the guard, was the faithful Bernouin, a Cerberus whom no speech could soften; no wand, even of gold, could charm.

It was, therefore, at the third door, that those who solicited or were bid to an audience, underwent a formal interrogatory.

The young man, having left his horse tied to the gate in the court, mounted the great staircase, and addressed the guard in the first chamber.

"Cardinal Mazarin," said he.

"Pass on," replied the guard.

The cavalier entered the second hall, which was guarded by the musketeers.

"Have you a letter of audience?" asked an officer, advancing to the new arrival.

"I have one, but not from Cardinal Mazarin."

"Enter, and ask for Monsieur Bernouin," said the officer, opening the door of the third room. Whether he but held his usual post, or whether it might be by accident, but Monsieur Bernouin was found standing behind the door, and must have heard all that was said.

"You seek me, sir?" said he. "From whom may the letter be that you bear to his Eminence?"

"From General Oliver Cromwell," said the newcomer. "Be so good as to mention this name to his Eminence, and to bring me word whether he will receive me—yes or no."

Saying which, he resumed the dark and proud bearing peculiar at that time to the Puritans. Bernouin cast an inquisitorial glance at the person of the young man, and entered the cabinet of the Cardinal, to whom he transmitted the messenger's words.

"A man bringing a letter from General Cromwell?" said Mazarin. "And what kind of a man?"

"A true Englishman, your Eminence. Hair sandy-red—more red than sandy; grey-blue eyes—more grey than blue; and for the rest, stiff and arrogant."

"Let him hand in his letter."

"His Eminence asks for the letter," said Bernouin, passing back into the antechamber.

"His Eminence cannot see the letter without the bearer of it," replied the young man; "but to convince you that I am really the bearer of a letter, see, here it is; and add," continued he, "that I am not a simple messenger, but an envoy extraordinary."

Bernouin re-entered the cabinet, and returning in a few seconds, —"Enter, sir," said he.

The young man appeared on the threshold of the minister's closet; in one hand holding his hat, in the other the letter. Mazarin rose. "Have you, sir," asked he, "a letter accrediting you to me?"

"Here it is, my lord," said the young man.

Mazarin took the letter, and read:

"Mr. Mordaunt, one of my secretaries, will remit this letter of introduction to his Eminence, the Cardinal Mazarin, in Paris. He is also the bearer of a second confidential epistle for his Eminence.

"OLIVER CROMWELL."

"Very well, Monsieur Mordaunt," said Mazarin, "let me have the second letter, and sit down."

Mordaunt drew from his pocket the second letter, presented it to the Cardinal, and sat down. The Cardinal, however, did not unseal the letter at once, but continued to turn it again and again in his hand; then in accordance with his usual custom, and judging from experience that few people could hide anything from him when he began to question them, fixing his eyes upon them at the same time, he thus addressed the messenger:

"You are very young, Monsieur Mordaunt, for this difficult task of ambassador, in which the oldest diplomatists sometimes fail."

"My lord, I am twenty-three years of age; but your Eminence is mistaken in saying that I am young. I am older than your Eminence, although I possess not your wisdom. Years of suffering, in my opinion, count double, and I have suffered for twenty years."

"Ah, yes, I understand," said Mazarin; "want of fortune, perhaps. You are poor—are you not?" Then he added to himself—"These English revolutionists are all beggars and ill-bred."

"My lord, I ought to have a fortune of five hundred a year, but it has been stolen from me."

"You are not then a man of the people?" said Mazarin, astonished.

"If I bore my title I should be a lord. If I bore my name, you would have heard one of the most illustrious names of England."

"What is your name, then?" asked Mazarin.

"My name is Mordaunt," replied the young man, bowing.

Mazarin now understood that Cromwell's envoy desired to retain his incognito. He was silent for a moment, and during that time he scanned the young man even more attentively than he had at first. The messenger was unmoved.

"Devil take these Puritans," said Mazarin aside; "they are made of marble." Then he added aloud, "But you have relations left to you?"

"I have one remaining, and three times I have presented myself to him to ask his support, and three times he has desired his servants to turn me away."

"Oh, *mon Dieu!* my dear Monsieur Mordaunt," said Mazarin, hoping, by a display of affected pity, to catch the young man in a snare, "how extremely your history interests me! You know not, then, anything of your birth, you have never seen your mother?"

"Yes, my lord; she came three times, while I was a child, to my nurse's house; I remember the last time she came as well as if it were to-day."

"You have a good memory," said Mazarin.

"Oh, yes, my lord!" said the young man, with such peculiar emphasis that the Cardinal felt a shudder run through all his veins.

"And who brought you up?" he asked again.

"A French nurse, who sent me away when I was five years old, because no one paid for me, telling me the name of a relation, whom she had heard my mother often mention."

"What then befell you?"

"As I was weeping and begging on the high-road, a minister from Kingston took me in, instructed me in the Calvinistic faith, taught me all he knew himself, and aided me in my researches after my family."

"And these researches?"

"Were fruitless; chance accomplished everything."

"You discovered what had become of your mother?"

"I learnt that she had been assassinated by my relation, aided by four friends, but I already knew that I had been robbed of my wealth, and degraded from my nobility, by King Charles I."

"Oh! I now understand why you are in the service of Cromwell; you detest the king."

"Yes, my lord, I hate him!" said the young man.

Mazarin marked, with surprise, the diabolical expression with which the young man uttered these words; as, in general, ordinary countenances are coloured by the blood—his face seemed dyed by hatred, and became livid.

"Your history is a terrible one, Monsieur Mordaunt, and touches me keenly; but, happily for you, you serve an all-powerful master, he ought to aid you in your search; we have so many means of gaining information."

"My lord, to a dog of good breed it is only necessary to show but one end of a track, that he may be certain to reach the other end."

"But this relation whom you mention, do you wish me to speak to him?" said the Cardinal, who was anxious to make a friend about Cromwell's person.

"Thanks, my lord, I will speak to him myself; he will treat me better the next time I see him."

"You have the means, then, of touching him?"

"I have the means of making myself feared."

Mazarin looked at the young man, but at the fire which shot from his glance, he bent down his head; then, embarrassed how to continue such a conversation, he opened Cromwell's letter. It was lengthy, and began by alluding to the situation of England, and announcing that he was on the eve of a decisive engagement with King Charles, and certain of success. He then adverted to the hospitality and protection afforded by France to Henrietta Maria, and continued:

"As regards King Charles, the question must be viewed differently; in receiving and aiding him France will censure the acts of the English nation, and thus so essentially do harm to England, and especially to the progress of the Government which she reckons upon forming, so that such a proceeding will be equal to flagrant hostilities."

At this moment Mazarin became very uneasy at the turn which the letter was taking, and paused to glance under his eyes at the young man. The latter continued engaged in thought. Mazarin resumed his reading of the general's epistle, which ended by demanding perfect neutrality from France:

"A neutrality," it said, "which was solely to consist in excluding King Charles from the French territories, nor to aid a king so entirely a stranger, either by arms, money, or troops. Farewell, sir; should we not receive a reply in the space of fifteen days, I shall presume my letter will have miscarried.

"OLIVER CROMWELL."

"Monsieur Mordaunt," said the Cardinal, raising his voice, as if to arouse the thinker, "my reply to this letter will be most satisfactory to General Cromwell if I am convinced that all are ignorant of my having given one; go, therefore, and await it at Boulogne-sur-Mer, and promise me to set out to-morrow morning."

"I promise, my lord," replied Mordaunt: "but how many days will your Eminence oblige me to wait your reply?"

"If you do not receive it in ten days, you can leave."

Mordaunt bowed.

"It is not all, sir," continued Mazarin; "your private adventures have aroused my interest; besides, the letter from General Cromwell makes you an important person in my eyes as ambassador; come, tell me what can I do for you?"

Mordaunt reflected a moment, and, after some hesitation, was about to speak, when Bernouin entered hastily, and, bending down to the ear of the Cardinal, whispered to him:

"My lord, the Queen Henrietta Maria, accompanied by an English noble, is just entering the Palais Royal at this moment."

Mazarin bounded from his chair, which did not escape the attention of the young man, and repressed the confidence he was about to make.

"Sir," said the Cardinal, "you have heard me? I fix on Boulogne because I presume that every town in France is indifferent to you; if you prefer another, name it; but you can easily conceive that, surrounded as I am by influence from which I can escape alone by means of discretion, I desire your presence in Paris to be ignored."

"I shall go, sir," said Mordaunt, advancing a few steps to the door by which he had entered.

"No, not that way, I beg," quickly exclaimed the Cardinal; "be so good as to pass by that gallery, by which you can gain the hall; I do not wish you to be seen leaving—our interview must at present remain a secret."

Mordaunt followed Bernouin, who conducted him through a neighbouring chamber, and left him after showing him the way out.

He then returned in haste to his master, to introduce Queen Henrietta, who was already crossing the glazed gallery.

38

HENRIETTA AND MAZARIN

THE Cardinal rose, and advanced in haste to receive the Queen of England. He showed the more respect to this queen, deprived of all pomp, and without followers, as he felt some self-reproach for his own want of heart and his avarice. But suppliants for favour know how to vary the expression of their features, and the daughter of Henry IV. smiled as she advanced to meet one whom she hated and despised.

"Ah!" said Mazarin to himself, "what a noble face! does she come to borrow money of me?"

And he threw an uneasy glance at his strong box; he even turned inside the bevel of the magnificent diamond ring, the brilliancy of which drew every eye upon his hand, which indeed was handsome and white.

"Your Eminence," began the august visitor, "it was my first intention to speak of the affairs which have brought me here, to the queen, my sister, but I have reflected that political matters are more especially the concerns of men."

"Madame," said Mazarin, "be assured that your majesty overwhelms me with this flattering distinction."

"He is very gracious," thought the queen; "has he guessed my errand, then?"

"Give," resumed the Cardinal, "your commands to the most obedient of your servants."

"Alas, sir," replied the queen, "I have lost the habit of giving commands, and have adopted instead that of making petitions; I am come to petition you, too happy should my prayer be heard favourably."

"I listen, madam, with interest," said Mazarin.

"Your Eminence, it concerns the war which the king, my husband, now sustains against his rebellious subjects. You are, perhaps, ignorant that they are fighting in England," added she, with a melancholy smile, "and that, in a short time, they will fight in a much more decided fashion than they have done hitherto."

"I am completely ignorant of it, madame," said the Cardinal, accompanying his words with a slight shrug of the shoulders; "alas, our own wars have quite absorbed the time and the mind of a poor, incapable, and infirm minister like myself."

"Well, then, your Eminence," said the queen, "I must inform you that Charles I., my husband, is on the eve of a decisive engagement. In case of a check (Mazarin made a slight movement), one must foresee everything; in case of a check, he desires to retire into France, and to live here as a private individual. What do you say to such a project?"

The Cardinal had listened without permitting a single fibre of his face to betray what he felt, and his smile remained as it ever was—false and flattering, and, when the queen finished speaking, he said:

"Do you think, madame, that France, agitated and disturbed as it is, would be a safe refuge for a dethroned king? How will the crown, which is so recently placed on the head of Louis XIV., support a double weight?"

"This weight was not so heavy when I was in peril," interposed the queen, with a sad smile, "and I ask no more for my husband than what was done for me; you see that we are very humble monarchs, sir."

"Oh, you, madame, you," the Cardinal hastened to say, in order to cut short the explanations which he foresaw were coming, "with regard to you, that is another thing; a daughter of Henry IV., of that great, that sublime sovereign——"

"All which does not prevent you refusing hospitality to his son-in-law, sir! Nevertheless, you ought to remember that that great, that sublime monarch, when proscribed at one time, as my husband may be, demanded aid from England, and that England accorded it to him; and it is but just to say that Queen Elizabeth was not his niece."

"*Peccato!*" said Mazarin, writhing beneath this simple eloquence, "your majesty does not understand me; you judge my intentions wrongly, and that is because doubtless I explain myself ill in French."

"Speak Italian, sir; ere the Cardinal, your predecessor, sent our mother, Marie de Medicis, to die in exile, she taught us that language. If anything yet remains of that great, that sublime king, Henry, of whom you have just spoken, he would be much surprised at so little pity for his family being united to such a profound veneration of himself."

The perspiration hung in large drops upon Mazarin's brow.

"That admiration is, on the contrary, so great, so real, madame," returned Mazarin, without noticing the change of language offered to him by the queen, "that if the king, Charles I., whom Heaven protect from evil! came into France, I would offer him my house—my own house—but, alas! it would be but an insecure retreat. Some day the people will burn that house, as they burnt that of the Maréchal d'Ancre. Poor Concino Concini! and yet he but desired the good of the people."

"Yes, my lord, even as yourself!" said the queen, ironically.

Mazarin pretended not to understand the double meaning of his own sentence, but continued to compassionate the fate of Concino.

"Well, then, your Eminence," said the queen, becoming impatient, "what is your answer?"

"Madame," cried Mazarin, more and more moved, "will your majesty permit me to give you counsel?"

"Speak, sir," replied the queen; "the counsels of so prudent a minister as yourself ought certainly to be beneficial."

"Madame, believe me, the king ought to defend himself to the last."

"He has done so, sir, and this last battle, which he encounters with resources much inferior to those of the enemy, proves that he will not yield without a struggle; but, in case he is beaten?"

"Well, madame, in that case my advice—I know that I am very bold to offer advice to your majesty—my advice is that the king should not leave his kingdom. Absent kings are very soon forgotten; if he comes to France his cause is lost."

"But, then," persisted the queen, "if such be your advice, and you have his interest at heart, send him some help of men and money, for I can do nothing for him: I have sold even to my last diamond to aid him. If I had had a single ornament left, I should have purchased wood this winter to make a fire for my daughter and myself."

"Oh, madame," said Mazarin, "your majesty knows not what you ask. On the day when foreign succour follows in the train of a king to replace him on his throne, it is an avowal that he no longer possesses the help and the love of his subjects."

"To the point, sir," said the queen, "to the point, and answer me, yes or no; if the king insists upon remaining in England, will you send him succour? If he comes to France, will you accord him hospitality? What do you intend to do?—answer."

"I will go this instant and consult the queen, and we will refer the matter at once to the parliament."

"With which you are at war, is it not so? You will charge Broussel to report it. Enough, sir, enough. I understand you, or rather, I am wrong. Go to the parliament; for it was from this parliament, the enemy of monarchs, that the daughter of the great, the sublime Henry IV., whom you so much respect, received the only relief this winter, which prevented her from dying of hunger and cold!"

And with these words Henrietta rose in majestic indignation, whilst the Cardinal, raising his hands clasped towards her, exclaimed, "Ah, your majesty, how little you know me, *mon Dieu!*"

"It signifies little," said Mazarin, when he was alone; "it gave me pain, and it is an ungracious part to play. But I have said nothing either to the one or to the other. Bernouin!"

Bernouin entered.

"Ascertain if the young man with the black doublet and the short hair, who was with me just now, is still in the palace."

Bernouin went out, and soon returned with Comminges, who was on guard.

"Your Eminence," said Comminges, "as I was reconducting the young man for whom you have asked, he approached the glass door of the gallery, and gazed intently upon some object, doubtless the picture by Raphael, which is opposite the door. He thought for a second, and then went down the stairs. I believe I saw him mount on a grey horse and leave the palace court. But is not your Eminence going to the queen?"

"For what purpose?"

"Monsieur de Guitant, my uncle, has just told me that her majesty has received news of the army."

"It is well—I will go."

Comminges had seen rightly, and Mordaunt had really acted as he had related. In crossing the gallery parallel to the large glass gallery, he perceived de Winter, who was waiting until the queen had finished her negotiation.

At this sight the young man stopped short, not in admiration of Raphael's picture, but as if fascinated by the sight of some terrible object. His eyes dilated, and a shudder ran through his body. One would have said that he longed to break through the glass which divided him from his enemy; for if Comminges had seen with what an expression of hatred the eyes of this young man were fixed upon de Winter, he would not have doubted for an instant but that the English lord was his mortal foe.

But he stopped—doubtless to reflect; and, instead of allowing his first impulse to carry him away, which had been to go straight to Lord de Winter, he leisurely descended the staircase, left the palace with his head bent, mounted his horse, which he reined in at the corner of the Rue Richelieu, and with his eyes fixed on the gate, he waited until the queen's carriage had left the court.

He did not wait long, for the queen scarcely remained a quarter of an hour with Mazarin; but this quarter of an hour of expectation appeared a century to him. At last the heavy machine, which in those days was styled a chariot, came out, rumbling against the gates, and de Winter, still on horseback, bent again to the door to converse with her majesty.

The horses started into a trot, and took the road to the Louvre, which they entered. Before leaving the convent of the Carmelites, Henrietta had desired her daughter to attend her at the palace, which she had inhabited for a long time, and which she had only left because their poverty seemed to them more difficult to bear in gilded chambers.

Mordaunt followed the carriage, and when he had watched it drive under the sombre arches, he went and placed himself under a wall over which the shadow was extended, and remained motionless, amidst the mouldings of Jean Goujon, like a bas-relief representing an equestrian statue.

39

HOW THE WRETCHED SOMETIMES TAKE CHANCE FOR PROVIDENCE

"'Well, madame," said de Winter, when the queen had dismissed her attendants.

"Well, my lord, what I had foreseen has come to pass."

"What? does the Cardinal decline to receive the king? France refuse hospitality to an unfortunate prince? But it is for the first time, madame!"

"I did not mean France, my lord, I meant Mazarin, and he is not even a Frenchman."

"But did you see the queen?"

"It is useless," replied Henrietta; "the queen will not say 'yes' when the Cardinal has said 'no.' Are you not aware that this Italian directs everything, both indoors and out? And, moreover, I should not be astonished had we been forestalled by Cromwell; he was embarrassed whilst speaking to me, and yet quite firm in his determination to refuse. Then, did you not observe the agitation in the Palais Royal, the passing to and fro of busy people? Can they have received any news, my lord?"

"Not from England, madame. I made such haste that I am certain of not having been forestalled. I set out three days ago, passing miraculously through the Puritan army, and I took post-horses with my servant Tony: the horses on which we rode were bought in Paris. Besides, the king, I am sure, awaits your majesty's reply before risking anything."

"You will tell him, my lord," resumed the queen despairingly, "that I can do nothing: that I have suffered as much as himself—more than he has—obliged as I am to eat the bread of exile, and to ask hospitality from false friends who smile at my tears; and as regards his royal person, he must sacrifice it generously, and die like a king. I shall go and die by his side."

"Madame, madame!" exclaimed de Winter, "your majesty abandons yourself to despair: and yet, perhaps, there still remains some hope."

"No friends left, my lord; no other friend left in the whole world but yourself! O God!" exclaimed the queen, raising her eyes to heaven, "have you indeed taken back all the generous hearts which existed in the world?"

"I hope not, madame," replied de Winter thoughtfully; "I once spoke to you of four men."

"What can be done with four men?"

"Four devoted, resolute men can do much, be assured, madame; and those of whom I speak have done much at one time."

"And these men were your friends?"

"One of them held my life in his hands, and gave it to me. I know not whether he is still my friend; but since that time I have remained his."

"And these men are in France, my lord?"

"I believe so."

"Tell me their names; perhaps I have heard them mentioned, and might be able to aid you in your search for them."

"One of them was called the Chevalier d'Artagnan."

"Oh! my lord, if I do not mistake, the Chevalier d'Artagnan is a lieutenant of the guards; but take care, for I fear that this man is devoted entirely to his Eminence."

"That would be a misfortune," said de Winter, "and I shall begin to think that we are really doomed."

"But the others," said the queen, who clung to this last hope as a shipwrecked man clings to the remains of his vessel: "the others, my lord!"

"The second—I heard his name by accident; for before fighting us, these four gentlemen told us their names; the second was called the Count de la Fère. As for the two others, I had so much the habit of calling them by nicknames, that I have forgotten their real ones."

"Oh, my God, it is a matter of great urgency to find them out," said the queen, "since you think these worthy gentlemen might be of service to the king."

"Oh, yes," said de Winter, "for they are the same men."

"Well then, my lord, they must be found; but what can four men, or rather three men do?—for I assure you, you must not count on Monsieur d'Artagnan."

"It will be one valiant sword the less, but there will remain still three, without reckoning my own. Now, four devoted men round the king to protect him from his enemies, to be at his side in battle, to aid him in counsel, to escort him in flight, are sufficient, not to make the king a conqueror, but to save him if conquered; and whatever Mazarin may say—once on the shores of France, your royal husband may find as many retreats and asylums as the sea-birds find in storms."

"Seek them, my lord, seek these gentlemen; and if they will consent to go with you to England, I will give to each a duchy the day that we reascend the throne, besides as much gold as would pave Whitehall. Find them, my lord. Find them, I entreat you."

"I will search for them well, madame," said de Winter, "and doubtless I shall find them—but time fails me. Has your majesty forgotten that the king expects your reply, and awaits it in agony?"

"Then, indeed, we are lost," cried the queen, in the fullness of a broken heart.

At this moment the door opened, and the young Henrietta appeared. Then the queen, with that wonderful strength which is heroism in a mother, repressed her tears, and motioned to de Winter to change the subject of conversation.

"What do you want, Henrietta?"

"My mother," replied the young princess, "a cavalier has just entered the Louvre, and wishes to present his respects to your majesty; he arrives from the army, and has, he says, a letter to remit to you on behalf of the Maréchal de Grammont, I think."

"Ah!" said the queen to de Winter, "he is one of my most faithful friends; but do you not observe, my dear lord, that we are so poorly served that it is my daughter who fills the office of introducer?"

"Madame, have pity on me," exclaimed de Winter; "you break my heart!"

"And who is this cavalier, Henrietta?" asked the queen.

"I saw him from the window, madame; he is a young man who appears scarcely sixteen years of age, and who is called the Vicomte de Bragelonne."

The queen smiled, and made a sign with her hand; the young princess opened the door, and Raoul appeared on the threshold.

Advancing a few steps towards the queen, he knelt down.

"Madame," said he, "I bear to your majesty a letter from my friend the Count de Guiche, who informed me he had the honour of being your servant; this letter contains important news, and the expression of his respect."

At the name of the Count de Guiche, a blush spread over the cheeks of the young princess, and the queen glanced at her with some degree of severity.

"You told me that the letter was from the Maréchal de Grammont, Henrietta!" said the queen.

"I thought so, madame," stammered the young girl.

"It is my fault, madame," said Raoul. "I did announce myself, in truth, as coming on the part of the Maréchal de Grammont; but being wounded in the right arm, he was unable to write, and therefore the Count de Guiche acted as his secretary."

"There has been fighting, then?" asked the queen, motioning to Raoul to rise.

"Yes, madame," answered the youth.

At this announcement of a battle having taken place, the young princess opened her mouth as if to ask a question; but her lips closed again without articulating a word, while the colour gradually faded from her cheeks.

The queen saw this, and doubtless her maternal heart translated this emotion, for addressing Raoul again:

"And no evil has happened to the young Count de Guiche?" she asked; "for not only is he our servant, as you say, sir, but more; he is one of our friends."

"No, madame," replied Raoul; "on the contrary, he gained great glory on that day, and had the honour of being embraced by his highness the prince on the field of battle."

The young princess clasped her hands; and then, as if ashamed of having been betrayed into such a demonstration of joy, she turned away, and bent over a vase of roses, as if to inhale their odour.

"Let us see," said the queen, "what the count says." And she opened the letter and read:

"MADAME,—Not being able to have the honour of writing to you myself, by reason of a wound which I have received in the right hand, I have commanded my son, the Count de Guiche, who, with his father, is equally your humble servant, to write to you that we have just gained the battle of Lens, and that this victory cannot fail to afford great power to the Cardinal Mazarin and to the queen over the affairs of Europe. If her majesty will have faith in my counsels, she will profit by this event to address at this moment, in favour of her august husband, the court of France. The Vicomte de Bragelonne, who will have the honour of remitting this letter to your majesty, is the friend of my son, to whom he owes his life; he is a gentleman in whom your majesty can confide entirely, in the case when your majesty may have some verbal or written order to forward to me.

"I have the honour to be, with respect, etc.,
"DE GRAMMONT."

At the moment when mention occurred of his having rendered a service to the count, Raoul could not help turning his eyes towards the young princess, and then he saw in her eyes an expression of infinite gratitude to the young man; he no longer doubted that the daughter of King Charles the First loved his friend.

"The battle of Lens gained!" said the queen; "they are lucky indeed for me—they can gain battles! Yes, the Maréchal de Grammont is right; this will alter the aspect of affairs; but I much fear it will do nothing for ours, even if it does not harm them. This is recent news, sir," continued she, "and I thank you for having made much haste to bring it to me; without this letter, I should not have heard it till to-morrow, perhaps after to-morrow, the last of all Paris."

"Madame," said Raoul, "the Louvre is but the second place which this news has reached: it is as yet unknown to all, and I had sworn to the Count de Guiche to remit this letter to your majesty ere even I should embrace my guardian."

"Your guardian! is he too a Bragelonne?" asked Lord de Winter. "I knew formerly a Bragelonne—is he still alive?"

"No, sir, he is dead; and I believe it is from him that my guardian, whose near relation he was, inherited the estate from which I take my name."

"And your guardian, sir," asked the queen, who could not help feeling interest for the handsome young man before her, "what is his name?"

"The Count de la Fère, madame," replied the young man, bowing.

De Winter made a gesture of surprise, and the queen turned to him with a start of joy.

"The Count de la Fère!" cried de Winter, in his turn. "Oh, sir, reply, I entreat you—is not the Count de la Fère a noble, whom I remember handsome and brave, a musketeer under Louis XIII., and who must be now about forty-seven or forty-eight years of age?"

"Yes, sir, you are right in every respect."

"And who served under a 'nom-de-guerre'?"

"Under the name of Athos. Lately I heard his friend Monsieur d'Artagnan address him by that name."

"That is it, madame, that is the same. God be praised! And he is in Paris?" continued he, turning to Raoul; then speaking to the queen—"We must still hope. Providence has declared for us, since I have found this brave man again in so miraculous a manner. And, sir, where does he reside, pray?"

"The Count de la Fère lodges in the Rue Guénégaud, Hôtel du Grand Roi Charlemagne."

"Thanks, sir. Request this excellent friend to remain at home. I shall go and see him instantly."

"Sir, I obey with pleasure, if her majesty will permit me to retire."

"Go, Monsieur de Bragelonne," said the queen, "and be assured of our affection."

Raoul bent respectfully before the queen and the princess, and, saluting de Winter, departed.

The queen and de Winter continued to converse for some time in low voices, in order that the young princess should not overhear them; but the precaution was needless; she was in deep converse with her own thoughts.

Then, when de Winter rose to take leave,—

"Listen, my lord," said the queen; "I have preserved this diamond cross which came from my mother, and this order of St. Michael, which came from my husband. They are worth about fifty thousand pounds. I had sworn to die, rather than to part with these precious jewels; but now that these ornaments may be useful to him or to his defenders, everything must be sacrificed to the hope of it. Take them, and if you need money for your expedition, sell them fearlessly, my lord. But should you find the means of keeping them, remember, my lord, that I shall esteem you as having rendered the greatest service which a gentleman can render to a queen; and in the day of my prosperity, he who brings me this order and this cross will be blessed by me and my children."

"Madame," replied de Winter, "your majesty will be served by a man devoted to you. I hasten to deposit these two objects in a safe place, nor should I accept them if the resources of our ancient fortune were left to us; but our estates are confiscated, our ready money is exhausted, and we are reduced to turn into resources everything we possess. In an hour hence I shall be with the Count de la Fère, and to-morrow your majesty shall receive a definite answer."

The queen held out her hand to Lord de Winter, who kissed it respectfully, and turning to her daughter,—

"My lord," said she, "you are charged with something from this child for her father."

De Winter was astonished; he did not know what the queen meant. The young Henrietta came forward, smiling and blushing, and presented her forehead.

"Tell my father that, as a fugitive king, as a conqueror or as conquered," said the young princess, "he has in me the most affectionate and obedient of daughters."

"I know it, madame," replied de Winter, touching Henrietta's forehead with his lips.

He then departed, crossing without a conductor those vast, deserted, and dark chambers, wiping away the tears which, deadened as his heart was by fifty years of a courtier's life, he could not refrain from shedding, at the spectacle of royal misfortune, so dignified and so severe.

40

UNCLE AND NEPHEW

DE WINTER's horse and lackey were waiting for him at the gate. He directed his course towards his hotel absorbed in thought, looking back occasionally at the silent and dark façade of the Louvre. It was then that he saw a horseman, as it were, detach himself from the wall and follow him at a short distance. In leaving the Palais Royal he remembered to have observed a similar shadow.

"Tony," he said, motioning his groom to approach.

"Here I am, my lord."

"Did you remark that man who is following us?"

"Yes, my lord."

"Who is he?"

"I do not know, only he has followed your lordship from the Palais Royal, stopped at the Louvre to wait for you, and now leaves the Louvre with you."

"Some spy of the Cardinal," said de Winter to him. "Let us affect not to notice that he is watching us."

And spurring on, he pursued the labyrinth of streets which led to his hotel, situated near the Marais, for, having for so long a time lived near the Place Royale, Lord de Winter naturally returned to lodge near his old dwelling-place.

The unknown put his horse into a gallop.

De Winter dismounted at his hotel, went up into his apartment, intending to watch the spy; but as he was about to place his gloves and hat on the table, he saw reflected in a glass opposite to him a figure which stood on the threshold of the room. He turned round, and Mordaunt stood before him.

There was a moment of frozen silence between these two men.

"Sir," said de Winter, "I thought I had already made you aware that I am tired of this persecution; withdraw, then, or I shall call, and have you turned out, as you were in London. I am not your uncle; I know you not."

"My uncle," replied Mordaunt, in a harsh and bantering tone, "you are mistaken; you will not have me turned out this time, as you did in London; you dare not. As for denying that I am your nephew, you will think twice about it, now that I have learnt some things of which until a few days ago I was ignorant."

"And how doth it concern me what you have learnt?" said de Winter.

"Oh, it concerneth you much, my uncle, I am sure; and you will soon be of my opinion," added he, with a smile which sent a shudder through the veins of him whom he addressed. "When I presented myself before you for the first time in London, it was to ask you what had become of my wealth; the second time it was to demand who had sullied my name; and this time I come before you to ask a question far more terrible than any other: to ask you, my lord, what have you done with your sister—your sister, who was my mother?"

De Winter shrank back from the fire of those scorching eyes.

"Your mother?" he said.

"Yes, my lord, my mother," replied the young man, advancing into the room until he was face to face with Lord de Winter, and crossing his arms. "I have asked the headsman of Béthune," he said, his voice hoarse and his face livid with passion and grief; "and the headsman of Béthune gave me a reply."

De Winter fell back into a chair as if struck by a thunderbolt, and vainly sought an answer.

"Yes," continued the young man, "all is now explained; with this key the abyss is opened. My mother had inherited an estate from her husband, and you have assassinated my mother; my name would have secured to me the paternal estate, and you have despoiled me of my name, you have deprived me of my fortune. I am no longer astonished that you knew me not. I am not surprised that you refused to recognise me. When a man is a robber, it is unbecoming to call him a nephew whom one has impoverished; when one is a murderer, to term that man whom one has made an orphan a relative."

These words produced a contrary effect to what Mordaunt had anticipated. De Winter remembered the monster that milady had been: he rose, dignified and calm, restraining by the severity of his look the wild glances of the young man.

"You desire to fathom this terrible secret?" said de Winter; "well, then, so be it. Know, then, what that woman was for whom to-day you come to call me to account. That woman had, in all probability, poisoned my brother, and that she might inherit from me she was about to assassinate me in my turn. I have proof of it. What say you to that?"

"I say that she was my mother."

"She caused the unfortunate Duke of Buckingham to be

stabbed by a man who was, ere that, honest, good, and true. What say you to that crime, of which I have the proof?"

"She was my mother!"

"On our return to France she had a young woman, who was attached to one of her foes, poisoned in the convent of the Augustines at Béthune. Will this crime persuade you of the justice of her punishment? Of this I have the proofs."

"Silence, sir—she was my mother," exclaimed the young man, his face running with sweat, his hair standing upon his forehead, and raging with fury; "she was my mother! Her crimes, I know them not—her disorders, I know them not—her vices, I know them not; but this I know, that I had a mother, that five men leagued against one woman, murdered her clandestinely by night—silently—like cowards. I know that you were one of them, my uncle, and that you cried louder than the others, 'She must die.' Therefore I warn you—and listen well to my words, that they may be engraved on your memory, never to be forgotten—this murder, which has deprived me of everything—this murder, which has divested me of my name—this murder, which has impoverished me—this murder, which has made me corrupt, wicked, implacable—I shall summon you to account for it first, and then those who were your accomplices—when I discover them!"

With hatred in his eyes, foaming at his mouth, and his hand extended, Mordaunt had advanced one more step—a threatening, terrible step—towards de Winter. The latter put his hand to his sword, and said, with the smile of a man who for thirty years has jested with death:

"Would you assassinate me, sir? Then I shall recognise you as my nephew, for you are a worthy son of such a mother."

"No," replied Mordaunt, forcing all the veins in his face and the muscles of his body to resume their usual places and to be calm; "no, I shall not kill you—at least, not at this moment, for without you I could not discover the others. But when I have found them, then tremble, sir. I have stabbed the headsman of Béthune—stabbed him without pity or remorse, and he was the least guilty of you all."

With these words the young man went out, and descended the stair sufficiently calm to pass unobserved; then upon the lowest landing-place he passed Tony leaning over the balustrade, waiting only for a call from his master to rush to his room.

But de Winter did not call; crushed, enfeebled, he remained standing, and with listening ear; then only, when he had heard the step of the horse going away, he fell back on a chair saying:

"My God, I thank Thee that he knows me alone."

41

PATERNAL AFFECTION

WHILE this dreadful scene was passing at Lord de Winter's, Athos, seated near the window, his elbow on the table, and his head supported on his hand, was listening intently to Raoul's account of the adventures he met with on his journey, and the details of the battle.

Listening to the relation of those first emotions, so fresh and pure, the fine, noble face of Athos betrayed indescribable pleasure; he inhaled the tones of that young voice as harmonious music. He forgot all that was dark in the past, and what was cloudy in the future. It almost seemed as if the return of this much-loved boy had changed his fears into hopes. Athos was happy—happier than he had ever been before.

"And you assisted and took part in this great battle, Bragelonne?" he said.

"Yes, sir."

"And it was a difficult one?"

"His highness the prince charged eleven times in person."

"He is a great commander, Bragelonne."

"He is a hero, sir; I did not lose sight of him for an instant. Oh! how fine it is to be called Condé, and to be so worthy of such a name!"

"He is calm and radiant, is he not?"

"As calm as at parade; as radiant as at a fête. When we went up to the enemy, it was slowly; we were forbidden to draw first, and we were marching towards the Spaniards, who were on a height with lowered muskets. When we arrived about thirty paces from them, the prince turned round to the soldiers, 'Comrades,' he said, 'you are about to suffer a furious discharge; but——' There was such a dead silence that friends and enemies could have heard these words; then raising his sword, 'Sound trumpets!' he cried."

"Well, very good: you will do as much when the opportunity occurs—will you, Raoul?"

"I know not, sir, but it was very fine and grand!"

"Were you afraid, Raoul?" asked the count.

"Well, sir," replied the young man naïvely; "I felt a great chill at my heart, and at the word 'fire,' which resounded in Spanish from the enemy's flanks, I closed my eyes and thought of you."

"In honest truth, Raoul?" said Athos, pressing his hand.

"Yes, sir; and then there was such a firing that one might have supposed that the infernal regions were opened, and those who were not killed felt the heat of the flames. I opened my eyes, astonished at being alive, or at least unhurt; a third of the squadron were lying on the ground, mutilated and bloody. At this moment I caught the eye of the prince, and I had but one thought, and that was that he was observing me. I spurred on, and found myself in the enemy's ranks."

"And the prince was pleased with you?"

"He told me so, at least, sir, when he desired me to return to Paris with Monsieur de Châtillon, who was charged to carry the news to the queen, and to bring the colours we had taken. 'Go,' said he, 'the enemy will not rally for fifteen days, and until that time I have no need of your service. Go and see those whom you love, and who love you, and tell my sister de Longueville that I thank her for the present she made me of you.' And I came, sir," added Raoul, gazing at the count with a smile of true affection, "for I thought you would be glad to see me again."

Athos drew the young man towards him, and pressed his lips to his brow, as he would have done to a young daughter.

"And now, Raoul," said he, "you are launched; you have dukes for friends, a marshal of France for a godfather, a prince of the blood as commander, and on the day of your return you have been received by two queens; it is rather well for a novice."

"Oh, sir!" said Raoul suddenly, "you recall something to me, which, in my haste to relate my exploits, I had forgotten; it is that there was with her majesty the Queen of England, a gentleman who, when I made mention of your name, uttered a cry of surprise and joy; he said he was a friend of yours—asked your address, and is coming to see you."

"What is his name?"

"I did not dare ask, sir; he spoke elegantly, although I thought from his accent he was an Englishman."

"Ah!" said Athos, leaning down his head, as if to remember who it could be. Then, when he raised it again, he was struck by the presence of a man who was standing at the open door, and was gazing at him with a compassionate air.

"Lord de Winter!" exclaimed the count.

"Athos, my friend!"

And the two gentlemen were for an instant locked in each other's arms; then Athos, looking into his friend's face, and taking him by both hands, said:

"What ails you, my lord? you appear as unhappy as I am happy."

"Yes, truly, dear friend; and I may even say that the sight of you increases my dismay."

And de Winter glancing round him, Raoul quickly understood that the two friends wished to be alone, and he therefore left the room.

"Come, now that we are alone," said Athos, "let us talk of yourself."

"Whilst we are alone let us speak of ourselves," replied de Winter. "He is here."

"Who?"

"Milady's son."

Athos, who was again struck by this name, which seemed to pursue him like an echo, hesitated for a moment, then slightly knitting his brows, he calmly said:

"I know it; Grimaud met him between Béthune and Arras, and then came here to warn me of his presence."

"Does Grimaud know him, then?"

"No; but he was present at the deathbed of a man who knew him."

"The headsman of Béthune?" exclaimed de Winter.

"You know about that?" said Athos, astonished.

"He has just left me," replied de Winter, "after telling me all. Ah! my friend! what a horrible scene! Why did we not destroy the child with the mother?"

"What need is there to fear?" said Athos, recovering, by the aid of reason, from the instinctive fear he had at first experienced; "are we not able to defend ourselves? Is this young man an assassin by profession—a murderer in cold blood? He has killed the executioner of Béthune in an impulse of passion, but now his fury is assuaged."

De Winter smiled mournfully, and shook his head.

"Do you not then know the race?"

"Pooh!" said Athos, trying to smile in his turn. "It must have lost its ferocity in the second generation. Besides, my friend, Providence has warned us that we may be on our guard. All we can do is to wait. Let us wait; and, as I said before, let us speak of yourself. What brings you to Paris?"

"Affairs of importance which you shall know later. But what is this that I hear from her majesty the Queen of England? Monsieur d'Artagnan is with Mazarin! Pardon my bluntness, dear friend. I neither hate nor blame his Eminence, and your opinions will be held ever sacred by me; do you happen to belong to this man?"

"Monsieur d'Artagnan," replied Athos, "is in the service; he is a soldier, and obeys the constituted authority. Monsieur d'Artagnan is not rich, and has need of his position as lieutenant to enable him to live. Millionaires like yourself, my lord, are rare in France."

"Alas!" said de Winter, "I am at this moment as poor as he is, if not poorer; but to return to our subject."

"Well, then, you wish to know if I am of Mazarin's party. No. Pardon my bluntness, also, my lord."

"I am obliged to you, count, for this pleasing intelligence! You make me young and happy again by it. Ah! so you are not a Mazarinist? Delightful! Indeed, you could not belong to him. But pardon me, are you free?"

"What mean you by free?"

"I mean to ask if you be not married?"

"Ah! as to that, no," replied Athos, laughing.

"Because that young man—so handsome, so elegant, so polished——"

"He is a lad that I have adopted, and who does not even know the name of his father."

"Very well—you are always the same, Athos, great and generous. Are you still friends with Monsieur Porthos and Monsieur Aramis?"

"And add Monsieur d'Artagnan, too, my lord. We still remain four friends devoted to each other; but when it becomes a question of serving the Cardinal, or of fighting, of being Mazarinists or Frondists, then we are only two."

"Is Monsieur Aramis with d'Artagnan?" inquired Lord de Winter.

"No," answered Athos: "Monsieur Aramis does me the honour to share my opinions."

"Could you put me in communication with your witty and agreeable friend? Has he altered?"

"He has become an abbé, that is all."

"You alarm me; his profession must have made him renounce any great undertakings."

"On the contrary," said Athos, smiling, "he has never been so much a musketeer as since he became an abbé, and you will find him a veritable soldier."

"Could you engage to bring him to me to-morrow morning at ten o'clock, on the Pont du Louvre?"

"Oh, oh!" exclaimed Athos, smiling, "you have a duel in prospect."

"Yes, Count, and a splendid duel, too; a duel in which I hope you will take a part."

"Where are we to go to, my lord?"

"To Her Majesty the Queen of England, who has desired me to present you to her."

"This is an enigma," said Athos; "but it matters not; from the moment that you have guessed the word, I ask no further. Will your lordship do me the honour to sup with me?"

"Thanks, count, no," replied de Winter. "I own to you that that young man's visit has taken away my appetite, and will probably deprive me of sleep. What purpose can have brought him to Paris? It was not to meet me that he came, for he was ignorant of my journey. This young man terrifies me, for there lies in him a sanguinary predisposition."

"What occupies him in England?"

"He is one of Cromwell's most enthusiastic followers."

"But what has attached him to this cause? His father and mother were Catholics, I believe?"

"His hatred of the king, who deprived him of his estates, and forbade him to bear the name of de Winter."

"Well; what is he called now?"

"Mordaunt."

"A puritan, yet, disguised as a monk, he travels alone in France."

"Do you say as a monk?"

"It was thus, and by mere accident—may God pardon me if I blaspheme!—that he heard the confession of the executioner of Béthune."

"Then I see it all; he has been sent by Cromwell to Mazarin, and the queen guessed rightly; we have been forestalled. Everything is clear to me now. Adieu, count, till to-morrow."

"But the night is dark," said Athos, observing that Lord de Winter seemed more uneasy than he wished to show; "and you have no attendant."

"I have Tony, a good but simple young man."

"Halloa there, Grimaud, Olivain, and Blaisois, call the viscount here, and take your musket with you."

Blaisois was the tall youth, whom we saw at the Château de Bragelonne, whom Athos had christened by the name of his province.

"Viscount," said Athos to Raoul as he entered, "you will conduct my lord as far as his hotel, and permit no one to approach him."

"Oh! count," said de Winter, "for whom do you take me?"

"For a stranger who does not know Paris," said Athos, "and to whom the viscount will show the way."

De Winter shook him by the hand.

"Grimaud," said Athos, "put yourself at the head of the troop, and beware of the monk."

Grimaud shuddered, and nodding, awaited the departure, regarding the butt of his musket with silent eloquence. Then, obeying the orders given him by Athos, he headed the little procession, bearing the torch in one hand and the musket in the other, until it reached the door of de Winter's inn, when, striking on the door with his fist, he bowed to the Englishman without saying a word.

The same order was pursued in returning; nor did Grimaud's searching glance discover anything of a suspicious appearance, save a dark shadow in hiding at the corner of the Rue Guénégaud du Quai. He thought also that in going he had already observed the street watcher who had attracted his attention. He pushed on towards him, but before he could reach it the shadow had disappeared into an alley, in which Grimaud deemed it scarcely prudent to pursue it.

The next day, on awakening, the count perceived Raoul by his bedside. The young man was already dressed, and was reading a new book by M. Chapelain.

"Already up, Raoul?" said the count.

"Yes, sir," replied Raoul, with a slight hesitation. "I did not sleep well."

"You, Raoul, not sleep well! then you must have something on your mind!" said Athos.

"Sir, you will, perhaps, think that I am in great haste to leave you, when I have only just arrived, but——"

"Have you only two days of leave, Raoul?"

"On the contrary, sir, I have ten; nor is it to the camp that I wish to go."

"Where then?" said Athos, smiling, "if it be not a secret. You are now almost a man, since you have made your first passage of arms, and have acquired the right to go where you will without telling me."

"Never, sir," said Raoul, "as long as I possess the happiness of having you for a protector, shall I deem I have the right of freeing myself from a guardianship which is so valuable to me. I have, therefore, the wish to go and pass a day only at Blois. You look at me, and are going to laugh at me."

"No; on the contrary, I am not inclined to laugh," said Athos, suppressing a sigh. "You wish to see Blois again; it is but very natural."

"Then you permit me to go, and you are not angry in your heart!" exclaimed Raoul.

"Certainly; and why should I regret what will give you pleasure?"

"Oh! how good you are," exclaimed the young man, pressing his guardian's hand; "and I can start now?"

"When you like, Raoul."

"Sir," said Raoul, as he turned to leave the room, "I have thought of one thing, and that is about the Duchess of Chevreuse, who was so kind to me, and to whom I owe my introduction to the prince."

"And you ought to thank her, Raoul. Well, go to the Hôtel du Luynes, Raoul, and ask if the duchess can receive you. I am glad to see that you pay attention to the customs of the world. You must take Grimaud and Olivain."

"Both, sir?" asked Raoul, astonished.

"Both."

Raoul went out, and when Athos heard his young, joyous voice calling to Grimaud and Olivain he sighed.

"It is very soon to leave me," he thought, "but he follows the ordinary path. Nature has made us thus: she looks on before her. He certainly likes that child, but will he love me less because he loves others?"

And Athos confessed to himself that he was unprepared for so prompt a departure; but Raoul was so happy that this consideration effaced all other things from the mind of his guardian.

Everything was ready at ten o'clock for their journey, and as Athos saw Raoul mount, a groom rode up from the Duchess de Chevreuse, He was charged to tell the Count de la Fère that she had learnt the return of her youthful protégé, and also the manner he had conducted himself on the field, and she added that she should be very glad to offer him her congratulations.

"Tell her grace," replied Athos, "that the viscount has just mounted his horse to proceed to the Hôtel du Luynes."

Then, with renewed instructions to Grimaud, Athos signified to Raoul that he could depart, and ended by reflecting that it was, perhaps, better that Raoul should be away from Paris at that moment.

42

ANOTHER QUEEN SEEKS HELP

ATHOS had sent to Aramis early in the morning, and had given his letter to Blaisois, the only serving-man whom he had left. Blaisois found Bazin donning his beadle's gown, his services being required that day at Notre Dame.

Athos had desired Blaisois to try to speak to Aramis himself. Blaisois, a tall, simple youth, who understood nothing but what he was told, asked, therefore, for the Abbé d'Herblay, and in spite of Bazin's assurances that his master was not at home, he persisted in such a manner as to put Bazin into a passion. Blaisois seeing Bazin in clerical guise, was little discomposed at his denials, and wanted to pass at all risks, believing, too, that he with whom he had to do was endowed with the virtues of his cloth—namely, patience and Christian charity.

But Bazin was still the servant of a musketeer. In a moment the blood mounted to his fat cheeks, and he seized a broomstick and began thumping Blaisois, saying:

"You insulted the Church; my friend, you have insulted the Church!"

At this moment Aramis, aroused by this unusual disturbance, cautiously opened the door of his room; and Blaisois, looking reproachfully at the Cerberus, drew the letter from his pocket, and presented it to Aramis.

"From the Count de la Fère," said Aramis. "All right." And he retired into his room without even asking the cause of so much noise.

Blaisois returned disconsolate to the hotel of the Grand Roi Charlemagne, and when Athos inquired if his commission was executed, he related his adventure.

"You foolish fellow!" said Athos, laughing. "And you did not tell him that you came from me?"

"No, sir."

At ten o'clock, Athos, with his habitual exactitude, was waiting on the Pont du Louvre, and was almost immediately joined by Lord de Winter.

They waited some little time, and then his lordship began to fear that Aramis was not coming to join them.

"Patience," said Athos, whose eyes were fixed in the direction of the Rue du Bac, "patience; I see an abbé giving a cuff to a man, and a bow to a woman; that must be Aramis."

It was he, in truth; having run against a young shopkeeper who was gaping at the birds, and who had splashed him, Aramis with one blow of his fist had distanced him ten paces.

At this moment one of his penitents passed, and, as she was young and pretty, Aramis took off his cap to her, with his most gracious smile.

A most affectionate greeting took place between him and Lord de Winter.

"Where are we going?" inquired Aramis; "are we going to fight there, faith? I carry no sword this morning, and cannot return home to procure one."

"No," said Lord de Winter, "we are going to pay a visit to her majesty the Queen of England."

"Oh, very well," replied Aramis; then, bending his face down to Athos's ear, "what is the object of this visit?"

"I'faith, I know not; some evidence required from us, perhaps."

"May it not be about that cursed affair?" asked Aramis, "in which case I do not greatly care to go, for it will be to pocket some reproofs; and since I am used to give it to so many, I do not like to receive it myself."

"If it were so," answered Athos, "we should not be taken there by Lord de Winter, for he would come in for his share; he was one of us."

"True; yes, let us go."

On arriving at the Louvre, Lord de Winter entered first; indeed, there was but one porter to receive them at the gate.

It was impossible, in daylight, for the impoverished state of the habitation, which avaricious charity had conceded to an unfortunate queen, to pass unnoticed by Athos, Aramis, and even the Englishman. Large rooms, completely naked of furniture, bare walls, upon which, here and there, shone the old gold mouldings which had resisted time and neglect, windows with broken panes (which it was impossible to fasten), no carpets, nor guards, nor servants; this is what at first met the eyes of Athos, to which he, touching his companion's elbow, directed his attention by his glances.

"Mazarin is better housed," said Aramis.

"Mazarin is almost king," answered Athos; "and Madame Henrietta is almost no longer queen."

"If you would condescend to be clever, Athos," observed Aramis, "I really do think you would be more so than poor Monsieur de Voiture."

Athos smiled.

The queen appeared to be impatiently awaiting them, for at the first slight noise which she heard in the hall leading to her room, she came herself to the door to receive the courtiers of the days of misfortune.

"Enter and be welcome, gentlemen," she said.

The gentlemen went in and remained standing, but at a sign from the queen they seated themselves. Athos was calm and grave, but Aramis was furious; the sight of such royal misery exasperated him, and his eyes examined every new trace of poverty which presented itself.

"You are examining the luxury I enjoy?" said the queen, glancing sadly around her.

"Madame," replied Aramis, "I must ask your pardon, but I know not how to hide my indignation at seeing how a daughter of Henry IV. is treated at the court of France."

"Monsieur Aramis is not an officer?" asked the queen of Lord de Winter.

"That gentleman is the Abbé d'Herblay," replied he.

Aramis coloured. "Madame," he said, "I am an abbé, it is true, but I am so against my will; I never had a vocation for the bands; my cassock is fastened by one button only, and I am ready to become a musketeer again at any moment. This morning, being ignorant that I should have the honour of seeing your majesty, I encumbered myself with this dress, but you will find me no less a man devoted to your majesty's service, in whatever you see fit to command me."

"The Abbé d'Herblay," resumed de Winter, "is one of those gallant musketeers belonging to his majesty King Louis XIII., of whom I have spoken to you, madame." Then, turning towards Athos, he continued: "And this gentleman is that noble Count de la Fère, whose high reputation is so well known to your majesty."

"Gentlemen," said the queen, "a few years ago I had around me gentlemen, treasures, and armies; and by the lifting of a finger all these were occupied in my service. To-day, look around you, and it may astound you, that in order to accomplish a plan which is dearer to me than life, I have only Lord de Winter, the friend of twenty years, and you, gentlemen, whom I see for the first time, and whom I know but as my countrymen."

"It is enough," said Athos, bowing low, "if the life of three men can purchase yours, madame."

"I thank you, gentlemen. But hear me," continued she. "I am not only the most miserable of queens, but the most unhappy of mothers, the most despairing of wives. My children—two of them at least—the Duke of York and the Princess Elizabeth, are far away from me, exposed to the blows of the ambitious and our foes; my husband, the king, is leading in England so wretched an existence, that it is no exaggeration to say that he seeks death, as a thing to be desired. Hold! gentlemen, there is the letter conveyed to me by Lord de Winter. Read it."

Obeying the queen, Athos read aloud the letter, which we have already seen, in which King Charles solicited that the hospitality of France should be accorded to him.

"Well?" asked Athos, when he had closed the letter.

"Well," said the queen, "it has been refused."

The two friends exchanged a smile of contempt.

"And now," said Athos, "what is to be done? I have the honour to inquire from your majesty, what you desire Monsieur d'Herblay and myself to do in your service. We are ready."

"Ah! sir, you have a noble heart," exclaimed the queen, with a burst of gratitude; whilst Lord de Winter turned to her with a glance which said, "Did I not answer for them to you?"

"But you, sir?" said the queen to Aramis.

"I, madame," replied he, "follow Monsieur de la Fère wherever he leads, even were it to death, without seeking any explanation; but when it concerns your majesty's service, then," added he, looking at the queen with all the grace of his former days, "I precede the count."

"Well, then, gentlemen," said the queen, "since it is thus, and since you are willing to devote yourselves to the service of a queen whom the whole world has abandoned, this is what is required to be done for me. The king is alone with a few gentlemen, whom he fears to lose every day; surrounded by the Scotch, whom he distrusts, although he be himself a Scotchman. Since Lord de Winter left him I am distracted, sirs. I ask much, too much perhaps, for I have no right to ask it. Go to England, join the king, be his friends, his protectors, march to battle at his side, and be near him in the interior of his house, where conspiracies, more dangerous than the perils of war, increase every day. And in exchange for the sacrifice that you make, gentlemen, I promise—not to reward you, I believe that word would offend you—but to love you as a sister, to prefer you next to my husband and my children, to every one. I swear it before heaven."

And the queen raised her eyes solemnly upwards.

"Madame," said Athos, "you have but to command."

"You consent, then?" exclaimed the queen joyfully.

"Yes, madame; only it seems to me that your majesty goes too far in engaging to load us with a friendship so far above our merit. We do service to God, madame, in serving a prince so unfortunate, and a queen so virtuous. Madame, we are yours, body and soul."

"Oh, sirs," said the queen, moved to tears, "this is the first time for five years that I have felt anything like joy and hope. God—who understands my heart, knows all the gratitude I feel—will reward you! Save my husband! Save the king, and although you care not for the price which is placed upon a good action in this world, leave me the hope that we shall meet again, when I may be able to thank you myself. In the meantime I remain here. Have you any counsel and advice to offer me? From this moment I become your friend, and since you are engaged in my affairs, I ought to occupy myself in yours."

"Madame," replied Athos, "I have only to ask your majesty's prayers."

"And I," said Aramis, "I am alone in the world, and seek only to serve your majesty."

The queen held out her hand, which they kissed, and having two letters prepared for the king—one from herself, and one written by the Princess Henrietta—she gave one to Athos and the other to Aramis, lest, should they be separated by any chance, they might make themselves known to the king; after which they withdrew.

At the foot of the staircase de Winter stopped.

"Not to arouse suspicions, gentlemen," said he, "go your way, and I will go mine, and this evening at nine o'clock we will meet again at the gate St. Denis. We will travel on horseback as far as our horses can go, and afterwards we can take the post. Once more permit me to thank you, my good friends; to thank you in my own name, and in that of the queen."

The three gentlemen separated, Lord de Winter taking the Rue St. Honoré, and Athos and Aramis remaining together.

"Well," said Aramis, when they were alone, "what do you think of this business, my dear count?"

"Bad," replied Athos, "very bad."

"But you received it with enthusiasm."

"As I shall ever receive the defence of a great principle, my dear d'Herblay. Monarchs are only strong by the aid of the aristocracy, but aristocracy cannot exist without monarchs. Let us then support monarchy in order to support ourselves."

"We shall be murdered there," said Aramis. "I hate the English—they are coarse, like all people who drink beer."

"Would it be better to stay here?" said Athos, "and take a turn in the Bastille, or in the dungeon of Vincennes, for having favoured

9

the escape of Monsieur de Beaufort? Oh! i'faith, Aramis, believe me there is little left to regret. We avoid imprisonment, and we take the part of heroes—the choice is easy."

"It is true; but in everything, friend, one must always return to the same question—a stupid one I admit—but very necessary; have you any money?"

"Something like a hundred pistoles, that my farmer sent to me the day before I left Bragelonne; but out of that sum, I ought to leave fifty for Raoul—a young man must live respectably. I have then about fifty pistoles. And you?"

"As for me, I am quite sure that after turning out all my pockets and emptying my drawers, I shall not find ten louis at home. Fortunately, Lord de Winter is prosperous."

"Lord de Winter is ruined for the moment, for Cromwell claims all his resources."

"Now is the time when Lord Porthos would be useful!"

"Now it is that I regret d'Artagnan."

"Let us entice them away."

"This secret, Aramis, does not belong to us; take my advice, then, and put no one into our confidence. And, moreover, in taking such a step, we should appear to be doubtful of ourselves. Let us regret to ourselves for our own sakes, but not speak of it."

"You are right; but what are you going to do till this evening; I have two things that must be held over."

"And what are they?"

"First, a thrust with the Coadjutor, whom I met last night at Madame de Rambouillet's, and whom I found insulting in his remarks concerning me."

"Oh, fye—a quarrel between priests, a duel between allies!"

"What can I do, friend; he is a bully, and so am I; his cassock is a load upon him, and I think I have had enough of mine; in fact, there is so much resemblance between us, that I sometimes believe he is Aramis, and I am the Coadjutor. This kind of life fatigues and oppresses me; besides, he is a turbulent fellow who will ruin our party. I am convinced that if I gave him a box on the ear, such as I gave this morning to the little citizen who splashed me, it would change the appearance of things."

"And I, my dear Aramis," quietly replied Athos, "I think it would only change Monsieur de Retz's appearance. Take my advice, leave things as they are; besides, you are neither of you now your own masters; he belongs to the Fronde, and you to the Queen of England. But now we must part. I have one or two calls to make, and a letter to write. Call for me at eight o'clock, or shall I wait supper for you at seven?"

"That will do very well," said Aramis. "I have twenty calls to make, and as many letters to write."

They then separated. Athos went to pay a visit to Madame de Vendôme, left his name at Madame de Chevreuse's, and wrote the following letter to d'Artagnan:—

"DEAR FRIEND,—I am about to set off with Aramis on important business. I wished to make my adieux to you, but time is too pressing. Remember that I write to you now to repeat how much affection I have for you.

"Raoul is gone to Blois, and is not aware of my departure; watch over him in my absence as much as you possibly can, and if it should happen that you receive no news of me in three months from now, tell him to open a packet which he will find addressed to him in my bronze casket at Blois, and of which I send you the key.

"Embrace Porthos from Aramis and myself. *Adieu*, perhaps farewell."

At the hour agreed Aramis arrived; he was dressed as an officer, and had his old sword at his side which he had drawn so often, and which he was more than ever ready to draw.

"By the bye," he said, "I think that we are decidedly wrong to depart thus, without leaving a line for Porthos and d'Artagnan."

"The thing is done, dear friend," said Athos; "I foresaw that, and have embraced them both from you and myself."

"You are a wonderful man, my dear count," said Aramis; "you think of everything."

"Well, have you made up your mind to this journey?"

"Quite; and now that I reflect about it, I am glad to leave Paris at this moment."

"And so am I," replied Athos; "my only regret is not having seen d'Artagnan; but that rascal is so cunning, he might have guessed our project."

When supper was over Blaisois entered. "Sir," said he, "here is Monsieur d'Artagnan's answer."

"But I did not tell you there was an answer, stupid!" said Athos.

"And I set off without waiting for one, but he called me back and gave me this;" and he presented a little bag made of leather, round, and having a ringing sound.

Athos opened it, and began by drawing from it a little note, written in these terms:—

"My Dear Friend,—When one travels—and especially for three months—one has never enough money. Now, recalling our former time of distress, I send you the half of my purse; it is money to obtain which I made Mazarin sweat. Don't make a bad use of it I entreat you.

"As to what you say about not seeing you again, I don't believe a word of it; with your heart and your sword one might pass through anything. *Au revoir*, then, and not farewell.

"It is unnecessary to say that from the day I saw Raoul I loved him; nevertheless, believe that I heartily pray to God that I may not become his father, however much I might be proud of such a son.

"John d'Artagnan."

"P.S.—I would wish you to understand that the fifty louis which I send are equally for Aramis as for you, and for you as for Aramis."

Athos smiled, and his fine eye was dimmed by a tear. D'Artagnan, who had loved him so tenderly, loved him still, Mazarinist though he was.

"There are the fifty louis, i'faith," said Aramis, emptying the purse on the table, "all bearing the effigy of Louis XIII. Well, what shall you do with this money, count; shall you keep it, or send it back?"

"I shall keep it, Aramis; and even had I no need of it, I should keep it all the same. What is offered from a generous heart should be accepted generously. Take twenty-five of them, Aramis, and give me the remaining twenty-five."

"Very well; I am glad to see that you are of my opinion. There now, shall we start?"

"When you like; but have you no groom?"

"No! that idiot Bazin was fool enough to make himself verger, as you know, and therefore cannot leave Notre Dame."

"Very well, take Blaisois, with whom I know not what to do since I have had Grimaud."

"Willingly," said Aramis.

At this moment Grimaud appeared at the door. "Ready," said he laconically.

"Let us go then," said Athos.

The two friends mounted, as did their servants. At the corner of the Quai they encountered Bazin, who was running breathlessly.

"Oh, sir!" cried he, "thank heaven I have arrived in time. Monsieur Porthos has just been to your house, and has left this for you, saying that the thing was important, and ought to be given to you before you left.''

''Good,'' said Aramis, taking a purse which Bazin presented to him. ''What is this?''

''Wait, your reverence, there is a letter.''

''You know that I have already told you that if you ever call me anything but chevalier I will break your bones. Give me the letter.''

''How can you read?'' asked Athos; ''it is as dark as pitch.''

''Wait,'' said Bazin, striking a light, and lighting a twisted wax-light, with which he lighted the church candles. By this light Aramis read the following letter:

''MY DEAR D'HERBLAY,—I learn from d'Artagnan, who has embraced me on the part of the Count de la Fère and yourself, that you are setting out on a journey which may perhaps last two or three months. As I know that you do not like to ask money of your friend, I send to you. Here are two hundred pistoles, of which you can dispose, and return to me when an opportunity occurs. Do not fear that you put me to inconvenience; if I want money, I can send for some from one of my châteaux; at Bracieux alone I have twenty thousand francs in gold. So, if I do not send you more, it is because I fear you would not accept a large sum.

''I address you, because you know, that although I esteem him from my heart, I am a little awed by Count de la Fère; but it is understood, that what I offer to you I offer to him at the same time.—I am, as I trust you do not doubt, your devoted friend,

''DU VALON DE BRACIEUX DE PIERREFONDS.''

''Well,'' said Aramis, ''what do you say to that?''

''I say, my dear d'Herblay, that it is almost sacrilege to distrust Providence when one has such friends, and therefore we will divide the pistoles from Porthos, as we divided the louis sent by d'Artagnan.''

The division being made, the two friends continued their road, and a quarter of an hour later they had joined Lord de Winter at the Porte St. Denis.

43

WHEREIN IT IS PROVED THAT FIRST IMPULSES ARE ALWAYS THE BEST

THE three gentlemen took the road to Picardy—a road so well known to them, and which recalled to Athos and Aramis some of the most picturesque adventures of their youthful days.

"If Mousqueton were with us," observed Athos, on reaching the spot where they had had a dispute with the paviers, "how he would tremble at passing this! Do you remember, Aramis, that it was here he received that famous ball?"

"By my faith, I do not wonder at that," replied Aramis; "for even I feel a shudder at the recollection; hold, just above that tree is the little spot where I thought I was killed."

It was soon time for Grimaud to recall the past. Arriving before the inn at which his master and himself had made such an enormous repast, he approached Athos, and said, showing him the airhole of the cellar:

"Sausages!"

Athos began to laugh, and this youthful folly of his appeared to be as amusing as if some one had related it of another person.

At last, after two days and one night, they arrived at Boulogne towards the evening, favoured by glorious weather. Boulogne was a strong position, and then almost a deserted town, built entirely on the heights, and what is now called the lower town was not then in existence.

"Gentlemen," said de Winter, on reaching the gate of the town, "let us do here as at Paris—let us separate to avoid suspicion. I know an inn, little frequented, but of which the host is entirely devoted to me. I will go there, where I expect to find letters, and you go to the first tavern in the town, to L'Épée du Grand Henri, for instance, refresh yourselves, and in two hours be upon the jetty. A boat is waiting there for us."

The matter being thus decided, the two friends found, about two hundred paces farther, the tavern indicated to them. The horses were fed, but not unsaddled; the grooms supped, for it was already late; and their two masters, impatient to return, appointed a place of meeting with them on the jetty, and desired them on no account to speak a word with any one. It is needless to say that this caution concerned Blaisois alone : it was long since it had become a necessary one to Grimaud.

Athos and Aramis walked down towards the port. From their dress, covered with dust, and from a certain easy manner by which a man accustomed to travel is always recognised, the two friends excited the attention of a few people. There was more especially one upon whom their arrival had produced a decided impression. This man, who they had observed from the first for the same reason as they had themselves been remarked by others, walked in a melancholy way up and down the jetty. From the moment he perceived them he did not cease to look at them, and seemed to be greatly inclined to speak to them.

On reaching the jetty, Athos and Aramis stopped to look at a little boat fastened to a stake, and ready rigged as if waiting to start.

"That is, doubtless, our boat," said Athos.

"Yes," replied Aramis, "and the sloop sailing about there must be that which is to take us to England; now," continued he, "if only de Winter does not keep us waiting. It is not at all amusing here—there is not a single woman passing."

"Hush !" said Athos, "we are overheard."

In truth, the man who, during the observations of the two friends, had passed and repassed behind them several times, stopped at the name of de Winter; but as his face betrayed no emotion at the mention of this name, it might have been by chance that he had stopped.

"Gentlemen," said the man, who was young and pale, bowing with much ease and politeness, "pardon my curiosity, but I see you come from Paris, or at least that you are strangers at Boulogne."

"We come from Paris, yes," replied Athos, with the same courtesy; "can we be of any service to you?"

"Sir," said the young man, "will you be so good as to tell me if it be true that Cardinal Mazarin is no longer minister?"

"That is a strange question," said Aramis.

"He is and he is not," replied Athos; "that is to say, he is dismissed by one half of France; and that by means of intrigues and promises, he makes the other half retain him; you will observe that this may last a long time."

"However, sir," said the stranger, "he has neither fled, nor is in prison?"

"No, sir, at least not when we left."

"Sirs, accept my thanks for your politeness," said the young man, retreating.

"What do you think of that interrogator?" asked Aramis.

"I think he is either a provincial person who is dull, or a spy wishing for information."

"And you replied to him with that notion?"

"Nothing warranted me to answer him otherwise: he was polite to me, and I was compelled to be so to him."

"But if he be a spy——"

"What do you think a spy would be about here? We are not living in the time of Cardinal Richelieu, who would have closed the ports on a bare suspicion."

"It matters not; you were wrong to reply to him as you did," continued Aramis, following with his eyes the young man disappearing behind the cliffs.

"And you," said Athos, "you forget that you committed a very different kind of imprudence in pronouncing Lord de Winter's name. Did you not see that at that name the young man stopped?"

"More reason, then, when he spoke to you for sending him about his business."

"A quarrel?" inquired Athos.

"And since when have you become afraid of a quarrel?"

"I am always afraid of a quarrel when I am expected at any place, and that such a quarrel might possibly prevent my reaching it. Besides, let me own something to you. I am anxious to see that young man nearer."

"And wherefore?"

"Aramis, you will certainly laugh at me; you will say that I am always repeating the same thing; you will call me the most timorous of visionaries; but to whom do you see a resemblance in that young man?"

"In beauty, or on the contrary?" asked Aramis, laughing.

"In ugliness, and as far as a man can resemble a woman?"

"Ah, egad!" cried Aramis, "you have made me think. No, in truth, you are no visionary, my dear friend, and now that I think of it—you—yes, i'faith, quite right—that delicate and compressed mouth, those eyes which seem always at the command of the intellect, and never of the heart! Yes, it is one of milady's sons!"

"You laugh, Aramis."

"Only from habit; for I swear to you, I should like no better than yourself to remove that viper from my path."

"Ah! here is de Winter coming," said Athos.

"Good, one thing now is only wanting, and that is that our grooms should keep us waiting."

"No," said Athos, "I see them about twenty paces behind my

lord. I recognise Grimaud by his long legs and stiff gait. Tony carries our muskets."

"Then we shall sleep on board to-night?" asked Aramis, glancing towards the west, where the sun had left but one golden cloud, which, dipping into the ocean, appeared by degrees to be extinguished.

"Probably so," said Athos.

"*Diable!*" remarked Aramis; "I have little fancy for the sea by day, but still less at night; the sounds of the winds and waves, the frightful motion of the vessel—I confess that I prefer to be in the convent of Noisy."

Athos smiled sadly, for it was evident that he was thinking of other things as he listened to his friend, and he moved towards de Winter.

"What is the matter with my friend?" said Aramis; "he resembles one of Dante's damned people, whose neck Satan has dislocated, and who always look at their heels. What on earth makes him look thus behind him?"

When de Winter perceived them, in his turn he advanced towards them with surprising rapidity.

"Is anything the matter, my lord?" said Athos; "you are out of breath."

"No," replied de Winter, "no; and yet in passing the heights it seemed to me——" and he again turned round.

Athos looked at Aramis.

"But let us go," continued de Winter; "let us be off; the boat must be waiting for us, and there is our sloop at anchor—do you see it there? I wish I were on board already,"—and he looked back again.

"He has seen him," said Athos, in a low tone to Aramis.

They had now reached the ladder which led to the boat. De Winter made the grooms who conveyed the arms, and the porters with the luggage, descend first, and was about to follow them.

At this moment, Athos perceived a man walking on the seashore parallel to the jetty, and hastening his steps as if to reach the other side of the port, scarcely twenty steps from the place of embarking. He fancied in the darkness that he recognised the young man who had questioned him. Athos now descended the ladder in his turn, without losing sight of the young man. The latter, to make a short cut, had appeared on a sluice.

"He certainly bodes us no good," said Athos; "but let us embark —once out at sea, let him come."

And Athos sprang into the boat, which was immediately pushed off, and which soon distanced the shore under the efforts of four strong rowers.

But the young man had begun to follow or rather to advance before the boat. It was obliged to advance between the point of the jetty, surmounted by a beacon, just lighted, and a rock which jutted out. They saw him in the distance climbing the rock, in order to look down upon the boat as it passed.

"Ay, but," said Aramis, "that young man is decidedly a spy."

"Which is the young man?" asked de Winter, turning round.

"He who followed us, and spoke to us, and awaits us there— see!"

De Winter turned, and followed the direction of Aramis's finger. The beacon bathed its light upon the little strait through which they were about to pass, and the rock where the young man stood with bare head and folded arms.

"It is he!" exclaimed de Winter, clutching the arm of Athos; "it is he! I thought I recognised him, and I was not mistaken."

"Who—him?" asked Aramis.

"Milady's son," replied Athos.

"The monk!" exclaimed Grimaud.

The young man heard the words, and bent so forward over the rock that one might have supposed he was about to precipitate himself from it.

"Yes, it is I, my uncle. I, the son of milady—I, the monk—I, the secretary and friend of Cromwell—and I know you, both you and your companions."

There were in that boat three men, undoubtedly brave, and whose courage no man would have dared to dispute; nevertheless, at that voice, that accent, and those gestures, they felt a shudder run through their veins. As for Grimaud, his hair stood on end, and drops of sweat proceeded from his brow.

"Ah!" exclaimed Aramis, "that is the nephew, the monk, and the son of milady, as he says himself."

"Alas! yes," murmured de Winter.

"Then, wait," said Aramis; and with the terrible coolness which he showed on important occasions, he took one of the muskets from Tony, shouldered and aimed it at the young man, who stood, like the accusing angel, upon the rock.

"Fire!" cried Grimaud unconsciously.

Athos threw himself on the mouth of the gun, and thus stayed the shot which was about to be fired.

"The devil take you," said Aramis, "I had him so well at the point of my gun, I should have sent a ball into his breast."

"It is enough to have slain the mother," said Athos hoarsely.

"The mother was a wretch, who struck at us all, and at those dear to us."

"Yes, but the son has done us no harm."

Grimaud, who had risen to watch the effect of the shot, fell back, wringing his hands.

The young man burst into a laugh.

"Ah, it is certainly you," he cried, "and I know you now."

His mocking laugh and threatening words passed over their heads, carried on by the breeze, until lost in the depths of the horizon. Aramis shuddered.

"Be calm!" exclaimed Athos, "for Heaven's sake;—have we ceased to be men?"

"No," said Aramis, "but that being is a fiend; and ask the uncle if I was wrong to rid him of his nephew."

De Winter answered only by a groan.

"It was all up with him," continued Aramis, "ah, I much fear that, with your wisdom, you have made me commit a great folly."

Athos took Lord de Winter's hand, and tried to turn the conversation.

"When shall we land in England?" he questioned; but de Winter seemed not to hear his words, and made no reply.

"Hold, Athos," said Aramis, "perhaps there is still time. See if he is still in the same place."

Athos turned round with an effort; the sight of the young man was evidently painful to him, and there he still was, in fact, on the rock, the beacon shedding round him, as it were, a halo of light.

"Decidedly, Aramis," said Athos; "I think I was wrong not to let you fire."

"Hold your tongue," replied Aramis; "you will make me weep if it were possible."

At this moment they were hailed by a voice from the sloop, and a few seconds later, men, servants, and baggage were on deck. The captain had been only awaiting his passengers, and hardly had they put foot on board ere her head was turned towards Hastings, where they were to disembark. At this instant the three friends turned, in spite of themselves, a last look on the rock, upon the menacing figure which pursued them and stood out boldly. Then a voice reached them once more, sending out this threat: "We shall meet in England, gentlemen."

44

THE TE DEUM FOR THE VICTORY OF LENS

THE commotion which had been observed by Henrietta Maria, and for which she had vainly sought to discover a reason, was occasioned by the battle of Lens, announced by the prince's messenger, the Duc de Châtillon, who had taken such a noble part in the engagement; he was, besides, commissioned to hang twenty-five flags taken from the Lorraine party, as well as from the Spaniards, upon the arches of Notre Dame.

This news was decisive; it destroyed, in favour of the court, the struggle commenced with the parliament. The motive given for all the taxes summarily imposed, and to which the parliament had made opposition, was the necessity of sustaining the honour of France, and upon the uncertain hope of subduing the enemy. Now, since the affair of Nordlingen, they had but experienced reverses; the parliament had a plea for calling Mazarin to account for all the victories—always promised and always deferred; but this time there had really been fighting, there had been a triumph and a complete one. And this all knew so well, that it was a double victory for the court—a victory interior and exterior, so that even when the young king learned the news, he exclaimed, "Ah, gentlemen of the parliament, we shall see what you will say now." Upon which the queen had pressed to her heart the royal child, whose proud and unruly sentiments were in such harmony with her own. A council was called the same evening, but nothing further was known of its decision than that, on the following Sunday, a "Te Deum" would be rendered at Notre Dame in honour of the victory of Lens.

The following Sunday, then, the Parisians arose with joy; at that period a "Te Deum" was a grand affair; this kind of ceremony had not then been made an abuse of, and it produced a great effect. The shops were closed, the houses deserted: every one wished to see the young king with his mother, and the famous Cardinal Mazarin, whom they detested so much, that no one wished to be deprived of his presence. Moreover, great liberty prevailed among this immense crowd; every opinion was openly expressed, and rang out, so to speak, insurrection, as the thousand bells of all the Paris churches rang out the "Te Deum." The police belonging to the city being formed by the city itself, nothing threatening presented itself to disturb the concert of universal hatred, or to freeze words between slandering lips.

Nevertheless, at eight o'clock in the morning, the regiment of the queen's guards, commanded by Guitant, under whom was his nephew Comminges, marched, preceded by drums and trumpets, to file off from the Palais Royal as far as Notre Dame, a manœuvre which the Parisians witnessed quietly, delighted as they were with military music and brilliant uniforms.

Friquet had put on his Sunday clothes, under the pretext of having a cold, which he had managed to procure momentarily, by introducing an infinite number of cherry nuts into one side of his mouth, and had procured a whole holiday from Bazin. On leaving Bazin, Friquet started off to the Palais Royal, where he arrived at the moment of the turning out of the regiment of guards, and as he had only gone there for the enjoyment of seeing it and hearing the music, he took his place at their head, beating the drum on two pieces of slate, and passing from that exercise to that of the trumpet, which he counterfeited naturally with his mouth in a manner which had more than once called forth the praises of amateurs of imitative harmony.

This amusement lasted from the Barrière des Sergens to the place of Notre Dame; and Friquet found in it true enjoyment; but when at last the regiment separated, penetrated to the heart of the city, and placed itself at the extremity of the Rue St. Christophe, near the Rue Cocatrix, in which Broussel lived, then Friquet remembered that he had not had breakfast; and after thinking to which side he had best turn his steps in order to accomplish this important act of the day, he reflected deeply, and decided that it should be Councillor Broussel who should bear the cost of his repast.

In consequence he started hurriedly and arrived breathlessly at the councillor's door, and knocked violently.

His mother, the councillor's old servant, opened it.

"What dost thou here, good-for-nothing?" she said, "and why art thou not at Notre Dame?"

"I have been there, mother," answered Friquet, "but I saw things happen of which Master Broussel ought to be acquainted, and so with Monsieur Bazin's permission, I came to speak to Monsieur Broussel."

"And what hast thou to say, boy, to Monsieur Broussel?"

"I wish to tell him," replied Friquet, screaming with all his might, "that there is a whole regiment of guards coming this way. And, as I hear everywhere that at the court they are ill-disposed to him, I wish to warn him, that he may be on his guard."

Broussel heard the scream of the young oddity; and, enchanted with such excess of zeal, came down to the first floor, for he was, in truth, working in his room on the second.

"Well!" said he, "friend—what matters the regiment of guards to us, and art thou not mad to make such a disturbance? Knowest thou not that it is the custom of these soldiers to act thus, and that it is usual for the regiment to form themselves into a hedge where the king passes?"

Friquet counterfeited surprise—and turning his new cap round his fingers, said:

"It is not surprising for you to know it, Monsieur Broussel, who knows everything;—but me, by the holy truth, I do not know it, and I thought I would give you good advice:—you must not be angry with me for that, Monsieur Broussel."

"On the contrary, my boy; on the contrary, I am pleased with your zeal. Dame Nanette, look for those apricots which Madame de Longueville sent to us yesterday from Noisy, and give half a dozen of them to your son, with a crust of new bread."

"Oh, thank you, sir, thank you, Monsieur Broussel," said Friquet; "I am so fond of apricots!"

Broussel then went to his wife's room, and asked for breakfast; it was nine o'clock. The councillor placed himself at the window. The street was completely deserted; but in the distance was heard, like the noise of the tide rushing in, the deep hum of the popular waves which increased around Notre Dame.

This noise redoubled, when d'Artagnan, with a company of musketeers, placed himself at the gate of Notre Dame to secure the service of the church. He had told Porthos to profit by this opportunity to see the ceremony; and Porthos, in full dress, mounted his finest horse, acting the part of an honorary musketeer, as d'Artagnan had so often done formerly. The sergeant of this company, an old veteran of the Spanish wars, had recognised Porthos, his old companion, and very soon all those who served under him had been placed in possession of startling facts concerning the honour of the famous musketeers of Tréville. Porthos had not only been well received by the company, but he was, moreover, looked upon with great admiration.

At ten o'clock the guns of the Louvre announced the departure of the king, and then a movement, similar to that of trees in a stormy wind bending and agitating their tops, ran through the multitude, which was compressed behind the immovable muskets of the guards. At last the king appeared with the queen in a gilded carriage. Ten other carriages followed containing the ladies of honour, the officers of the royal household, and the remainder of the court.

"God save the king!" was the cry in every direction; the young monarch gravely put his head out of the window, looked sufficiently grateful, and even bowed slightly: at which the cries of the multitude were renewed.

Just as the company was being placed in the cathedral, a carriage, bearing the arms of Comminges, quitted the line of court carriages and proceeded slowly to the end of the Rue St. Christophe, now entirely deserted. When it arrived there four guards and a police-officer who accompanied it, mounted into the heavy vehicle, and drew the blinds; then, with a judicious admittance of the light, the policeman began to watch the length of the Rue Cocatrix, as if he was waiting for some one.

All the world was occupied with the ceremony, so that neither the chariot, nor the precautions taken by those who were within it, had been observed. Friquet, whose eye, always on the alert, could alone have discovered them, had gone to devour his apricots upon the entablature of a house in the square of Notre Dame. Thence, he saw the king, the queen, and Monsieur Mazarin, and heard the mass, as well as if he had been on service.

Towards the end of the service, the queen, seeing Comminges standing near her, waiting for a confirmation of the order she had given him before quitting the Louvre, said, in a whisper:

"Go, Comminges, and may God aid you!"

Comminges immediately left the church, and entered the Rue St. Christophe. Friquet, seeing this fine officer thus walk away, followed by two guards, amused himself by following them, and did this so much the more joyfully, since the ceremony ended at that moment, and the king regained his carriage.

Hardly had the police-officer observed Comminges at the end of the Rue Cocatrix, than he said one word to the coachman, who at once put his vehicle into motion, and drove up before Broussel's door. Comminges knocked at the door at the same moment, and Friquet was waiting behind Comminges until the door should be opened.

"What dost thou there, rascal?" asked Comminges.

"I want to go into Monsieur Broussel's house, captain," replied Friquet, in that coaxing tone which the gamins of Paris know so well how to assume when necessary.

"And on what floor does he live?" asked Comminges.

"In the whole house," said Friquet; "the house belongs to him; he occupies the second floor when he works, and descends to the first to take his meals; he must be at dinner now—it is noon."

"Good," said Comminges.

Just then the door was opened, and having questioned the servant, the officer learnt that Monsieur Broussel was at home, and at dinner.

Broussel was seated at the table with his family, having his wife opposite to him, his two daughters by his side, and his son, Louvières, whom we have already seen when the accident happened to the councillor—an accident from which he had quite recovered—at the bottom of the table. The worthy man, again in perfect health, was eating the fine fruit which Madame de Longueville had sent to him.

At the sight of the officer, Broussel was somewhat moved; but on seeing him bow politely, he rose and bowed also. Still, in spite of this reciprocal politeness, the countenances of the women betrayed some uneasiness; Louvières became very pale, and waited impatiently for the officer to explain himself.

"Sir," said Comminges, "I am the bearer of an order from the king."

"Very well, sir," replied Broussel; "what is this order?" And he held out his hand.

"I am commissioned to seize your person, sir," said Comminges, in the same tone, and with the same politeness; "and if you will believe me, you will spare yourself the trouble of reading that long letter, and follow me."

A thunderbolt falling in the midst of these good people, so peacefully assembled there, would not have produced a more appalling effect. It was a terrible thing at that period to be imprisoned by the enmity of the king. Louvières sprang forward to take his sword, which was hung up in a corner of the room; but a look from the worthy Broussel, who in the midst of it all did not lose his presence of mind, checked this action of despair. Madame Broussel, separated by the width of the table from her husband, burst into tears, and the young girls clung to their father's arms.

"Come, sir," said Comminges, "be quick; you must obey the king."

"Sir," said Broussel, "I am in bad health, and cannot give myself up a prisoner in this state; I ask for time."

"It is impossible," said Comminges; "the order is strict, and must be put into execution at once."

"Impossible!" said Louvières; "sir, beware of driving us to despair."

"Impossible!" cried a shrill voice from the bottom of the room.

Comminges turned and saw Dame Nanette, her eyes flashing with anger, and a broom in her hand.

"My good Nanette, be quiet, I beseech you," said Broussel.

"Me! keep quiet while my master is arrested; he, the support—the liberator—the father of the poor! Ah! well, yes—you have to know me yet. Are you going?" added she to Comminges.

The latter smiled.

"Come, sir," said he to Broussel, "silence that woman, and follow me."

"Silence me!—me! me!" said Nanette. "Ah! yet one wants some beside you for that, my fine officer. You shall see." And Dame Nanette sprang to the window, threw it open, and in such a piercing voice that it might have been heard in the square of Notre Dame:

"Help!" she screamed, "my master is being arrested! the Councillor Broussel is arrested—help!"

"Sir," said Comminges, "declare yourself at once; will you obey, or do you intend to rebel against his majesty?"

"I obey—I obey, sir," cried Broussel, trying to disengage himself from the grasp of his two daughters, and to restrain, by his look, his son, always ready to escape from it.

"In that case," said Comminges, "silence that old woman."

"Ah! old woman!" screamed Nanette.

And she began to shriek loudly, clinging to the bars of the window.

"Help! help! for Monsieur Broussel, who is arrested because he has defended the people—help!"

Comminges seized the servant round the waist, and would have dragged her from her post; but at that instant a treble voice was heard screeching:

"Murder! fire! assassins! Monsieur Broussel is being killed; Monsieur Broussel is being murdered."

It was Friquet's voice; and Dame Nanette, feeling herself supported, recommenced with all her strength to make a chorus.

Many curious faces had already appeared at the windows, and the people, attracted to the end of the street, began to run—first men, then groups, and then a crowd of people; hearing cries, and seeing a chariot, they could not understand it; but Friquet sprang on to the top of the carriage.

"They want to arrest Monsieur Broussel," he cried; "the guards are in the carriage, and the officer is upstairs!"

The crowd began to murmur, and approached the house. The two guards who had remained in the lane went to the aid of Comminges; those who were in the chariot opened the doors and presented arms.

"Don't you see them?" shouted Friquet, "don't you see?—there they are!"

The coachman turned round, and gave Friquet a cut with his whip, which made him scream with pain.

"Ah! devil's coachman!" cried Friquet, "you're meddling too—wait!"

And getting beyond the reach of the whip, he overwhelmed the coachman with every projectile he could lay hands on.

The tumult now increased; the street was not able to contain the spectators, who assembled from every direction; the crowd invaded the space which the dreaded pikes of the guards kept clear, between them and the carriage. The soldiers, pushed back by these living walls, were about to be crushed against the wheels and the panels of the carriage. The cries which the police-officer repeated twenty times, of "In the king's name," were powerless against the formidable multitude, and seemed on the contrary to exasperate it still more; when, at the cries, "In the name of the king," an officer ran up, and seeing the uniforms much ill-treated, he sprang into the scuffle, sword in hand, and brought unexpected help to the guards. This gentleman was a youth, scarcely sixteen years of age, perfectly pale with anger. He sprang on foot, as the other guards, placed his back against the shaft of the carriage, making a rampart of his horse, drew his pistols from their holsters, and fastened them to his belt, and began to fight with the flat of his sword, like a man accustomed to the handling of his weapon.

For ten minutes he alone kept the crowd at bay; at last Comminges appeared, pushing Broussel before him.

"Let us break the carriage!"

"In the king's name!" cried Comminges.

"The first who advances is a dead man!" cried Raoul, for it was in fact he, who, feeling himself pressed and almost crushed by a kind of giant, pricked him with the point of his sword, and sent him back groaning.

Comminges, so to speak, threw Broussel into the carriage, and sprang in after him. At this moment a shot was fired, and a ball passed through the hat of Comminges, and broke the arm of one of the guards. Comminges looked up, and saw among the smoke the threatening face of Louvières, appearing at the window of the second floor.

"Very well, sir," said Comminges, "you shall hear of me again."

"And you of me too, sir," said Louvières; "and we shall see who can speak the loudest."

Friquet and Nanette continued to shout; the cries, the noise of the shot, and the smell of the powder, produced their effect.

"Down with the officer! down with him!" was the cry.

"One step nearer," said Comminges, putting down the sashes that the interior of the carriage might be well seen, and placing his sword to his prisoner's breast, "one step nearer, and I kill the prisoner; my orders were to bring him off alive or dead. I will take him dead, that's all."

A terrible cry was heard, and the wife and daughters of Broussel held up their hands in supplication to the people; the latter knew that this officer, who was so pale, but who appeared so determined, would keep his word; they continued to threaten, but they began to disperse.

"Drive to the palace," said Comminges to the coachman, more dead than alive.

The man whipped his horses, which cleared a way through the crowd; but on arriving on the Quai, they were obliged to stop; the carriage was upset, the horses were carried off, stifled, mangled by the mob. Raoul, on foot, for he had not had time to reach his horse again, tired, like the guards, of distributing blows with the flat of his sword, had recourse to its point. But this last and dreaded resource served only to exasperate the people. From time to time a shot from a musket, or the blade of a rapier, flashed among the crowd; the projectiles continued to rain from the windows, and some shots were heard, the echo of which, though they were probably fired in the air, made all hearts vibrate. Voices, which are heard but on days of revolution, were distinguished; faces were seen that only appeared on days of bloodshed. Cries of "Death! —death to the guards!—to the Seine with the officer!" were heard above all the din, deafening as it was. Raoul, his hat torn to pieces, and his face bleeding, felt not only his strength, but also his reason going; a red mist covered his sight, and through this mist he saw a hundred threatening arms stretched over him, ready to seize upon him when he fell. The guards were unable to help any one—for each was occupied with his personal safety. All was over; carriage, horses, guards, and perhaps even the prisoner, were about to be torn to shreds, when all at once a voice well known to Raoul was heard, and suddenly a large sword glistened in the air; at the same time the crowd opened—upset, trodden down—and an officer of the musketeers, striking and cutting right and left, rushed up to Raoul, and took him in his arms, just as he was about to fall.

"My faith," cried the officer, "they have killed him? Woe to them if it be so."

And he turned round, so stern with anger, strength, and threat.

that the most excited rebels hustled back against one another, in order to escape, and some of them even rolled into the Seine.

"Monsieur d'Artagnan!" murmured Raoul.

"Yes, in person, and fortunately it seems for you, my young friend. Come on—here—you others," he continued, rising in his stirrups and raising his sword, and addressing those musketeers who had not been able to follow his rapid pace, "come, sweep away all that for me—shoulder muskets—present arms—aim——"

At this command the mountains of populace thinned so suddenly that d'Artagnan could not repress a burst of Homeric laughter.

"Thank you, d'Artagnan," said Comminges, displaying half of his body through the window of the broken vehicle, "thanks, my young friend; your name?—that I may give it to the queen."

Raoul was about to reply, when d'Artagnan bent down to his ear.

"Hold your tongue," said he, "and let me answer. Do not lose time, Comminges," he continued; "get out of the carriage, if you can, and make another attempt; be quick, or in five minutes all the mob will be back with swords and muskets, you will be killed, and your prisoner freed. Hold—there is a carriage coming down there."

Then, turning again to Raoul, he whispered, "Above all things, don't tell your name."

"That's right. I will go," said Comminges; "and if they come back, fire!"

"Not at all—not at all," replied d'Artagnan; "let no one move. On the contrary, one shot at this moment would be paid for dearly to-morrow."

Comminges took four guards and as many musketeers, and ran to the carriage, from which he made the people inside dismount, and brought them to the vehicle which had been upset. But when it was necessary to convey the prisoner from one carriage to the other, the people, catching sight of him whom they called their liberator, uttered all kinds of cries, and knotted once more against the vehicle.

"Off with you!" said d'Artagnan. "There are ten men to accompany you. I will keep twenty to hold in the mob: go, and lose not a moment. Ten men for Monsieur de Comminges!"

As the carriage started off the cries were redoubled, and more than ten thousand were hurried on the Quai, and encumbered the Pont Neuf and the adjacent streets. A few shots were fired, and a musketeer wounded.

"Forward!" cried d'Artagnan, driven to extremities, and biting his moustache; and then he charged with his twenty men, and dispersed them in fear. One man alone remained in his place, gun in hand.

"Ah!" he exclaimed, "it is thou who wouldst have him assassinated?—wait an instant." And he pointed his gun at d'Artagnan, who was riding towards him at full gallop. D'Artagnan bent down to his horse's neck, the young man fired, and the ball severed the feather from his hat. The horse, startled, brushed against the imprudent man, who thought by his strength alone to avert the tempest, and he fell against the wall. D'Artagnan pulled up his horse, and while his musketeers continued to charge, he returned, and bent with drawn sword over the man whom he had knocked down.

"Oh, sir!" exclaimed Raoul, recognising the young man as having seen him in the Rue Cocatrix—"spare him—it is his son!"

D'Artagnan's arm dropped to his side, "Ah, you are his son!" he said—"that is a different thing."

"Sir, I surrender," said Louvières, presenting his unloaded gun to the officer.

"Eh, no; do not surrender, egad! No! be off, and quickly. For if I take you, you will be hung."

The young man waited not to be told twice; but, passing under the horse's head, disappeared at the corner of the Rue Guénégaud.

"I'faith!" said d'Artagnan to Raoul, "you were just in time to stay my hand. He was a dead man; and, by my faith, if I had discovered that it was his son, I should have been sorry for having killed him."

"Ah! sir," said Raoul, "allow me, after thanking you for that poor fellow, to thank you on my own account. I too, sir, was almost dead when you arrived."

"Wait—wait, young man, and do not fatigue yourself with speaking. We can talk of it afterwards."

Then, seeing that the musketeers had cleared the Quai from the Pont Neuf to the Quai St. Michael, and that they had returned, he raised his sword for them to double their speed. The musketeers trotted up, and at the same time the ten men whom d'Artagnan had given to Comminges appeared.

"Holloa!" cried d'Artagnan; "has something fresh happened?"

"Yes, sir!" replied the sergeant, "their vehicle has broken down a second time—it is really doomed."

"They are bad managers," said d'Artagnan, shrugging his shoulders. "When a carriage is chosen, it ought to be strong. The carriage in which a Broussel is to be arrested ought to be able to bear ten thousand men."

"What are your commands, lieutenant?"

"Take the detachment, and conduct him to his place."

"But you will be left alone?"

"Certainly. Do you imagine I have need of an escort? Go." The musketeers set off, and d'Artagnan was left alone with Raoul.

"Now," he said, "are you in pain?"

"Yes, my head is hot and heavy."

"What's the matter with this head?" said d'Artagnan, raising the battered hat. "Ah! ah! a bruise."

"Yes, I think I received a flower-pot upon my head."

"Brutes!" said d'Artagnan. "But were you not on horseback? —you have spurs."

"Yes, but I got down to defend Monsieur de Comminges, and my horse was taken from me. Here it is, I see."

At this very moment Friquet passed, mounted on Raoul's horse, waving his parti-coloured cap, and crying, "Broussel! Broussel!"

"Holloa! stop, gamin!" cried d'Artagnan. "Bring hither that horse."

Friquet heard perfectly, but he pretended not to do so, and attempted to continue his road. D'Artagnan felt inclined for an instant to pursue Master Friquet, but not wishing to leave Raoul alone, he contented himself with taking a pistol from the holster, and cocking it.

Friquet had a quick eye and a fine ear. He saw d'Artagnan's movement; heard the sound of the click, and stopped at once.

"Ah! it is you, your honour," he said, advancing towards d'Artagnan; "I am truly pleased to meet you."

D'Artagnan looked attentively at Friquet, and recognised the boy of the Rue de la Calandre.

"Ah, 'tis thou, rascal!" said he, "come here. So thou hast changed thy trade; thou art no longer a choir-boy, or a tavern-boy; thou art then become a horse-stealer?"

"Ah, your honour, how can you say so!" exclaimed Friquet. "I was seeking the gentleman to whom this horse belongs—an officer, brave and handsome as a Cæsar"—then, pretending to see Raoul for the first time,—

"Ah! but if I mistake not," continued he, "here he is; you won't forget the boy, sir?"

Raoul put his hand to his pocket.

"What are you about?" asked d'Artagnan.

"To give ten francs to this honest fellow," replied Raoul, taking a pistole from his pocket.

"Ten kicks on his back!" said d'Artagnan; "be off, you little rascal, and forget not that I have your address."

Friquet, who did not expect to be let off so easily, made but one spring to the Quai à la Rue Dauphine, and disappeared. Raoul mounted his horse, and both leisurely proceeded to the Rue Tiquetonne.

D'Artagnan protected the youth as if he were his own son.

They arrived without accident at the Hôtel de la Chevrette.

The beautiful Madeleine announced to d'Artagnan that Planchet had returned, bringing Mousqueton with him, who had heroically borne the extraction of the ball, and was as well as his state would permit.

D'Artagnan desired Planchet to be summoned, but he had disappeared.

"Then bring some wine," said d'Artagnan. "You are much pleased with yourself?" said he to Raoul, when they were alone, "are you not?"

"Well, yes," replied Raoul; "it appears to me that I did my duty. I defended the king."

"And who told you to defend the king?"

"The Count de la Fère himself!"

"Yes, the king; but to-day you have not fought for the king, you have fought for Mazarin; it is not quite the same thing."

"But you yourself?"

"Oh, for me; it is another matter. I obey my captain's orders. As for you, your captain is the prince. Understand that rightly; you have no other. But has one ever seen such a wild fellow," continued he, "making himself a Mazarinist, and helping to arrest Broussel! Breathe not a word of that, or the Count de la Fère will be furious."

"You think that the count will be angry with me?"

"Do I think it?—I am sure of it; were it not for that, I should thank you, for you have worked for us. However, I scold you instead of him, and in his place; the storm will blow over more easily, believe me. And, moreover, my dear lad," continued d'Artagnan, "I am making use of the privilege conceded to me by your guardian."

"I do not understand you, sir," said Raoul.

D'Artagnan rose, and taking a letter from his writing-desk, presented it to Raoul. The face of the latter became serious when he had cast his eyes on the paper.

"Oh, *mon Dieu!*" he said, lifting his fine eyes to d'Artagnan, moist with tears, "the count has then left Paris without seeing me?"

"He left four days ago," said d'Artagnan.

"But his letter seems to intimate that he is about to incur danger, perhaps of death."

"He—he—incur danger of death!—no—be not anxious; he is travelling on business, and will return before long. I hope you have no repugnance to accept me as a guardian in the interim?"

"Oh, no, Monsieur d'Artagnan," said Raoul, "you are such a brave gentleman, and the Count de la Fère has so much affection for you!"

"Eh, egad! love me too; I will not torment you much, but only on condition that you become a Frondist, my young friend, and a hearty Frondist, too."

"Well, sir, I will obey you, although I do not understand you."

"It is unnecessary for you to understand; hold," continued d'Artagnan, turning towards the door, which had just opened, "here is Monsieur du Valon, who comes with his coat torn."

"Yes, but in exchange," said Porthos, covered with perspiration and soiled in dust—"in exchange I have torn many skins. Those wretches wanted to take away my sword! Deuce take 'em, what a popular commotion!" continued the giant, in his quiet manner; "but I knocked down more than twenty with the hilt of Balizarde. A glass of wine, d'Artagnan."

"Oh, I'll answer for you," said the Gascon, filling Porthos's glass to the brim, "but, when you have drunk, give me your opinion."

"Upon what?" asked Porthos.

"Look here," resumed d'Artagnan; "here is Vicomte de Bragelonne, who determined, at all risks, to aid the arrest of Broussel, and whom I had great difficulty to prevent defending Monsieur de Comminges."

"The deuce! and the count, what would he have said to that?"

"Do you hear?" said d'Artagnan; "be a Frondist, my friend; belong to the Fronde, and remember that I fill the count's place in everything;" and he jingled his money.

"Will you come?" said he to Porthos.

"Where to?" asked Porthos, filling a second glass of wine.

"To present our respects to the Cardinal."

Porthos swallowed the second glass with the same ease with which he had drunk the first, took his hat, and followed d'Artagnan. As for Raoul, he remained bewildered with what he had seen, having been forbidden by d'Artagnan to leave the room until the disturbance was over.

45

THE BEGGAR AT THE CHURCH OF ST. EUSTACHE

D'ARTAGNAN had calculated that in not going at once to the Palais Royal he would give time to Comminges to arrive there before him, and consequently to make the Cardinal acquainted with the eminent services which he, d'Artagnan and his friend, had rendered to the queen in the morning.

They were indeed cordially received by Mazarin, who paid them numerous compliments, and announced that they were more than half on their way to obtain what they desired, namely, d'Artagnan his captaincy, and Porthos his barony.

Whilst the two friends were with the Cardinal, the queen sent for him. Mazarin, thinking that it would be the means of increasing the zeal of his two defenders if he procured them personal thanks from the queen, motioned to them to follow him. D'Artagnan and Porthos pointed to their dusty and torn dresses, but the Cardinal shook his head.

"Those costumes," he said, "are of more worth than most of those which you will see on the queen's courtiers; they are the costumes of true soldiers."

D'Artagnan and Porthos proudly obeyed. The court of Anne of Austria was full of gaiety and animation; for, after having secured a conquest over the Spaniards, it had just gained a victory over the people. Broussel had been conducted out of Paris without resistance, and was at this time in the prison of St. Germain; and Blancmesnil, who was arrested at the same time, but whose arrest had been made without difficulty or noise, was safe in the Castle of Vincennes.

Comminges was near the queen, who was questioning him upon the details of his expedition, and every one was listening to his account, when d'Artagnan and Porthos were perceived at the door behind the Cardinal.

"Eh, madame," said Comminges, approaching d'Artagnan, "here is one who can tell you far better than myself, for he is my protector. Without him I should probably, at this moment, be caught in the nets of St. Cloud, for it was a question of nothing less than throwing me into the river. Speak, d'Artagnan, speak."

D'Artagnan had been a hundred times in the same room with

the queen since he had become lieutenant of the musketeers, but
her majesty had never once spoken to him.

"Well, sir," at last said Anne of Austria, "you are silent, after
rendering such a service?"

"Madame," replied d'Artagnan, "I have nothing to say, but
that my life is ever at your majesty's service; and that I shall only
be happy the day that I lose it for you."

"I know that, sir; I have known that," said the queen, "a long
time; therefore I am delighted to be able thus publicly to mark
my gratitude and my esteem."

"Permit me, madame," said d'Artagnan, "to reserve a portion
for my friend; like myself"—(he laid an emphasis on these words)
—"an old musketeer of the company of Tréville, and he has done
wonders."

"His name?" asked the queen.

"In the regiment," said d'Artagnan, "he is called Porthos"
(the queen started), "but his true name is the Chevalier du
Valon."

"De Bracieux de Pierrefonds," added Porthos.

"These names are too numerous for me to remember, and I will
content myself with the first," said the queen graciously. Porthos
bowed. At this moment the Coadjutor was announced; a cry of
wonder ran through the royal assemblage. Although the Coadjutor
had preached that same morning, it was well known that he
inclined much to the side of the Fronde; and Mazarin, in requesting the Archbishop of Paris to make his nephew preach, had
evidently the intention of administering to Monsieur de Retz one
of those Italian knocks which he so much enjoyed giving.

The fact was, in leaving Notre Dame the Coadjutor had learnt
the event of the day. Although almost engaged to the leaders of
the Fronde, he had not gone so far but that retreat was possible,
should the court offer him the advantages for which he was
ambitious, and to which the Coadjutorship was but a stepping-
stone. Monsieur de Retz wished to be archbishop in his uncle's
place, and cardinal, like Mazarin; and the popular party
could with difficulty accord to him favours so entirely royal. He,
therefore, hastened to the palace to congratulate the queen
on the battle of Lens, determined beforehand to act with or
against the court, according as his congratulations were well or
ill received.

The Coadjutor had, perhaps, in his own person, as much wit as
all those together who were assembled at the court to laugh at
him. His speech, therefore, was so well turned, that in spite of the
great wish felt by the courtiers to laugh, they could find no way in

which to vent their ridicule. He ended by saying that he placed his feeble influence at her majesty's command.

During the whole time that he was speaking the queen appeared to be well pleased with the Coadjutor's address; but terminating as it did with such a phrase, the only one which could be caught at by the jokers, Anne turned round and directed a glance towards her favourites, which announced that she had delivered up the Coadjutor to their tender mercies. Immediately the wits of the court plunged into irony. Nogent-Beautin, the fool of the court, exclaimed that "the queen was very happy to have the succour of religion at such a moment." This caused a universal burst of laughter. The Count de Villeroy said "that he did not know how any fear could be entertained for a moment when the court had, to defend itself against the parliament and the citizens of Paris, his holiness the Coadjutor, who by a signal could raise an army of curates, church porters, and vergers;" and so on.

During this storm, Gondy, who had it in his power to make it fatal to the jesters, remained calm and stern. The queen at last asked him if he had anything to add to the fine discourse which he had just made to her.

"Yes, madame," replied the Coadjutor; "I have to beg you to reflect twice ere you cause a civil war in the kingdom."

The queen turned her back, and the laughter recommenced.

The Coadjutor bowed and left the palace, casting upon the Cardinal such a glance as is best understood between deadly foes.

"Oh!" murmured Gondy, as he left the threshold of the palace, "ungrateful court! faithless court! cowardly court! I will teach you how to laugh to-morrow—but in another manner."

But whilst they were indulging in extravagant joy at the Palais Royal, to increase the hilarity of the queen, Mazarin, a man of sense, and whose fear, moreover, gave him foresight, lost no time in making idle and dangerous jokes; he left after the Coadjutor, settled his account, locked up his gold, and had confidential workmen to contrive hiding-places in his walls.

On his return home the Coadjutor was informed that a young man had come in after his departure, and was waiting for him; he started with delight when, on demanding the name of this young man, he learned that it was Louvières.

He immediately went to his apartment, and advancing towards him, held out his hand. The young man looked at him as if he would have read the secret of his heart.

"My dear Monsieur Louvières," said the Coadjutor, "believe me how truly concerned I am for the misfortune which has happened to you."

"Is that true, and do you speak sincerely?" asked Louvières.

"From the depth of my heart," said Gondy.

"In that case, my lord, the time for words has passed, and the hour for action has arrived. My lord, in three days, if you wish it, my father will be out of prison, and in six months you may be Cardinal."

The Coadjutor started.

"Oh! let us speak candidly," continued Louvières, "and act in a straightforward manner. Thirty thousand crowns in alms is not given—as you have done for the last six months—out of pure Christian charity; that would be too grand. You are ambitious, that is natural; you are a man of genius, and you know your worth. As for me, I hate the court, and have but one desire at this moment—it is for revenge. Give us the clergy and the people, of whom you can dispose, and I will bring you the citizens and the parliament: with these four elements Paris is ours in a week; and believe me, Monsieur Coadjutor, the court will give from fear what it will not give from good-will."

It was now the Coadjutor's turn to fix his piercing glance on Louvières.

"But Monsieur Louvières, are you aware that it is simply civil war that you propose to me?"

"You have been preparing it long enough, my lord, for it to be welcome to you now."

"Never mind," said the Coadjutor; "you must know that this requires reflection."

"And how many hours of reflection do you ask?"

"Twelve hours, sir; is it too long?"

"It is now noon: at midnight I will return."

"If I am not in, wait for me."

"Good! at midnight, my lord."

"At midnight, my dear Monsieur Louvières."

When once more alone, Gondy sent for all the curates with whom he had any connection, to attend his house. Two hours later, thirty officiating ministers from the most populous, and consequently the most disturbed, parishes of Paris, had assembled together there. Gondy related to them the insults he had received at the Palais Royal, and detailed the jests of Beautin, Count de Villeroy, and the Maréchal de la Meilleraie. The curates demanded what was to be done.

"Simply this," said the Coadjutor; "you are the directors of consciences. Well, undermine in them the miserable prejudice of respect and fear of kings. Teach to your flocks that the queen is a tyrant; and repeat, often and loudly, so that all may know it, that the misfortunes of France are caused by Mazarin, her lover and her destroyer. Begin this work to-day, this instant even, and in three days I shall expect the result. For the rest, if any one of you have good advice to give me, I shall listen to him with pleasure."

Three curates remained: those of St. Merri, St. Sulpice, and St. Eustache.

"You think, then, that you can help me more efficaciously than your brothers?" said Gondy.

"We hope so," answered the curates.

"Let us hear. Monsieur de St. Merri, you begin."

"My lord, I have in my parish a man who might be of extreme service to you."

"What is this man?"

"A shopkeeper in the Rue des Lombards, who has great influence upon the tradespeople of this quarter."

"What is his name?"

"He is named Planchet, who himself also caused a commotion about six weeks ago; but when he was searched for after this disturbance, he had disappeared."

"And could you find him?"

"I hope so. I think he has not been arrested, and as I am his wife's confessor, if she knows where he is, I shall know it too."

"Very well, sir; find this man, and when you have found him, bring him to me."

"We will be with you at six o'clock, my lord."

"Depart, my dear curate, and may God aid you!"

"And you, sir," continued Gondy, turning to the curate of St. Sulpice.

"I, my lord," said the latter, "I know a man who has rendered great service to a very popular prince, and who would make an excellent leader of a revolt, and whom I can put at your disposal; it is Count de Rochefort."

"I know him also, but unfortunately he is not in Paris."

"My lord, he has been for three days at the Rue Cassette."

"And wherefore has he not been to see me?"

"He was told—my lord will pardon me——?"

"Certainly; speak."

"That your lordship was on the point of treating with the court." Gondy bit his lips.

"They are mistaken; bring him here at eight o'clock, sir, and may Heaven bless you as I bless you!"

"And now 'tis your turn," said the Coadjutor, turning to the curate of St. Eustache, "have you anything as good to offer me as the two gentlemen who have left us?"

"Better, my lord."

"Faith! think what a solemn engagement you are making there; one has offered a shopkeeper, the other a count; you are going, then, to offer a prince, are you?"

"I offer you a beggar, my lord."

"Ah! ah!" said Gondy, reflecting, "you are right, sir; some one who could raise an army of paupers who choke up the crossings of Paris, some one who would know how to cry aloud to them, that all France might hear it, that it is Mazarin who has reduced them to the wallet——"

"Exactly your man."

"Bravo! and what is he?"

"A simple beggar, as I have said, my lord, who solicits alms, as he gives holy water, a practice he has carried on for about six years on the steps of the Church of St. Eustache."

"And you say that he has a great influence over his compeers?"

"Are you aware, my lord, that mendicity is an organised body, a kind of association of those who have not, against those who have; an association in which every one takes his share, and which elects a leader."

"Yes, I have heard that said," replied the Coadjutor.

"Well, the man whom I offer to you is a general authority."

"And what do you know of him?"

"Nothing, my lord, except that he is tormented with remorse."

"What makes you think so?"

"On the twenty-eighth of every month, he makes me say a mass for the repose of the soul of a person who died a violent death; yesterday I said this mass again."

"And his name?"

"Maillard; but I do not think it is his true name."

"And think you that we should find him at this hour at his post?"

"Yes, my lord."

"Let us go and see this beggar, sir, and if he is such as you describe him, you are right: it will be you who have found the true treasure."

Gondy dressed himself as an officer, put on a felt cap with a red feather, hung on a long sword, buckled spurs to his boots, wrapped himself in an ample cloak, and followed the curate.

On arriving at the Rue des Prouvaires, the curate pointed towards the square before the church.

"Stop!" he said, "there he is at his post."

Gondy looked at the spot indicated, and perceived a beggar seated in a chair, and leaning against one of the mouldings; a little basin was near him, and he held a holy-water brush in his hand.

"Is it by permission that he remains there?" asked Gondy.

"No, my lord; these places are bought and sold; I think that this man paid his predecessor a hundred pistoles for his."

"The rascal is rich, then?"

"Some of these men die worth twenty thousand, and twenty-five, and thirty thousand francs, and sometimes more."

"Hum!" said Gondy, laughing; "I was not aware that my alms were so well invested."

In the meantime they were advancing towards the square, and the moment the Coadjutor and the curate put their feet on the first church step, the mendicant rose and proffered his brush.

He was a man between sixty-six and sixty-eight years of age, short, rather stout, with grey hair, and light eyes. His countenance denoted the struggle between two opposite principles—a wicked nature subdued by determination, perhaps by repentance.

He started on seeing the Coadjutor with the curate. The latter and his companion touched the brush with the tips of their fingers and made the sign of the cross; the Coadjutor threw a piece of money into the hat, which was on the ground.

"Maillard," began the curate, "this gentleman and I have come to talk with you a little."

"With me!" said the mendicant; "it is a great honour for a simple giver of holy water."

There was an ironical tone in his voice, which he could not quite prevent, and which astonished the Coadjutor.

"Yes," continued the curate, apparently accustomed to his tone, "yes, we wish to know your opinion of the events of to-day, and what you have heard said by people going in and out of the church."

The mendicant shook his head.

"These are melancholy doings, your reverence, which always fall again upon the poor people. As to what is said, everybody is discontented—everybody complains—but——"

"Explain yourself, my good friend," said the Coadjutor.

"I mean that all these cries, all these complaints, these curses, produce nothing but storms and flashes, and that is all; but the lightning will not strike until there is a hand to guide it."

"My friend," said Gondy, "you seem to be a clever man; are you disposed to take a part in a little civil war, should we have one, and put at the command of the leader—should we find one—your personal influence, and the influence you have acquired over your comrades?"

"Yes, sir, provided this war was approved by the Church, and would advance the end I wish to attain—I mean the remission of my sins."

"This war will not only be approved of, but directed by the Church. As for the remission of your sins, we have the Archbishop of Paris, who has great power at the court of Rome, and even the Coadjutor, who possesses some particular indulgences—we will recommend you to him. And do you think your power as great with your fraternity as this reverend gentleman told me it was just now?"

"I think they have some esteem for me," said the mendicant, with pride, "and not only they will obey me, but that, wherever I go, they will follow me."

"And could you count upon fifty resolute men, from the un-employed, good, but active souls capable of bringing down the walls of the Palais Royal by crying 'Down with Mazarin,' as fell all those at Jericho?"

"I am certain," said the beggar, "that I can undertake things even more difficult, and more important than that."

"Ah, ha," said Gondy, "you will undertake, then, some night, to throw up some ten barricades."

"I will undertake to throw up fifty, and when the day comes to defend them."

"I'faith!" exclaimed Gondy, "you speak with a certainty that affords me pleasure; and since our reverend friend can answer for you——"

"I answer for him," said the curate.

"Here is a bag containing five hundred pistoles in gold. Make all your arrangements, and tell me where I shall be able to find you this evening at ten o'clock."

"It must be on some elevated place, whence a given signal may be seen in every quarter of Paris."

"Shall I give you a line for the Vicar of St. Jacques-de-la-Boucherie? he will let you into the rooms in his tower," said the curate.

"Capital," answered the beggar.

"Then," said the Coadjutor, "this evening, at ten o'clock; and if I am pleased with you, another bag of five hundred pistoles will be at your disposal."

The eyes of the mendicant flashed with cupidity, but he suppressed this emotion.

"This evening, sir," he replied, "all will be ready." And he carried his chair into the church, set his pail and sprinkler near the chair, went and took some holy water from the large receptacle as if he had no confidence in his own, and left the church.

46

THE TOWER OF ST. JACQUES-DE-LA-BOUCHERIE

AT a quarter to six o'clock, Monsieur de Gondy, having finished all his business, returned to the ecclesiastical palace.

At six o'clock the curate of St. Merri was announced.

The Coadjutor glanced rapidly behind and saw that he was followed by another man. The curate then entered, and with him, Planchet.

"Your holiness," said the curate, "here is the person of whom I had the honour of speaking to you."

"And you are disposed to serve the cause of the people?" asked Gondy.

"Most assuredly," said Planchet. "I am a Frondist from my heart. You see in me, such as I am, my lord, a person condemned to be hung."

"And on what account?"

"I rescued from the hands of Mazarin's police a noble lord, whom they were conducting again to the Bastille, where he had been for five years."

"Will you name him?"

"Oh, you know him well, my lord; it is Count de Rochefort."

"Ah! really, yes," said the Coadjutor, "I have heard this affair mentioned. You raised the whole district, they told me?"

"Very nearly," replied Planchet, with a self-satisfied air.

"And your business is——"

"That of a confectioner, in the Rue des Lombards."

"Tell me how it happens that, following so peaceful an occupation, you partake of such warlike inclinations."

"Why does my lord, belonging to the Church, now receive me in the dress of an officer, with a sword at his side and spurs to his boots?"

"Not badly answered, i'faith," laughed Gondy; "but I have, you must know, always had, in spite of my bands, warlike inclinations."

"Well, my lord, before I became a confectioner, I myself was three years sergeant in the Piedmontese regiment, and before I became sergeant I was for eighteen months the servant of Monsieur d'Artagnan."

"The lieutenant of the musketeers?" asked Gondy.

"Himself, my lord."

"But he is said to be a furious Mazarinist."

"Pshaw!"

"What do you mean by that?"

"Nothing, my lord; Monsieur d'Artagnan belongs to the service; Monsieur d'Artagnan makes it his business to defend the Cardinal, who pays him, as much as we make it ours—we citizens —to attack him, whom he robs."

"You are intelligent, my good friend; can we count upon you?"

"You may count upon me, my lord, provided you wish to make a total revolt of our citizens."

"'Tis that exactly. How many men, think you, you could collect together to-night?"

"Two hundred muskets, and five hundred halberds."

"Let there be only one man in every district who can do as much, and by to-morrow we shall have a tolerably strong army. Are you disposed to obey Count de Rochefort?"

"I would follow him to Hades; and that is not saying a little, as I believe him quite capable of descending there."

"Bravo!"

"By what sign to-morrow shall we be able to distinguish friends from foes?"

"Every Frondist must put a knot of straw in his hat."

"Good. Give the watchword."

"Do you want money?"

"Money never comes amiss at any time, my lord; if one has it not, one must do without it; but with it matters go on much better, and more rapidly."

Gondy went to a box and drew forth a bag.

"Here are five hundred pistoles," he said; "and if the action goes off well you may reckon on a similar sum to-morrow."

"I will give a faithful account of the sum to your lordship," said Planchet, putting the bag under his arm.

"That is right: I recommend the Cardinal to your attention."

"Make your mind easy, he is in good hands."

Planchet went out, and ten minutes later the curate of St. Sulpice was announced. As soon as the door of Gondy's study was opened, a man rushed in; it was Count de Rochefort.

"It is you, then, my dear count," cried Gondy, offering his hand.

"You are decided at last, my lord?" said Rochefort.

"I have ever been so," said Gondy.

"Let us speak no more on that subject: you tell me so—I believe you. Well, we are going to give a ball to Mazarin."

"I hope so."

"And when will the dance begin?"

"The invitations are given for this evening," said the Coadjutor, "but the music will only begin to play to-morrow morning."

"You may reckon upon me, and upon fifty soldiers which the Chevalier d'Humières has promised to me, whenever I might need them."

"Upon fifty soldiers?"

"Yes, he is making recruits, and he will lend them to me; if any are missing, when the fête is over, I shall replace them."

"Good, my dear Rochefort; but that is not all. What have you done with Monsieur de Beaufort?"

"He is in Vendôme, where he waits until I write to him to return to Paris."

"Write to him—now's the time."

"You are quite sure of your enterprise?"

"Yes, but he must hurry himself;—for hardly shall the people of Paris have revolted, than we shall have ten other princes wishing to be at their head: if he defers, he will find the place taken."

"And you will leave all command to him?"

"For the war, yes; but in politics——"

"You know it is not his element."

"He must leave me to negotiate for my cardinal's hat in my own way."

"You care for it so much?"

"Since they force me to wear a hat of a shape which does not become me," said Gondy, "I wish at least that the hat should be red."

"One must not dispute taste and colours," said Rochefort, smiling. "I answer for his consent."

"How soon can he be here?"

"In five days."

"Let him come, and he will find a change. I will answer for it. Therefore, go and collect your fifty men, and hold yourself in readiness."

"For what?"

"For everything."

"Is there any signal for rallying?"

"A knot of straw in the hat."

"Very good. Adieu, my lord."

"*Adieu*, my dear Rochefort."

"Ah! Monsieur Mazarin, Monsieur Mazarin!" said Rochefort, leading off his curate, who had not found an opportunity of uttering a single word during the foregoing dialogue, "you will see whether I am too old to be a man of action!"

It was half-past nine o'clock, and the Coadjutor required half an hour to go from the Archbishop's palace to the tower of St. Jacques-de-la-Boucherie. He remarked that a light was burning in one of the highest windows of the tower. "Good," said he, "our friend is at his post."

He knocked, and the door was opened.

The vicar himself awaited him, conducted him to the top of the tower, and when there pointed to a little door, placed the light which he had brought with him in a corner of the wall, that the Coadjutor might be able to find it on his return, and went down again. Although the key was in the door, the Coadjutor knocked.

"Come in," said a voice which he recognised as that of the mendicant, whom he found lying on a kind of truckle bed. He rose on the entrance of the Coadjutor, and at that moment ten o'clock struck.

"Well," said Gondy, "have you kept your word with me?"

"Not quite," replied the mendicant.

"How is that?"

"You asked me for five hundred men, did you not? Well, I shall have ten thousand for you."

"You are not boasting?"

"Do you wish me to prove it?"

"Well,—it would be as well."

There were three candles alight—each of which burned before a window—one looking upon the city, the other upon the Palais Royal, and a third upon the Rue St. Denis.

The man went silently to each of the candles, and blew them out one after the other.

"What are you about?" asked the Coadjutor.

"I have given the signal."

"For what?"

"For the barricades. When you leave this, you will see my men at their work. Only take care not to break your legs in stumbling over some chain, nor to fall into some hole."

"Good! there is your money,—a similar sum as that which you have received already. Now remember that you are a general, and do not go and drink."

"For twenty years I have tasted nothing but water."

The man took the bag from the hands of the Coadjutor, who heard the sound of his fingers counting and handling the gold pieces.

"Ah! ah!" said the Coadjutor, "you are avaricious, my good friend."

The mendicant sighed, and threw down the bag.

"Must I always be the same," said he, "and shall I never succeed in overcoming the old leaven? Oh, misery, oh, vanity!"

"You take it, however."

"Yes, but I make a vow in your presence, to employ all that remains to me in good works."

His face was pale and drawn, like that of a man who had just undergone an inward struggle.

"Singular man!" muttered Gondy, taking his hat to go away, when he saw the beggar between him and the door. His first idea was that this man intended to do him a mischief—but on the contrary, he fell on his knees before him, with his hands clasped.

"Your blessing, your holiness, before you leave, I beseech you!" he cried.

"Your holiness!" said Gondy; "my friend, you take me for some one else."

"No, your holiness, I take you for what you are; that is to say, the Coadjutor. I recognised you from the first."

Gondy smiled—"And you want my blessing?" he said.

"Yes, I have need of it."

The mendicant uttered these words in a tone of such great humility, and such earnest repentance, that Gondy placed his hand upon him, and gave him his benediction with all the unction of which he was capable.

"Now," said the Coadjutor, "there is a communion between us. I have blessed you, and you are sacred to me. Come, have you committed some crime, pursued by human justice, from which I can protect you?"

The beggar shook his head. "The crime which I have committed, my lord, has no call upon human justice, and you can only deliver me from it in blessing me frequently, as you have just done."

"Come, answer me truthfully," said the Coadjutor, "you have not all your life followed the trade which you do now?"

"No, my lord. I have pursued it for six years only."

"And, previously, where were you?"

"In the Bastille."

"And before you went to the Bastille?"

"I will tell you, my lord, on the day when you are willing to hear my confession."

"Good! at whatever hour of the day or of the night on which you present yourself, remember that I shall be ready to afford you absolution."

"Thank you, my lord," said the mendicant in a hoarse voice, "but I am not yet ready to receive it."

"Very well. Adieu."

"*Adieu*, your holiness," said the mendicant, opening the door, and bending low before the prelate.

47

THE RIOT

IT was about eleven o'clock at night. Gondy had not walked a hundred steps ere he perceived the strange change which had been made in the streets of Paris.

The whole city seemed peopled with fantastic creatures; silent shadows were seen unpaving the streets, and others dragging and upsetting great waggons, whilst others again dug ditches large enough to engulf whole regiments of horsemen. These active beings flitted here and there like so many demons completing some unknown labour—these were the beggars of the Court of Miracles—the agents of the giver of holy water in the square of St. Eustache—preparing the barricades for the morrow.

Gondy looked on these men of darkness—these nocturnal labourers, with a kind of fear: he questioned if, after having called forth these foul creatures from their dens, he should have the power of making them retire again. He felt almost inclined to cross himself when one of them chanced to approach him. He reached the Rue St. Honoré, and went towards the Rue de la Ferronière: there, the aspect was changed; here it was the trades-men who were running from shop to shop. Their doors seemed closed like their shutters; but they were only pushed to in such a manner as to open and allow the men, who seemed fearful of showing what they carried, to enter, closing immediately. These men were shopkeepers, who had arms to lend to those who had none.

One individual went from door to door, bending under the weight of swords, guns, muskets, and every kind of weapon, which he deposited as fast as he could. By the aid of a lantern the Coadjutor recognised Planchet.

On reaching the Pont Neuf, the Coadjutor found this bridge guarded, and a man approached him.

"Who are you?" asked the man; "I do not know you for one of us."

"Then it is because you do not know your friends, my dear Monsieur Louvières," said the Coadjutor, raising his hat.

Louvières recognised him and bowed.

Gondy continued his way, and went as far as the Tour de Nesle. There he saw a long line of people gliding under the walls. They might be said to be a procession of ghosts, for they were all wrapped in white cloaks. When they reached a certain spot, these men seemed to sink into nothingness, one after the other, as if the earth had opened under their feet. Gondy moved into a corner, saw them vanish from the first until the last but one. The last raised his eyes, to ascertain doubtless that neither his companions nor himself had been observed, and in spite of the darkness he perceived Gondy. He walked straight up to him, and placed a pistol to his head.

"Holloa, Monsieur de Rochefort," said Gondy, laughing, "do not play with firearms."

Rochefort recognised the voice.

"Ah, it is you, my lord," said he.

"Myself. What people are you leading thus into the bowels of the earth?"

"My fifty recruits from the Chevalier d'Humières, who are destined to enter the light cavalry, and who have only received for their equipment their white cloaks."

"And where are you going?"

"To one of my friends, a sculptor, only we descend by the trap through which he lets down his marble."

"Very good," said Gondy, shaking Rochefort by the hand, who descended in his turn, and closed the trap after him.

It was now one o'clock in the morning, and the Coadjutor went home. He opened a window and leant out to listen. A strange, incomprehensible, unearthly sound seemed to pervade the whole city; one felt that something unusual and terrible was happening in all the streets, now dark as abysses.

The work of revolt continued the whole night thus. The next morning, on awaking, Paris seemed to be startled at her own appearance. It was like a besieged town. Armed men, shouldering muskets, watched over the barricades with menacing looks; words of command, patrols, arrests, floggings even, were encountered at every step. Those bearing plumed hats and gold swords were stopped and made to cry, "Long live Broussel!" "Down with Mazarin!" and whoever refused to comply with this ceremony was hooted at, spat upon, and even beaten. They had not yet begun to slay, but it was well felt that the inclination to do so was not wanting.

The barricades extended as far as the Palais Royal, and the astonishment of Mazarin and of Anne of Austria was great when they were informed that the city, which the previous evening they had seen tranquil, had awakened so feverish and in such commotion; nor would either the one or the other believe the reports which were brought to them, and declared that they would rely on the evidence of their own eyes and ears. Then a window was opened, and when they saw and heard, they were convinced.

Mazarin shrugged his shoulders, and affected to despise the populace; but he turned visibly pale, and ran trembling to his closet, locked up his gold and jewels in his caskets, and put his finest rings on his fingers. As for the queen, furious, and left to her own guidance, she sent for the Maréchal de la Meilleraie, and desired him to take as many men as he pleased, and to go and see what was the cause of the commotion.

We have already said that Mazarin was in his closet, putting his affairs into order. He called for d'Artagnan, but in the midst of such tumult he little expected to see him, d'Artagnan not being on service.

In about ten minutes d'Artagnan appeared at the door, followed by Porthos.

"Ah, come—come in, Monsieur d'Artagnan," cried the Cardinal, "and be welcome, as well as your friend. But what is going on, then, in this accursed Paris?"

"What is going on, my lord? nothing good," replied d'Artagnan, shaking his head: "the town is in open revolt; and just now, as I was crossing the Rue Montorgueil with Monsieur du Valon, who is here, and is your humble servant, they wanted, in spite of my uniform, or, perhaps, because of my uniform, to make us cry, 'Long live Broussel!' and must I tell you, my lord, what they wished us to cry as well?"

"Speak, speak."

"'Down with Mazarin!' I'faith, it is out now."

Mazarin smiled, but became very pale.

"And you did cry?" he asked.

"I'faith, no," said d'Artagnan, "I was not in voice; Monsieur du Valon has a cold, and did not cry either. Then, my lord——"

"Then what?" asked Mazarin.

"Look at my hat and cloak."

And d'Artagnan displayed four gun-shot holes in his cloak and two in his headgear. As for Porthos' coat, a blow from a halberd had cut it open on one side, and a pistol-shot had split his feather in two.

"Faith!" said the Cardinal pensively, gazing at the two friends with lively admiration; "I should have cried, I should."

At this moment the tumult was heard nearer.

Mazarin wiped his forehead and looked around him. He had a strong desire to go to the window, but he dared not.

"See what is going on, Monsieur d'Artagnan," said he.

D'Artagnan went to the window, with his habitual composure.

"Oh, oh!" said he, "what is that? Maréchal de la Meilleraie returning without a hat, Fontrailles with his arm in a sling, wounded guards, horses bleeding, eh, then, what are the sentinels about? they are aiming; they are going to fire!"

"They have received orders to fire on the people, if they approach the Palais Royal!" exclaimed Mazarin.

"But if they fire, all is lost!" cried d'Artagnan.

"We have the gates."

"The gates! to hold for five minutes—the gates, they will be torn down, bent, ground to powder! Good Lord, don't fire!" screamed d'Artagnan, throwing open the window.

In spite of this recommendation, which, owing to the noise, could not have been heard, two or three musket-shots resounded, which was succeeded by a terrible discharge. The balls might be heard pounding the façade of the Palais Royal, and one of them, passing under d'Artagnan's arm, entered and broke a mirror, in which Porthos was complacently admiring himself.

"Alack, alack," cried the Cardinal; "a Venetian glass!"

"Oh, my lord," said d'Artagnan, quietly shutting the window, "it is not worth while weeping yet, for probably an hour hence there will not be one of your mirrors remaining in the Palais Royal, whether they be Venetian or Parisian."

"But what do you advise, then?" asked Mazarin, trembling.

"Eh, egad, to give up Broussel, as they demand! What the devil do you want with a member of the parliament? He is of no use for anything."

"And you, Monsieur du Valon, is that your advice? What would you do?"

"I should give up Broussel."

"Come, come with me, gentlemen!" exclaimed Mazarin. "I will go and discuss the matter with the queen."

He stopped at the end of the corridor, and said:

"I can rely upon you, gentlemen, can I not?"

"We do not give ourselves twice over," said d'Artagnan; "we have given ourselves to you—command, we shall obey."

"Very well, then," said Mazarin; "come into this closet and wait there."

And turning away, he entered the drawing-room by another door.

48

THE RIOT BECOMES AN INSURRECTION

THE room into which d'Artagnan and Porthos had been ushered was divided from the drawing-room where the queen was by tapestry curtains only, and this thin partition enabled them to hear all that passed in the adjoining room, while the aperture between the two hangings, small as it was, permitted them to see.

The queen was standing in the room, pale with anger; her self-control, however, was so great that it might have been supposed that she was calm. Comminges, Villequier, and Guitant were behind her, and the women again were behind the gentlemen. The Chancellor Séguier, who twenty years previously had persecuted her so violently, was before her, relating how his carriage had been broken, how he had been pursued, and had rushed into the Hôtel d'C——, that the hotel was immediately invested, pillaged, and devastated: happily, he had time to reach a closet hidden behind tapestry, in which he was secreted by an old woman, together with his brother, the Bishop of Meaux. Happily, however, he had not been taken; the people, believing that he had escaped by some back entrance, had retired, and left him to retreat at liberty. Then, disguised in the clothes of the Marquis d'C—— he had left the hotel, stumbling over the bodies of an officer and those of two guards who were killed whilst defending the street door.

During the recital Mazarin entered and glided noiselessly up to the queen to listen.

"Well," said the queen, when the chancellor had finished speaking; "what do you think of it all?"

"I think that matters look very gloomy, madame."

"But what advice do you offer me?"

"I could advise your majesty—but I dare not."

"You may, you may, sir," said the queen, with a bitter smile; "you were not so timid once."

The chancellor reddened, and stammered out a few words.

"It is not a question of the past, but of the present," said the queen; "you said you could give me advice—what is it?"

"Madame," said the chancellor, hesitating, "it would be to release Broussel."

The queen, although already pale, became even more so, and her face was contracted.

"Release Broussel!" she cried, "no; it is too much."

At this moment steps were heard in the anteroom, and, without any announcement, the Maréchal de la Meilleraie appeared at the door.

"Ah, there you are, maréchal," cried Anne of Austria joyfully. "I hope you have brought this rabble to reason."

"Madame," replied the maréchal, "I have left three men on the Pont Neuf, four at the Halle, six at the corner of the Rue de l'Arbre-Sec, and two at the door of your palace—fifteen in all. I have brought away ten or twelve wounded. I know not where I have left my hat, and in all probability I should have been left with my hat, had the Coadjutor not arrived in time to rescue me."

"Ah, indeed!" said the queen, "it would have astonished me if that low fellow, with his distorted legs, had not been mixed up with it."

"Madame," said La Meilleraie, "do not say too much against him before me, for the service he rendered me is still fresh."

"Very good," said the queen, "be as grateful as you like, it does not matter to me; you are here safe and sound, that is all I wished for, therefore you are not only welcome, but welcome back."

"Yes, madame; but I only came back on one condition—that I would transmit to your majesty the will of the people."

"The will!" exclaimed the queen, frowning. "Oh! oh! Monsieur Maréchal, you must indeed have found yourself in great peril to have undertaken so strange a commission!"

The irony with which these words were uttered did not escape the maréchal.

"Pardon, madame," he said, "I am not a lawyer, I am a mere soldier, and probably, therefore, I do not quite comprehend the value of certain expressions; I ought to have said the wishes, and not the will, of the people. As for what you do me the honour to say, I presume that you mean that I felt fear."

The queen smiled.

"Well, then, madame, yes, I did feel fear; and though I have seen twelve pitched battles, and I know not how many fights and skirmishes, I own that, for the third time in my life, I was afraid. Yes; and I would rather face your majesty, however threatening your smile, than face those hell-demons who accompanied me hither, and who sprang from I know not where."

"Bravo," said d'Artagnan, in a whisper to Porthos; "boldly put."

"Well," said the queen, biting her lips, whilst her courtiers looked at each other with surprise, "what is the desire of my people?"

"That Broussel should be given up to them, madame."

"Never!" said the queen, "never!"

"Your majesty is mistress," said La Meilleraie, retreating a few steps.

"Where are you going, maréchal?" asked the queen.

"To give your majesty's reply to those who await it."

"Stay, maréchal; surely it is beneath the dignity of a queen to treat with rebellious subjects?"

"Madame, I have given my word; and unless you order me to be arrested, I shall be forced to return."

Anne of Austria's eyes glittered fiercely.

"Oh! that is no impediment, sir," said she; "I have had greater men than you arrested.—Guitant!"

Mazarin sprang forward.

"Madame," said he, "if I dared in my turn advise——"

"Would it be to give up Broussel, sir? If so, you can spare yourself the trouble."

"No," said Mazarin; "although, perhaps, that is as good a counsel as any other."

"Then what may it be?"

"To call for the Coadjutor."

"And stay, madame," suggested Comminges, who was near a window, out of which he could see; "hold, the moment is a happy one, for there he is now giving his blessing in the square of the Palais Royal."

The queen advanced to the window.

"It is true," she said; "the arch-hypocrite!—see!"

"I see," said Mazarin, "that everybody kneels before him, although he be but Coadjutor, whilst I—were I in his place—though I be Cardinal, should be torn to pieces. I persist, then, madame, in my wish" (he laid emphasis on the word) "that your majesty should receive the Coadjutor."

"And wherefore say you not, like the rest, your will?" replied the queen, in a quivering voice.

Mazarin bowed.

"Monsieur le Maréchal," said the queen, after a moment's reflection, "go and find the Coadjutor, and bring him to me."

"And what shall I say to the people?"

"That they must have patience," said Anne, "as I have."

The Maréchal bowed and departed; and, during his absence, Anne of Austria approached Comminges, and conversed with him in a subdued tone, whilst Mazarin glanced uneasily at the corner occupied by d'Artagnan and Porthos. Ere long the door opened, and the maréchal entered, followed by the Coadjutor.

"There, madame," he said, "is Monsieur Gondy, who hastens to obey your majesty's summons."

The queen advanced a few steps to meet him, and then stopped, cold, severe, and unmoved, and her lower lip scornfully projected. Gondy bowed respectfully.

"Well, sir," said the queen, "what is your opinion of this riot?"

"That it is no longer a riot, madame," he replied, "but a revolt."

"The revolt is in those who think that my people can revolt," cried Anne, unable to dissimulate before the Coadjutor, whom she suspected—and perhaps with reason—as the promoter of the tumult. "Revolt! thus is it called by those who have wished for this demonstration, and who are perhaps responsible for it; but wait, wait! the king's authority will put it all to rights."

"Was it to tell me that, madame," coldly replied Gondy, "that your majesty admitted me to the honour of entering your presence?"

"No, my dear Coadjutor," said Mazarin; "it was to ask your advice in the unhappy dilemma in which we find ourselves."

"Is it true?" asked Gondy, feigning astonishment, "that her majesty summoned me to ask for my advice?"

"Yes," said the queen, "it was so requested."

The Coadjutor bowed.

"Your majesty wishes then——"

"You to state what you would do in her place," Mazarin hastened to reply.

The Coadjutor looked at the queen, who replied by a sign in the affirmative.

"Were I in your majesty's place," said Gondy coldly, "I should not hesitate, I should at once release Broussel."

"And if I do not give him up, what think you would be the result?" exclaimed the queen.

"I believe that not a stone in Paris will remain unturned," said the maréchal.

"It was not your opinion that I asked," said the queen sharply without even turning round.

"If it is I whom your majesty interrogates," replied the

Coadjutor, in the same calm manner, "I reply that I hold Monsieur le Maréchal's opinion in all respects."

The colour had mounted to the queen's face; her fine blue eyes seemed to start out of her head, and her carmine lips, compared by all the poets of the day to a pomegranate in flower, were white and trembling with anger. Mazarin himself, who was accustomed to the domestic outbreaks of this disturbed household, was alarmed.

"Give up Broussel!" she cried; "a wise counsel, indeed. Upon my word! one can easily perceive that it comes from a priest."

Gondy remained firm; and the abuse of the day seemed to glide over his head as the sarcasms of the evening before had done; but hatred and revenge were accumulating in the depth of his heart, silently, and drop by drop.

"Madame," he said, "if the humble opinion I have submitted to you is not to your taste, it is doubtless because you have better counsels to follow. I know too well the wisdom of the queen, and that of her advisers, to suppose that they will leave the capital long in trouble that might lead to a revolution."

"Thus, then, it is your opinion," said Anne of Austria, with a sneer, and biting her lips with rage, "that yesterday's riot, which, as to-day, is already a rebellion, to-morrow might become a revolution."

"Yes, madame," replied the Coadjutor gravely.

"But, if I believe you, sir, our people seem to have thrown off all restraint."

"It is a bad day for monarchs," said Gondy, shaking his head, "look at England, madame."

"Yes; but fortunately we have no Oliver Cromwell in France," replied the queen.

"Who knows?" said Gondy; "these men are like thunderbolts —one recognises them only when they have struck."

Every one shuddered; and there was a moment of silence, during which the queen pressed her hand to her side, evidently to still the beatings of her heart. At last she made a sign for every one except Mazarin to quit the room; and Gondy bowed as if to depart with the rest.

"Stay, sir," said Anne to him.

"Good," thought Gondy, "she is going to yield."

"She is going to have him killed," said d'Artagnan to Porthos, "but, at all events, it shall not be by me. I swear to Heaven, on the contrary, that if they fall upon him, I will fall upon them."

"And I too," said Porthos.

"Good," muttered Mazarin, sitting down, "we shall see something new."

The queen's eyes followed the retreating figures, and when the last had closed the door, she turned away. It was evident that she was making unnatural efforts to subdue her anger; she fanned herself, clenched her hands nervously, and walked up and down. Gondy, who began to feel uneasy, examined the tapestry with his eyes, touched the coat of mail which he wore under his long gown, and felt from time to time to see if the handle of a good Spanish dagger, which was hidden under his cloak, was well within reach of his hand.

"And now," at last said the queen, "now that we are alone, repeat your counsel, Monsieur le Coadjuteur."

"It is this, madame; that you should appear to have reflected, and publicly acknowledged an error,—which constitutes the strength of a strong government,—release Broussel from prison, and restore him once more to the people."

"Oh!" cried Anne, "to humble myself thus! Am I, or am I not, the queen? This screaming mob, are they, or are they not, my subjects? Have I friends? Have I guards? Ah! by Notre Dame! as Queen Catherine used to say," continued she, excited by her own words, "rather than give up this infamous Broussel to them, I will strangle him with my own hands."

And she sprang towards Gondy, whom without doubt at that moment she hated more than Broussel, with outstretched arms. The Coadjutor remained immovable, and not a muscle of his face was discomposed: only his glance flashed like a sword, in returning the furious looks of the queen.

"He were a dead man," said the Gascon, "if there were still a Vitry at the court, and if Vitry entered at this moment: but for my part, before he could reach the good prelate, I would kill Vitry at once; the Cardinal would be infinitely pleased with me."

"Hush!" said Porthos, "and listen."

"Madame," cried the Cardinal, seizing hold of Anne and drawing her back—"madame, what are you doing?"

Then he added in Spanish, "Anne, are you mad? You a queen and behaving thus like a shopwoman! And do you not perceive that in the person of this priest is represented the whole people of Paris, and that it is dangerous to insult him at this moment, and that if this priest wished it, in an hour you would be without a crown? Come, then, on another occasion you can be firm and strong; but to-day is not the proper time; to-day you must flatter and caress, or you will be but an ordinary person."

This strong appeal, marked by the eloquence which characterised Mazarin when he spoke in Italian or Spanish, and which he lost entirely in speaking French, was uttered with such impenetrable expression that Gondy, cunning physiognomist as he was, had no suspicion of its being more than a simple warning to be more subdued.

The queen, on her part, thus chided, softened immediately, and sat down, and in an almost weeping voice, letting her arms fall by her sides, said:

"Pardon me, sir, and attribute this violence to what I suffer. A woman, and consequently subject to the weaknesses of my sex, I am alarmed at the idea of civil war; a queen, and accustomed to be obeyed, I am excited at the first opposition."

"Madame," replied Gondy, bowing, "I fear I do not express myself correctly; for I had not the slightest thought that your majesty would look upon my sincere advice as opposition to your wishes. As a fact, madame, your subjects are nothing but respectful and submissive. It is not the queen with whom the people are displeased; they ask for Broussel, and are only too happy, if you release him to them, to live under your government."

Mazarin, who at the words "It is not the queen with whom the people are displeased," had pricked up his ears, thought that the Coadjutor was about to speak of the cries, "Down with Mazarin!" and pleased with Gondy's suppression of this fact, he said, in his sweetest tones, and his most gracious expression:

"Madame, believe the Coadjutor, who is one of the most able politicians that we have; the first vacant cardinal's hat seems to belong to his noble head."

"Ah! how much you have need of me, artful rogue," thought Gondy.

"And what will he promise us?" said d'Artagnan. "*Peste*, if he is giving away hats like that, Porthos, let us look out, and each ask a regiment to-morrow. *Corbleu*, let the civil war last but one year, and I will have a constable's sword gilt for me."

"And for me?" said Porthos.

"For you! I will give you the *baton* of the Maréchal de la Meilleraie, who does not seem to be much in favour just now."

"And so, sir," said the queen, "you are seriously afraid of a public tumult?"

"Seriously," said Gondy, astonished at not having further advanced; "I fear that when the torrent has broken down its embankment it will cause fearful destruction."

"And I," said the queen, "think that in such a case new embankments must be raised to oppose it. Go—I will reflect."

Gondy looked at Mazarin, astonished, and Mazarin approached

the queen to speak to her, but at this time a frightful tumult arose from the square of the Palais Royal.

Gondy smiled, the queen's colour rose, and Mazarin became very white.

"What is that again?" he asked.

At this moment Comminges rushed into the room.

"Pardon, your majesty," he cried, "but the people have crushed the sentinels against the gates and they are now forcing the doors; what are your commands, for time is urgent."

"How many men have you about at the Palais Royal?"

"Six hundred men."

"Place a hundred men round the king, and with the rest sweep away this rabble."

"Madame," cried Mazarin, "what are you about?"

"Go," said the queen.

Just then a terrible crash was heard. One of the gates began to yield.

"Oh! madame," cried Mazarin, "you have lost us all; the king, yourself, and me."

At this cry from the soul of the frightened Cardinal, Anne became alarmed in her turn, and would have recalled Comminges.

"It is too late!" said Mazarin, tearing his hair, "too late!"

The gate had given way, and shouts were heard from the mob. D'Artagnan put his hand to his sword, motioning to Porthos to follow his example.

"Save the queen!" cried Mazarin to the Coadjutor.

Gondy sprang to the window and threw it open; he recognised Louvières at the head of a troop of about three or four thousand men.

"Not a step farther," he shouted, "the queen is signing!"

"What did you say?" asked the queen.

"The truth, madame," said Mazarin, placing a pen and a paper before her; "you must;" then he added, "sign, Anne, I implore you—I command you."

The queen fell into a chair, took the pen and signed.

The people, kept back by Louvières, had not made another step forward; but the awful murmuring, which indicates an angry mob, continued.

The queen had written, "The keeper of the prison of St. Germain will put Councillor Broussel at liberty;" and she had signed it.

The Coadjutor, whose eyes devoured her slightest movements, seized the paper immediately the signature had been affixed, returned to the window, and waved it in his hand.

"This is the order," he said.

All Paris seemed to shout with joy; and then the air resounded with the cries of "Long live Broussel!" "Long live the Coadjutor!"

"Long live the queen!" cried de Gondy: but the cries which replied to his were poor and weak; and it is reasonable to assume that he had but uttered it to cause the queen to be cognisant of her own decreasing popularity.

"And now that you have obtained what you want, go," said she, "Monsieur de Gondy."

"Whenever her majesty has need of me," replied the Coadjutor, bowing, "her majesty knows that I am at her command."

"Ah, cursed priest!" cried Anne, when he had retired, stretching out her arm to the scarcely closed door, "one day I will make you drink the remains of the gall which you have poured out on me to-day."

Mazarin went to approach her. "Leave me!" she exclaimed; "you are not a man!" and she haughtily left the room.

"It is you who are not a woman," muttered Mazarin.

Then, after a moment of thought, he remembered where he had left d'Artagnan and Porthos, and that they must have overheard everything. He knit his brows, and went direct to the tapestry, which he pushed aside. The closet was empty.

At the queen's last word, d'Artagnan had dragged Porthos into the gallery. Thither Mazarin went in his turn, and found the two friends walking up and down.

"Why did you leave the closet, Monsieur d'Artagnan?" asked the Cardinal.

"Because," replied d'Artagnan, "the queen desired every one to leave, and I thought that this command was intended for us as well as for the rest."

"And you have been here since——"

"About a quarter of an hour," said d'Artagnan, motioning to Porthos not to contradict him.

Mazarin saw the sign, and remained convinced that d'Artagnan had seen and heard everything; but he was pleased with his falsehood.

"Decidedly, Monsieur d'Artagnan, you are the man I have been seeking, and you may reckon upon me as your friend, too."

Then, bowing to the two friends, with his most gracious smile, he re-entered his closet more calmly, for on the departure of de Gondy, the tumult had ceased as if by enchantment.

49

MISFORTUNE REFRESHES THE MEMORY

ANNE retired to her oratory, quite furious at the part she had been forced to play.

"What!" she cried, folding her beautiful arms, "what! the people have seen Monsieur de Condé, a prince of the blood royal, arrested by my mother-in-law, Marie de Medicis; they saw my mother-in-law, their former regent, expelled by the Cardinal; they saw Monsieur de Vendôme, that is to say, the son of Henry IV., a prisoner at Vincennes; and whilst these great personages were imprisoned, insulted, and threatened, they said nothing; and now for a Broussel—good God—what then is become of royalty!"

Her majesty had unconsciously touched here upon the very vitals of the situation. The people had made no demonstration for the princes, but they had risen for Broussel; they were taking the part of a plebeian, and in defending Broussel, they instinctively felt that they were defending themselves.

During this time Mazarin walked up and down his study, glancing from time to time at his beautiful Venetian mirror, starred all over. "Ah!" he said, "it is indeed vexing, to be forced to yield thus; but, bah! we shall have our revenge; what matters it about Broussel. It is a name, not a thing."

Mazarin, like many another clever politician, was in this matter entirely mistaken; Broussel was a thing, not a name.

The next morning, therefore, when Broussel made his entrance into Paris in a large carriage, having his son Louvières at his side, and Friquet behind the vehicle, the people threw themselves in his way, and cries of "Long live Broussel!" "Long live our father!" resounded from all parts, and was death to Mazarin's ears; and the Cardinal's spies brought bad news from every direction, which greatly agitated the minister, but were calmly received by the queen. The latter seemed to be maturing in her mind some great stroke—a fact which increased the uneasiness of the Cardinal, who knew the proud princess, and who dreaded much the determination of Anne of Austria.

The Coadjutor returned to parliament more a monarch than the King, Queen, and Cardinal were, all three together. By his advice, a decree from parliament had summoned the citizens to lay down their arms, and to demolish the barricades. They now knew that it required but one hour to take up arms again, and only one night to reconstruct the barricades.

D'Artagnan profited by a moment of calm to send away Raoul, whom he had had great difficulty in keeping in confinement during the riot, and who wanted most positively to strike a blow for one party or the other. Raoul had offered some opposition at first; but d'Artagnan made use of Count de la Fère's name, and, after paying a visit to Madame de Chevreuse, Raoul started to rejoin the army.

Rochefort alone was discontented with the termination of affairs. He had written to the Duc de Beaufort to come, and the duke was about to arrive, and he would find Paris tranquil. He went to the Coadjutor to consult with him whether it were not better to send word to the duke to stop on the road, but Gondy reflected for a moment, and then said:

"Let him continue his journey."

"But all is not then at an end?" asked Rochefort.

"No, my dear count; we have only just begun."

"What induces you to think so?"

"The knowledge that I have of the queen's heart; she will not rest satisfied."

"Come, let us see what you know."

"I know that she has communicated to the prince to return in haste from the army."

"Ah! ah!" said Rochefort, "you are right. We must let Monsieur de Beaufort come."

In fact, the evening after this conversation, it was reported that the Prince Condé had arrived. It was a very simple and natural circumstance, and yet it created a vast sensation. It was said that Madame de Longueville, for whom the prince had more than a brother's affection, and in whom he had confided, had been indiscreet. His confidence had unveiled the sinister projects of the queen. Even on the night of the prince's return, some citizens, more bold than the rest, such as the sheriffs, the captains, and the quartermasters, went from house to house among their friends, saying:

"Why do we not take the king and place him in the Hôtel de Ville? It is a shame to leave him to be educated by our enemies, who will give him evil counsels; whereas, brought up by the Coadjutor, for instance, he would imbibe national principles and love his people."

That night was secretly agitated, and on the morning the grey and black cloaks, the patrols of armed shop-people, and the bands of mendicants had reappeared.

The queen had passed the night in conference alone with the prince, who had entered her oratory at midnight, and did not leave till five o'clock in the morning.

At five o'clock Anne went to the Cardinal's room. If she had not yet taken any repose, he at least was already occupied. Six days had already passed out of the ten he had asked from Mordaunt; he was therefore occupied in correcting his reply to Cromwell, when some one knocked gently at the door of communication with the queen's apartments. Anne of Austria alone was permitted to enter by that door. The Cardinal therefore rose to open it.

The queen was in a morning gown, and it became her well; for, like Diana of Poitiers and Ninon, Anne of Austria enjoyed the privilege of remaining ever beautiful; nevertheless this morning she looked more handsome than usual, for her eyes had all the sparkle which inward satisfaction added to their expression.

"What is the matter, madame?" said Mazarin uneasily, "You have quite a proud look."

"Yes, Giulio," she said, "proud and happy; for I have found the means of stifling this hydra."

"You are a great politician, my queen," said Mazarin; "let us see the means." And he hastily concealed what he had written by sliding the letter under a sheet of white paper.

"You know," said the queen, "that they want to take the king away from me."

"Alas! yes, and to take my life!"

"They shall not have the king."

"Nor kill me."

"Listen. I want to carry off my son from them—with yourself and myself. I wish that this event, which, on the day it is known, will completely change the aspect of affairs, should be accomplished without the knowledge of any others but yourself, myself, and a third person."

"And who is this third person?"

"Monsieur le Prince."

"And you have seen him?"

"He has just left me."

"And will he aid this project?"

"The plan is his own."

"And Paris?"

"He will starve it out and force it to surrender at discretion."

"The plan is wanting not in grandeur, but I only see one impediment to it."

"What is it?"

"Impossibility."

"A meaningless word; nothing is impossible. Have we money?"

"A little," said Mazarin, trembling lest Anne should ask to draw upon his finances.

"Have we troops?"

"Five or six thousand men."

"Have we courage?"

"Much."

"Then the thing is easy. Oh! do think of it, Giulio! Paris, this odious Paris, awaking one morning without queen or king, surrounded, besieged, famished—having, as an only resource, its vapid parliament, and their Coadjutor, with crooked limbs!"

"Charming! charming!" said Mazarin. "I see the effect, but I do not see the way to obtain it."

"I will find it out myself."

"You are aware that it will be war—civil war—furious, burning, and implacable?"

"Oh! yes, yes, war," said Anne of Austria. "Yes, I will reduce this rebellious city to ashes. I will extinguish the fire by blood! I will perpetuate the crime and the punishment by making a frightful example. Paris!—I hate it!—I detest it!"

"Very fine, Anne. You are now sanguinary; but take care. We are not in the time of the Malattesta and the Castrucio Castracani. You will get yourself decapitated, my beautiful queen, and that would be a pity."

"You laugh."

"Faintly. It is disastrous to go to war with a whole nation. Look at your brother monarch, Charles I. He is badly off—very badly."

"We are in France, and I am Spanish."

"So much the worse; I would much rather you were French, and myself also—they would hate us both less."

"Nevertheless, you consent?"

"Yes, if the project be a possible one."

"It is; it is I who tell you so; make your preparations for departure."

"I! I am always prepared to go, only you know I never do go and, perhaps, shall do this time as little as before."

"But, if I go, will you go too?"

"I shall attempt it, at least."

"You torment me, Giulio, with your fears; and what are you afraid of, then?"

"Of many things."

Mazarin's face, smiling as it was, became clouded.

"Anne," said he, gravely, "after all, you are but a woman, and as a woman you may insult men at your ease, knowing that you can do it with impunity; you accuse me of fear; I have not so much as you have, since I do not fly as you do. Against whom do they cry out? is it against you, or against myself? Whom would they slay—yourself or me? Well, I can weather the storm;—I—whom, notwithstanding, you tax with fear—not with bravado, that is not my way, but I am firm. Imitate me; make less noise, and do more. You cry very loud, you end by doing nothing; you talk of flying——"

Mazarin shrugged his shoulders, and taking the queen's hand led her to the window.

"Look!"

"Well?" said the queen, blinded by her obstinacy.

"Well, what do you see from this window? If I am not mistaken, those are citizens, helmeted and mailed, armed with good muskets, as in the time of the League, and whose eyes are so intently fixed on this window, that they will see you if you raise that curtain much; and now come to the other side—what do you see? Creatures of the people, armed with the halberds, guarding your doors. You will see the same at every opening from this palace to which I should lead you. Your doors are guarded, the airholes of your cellars are guarded, and I could say to you, as that good La Ramée said to me of the Duc de Beaufort, you must either be bird or mouse to get away."

"He did get away, however."

"Do you think of escaping in the same manner."

"I am a prisoner, then?"

"*Parbleu!*" said Mazarin, "I have been proving it to you this last hour."

And he quietly resumed his despatch at the place where he had been interrupted.

Anne, trembling with anger, and red with humiliation, left the room, shutting the door violently after her. Mazarin did not even turn round. When once more in her own apartment, Anne fell into a chair and wept bitterly; then suddenly struck with an idea:

"I am saved!" she exclaimed, rising; "oh, yes! yes! I know a man who will find the means of taking me from Paris; a man whom I have too long forgotten." Then, falling into a reverie, she added, however, with an expression of joy, "Ungrateful woman that I am, for twenty years I have forgotten this man, whom I ought to have made maréchal of France. My mother-in-law expended gold, caresses, and dignities on Concini, who ruined her; the king made Vitry maréchal of France for an assassination; while

I have left in obscurity, in poverty, that noble d'Artagnan who saved me!"

And she ran to a table upon which were paper, pens, and ink, and began to write.

50

THE INTERVIEW WITH THE QUEEN

THAT morning d'Artagnan was sleeping in Porthos's chamber. It was a custom that the two friends had adopted since the disturbances. Their swords were under the bolster, and their pistols were on a table within reach of their hands. D'Artagnan was still asleep, and dreaming that the sky was covered by a yellow cloud, that a shower of gold was falling from this cloud, and that he was holding his hat under a rain-spout. As for Porthos, he dreamed that the panels of his carriage had not sufficient breadth to contain the armorial bearings which he had ordered to be painted upon them. They were both aroused at seven o'clock by the entrance of an unliveried servant, who had brought a letter to d'Artagnan.

"From whom?" asked the Gascon.

"From the queen," replied the servant.

"Ho!" said Porthos, raising himself in his bed, "what does she say?"

D'Artagnan told the servant to wait in the next room, and when the door was closed, he sprang up from his bed, and read rapidly, whilst Porthos looked at him with open eyes, not daring to ask a single question.

"Friend Porthos," said d'Artagnan, handing the letter to him, "this time, at least, you are sure of your title of baron, and I of my captaincy. There, read and judge."

Porthos took the letter, and with a faltering voice read the following words:

"The queen wishes to speak to Monsieur d'Artagnan, who must accompany the bearer."

"Well!" exclaimed Porthos, "I see nothing in that very extraordinary."

"But I see much that is extraordinary in it," replied d'Artagnan. "It is plain, by their sending for me, that matters are becoming complicated. Just reflect a little what an agitation the queen's mind must be in, for her to have remembered me after twenty years."

"It is true," said Porthos.

"Sharpen your sword, baron, load your pistols, and give some corn to the horses, for I will give you my word that something new will happen before to-morrow."

"But stop; do you think it can be a trap that they are laying for us?" suggested Porthos, incessantly thinking how his greatness must be irksome to other people.

"If it is a snare," replied d'Artagnan, "I shall scent it out, be assured. If Mazarin be an Italian, I am a Gascon."

And d'Artagnan dressed himself at once.

Whilst Porthos, still in bed, was hooking on his cloak for him, a second knock was heard.

"Come in," cried d'Artagnan; and another servant entered.

"From his Eminence, Cardinal Mazarin," he said, presenting a letter.

D'Artagnan looked at Porthos, and said:

"It is arranged capitally; his Eminence expects me in half an hour."

"Good."

"My friend," said d'Artagnan, turning to the servant, "tell his Eminence that in half an hour I shall be at his command."

"It is very fortunate," resumed the Gascon, when the valet had retired, "that he did not meet the other one."

"Do you not think that they have sent for you, both for the same purpose?"

"I do not think it, I am sure of it."

"Quick, quick, d'Artagnan. Remember that the queen awaits you; and after the queen, the cardinal; and after the cardinal, myself."

D'Artagnan summoned Anne of Austria's servant, and answered that he was ready to follow him.

The servant conducted him by the Rue des Petits-Champs, and turned to the left, entered the little garden gate leading into the Rue Richelieu; then they gained the private staircase, and d'Artagnan was ushered into the oratory. A certain emotion, for which he could not explain, made the lieutenant's heart beat; he had no longer the assurance of youth, and experience taught him all the importance of past events. Formerly, he would have approached the queen, as a young man who bends before a woman; but now it was a different thing; he answered her summons as a humble soldier obeys an illustrious general.

The silence of the oratory was at last disturbed by a slight rustling sound, and d'Artagnan started when he perceived the tapestry raised by a white hand, which, by its form, its colour, and its beauty, he recognised as that royal hand, which had one day been presented to him to kiss. The queen entered.

"It is you, Monsieur d'Artagnan," she said, fixing a gaze full of melancholy interest on the countenance of the officer, "and I know you well. Look at me well in your turn. I am the queen; do you recognise me?"

"I have the honour of awaiting your majesty's commands," replied d'Artagnan in a subtle tone.

"Then you are not aware," continued Anne, giving that sweet expression to her voice which she could do at will, "that in former days the queen had once need of a young, brave, and devoted cavalier; that she found this cavalier; and that although he might have thought that she had forgotten him, she had kept a place for him in the depths of her heart."

"No, madame, I was ignorant of that," said the musketeer.

"So much the worse, sir," said Anne of Austria, "so much the worse, at least for the queen; for to-day she has need of the same courage, and of that same devotion."

"What!" exclaimed d'Artagnan, "does the queen, surrounded as she is by such devoted servants, such wise counsellors, men who are so great by their merit or their position—does she deign to cast her eyes on an obscure soldier?"

Anne understood this covert reproach, and was more moved than irritated by it. She had many a time felt humiliated by the self-sacrifice and disinterestedness shown by the Gascon gentleman, and she had allowed herself to be exceeded in generosity.

"All that you tell me of those by whom I am surrounded, Monsieur d'Artagnan, is doubtless true," said the queen, "but I have confidence in you alone. I know that you belong to the Cardinal—but you belong to me as well—and I will take upon myself the making of your fortune. Come, will you do to-day what formerly the gentleman whom you affect to have forgotten, did for the queen?"

"I will do everything which your majesty commands," replied d'Artagnan.

The queen reflected for a moment, and then, seeing the cautious demeanour of the musketeer—

"Perhaps you like repose?" she said.

"I do not know, for I have never had it, madame."

"Have you any friends?"

"I had three, two of whom have left Paris, to go I know not where. One alone is left to me, but he is one of those known, I believe, to the cavalier, of whom your majesty did me the honour to speak to me."

"Very good," said the queen, "you and your friend are worth an army."

"What am I to do, madame?"

"Return at five o'clock, and I will inform you: but do not breathe to a living soul, sir, the rendezvous which I give you."

"No, madame."

"Swear it by Christ."

"Madame, I have never been false to my word—when I say no, it means no."

The queen, although astonished at this language, to which she was not accustomed from her courtiers, argued from it a happy omen of the zeal with which d'Artagnan would serve her in the accomplishment of her project. It was one of the Gascon's artifices to conceal his deep cunning occasionally under an appearance of rough loyalty.

"Has the queen any further commands for me at present?" asked d'Artagnan.

"No, sir," replied Anne of Austria, "and you may retire until the time that I mentioned to you."

D'Artagnan bowed and went out.

"Faith!" he exclaimed, when the door was closed, "they seem to have great need of me here."

Then, as the half-hour had already expired, he crossed the gallery, and knocked at the Cardinal's door.

"I come for your commands, my lord," he said.

And according to his custom, d'Artagnan glanced rapidly round him, and remarked that Mazarin had a sealed letter before him.

"You come from the queen?" said Mazarin, looking keenly at d'Artagnan.

"I! my lord, who told you that?"

"Nobody, but I know it."

"I regret, infinitely, to tell you, my lord, that you are in error," replied the Gascon impudently, firm to the promise he had just made to Anne of Austria.

"I opened the door of the anteroom myself, and I saw you enter at the end of the corridor."

"Because I was shown up the private stairs."

"How so?"

"I know not, it must have been a mistake."

Mazarin was aware that it was not easy to make d'Artagnan reveal anything which he was desirous of keeping back, so he therefore gave up, for the time, the discovery of the mystery which the Gascon made.

"Let us speak of my affairs," said Mazarin, "since you will tell me nothing of yours. Do you delight in travelling?"

"My life has been passed on the high-roads."

"Would anything retain you particularly in Paris?"

"Nothing but an order from a superior would retain me in Paris."

"Very well. Here is a letter which must be taken to its address."

"To its address, my lord? But it has none."

"I forgot to mention," resumed Mazarin, "that it is in a double envelope."

"I understand; and I am only to take off the first one when I have reached a certain place?"

"Just so. Take it and go. You have a friend, Monsieur du Valon, whom I like much; let him accompany you."

"The devil!" said d'Artagnan to himself. "He knows that we overheard his conversation yesterday, and he wants to send us away from Paris."

"Do you hesitate?" asked Mazarin.

"No, my lord, and I will set out at once. There is one thing only which I must request."

"What is it? speak."

"That your Eminence will at once seek the queen."

"What for?"

"Merely to say these words: 'I am going to send Monsieur d'Artagnan away, and I wish him to set out directly.'"

"I told you," said Mazarin, "that you had seen the queen."

"I had the honour of assuring your Eminence that there had been some mistake."

"Very well; I will go. Wait here for me." And looking attentively around him, to see if he had forgotten any keys in his closet, Mazarin went out. Ten minutes elapsed ere he returned, pale, and evidently thoughtful. He seated himself at his desk, and d'Artagnan proceeded to examine his face, as he had just examined the letter he held; but the envelope which covered his countenance was almost as impenetrable as that which covered the letter.

"Eh! eh!" thought the Gascon; "he looks displeased. Can it be with me? He meditates. Is it about sending me to the Bastille? All very fine, my lord; but at the very first hint you give of such a thing, I will strangle you and become a Frondist. I should be carried in triumph like Monsieur Broussel, and Athos would proclaim me the French Brutus. It would be droll."

The Gascon, with his vivid imagination, had already seen the advantage to be derived from his situation; Mazarin gave, however, no order of the kind, but, on the contrary, began to be insinuating.

"You were right," he said, "my dear Monsieur d'Artagnan, and you cannot go just yet. I beg you to return me that despatch."

D'Artagnan obeyed, and Mazarin ascertained that the seal was intact.

"I shall require you this evening," he said. "Return in two hours."

"My lord," said d'Artagnan, "I have an appointment in two hours, which I cannot miss."

"Do not be uneasy," answered Mazarin; "it is the same."

"Good!" thought d'Artagnan: "I fancied it was so."

"Return then at five o'clock, and bring the worthy Monsieur du Valon with you. Only, leave him in the anteroom, as I wish to speak to you alone."

D'Artagnan bowed, and thought, "Both at the same hour; both commands alike; both at the Palais Royal, I guess. Ah! Monsieur de Gondy would pay a hundred thousand francs for such a secret!"

"You are thoughtful," said Mazarin uneasily.

"Yes; I was thinking whether we ought to come armed or not."

"Armed to the teeth!" replied the Cardinal.

"Very well, my lord, it shall be so."

D'Artagnan bowed, left the room, and hastened to repeat Mazarin's flattering promises, which put Porthos into the highest spirits.

51

FLIGHT

THE Palais Royal, notwithstanding the agitation which prevailed in the city, when d'Artagnan went thither about five o'clock in the evening, presented a spectacle of the most cheerful kind. Nor was that surprising. The queen had restored Broussel and Blancmesnil to the people, and had therefore nothing to fear, since the people had nothing more to ask for. The return also of the conqueror of Lens was the pretext for giving a grand banquet. The princes and princesses were invited, and their carriages had crowded the court since noon; then after dinner the queen was to form her pool of quadrille. Anne of Austria had never appeared more brilliant than on that day—radiant with grace and wit. Mazarin disappeared as they rose from table. He found d'Artagnan waiting for him already at his post in the anteroom. The Cardinal advanced to him with a smile, and taking him by the hand, led him into his study.

"My dear Monsieur d'Artagnan," said the Cardinal, sitting down, "I am about to give you the greatest proof of confidence that a minister can give to an officer."

"I hope," said d'Artagnan bowing, "that you give it, my lord, without hesitation, and with the conviction that I am worthy of it."

"More worthy than any one, my dear friend; therefore I apply to you. You are about to leave this evening," continued Mazarin. "My dear Monsieur d'Artagnan, the welfare of the state is reposed in your hand." He paused.

"Explain yourself, my lord; I am listening."

"The queen has resolved to make a little excursion with the king to St. Germain."

"Ah! ah! ah!" said d'Artagnan, "that is to say, the queen wishes to leave Paris."

"A woman's caprice—you understand."

"Yes, I understand perfectly," said d'Artagnan.

"It was for this that she summoned you this morning, and that she told you to return at five o'clock."

"Was it worth while to wish me to swear this morning that I would mention the appointment to no one?" muttered d'Artagnan. "Oh, women! women! whether queens or not, they are always the same."

"Do you disapprove of this journey, my dear Monsieur d'Artagnan?" asked Mazarin anxiously.

"I, my lord?" said d'Artagnan; "and why?"

"Because you shrug your shoulders."

"It is a habit I have in speaking to myself. I neither approve nor disapprove, my lord; I merely await your commands."

"Good; it is you, therefore, that I have selected to conduct the king and queen to St. Germain."

"Liar!" said d'Artagnan to himself.

"You see, therefore," resumed Mazarin, perceiving d'Artagnan's composure, "that, as I have told you, the welfare of the state is placed in your hands."

"Yes, my lord, and I feel the full responsibility of such a charge."

"Do you think the thing possible?"

"Everything is."

"Shall you be attacked on the road?"

"It is probable."

"And in that event, what would you do?"

"I shall pass through those who attack me."

"And suppose you cannot pass through them?"

"So much the worse for them. I must pass over them."

"And you will place the king and queen in safety also, and at St. Germain?"

"Yes."

"On your life."

"On my life."

"You are a hero, my friend," said Mazarin, gazing at the musketeer with admiration.

D'Artagnan smiled.

"And I?" asked Mazarin, after a moment's silence.

"How?—and you, my lord?"

"If I wish to leave?"

"That would be much more difficult."

"Why so?"

"Your Eminence might be recognised."

"Even under this disguise?" asked Mazarin, raising a cloak which covered an arm-chair, upon which lay a complete dress for an officer, of pearl-grey and red, entirely embroidered with silver.

"If your Eminence is disguised, it will be more easy."

"Ah!" said Mazarin, breathing more freely.

"But it will be necessary for your Eminence to do what the other day you declared you would have done in our place—cry, 'Down with Mazarin!'"

"I will cry it."

"In French—in good French, my lord—take care of your accent; they killed six thousand Angerines in Sicily, because they pronounced Italian badly. Take care that the French do not take their revenge on you for the Sicilian vespers."

"I will do my best."

"The streets are full of armed men," continued d'Artagnan. "Are you sure that no one is aware of this project of the queen's?"

Mazarin reflected.

"This affair would give a fine opportunity for a traitor, my lord; the chance of being attacked would be an excuse for everything."

Mazarin shuddered; but he reflected that a man who had an intention to betray him was not likely to warn him first.

"And, therefore," added he quietly, "I have not confidence in every one; the proof of which is, that I have fixed upon you to escort me."

"Shall you not go with the queen?"

"No," replied Mazarin.

"Then you will start after the queen?"

"No," said Mazarin again.

"Ah!" said d'Artagnan, who began to understand.

"Yes," continued the Cardinal. "I have my plan;—with the queen, I double her risk,—after the queen, her departure would double mine—then, the court once safe, I might be forgotten; the great are often forgetful."

"Very true," said d'Artagnan, fixing his eyes, in spite of himself, on the queen's diamond, which Mazarin wore on his finger. Mazarin followed the direction of his eyes, and gently turned the hoop of the ring inside.

"I wish," he said, with a cunning smile, "to prevent them from being forgetful to me."

"It is but Christian charity," replied d'Artagnan, "not to lead one's neighbours into temptation."

"It is for that reason," said Mazarin, "that I wish to start before them."

D'Artagnan smiled—he was the exact man to understand the astute Italian. Mazarin saw the smile, and profited by the moment.

"You will begin, therefore, by taking me first out of Paris, will you not, my dear Monsieur d'Artagnan?"

"A difficult commission, my lord," replied d'Artagnan, resuming his serious manner.

"But," said Mazarin, "you did not make so many difficulties with regard to the king and queen."

"The king and the queen are my king and queen, my lord," replied the musketeer, "my life is theirs, and I ought to give it to them. They ask it; and I have nothing to say."

"That is true," murmured Mazarin, in a low tone, "but as thy life is not mine, I suppose I must buy it, must I not?" and sighing deeply, he began to turn the hoop of his ring outside again; d'Artagnan smiled once more. These two men met at one point, and that was, cunning; had they been actuated alike by courage, the one would have done great things for the other.

"But also," said Mazarin, "you must understand that if I ask this service from you it is with the intention of being grateful."

"Is it still only in intention, my lord?" asked d'Artagnan.

"Stay," said Mazarin, drawing the ring from his finger, "my dear Monsieur d'Artagnan—here is a diamond which belonged to you formerly, it is but just that it should return to you—take it, I pray."

D'Artagnan spared Mazarin the trouble of insisting, and after looking to see if the stone were the same, and assuring himself of the purity of its water, he took it, and passed it on to his finger with indescribable pleasure.

"I valued it much," said Mazarin, giving a last look at it; "nevertheless I give it to you with great pleasure."

"And I, my lord," said d'Artagnan, "accept it in the same spirit as it is given. Come, let us speak of your little affairs. You wish to leave before everybody, and at what hour?"

"At ten o'clock."

"And the queen, at what time does she wish to start?"

"At midnight."

"Then it is possible. I can get you out of Paris and leave you beyond the '*barrière*,' and can return for her majesty."

"Capital, but how will you take me out of Paris?"

"Oh! as to that, you must leave it to me."

"I give you full power, therefore take as large an escort as you like."

D'Artagnan shook his head.

"It seems to me, however," said Mazarin, "the safest method."

"Yes, for you, my lord, but not for the queen; you must leave it to me, and give me the entire control of the undertaking."

"Nevertheless——"

"Or find some one else," continued d'Artagnan, turning his back.

"Oh!" muttered Mazarin; "I do believe he is going off with the diamond!"

"Monsieur d'Artagnan, my dear Monsieur d'Artagnan;" he called out in a coaxing voice, "will you answer for everything?"

"I will answer for nothing, but I will do my best."

"Well, then, let us go; I must trust to you."

"It is very fortunate," said d'Artagnan to himself.

"You will be here at half-past nine?"

"And I shall find your Eminence ready?"

"Certainly, quite ready."

"Well, then, it is a settled thing; and now, my lord, will you obtain for me an audience of the queen?"

"For what purpose?"

"I wish to receive her majesty's commands from her own lips."

"She desired me to give them to you."

"There may be something she has forgotten."

"You really wish to see her!"

"It is indispensable, my lord."

Mazarin hesitated for one instant, whilst d'Artagnan remained firm. "Come, then," said the minister; "I will conduct you to her majesty—but, remember, not one word of our conversation."

"What has passed between us concerns us alone, my lord," replied d'Artagnan.

"Swear to be mute."

"I never swear, my lord, I say yes or no; and, as I am a gentleman, I keep my word."

"Come, then, I see that I must trust unreservedly to you."

"Believe me, my lord, it will be the best plan."

"Come," said Mazarin, conducting d'Artagnan into the queen's oratory, and desiring him to wait there. He did not wait long, for in five minutes the queen entered in full court costume. Thus dressed, she scarcely appeared thirty-five years of age, and was still handsome.

"Is it you, Monsieur d'Artagnan," she said, smiling graciously, "I have to thank you for having insisted on seeing me."

"I ought to ask your majesty's pardon; but I wished to receive your commands from your own mouth."

"Will you accept the commission which I have entrusted to you?"

"With gratitude."

"Very well, be here at midnight."

"I will not fail."

"Monsieur d'Artagnan," continued the queen, "I know your disinterestedness too well to speak of my gratitude at this moment; but I swear to you that I shall not forget this second service as I forgot the first."

"Your majesty is free to forget or to remember as it pleases you," said d'Artagnan, bowing.

"Go, sir," said the queen, with her most bewitching smile, "go and return at midnight."

And d'Artagnan retired, but as he passed out he glanced at the curtain through which the queen had entered, and at the bottom of the tapestry he remarked the tip of a velvet slipper.

"Good," thought he; "Mazarin has been listening to discover whether I had betrayed him. In truth he does not deserve the services of an honest man."

D'Artagnan was not less exact to his appointment, and at half-past nine o'clock he entered the anteroom.

He found the Cardinal dressed as an officer, and he looked very well in that costume, which, as we have already stated, he wore elegantly, only he was extremely pale, and trembled a little.

"Quite alone?" he asked.

"Yes, my lord."

"And that worthy Monsieur du Valon, are we to enjoy the pleasure of his society?"

"Certainly, my lord, he is waiting in his carriage at the gate of the garden of the Palais Royal."

"And we depart in his carriage then?"

"Yes, my lord."

"And with us no other escort but you two?"

"Is it not enough? One of us would suffice."

"Really, my dear Monsieur d'Artagnan," said the Cardinal, "your coolness startles me."

"I should have thought, on the contrary, that it ought to have inspired you with confidence."

"And Bernouin, do I not take him with me?"

"There is no room for him; he will rejoin your Eminence."

"Let us go," said Mazarin, "since everything must be ready—do you wish it?"

"My lord, there is yet time to draw back," said d'Artagnan, "and your Eminence is perfectly free."

"Not at all, not at all," said Mazarin; "let us be off."

And they both descended the private stair, Mazarin leaning on the arm of d'Artagnan, an arm which the musketeer felt trembling upon his own. At last, after crossing the courts of the Palais Royal, where there still remained some of the conveyances of late guests, they entered the garden and reached the little gate. Mazarin attempted to open it by a key which he took from his pocket, but his hand trembled so much that he could not find the keyhole.

"Give it to me," said d'Artagnan, who, when the gate was opened, deposited the key in his pocket, reckoning upon returning by that means.

The steps were already down, and the door open. Mousqueton held open the door, and Porthos was inside the carriage.

"Mount, my lord," said d'Artagnan to Mazarin, who sprang into the carriage without waiting for a second bidding. D'Artagnan followed him; and Mousqueton, having closed the door, mounted behind the carriage with many groans. He had made some difficulties about going, under pretext that he still suffered from his wound, but d'Artagnan had said to him:

"Remain if you like, my dear Monsieur Mouston, but I warn you that Paris will be burnt down to-night;" upon which Mousqueton had declared, without asking anything further, that he was ready to follow his master and Monsieur d'Artagnan to the end of the world.

The carriage started at a moderate pace, without betraying in the least that it contained people in a hurry. The Cardinal wiped his forehead with his handkerchief, and looked around him. On his left was Porthos, whilst d'Artagnan was on his right; each guarded a door, and served as a rampart to him on either side. Before him, on the front seat, lay two pairs of pistols—one before Porthos, and the other before d'Artagnan. About a hundred paces from the Palais Royal a patrol stopped the carriage.

"Who goes there?" asked the captain.

"Mazarin!" said d'Artagnan, laughing loudly. The Cardinal's hair stood on end. But the joke appeared excellent to the citizens, who, seeing the conveyance without escort and unarmed, would never have believed in the reality of so great an imprudence.

"A good journey to you!" they cried, making way for it to pass.

"Hem!" said d'Artagnan, "what does my lord think of that answer?"

"I congratulate you on your readiness; you are unquestionably a man of talent!" cried Mazarin.

"In truth," said Porthos, "I understand; but now——"

About the middle of the Rue des Petits-Champs they were stopped by a second patrol.

"Who goes there?" inquired the captain of the patrol.

"Keep back, my lord," said d'Artagnan. And Mazarin buried himself so far behind the two friends that he disappeared, completely hidden between them.

"Who goes there?" cried the same voice impatiently, whilst d'Artagnan perceived that they had rushed to the horses' heads. But, putting his head half out of the carriage—

"Eh! Planchet," said he.

The chief approached, and it was indeed Planchet; d'Artagnan had recognised the voice of his old attendant.

"How, sir!" said Planchet, "is it you?"

"Eh! *mon Dieu!* yes, my good friend, this worthy Porthos has just received a severe sword thrust, and I am taking him to his country house at St. Cloud."

"Oh! really," said Planchet.

"Porthos," said d'Artagnan, "if you can still speak, say a word, my dear Porthos, to this good Planchet."

"Planchet, my friend," said Porthos, in a melancholy voice. "I am very ill; should you meet a doctor, you will do me a favour by sending him to me."

"Oh! good Heaven," said Planchet, "what a misfortune; and how did it occur?"

"I will tell you all about it," replied Mousqueton.

Porthos uttered a deep groan.

"Make way for us, Planchet," said d'Artagnan, in a whisper to him, "or he will not arrive alive; the lungs are affected, my friend."

Planchet shook his head with the air of a man who says: "In

that case, things look ill." Then he turned to his men, "Let them
pass; they are friends."

The carriage resumed its course, and Mazarin, who had held
his breath, ventured to breathe again.

"A narrow squeak," muttered he.

A few steps in advance of the gate of St. Honoré, they met a
third troop; this party was composed of ill-looking fellows, who
resembled bandits more than anything else; they were the men of
the beggar of St. Eustache.

"Attention, Porthos!" cried d'Artagnan. Porthos placed his
hand on the pistols.

"What is it?" asked Mazarin.

"My lord, I think we are in bad company."

A man advanced to the door with a scythe in his hand.

"Eh, rascal!" said d'Artagnan, "do you not know his highness
the prince's carriage?"

"Prince or not," said the man, "open; we are here to guard the
gate, and no one whom we do not know shall pass."

"What is to be done?" said Porthos.

"*Pardieu!* to pass," replied d'Artagnan.

"But how pass?" asked Mazarin.

"Through or over; coachman, gallop on."

"Not a step farther," said the man, who appeared to be the
captain, "or I will hamstring your horses."

"*Peste!*" said Porthos, "it would be a pity; horses which cost me
a hundred pistoles each."

"I will pay you two hundred for them," said Mazarin.

"Yes, but when once they are hamstrung, our necks will be
strung next."

"If one of them comes to my side," asked Porthos, "must I kill
him?"

"Yes, by a blow of your fist, if you are able; we will not fire but
at the last extremity."

"All right," said Porthos.

"Come and open then," cried d'Artagnan to the man with the
scythe, taking one of the pistols up by the muzzle, and preparing
to strike with the handle. And as the man approached, d'Artagnan
in order to have more freedom for his actions, leant half out of the
door; his eyes were fixed upon those of the mendicant, which were
lighted up by a lantern. Doubtless he recognised d'Artagnan, for
he became deadly pale; doubtless the musketeer knew him, for his
hair stood up on his head.

"Monsieur d'Artagnan!" he cried, starting back, "Monsieur
d'Artagnan! let him pass."

D'Artagnan was, perhaps, about to reply, when a blow similar to that of a mallet falling on the head of an ox was heard; it was Porthos, who had just knocked down his man.

D'Artagnan turned round and saw the unfortunate man writhing about four steps off.

"'Sdeath!" cried he to the coachman. "Hasten your horses! whip! get on!"

The coachman bestowed a heavy blow of the whip upon his horses; the noble animals reared, then cries of men who were knocked down were heard; then a double concussion was felt, and two of the wheels had passed over a round and flexible body. There was a moment's silence; the carriage had cleared the gate.

"To Cours la Reine!" cried d'Artagnan to the coachman; then turning to Mazarin, he said, "Now, my lord, you can say five *paters* and five *aves*, to thank Heaven for your deliverance. You are safe, you are free."

Mazarin replied only by a groan; he could hardly believe in such a miracle. Five minutes later the carriage stopped, having reached Cours la Reine.

"Is my lord satisfied with his escort?" asked d'Artagnan.

"Enchanted, Chevalier," said Mazarin, putting his head out of the window; "and now do as much for the queen."

"It will be less difficult," replied d'Artagnan, springing to the ground. "Monsieur du Valon, I commend his Eminence to your care."

"Be quite at ease," said Porthos, holding out his hand, which d'Artagnan took and shook in his.

"Oh!" said Porthos.

D'Artagnan looked with surprise at his friend.

"What is the matter, then?" he asked.

"I think I have sprained my wrist," said Porthos.

"The deuce! why did you strike like a blind or a deaf man."

"It was necessary; my man was going to fire at me. But you, how did you get rid of yours?"

"Oh! mine," replied d'Artagnan, "was not a man."

"What was it, then?"

"It was an apparition."

"And——"

"I charmed it away."

Without further explanation, d'Artagnan took the pistols which were upon the front seat, and placed them in his belt, settled himself in his cloak, and, not wanting to enter by the same gate as that by which they had left, he took his way towards the Richelieu Gate.

52

THE COADJUTOR'S CARRIAGE

INSTEAD of returning, then, by the St. Honoré gate, d'Artagnan, who had time before him, walked round and entered by the Porte Richelieu. He was approached to be examined; and when it was seen by his plumed hat and his laced coat that he was an officer of the musketeers, he was surrounded, with an intention to make him cry "Down with Mazarin!" Their first demonstration did not fail to make him uneasy; but when he knew what it concerned, he shouted in such a fine voice that even the most exacting were satisfied. He walked down the Rue Richelieu, meditating how he should carry off the queen in her turn—for to take her in a carriage bearing the Royal arms was not to be thought of—when he perceived an equipage standing at the door of the hotel belonging to Madame de Guéménée.

He was struck by a sudden idea.

"Ah, *pardieu!*" he exclaimed; "that would be fair play."

And approaching the carriage, he examined the arms on the panels, and the livery of the coachman on his box. This scrutiny was so much the more easy, the coachman being asleep with the reins in his hands.

"It is, in truth, Monsieur le Coadjuteur's carriage," said d'Artagnan; "upon my honour, I begin to think that Heaven is prospering us."

He entered quietly into the chariot, and pulled the silk cord which was attached to the coachman's little finger.

"To the Palais Royal," he called out.

The coachman awoke with a start, and drove off in the direction he was desired, never doubting but that the order had come from his master. The porter at the palace was about to close the gates, but seeing such a handsome equipage, he thought that it was some visit of importance, and the carriage was allowed to pass, and to stop under the porch. It was then only that the coachman perceived that the grooms were not behind the vehicle; he fancied Monsieur le Coadjuteur had sent them back, and without leaving the reins he sprang from his box to open the door. D'Artagnan sprang in his turn to the ground, and just at the moment when the coachman, alarmed at not seeing his master, fell back a step, he seized him by his collar with the left, whilst with the right he placed a pistol to his head.

"Try to pronounce one single word," muttered d'Artagnan, "and you are a dead man."

The coachman saw at once, by the expression in the countenance of the man who thus addressed him, that he had fallen into a trap, and he remained with his mouth and eyes open to their fullest extent.

Two musketeers were pacing the court, to whom d'Artagnan called by their names.

"Monsieur Bellière," said he to one of them, "do me the favour to take the reins from the hands of this worthy man, to mount upon the box, and to drive to the door of the private stair, and to wait for me there; it is on an affair of importance which is for the service of the king."

The musketeer, who knew that the lieutenant was incapable of jesting with regard to the service, obeyed without saying a word, although he thought it a curious order. Then turning towards the second musketeer, d'Artagnan said:

"Monsieur de Verger, help me to put this man in a place of safety."

The musketeer, thinking that his lieutenant had just arrested some prince in disguise, bowed, and drawing his sword, signified that he was ready. D'Artagnan mounted the staircase, followed by his prisoner, who in his turn was followed by the soldier, and entered Mazarin's anteroom. Bernouin was waiting there, impatient for news of his master.

"Yes, sir?" he said inquiringly.

"Everything goes well, my dear Monsieur Bernouin, but here is a man whom I must beg you to put in a safe place."

"Where then, sir?"

"Where you like, provided that the place which you shall choose has shutters secured by padlocks and a door which can be locked."

"We have that, sir," replied Bernouin; and the unfortunate coachman was conducted to a chamber, the windows of which were barred, and which looked very much like a prison.

"And now, my good friend," said d'Artagnan to him, "I must ask you to deprive yourself, for my sake, of your hat and cloak."

The coachman, as we can well understand, made no resistance; in fact, he was so astonished at what had happened to him that he stammered and reeled like a drunken man. D'Artagnan deposited his clothes under the arm of one of the valets.

"And now, Monsieur Verger," he said, "shut yourself up with this man until Monsieur Bernouin returns to open the door. Your office will be tolerably long and not very amusing, I know;

but," added he seriously, "you understand, it is on the king's service."

"At your command, lieutenant," replied the musketeer, who saw that the business was a serious one.

"Bye the bye," continued d'Artagnan, "should this man attempt to fly or call out, pass your sword through his body."

The musketeer signified that the commands should be obeyed to the letter, and d'Artagnan went out, followed by Bernouin. Midnight struck.

"Lead me into the queen's oratory," said d'Artagnan, "announce to her I am there, and put this parcel, with a well-loaded musket, under the seat of the carriage which is waiting at the foot of the private stair."

Bernouin conducted d'Artagnan to the oratory, where he sat down pensively. Everything had gone on as usual at the Palais Royal. As we said before, at ten o'clock almost all the guests had dispersed; those who had to fly with the court had the word of command, and they were each severally desired to be from twelve o'clock to one at Cours la Reine.

At ten o'clock Anne of Austria had entered the king's room. *Monsieur* had just retired, and the youthful Louis, remaining the last, was amusing himself by placing some lead soldiers in a line of battle, a game which delighted him much. Two royal pages were playing with him.

"La Porte," said the queen, "it is time for his majesty to go to bed."

The king asked to remain up, having, he said, no wish to sleep; but the queen was steadfast.

"Are you not going early to-morrow morning to bathe at Conflans, Louis? I think you asked to do so yourself."

"You are right, madame," said the king, "and I am ready to retire to my room when you have kissed me. La Porte, give the light to Monsieur the Chevalier de Cosilin."

The queen touched with her lips the white, smooth brow which the royal child presented to her with the gravity which already partook of etiquette.

"Go to sleep soon, Louis," said the queen, "for you must be woke very early."

"I will do my best to obey you, madame," said the youthful king, "but I have no desire to sleep."

"La Porte," said Anne of Austria, in a whisper, "find some very dull book to read to his Majesty, but do not undress yourself."

The king went out, accompanied by the Chevalier de Cosilin bearing the candlestick, and then the queen returned to her own apartment. Her ladies—that is to say, Madame de Brey, Mademoiselle de Beaumont, Madame de Motteville, and Socraytine, her sister, so called on account of her sense, had just brought into her dressing-room the remains of the dinner, upon which, according to her usual custom, she partook. The queen then gave her orders, spoke of a banquet which the Marquis de Villequier was to give to her on the day after the morrow, indicated the person whom she should admit to the honour of being at it, announced another visit on the following day to Val-de-Grace, where she intended to pay her devotions, and gave her commands to her senior valet to accompany her. When the ladies had finished their supper, the queen feigned extreme fatigue, and passed into her bedroom. Madame de Motteville, who was on especial duty that evening, followed to aid and undress her. The queen then began to read, and, after conversing with her affectionately for a few minutes, dismissed her.

It was at this moment that d'Artagnan entered with the Coadjutor's carriage into the courtyard of the palace, and a few minutes later the carriage of the ladies-in-waiting drove out, and the gates were shut after them.

Just after twelve o'clock Bernouin knocked at the queen's bedroom door, having come by the Cardinal's secret corridor. Anne of Austria opened the door herself. She was undressed—that is to say, she had drawn on her stockings again, and was wrapped in a long dressing-gown.

"It is you, Bernouin," she said. "Is Monsieur d'Artagnan there?"

"Yes, madame, in your oratory; he is awaiting the orders of your majesty."

"I am ready. Go and tell La Porte to wake and dress the king, and then pass on to the Maréchal de Villeroy and summon him to me."

Bernouin bowed and retired.

The queen entered her oratory, which was lighted by a single lamp of Venetian crystal. She saw d'Artagnan, who stood expecting her.

"Is it you?" she said.

"Yes, madame."

"Are you ready?"

"I am."

"And his Eminence, the Cardinal."

"Has got off without any accident. He is awaiting your majesty at Cours la Reine."

"But in what carriage do we start?"

"I have provided for everything; a carriage is waiting below for your majesty."

"Let us go to the king."

D'Artagnan bowed, and followed the queen. The young king was already dressed, with the exception of his shoes and doublet; he had allowed himself to be dressed in great astonishment, overwhelming with questions La Porte, who replied only in these words:

"Sire, it is by the order of the queen."

The bed was open, and the sheets were so worn that holes could be seen in some places—another evidence of the meanness of Mazarin.

The queen entered, and d'Artagnan remained at the door. As soon as the child saw the queen escaped from La Porte, and ran to meet her. Anne then motioned to d'Artagnan to approach, and he obeyed.

"My son," said Anne of Austria, pointing to the musketeer, standing calm and uncovered, "here is Monsieur d'Artagnan, who is as brave as one of those ancient heroes concerning whom you like so much to hear. Remember his name well, and look at him well, that his face may not be forgotten, for this evening he is going to render us a great and glorious service."

The young king looked at the officer with his full, proud eye, and repeated:

"Monsieur d'Artagnan."

"That is it, my son."

The young king slowly raised his hand, and held it out to the musketeer; the latter bent on his knee, and kissed it.

"Monsieur d'Artagnan," repeated Louis; "very well, madame."

Just then they were startled by a noise as if a tumult were approaching.

"What is that?" exclaimed the queen.

"Oh, oh!" replied d'Artagnan, straining both at the same time his quick ear and his intelligent glance, "it is the sound of the people revolting."

"We must proceed," said the queen.

"Your majesty has given me the control of this business; we must wait and see what they want."

"Monsieur d'Artagnan!"

"I will answer for everything."

Nothing is so catching as confidence. The queen, full of strength and courage, was quickly alive to those two virtues in others.

"Do as you like," she said, "I rely upon you."

"Will your majesty permit me to give orders in your name in this whole business?"

"Command, sir."

"What do the people require?" asked the king.

"We are about to know, sire," replied d'Artagnan, as he rapidly left the room.

The tumult continued to increase, and seemed to surround the Palais Royal entirely. Cries were heard from the interior, of which they could not comprehend the sense. It was plain that there was clamour and sedition.

The king, half-dressed, the queen and La Porte remained each in the same state, and almost in the same place, where they were listening and waiting. Comminges, who was on guard that night at the Palais Royal, ran in. He had about two hundred men in the courtyards and stables, and he placed them at the queen's disposal.

"Well," asked Anne of Austria, when d'Artagnan reappeared, "what is it?"

"It is, madame, that the report has spread that the queen has left the Palais Royal, carrying off the king, and the people ask to have proof to the contrary, or threaten to demolish the Palais Royal."

"Oh, this time it is too much," exclaimed the queen, "and I will prove to them that I have not left."

D'Artagnan saw from the expression of the queen's face that she was about to give some violent command. He went to her, and said, in a low voice:

"Has your majesty still confidence in me?"

His voice startled her. "Yes, sir," she replied, "every confidence—speak."

"Will the queen deign to follow my advice?"

"Speak."

"Let your majesty dismiss M. de Comminges, and desire him to shut himself up with his men, in the guard-house and in the stables."

Comminges glanced at d'Artagnan, with the envious look with which every courtier sees a new favourite spring up.

"You hear, Comminges?" said the queen.

D'Artagnan approached him; with his usual alertness he had caught the anxious glance.

"Monsieur de Comminges," he said, "pardon me; we are both the queen's servants, are we not? it is my turn to be of use to her; do not envy me this happiness."

Comminges bowed and left.

"Come," thought d'Artagnan, "that is one more enemy for me there."

"And now," said the queen, addressing d'Artagnan, "what is to be done? for you hear that, instead of decreasing, the noise becomes louder."

"Madame," said d'Artagnan, "the people want to see the king, and they must see him."

"How! they must see him! where, on the balcony?"

"Not at all, madame, but here, sleeping in his bed."

"Oh, your majesty," exclaimed La Porte, "Monsieur d'Artagnan is right."

The queen became thoughtful, and smiled, like a woman to whom duplicity is no stranger.

"Without doubt," she murmured.

"Monsieur La Porte," said d'Artagnan, "go and announce to the people through the grating that they are going to be satisfied, and that in five minutes they shall not only see the king, but they shall see him in bed; and that the king sleeps, and that the queen begs that they will keep silence, so as not to awaken him."

"But not every one; a deputation of two or four people."

"Every one, madame."

"But reflect, they will keep us here till daybreak."

"It shall take but a quarter of an hour. I answer for everything, madame; believe me, I know the people—they are like a great child, who simply wants humouring. Before the sleeping king, they will be mute, gentle, and timid as lambs."

"Go, La Porte," said the queen.

The young king approached his mother and said: "Why do as these people ask?"

"It must be so, my son," said Anne of Austria.

"But then, are the people to say 'it must be' to *me*; am I not the king? and is not the will of the king supreme and highest of all?"

The queen remained silent.

"Sire," said d'Artagnan, "will your majesty permit me to ask you a question?"

Louis XIV. turned round, astonished that any one should dare to address *him*. But the queen pressed the child's hand.

"Yes, sir," he said.

"Does your majesty remember when playing in the park of Fontainebleau, or in the palace courts at Versailles, to have seen the sky suddenly become dark, and have heard the sound of thunder?"

"Yes, certainly."

"Well, then, this noise of thunder, however much your majesty may have wished to play on, has said: 'Go in, sire.' You must do so."

"Certainly, sir; but they tell me that the noise of thunder is the voice of God."

"Well, then, sire," continued d'Artagnan, "listen to the voice of the people, and you will see that it very much resembles that of thunder, which, as your majesty truly observes, is the voice of God."

In truth, at that moment a terrible murmur was wafted to them by the night breeze; then all at once it ceased.

"Hold, sire," said d'Artagnan, "they have just told the people that you are asleep; you see that you *are* the king."

The queen looked with surprise at this strange man, whose brilliant courage made him the equal of the bravest, and who was, by his fine and ready intelligence, the equal of all.

La Porte entered. "Well, La Porte," asked the queen.

"Madame," he replied, "Monsieur d'Artagnan's prediction has been accomplished; they were calmed as if by magic. The doors are about to be opened, and in five minutes they will be here."

"La Porte," said the queen, "suppose you substitute one of your sons in the king's place; we might be away during the time."

"If your majesty desires it," said La Porte, "my sons, like myself, are at the queen's service."

"Not at all," said d'Artagnan; "for should one of them know his majesty, and discover the substitute, all would be lost."

"You are right! chevalier—always right," said Anne of Austria. "La Porte, place the king in bed."

La Porte placed the king, dressed as he was, in the bed, and then covered him as far as the shoulders with the sheet. The queen bent over him, and kissed his forehead.

"Pretend to sleep, Louis," said she.

"Yes," said the king, "but I wish not to be touched by one of those men."

"Sire, I am here," said d'Artagnan, "and I give you my word that if a single man has the audacity, his life shall pay for it."

"And now what is to be done?" asked the queen, "for I hear them."

"Monsieur La Porte, go to them, and again recommend silence. Madame, stand by the door, whilst I shall be at the head of the king's bed ready to die for him."

La Porte went out; the queen remained near the hangings, whilst d'Artagnan glided behind the curtains.

Then the heavy and collected steps of a multitude of men were heard, and the queen herself raised the tapestry hangings, and put her finger on her lips.

On seeing the queen, the men stopped short, respectfully.

"Enter, gentlemen; enter," said the queen.

There was then amongst that crowd a moment's hesitation, which looked like shame. They had expected resistance—they had expected to be thwarted—to have to force the gates, and to over-turn the guards. The gates had opened of themselves; and the king, ostensibly at least, had no other guard at his bed-head but his mother. The foremost of them stammered, and attempted to fall back.

"Enter then, gentlemen," said La Porte, "since the queen per-mits you to do so."

Then one more bold than the rest ventured to pass the door, and to advance on tiptoe. This example was imitated by the rest, until the room filled silently, as if these men had been the most humble and devoted courtiers. Far beyond the door, the heads of those who were not able to enter could be seen, all rising on the tips of their feet.

D'Artagnan saw it all through an opening that he had made in the curtain, and in the first man who had entered he had recog-nised Planchet.

"Sir," said the queen to him, thinking that he was the leader of the band, "you wished to see the king, and therefore I determined to show him to you myself. Approach, and look at him, and say if we have the appearance of people who wish to escape."

"No, certainly," replied Planchet, taken aback at the un-expected honour conferred upon him.

"You will say, then, to my good and faithful Parisians," con-tinued Anne, with a smile, the expression of which did not deceive d'Artagnan, "that you have seen the king in bed and asleep, and the queen also ready to retire."

"I shall tell them, madame, and those who accompany me will say the same thing, but——"

"But what?" asked Anne of Austria.

"Will your majesty pardon me," said Planchet; "but is it really the king who is lying there."

Anne of Austria started. "If," she said, "there is one among you who knows the king, let him approach, and say whether it is really his majesty lying there?"

A man wrapped in a cloak, in the folds of which his face was hidden, approached, and bent over the bed.

For a moment d'Artagnan thought the man had some evil design, and he put his hand to his sword; but in the movement made by the man in stooping, a portion of his face was uncovered, and d'Artagnan recognised the Coadjutor.

"It is the king, undoubtedly," said the man, rising again. "God bless his majesty!"

"Yes," repeated the leader in a whisper, "God bless his majesty!" and all these men who had entered furious, passed from anger to pity, and blessed the royal infant in their turn.

"Now," said Planchet, "let us thank the queen. My friends, retire."

They all bowed, and retired by degrees, as noiselessly as they had entered.

Planchet, who had been the first to enter, was the last to leave. The queen stopped him.

"What is your name, my friend?" she said.

Planchet turned round, very much astonished at the question.

"Yes," continued the queen, "I think myself as much honoured to have received you this evening as if you had been a prince, and I wish to know your name."

"Yes," thought Planchet, "to treat me as a prince. No, thank you."

D'Artagnan trembled lest Planchet, infatuated like the crow in the fable, should mention his name, and that the queen possessed of such information, would discover that Planchet was connected with him.

"Madame," replied Planchet respectfully, "I am called Dulaurier, at your service."

"Thank you, Monsieur Dulaurier," said the queen; "and what is your business?"

"Madame, I am a clothier in the Rue Bourdonnais."

"That is all that I wished to know," said the queen. "I am obliged to you, Monsieur Dulaurier. You will hear again from me."

"Come, come," thought d'Artagnan, emerging from behind the curtain; "decidedly Monsieur Planchet is no fool, and it is evident he has been brought up in a good school."

The different actors in this strange scene remained facing one another, without uttering a single word; the queen standing near the door—d'Artagnan half out of his hiding-place—the king raised on his elbow, ready to fall down on his bed again, at the slightest sound which should indicate the return of the multitude; but instead of approaching, the noise became more and more distant, and finished by dying away entirely.

The queen breathed more freely. D'Artagnan wiped his damp forehead, and the king slid off his bed, saying, "Let us go."

At this moment La Porte reappeared.

"Well?" asked the queen.

"Well, madame!" replied the valet; "I followed them as far as the gates. They announced to all their comrades that they had seen the king, and that the queen had spoken to them; and, in fact, they have gone off quite proud and happy."

"Oh, the miserable wretches!" murmured the queen, "they shall pay dearly for their boldness, and it is I who promise it to them."

Then turning to d'Artagnan, she said:

"Sir, you have given me this evening the best advice that I have ever received. Continue, and say what we must do now."

"Monsieur La Porte," said d'Artagnan, "finish dressing his majesty."

"We may depart then?" asked the queen.

"When your majesty pleases. You have only to descend by the private stairs, and you will find me at the door."

"Go, sir," said the queen; "we will follow you."

D'Artagnan went down, and found the carriage, and the musketeer on the box. D'Artagnan took out the parcel, which he had desired Bernouin to place under the seat. It may be remembered that it was the hat and cloak belonging to Monsieur de Gondy's coachman.

He put the cloak on his shoulders, and the hat on his head, whilst the musketeer got off the box.

"Sir," said d'Artagnan, "you will go and release your companion, who is guarding the coachman. You must mount your horse, and proceed to Rue Tiquetonne, Hôtel de la Chevrette, whence you will take my horse, and that of Monsieur du Valon, which you must saddle and equip as if for war, and then you will leave Paris, bringing them with you to Cours la Reine. If, when you arrive at Cours la Reine, you find no one, you must go on to St. Germain. On the king's service."

The musketeer touched his hat, and went away to execute the orders that had been given him.

D'Artagnan mounted on the box, having a pair of pistols in his belt, a musket under his feet, and a naked sword behind him.

The queen appeared, and was followed by the king and the Duc d'Anjou, his brother.

"Monsieur the Coadjutor's carriage!" she exclaimed, falling back.

"Yes, madame," said d'Artagnan; "but get in fearlessly, for I drive you."

The queen uttered a cry of surprise, and entered the carriage, and the king and Monsieur took their places at her side.

"Come, La Porte," said the queen.

"How, madame!" said the valet, "in the same carriage as your majesties?"

"It is not a matter of royal etiquette this evening, but of the king's safety. Get in, La Porte."

La Porte obeyed.

"Pull down the blinds," said d'Artagnan.

"But will that not excite suspicion, sir?" asked the queen.

"Your majesty's mind may be quite at ease," replied the officer. "I have my answer ready."

The blinds were pulled down, and they started at a gallop by the Rue Richelieu. On reaching the gate, the captain of the post advanced at the head of some ten men, holding a lantern in his hand.

D'Artagnan signed to them to draw near.

"Do you recognise the carriage?" he asked the sergeant.

"No," replied the latter.

"Look at the arms."

The sergeant put the lantern near the panel.

"They are those of Monsieur le Coadjuteur," he said.

"Open the gate," he continued. "It is all right, it is Monsieur le Coadjuteur."

The order was at once complied with, the gate groaned on its hinges, and d'Artagnan, seeing the way cleared, whipped on his horses, who started at a canter, and five minutes later they had rejoined the Cardinal.

"Mousqueton!" exclaimed d'Artagnan, "draw up the blinds of his majesty's carriage."

"It is he!" cried Porthos.

"As a coachman!" exclaimed Mazarin.

"And with the Coadjutor's carriage!" said the queen.

"*Corpo di Dio!* Monsieur d'Artagnan," said Mazarin, "you are orth your weight in gold."

53

WHAT D'ARTAGNAN AND PORTHOS EARNED BY THE SALE OF STRAW

MAZARIN was anxious to set out instantly for St. Germain; but the queen declared that she should wait for the people whom she had appointed to meet her. However, she offered the Cardinal La Porte's place, which he accepted, and went from one carriage to the other.

It was not without foundation that a report of the king's intending to leave Paris by night had been circulated. Ten or twelve persons had been in the secret since six o'clock, and how great soever their prudence might be, they could not issue the necessary orders for the departure without the thing transpiring a little. Besides, each individual had some one or two others interested in him; and as there could be no doubt but that the queen was leaving Paris full of terrible projects of vengeance, every one had warned parents and friends of what was going to happen; so that the news of the approaching exit ran like a train of lighted gunpowder through the streets.

The first carriage which arrived after that of the queen was that of the Prince de Condé, who, with the princess and dowager-princess, was in it. Both these ladies had been awakened in the middle of the night, and did not know what it was all about. The second contained the Duke and Duchess of Orléans, the tall young Mademoiselle, and the Abbé de la Rivière; and the third, the Duc de Longueville and the Prince de Conti, brother and brother-in-law of Condé. They all alighted, and hastened to pay their respects to the king and queen in their coach. The queen fixed her eyes upon the carriage they had left, and seeing that it was empty, she said:

"But where is Madame de Longueville?"

"Ah, yes, where is my sister?" inquired the prince.

"Madame de Longueville is ill," said the duke, "and she desired me to present her excuses to your majesty."

Anne gave a quick glance at Mazarin, who replied by an almost imperceptible shake of his head.

"What do you say of this?" asked the queen.

"I say that she is an hostage for the Parisians," answered the Cardinal.

"Why has she not come?" asked the prince in a low voice, addressing his brother.

"Silence," whispered the duke; "she has her reasons."

"She will ruin us!" replied the prince.

"She will save us," said Conti.

Carriages now arrived in crowds: those of the Maréchal de Villeroy, Guitant, Villequier, and Comminges came into the line. The two musketeers arrived in their turn, holding the horses of d'Artagnan and Porthos in their hands. These two instantly mounted; the coachman of the latter replacing d'Artagnan on the box of the royal coach. Mousqueton took the place of the coachman, and drove standing—for reasons known alike to the reader and himself—like the Phaeton of antiquity.

The queen, though occupied by a thousand details, tried to catch the Gascon's eye; but he, with his wonted prudence, had mingled with the crowd.

"Let us be the vanguard," said he to Porthos, "and find out good quarters at St. Germain; nobody will think of us, and for my part, I am extremely tired."

"As for me," replied Porthos, "I'm falling asleep, considering that we have not had any fighting; truly, the Parisians are idiots."

"Or rather, we are very clever," said d'Artagnan.

"Perhaps."

"And your wrist—how is it?"

"Better—but do you think that we've got them this time?"

"Got what?"

"You, your promotion—and I, my title."

"I'faith! yes—I should expect so—besides, if they forget, I shall take the liberty of reminding them."

"The queen's voice! She is speaking," said Porthos; "I think she wants to ride on horseback."

"Oh, she would like it—she would—but——"

"But what?"

"His Eminence won't allow it. Gentlemen," he said, addressing the two musketeers, "be so kind as to accompany the royal carriage; we shall seek for lodgings."

"Let us depart, gentlemen," said the queen.

And the royal carriage drove on, followed by the other coaches and about fifty horsemen.

They reached St. Germain without any incident; on descending the footstep, the queen found the prince awaiting her, bareheaded, to offer her his hand.

"What an alarum for the Parisians!" said the queen.

"It is war!" was the emphatic remark of the prince.

"Well, then, let it be war! Have we not on our side the conqueror of Rocroy, of Nordlingen, of Lens?"

The prince bowed low.

It was then nine o'clock in the morning. The queen walked first into the château; every one followed her. About two hundred persons had followed her in her flight.

"Gentlemen," said the queen, laughing, "pray take up your abode in the château; it is large, and there will be no want of room for you all; but, as we never thought of coming here, I am informed that there are, in all, only three beds here, one for the king, one for me——"

"And one for the Cardinal," muttered the prince.

"Am I—am I then to sleep on the floor?" asked Gaston d'Orléans, with a forced smile.

"No, my prince," replied Mazarin, "for the third bed is intended for your highness."

"But your Eminence?" replied the prince.

"I"—answered Mazarin—"I shall not sleep at all; I have work to do."

Gaston desired that he should be shown into the room where he was to sleep, without in the least concerning himself as to where his wife and daughter were to repose.

"Well, for my part, I shall go to bed," said d'Artagnan; "come, Porthos."

Porthos followed the lieutenant with that profound confidence which he had in the wisdom of his friend. They went from one end of the château to the other, Porthos looking with wondering eyes at d'Artagnan, who was counting on his fingers.

"Four hundred, at a pistole each—four hundred pistoles."

"Yes," interposed Porthos, "four hundred pistoles; but who is to make four hundred pistoles?"

"A pistole is not enough," said d'Artagnan, "'tis worth a louis."

"What is worth a louis?"

"Four hundred, at a louis each, make four hundred louis."

"Four hundred!" exclaimed Porthos.

"Listen!" cried d'Artagnan.

But as there were all kinds of people about, who were in a state of wonderment at the arrival of the court, which they were watching, he murmured in his friend's ear.

"I understand," answered Porthos, "I understand you perfectly, on my honour: two hundred louis, each of us would be making a pretty good thing of it; but what will people say?"

"Let them say what they will; besides, how will they know it's us?"

"But who will distribute these things?" asked Porthos.

"I, and Mousqueton there."

"But he wears my livery; my livery will be known," replied Porthos.

"He can turn his coat inside out."

"You are always in the right, my dear friend," cried Porthos; "but where the dickens do you discover all the notions you put into practice?"

D'Artagnan smiled. The two friends turned down the first street they came to. Porthos knocked at the door of a house to the right, whilst d'Artagnan knocked at the door of a house to the left.

"Some straw," they asked.

"Sir, we don't keep it," was the reply of the people who opened the doors; "but ask, please, at the hay-dealer's."

"Where is the hay-dealer's?"

"At the last door in the street."

"Are there any other people in Saint Germain who sell straw?"

"Yes; there's the landlord of the Lamb, and Gros-Louis, the farmer—they live in the Rue des Ursulines."

"Very well."

D'Artagnan went immediately to the hay-dealer, and agreed with him for a hundred and fifty trusses of straw, which he had at the rate of three pistoles each. He went afterwards to the inn-keeper, and bought from him two hundred trusses at the same price. Finally, Farmer Louis sold them eighty trusses, making in all four hundred and thirty.

There was no more to be had in Saint Germain. This foraging did not occupy more than half an hour. Mousqueton, duly instructed, was put at the head of this sudden and new business. He was ordered not to let a bit of straw out of his hands under a louis a truss, and they entrusted to him straw to the amount of four hundred and thirty louis. D'Artagnan, taking with him three trusses of straw, returned to the château, where everybody, freezing with cold and falling asleep, envied the king, the queen, and the Duke of Orléans on their camp-beds. The lieutenant's entrance produced a burst of laughter in the drawing-room; but he did not appear to notice that he was the object of general attention, but began to prepare, with so much cleverness, nicety, and gaiety, his straw bed, that the mouths of all these sleepy creatures, who could not go to sleep, began to water.

"Straw!" they all cried out, "straw! where is there any to be found?"

"I can show you," answered the Gascon.

And he conducted them to Mousqueton, who distributed

lavishly the trusses at a louis a piece. It was thought rather dear, but people wanted to go to sleep, and who would not give even two or three louis for some hours of sound sleep?

Mousqueton, who knew something of what was going on in the château, wondered that the idea had not occurred to him sooner. D'Artagnan put the gold in his hat, and, in going back to the château, settled the reckoning with Porthos; each of them had cleared two hundred and fifty louis.

Porthos, however, found that he had no straw left for himself. He returned to Mousqueton, but the steward had sold the last wisp. He then repaired to d'Artagnan, who, thanks to his three trusses of straw, was in the act of making up and of tasting, by anticipation, the luxury of a bed so soft, so well stuffed at the head, so well covered at the foot, that it would have excited the envy of the king himself, if his majesty had not been fast asleep in his own. D'Artagnan could not on any account consent to pull his bed to pieces again for Porthos, but for a consideration of four louis that the latter paid him for it, he consented that Porthos should share his couch with him. He laid his sword at the head, his pistols by his side, stretched his cloak over his feet, placed his felt hat on the top of his cloak, and extended himself luxuriously on the straw, which rustled under him. He was already enjoying the sweet dreams engendered by the possession of two hundred and nineteen louis, made in a quarter of an hour, when a voice was heard at the door of the hall, which made him stir.

"Monsieur d'Artagnan!" it cried.

"Here!" cried Porthos, "here!"

Porthos foresaw that if d'Artagnan was called away he should remain sole possessor of the bed. An officer approached.

"I am come to fetch you, Monsieur d'Artagnan."

"From whom?"

"His Eminence."

"Tell my lord that I'm going to sleep, and I advise him, as a friend, to do the same."

"His Eminence is not gone to bed, and will not go to bed, and wants you immediately."

"The devil take Mazarin, who does not know when to sleep at the proper time. What does he require of me now? Is it to make me a captain? In that case he has my pardon."

And the musketeer rose, grumbling, took his sword, hat, pistols, and cloak, and followed the officer, whilst Porthos, alone, and sole possessor of the bed, endeavoured to follow the good example of falling asleep, which his predecessor had set him.

"Monsieur d'Artagnan," said the Cardinal, on perceiving him,

"I have not forgotten with what zeal you have served me. I am going to prove to you that I have not."

"Good," thought the Gascon, "this begins well."

"Monsieur d'Artagnan," he resumed, "do you wish to become a captain?"

"Yes, my lord."

"And your friend still wishes to be made a baron?"

"At this very moment, my lord, he's dreaming that he is one."

"Then," said Mazarin, taking from his portfolio the letter which he had already shown d'Artagnan, "take this despatch, and carry it to England."

D'Artagnan looked at the envelope; there was no address on it.

"Am I not to know to whom it is addressed?"

"You will know when you reach London: at London you may tear off the outer envelope."

"And what are my instructions?"

"To obey, in every particular, him to whom this letter is sent. You must set out for Boulogne. At the Royal Arms of England you will find a young gentleman, named Mordaunt."

"Yes, my lord; and what am I to do with this young gentleman?"

"To follow him wherever he leads."

D'Artagnan looked at the Cardinal with a puzzled air.

"There are your instructions," said Mazarin; "go!"

"Go! 'tis easy to say so, but that requires money, and I haven't any."

"Ah!" replied Mazarin, "so you've no money?"

"None, my lord."

"But the ring I gave you yesterday?"

"I wish to keep it in remembrance of your Eminence."

Mazarin heaved a sigh.

"'Tis very dear living in England, my lord, especially as envoy extraordinary."

"Zounds!" replied Mazarin, "the English people are very sedate, and their habits simple, since the revolution; but no matter."

He opened a drawer, and took out a purse.

"What do you say to a thousand crowns?"

D'Artagnan pouted his lower lip in a most extraordinary manner.

"I reply, my lord, 'tis but a little, as certainly I shall not go alone."

"I suppose not. Monsieur du Valon, that worthy gentleman, for, with the exception of yourself, Monsieur d'Artagnan, there's not a man in France that I esteem and love so much as him——"

"Then, my lord," replied d'Artagnan, pointing to the purse which Mazarin still held, "if you love and esteem him so much, you—understand me?"

"Be it so! on his account I add two hundred crowns."

"Scoundrel!" muttered d'Artagnan—"but on our return," he said aloud, "may we, that is, my friend and I, depend on having, he his barony, and I my promotion?"

"On the honour of Mazarin."

"I should like another sort of oath better," said d'Artagnan to himself—then aloud, "May I not offer my duty to her majesty the queen?"

"Her majesty is asleep, and you must set off at once," answered Mazarin, "go, pray, sir——"

"One word more, my lord; if there's any fighting where I'm going, ought I to fight?"

"You are to obey the commands of the personage to whom the letter is addressed."

"'Tis well," said d'Artagnan, holding out his hand for the money. "I offer my best respects and services to you, my lord."

D'Artagnan then, returning to the officer, said:

"Sir, have the goodness also to awaken Monsieur du Valon, and to say 'tis by his Eminence's orders, and that I shall wait for him at the stables."

The officer went off with an eagerness that showed the Gascon that he had some personal interest in the matter.

Porthos was comfortably sleeping, when some one touched him on the shoulder.

"I come from the Cardinal," said the officer.

"Heigho!" said Porthos, opening his large eyes; "what do you say?"

"I say that his Eminence has ordered you to go to England, that Monsieur d'Artagnan is waiting for you in the stables."

Porthos sighed heavily—arose, took his hat, his pistols, and his cloak, and departed, casting a look of regret on the bed where he had hoped to sleep so well.

Scarcely had he turned his back than the officer laid himself down in it, and he had not crossed the threshold of the door, before his successor, in his turn, snored immoderately, which was natural, he being the only man in the whole assemblage, except the king, the queen, and the Duke of Orléans, who slept gratis.

54

NEWS FROM ARAMIS

D'ARTAGNAN had gone straight to the stables. Day was just dawning. He found his horse and that of Porthos fastened to the manger, but to an empty manger. He took pity on these poor animals, and went to a corner of the stable, where he saw a little straw, but in doing so he struck his foot against a round body, which uttered a cry, and arose on its knees, rubbing its eyes. It was Mousqueton, who, having no straw to lie upon himself, had helped himself to that of the horses.

"Mousqueton," cried d'Artagnan, "come, come, let us be off!"

Mousqueton, recognising the voice of his master's friend, got up suddenly, and in doing so, let fall some louis which he had appropriated to himself illegally during the night.

"Ho! ho!" exclaimed d'Artagnan, picking up a louis and displaying it; "here's a louis that smells of straw a little."

Mousqueton became so confused that the Gascon began to laugh at him, and said:

"Porthos would be angry, my dear Monsieur Mouston, but I pardon you; only let us remember that this gold must serve us as a jest—so be gay—come on."

Mousqueton instantly assumed a most jovial countenance, saddled the horses quickly, and mounted his own without making faces over it.

Whilst this went on, Porthos arrived with a very cross look on his face, and was astonished to find the lieutenant resigned, and Mousqueton almost merry.

"Ah, that's it," he cried, "you have your promotion, and I my barony."

"We are going to fetch our brevets," said d'Artagnan, "and when we come back, Mazarin will sign them."

"And where are we going?" asked Porthos.

"To Paris first—I have affairs to settle."

And they both set out for Paris.

On arriving at its gates they were astounded to see the threatening aspect of the capital. Around two broken-down carriages the people were uttering imprecations, whilst the persons who had attempted to escape were made prisoners—that is to say, an old man and two women. On the other hand, when the two friends wanted to enter, they showed them every kind of civility, thinking them deserters from the royal party, and wishing to bind them to their own.

"How is the king?" they asked.

"He is sleeping."

"And the queen?"

"She's dreaming."

"And the Cardinal?"

"He is awake, so keep on the watch—as they are gone away, it's for some purpose, rely on it. But as you are the strongest after all," continued d'Artagnan, "don't be furious with old men and women, and keep your wrath for proper occasions."

The people listened to these words, and let go the ladies, who thanked d'Artagnan with an appealing look.

"Now! onward!" cried the Gascon.

And they continued their way, crossing the barricades, getting the chains about their legs, pushed about, questioning, and questioned.

In the place of the Palais Royal d'Artagnan saw a sergeant, who was drilling six or seven hundred citizens. It was Planchet, who brought into play profitably the recollections of his former military days. He recognised his old master, and, staring at him with wondering eyes, stood still. The first row, seeing their sergeant stop, stopped also, and soon to the very last.

"These citizens are awfully ridiculous," observed d'Artagnan to Planchet, and went on his way.

Five minutes afterwards he entered the hotel of La Chevrette, where pretty Madeleine, the hostess, came to him.

"My dear Mistress Turquanie," said the Gascon, "if you happen to have any money, lock it up quickly. If you happen to have any jewels, hide them directly; if you happen to have any debtors, make them pay you, or have any creditors, don't pay them."

"Why, prithee?" asked Madeleine.

"Because Paris is about to be reduced to dust and ashes like Babylon, of which you have heard tell."

"And you are going to leave me at such a time?"

"This very instant."

"And where are you going?"

"Ah, if you could tell me that you'd be doing me a service."

"Ah, me! ah, me!"

"Have you any letters for me?" inquired d'Artagnan, wishing to signify to the hostess that he did not require her lamentations and that she had better spare him the demonstrations of her grief.

"There's one just arrived."

"From Athos," and he read as follows:

" 'DEAR D'ARTAGNAN, DEAR DU VALON,—My good friends, perhaps this may be the last time that you will ever hear from me. Let God, our courage, and the remembrance of our friendship, support you always. I entrust to you certain papers which are at Blois, and in two months and a half, if you do not hear of us, take possession of them.

Embrace, with all your heart, the vicomte, for your devoted friend, ATHOS.' "

"I believe, by heaven," said d'Artagnan, "that I shall embrace him, since he's upon our road; and if he is so unfortunate as to lose our dear Athos, from this very day he becomes my son."

"And I," said Porthos, "shall make him my sole heir."

"Let us see, what more does Athos say?"

" 'Should you meet on your journey a certain Monsieur Mordaunt, distrust him—in a letter I cannot say more.' "

"Monsieur Mordaunt!" exclaimed the Gascon, astonished.

"Monsieur Mordaunt! 'tis well," said Porthos; "we shall remember that—but look, there's a postscript from Aramis."

" 'We conceal the place where we are, dear friend, knowing your brotherly affection, and that you would come and die with us were we to reveal it.' "

"Confound it," interrupted Porthos, with an explosion of passion which sent Mousqueton to the other end of the room; "are they in danger of dying?"

D'Artagnan went on:

" 'Athos bequeaths to you Raoul, and I bequeath to you my revenge. If by any good luck you come across a certain man named Mordaunt, tell Porthos to take him into a corner, and to wring his neck. I dare not say more in a letter.' "

"If that is all, Aramis, it is easily done," said Porthos.

"On the contrary," observed d'Artagnan, with a vexed look; "it would be impossible."

"How so?"

"That is precisely this Monsieur Mordaunt, whom we are going to join at Boulogne, and with whom we cross to England."

"Well, suppose instead of joining this Monsieur Mordaunt, we were to go and join our friends?" said Porthos, with a gesture fit to frighten a whole army.

"I did think of it, but this letter has neither date nor postmark."

"True," said Porthos. And he began to wander about the room

like a man beside himself, gesticulating, and half drawing his sword from the scabbard.

As to d'Artagnan, he remained standing like a man in consternation, with the deepest affliction depicted on his face.

"Ah, 'tis not right; Athos insults us; he wishes to die alone—that's too bad."

Mousqueton, witnessing this despair, melted into tears, in a corner of the room.

"Stop—an idea!" cried Porthos; "indeed, my dear d'Artagnan, I don't know how you manage, but you are always full of ideas; let us go and embrace Raoul."

"Woe to that man who should happen to contradict my master at this moment," said Mousqueton to himself, "I wouldn't give much for his skin."

They set out. On arriving at St. Denis, the friends found a vast concourse of people. It was the Duc de Beaufort who was coming from the Vendômois, and whom the Coadjutor was showing to the Parisians, intoxicated with joy. With the aid of the duke, they considered themselves already as invincible.

"Is it true," said the guard to the two cavaliers, "that the Duc de Beaufort has arrived in Paris?"

"Nothing more certain; and the best proof of it is," said d'Artagnan, "that he has despatched us to meet the Duc de Vendôme, his father, who is coming in his turn."

"Long live de Beaufort!" cried the guards, and they drew back respectfully to let the two friends pass.

Once across the barriers, these two knew neither fatigue nor fear. Their horses flew, and they never ceased speaking of Athos and Aramis.

The camp had entered Saint Omer: the friends made a little round, and went to the camp, and gave the army an exact account of the flight of the king and queen. They saw Raoul near his tent, reclined upon a truss of hay, of which his horse stole some mouthfuls; the young man's eyes were red, and he seemed dejected. The Maréchal de Grammont and the Duc de Guiche had returned to Paris, and he was quite lonely. When he saw the two cavaliers, he ran to them with open arms.

"Oh, is it you, dear friends? Do you come here to fetch me? Shall you take me away with you? Do you bring me tidings of my guardian?"

"Have you not received any?" said d'Artagnan.

"Alas! sir, no—and I do not know what has become of him—so that I am really so unhappy as to weep."

In fact, tears rolled down his cheeks.

Porthos turned aside, in order not to show on his good round face what was passing in his mind.

"Deuce take it," cried d'Artagnan, more moved than he had been for a long time—"don't despair, my friend, if you have not received any letters from the count, we have received—we—one."

"Oh, really!" cried Raoul.

"And a comforting one, too," added d'Artagnan, seeing the delight that this intelligence gave the young man.

"Have you got it?" asked Raoul.

"Yes—that is, I had it," replied the Gascon, making believe to try and find it. "Wait, it ought to be there, in my pocket; it speaks of his return, does it not, Porthos?"

"Yes," replied Porthos, smiling.

"Eh! I read it not long since. Can it be lost? Ah! confound it! my pocket has a hole in it."

"Oh, yes, Monsieur Raoul!" said Mousqueton; "the letter was very consoling. These gentlemen read it to me, and I wept for joy."

"But then, at any rate, you know where he is, Monsieur d'Artagnan?" asked Raoul, somewhat comforted.

"Ah! that's the thing!" replied the Gascon. "Undoubtedly I know it, but it is a mystery."

"Not to me, I hope?"

"No, not to you, so I am about to tell you where he is."

Porthos looked at d'Artagnan with his large wondering eyes.

"Where the devil shall I say he is, so that he cannot try to rejoin him?" thought d'Artagnan.

"Well, where is he, sir?" asked Raoul, in a soft and coaxing voice.

"He is at Constantinople."

"Among the Turks!" exclaimed Raoul, alarmed. "Good heavens! how can you tell me that?"

"Does that alarm you?" cried d'Artagnan. "Pooh! what are the Turks to such men as the Count de la Fère and the Abbé d'Herblay?"

"Ah, his friend is with him!" said Raoul; "that consoles me a little."

"Has he not wit—this demon d'Artagnan?" said Porthos, astonished at his friend's deception.

"Now, sir," said d'Artagnan, wishing to change the conversation, "here are fifty pistoles that the count has sent you by the same courier. I suppose you have no more money, and that they will be welcome."

"I have still twenty pistoles, sir."

"Well, take them; that makes seventy."

"And if you wish for more——" said Porthos, putting his hand to his pocket.

"Thank you, sir," replied Raoul, reddening; "thank you a thousand times."

At this moment Olivain appeared. "Apropos," said d'Artagnan, loud enough for the servant to hear him, "are you satisfied with Olivain?"

"Yes, in most respects, pretty well."

"What fault do you find with the fellow?"

"He is a glutton."

"Oh, sir," cried Olivain, at this accusation.

"And somewhat of a thief."

"Oh, sir! oh!"

"And, more especially, a great coward."

"Oh, oh, sir! you really vilify me!" cried Olivain.

"The deuce!" cried d'Artagnan. "Pray learn, Monsieur Olivain, that people like us are not to be served by cowards. You rob your master—you eat his sweetmeats and drink his wine; but, by Jove! don't be a coward, or I shall lop off your ears. Look at Monsieur Mouston, see the honourable wounds he has received, and look how his habitual valour has given dignity to his countenance."

Mousqueton was in the third heaven, and would have embraced d'Artagnan had he dared; meanwhile, he resolved to sacrifice his life for him on the next occasion that presented itself.

"Send away that fellow, Raoul," said the Gascon; "for if he's a coward he will disgrace you some day."

"Monsieur says I am a coward," cried Olivain, "because he wanted the other day to fight a cornet in Grammont's regiment, and I refused to accompany him."

"Monsieur Olivain, a servant ought never to disobey," said d'Artagnan sternly. Then, taking him aside, he whispered to him, "Thou hast done right; thy master was wrong; here's a crown for thee; but should he ever be insulted, and thou dost not let thyself be cut in quarters for him, I will cut out thy tongue. Remember that well."

Olivain bowed, and slipped the crown into his pocket.

"And now, Raoul," said the Gascon, "Monsieur du Valon and I are going away as ambassadors—where, I know not; but should you want anything, write to Madame Turquainie, at La Chevrette, Rue Tiquetonne, and draw upon her money as on a banker—with economy; for it is not so well filled as that of Monsieur St. Emery."

And having, meantime, embraced the youth, he passed him

into the robust arms of Porthos, who lifted him up from the ground and held him a moment suspended, near the noble heart of that formidable giant.

"Come," said d'Artagnan, "let us go."

And they set out for Boulogne, where, towards evening, they arrived, their horses covered with foam and sweat.

At ten steps from the place where they halted was a young man in black, who seemed waiting for some one, and who, from the moment he saw them enter the town, never took his eyes off them.

D'Artagnan approached him, and seeing him gaze so fixedly, said:

"Well, friend! I don't like people to stare at me!"

"Sir," said the young man, "do you not come from Paris, if you please?"

D'Artagnan thought it was some gossip who wanted news from the capital.

"Yes, sir," he said, in a softened tone.

"Are you not to lodge at the Arms of England?"

"Yes, sir."

"Are you not charged with a mission from his Eminence, Cardinal Mazarin!"

"Yes, sir."

"In that case I am the man you have do with. My name is Mordaunt."

"Ah!" thought d'Artagnan, "the man I am warned against by Athos."

"Ah!" thought Porthos, "the man Aramis wants me to strangle."

"Well, gentlemen," resumed Mordaunt, "we must set off without delay; to-day is the last day granted me by the Cardinal. A ship is waiting, and had you not arrived this day, I must have set off without you, for General Cromwell expects my return impatiently."

"So!" thought the lieutenant, "'tis to General Cromwell that our despatches are addressed."

"Have you no letter to him?" asked the young man.

"I have one, the seal of which I was not to break till I reached London; but since you tell me to whom it is addressed, 'tis useless to wait till then."

D'Artagnan tore open the envelope of the letter. It was directed to "General Oliver Cromwell."

"Ah!" said d'Artagnan, "a singular commission."

"Who is this Monsieur Oliver Cromwell?" asked Porthos.

"Formerly a brewer," replied the Gascon.

"Perhaps Mazarin wishes to make a speculation in beer, as we have in straw," said Porthos.

"Come, come, gentlemen," said Mordaunt impatiently, "let us depart."

"What!" cried Porthos, "without supper? Cannot Monsieur Cromwell wait a little?"

"Yes, but I cannot," replied Mordaunt.

"Oh! as to you, that is not my affair, and I shall sup either with or without your permission."

The young man's eyes kindled a little, but he restrained himself.

"Just as you please, gentlemen, provided we set sail," he said.

"The name of your ship?" inquired d'Artagnan.

"The *Standard*."

"Very well; in half an hour we shall be on board." And the friends, spurring on their horses, rode to the hotel, the Arms of England, where they supped with hearty appetite, and then at once proceeded to the port.

There they found a brig ready to sail, upon the deck of which they recognised Mordaunt, walking to and fro impatiently.

"It is indeed strange," said d'Artagnan, whilst the boat was taking them to the *Standard*, "it is astonishing how that young man resembles some one whom I have known—but whom I cannot name."

A few minutes later they were on board; but the embarkation of the horses was a longer matter than that of the men, and it was eight o'clock before they raised the anchor.

55

THE FAITHLESS SCOT

AND now our readers must leave the *Standard* to sail peaceably, not towards London, where d'Artagnan and Porthos believed they were going, but to Durham, whither Mordaunt had been ordered to repair by the letter he had received during his sojourn at Boulogne, and accompany us to the Royalist camp, on this side of the Tyne, near Newcastle.

There, placed between two rivers on the borders of Scotland, but still on English soil, were the tents of a little army extended. It was midnight. Some Highlanders were keeping watch. The moon, which was partly obscured by two heavy clouds, now and then lit up the muskets of the sentinels, or silvered the walls, the roofs, and the spires of the town that Charles I. had just surrendered to the parliamentary troops, whilst Oxford and Newark still held out for him, in the hopes of coming to some arrangement.

At one of the extremities of the camp, near an immense tent, in which the Scottish officers were holding a kind of council, presided over by Lord Leven, lay their commander, a man dressed as a cavalier, sleeping on the turf, his right hand extended over his sword.

About fifty paces off, another man, also dressed as a cavalier, was talking to a Scotch sentinel, and, though a foreigner, he seemed to understand, without much difficulty, the answers given him in broad Perthshire dialect.

As the town clock of Newcastle struck one the sleeper awoke, and, with all the gestures of a man rousing himself out of a deep sleep, he looked closely about him. Perceiving that he was alone, he rose, and making a little circuit passed close to the man who was speaking to the sentinel. The former had, no doubt, finished his questions, for a moment after he said good-night, and carelessly followed the same path taken by the first cavalier.

In the shadow of a tent the former was awaiting him.

"*Eh bien, mon cher ami,*" said he, in as pure French as has ever been uttered between Rouen and Tours. "*Eh bien, mon ami*; there is not a moment to be lost; we must let the king know at once."

"Why, what is the matter?"

"It is too long to tell you; besides, you wish to hear it all directly, and the least word dropped here might ruin all. We must go and find Lord de Winter."

They both set off to the other end of the camp, but as it did not cover more than a surface of five hundred feet, they quickly arrived at the tent they were looking for.

"Tony, is your master asleep?" said one of the two cavaliers to a servant who was lying in the outer compartment, which served as a kind of anteroom.

"No, Monsieur le Comte," replied the servant, "I think not; or at least, he has not long been so, for he was pacing up and down for more than two hours after he left the king, and the sound of his footsteps has only ceased during the last ten minutes; however, you may look and see," added the servant, raising the curtained entrance of the tent.

As he had said, Lord de Winter was seated near the aperture, arranged as a window to let in the night air, his eyes mechanically following the course of the moon, hidden, as we before observed, by heavy black clouds. The two friends approached de Winter, who, leaning his head on his hand, was gazing at the heavens: he did not hear them enter, and remained in the same attitude till he felt a hand placed on his shoulder.

He turned round, recognised Athos and Aramis, and held out his hand to them.

"Have you noticed," said he to them, "what a blood-red colour the moon is to-night?"

"No," replied Athos; "I thought she appeared much the same as usual."

"Look again, chevalier," returned Lord de Winter.

"I must own," said Aramis, "I am like the Count de la Fère, I can see nothing remarkable about it."

"My lord," said Athos, "in a position so precarious as ours, we must examine the earth, and not the heavens. Have you studied our Scotch troops, and have you confidence in them?"

"The Scotch!" inquired de Winter. "What Scotch?"

"Ours! Egad!" exclaimed Athos, "Those to whom the king has confided Lord Leven's Highlanders."

"No," said de Winter, then he paused; "but tell me, can you not perceive the roseate tint which covers the heavens?"

"Not the least in the world," said Aramis and Athos at once.

"Tell me," continued de Winter, always possessed by the same idea, "is there not a tradition in France that Henry IV., the evening before the day he was assassinated, when he was playing at chess with M. de Bassompierre, saw marks of blood on the chess-board?"

"Yes," said Athos, "and the Maréchal has often told me so himself."

"Then it was so," murmured de Winter, "and the next day Henry IV. was slain."

"But what has this vision of Henry IV. to do with you, my lord?" inquired Aramis.

"Nothing; and, indeed, I am wrong to amuse you with such trifles, when your coming to my tent at such an hour announces that you are the bearers of important news."

"Yes, my lord," said Athos. "I wish to speak to the king."

"To the king! but the king is sleeping."

"I have something important to reveal to him."

"Cannot that be put off till to-morrow?"

"He must know it this moment; and, perhaps, it is already too late."

"Come, then," said Lord de Winter.

Lord de Winter's tent was pitched by the side of the royal one; a kind of corridor communicating between the two. This corridor was guarded, not by a sentinel but by a confidential servant, through whom in any case of urgency the king could communicate instantly with his faithful subject.

"These gentlemen are with me," said de Winter.

The servant bowed and let them pass. As he had said, on a camp-bed, dressed in his black doublet, booted, unbelted, with his felt hat beside him, lay the king, overcome by sleep and fatigue. They advanced, and Athos, who was first to enter, gazed a moment in silence on that pale and noble face, encircled by his long and matted dark hair, the blue veins showing through his transparent skin; his eyes seemingly swollen by tears.

Athos sighed deeply; the sigh awoke the king—so lightly did he sleep.

He raised his eyes.

"Ah!" said he, drawing himself up, "is it you, Count de la Fère?"

"Yes, sire," replied Athos.

"You were watching me while I slept, and you come to bring me some news?"

"Alas! sire," answered Athos, "your majesty has guessed correctly."

"Then it is bad news?"

"Yes, sire."

"Never mind! the messenger is welcome, and you never come here without giving me pleasure. You, whose devotion recognises neither country nor misfortune—you who are sent to me by Henrietta; whatever news you bring, speak out."

"Sire, Cromwell has arrived this night at Newcastle."

"Ah!" exclaimed the king, "to fight?"

"No, sire, but to buy your majesty!"

"What did you say?"

"I said, sire, that he owes four hundred thousand pounds to the Scottish army."

"For unpaid wages, yes, I am aware of it. For the last year my faithful Highlanders have fought for honour alone."

Athos smiled.

"Well, sire! although honour is a fine thing, they are tired of fighting for it, and to-night they have sold you for two hundred thousand pounds—that is to say, the half of what is owing to them."

"Impossible!" cried the king; "the Scotch sell their king for two hundred thousand pounds? and who is the Judas who has concluded this infamous bargain?"

"Lord Leven."

"Are you certain of it, sir?"

"I heard it with my own ears."

The king sighed deeply, as if his heart would break, and then buried his face in his hands.

"Oh! the Scotch," he exclaimed—"the Scotch that I called 'my faithful,' to whom I trusted myself, when I could have fled to Oxford—the Scotch!—my countrymen—the Scotch! my brothers! But are you well assured of it, sir?"

"Lying behind the tent of Lord Leven, I raised it, and saw all—heard all!"

"And when is this to be completed?"

"To-day, in the morning; so your majesty must perceive there is no time to lose!"

"To do what? since you say I am sold."

"To cross the Tyne, reach Scotland, rejoin Lord Montrose, who will not sell you."

"And what shall I do in Scotland? a war of partisans, unworthy of a king."

"Robert Bruce's example will absolve you, sire."

"No! no, I have fought too long; they have sold me, they shall give me up, and the eternal shame of their treason shall fall on their heads."

"Sire," said Athos, "perhaps a king should act thus, but not a husband and a father. I have come in the name of your wife and daughter and two other children you have still in London, and I say to you, 'Live, sire, God wills it!'"

The king raised himself, buckled on his belt, and passing his handkerchief over his moist forehead, inquired:

"Well, what is to be done?"

"Sire, you have in the army only one regiment on which you can rely."

"Winter," said the king, "do you believe in the faithfulness of yours?"

"Sire, they are but men, and men are become both weak and wicked. I will not answer for them. I would confide my life to them, but I should hesitate ere I confided to them that of your majesty."

"Well!" said Athos, "since you have not a regiment, we three devoted men are enough. Let your majesty mount on horseback, and place yourself in the midst of us, and we will cross the Tyne, reach Scotland, and you are saved."

"Do you counsel this also, Winter?" inquired the king.

"Yes, sire!"

"And you, Monsieur d'Herblay?"

"Yes, sire!"

"As you wish, then. Winter, give all the necessary orders."

De Winter left the tent; in the meantime the king finished his toilette. The first rays of daybreak penetrated through the apertures of the tent as de Winter re-entered it.

"All is ready, sire," he said.

"For us also?" inquired Athos.

"Grimaud and Blaisois are holding your horses, ready saddled."

"In that case," exclaimed Athos, "let us not lose an instant in setting off."

"Come," added the king.

"Sire," said Aramis, "will not your majesty acquaint some of your friends of this?"

"My friends!" replied the king sadly, "I have but three—one of twenty years, who has never forgotten me, and two of a week's standing, whom I shall never forget. Come, gentlemen, come."

The king quitted his tent, and found his horse ready waiting for him. It was a chestnut that the king had ridden for three years, and of which he was very fond.

The horse neighed with joy at seeing him.

"Ah!" said the king, "I was unjust; here is a creature that loves me. You, at least, will be faithful to me, Arthur."

The horse, as if it had understood those words, bent its red nostrils towards the king's face, and parting its lips, displayed all its white teeth as if with pleasure.

"Yes, yes," said the king, patting it with his hand, "yes, my Arthur, thou art a good creature."

And then the king threw himself into the saddle, and, turning to Athos, Aramis, and de Winter, said:

"Now, gentlemen, I am ready."

But Athos was standing with his eyes fixed on a black line which bordered the banks of the Tyne, and seemed to extend double the length of the camp.

"What is that line?" cried Athos, whose vision was still rather obscured by the uncertain light of daybreak. "What is that line? I did not perceive it yesterday."

"It must be the fog rising from the river," said the king.

"Sire, it is something thicker than the fog."

"Indeed," said de Winter. "It appears to me like a bar of red colour."

"It is the enemy, who have made a sortie from Newcastle, and are surrounding us!" exclaimed Athos.

"The enemy!" cried the king.

"Yes, the enemy. It is too late. Stay a moment; does not that sunbeam yonder, just by the side of the town, glitter on the Ironsides?"

This was the name given to the regiment whom Cromwell had made his bodyguard.

"Ah!" said the king, "we shall soon see whether our highlanders are traitors or not."

"What shall you do?" asked Athos.

"Give them the order to charge, and run down these miserable rebels."

And the king, putting spurs to his horse, set off to the tent of Lord Leven.

"Follow him," said Athos.

"Come," exclaimed Aramis.

"Is the king wounded?" cried Lord de Winter. "I see spots of blood on the ground,"—and he set off to follow the two friends.

He was stopped by Athos.

"Go and call out your regiment," said he, "I can foresee that we shall have need of it directly."

De Winter turned his horse, and the two friends rode on. It had taken but two minutes for the king to reach the tent of the Scottish commander; he dismounted and entered.

"The king!" they exclaimed, as they all rose in bewilderment.

Charles was indeed in the midst of them; his hat on his head, his brows bent, striking his boot with his riding-whip.

"Yes, gentlemen, the king in person, the king who has come to ask some account of all that has happened."

"What is it, sire?" exclaimed Lord Leven.

"It is, sir," said the king angrily, "that General Cromwell has arrived at Newcastle; that you knew it, and I have not been informed of it; that the enemy have gone from the town, and are now closing the passages of the Tyne against us; that our sentinels have seen this movement, and I have been left ignorant of it. It is that, by an infamous treaty, you have sold me for two hundred thousand pounds to the parliament. Of this treaty at least I have been warned. This is the matter, gentlemen; answer and exculpate yourselves, for I stand here to accuse you."

"Sire," said Lord Leven, with hesitation, "sire, your majesty has been deceived by a false report."

"My own eyes have seen the enemy extend itself between myself and Scotland. With my own ears I have heard the clauses of the treaty debated."

The Scotch chieftains looked at each other in their turn with frowning brows.

"Sire," murmured Lord Leven, crushed by shame; "sire, we are ready to give every proof of our fidelity."

"I ask but one," said the king; "put the army into battle array and face the foe."

"That cannot be, sire," said the earl.

"How—cannot be? and what stays it?"

"Your majesty is well aware that there is a truce between us and the English army."

"And if there is a truce, the English army has broken it in leaving the town, contrary to the agreement which kept it there. Now, I tell you, you must pass with me through this army across to Scotland, and if you refuse, you may choose between two names —which the contempt of all honest men will brand you with, you are either cowards or traitors!"

The eyes of the Scotch flashed fire; and, as often happens on such occasions, from shame they passed to extreme effrontery, and two heads of the clans advanced towards the king.

"Yes," said they, "we have agreed to deliver Scotland and England from him who for the last five-and-twenty years has sucked the blood and gold of Scotland and England. We have promised, and we will keep our promise. Charles Stuart, you are our prisoner."

And both extended their hands as if to seize the king; but before they could touch him with the tips of their fingers both had fallen —one dead and the other stunned.

Aramis had passed his sword through the body of the first, and Athos had knocked down the other with the butt-end of his pistol.

Then, as Lord Leven and the other chieftains retired, alarmed at this unexpected aid, which seemed to fall from heaven for him they believed already their prisoner, Athos and Aramis dragged the king from the perjured assembly, into which he had so imprudently ventured, and throwing themselves on horseback, all three returned at full gallop to the royal tent.

On their way they perceived Lord de Winter hurrying up with his regiment. The king made him a sign to accompany them.

56

THE AVENGER

ALL four entered the tent. They had no plan arranged; one must be matured at once.

The king threw himself into an arm-chair.

"I am lost," he exclaimed.

"No, sire," replied Athos; "you are only betrayed."

The king sighed heavily.

"Betrayed! yes—betrayed by the Scotch, amongst whom I was born; whom I have always loved even more so than the English. Oh, traitors that ye are!"

"Sire," said Athos, "this is not the time for recrimination, but a time to show yourself a king and a gentleman. Up, sire, up! for you have here at least three men who will not betray you. Ah! if we had been five!" murmured Athos, thinking of d'Artagnan and Porthos.

"What are you saying?" inquired the king, rising.

"I said, sire, there is more than one thing open. Lord de Winter answers for his regiment, or at least very nearly so—we will not split straws about words—let him place himself at the head of his men, we will place ourselves at the side of your majesty, and let us cut through Cromwell's army and reach Scotland."

"There is another mode," said Aramis. "Let one of us put on the dress, and mount the king's horse. Whilst they pursue him the king might escape."

"It is good advice," said Athos, "and if the king will do us the honour, we will be truly grateful to him."

"What do you think of this counsel, Winter?" asked the king, looking with admiration at these two men, whose chief idea seemed to be how they could take on their own shoulders all the dangers which threatened him.

"I think that the only chance of saving your majesty has just been proposed by Monsieur d'Herblay. I humbly entreat your majesty to choose quickly, for we have not a moment to lose."

"But if I accept, it is death, or at least imprisonment, for him who takes my place."

"It is the glory of having saved his king," cried de Winter.

The king looked at his old friend with tears in his eyes, un-fastened the order of the Saint-Esprit which he wore, to honour

the two Frenchmen who were with him, and passed it round
de Winter's neck, who received, on his knees, this striking proof of
his sovereign's confidence and friendship.

"It is right," said Athos; "he has served your majesty longer
than we have."

The king overheard these words, and turned round, with tears
in his eyes.

"Wait a moment, sirs," said he; "I have an order for each of
you also."

He turned to a closet where his own orders were locked up, and
took out two ribbons of the Order of the Garter.

"These cannot be for us?" said Athos.

"Why not, sir?" asked the king.

"Such are for royalty, and we are simple gentlemen."

"Speak not of crowned heads. I shall not find amongst them
such noble hearts as yours. No, no, you do yourselves injustice;
but I am here to do justice to you. On your knees, count."

Athos knelt down, and the king passed the ribbon from left to
right as usual, and said: "I make you a knight. Be brave, faithful,
and loyal. You are brave, faithful, and loyal. I knight you,
Monsieur le Comte."

Then, turning to Aramis, he said:

"It is now your turn, Monsieur le Chevalier."

The same ceremony recommenced, with the same words, whilst
de Winter unlaced his leather cuirass, that he might disguise himself
like the king, who, having finished with Aramis the same as Athos,
embraced them both.

"Sire," said de Winter, who in this trying emergency felt
strangely excited, "we are ready."

The king looked at the three gentlemen. "Then we must fly!"
said he.

"Fly through an army, sire?" said Athos.

"Then I shall die sword in hand," said Charles I. "Monsieur
le Comte, Monsieur le Chevalier, if ever I am king——"

"Sire, you have already honoured us more than simple gentlemen could ever aspire to, therefore gratitude is on our side. But we
must not lose time; we have already wasted too much."

The king again shook hands with all three, exchanged hats with
de Winter, and went out.

De Winter's regiment was situated on some high ground above
the camp. The king, followed by the three friends, turned his steps
that way. The Scotch camp seemed as if at last awakened; the
soldiers had come out of their tents, and taken up their station in
battle array.

"Do you see that?" said the king. "Perhaps they are penitent, and preparing to march."

"If they are penitent," said Athos, "they will follow us."

"Well!" said the king, "what shall we do?"

"Let us examine the enemy's army."

At the same instant the eyes of the little group were fixed on the same line which at daybreak they had mistaken for fog, and which the morning sun now plainly showed was an army in order of battle. The air was soft and clear, as it always is at this hour of the morning. The regiments, the standards, and even the colours of the horses and uniforms were now clearly distinct.

On the summit of a rising ground, a little in advance of the enemy, appeared a short and heavy-looking man; this man was surrounded by officers. He turned a spy-glass towards the little group amongst which the king stood.

"Does this man know your majesty personally?" inquired Aramis.

The king smiled.

"That man is Cromwell," said he.

"Ah!" said Athos, "how much time we have lost."

"Now," said the king, "give the word, and let us away."

"Will you not give it, sire?" asked Athos.

"No; I make you my lieutenant-general," said the king.

"Listen, then, Lord de Winter. Proceed sire, I pray. What we are going to say does not concern your majesty."

The king, smiling, turned a few steps back.

"This is what I propose doing," said Athos. "We will divide our regiment into two squadrons. You will put yourself at the head of the first; we and his majesty at the head of the second. If no obstacle happens, we will both charge together, force the enemy's line, and throw ourselves into the Tyne, which we must cross, either by fording or swimming; if, on the contrary, any repulse should take place, you and your men must fight to the last man, whilst we and the king proceed on our way. Once arrived at the brink of the river, should we even find them three ranks deep, as long as you and your regiment do your duty, we will look to the rest."

"To horse!" said Lord de Winter.

"To horse!" re-echoed Athos; "all is arranged and decided."

"Now, gentlemen," cried the king, "forward! and rally to the old cry of France—Montjoy and St. Denis. The war-cry of England is too often in the mouths of those traitors."

The Scotch army stood motionless and silent with shame on viewing these preparations.

Some of the chieftains left the ranks, and broke their swords in two.

"There," said the king, "that consoles me; they are not all traitors."

At this moment de Winter's voice was raised with the cry of "Forward!"

The first squadron moved off; the second followed it, and descended from the platform. A regiment of cuirassiers, nearly equal as to numbers, came from behind the hill, and at full speed towards it.

The king pointed this out.

"Sire," said Athos, "we foresaw this, and if Lord de Winter's men do their duty, we shall be saved instead of lost."

At this moment they heard, above all the galloping and neighing of the horses, de Winter's voice crying out:

"Sword in hand."

At these words every sword was drawn, and glittered in the air like lightning.

"Now, gentlemen," said the king, excited by this sight, and the sound of it, "come, gentlemen, sword in hand."

But it was only Aramis and Athos who obeyed this command and the king's example.

"We are betrayed," said the king, in a low voice.

"Wait a moment," said Athos, "perhaps they do not recognise your majesty's voice, and await the order of their captain."

"Have they not heard that of their colonel? But look! look!" cried the king, drawing up his horse with a sudden jerk, which threw it back on its haunches, and seizing the bridle of Athos' horse.

"Ah, cowards! ah, traitors!" cried out Lord de Winter, whose voice they heard, whilst his men, quitting their ranks, dispersed all over the plain.

About fifteen men were ranged around him, and awaited the the charge of Cromwell's cuirassiers.

"Let us go and die with them!" said the king.

"Let us go," said Athos and Aramis.

"All faithful hearts with me!" cried out de Winter.

This voice was heard by the two friends, who set off at a full gallop.

"No quarter," cried out a voice in French, answering to that of de Winter, which made them tremble.

It was the voice of a cavalier mounted on a magnificent black horse, who was charging at the head of the English regiment, of which, in his ardour, he was ten steps in advance.

"'Tis him!" murmured de Winter; his eyes glaring, and letting his sword fall to his side.

"The king! the king!" cried out several voices, deceived by the blue ribbon, and chestnut horse of de Winter; "take him alive."

"No! it is not the king!" exclaimed the cavalier. "Lord de Winter, you are not the king; you are my uncle."

At the same time Mordaunt, for it was he, cocked his pistol at de Winter, the fire flashed, and the ball entered the heart of the old cavalier, who, with one bound on his saddle, fell back into the arms of Athos, murmuring, "He is revenged."

"Think of my mother!" shouted Mordaunt, as his horse plunged and darted off at full gallop.

"Wretch!" exclaimed Aramis, raising his pistol, as he passed by him; but the fire flashed in the pan and did not go off.

At this moment the whole regiment came up, and they fell upon the few men who had held out, surrounding the two Frenchmen.

Athos, after making sure that Lord de Winter was really dead, let fall the body and said:

"Come, Aramis, now for the honour of France," and the two Englishmen, who were nearest to them, fell mortally wounded.

At the same moment a wild "hurrah!" rent the air, and thirty blades glittered above their heads.

Suddenly a man leaped out of the English ranks, fell upon Athos, entwined his muscular arms around him, and tearing his sword from him, said in his ear:

"Silence! yield yourself—you yield to me; do you not?"

A giant had also seized Aramis' hands, and he struggled in vain to release himself from this formidable grasp.

"D'Art——" exclaimed Athos, whilst the Gascon covered his mouth with his hand.

"I yield myself prisoner," said Aramis, giving up his sword to Porthos.

"Fire, fire," cried out Mordaunt, returning to the group of friends.

"And wherefore fire?" said the colonel; "they have all yielded."

"It is the son of milady," said Athos to d'Artagnan. "I recognised him."

"It is the monk," whispered Porthos to Aramis.

"I know it."

And now the ranks began to open. D'Artagnan held the bridle of Athos' horse, and Porthos that of Aramis. Both of them attempted to lead his prisoner off the battlefield.

This movement revealed the spot where de Winter's body had

fallen. Mordaunt had found it out, and was gazing at it with a bitter expression of hatred.

Athos, though now quite cool and collected, put his hand to his belt, where his loaded pistols still remained.

"What are you about?" said d'Artagnan.

"Let me kill him."

"We are all four lost, if, by the least gesture, you disclose any knowledge of him."

Then, turning to the young man, he exclaimed:

"A fine prize! a fine prize, friend Mordaunt; we have, both myself and Monsieur du Valon, taken two Knights of the Garter, nothing less."

"But," said Mordaunt, looking at Athos and Aramis with bloodshot eyes, "these are Frenchmen, I imagine."

"I'faith, I don't know. Are you French, sir?" said he to Athos.

"I have that honour."

"Very well, my dear sir! you are the prisoner of a fellow countryman."

"But the king—where is the king?" exclaimed Athos anxiously.

"Ah! we have got him."

"Yes," said Aramis, "through an infamous act of treason."

Porthos pressed his friend's hand, and said:

"Yes, sir, all is fair in war—stratagem as well as force. Look yonder!"

At this instant the squadron—that ought to have protected the royal retreat—was advancing to meet the English regiments. The king, who was entirely surrounded, walked alone on foot. He appeared calm, but it was evidently not without a great effort. Drops of perspiration rolled down his face; and from time to time he put a handkerchief to his mouth, to wipe off the blood that flowed from it.

"Behold Nebuchadnezzar!" exclaimed an old Puritan soldier, whose eyes flashed at the sight of one whom he called the tyrant.

"Do you call him Nebuchadnezzar?" said Mordaunt, with a terrible smile; "no it is Charles the First, the king, the good king Charles, who despoils his subjects to enrich himself."

Charles I. glanced a moment at the insolent creature who uttered this, but he did not recognise him. Nevertheless, the calm and religious dignity of his countenance abashed Mordaunt.

"Good-bye, messieurs," said the king to the two gentlemen who were held by d'Artagnan and Porthos. "The day has been unfortunate, but it is not your fault, thank God! But where is my old friend, Winter?"

The two gentlemen turned away their heads in silence.

"Look for him with Strafford," said Mordaunt mockingly.

The king shuddered. The demon had known how to wound him. The remembrance of Strafford was a source of lasting remorse to him, the shadow that haunted him by day and night. The king looked around him. He saw a corpse at his feet; it was de Winter's. He uttered no word nor shed any tear, but his face became deadly pale; he knelt down on the ground, raised de Winter's head, and unfastening the order of the Saint-Esprit placed it on his own breast.

"Lord de Winter is dead, then?" inquired d'Artagnan, fixing his eyes on the corpse.

"Yes," said Athos, "killed by his own nephew."

"Come, he was the first of us to go; peace be to him! he was an honest man," said d'Artagnan.

"Charles Stuart," said the colonel of the English regiment approaching the king, who had just put on the insignia of royalty, "do you yield yourself a prisoner!"

"Colonel Tomlinson," said Charles I., "the king cannot yield! the man alone submits to force."

"Your sword."

The king drew his sword and broke it on his knee.

At this moment a horse without a rider, covered with foam, his nostrils extended, and eyes all fire, galloped past, and recognising his master, stopped and neighed with pleasure; it was Arthur.

The king smiled, caressed it with his hand, and then sprang lightly into the saddle.

"Now, gentlemen," said he, "conduct me where you will."

Turning back again, he said, "I thought I saw Winter move; if he still lives, by all you hold most sacred, do not abandon him."

"Never fear, King Charles," said Mordaunt, "the ball pierced his heart."

"Do not breathe a word, nor make the least sign to me or Porthos," said d'Artagnan to Athos and Aramis, "that you recognise this man, for milady is not dead; her soul lives in the body of this demon."

The detachment now moved towards the town with the royal captive; but on the road an aide-de-camp from Cromwell sent orders that Colonel Tomlinson should conduct him to Holdenby Castle.

At the same time couriers started in all directions over England and Europe, to announce that Charles Stuart, King of England, was now the prisoner of Oliver Cromwell.

57

OLIVER CROMWELL

"HAVE you been to the general?" said Mordaunt to d'Artagnan and Porthos; "you know he sent for you after the action."

"We went first to put our prisoners in a safe place," replied d'Artagnan. "Do you know, sir, these gentlemen are each of them worth fifteen hundred pounds?"

"Oh! be assured," said Mordaunt, looking at them with an expression he in vain endeavoured to soften, "my soldiers will guard them—and guard them securely, I promise you."

"I shall take better care of them myself," answered d'Artagnan; "besides, all they require is a good room, with sentinels, from which their parole is enough that they will not attempt to escape. I will go and see about that, and then we shall have the honour of presenting ourselves to your general, and receiving his commands for his Eminence."

"You are thinking of returning soon, then?" inquired Mordaunt.

"Our mission is at an end, and there is nothing more to detain us now but the good pleasure of the great man to whom we have been sent."

The young man bit his lips, and whispered to his sergeant,

"You will follow these men, and not lose sight of them; when you have found out where they lodge, come and await me at the town gate."

The sergeant signified that he should be obeyed.

Instead of following the mass of prisoners that were being taken into the town, Mordaunt turned his steps towards the rising ground from whence Cromwell had witnessed the battle, and on which he had just had his tent pitched.

Cromwell had given orders that no one was to enter it; but the sentinel, who knew that Mordaunt was one of the most confidential friends of the general, thought the order did not extend to the young man. Mordaunt, therefore, raised the canvas, and saw Cromwell seated before a table, his head buried in his hands; his back was turned to him.

Whether he heard Mordaunt or not as he entered, Cromwell did not move. Mordaunt remained standing near the door. At last, after a few moments, Cromwell raised his head, and, as if he divined that some one was there, he turned slowly round.

"I said I wished to be alone!" he said, on seeing the young man.

"They thought this order did not concern me, sir; nevertheless, if you wish it, I will leave."

"Ah! it is you, Mordaunt!" said Cromwell, the cloud passing away from over his face; "since you are here, it is well, you may remain."

"I come to congratulate you."

"To congratulate me—what for?"

"On the capture of Charles Stuart. You are now master of England."

"I was much more really so two hours ago."

"How so, general?"

"Because England had need of me to take the tyrant, and now the tyrant is taken. Have you seen him?"

"Yes, sir," said Mordaunt.

"What is his bearing?"

Mordaunt hesitated; but he seemed as if compelled to speak the truth.

"Calm and dignified," said he.

"Did he say anything?"

"Merely a few parting words to his friends."

"His friends!" murmured Cromwell. "Has he any friends?" Then he said aloud, "Did he make any resistance?"

"No, sir; with the exception of two or three friends, every one deserted him; he had no means of resistance."

"To whom did he give up his sword?"

"He did not give it up—he broke it."

"He did well; but, instead of breaking it, he might have used it to more advantage."

There was a momentary pause.

"I heard that the colonel of the regiment that escorted the king was killed?" said Cromwell, gazing very fixedly at Mordaunt.

"Yes, sir."

"By whom?" inquired Cromwell.

"By me."

"What was his name?"

"Lord de Winter."

"Your uncle?" exclaimed Cromwell.

"My uncle," answered Mordaunt; "but traitors to England are not of my family."

Cromwell gazed at the young man a moment in silence, and then added:

"Mordaunt, you are strong among the strong ones. And the Frenchmen, how did they behave?"

"Most fearlessly."

"Yes, yes," murmured Cromwell, "the French always fight well; and if my glass was good, and I mistake not, they were foremost in the affray."

"They were," replied Mordaunt.

"After you, however," said Cromwell.

"The fault was not theirs, it was caused by their horses."

Another pause.

"And the Scotch?"

"They kept their word, and never moved," said Mordaunt.

"Wretched men!"

"Their officers wish to see you, sir."

"I have no time for them. Have they been paid?"

"Yes, to-night."

"Let them set off and return to their mountains, and there hide their shame, if their mountains are high enough. I have nothing more to do with them, or they with me. And now, go, Mordaunt."

"Before I go," said Mordaunt, "I have some questions and a favour to ask you, sir."

"A favour from me?"

Mordaunt bowed.

"I come to you, my leader, my head, my father, and I ask you, master, are you satisfied with me?"

Cromwell looked at him with astonishment. The young man remained immovable.

"Yes," said Cromwell; "you have done, since I knew you, not only your duty, but more than your duty; you have been a faithful friend, a clever negotiator, and a good soldier."

"Do you remember, sir, it was my idea, the Scotch treaty, for giving up the king?"

"Yes, the idea was yours. I had not such a contempt for men before that."

"Was I not a good ambassador in France?"

"Yes, for Mazarin has granted what I desired."

"Have I not always fought for your honour and interests?"

"Too ardently, perhaps; it is what I have just reproached you for; but what is the meaning of all these questions?"

"To tell you, my lord, that the moment has now arrived when, with a single word, you may recompense me for these services."

"Oh!" said Cromwell, with a slight curl of his lip, "I forgot that every service merits some reward, and that up to this moment you have served me for nothing."

"Sir, you can give me in a moment all I look for."

"What is it? Have they offered you money? Do you wish a step? or some place in the government?"

"Sir, will you grant me my request?"

"Let us hear what it is first."

"Sir, when you have told me to obey an order, have I ever inquired what it is first? I cannot inform you."

"But such a request made——"

"Ah! do not fear, sir," said Mordaunt, with apparent simplicity, "it will not ruin you."

"Well, then," said Cromwell, "I promise, as far as lies in my power, to grant your request. Proceed."

"Sir, two prisoners were taken this morning; will you let me have them?"

"For their ransom? Have they, then, offered a large one?" inquired Cromwell.

"On the contrary, I think they are poor, sir."

"They are friends of yours, then?"

"Yes, sir," exclaimed Mordaunt, "they are friends, dear friends of mine, and I would lay down my life for them."

"Very well, Mordaunt," said Cromwell, pleased at having his opinion of the young man once more upheld, "I will give them to you; I will not even ask who they are—do as you like with them."

"Thank you, sir!" exclaimed Mordaunt, "thank you; my life is always at your service, and should I lose it, I should still owe you something; thank you—you have, indeed, repaid me munificently for my services."

And he threw himself at the feet of Cromwell; and in spite of the efforts of the Puritan general, who did not like this almost kingly homage, he took his hand and kissed it.

"What!" said Cromwell, arresting him for a moment as he rose, "is there nothing more you wish? neither gold nor rank?"

"You have given me all that I desire, and from to-day your debt is paid."

And Mordaunt darted out of the general's tent, his heart beating, and his eyes sparkling with joy.

Cromwell gazed a moment after him.

"He has killed his uncle!" he murmured. "Alas! what are my servants? Perhaps those who ask nothing, or seem to ask nothing, have asked more in the eyes of Heaven than those who tax the country, and steal the bread of the poor. Nobody serves me for nothing! The king, who is my prisoner, may still have friends; but I have none!"

And with a deep sigh he resumed his reverie which had been interrupted by Mordaunt.

58

D'ARTAGNAN'S STRATAGEM

WHILST Mordaunt was on his way to Cromwell's tent, d'Artagnan and Porthos were leading their prisoners to the house that had been assigned to them as their dwelling at Newcastle.

The two friends made the prisoners enter the house first, whilst they stood at the door, desiring Mousqueton to take all the four horses to the stable.

"Why don't we go in with them?" asked Porthos.

"We must first see what the wishes of the sergeant are," replied d'Artagnan, and he then made inquiry of the sergeant.

"We have had orders," answered the man, "to help you to take care of those prisoners."

There could be no fault found with this arrangement; on the contrary, it seemed to be a delicate attention to be received gratefully. D'Artagnan, therefore, thanked the man, and gave him a crown piece to drink to General Cromwell's health.

The sergeant answered that Puritans never drank, but put the crown piece into his pocket.

"Ah!" said Porthos, "what a fearful day, my dear d'Artagnan."

"What! a fearful day, when we have to-day found our friends."

"Yes; but under what circumstances?"

"'Tis true that our position is an awkward one; but let us go in and see more clearly what is to be done."

"Things look very bad," replied Porthos; "I see now why Aramis advised me to strangle that horrible Mordaunt."

"Silence!" cried the Gascon; "do not utter that name."

"But," argued Porthos, "I speak French, and they are all English."

D'Artagnan looked at Porthos with that air of wonder which a sensible man cannot help feeling at stupidity in every degree.

But, as Porthos on his side could not comprehend his astonishment, he merely pushed him indoors, saying: "Let us go in."

They found Athos in a profound despondency. Aramis looked first at Porthos and then at d'Artagnan, without speaking; but the latter understood his meaning look.

"You want to know how we came here; 'tis easily guessed. Mazarin sent us with a letter to General Cromwell."

"But how came you to fall into the society of Mordaunt, whom I bade you distrust?" asked Athos.

"Mazarin again. Cromwell had sent him to Mazarin. Mazarin sent us to Cromwell. There has been a fate in it."

"Yes, you are right, d'Artagnan—a fate which will separate and ruin us; so, my dear Aramis, say no more about it, and let us prepare to submit to our destiny."

"Zounds! let us speak about things, on the contrary!—for we always agreed to keep on the same side; and here we are engaged in conflicting parties."

"Yes," added Athos, "I now ask you, d'Artagnan, what side you are on? Ah! behold for what end the wretched Mazarin has made use of you. Do you know in what crime you are to-day concerned? In the capture of a king, in his degradation, in his death."

"Oh! oh!" cried Porthos, "do you say so?"

"You are exaggerating, Athos; we are not so far gone as that," replied the lieutenant.

"Good Heavens! we are on the very verge of it. I say why is the king taken prisoner? Those who wish to respect him as a master, would not buy him as a slave."

"I don't say to the contrary," said d'Artagnan. "But what's that to us? I am here, because I am a soldier, and have to obey orders; I have taken an oath to obey, and I do obey; but you, who have taken no oath, why are you here, and what cause do you serve?"

"That most sacred in the world," said Athos; "the cause of misfortune, of religion, of royalty. A friend, a wife, a daughter, have done us the honour to call us to their aid. We have served them to the best of our poor ability, and God will recompense the will, and forgive the want of power: you may see matters differently, d'Artagnan, and think otherwise. I do not attempt to argue with you, but I blame you."

"Hey-day!" cried d'Artagnan; "what matters it to me, after all, if Cromwell, who's an Englishman, revolts against his king, who is a Scotchman? I am myself a Frenchman, I have nothing to do with these things—why make me responsible for them?"

"Why you? Because you, d'Artagnan, a man sprung from the ancient nobility of France, bearing a good name, carrying a sword, have helped to give up a king to beersellers, shopkeepers, and carters. Ah! d'Artagnan! perhaps you have done your duty as a soldier, but, as a gentleman, I say that you are culpable, to the extreme."

D'Artagnan was chewing the stalk of a flower, unable to reply, and feeling very uncomfortable.

"And you, Porthos—you, a gentleman in manners, in tastes, in courage, are as much to blame as d'Artagnan."

Porthos coloured, and hanging his head, said:

"Yes, yes, my dear count, I feel that you are right."

Athos rose.

"Come," he said, stretching out his hand to d'Artagnan, "come, don't be sullen, my dear son, for I have said all this to you, if not in the tone, at least with the feeling of a father. It would have been easier to me merely to have thanked you for preserving my life, and not to have uttered a word of all this."

"Doubtless, doubtless, Athos. But this is it—you have sentiments, the devil knows what, such as every one can't possess. Who could suppose that a sensible man could leave his château, France, his ward—a charming youth, for we saw him in the camp —to fly to the aid of a rotten, worm-eaten royalty, which one day is sure to crumble like the walls of an old castle? The sentiments you sport are certainly fine, so fine—that they are superhuman."

"However that may be, d'Artagnan," replied Athos, without falling into the snare which his Gascon friend had prepared for him by an appeal to his parental love, "you know, in the bottom of your heart, that it is true; but I am coming to dispute with my superiors. D'Artagnan, I am your prisoner—treat me as such."

D'Artagnan said nothing; but, after gnawing the flower-stalk, he began to bite his nails. At last,—

"Do you imagine," he resumed, "that they mean to kill you? And wherefore should they do so? What interest have they in your death? Moreover, you are *our* prisoners."

"Fool!" cried Aramis; "knowest thou not, then, Mordaunt? I have merely exchanged with him one look, but that look convinced me that we were doomed."

"The truth is, I'm very sorry that I did not strangle him as you advised me to do," said Porthos.

"Stop," cried Athos, extending his hand to one of the grated windows by which the room was lighted; "you will soon know, for here he is."

In fact, looking at the place to which Athos pointed, d'Artagnan saw a cavalier coming towards the house at full gallop.

It was Mordaunt.

D'Artagnan left the room.

Porthos was about to follow him.

"Stay," said d'Artagnan, "and do not come till you hear me beat like a drum with my fingers upon the door."

When Mordaunt arrived opposite the house he saw d'Artagnan upon the threshold, and the soldiers lying on the grass, here and there, with their arms.

"Hallo!" he cried, "are the prisoners still there?"

"Yes, sir," answered the sergeant, removing his hat.

"'Tis well: order four men to conduct them to my lodging."

Four men prepared to do so.

"What do you want, sir?" asked d'Artagnan.

"Sir," replied Mordaunt, "I have ordered the two prisoners that we made this morning to be conducted to my lodging."

"Wherefore, sir? Excuse my curiosity, but I wish to be enlightened on the subject."

"Because these prisoners, sir, are at my disposal, and I choose to dispose of them as I like."

"Allow me—allow me, sir," said d'Artagnan, "to observe you are in error. The prisoners belong to those who took them, and not to those who only saw them taken. You might have taken Lord de Winter prisoner, who is said to be your uncle, but you preferred killing him; 'tis well. We, that is Monsieur du Valon and I, could have killed our prisoners, we preferred taking them."

Mordaunt's very lips were white with rage.

D'Artagnan now saw that affairs were growing worse, and he beat the guard's march upon the door. At the first beat Porthos came out, and stood on the opposite side of the door.

This movement was observed by Mordaunt.

"Sir!" he thus addressed d'Artagnan, "your resistance is useless—these prisoners have just been given to me by my illustrious patron, Oliver Cromwell."

These words struck d'Artagnan like a thunderbolt. The blood mounted to his temples, his eyes became dim; he saw from what source the ferocious hopes of the young man arose. He put his hand to the hilt of his sword.

As to Porthos, he looked inquiringly at d'Artagnan.

This look of Porthos's made the Gascon regret that he had ordered the brute force of his friend to aid him in an affair which seemed to require chiefly cunning.

"Violence," he said to himself, "would spoil all; d'Artagnan, my friend, prove to this young serpent that thou art not only stronger, but more subtle than himself."

"Ah!" he said, making a low bow, "why did you not begin by saying that, Monsieur Mordaunt? What! are you sent by General Oliver Cromwell, the most illustrious captain of his age?"

"I have this instant left him," replied Mordaunt, jumping off his horse.

"Why did you not say so at once, my dear sir! all England is with Cromwell; and since you ask for my prisoners, I bow to your wishes. They are yours; take them."

Mordaunt, delighted, advanced—Porthos looking at d'Artagnan

with open-mouthed astonishment. Then d'Artagnan trod on his foot, and Porthos began to understand that this was simply byplay.

Mordaunt put his foot on the first step of the door, and, with his hat in his hand, prepared to pass by the two friends, motioning to the four men to follow him.

"But, pardon me," he said, stopping short, "since the illustrious general has given my prisoners into your hands, he has of course confirmed that act in writing."

Mordaunt stood still, then retreated—cast a terrible glance at d'Artagnan, which was answered by the most amicable and friendly manner that could be imagined.

"Speak out, sir," said Mordaunt.

"Monsieur du Valon, yonder, is rich, and has forty thousand francs yearly, so he does not care about money. I do not speak for him, but for myself."

"Well, sir? What more?"

"Well—I—I'm not rich. In Gascony 'tis no dishonour, sir, nobody is rich; and Henry IV., of glorious memory, who was the king of the Gascons, as his majesty Philip IV. is the king of the Spaniards, never had a penny in his pocket."

"Go on, sir. I see where you wish to come to; and if it is what I think that stops you, I can remedy that evil."

"Ah, I knew well," said the Gascon, "that you were a man of talent. Well, here's the case; here's where the saddle hurts me, as we French say. I am an officer of fortune, nothing else; I have nothing but what my sword brings me in—that is to say, more blows than bank-notes. Now, on taking prisoners this morning two gentlemen, who seemed to me of high birth—in short, two Knights of the Garter—I said to myself, my fortune is made."

Mordaunt, completely deceived by this mundane policy of d'Artagnan, smiled like a man who understands perfectly the reasons given him, and said:

"I shall have the order signed directly, sir, and with it two thousand pistoles; meanwhile, let me take these men away."

"No," replied d'Artagnan; "what signifies a delay of half an hour? I am a man of order, sir; let us do things in order."

"Nevertheless," replied Mordaunt, "I could compel you; I command here."

"Ah, sir!" said d'Artagnan, "I see that although we have had the honour of travelling in your company, you do not know us. We are gentlemen; we are, both of us, able to kill you and your eight men; we two only. For heaven's sake don't be obstinate, for when others are obstinate, I am obstinate likewise, and then I become savage and headstrong; and there's my friend, who is even more headstrong and savage than I am; besides, we are sent here by Cardinal Mazarin, and at this moment represent both the king and the cardinal, and are therefore, as ambassadors, able to act with impunity, a thing that General Oliver Cromwell, who is assuredly as great a politician as he is a general, is quite a man to understand. Ask him then for the written order. What will that cost you, my dear Monsieur Mordaunt?"

"Yes, the written order," said Porthos, who now began to comprehend what d'Artagnan was aiming at; "we must have the order in writing."

However anxious Mordaunt was to have recourse to violence, he quite understood the reasons given him by d'Artagnan; and, besides, completely ignorant of the friendship which existed between the four Frenchmen, all his uneasiness disappeared when he heard of the plausible motive of the ransom. He decided, therefore, not only to fetch the order, but the two thousand pistoles at which he estimated the prisoners. He therefore remounted his horse and disappeared.

"Good!" thought d'Artagnan; "a quarter of an hour to go to the tent, a quarter of an hour to return;" then turning, without the least change of countenance to Porthos, he said, looking him full in the face, "Friend Porthos, listen to this: first, not a syllable to either of our friends about the service we are going to render them."

"Very well; I understand."

"Go to the stable; you will find Mousqueton there. Saddle your horses, put your pistols in your saddle-bags, take out the horses, and lead them to the street below this, so that there will be nothing to do but to mount them; all the rest is my business."

Porthos made no reply, but obeyed, with the sublime confidence that he had in his friend. He then proceeded with his usual calm gait to the stable, and went into the very midst of the soldiery, who could not help admiring his height and the strength of his powerful limbs.

At the corner of the street he met Mousqueton and took him with him.

D'Artagnan, meantime, went into the house, whistling a tune which he had begun before Porthos went away. "My dear Athos, I have reflected on your arguments, and am convinced. I am sorry to have had anything to do with this matter. As you say, Mazarin is a knave. I have resolved to fly with you; not a word; be ready; your swords are in the corner; do not forget them, they are, in many circumstances, very useful; there's Porthos' purse, too."

He took it up and placed it in his pocket. The two friends were perfectly stupefied.

"Well—pray, what is there to be surprised at?" he said. "I was blind; Athos made me see clearly; that's all. Come here."

The two friends went near him.

"Do you see that street? There are the horses. Go out by the door, turn to the right, jump into your saddles, all will be right; don't be uneasy at anything except mistaking the signal. That will be the signal when I call out 'Lord have mercy!'"

"But you give us your word that you will come too, d'Artagnan," said Athos.

"I swear I will, by heaven!"

"'Tis settled," said Aramis; "at the cry, 'Lord have mercy!' we go out, upset all that stands in our way, run to our horses, jump into our saddles, spur them—is that so?"

"Exactly."

"See, Aramis, as I have told you, d'Artagnan is the best of us all," said Athos.

"Very true," replied the Gascon, "but I always run away from compliments. Don't forget the signal—'Lord have mercy!'" and he went out as he came in, whistling the air that he had been whistling when he entered.

The soldiers were playing or sleeping; two of them were singing in a corner, out of tune, the psalm—"On the rivers of Babylon."

D'Artagnan called the sergeant. "My dear friend, General Cromwell has sent Monsieur Mordaunt to fetch me. Guard the prisoners well, I beg of you."

The sergeant made a sign, as much as to say he did not understand French, and d'Artagnan tried to make him comprehend him by signs and gestures. Then he went into the stable; he found the five horses and his own, among others, saddled. He gave his instructions, and Porthos and Mousqueton went to their post accordingly.

Then d'Artagnan, being alone, struck a light and lighted a small bit of the tinder, mounted his horse, and stopped at the door in the midst of the soldiers.

Then pretending to pat the animal with his hand, he put this bit of burning tinder into his ear.

It was necessary to be as good a horseman as he was to risk such a scheme; for hardly had the animal felt the burning tinder than he uttered a cry of pain, and reared and jumped as if he had been mad.

The soldiers, whom he nearly trampled upon, ran away from him.

"Help! help!" cried d'Artagnan; "stop, my horse has the staggers."

In an instant blood came from his eyes, and he was white with foam.

"Help!" cried d'Artagnan. "What! will you see me killed? 'Lord have mercy!'"

Scarcely had he uttered this cry than the door was opened, and Athos and Aramis rushed out. The coast, owing to the Gascon's stratagem, was clear.

"The prisoners are escaping! the prisoners are escaping!" cried the sergeant.

"Stop! stop!" cried d'Artagnan, giving rein to his maddened horse, which, darting forth, overturned several men.

"Stop! stop!" cried the soldiers, and ran for their arms.

But the prisoners were in their saddles, and lost no time, hastening to the nearest gate.

In the middle of the street they saw Grimaud and Blaisois, who were looking for their masters. With one wave of his hand, Athos made Grimaud, who followed the little troop, understand everything, and they passed on like a whirlwind, d'Artagnan still directing them from behind with his voice.

They passed through the gate like apparitions, without the guards thinking of detaining them, and reached the open country.

All this while the soldiers were calling out "Stop! stop!" and the sergeant, who began to see that he was the victim of an artifice, was almost in a frenzy of despair: whilst all this was going on, a cavalier in full gallop was seen approaching. It was Mordaunt with the order in his hand.

"The prisoners!" he exclaimed, jumping off his horse.

The sergeant had not the courage to reply; he showed him the open door and the empty room. Mordaunt darted to the steps— understood all, uttered a cry as if his very heart were pierced, and fell fainting on the steps.

59

GREAT HEARTS NEVER LOSE THEIR COURAGE, NOR GOOD STOMACHS THEIR APPETITES

THE little troop, without looking behind them, or exchanging a single word, fled at a rapid gallop, crossing on foot a little stream, of which none of them knew the name, and leaving on their left a town, which Athos declared to be Durham. At last they came in sight of a small wood, and spurring their horses afresh, they rode towards it.

As soon as they had disappeared behind a green curtain sufficiently thick to conceal them from the sight of any who might be in pursuit of them, they drew up to hold a council together. The two grooms held the horses, that they might take rest without being unsaddled, and Grimaud was posted as sentinel.

"Come, first of all," said Athos to d'Artagnan, "my friend, that I may shake hands with you—you, our rescuer; you, the true hero among us all."

"Athos is right, and you have my admiration," said Aramis, in his turn pressing his hand; "to what are you not equal? with superior intelligence, and an infallible eye; an arm of iron, and an enterprising mind!"

"Now," said the Gascon, "that is all right, I accept for Porthos and myself everything—thanks and embracings—we have plenty of time to spare."

The two friends, recalled by d'Artagnan to what was also due to Porthos, pressed his hand in their turn.

"And now," said Athos, "it is not our plan to run anywhere, and like madmen; but we must arrange some plan. What shall we do?"

"What shall we do, i'faith? It is not very difficult to answer!"

"Tell us then, d'Artagnan."

"We are going to reach the nearest seaport, unite our little resources, hire a vessel, and return to France. Life is the greatest treasure, and, speaking candidly, ours is only held by a thread."

"What do you say to this, du Valon?"

"I," said Porthos—"I am entirely of d'Artagnan's opinion; this is a beastly country—this England."

"You have made up your mind then to leave it?" asked Athos of d'Artagnan.

"Egad! I don't see what is to keep me here."

A glance was exchanged between Athos and Aramis.

"Go, then, my friends," said the former, sighing.

"How, go then?" exclaimed d'Artagnan. "Let us go, you mean!"

"No, my friend," said Athos, "you must leave us."

"Leave you!" cried d'Artagnan, quite bewildered at this unexpected announcement.

"Bah!" said Porthos, "why separate, since we are all together?"

"Because you can, and you ought, to return to France; your mission is finished, but ours is not."

"Your mission is not accomplished!" exclaimed d'Artagnan, looking in amazement at Athos.

"No, my good friend," replied Athos, in his gentle, but decided voice, "we came here to defend King Charles; we have but ill defended him, it remains for us to save him."

"To save the king?" said d'Artagnan, looking at Aramis as he had looked at Athos.

Aramis made a sign with his head.

D'Artagnan's countenance took an expression of the deepest sorrow.

"You cannot be speaking seriously, Athos?" said he; "the king is surrounded by an army, which is conducting him to London. This army is commanded by a butcher, or the son of a butcher—it matters little—Colonel Harrison. His majesty, I can assure you, is about to be tried on his arrival in London; I have heard enough from the lips of M. Oliver Cromwell to know what to expect."

A second look was exchanged between Athos and Aramis.

"And when his trial is ended, there will be no delay in putting the sentence into execution," continued d'Artagnan.

"And to what penalty do you think the king will be condemned?" asked Athos.

"To the penalty of death, I much fear; they have gone too far for him to pardon them, and there is nothing left to them but one thing—and that is to kill him. Do you not know Oliver Cromwell's speech when he came to Paris, and when he was shown the dungeon at Vincennes where Monsieur de Vendôme was imprisoned?"

"What was the speech?" asked Porthos.

"Princes must be knocked on the head."

"I remember it," said Athos.

"And you think he will not put his maxim into practice, now that he has hold of the king?"

"On the contrary, I am certain he will do so; but then there is the more reason why we must not abandon the august head so threatened."

"Well, you know beforehand that you must perish!" said d'Artagnan.

"We fear so, and our only regret is, to die so far from you both."

"What will you do in a foreign land—an enemy's country?"

"I have travelled in England when young; I speak English like an Englishman; and Aramis, too, knows something of the language. Ah! if we had you, my friends! With you, d'Artagnan, with you, Porthos, all four, and reunited for the first time for twenty years, we would dare, not only England, but the three kingdoms together!"

"And did you promise the queen," resumed d'Artagnan petulantly, "to storm the Tower of London with a hundred thousand soldiers, to fight victoriously against the wishes of a nation and the ambition of a man, and when that man is called Cromwell? Do not overestimate your duty. In Heaven's name, my dear Athos, do not make a useless sacrifice. When I see you merely, you look like a reasonable being; yet when you speak, I seem to have to do with a fanatic. Come, Porthos, join me; say, frankly, what do you think of this business?"

"Nothing good," replied Porthos.

"Come," continued d'Artagnan, who, irritated that instead of listening to him Athos seemed to be attending to his own thoughts, "you have never found yourself the worse for my advice. Well, then, believe me, Athos, your mission is ended, and ended nobly; return to France with us."

"Friend," said Athos, "our resolution is unchangeable."

"Then you have some other motive unknown to us?"

Athos smiled, and d'Artagnan struck his heels in anger, and uttered the most convincing reasons that he could discover; but to all these reasons Athos contented himself by replying with a calm sweet smile, and Aramis by nodding his head.

"Very well," cried d'Artagnan at last, furious,—"very well—since you wish it, let us leave our bones in this beggarly land, where it is always cold, where the fine weather comes after a fog, and a fog after rain, and the rain after the deluge, where the sun resembles the moon, and the moon a cream cheese; in truth, whether we die here or elsewhere, matters little since we must die."

"Only think, my good friend," said Athos, "it is but dying rather sooner."

"Pooh! a little sooner, or a little later, that isn't worth quarrelling about."

"But your future career, d'Artagnan?—your ambition, Porthos?"

"Our future, our ambition!" replied d'Artagnan, "need we think of that since we are to save the king? The king saved, we shall assemble our friends together; we will head the Puritans, reconquer England; we shall re-enter London, place him securely on his throne——"

"And he will make us dukes and peers," said Porthos, whose eyes sparkled with joy at this imaginary prospect.

"Or he will forget us," added d'Artagnan.

"Well! then," said Athos, offering his hand to d'Artagnan.

"'Tis settled," replied d'Artagnan. "I find England a charming country, and I stay—but only on one condition."

"What is it?"

"That I am not forced to study English."

"Well then, now," said Athos fervently, "I swear to you, my friend, by the God who hears us, I believe that there is a power watching over us, and I hope we shall all four meet in France."

"So be it!" said d'Artagnan, "but I—I confess I have quite a contrary conviction."

"Our good friend d'Artagnan," said Aramis, "represents among us the opposition in parliament, which says always *no*, and does always *aye*."

"But which in the meantime saves the country," added Athos.

"Well, now that everything is settled," cried Porthos, rubbing his hands, "suppose we think of dinner! It seems to me that in the most critical positions of our lives we have always dined."

"Oh! yes, speak of dinner in a country where for a feast they eat boiled mutton, and where as a treat they drink beer. What the deuce did you come to such a country for, Athos?"

"But, I forgot," added the Gascon, smiling, "pardon, I forgot you are no longer Athos; but never mind, let us hear your plan for dinner, Porthos."

"My plan!"

"Yes; have you a plan?"

"No! I am hungry, that is all."

"*Pardieu*, if that is all, I am hungry too; but it is not everything to be hungry; one must find something to eat, unless we browse on the grass, like our horses——"

"Ah!" said Aramis, who was not quite so indifferent to the good things of the earth as Athos, "do you remember, when we were at Gravesend, the beautiful oysters that we ate?"

"And the legs of mutton of the salt marshes," said Porthos, smacking his lips.

"But," suggested d'Artagnan, "have we not our friend Mousqueton, he who managed for us so well at Chantilly, Porthos?"

"By the bye," said Porthos, "we have Mousqueton, but since he has been steward, he has become very portly; never mind, let us call him: and to make sure that he will reply agreeably— Here! Mouston," cried Porthos.

Mouston appeared, with a very wry face.

"What is the matter, my dear Mouston?" asked d'Artagnan. "Are you ill?"

"Sir, I am very hungry!" replied Mouston.

"Well, it is just for that reason that we have called you, my good Mouston. Could you not get us a few of those nice little rabbits and some of those delicious partridges, of which you used to make fricassées at the hotel——? Faith, I do not remember the name of the hotel."

"At the hotel of——," said Porthos; "by my faith—nor do I remember it either."

"It does not matter; and a few of those bottles of old Burgundy wine, which cured your master so quickly of his sprain!"

"Alas! sir," said Mousqueton, "I much fear that what you ask for are very rare things in this execrable country, and I think we should do better to go and seek hospitality from the owner of a little house that we see at the extremity of the wood."

"How! is there a house in the neighbourhood?" asked d'Artagnan.

"Yes, sir!" replied Mousqueton.

"Well, let us, as you say, go and ask a dinner from the master of that house. What is your opinion, gentlemen, and does not Monsieur Mouston's suggestion appear to you full of sense?"

"Oh! oh!" said Aramis, "suppose the master is a Puritan?"

"So much the better, *Mordieux*!" replied d'Artagnan; "if he is a Puritan, we will tell him of the king's capture, and in honour of the news he will kill for us his white hens."

"But if he should be a cavalier?" said Porthos.

"In that case, we will put on an air of mourning, and he will pluck his black fowls."

"You are very happy," exclaimed Athos, laughing, in spite of himself, at the sally of the irresistible Gascon; "for you see the bright side of everything."

"What would you have?" said d'Artagnan. "I come from a land where there is not a cloud in the sky."

"It is not like this, then," said Porthos, stretching out his hand to assure himself whether a sensation of freshness which he had just felt on his cheek was not really caused by a drop of rain.

"Come, come," said d'Artagnan, "more reason why we should commence our journey—halloa, Grimaud!"

Grimaud appeared.

"Well, Grimaud, my friend, have you seen anything?" asked the Gascon.

"Nothing!" replied Grimaud.

"Those idiots!" cried Porthos, "they have not even pursued us. Oh! if we had been in their place!"

"Yes, they are wrong," said d'Artagnan. "I would willingly have said two words to Mordaunt in this little Thebes. See what a splendid place for bringing down a man properly."

"I think, decidedly," observed Aramis, "gentlemen, that the son is not quite so bad as his mother."

"What, my good fellow!" replied Athos; "wait awhile, we have scarcely left him two hours ago—he does not know yet in what direction we came, nor where we are. We may say that he is not equal to his mother when we put foot in France, if we are not poisoned or killed before then."

"Meanwhile, let us have dinner," suggested Porthos.

"I'faith, yes!" said Athos, "for I am very hungry."

"Look out for the black fowls!" said Aramis.

And the four friends, guided by Mousqueton, went quickly towards the house, already almost restored to their former gaiety; for they were now, as Athos had said, all four united and of one mind.

60

HEALTH TO FALLEN MAJESTY

As our fugitives approached the house, they found the ground cut up, as if a considerable body of horsemen had preceded them. Before the door, the traces were yet even more apparent; these horsemen, whoever they might be, had halted there.

"Egad!" cried d'Artagnan, "it's quite clear that the king and his escort have been here."

He pushed the door open, and found the first room empty and deserted.

"Well!" cried Porthos.

"I can't see anybody," said d'Artagnan. "Aha!"

"What?"

"Blood!"

At this word the three friends leapt from their horses, and entered. D'Artagnan had already opened the door of the second room, and, from the expression of his face, it was clear that he there beheld some extraordinary object.

The three friends drew near, and discovered a young man stretched on the ground, and bathed in a pool of blood. It was evident that he had attempted to gain his bed, but had not had the strength to do so.

Athos, who imagined that he saw him move, was the first to go to him.

"Well?" inquired d'Artagnan.

"Well, if he is dead," said Athos, "he has not been so long, for he is still warm. But no, his heart is beating. Eh! there, my friend."

The wounded man heaved a sigh. D'Artagnan took some water in the hollow of his hand, and dashed it upon his face. The man opened his eyes, made an effort to raise his head, and fell back again. The wound was in the top of the head, and the blood was flowing freely.

Aramis dipped a cloth in the water, and applied it to the gash. Again the wounded man opened his eyes, and looked in astonishment at these strangers, who appeared to pity him.

"You are among friends," said Athos compassionately; "so cheer up, and tell us, if you have the strength to do so, what has happened."

"The king," muttered the wounded man, "the king is a prisoner."

"Make your mind easy," resumed Athos, "we are all faithful servants of his majesty."

"Is what you tell me true?" asked the wounded man.

"On our honour as gentlemen."

"Then I may tell you all. I am the brother of Parry, his majesty's valet."

Athos and Aramis remembered that this was the name by which de Winter had called the man whom they had found in the passage of the king's tent.

"We know him," said Athos; "he never left the king."

"Yes, that is he; well, he thought of me, when he saw that the king was taken, and as they were passing before the house here, he begged in the king's name that they would stop, as the king was hungry. They brought him into this room, and placed guards at the doors and windows. Parry knew this room, as he had often been to see me when the king was at Newcastle. He knew that there was a trap-door communicating with the cellar, from which one could get into the garden. He made me a sign, which I understood, but the king's guards must have noticed it, and put themselves on the alert. I went out, as if to fetch wood, passed through the subterranean passage into the cellar, and while Parry was gently bolting the door, pushed up the board and beckoned the king to follow me. Alas! he would not. But Parry clasped his hands and implored him, and at last he agreed. I went on first, quite delighted. The king was a few steps behind me, when suddenly I saw something rise up in front of me, like a huge shadow. I wanted to cry out to warn the king, but the same moment I felt a blow as if the house were falling on my head, and fell insensible. When I came to myself again, I was stretched in the same place. I dragged myself as far as the yard. The king and his escort had vanished."

"And now what can we do for you?" asked Athos.

"Help me to get on to the bed; that will ease me."

They helped him on to the bed, and, calling Grimaud to dress his wound, returned to the outer room for consultation.

"Now," said Aramis, "we know how the case stands. The king and his escort have been this way; we had better take the opposite direction, eh?"

"Yes," said Porthos; "if we follow the escort we shall find everything devoured, and die of hunger. What a confounded country this England is! This is the first time I shall have lost my dinner, and it's my best meal."

"What do you say about it, d'Artagnan?" said Athos.

"Just the contrary to Aramis."

"What! follow the escort?" cried Porthos, quite alarmed.

"No, but join them. They will never look for us among the Puritans!"

"A good idea," said Athos, "they will think we want to leave England, and seek us in the ports. Meanwhile we shall reach London with the king, and once there, it will not be difficult to conceal ourselves."

"But," said Aramis, "shall we not be suspected by Colonel Harrison?"

"Egad!" cried d'Artagnan, "he's just the man I count upon. Colonel Harrison is one of our friends. We have met him twice at General Cromwell's. He is aware that we were sent from France by Monsieur Mazarin; he will think us brothers. Besides, is he not a butcher's son? Well, then, Porthos will show him how to knock down an ox with a blow of the fist; and I, how to trip up a *bull* by taking him by the horns. That will ensure his confidence."

Athos smiled.

At this moment Grimaud came in. He had staunched the wound and the man was better.

The little troop again started on their march, and, at the end of two hours, perceived a considerable body of horsemen about half a league ahead.

"My dear friends," said d'Artagnan, "give your swords to Monsieur Mouston, who will return them to you in proper time and place, and do not forget you are our prisoners."

It was not long ere they joined the escort. The king was in the front, surrounded by troopers, and when he saw Athos and Aramis a glow of pleasure lighted up his wan cheeks.

D'Artagnan passed to the head of the column, and, leaving his friends under the guard of Porthos, went straight to Harrison, who recognised him as having met him at Cromwell's, and received him as politely as a man of his breeding and disposition could. It turned out as d'Artagnan had foreseen. The colonel neither had nor could have any suspicion.

They halted for the king to dine. This time, however, due precautions were taken to prevent any attempt at escape. In the large room of the hotel a small table was placed for him, and a large one for the officers.

"Will you dine with me?" asked Harrison of d'Artagnan.

"'Gad, I should be very happy, but I have my companion, Monsieur du Valon, and the two prisoners, whom I cannot leave. Let us arrange it better. Have a table set for us in a corner, and hand us whatever you like from yours."

"Good," answered Harrison.

The table at which the Puritan officers were seated was round, and whether by chance or a coarse intention, Harrison had his back turned to the king.

The king saw the four gentlemen enter, but appeared to take no notice of them.

They sat down in such a manner as not to turn their backs upon anybody.

"I'faith, colonel," said d'Artagnan, "we are very grateful for your gracious invitation; for, without you, we ran the risk of going without dinner, as we have without breakfast. My friend here, Monsieur du Valon, shares my gratitude, for he was particularly hungry."

"And I am so still," said Porthos, bowing to Harrison.

"And how," said Harrison, laughing, "did this serious calamity of going without breakfast happen?"

"In a very simple manner, colonel," said d'Artagnan. "I was

in a hurry to join you, and took the road you had already gone by. You can understand our disappointment when, arriving at a pretty little house on the skirts of a wood, which at a distance had quite a gay appearance with its red roof and green shutters, we found nothing but a poor wretch bathed—— Ah! colonel, pay my respects to the officer of yours who struck that blow."

"Yes," said Harrison, laughing, and looking over at one of the officers seated at his table. "When Groslow undertakes this kind of thing, there's no occasion to go over the ground after him."

"Ah! it's that gentleman?" said d'Artagnan, bowing to the officer. "I am sorry he does not speak French, that I might offer him my compliments."

"I am ready to receive and return them, sir," said the officer, in fairly good French. "For I lived three years in Paris."

"Then, sir, allow me to assure you that your blow was so well directed that you have nearly killed your man."

"Nearly? I thought it was quite," said Groslow.

"No. It was a very near thing, but he is not dead."

As he said this, d'Artagnan gave a glance at Parry, who was standing in front of the king, to show him that the news was intended for him.

The king, too, who had listened in the greatest agony, now breathed again.

"Hang it," said Groslow, "I thought I had succeeded better. If it were not so far from here to the house, I would return and complete the job."

"And you would do well, if you are afraid of his recovering; for, you know, if a wound in the head does not kill at once, it is cured in a week."

And d'Artagnan threw a second glance towards Parry, on whose face such an expression of joy was manifested that the king stretched out his hand to him, smiling.

Parry bent over his master's hand, and kissed it respectfully.

"I have a great desire to drink the king's health," said Athos.

"Let me propose it, then," said d'Artagnan.

Porthos looked at d'Artagnan, quite amazed at the resources with which his companion's Gascon sharpness continually supplied him.

D'Artagnan took his cup, filled it, and rose.

"Gentlemen," said he, "let us drink to him who presides at our repast. Here's to our colonel, and let him know that we are always at his commands, as far as London, and farther."

And as d'Artagnan, as he spoke, looked at Harrison, the colonel imagined the toast was for himself. He rose and bowed to the four friends, whose eyes were fixed on the king, while Harrison emptied his glass without the slightest misgiving.

The king, in return, looked at the four gentlemen, and drank, with a smile full of nobleness and gratitude.

"Come, gentlemen," cried Harrison, quite regardless of his illustrious captive, "we must be moving."

"Where do we lodge, colonel?"

"At Thirsk," replied Harrison.

"Parry," said the king, rising too, "my horse; I desire to go to Thirsk."

"Egad," said d'Artagnan to Athos; "your king has thoroughly taken me, and I am quite at his service."

"If what you say is sincere," replied Athos, "he will never reach London."

"How so?"

"Why, because before then we shall have rescued him."

"Well, this time, Athos," said d'Artagnan, "upon my word you are mad."

"Have you any idea in your head, then?" asked Aramis.

"Ay," said Porthos, "the thing would not be impossible with a good plan."

"I have none," said Athos, "but d'Artagnan will surely find one."

D'Artagnan shrugged his shoulders, and they resumed their journey.

61

D'ARTAGNAN DISCLOSES A PLAN

ATHOS, perhaps, knew d'Artagnan better than d'Artagnan knew himself. He knew that in an adventurous mind like that of the Gascon, it was only necessary to let a thought fall, as in a rich and fertile soil it is only requisite to drop a seed in. He had therefore allowed his friend to shrug his shoulders without a remark, and rode quietly beside him, talking of Raoul; a subject of conversation which he had formerly shunned.

As night closed in they arrived at Thirsk. D'Artagnan was thoughtful, and seemed for the moment to have lost his usual loquacity. Porthos, who could not see anything that was not self-evident, talked to him as usual. He answered in monosyllables, and Athos and Aramis looked significantly at one another.

Next morning, d'Artagnan was the first to rise. He had gone down to the stables, had already had a look at the horses, and given the necessary orders for the day, while Athos and Aramis were still in bed, and Porthos sleeping soundly.

At eight o'clock, the march was resumed in the same order as the night before, except that d'Artagnan left his friends and began to renew the acquaintance which he had already struck up with Monsieur Groslow.

"Really, sir," d'Artagnan said to him, "I am happy to find some one with whom to talk in my own poor tongue. My friend, Monsieur du Valon, is of a very mournful disposition—so much so, that one can scarcely get three words a day out of him. As for our two prisoners, you can imagine that they are but little in the humour for conversation."

"They are hot Royalists," said Groslow.

"The more reason they should be sullen with us for having captured the Stuart, for whom, I hope, you are preparing a pretty trial."

"Why," said Groslow, "that's just what we are taking him to London for."

"And you don't lose sight of him, I presume?"

"I should think not, indeed. You see he has a truly royal escort."

"Ay, there's no chance in the daytime; but at night."

"We double our precautions."

"And what method of surveillance do you employ?"

"Eight men remain constantly in his room."

"The deuce, he is well guarded then. But, besides these eight men, you doubtless place some guard outside?"

"Oh, no! Just think. What would you have two men without arms do against eight armed men?"

"Two men—how do you mean?"

"Yes, the king and his valet."

"Oh! then they allow the valet to remain with him?"

"Yes; Stuart begged for this favour, and Harrison consented. Under pretence that he's a king, it appears he cannot dress or undress without assistance."

"Really, captain," said d'Artagnan, determined to continue on the laudatory tack on which he had commenced—"the more I listen to you, the more surprised I am at the easy and elegant manner in which you speak French. You resided three years in Paris? May I ask what you were doing there?"

"My father, who is a merchant, placed me with his correspondent, who, in turn, sent his son to my father's."

"Did you care for Paris, sir?"

"Yes; but you are much in want of a revolution like ours; not against your king, who is merely a child, but against that Italian, the queen's favourite."

"Ah! I am quite of your opinion, sir; and we should soon make an end of Mazarin, if we had only a dozen officers like yourself, without prejudices, vigilant, and incorruptible."

"But," said the officer, "I thought you were in his service, and that it was he who had sent you to General Cromwell?"

"That is to say I am in the king's service, and that knowing he wanted to send some one to England, I solicited the appointment, so great was my desire to know the man of genius who now governs the three kingdoms. So that when he proposed to us to draw our swords in honour of England, you see how we snatched at the proposition."

"Yes, I know that you charged by the side of Mordaunt."

"On his right and left, sir. Ah! that's another brave and excellent young man."

"Do you know him?" asked the officer.

"Yes, very well. Monsieur du Valon and myself came from France with him."

"It appears, too, you kept him waiting a long time at Boulogne."

"What would you have? I was like you, and had a king in keeping."

"Ah!" said Groslow; "what king?"

"Our own, to be sure; the little one, Louis XIV."

"And how long had you to take care of him?"

"Three nights; and, by my troth, I shall always remember those three nights with pleasure."

"How do you mean?"

"I mean that my friends, officers in the guards and 'mousquetaires,' came to keep me company, and we passed the night in eating and gambling."

"Ah! true," said the Englishman, with a sigh, "you Frenchmen are jovial boon companions."

"And don't you play, too, when you are on guard?"

"Never," said the Englishman.

"In that case you must be horribly bored, and I am sorry for you."

"The fact is, I look to my turn for keeping guard with horror. It's tiring work to keep awake a whole night."

"Yes; but with a jovial partner, and the gold and dice rolling on the table, the night passes like a dream. You don't like playing, then?"

"On the contrary, I do."

"Lansquenet, for instance?"

"I'm devoted to it. I used to play almost every night in France."

"But since you have returned to England?"

"I have not handled a single card or dice-box."

"I sincerely pity you," said d'Artagnan, with an air of profound compassion.

"Look here!" said the Englishman.

"Well?"

"To-morrow I am on guard."

"In Stuart's room?"

"Yes; come and spend the night with me."

"Impossible!"

"Impossible! why so?"

"I play with Monsieur du Valon every night. Sometimes we don't go to bed at all."

"Well, what of that?"

"Why, he would not like it if I did not play with him!"

"Does he play well?"

"I have seen him lose as much as two thousand pistoles—laughing all the while till the tears rolled down his face."

"Bring him with you, then."

"But how about our prisoners?"

"Let your servants guard them."

"Yes, and give them a chance of escaping," said d'Artagnan. "Why, one of them is a rich lord from Touraine, and the other a knight of Malta, of noble family. We have arranged the ransom of each of them—two thousand pounds on our arrival in France."

"Aha!" exclaimed Groslow. "But come," he continued, "are they dangerous men?"

"In what respect?"

"Are they capable of attempting violence?"

D'Artagnan burst out laughing at the idea.

"Well, then," said Groslow, "bring them with you."

"But really——" said d'Artagnan.

"I have eight men on guard, you know. Four of them can guard the king, and the other four your prisoners. I shall see to it somehow."

"But," said d'Artagnan, "now I think of it, what is to prevent our beginning to-night?"

"Nothing at all," said Groslow.

"Just so. Come to us this evening, and to-morrow we'll return your visit."

"Capital! This evening with you, to-morrow at Stuart's, the next day with me."

"Yes, one can lead a merry life everywhere," said d'Artagnan.

"Ah! with Frenchmen, and Frenchmen like you."

"And Monsieur du Valon," added the other. "You will see what a fellow he is; a man who nearly smashed Mazarin between two doors. They employ him because they are afraid of him. Ah, there he is, calling me now. You'll excuse me, I know."

They exchanged bows, and d'Artagnan returned to his companions.

"What on earth can you have been saying to that bulldog?" exclaimed Porthos.

"My dear fellow, don't speak like that of Monsieur Groslow. He's one of my intimate friends."

"One of your friends!" cried Porthos; "this butcher of peasants!"

"Hush! my dear Porthos. Monsieur Groslow is certainly rather quick, it's true, but at bottom I have discovered good qualities in him. He is conceited and stupid."

Porthos opened his eyes in astonishment; Athos and Aramis looked at one another and smiled.

"But," continued d'Artagnan, "you shall judge of him for yourself. He is coming to play with us this evening."

"Oh!" said Porthos, his eyes glistening at the news. "Is he rich?"

"He's the son of one of the wealthiest merchants in London."

"And knows lansquenet?"

"He adores it."

"Basset?"

"His mania."

"Bribi?"

"He glories in it."

"Good," said Porthos; "we shall pass an agreeable evening."

"The more so, as it will be the prelude to a better."

"How so?"

"We invite him to play to-night; he has invited us in return for to-morrow. But wait. To-night we stop at Derby; and if there is a bottle of wine in the town, let Mousqueton buy it. It will be well to prepare a light supper, of which you, Athos and Aramis, are not to partake. Athos, because I told him you had a fever; Aramis, because you are a knight of Malta, and won't mix with people like us. Do you comprehend?"

"Yes," said Porthos; "but deuce take me if I comprehend at all."

"Porthos, my friend, you know that I am descended on the father's side from the Prophets, and on the mother's from the Sybils, and that I only speak in parables and riddles. That is all I can say for the present."

"The fact is," said Porthos, with an air of finesse, "I am rather incredulous."

D'Artagnan gave him a slap on the shoulder, and as they had reached the station where they were to breakfast, the conversation ended there.

At five in the evening they sent Mousqueton on before, as they had agreed upon.

In crossing the principal street in Derby, the four friends perceived their man standing in the doorway of a handsome house. It was there that their lodging was prepared for them.

At the hour agreed upon Groslow came. D'Artagnan received him as he would have done a friend of twenty years' standing. Porthos looked at him from head to foot, and smiled when he discovered, that in spite of the blow he had administered to Parry's brother, he was not so strong as himself.

Athos and Aramis kept to the parts they had to play, and at midnight they retired to their room, leaving the door open. D'Artagnan accompanied them, and left Porthos to win fifty pistoles of Groslow, and to come to the conclusion when he left, that he was not such bad company as he had first imagined.

Groslow left with the determination of regaining his losses the next night, and reminded the Gascon of the appointment.

The day passed as usual. In his ordinary relations d'Artagnan was the same as ever; but with his friends, that is to say, Athos and Aramis, his gaiety was at fever-heat.

Arrived at Ryston, d'Artagnan assembled his friends. His face had lost the expression of careless gaiety which it had worn like a mask the whole day. Athos pinched Aramis' hand.

"The moment is at hand," he said.

"Yes," said d'Artagnan, who had overheard him, "to-night, gentlemen, we rescue the king."

"D'Artagnan," said Athos, "you are not jesting, I trust? It would quite cut me up."

"You are very odd, Athos," he replied, "to doubt me thus. Where and when have you seen me trifle with a friend's heart and a king's life? I have told you, and I repeat it, that to-night we rescue Charles I. You left it to me to discover the means of doing so, and I have done so."

Porthos looked at d'Artagnan with an expression of profound admiration. Aramis smiled as one who hopes. Athos was pale, and trembled in every limb.

"Speak," said Athos.

"We are invited," replied d'Artagnan, "to spend the night with M. Groslow. But do you know where?"

"No."

"In the king's room."

"The king's room?" cried Athos.

"Yes, gentlemen, in the king's room. Groslow is on guard there this evening, and to pass his time, has requested us to keep him company."

"Aha!" exclaimed Aramis.

"We are going, then—we two with our swords, you with daggers. We four are to make ourselves masters of these eight fools and their stupid captain. Monsieur Porthos, what do you say to it?"

"That it is simple enough," answered Porthos.

"We dress the king in Groslow's clothes. Mousqueton, Grimaud, and Blaisois have our horses saddled at the end of the first street. We mount them, and before daylight are twenty leagues distant."

Athos placed his two hands on d'Artagnan's shoulders, and gazed at him with his calm, mild smile.

"I declare, my friend," said he, "that there is not a creature under the sun who equals you in prowess and courage."

"And to think that I couldn't find that out," said Porthos, scratching his head; "it is so easy."

"But," said Aramis, "if I understand rightly, we are to kill them all, eh?"

Athos shuddered and turned pale.

"*Mordieux*," answered d'Artagnan; "I believe we must. I confess I can see no help for it."

"Let us see," said Aramis, "how are we to act?"

"I have arranged two plans. Firstly, at a given signal, which shall be the words 'At last,' you each plunge a dagger into the heart of the soldier nearest to you. We, on our side, do the same. That will be four killed. We shall then be matched—four against the remaining five. If those five give themselves up we gag them, if they do not, we kill them."

"Very good," said Porthos; "it will be a nice little throat-cutting."

"Horrible, horrible," exclaimed Athos.

"Nonsense," said d'Artagnan; "you would do as much, Monsieur Sensitive, in a battle. But, if you think the king's life is not worth what it must cost, there's an end of the matter, and I send to Groslow to say I am ill."

"No, you are correct," said Athos.

At this moment a soldier entered to inform them that Groslow was waiting for them.

"Where?" asked d'Artagnan.

"In the room of the English Nebuchadnezzar," replied the staunch Puritan.

"Good," replied Athos, whose blood mounted to his face at the insult offered to royalty; "tell the captain we are coming."

The Puritan went out. Orders had been given to the lackeys to saddle eight horses, and to wait with them, without separating or dismounting, at the corner of a street situated at about twenty paces from the house in which the king lodged.

62

THE CARD-PARTY

IT was now nine in the evening. The guard had been relieved at eight, and Captain Groslow's guard had commenced an hour before. D'Artagnan and Porthos, armed with their swords, and Athos and Aramis, with each a poignard concealed in his clothes, made their way towards the house where Charles Stuart was to lodge for the night. The two latter followed their conquerors, humble and disarmed in appearance, as captives.

"Faith," said Groslow, as the four friends entered, "I had almost given you up."

D'Artagnan went up to him, and whispered in his ear:

"The fact is we, that is, Monsieur du Valon and I, hesitated a little."

"And why?"

D'Artagnan looked significantly towards Athos and Aramis.

"Aha," said Groslow, "on account of opinions? No matter. On the contrary," he added, laughing, "if they want to see their Stuart they shall see him."

"Do we pass the night in the king's room?" asked d'Artagnan.

"No, but in the one next to it; and as the door will remain open, it's the same thing. Have you provided yourself with money? I assure you I intend to play the devil's game to-night."

D'Artagnan rattled some gold in his pockets.

"Very good," said Groslow, and opened the door of the room.

"I will show you the way," and he went in first.

D'Artagnan turned to look at his friends. Porthos was perfectly indifferent; Athos pale, but resolute. Aramis was wiping a slight moisture from his brow.

The eight guards were at their posts—four in the king's room, two at the door between the rooms, and two at that by which the friends had entered. Athos smiled when he saw their naked swords; he felt it was no longer to be a butchery but a fight, and his usual good humour returned to him.

The king was perceived through the door, lying dressed upon his bed, at the head of which Parry was seated, reading, in a low voice, a chapter from the Bible.

A candle of coarse tallow on a black table lit up the resigned face of the king, and that of his faithful retainer, far less calm.

From time to time Parry stopped, thinking the king, whose eyes were closed, was really asleep, but the king would open his eyes, and say with a smile:

"Go on, my good Parry, I am listening."

Groslow advanced to the entrance of the king's room, replaced on his head the hat which he had taken off to receive his guests, looked for a moment contemptuously at this simple and touching scene, and, turning again to d'Artagnan, assumed an air of triumph at what he had achieved.

"Capital," cried the Gascon, "you would make a distinguished general."

"And do you think," asked Groslow, "that the Stuart will ever escape while I am on guard?"

"No, to be sure," replied d'Artagnan; "unless, forsooth, the sky rains friends upon him."

Groslow's face brightened.

It is impossible to say whether the king, who kept his eyes constantly closed, had noticed the insolence of the Puritan captain, but the moment he heard the clear tone of d'Artagnan's voice, his eyelids rose in spite of himself.

Parry, too, started and stopped reading.

"What are you thinking about?" said the king; "go on, my good Parry, unless, at least, you are fatigued."

Parry resumed his reading.

On a table in the next room were lighted candles, cards, two dice-boxes and dice.

"That's it," said d'Artagnan; "you, Monsieur le Comte de la Fère, to the right of Monsieur Groslow. You, Chevalier d'Herblay, to his left. Du Valon next me. You'll bet for me, and those gentlemen for Monsieur Groslow."

By this arrangement, d'Artagnan could nudge Porthos with his knee, and make signs with the eyes to Athos and Aramis.

At the names of Comte de la Fère and Chevalier d'Herblay, the king opened his eyes, and, raising his noble head in spite of himself, threw a glance at all the actors in the scene.

"You asked me just now if I was in funds," said d'Artagnan, placing some twenty pistoles upon the table; "well, in my turn I advise you to keep a sharp lookout on your *treasure*, my dear Monsieur Groslow, for I can tell you we shall not leave this room without robbing you of it."

"Nor without my defending it," said Groslow.

"So much the better," said d'Artagnan. "Fight, my dear captain, fight. You know, or you don't know, that that is what we ask of you."

"Oh! yes," said Groslow, bursting into his usual hoarse laugh, "I know you Frenchmen want nothing but cuts and bruises."

The king had heard and understood it all. A slight colour mounted to his cheeks. The soldiers then saw him stretch his limbs little by little, and under the pretence of much heat, throw off the Scotch shawl which covered him.

Athos and Aramis started with joy to find that the king was lying with his clothes on.

The game began. The luck had turned, and Groslow having won some hundred pistoles, was in the merriest possible humour.

Porthos, who had lost the fifty pistoles he had won the night before, and thirty more besides, was very cross, and questioned d'Artagnan with a nudge of the knee, as to whether it would not soon be time to change the game. But d'Artagnan remained impassible.

It struck ten. They heard the guard going its rounds.

"How many rounds do they make a night?" asked d'Artagnan, drawing more pistoles from his pocket.

"Five," answered Groslow, "one every two hours."

D'Artagnan glanced at Athos and Aramis, and for the first time replied to Porthos's nudge of the knee by a nudge responsive. Meanwhile the soldiers, whose duty it was to remain in the king's room, attracted by that love of play so powerful in most men, had stolen little by little towards the table, and standing on tiptoe, were watching the game over the shoulders of d'Artagnan and Porthos.

Those on the other side had followed their example, thus favouring the views of the four friends.

D'Artagnan turned, mechanically looking behind him, and between the figures of two soldiers he could see Parry standing up, and the king leaning on his elbow, with his hands clasped, and apparently offering a fervent prayer to God.

D'Artagnan saw that the moment was come. He darted a preparatory glance at Athos and Aramis, who gently pushed back their chairs a little so as to leave themselves space for action. He gave Porthos a second nudge of the knee; and Porthos got up as if to stretch his legs, and took care at the same time to see that his sword could be drawn easily from the scabbard.

"Hang it," cried d'Artagnan; "another twenty pistoles lost. Really, Captain Groslow, you are too much in luck's way. This can't last;" and he drew another twenty from his pocket. "One more turn, captain, twenty pistoles on one throw—only one, the last."

"Done for twenty," replied Groslow.

And he turned up two cards as usual, a king for d'Artagnan, and an ace for himself.

"A king," said d'Artagnan; "it's a good sign, Master Groslow, look out for the king."

And in spite of his power over himself, there was a strange vibration in the Gascon's voice, which startled his partner.

Groslow began turning the cards one after another. If he turned up an ace first he won; if a king he lost.

He turned up a king.

"At last!" cried d'Artagnan.

At this word Athos and Aramis sprang up. Porthos drew back a step. Daggers and swords were just about to be drawn, when suddenly the door was thrown open, and Harrison appeared in the doorway, accompanied by a man covered with a large cloak. Behind this man could be seen the glistening muskets of five or six soldiers.

Groslow jumped up, ashamed at being surprised in the midst of wine, cards, and dice. But Harrison paid no attention to him, and, entering the king's room, followed by his companion—

"Charles Stuart," said he, "an order has come to conduct you to London without stopping day or night. Prepare yourself, then, to start at once."

"And by whom is this order given?" asked the king.

"By General Oliver Cromwell. And here is Mr. Mordaunt, who has brought it, and is charged with its execution."

"Mordaunt!" muttered the four friends, exchanging looks.

D'Artagnan swept up the money that he and Porthos had lost, and buried it in his pocket. Athos and Aramis placed themselves behind him. At this moment Mordaunt turned round, recognised them, and uttered an exclamation of savage delight.

"I'm afraid we are taken," whispered d'Artagnan to his friends.

"Not yet," replied Porthos.

"Colonel, colonel," cried Mordaunt, "you are betrayed. These four Frenchmen have escaped from Newcastle, and no doubt want to carry off the king. Arrest them."

"Ah! my young man," said d'Artagnan, drawing his sword, "that is an order sooner given than executed. Fly, friends, fly," he added, swinging his sword around him.

The next moment he darted to the door and knocked down two of the soldiers who guarded it, before they had time to cock their muskets. Athos and Aramis followed him. Porthos brought up the rear, and before soldiers, officers, or colonel had time to recover their surprise, all four were in the street.

"Fire!" cried Mordaunt; "fire on them."

Three or four shots were fired, but with no other result than to show the four fugitives turning the corner of the street safe and sound.

The horses were at the stated place, and they leapt lightly into their saddles.

"Forward!" cried d'Artagnan, "and spur well your horses."

They rode on, and took the road they had come by in the morning, namely, in the direction towards Scotland. A few yards beyond the town d'Artagnan drew up.

"Halt!" he cried; "this time we shall be pursued. We must let them leave the village and ride after us on the northern road, and when they are past we shall take the opposite direction."

There was a stream close by, and a bridge across it. D'Artagnan led his horse under the arch of the bridge. The others followed.

They had not been there ten minutes before they heard the rapid gallop of a troop of horsemen. In five minutes more this troop had passed over their heads, little imagining that they had been separated from those they sought only by the thickness of the arch of the bridge.

63

LONDON

WHEN the noise of the horses had died away, d'Artagnan regained the banks of the stream, and began to make all speed across the plain, directing his course as much as possible towards London. His three friends followed him in silence, until, by making a large detour, they had left the town far behind them.

"This time," said d'Artagnan, when they were sufficiently distant to proceed at a trot, "I think all is lost, and we have nothing better to do than to reach France. What do you think, Athos?"

"True," said Athos; "but we ought, I think, to see this great tragedy played out. Do not let us leave England before the crisis. Don't you agree with me, Aramis?"

"Entirely, my dear count. Then, too, I confess I should not be sorry to come across Mordaunt again. It seems to me that we have an account to settle with him, and that it is not our custom to leave a place without paying our debts, of this kind at least."

"Ah! that's another thing," said d'Artagnan; "and I should not mind stopping in London a whole year for a chance of meeting this Mordaunt in question. Only let us lodge with some one on whom we can count; for I imagine that, just now, M. Cromwell would not be inclined to trifle with us. Athos, do you know any inn in the whole town where one can find white sheets, roast beef agreeably cooked, and wine which is not made of hops or gin?"

"I think I know what you want," replied Athos. "De Winter took us to the house of a Spaniard, who, he said, had been naturalised in England by his new fellow-countrymen's guineas."

"Well, we must take every precaution."

"Yes, and among others, that of changing our clothes."

"Changing our clothes!" exclaimed Porthos. "I don't see why; we are very comfortable in those we have on."

"To prevent recognition," said d'Artagnan. "Our clothes have a cut which would denounce the Frenchman at first sight. Now, I don't care sufficiently about the cut of my jerkin to risk being hung at Tyburn, or sent for change of scene to the Indies. I shall buy a chestnut-coloured suit. I've remarked that your Puritans glory in that colour."

"But can you find your man?" said Aramis to Athos.

"Oh! to be sure, yes. He lives at the Bedford Tavern, Green Hall Street. Besides, I can find my way about the city with my eyes shut."

Athos was right. He went direct to the Bedford Tavern, and the host, who recognised him, was delighted to see him again with such a worthy and numerous company.

Though it was scarcely daylight, our four travellers found the town in a great bustle, owing to the rumoured approach of Harrison and the king.

The plan of changing their clothes was unanimously adopted. The landlord sent out for every description of garment, as if he wanted to fit up his wardrobe. Athos chose a black coat, which gave him the appearance of a respectable citizen. Aramis, not wishing to part with his sword, selected a dark one of a military cut. Porthos was tempted by a red doublet with green pockets. D'Artagnan, who had fixed on his colour beforehand, had only to select the shade, and looked in his chestnut suit exactly like a retired grocer.

"Now," said d'Artagnan, "for the actual man. We must cut our hair, that the populace may not insult us. As we no longer wear the sword of the gentleman, we may as well have the head of the Puritan. This, as you know, is the important point of distinction between the Covenanter and the Cavalier."

"We look frightful," said Athos.

"And smack of the Puritan to an awful extent," said Aramis.

"My head feels quite cool," said Porthos.

"And as for me, I feel anxious to preach a sermon," said d'Artagnan.

"Now," said Athos, "that we cannot even recognise one another, and have, therefore, no fear of others recognising us, let us go and see the king's entrance."

They had not been long in the crowd before loud shouts announced the king's arrival. A carriage had been sent to meet him; and the gigantic Porthos, who stood a head above all the other heads, soon announced that he saw the royal equipage approaching. D'Artagnan poised himself on tiptoe, and as the carriage passed, saw Harrison at one window and Mordaunt at the other.

The next day, Athos leaning out of his window, which looked upon the most populous part of the city, heard the Act of Parliament, which summoned the late king, Charles I., to the bar, publicly cried.

"The parliament, indeed!" cried Athos. "Parliament can never have passed such an act as that."

At this moment the landlord came in.

"Did parliament pass this act?" Athos asked of him in English.

"Yes, my lord, the pure parliament."

"Come," said d'Artagnan, "as I don't understand English, suppose you speak to us in Spanish, which we all understand."

"Do you mean to say, then," resumed Athos, "that there are two parliaments, one pure, and the other impure?"

"When I speak of the pure parliament," resumed the host, "I mean the one which Colonel Bridge has weeded."

"Ah! really," said d'Artagnan, "these people are very ingenious. When I go back to France I must suggest that to Cardinal Mazarin. One shall weed the parliament in the name of the court, and the other in the name of the people: so that there won't be any parliament left at all."

"And who is this Colonel Bridge?" asked Aramis.

"Colonel Bridge," replied the Spaniard, "is a retired wagoner, a man of great sense, who made one witty observation in driving his team, namely, that where there happened to be a stone on the road, it was much easier to remove the stone, than to try and make the wheel pass over it. Now, of two hundred and fifty-one members who composed the parliament, there were one hundred and ninety-one who were in his way, and might have upset his political wagon. He took them up, just as he formerly used to take up the stones from the road, and dropped them from out of the house."

"Smart," remarked d'Artagnan. "Extremely so!"

"And all these one hundred and ninety-one were Royalists?" asked Athos.

"Without doubt, sir; and, you understand, that they would have saved the king."

"To be sure," said Porthos, "they were in the majority."

"And you think," said Aramis, "he will consent to appear before such a tribunal?"

"He will be compelled to do so," answered the Spaniard.

"Now, Athos!" said d'Artagnan, "do you begin to believe that it's a ruined cause? and that what with your Harrisons, Bridges, and Cromwells, we shall never get the upper hand?"

"But," said Aramis, "if they dare to condemn their king, it can only be to exile or imprisonment."

D'Artagnan whistled a little air of incredulity.

"We shall see," said Athos, "for we shall go to the sittings, I presume."

"You will not have long to wait," said the landlord; "they begin to-morrow."

"So, then, they drew up the indictment before the king was taken?"

"Of course," said d'Artagnan; "they began the day he was sold."

"And you know," said Aramis, "that it was our friend Mordaunt who made, if not the bargain, at least the first overtures."

"And you know," added d'Artagnan, "that whenever I catch him, I kill him, this Mister Mordaunt."

"And I, too," exclaimed Porthos.

"And I, too," added Aramis.

"Touching unanimity!" cried d'Artagnan, "which well becomes good citizens like us. Let us take a turn round the town, and imbibe a little fog."

"Yes," said Porthos. "It will be a change from the beer."

And the four friends set out to take, as is commonly said, the air of the country.

64

THE TRIAL

THE next day a numerous guard conducted Charles I. before the high tribunal which was to try him. All London was crowding to the doors of the house. The throng was terrific; and it was not till after much crowding and some fighting that our four friends reached their destination. When they did so, they found the three lower rows of benches already filled; but, as they were not anxious to be too conspicuous, all, with the exception of Porthos, who was anxious to display his red doublet, were quite satisfied with their places, the more so as chance had brought them to the centre of their row, so that they were exactly opposite the arm-chair prepared for the royal captive.

Towards eleven o'clock the king entered the hall, surrounded by guards, but wearing his head covered, and with a calm expression turned to every side with a look of complete assurance, as if he were there to preside at an assembly of submissive subjects, rather than to reply to the accusations of a rebel court.

The judges, proud of having a monarch to humble, evidently prepared to employ the right they had arrogated to themselves, and sent an officer to inform the king that it was customary for the accused to uncover his head.

Charles I., without replying a single word, turned his head in another direction, and pulled his felt hat over it. Then, when the officer was gone, he sat down in the arm-chair opposite the president, and struck his boot with a little cane which he carried in his hand. Parry, who accompanied him, stood behind him.

D'Artagnan was looking at Athos, whose face betrayed all those emotions which the king, possessing more command over himself, had chased from his own. This agitation, in one so cool and calm as Athos, terrified him.

"I hope," he whispered to him, "that you will follow his majesty's example, and not get killed for your folly in this den."

"Set your mind at ease," replied Athos.

"Aha!" continued d'Artagnan, "it is evident that they are afraid of something or other; for, look, the sentinels are being re-inforced. They had only halberds before, and now they have muskets. The halberds were for the audience in the area. The muskets are for us."

"Thirty, forty, fifty, sixty-five men," said Porthos, counting the reinforcements.

"Ah!" said Aramis. "But you forget the officer."

D'Artagnan grew pale with rage. He had recognised Mordaunt, who, with bare sword, was marshalling the soldiers before the king, and opposite the benches.

"Do you think they have recognised us?" said d'Artagnan. "In that case I shall beat a retreat. I don't care to be shot in a box."

"No," said Aramis, "he has not seen us. He sees no one but the king. *Mon Dieu!* how he stares at him, the insolent dog! Does he hate his majesty as much as he does us?"

"*Pardi*," answered Athos, "we only carried off his mother, and the king has despoiled him of his name and property."

"True," said Aramis; "but silence! the president is speaking to the king."

"Stuart," Bradshaw was saying, "listen to the roll-call of your judges, and address to the court any observations you may have to make."

The king turned his head away, as if these words had not been intended for him. Bradshaw paused, and, as there was no reply, there was a moment of silence.

Out of the hundred and sixty-three members designated, there were only seventy-three present, for the rest, fearful of taking part in such an act, had remained absent.

When the name of Colonel Fairfax was called, one of those brief but solemn silences ensued, which announced the absence of the members who had no wish to take a personal part in the trial.

"Colonel Fairfax," repeated Bradshaw.

"Fairfax?" answered a laughing voice, the silvery tone of which betrayed it as that of a woman, "he is not such a fool as to be here."

A burst of laughter followed these words, pronounced with that boldness which women draw from their own weakness—a weakness which removes them beyond the power of retaliation.

"It is a woman's voice," cried Aramis; "faith, I would give a good deal for her to be young and pretty." And he mounted on the bench to try and get a sight of her.

"By my soul," said Aramis, "she is charming. Look, d'Artagnan: everybody is looking at her; and in spite of Bradshaw's gaze, she has not turned pale."

"It is Lady Fairfax herself," said d'Artagnan; "don't you remember, Porthos, we saw her at General Cromwell's?"

The roll-call continued.

"These rascals will adjourn when they find that they are not in sufficient force," said the Comte de la Fère.

"You don't know them, Athos; look at Mordaunt's smile. Is that the look of a man whose victim is likely to escape him. Ah, cursed basilisk, it will be a happy day for me when I can cross something more than a look with you."

"The king is really very handsome," said Porthos; "and look, too, though he is a prisoner, how carefully he is attired. The feather in his hat is worth at least fifty pistoles. Look at it, Aramis."

The roll-call being brought to an end, the president ordered them to read the act of accusation. Athos turned pale. A second time he was disappointed in his expectation.

"I told you so, Athos," said d'Artagnan, shrugging his shoulders. "Now take your courage in both hands, and hear what this gentleman in black is going to say about his sovereign, with full licence and privilege."

Never till then had a more brutal accusation or coarser insults tarnished the kingly majesty.

The king listened with marked attention, passing over the insults, noting the grievances, and, when hatred overflowed all bounds, and the accuser turned executioner beforehand, replying with a smile of contempt.

"The fact is," said d'Artagnan, "if men are punished for imprudence and triviality, this poor king deserves punishment. But it seems to me that that which he is just now undergoing is hard enough."

At this moment the accuser concluded with these words:—

"The present accusation is preferred by us in the name of the people of England."

At these words there was a murmur along the benches, and a second voice, not that of a woman, but a man's, stout and furious, thundered behind d'Artagnan:

"You lie," it cried, "and nine-tenths of the English people are horrified at what you say."

This voice was that of Athos, who, standing up with outstretched arm, and quite out of his mind, thus assailed the public accuser.

King, judges, spectators, all turned their eyes to the bench where the four friends were seated. Mordaunt did the same, and recognised the gentleman, around whom the three other Frenchmen were standing, pale and menacing. His eyes glittered with delight. He had discovered those to whose death he had devoted his life. A movement of fury called to his side some twenty of the riflemen, and, pointing to the bench where his enemies were,—"Fire on that bench," he cried.

But, rapid as thought, d'Artagnan seized Athos by the body, and, followed by Porthos with Aramis, leapt down from the benches, rushed into the passages, and, flying down the staircase, was lost in the crowd without, while the muskets within were pointed on some three thousand spectators, whose piteous cries and noisy alarms stopped the impulse already given to bloodshed.

Mordaunt, pale and trembling with rage, rushed from the hall, sword in hand, followed by six pikemen, pushing, inquiring, and panting in the crowd; and then, having found nothing, returned.

Quiet was at length restored.

"What have you to say in defence?" asked Bradshaw of the king.

Then, rising, with his head still covered, in the tone of a judge rather than a prisoner, the king began.

"Before questioning me," he said, "reply to my question. I was free at Newcastle, and had there concluded a treaty with both houses. Instead of performing your part of this contract, as I performed mine, you bought me from the Scotch—not dear, I know, and that does honour to the economy of your government. But because you have paid the price of a slave, do you expect that I have ceased to be your king? No. To answer you would be to forget it. I shall only reply to you when you have satisfied me of your right to question me. To answer you would be to acknowledge you as my judges, and I only acknowledge you as my executioners." And in the midst of a death-like silence, Charles, calm, lofty, and his head still covered, sat down again in his armchair.

"Why are not my Frenchmen here?" he murmured proudly, and turning his eyes to the benches where they had appeared for a moment; "they would have seen that their friend was worthy of their defence, while alive; and of their tears, when dead."

"Well," said the president, seeing that the king was determined to remain silent, "so be it. We will judge you in spite of your silence. You are accused of treason, of abuse of power, and murder. The evidence will support it. Go, and another sitting will accomplish what you have refused to do in this."

The king rose, and turned towards Parry, whose face was pallid, and his temples covered with moisture.

"Well, my dear Parry," said he, "what is the matter? and what can affect you in this manner?"

"Oh, my king," said Parry, with tears in his eyes, and in a tone of supplication, "pray do not look to the left as we leave the hall."

"And why, Parry?"

"Do not look, I entreat you, my king."

"What is the matter? speak," said the king, attempting to look across the cordon of guards which surrounded him.

"It is—but you will not look, will you?—it is, because they have had the axe, with which criminals are executed, brought and placed there on a table. The sight is hideous."

"Fools," said the king, "do they imagine me a coward like themselves? You have done well to warn me. Thank you, Parry."

When the moment arrived, the king followed the guards out of the hall. As he passed the table on which the axe was laid, he stopped, and turning with a smile, said:

"Ah! the axe, an ingenious device, and well worthy of those who know not what a gentleman is. You frighten me not, executioner's axe," added he, touching it with the cane which he held in his hand, "and I strike you now, waiting patiently and calmly for you to return the blow."

And, shrugging his shoulders with supreme contempt, he passed on. When he reached the door, a large concourse of people, who had been disappointed in not being able to get into the house, and to make amends had collected to see him come out, stood on each side as he passed, many among them glaring on him with threatening looks.

"How many people," thought he, "and not one true friend!" And as he uttered these words of doubt and depression within his mind, a voice near him said:

"Respect to fallen majesty."

The king turned quickly round, with tears in his eyes and heart. It was an old soldier of the guards, who could not see his king pass captive before him without rendering him this last homage. But the next moment the unfortunate man was nearly stunned with blows from the hilts of swords; and among those who set upon him the king recognised Captain Groslow.

"Alas!" said the king, "that is severe punishment for a very slight fault."

He continued his way; but he had scarcely gone a hundred paces, when a rough-looking fellow, leaning between two soldiers, spat in the king's face. Loud roars of laughter and sullen murmurs rose together. The crowd opened and closed again, undulating like a stormy sea; and the king imagined that he saw shining in the midst of this living wave the bright eyes of Athos.

The king wiped his face, and said, with a sad smile, "Poor wretch, for half a crown he would do as much to his own father."

The king was not wrong. Athos and his friends, again mingling with the throng, were taking a last look at the unfortunate king.

When the cowardly insulter had spat in the face of the captive monarch, Athos had grasped his dagger. But d'Artagnan stopped his hand, and in a hoarse voice cried, "Stay!"

Athos stopped. D'Artagnan, leaning on Athos, made a sign to Porthos and Aramis to keep near them, and then placed himself behind the man with the bare arms, who was still laughing at his own vile pleasantry, and receiving the congratulations of several others.

The man advanced toward the city. The four friends followed him. The fellow, who had the appearance of a butcher, descended a little steep and isolated street, looking on the river, with two of his friends. Arrived at the bank of the river, the three men perceived that they were followed, turned round, and looked insolently at the Frenchmen.

"Athos," said d'Artagnan, "will you interpret for me?"

At this, d'Artagnan walked up to the butcher, and touching him on the chest with the tip of his finger, said to Athos:

"Say to him in English, 'You are a coward. You have insulted a defenceless man. You have befouled the face of your king. You must die.'"

Athos, pale as a ghost, translated these words to the man, who, seeing the unpleasant preparations that were made, put himself in an attitude of defence. Aramis, at this movement, drew his sword.

"No," cried d'Artagnan, "no steel. Steel is for gentlemen."

And seizing the butcher by the throat—

"Porthos," said he, "knock this fellow down for me with a single blow."

Porthos raised his arm, which whistled through the air like a sling, and then fell with a dull noise on the skull of the coward, and broke it. The man fell like an ox under the mallet. His companions, horror-struck, could neither move nor cry out.

"Tell them this, Athos," resumed d'Artagnan; "'Thus shall all die who forget that a fettered man wears a sacred head.'"

The two men looked at the body of their companion, swimming in black blood; and then, recovering voice and legs together, ran shouting away.

"Justice is done," said Porthos, wiping his forehead.

"And now," said d'Artagnan to Athos, "do not have any doubts about me; I undertake everything that concerns the king."

65

WHITEHALL

THE parliament, as was foreseen, condemned Charles Stuart to death. Political judgments are generally merely vain formalities, for the same passions which give rise to the accusation give rise also to the condemnation. Such is the terrible logic of revolutions.

Meanwhile, before our four friends could concentrate their plans, they determined to put every possible obstacle in the way of the execution of the sentence. To this end they resolved to get rid of the executioner; for though, of course, another could be sent for, there would be still a delay of a day or two gained. D'Artagnan undertook this more than difficult task. The next thing was to warn the king of the attempt to be made to save him. Aramis undertook the perilous office. Bishop Juxon had received permission to visit the king in his prison at Whitehall; Aramis resolved to persuade the bishop to let him enter with him. Lastly, Athos was to prepare, in every emergency, the means of leaving England.

The palace of Whitehall was surrounded by three regiments of cavalry, and still more by the anxiety of Cromwell, who came and went, or sent his generals or his agents continually. Alone, in his usual room, lighted by two candles, the condemned monarch gazed sadly on the luxury of his past greatness, just as, at the last hour, one sees the image of life, milder and more brilliant than ever.

Parry had not left his master, and since his condemnation, had not ceased to weep. His majesty, leaning on a table, was gazing at a medallion of his wife and daughter; he was waiting first for Juxon, next for martyrdom.

"Alas!" he said to himself, "if I only had for a confessor one of those lights of the Church, whose soul has sounded all the mysteries of life, all the littlenesses of greatness, perhaps his voice would choke the voice that wails within my soul. But I shall have a priest of vulgar mind, whose career and fortune I have ruined by my misfortune. He will speak to me of God and of death, as he has spoken to many another dying man, not understanding that this one leaves his throne to a usurper and his children to starve."

And he raised the medallion to his lips.

It was a dull, foggy night. A neighbouring church clock slowly struck the hour. The pale light of the two candles raised flickering spectres in the lofty room. These spectres were the ancestors of King Charles, standing out from their gilt frames. A profound melancholy had possessed itself of the king. He buried his brow in his hands, and thought of all that was so dear to him, now to be left for ever. He drew from his bosom the diamond cross which Henrietta Maria had sent him by the hands of those generous Frenchmen, and kissed it, and remembered that she would not see it again till he was lying cold and mutilated in the tomb.

Suddenly the door opened, and an ecclesiastic, in episcopal robes, entered, followed by two guards, to whom the king waved an imperious gesture. The guards retired. The room resumed its obscurity.

"Juxon!" he cried, "Juxon, thank you, my last friend, you are come at a fitting moment."

The bishop looked anxiously at the sobbing man.

"Come, Parry," said the king, "dry your eyes."

"If it's Parry," said the bishop, "I have nothing to fear; so allow me to salute your majesty, and to tell you who I am, and for what I am come."

At this sight, and this voice, the monarch was about to cry out, when Aramis placed his finger on his lips, and bowed low to the King of England.

"The knight!" murmured the king.

"Yes, sire," interrupted Aramis, raising his voice, "the Bishop Juxon, faithful knight of Christ, and obedient to your majesty's wishes."

The ill-fated king clasped his hands, amazed and stupefied to find that these foreigners, without other motive than that which their conscience imposed on them, thus combated the will of a people, and the destiny of a king.

"You!" he said, "you! how did you penetrate hither? If they recognise you, you are lost."

"Care not for me, sire; think only of yourself. You see, your friends are wakeful. I know not what we shall do yet, but four determined men can do much. Meanwhile, do not be surprised at anything that happens; prepare yourself for every emergency."

The king shook his head.

"Do you know that I die to-morrow, at ten o'clock?"

"Something, your majesty, will happen, between now and then, to make the execution impossible."

At this moment, a sound, like the unloading of a cart, and followed by a cry of pain, was heard beneath the window.

"What is this noise and this cry?" said Aramis, perplexed.

"I know not who could have uttered that cry," said the king, "but the noise is easily understood. Do you know that I am to be decapitated outside this window? Well, this wood, that you hear fall, is the posts and planks to build my scaffold. Some workman must have been hurt in unloading them."

Aramis shuddered, in spite of himself.

"You see," said the king, "that it is useless for you to resist. I am condemned; leave me to my fate."

"My king," said Aramis, "they may well raise a scaffold, but they cannot make an executioner."

"What do you mean?" asked the king.

"I mean that, at this hour, the headsman is removed by force or persuasion. The scaffold will be ready by to-morrow, but the headsman will be absent, and they will put it off till the day after to-morrow."

"What then?" said the king.

"To-morrow night we shall save you."

"Oh! sir," cried Parry, "may you and yours be blessed!"

"I know nothing about it," continued Aramis, "but the cleverest, the bravest, the most devoted of us four, said to me, when I left him, 'Knight, tell the king, that to-morrow, at ten o'clock at night, we shall carry him off.' He has said it, and will accomplish it."

"You are really wonderful men," said the king; "take my hand, knight, it is that of a friend, who will love you to the last."

Aramis stooped to kiss the king's hand, but the king clasped his and pressed it to his heart.

At this moment a man entered, without even knocking at the door. Aramis attempted to withdraw his hand, but the king still held it. The man was one of those Puritans, half preacher and half soldier, who swarmed around Cromwell.

"What do you want, sir?" said the king.

"I desire to know if the confession of Charles Stuart is at an end?" said the stranger.

"And what is it to you?" replied the king; "we are not of the same religion."

"All men are brothers," said the Puritan. "One of my brothers is about to die, and I come to prepare him."

"Bear with him," whispered Aramis; "it is doubtless some spy."

"After my reverend Lord Bishop," said the king, to the man, "I shall hear you with pleasure, sir."

The man retired, but not before examining the supposed Juxon with an attention which did not escape the king.

"Knight," said the king, when the door was closed, "I believe you are right, and that this man only came here with evil intentions. Take care that no misfortune befalls you when you leave."

"I thank your majesty," said Aramis, "but, under my robes, I have a coat of mail and a dagger."

"Go, then, sir, and God keep you!"

The king accompanied him to the door, where Aramis pronounced his benediction upon him, and, passing through the anterooms, filled with soldiers, jumped into his carriage, and drove to the bishop's palace. Juxon was waiting for him impatiently.

Aramis resumed his own attire, and left Juxon with the assurance that he might again have recourse to him.

He had scarcely gone ten yards in the street, when he perceived that he was followed by a man, wrapped in a large cloak. He placed his hand on his dagger, and stopped. The man came straight towards him. It was Porthos.

"My dear friend," cried Aramis.

"You see, we had each our mission," said Porthos; "mine was to guard you, and I was doing so. Have you seen the king?"

"Yes, and all goes well."

"We are to meet our friends at the hotel, at eleven."

It was then striking half-past ten.

Arrived at the hotel, it was not long before Athos entered.

"All's well," he cried as he entered; "I have hired a little boat, as narrow as a canoe, and as light as a swallow. It is waiting for us at Greenwich, manned by a captain and four men, who, for the sum of fifty pounds sterling, will keep themselves at our disposition three successive nights. Once on board, we drop down the Thames, and, in two hours, are in the open sea. In case I am killed, the captain's name is Richards, and the boat is called the *Lightning*. A handkerchief tied at the four corners is to be the signal."

Next moment, d'Artagnan entered.

"Empty your pockets," said he, "I want a hundred pounds, and as for my own——" and he emptied them inside out.

The money was collected in a minute. D'Artagnan ran out, and returned directly after.

"There," said he, "it's done. Ough! and not without a deal of trouble too."

"Has the executioner left London?" asked Aramis.

"No, he is in the cellar."

"The cellar—what cellar?"

"Our landlord's, to be sure. Mousqueton is sitting by the door, and here's the key."

"Bravo!" said Aramis; "but how did you manage it?"

"Like everything else—with money; it cost me dear."

"How much?" asked Athos.

"Five hundred pounds."

"And where did you get all that from?" said Athos.

"The queen's famous diamond," answered d'Artagnan, with a sigh.

"Ah! true," said Aramis, "I recognised it on your finger."

"You bought it back, then, from Monsieur des Essarts?" asked Porthos.

"Yes, but it was fated that I should not keep it."

"Well, so much for the executioner," said Athos; "but, unfortunately, every executioner has his assistant, his man, or whatever he is called."

"And this one had his," said d'Artagnan; "but, as good luck would have it, just as I thought I should have two affairs to manage, my friend was brought home with a broken leg. In the excess of his zeal, he had accompanied the cart containing the scaffolding as far as the king's window, and one of the planks fell on his leg and broke it."

"Ah!" cried Aramis, "that accounts for the cry that I heard."

"Probably," said d'Artagnan; "but he is a young man of talent, he promised to send four expert workmen in his place to help those already at the scaffold, and wrote, the moment he was brought home, to Mister Jack Smith, an assistant carpenter and friend of his, to go down to Whitehall with three of his friends. Here's the letter he sent by a messenger for sixpence, who sold it to me for a guinea."

"And what on earth are you going to do with it?" asked Athos.

"Can you not guess, my dear Athos? You, who speak English like John Bull himself, are Mister Jack Smith, we, your three assistants. Do you understand now?"

66

THE WORKMEN

TOWARDS the middle of the night, Charles heard a great noise—hammers, axes, crowbars, and saws were all in full play.

Reclining dressed upon his bed, this noise awoke him with a start, and found a gloomy echo in his heart. He could not endure it, and sent Parry to ask the sentinel to beg the workmen to strike more gently, and not disturb the last slumber of one who had been their king. The sentinel was unwilling to leave his post, but allowed Parry to pass.

Arriving at the window, Parry perceived an unfinished scaffold, over which they were nailing a covering of black serge. Raised to the height of twenty feet, so as to be on a level with the window, it had two lower storeys. Odious as was this sight to him, Parry sought for those among some eight or ten workmen who were making the most noise, and fixed on two men who were loosening the last hooks of the iron balcony.

"My friends," said Parry, when he had mounted the scaffold and stood beside them, "would you work a little more quietly? The king wishes to get to sleep." One of the two, who was standing up, was of gigantic size, and was driving a pick with all his might into the wall, while the other kneeling beside him was collecting the pieces of stone. The face of the first was lost to Parry in the darkness, but as the second turned round and placed his finger on his lips, Parry started back in amazement.

"Very well, very well," said the workman aloud in excellent English. "Tell the king that if he sleeps badly to-night, he will sleep better to-morrow."

These blunt words, so terrible if taken literally, were received by the other workmen with a roar of laughter. But Parry withdrew, thinking he was dreaming.

"Sire," said he to the king, "do you know who these workmen are who are making so much noise?"

"I! no, how would you have me know?"

Parry bent his head and whispered to the king, "It is the Count de la Fère and his friend."

"Raising my scaffold," cried the king, astounded.

"Yes, and at the same time making a hole in the wall."

The king clasped his hands, and raised his eyes to heaven; then, starting from his bed, he went to the window, and pulling aside the curtain, tried to distinguish the figures outside, but in vain.

Parry was not wrong. It was Athos whom he had recognised, and it was Porthos who was boring a hole through the wall.

This hole communicated with a kind of low loft, the space between the floor of the king's room and the ceiling of the one below it. Their plan was to pass through the hole they were making into this loft, and cut out from below a piece of the flooring of the king's room, so as to form a kind of trap-door.

Through this the king was to escape the next night, and, hidden by the black covering of the scaffold, was to change his dress for that of a workman, slip out with his deliverers, pass the sentinels, who would suspect nothing, and so reach the boat that was waiting for him at Greenwich.

Day gilded the tops of the houses. The hole was completed, and Athos passed through it, carrying the clothes destined for the king, wrapped in a piece of black cloth, and the tools with which he was to open a communication with the king's room.

D'Artagnan returned to change his workman's clothes for his chestnut-coloured suit, and Porthos to put on his red doublet. As for Aramis, he departed to the bishop's palace to see if he could possibly pass in with Juxon to the king's presence. All three agreed to meet at noon in Whitehall Palace to see how things advanced.

Aramis found his two friends busy with a bottle of port and a cold chicken, and explained the arrangement to them.

"Bravo!" said Porthos, "besides, we shall be there at the time of the flight. What with d'Artagnan, Grimaud, and Mousqueton, we can manage to despatch eight of them. I say nothing about Blaisois, for he is only fit to hold the horses. Two minutes a man makes four minutes. Mousqueton will lose another, that's five; and in five minutes they can have galloped a quarter of a league."

Aramis hastily swallowed a mouthful, drank off a glass of wine, and then changed his clothes.

"Now," said he, "I'm off to the bishop's. Take care of the executioner, d'Artagnan."

"All right. Grimaud has relieved Mousqueton, and now has his foot on the cellar-door."

"Well, don't be inactive."

"Inactive, my dear fellow! Ask Porthos! I pass my life upon my legs, like a ballet-dancer."

Aramis again presented himself at the bishop's. Juxon consented the more readily to take him with him, as he would require an assistant priest, in case the king should wish to communicate.

Dressed as Aramis had been the night before, the bishop got into his carriage, and the former, more disguised by his pallor and sad countenance than his deacon's dress, got in by his side. The carriage stopped at the door of the palace.

It was about nine o'clock in the morning.

Nothing was altered. The anterooms were still filled with soldiers, the passages still lined by guards. The king was already sanguine, but when he perceived Aramis his hope turned to joy.

"Sire," said Aramis, the moment they were alone, "you are saved, the London executioner has vanished. His assistant broke his leg last night, beneath your majesty's window—the cry we heard was his—and there is no other executioner at present obtainable."

"But the Comte de la Fère?" asked the king.

"Two feet below you; take the poker from the fireplace, and strike three times on the floor. He will answer you."

The king did so, and the moment after, three dull knocks, answering the given signal, sounded beneath the floor.

"So," said the king, "he who knocks down there——"

"Is the Comte de la Fère, sire," said Aramis. "He is preparing a path for your majesty to escape by. Parry, for his part, will raise this slab of marble, and a passage will be opened."

"Oh! Juxon," said the king, seizing the bishop's two hands in his own, "promise that you will pray all your life for this gentleman, and for the other that you hear beneath your feet, and for two others again, who, wherever they may be, are vigilant, I am sure, for my safety."

"Sire," replied Juxon, "you shall be obeyed."

Meanwhile, the miner underneath was heard working away incessantly, when suddenly an unexpected noise resounded in the passage. Aramis seized the poker, and gave the signal to stop; the noise came nearer and nearer. It was that of a number of men steadily approaching. The four men stood motionless. All eyes were fixed on the door, which opened slowly, and with a kind of solemnity.

A parliamentary officer, clothed in black, and with a gravity that augured ill, entered, bowed to the king, and, unfolding a parchment, read him the warrant which is usually made to criminals before their execution.

"What is this?" said Aramis to Juxon.

Juxon replied with a sign which meant that he knew as little as Aramis about it.

"Then it is for to-day?" asked the king.

"Was not your majesty informed that it was to take place this morning?"

"Then I must die like a criminal by the hand of the common executioner?"

"The executioner has mysteriously disappeared, your majesty, but a man has offered his services instead. The execution will therefore only be delayed long enough for you to arrange your spiritual and temporal affairs."

A slight moisture on his brow was the only trace of emotion that the ill-starred monarch evinced as he learnt these tidings. But Aramis was livid. His heart almost ceased beating, he closed his eyes, and leant upon the table. The king perceived it, and took his hand.

"Come, my friend," said he, "courage." Then he turned to the officer. "Sir, I am ready. I have little to delay you. Firstly, I wish to communicate; secondly, to embrace my children, and bid them farewell for the last time. Will this be permitted me?"

"Certainly," replied the officer, and left the room.

Aramis dug his nails into his flesh and groaned aloud.

"Oh, my Lord Bishop!" he cried, seizing Juxon's hands, "where is God? where is God?"

"My son," replied the bishop, with firmness, "we see Him not, because the passions of the world conceal Him from our eyes."

"Be seated, Juxon," said the king, falling upon his knees. "I have now to confess to you. Remain, sir," he added to Aramis, who had moved to leave the room. "Remain, Parry. I have nothing to say that cannot be said before all."

Juxon sat down, and the king, kneeling humbly before him like the humblest of the faithful, began his confession.

67

REMEMBER!

WHEN the king had ended his confession, he partook of the Holy
Communion, and then asked to see his children. It was striking
ten o'clock; therefore, as the king had said, the delay had not been
great. Yet the people had already gathered. The king's children
then arrived—first, the Princess Elizabeth, a beautiful fair-haired
child, with tears in her eyes, and then the Duke of Gloucester, a
boy eight or nine years old, whose tearless eyes and curling lip
revealed a growing pride. He had wept all night long, but would
not show his grief to the people.

The king's heart melted within him. He turned to brush away
a tear, and then, summoning up all his firmness, drew his daughter
towards him, recommending her to be pious and resigned. Then
he took the boy upon his knee.

"My son," he said to him, "you saw a great number of people
in the streets as you came here. These men are going to take your
father's life. Do not forget that. Perhaps some day they will want
to make you king, instead of the Prince of Wales, or the Duke of
York, your elder brothers. But you are not the king, my son, and
can never be so while they are alive. Swear to me, then, never to
let them put the crown on your head. For one day—listen, my son
—one day, if you do so, they will throw it all down, head and
crown too, and then you will not be able to die calm and remorseless, as I die. Swear, my son."

The child stretched out his little hand towards that of his
father, and said, "I swear to your majesty."

"Henry, call me your father."

"Father," replied the child, "I swear to you that they shall kill
me sooner than make me king."

"Good, my child. Now kiss me, and you too, Elizabeth—never
forget me."

"Oh, never! never!" cried both the children, throwing their
arms round their father's neck.

"Farewell," said Charles I., "farewell, my children. Take them
away, Juxon; their tears will deprive me of courage."

Juxon led them away, and this time the doors were left open.

Meanwhile, Athos, in his concealment, waited in vain the signal
to recommence his work. Two long hours he waited in terrible

suspense. A deathlike silence reigned in the room above. At last he determined to ascertain the cause of this stillness. He crept from the hole, and stood, hidden by the black drapery, beneath the scaffold. Peeping out from the drapery, he could see rows of halberdiers round the scaffold, and the first ranks of the populace, swaying and groaning like a sea.

"What is the matter, then?" he asked himself, trembling more than the cloth he was holding back. "The people are hurrying on, the soldiers under arms, and among the spectators I see d'Artagnan. What is he waiting for? What is he looking at? Good God! have they let the headsman escape?"

Suddenly the dull beating of muffled drums filled the square. The sound of heavy steps was heard above his head. The next moment the very planks of the scaffold creaked with the weight of an advancing procession, and the eager faces of the spectators confirmed what a last hope at the bottom of his heart had prevented him believing till then. At the same moment a well-known voice above him pronounced these words:—

"Colonel, I wish to speak to the people."

Athos shuddered from head to foot. It was the king speaking from the scaffold. By his side stood a man wearing a mask, and carrying an axe in his hand, which he afterwards laid upon the block.

The sight of the mask excited a great amount of curiosity in the people, the foremost of whom strained their eyes to discover who it could be. But they could discern nothing but a man of middle height, dressed in black, apparently of an uncertain age, and the end of a dark beard peeped out from the bottom of the mask which concealed his features.

The king's request had undoubtedly been acceded to by an affirmative sign, for, in firm, sonorous accents, which vibrated in the depths of Athos' heart, the king began his speech, explaining his conduct, and counselling them for the welfare of England.

He was interrupted by the noise of the axe grating on the block.

"Do not touch the axe," said the king, and resumed his speech.

At the end of his speech, the king looked tenderly round upon the people. Then, unfastening the diamond ornament which the queen had sent him, he placed it in the hands of the priest who accompanied Juxon. Then he drew from his breast a little cross set in diamonds, which, like the order, had been the gift of Henrietta Maria.

"Sir," said he to the priest, "I shall keep this cross in my hand till the last moment. You will take it from me when I am dead."

He then took his hat from his head, and threw it on the ground.

One by one he unfastened the buttons of his doublet, took it off, and placed it by the side of his hat.

Then, as it was cold, he asked for his gown, which was brought to him.

All the preparations were made with a frightful calmness. One would have thought the king was going to bed, and not to his death.

"Will these be in your way?" he said to the executioner, raising his long locks; "if so they can be tied up."

The king accompanied these words with a look designed to penetrate the mask of the unknown headsman. His calm, noble gaze forced the man to turn away his head, and the question was again asked.

"It will do," replied the man, in a low voice, "if you separate them across the neck."

"This block is very low; is there no other to be had?"

"It is the usual block," answered the man in the mask.

"Do you think you can decapitate me with a single blow?" asked the king.

"I hope so," was the reply. There was something so strange in these three words that everybody except the king, shuddered.

"It is not my wish to be taken by surprise," added the king. "I shall kneel down to pray, do not strike then."

"When shall I strike?"

"When I shall lay down my head on the block, and say '*Remember!*'—then strike boldly."

"Gentlemen," said the king to those around him, "I must leave you to brave the tempest, and go before you to a kingdom which knows no storms. Farewell."

Then he knelt down, made the sign of the cross, and lowering his face to the planks, as if he would have kissed them, said in a low tone, in French, "Comte de la Fère, are you there?"

"Yes, your majesty," he answered, trembling.

"Faithful friend, noble heart!" said the king, "I should not have been rescued. I have addressed my people, and I have spoken to God: last of all I speak to you. To maintain a cause which I believe sacred, I have lost the throne, and my children their inheritance. A million in gold remains; I buried it in the cellar of Newcastle Keep. You only know that this money exists. Make use of it, then, whenever you think it will be most useful, for my eldest son's welfare. And now, farewell."

"Farewell, saintly, martyred majesty," said Athos, chilled with terror.

A moment's silence ensued, and then, in a full, sonorous voice, the king said, "*Remember!*"

He had scarcely pronounced the word when a heavy blow shook the scaffold, and where Athos stood immovable a warm drop fell upon his brow. He reeled back with a shudder, and the same moment the drops became a torrent.

Athos fell on his knees, and remained some moments as if bewildered or stunned. At last he rose, and taking his handkerchief, steeped it in the blood of the martyred king. Then, as the crowd gradually dispersed, he leapt down, crept from behind the drapery, gliding between two horses, mingled with the crowd, and was the first to arrive at the inn.

Having gained his room, he raised his hand to his forehead, and finding his fingers covered with the king's blood, fell down insensible.

68

THE MASKED MAN

THE snow was falling thick and frozen. Aramis was the next to come in, and to discover Athos almost unconscious. But at the first words he uttered, Athos roused himself from the kind of lethargy into which he had fallen.

"Are you wounded?" cried Aramis.

"No, this is his blood."

"Where were you, then?"

"Where you left me, under the scaffold."

"Did you see it all?"

"No, but I heard all. God preserve me from another such hour as I have just passed."

"Here is the order he gave me, and the cross I took from his hand; he desired they should be returned to the queen."

"Then here's a handkerchief to wrap them in," replied Athos, taking from his pocket the one he had steeped in the king's blood.

"And what," he continued, "has been done with the wretched body?"

"By order of Cromwell, royal honours will be accorded to it. The doctors are busy in embalming the corpse, and when ready it will be placed in a lighted chapel."

"Mockery," muttered Athos savagely; "royal honours to one whom they have murdered!"

"Well, cheer up," said a loud voice from the staircase, which Porthos had just ascended. "We are all mortal, my poor friends."

"Why are you so late, my dear Porthos?"

"Because, there were some people on the way who delayed me. The wretches were dancing. I took one of them by the throat, and think I throttled him a little. Just then a patrol rode up. Luckily the man I had most to do with was some minutes before he could speak, so I took advantage of his silence to walk off."

"Did you see d'Artagnan?"

"Yes, but we got separated in the crowd, and I could not find him again."

"Oh!" said Athos satirically, "I saw him. He was in the front row of the crowd, admirably placed for seeing; and as, on the whole, the sight was curious, he probably wished to stay to the end."

"Ah! Comte de la Fère," said a calm voice, though hoarse with running, "is it you who calumniate the absent?"

This reproof stung Athos to the heart, but as the impression produced by seeing d'Artagnan foremost in a coarse ferocious crowd had been very strong, he contented himself with exclaiming:

"I do not calumniate you, my friend. They were anxious about you here, and I explained to them where you were."

So saying, he stretched out his hand, but the other affected not to see it, and he let it drop again slowly by his side.

"Ugh! I am tired," cried d'Artagnan, sitting down.

"Drink a glass of port," said Aramis; "it will refresh you."

"Yes, let us drink," said Athos, anxious to make it up by hobnobbing glasses with d'Artagnan. "Let us drink, and get away from this hateful country."

"You are in a hurry, sir count," said d'Artagnan.

"But what would you have us do here, now that the king is dead?"

"Go, sir count," replied d'Artagnan, in a careless tone; "you see nothing to keep you a little longer in England? Well, for my part, I, a bloodthirsty ruffian, who can go and stand close to a scaffold, in order to observe better the king's execution—I remain."

Athos turned pale. Every reproach his friend made struck deeply into his heart.

"Hang it!" said Porthos, a little perplexed between the two, "I suppose, as I came with you, I must leave with you. I can't leave you alone in this abominable country."

"Thanks, my worthy friend. So then I have a little adventure to propose to you when the count is gone. I want to find out who was the man in the mask who so willingly offered to cut the king's throat."

"A man in a mask?" cried Athos. "You did not let the executioner escape, then?"

"The executioner is still in the cellar, where, I presume, he has had a few words' conversation with mine host's bottles. But you remind me. Mousqueton!"

"Sir," answered a voice from the depth of the earth.

"Let out your prisoner. All is over."

"But," said Athos, "who is the villain who has dared to raise his hand against his king?"

"An amateur headsman," replied Aramis, "who, however, does not handle the axe amiss."

"Did you not see his face?" asked Athos.

"He wore a mask."

"But you, Aramis, who were close to him?"

"I could see nothing but a dark beard under the bottom of the mask."

"Then you could not tell his age?"

"Oh!" said d'Artagnan, "that matters little. When one puts on a mask, it is not difficult to wear a beard under it."

"I am sorry I did not follow him," said Porthos.

"Well, my dear Porthos," said d'Artagnan, "that's the very thing which it came into my head to do."

Athos understood it all now.

"Forgive me, my friend," he said, offering his hand to d'Artagnan.

"Well," said d'Artagnan, "while I was looking on, the fancy led me to find out who this masked individual might be. Well, I looked about for Porthos, and as I did so, I saw near me a head which had been broken, but which, for better or worse, had been mended with black silk. 'Humph!' thought I, 'that looks like my cut; I fancy I must have mended that skull somewhere or other.' And, in fact, it was that unfortunate Scotchman, Parry's brother, you know, on whom Groslow amused himself by trying his strength. Well, this man was making signs to another at my left, and turning round, I recognised the honest Grimaud. 'Oh!' said I to him. Grimaud turned round with a jerk, recognised me, and pointed to the man in the mask. 'Eh?' said he, which meant, 'Do you see him?' '*Parbleu!*' I answered, and we perfectly understood one another. Well, everything finished you know how. The crowd dispersed. I made a sign to Grimaud and the Scotchman, and we all three retired into a corner of the square. I saw the executioner return into the king's room, change his clothes, put on a black hat and a large cloak, and disappear. Five minutes later he came down the grand staircase."

"You followed him?" cried Athos.

"I should think so, but not without much difficulty. Every minute he looked round, and thus obliged us to conceal ourselves. I might have gone up to him and killed him. But I am not covetous; and I thought it might console you all a little to have a share in the matter. So we allowed him to go through the lowest streets in the city, and in half an hour's time, he stopped before a small isolated house. Grimaud drew out a pistol. 'Eh?' said he, showing it. I held back his arm. The man in the mask stopped before a low door, and drew out a key; but before he placed it in the lock, he turned round to see if he was not followed. Grimaud and I had got behind a tree, and the Scotchman having nowhere to hide himself, threw himself on his face in the road. Next moment the door opened, and the man disappeared. I placed the Scotchman at the door by which he entered, making a sign to follow the man wherever he might go, if he came out again. Then going round the house, I placed Grimaud at the other exit, and here I am. Our game is up. Now for the tally-ho!"

Athos threw himself into d'Artagnan's arms.

"Humph!" said Porthos. "Don't you think the executioner might be Cromwell himself, who, to make certain of his work, undertook it himself?"

"Ah! just so. But Cromwell is short and stout, and this man lank and thin, and rather tall than otherwise."

"Some condemned soldier, perhaps," suggested Athos, "whom they have pardoned at the price of this deed."

"No, no," continued d'Artagnan. "It was not the measured step of a foot-soldier, nor the easy gait of a horseman. If I am not mistaken, it was a gentleman's walk."

"A gentleman!" exclaimed Athos. "Impossible! It would be a disgrace to his whole family."

"Fine sport, by Jove!" cried Porthos, with a laugh that shook the windows. "Fine sport!"

"Swords!" cried Aramis, "swords! and let us not lose a moment."

The four friends resumed their own clothes, girt on their swords, ordered Mousqueton and Blaisois to pay the bill, and to arrange everything for immediate departure, and, wrapped in their large cloaks, left in search of their game.

The night was dark, the snow still falling, and the streets deserted. D'Artagnan led the way, through the intricate windings and narrow lanes of the city, and ere long they had reached the house in question. For a moment d'Artagnan thought that Parry's brother had disappeared; but he was mistaken. The robust Scotchman, accustomed to the snows of his native hills, had stretched himself against a post, and like a fallen statue, insensible to the inclemencies of the weather, had allowed the snow to cover him. He rose, however, as they approached.

"Come," said Athos, "here's another good servant. Really, honest men are not so scarce as I thought."

"Don't be in a hurry to weave crowns for our Scotchman. I am sure that the fellow is here on his own account; for I have heard that these gentlemen born beyond the Tweed are very vindictive. I should not like to be Groslow, if he comes across him."

"Well?" said Athos to the man in English.

"Nobody has come out," he replied.

"Then Porthos and Aramis, will you remain with this man while we go round to Grimaud?"

Grimaud had made for himself a kind of sentry-box out of a hollow willow, and as they drew near, he put his head out and gave a low whistle.

"Oh!" said Athos.

"Yes," replied Grimaud.

"Well, has anybody come out?"

"No, but somebody has gone in."

"A man or a woman?"

"A man." At the same time he pointed to a window, through the shutters of which a faint light was to be seen.

They turned round the house to fetch Porthos and Aramis.

"Have you seen anything?" they asked.

"No, but we are going to," replied d'Artagnan, pointing to Grimaud, who had already climbed some five or six feet from the ground.

All four came up together. Grimaud continued to climb like a cat, and eventually succeeded in catching hold of a hook which served to keep one of the shutters back when opened. Then resting his foot on a small ledge, he made a sign to show that he was all right.

"Well?" asked d'Artagnan.

Grimaud showed his closed hand, with two fingers spread out.

"Speak," said Athos; "we cannot see your signs. How many are they?"

"Two. One opposite to me, the other with his back to me."

"Good. And the man opposite to you is——?"

"The man I saw go in."

"Do you know him?"

"I thought I recognised him, and was not mistaken. Short and stout."

"Who is it?" they all asked together, in a low tone.

"General Oliver Cromwell."

The four friends looked at each other.

"And the other?" asked Athos.

"Lank and thin."

"The executioner," said d'Artagnan and Aramis at the same time.

"I can't see anything but his back," resumed Grimaud. "But wait. He is moving; and if he has taken off his mask I shall be able to see. Ah!——"

And, as if struck in the heart, he let go the hook, and dropped with a groan.

"Did you see him?" they inquired.

"Yes," said Grimaud, with his hair standing on end.

"The thin and spare man?"

"Yes."

"The executioner?" asked Aramis.

"Yes."

"And who is it?" said Porthos.

"He—he——" murmured Grimaud, pale as death, and seizing his master's hand.

"Who? He?" asked Athos.

"Mordaunt!" moaned Grimaud.

D'Artagnan, Porthos, and Aramis uttered a cry.

Athos started back, and put his hand to his brow.

"Fate!" he muttered.

69

CROMWELL'S HOUSE

IT was really Mordaunt whom d'Artagnan had followed, without knowing it. On entering the house he had taken off his mask and the false beard, and mounting a staircase, had opened a door, and in a room lighted by a single lamp found himself face to face with a man behind a table.

This man was Cromwell.

Cromwell had two or three of these retreats in London, unknown except to the most intimate of his friends. Now Mordaunt was one of these.

"It is you, Mordaunt," he said. "You have arrived late."

"General, I wished to see the ceremony to the end, which delayed me."

"Ah! I scarcely thought you were so curious as that."

"I am always curious to see the downfall of your honour's enemies, and that one was not among the least of them. But you, general, were you not at Whitehall?"

"No," said Cromwell.

There was a moment's silence.

"Have you had any account of it?"

"None. I have been here since the morning. I only know that there was a conspiracy to rescue the king."

"Ah, you were aware of that," said Mordaunt.

"It matters little. Four men, disguised as workmen, were to get the king out of prison, and take him to Greenwich, where a boat was in waiting."

"And, knowing all that, your honour remained here, far from the city, calm and inactive?"

"Calm? yes," replied Cromwell. "But who told you I was inactive?"

"But—if the plot had succeeded?"

"I had hoped it would."

"I thought your excellence considered the death of Charles I. as a misfortune necessary to the welfare of England?"

"Yes, his death; but it would have been better not on the scaffold."

"Why so?" asked Mordaunt.

Cromwell smiled. "Because it could have been said that I had

had him condemned for the sake of justice, and had let him escape out of pity."

"But if he had escaped?"

"Impossible; my precautions were taken."

"And does your honour know the four men who undertook to rescue him?"

"The four Frenchmen, of whom two were sent by the queen to her husband, and two by Mazarin to me."

"And do you think Mazarin commissioned them to act in that manner?"

"It is possible. But he will not avow it."

"How so?"

"Because they did not succeed."

"Your honour gave me two of those Frenchmen when they were only fighting for Charles I. Now that they are guilty of a conspiracy against England, will your honour give me all four of them?"

"Yes, you can take them," said Cromwell.

Mordaunt bowed with a smile of triumphant ferocity.

"Did the people shout at all?" Cromwell asked.

"Very little, except 'Long live Cromwell!'"

"Where were you situated?"

Mordaunt tried for a moment to read in the general's face if this was simply an ordinary question, or whether he knew everything. But his piercing eye could not penetrate the sombre depths of Cromwell's.

"I was placed so as to hear and see everything," he answered.

It was now Cromwell's turn to look fixedly at Mordaunt, and Mordaunt's to make himself impenetrable.

"It appears," said Cromwell, "that this improvised executioner did his duty very well. The blow, so they told me at least, was struck with a master hand."

Mordaunt remembered that Cromwell had told him he had had no detailed account, and he was now quite convinced that the general had been present at the execution, hidden behind some curtain.

"Perhaps it was some one in the trade?" said Cromwell.

"Do you think so, sir? He did not look like an executioner."

"And who else than an executioner would have wished to fill that horrible office?"

"But," said Mordaunt, "it might have been some personal enemy, who may have made a vow of vengeance, and accomplished it in this way."

"Possibly."

"And if that were the case, would your honour condemn his action?"

"It is not for me to judge. It rests between him and God."

"But if your honour knew this man?"

"I neither know, nor wish to know him. Provided the king is dead, it is the axe, not the man, we must thank."

"And yet, without the man, the king would have been rescued."

Cromwell smiled.

"They would have carried him to Greenwich," he said, "and put him on board a boat, with five barrels of powder in the hold. Once out at sea,—you are too good a politician not to understand the rest."

"Yes, they would all have been blown up."

"Just so. The explosion would have done what the axe had failed to accomplish. They would have said that the king had escaped human justice, and been overtaken by God's arm. You see now why I did not care to know the gentleman in the mask."

Mordaunt bowed humbly. "Sir," he said, "you are a profound thinker, and your plan was sublime."

"Say absurd, since it is become useless. The only sublime ideas in politics are those which bear fruit. So, to-night, Mordaunt, go to Greenwich, and ask for the captain of the boat *Lightning*. Show him a white handkerchief knotted at the four corners, and tell the crew to disembark, and carry the powder back to the Arsenal, unless indeed——"

"Unless?"

"This boat might be of use to you for your personal projects."

"Oh, my lord, my lord!"

"That title," said Cromwell, laughing, "is all very well here, but take care a word like that does not escape in public."

"But your honour will soon be called so generally."

"I hope so, at least," said Cromwell, rising and putting on his hat.

"Then," said Mordaunt, "your honour gives me full power?"

"Certainly."

"Thank you, thank you."

Cromwell turned as he was going.

"Are you armed?" he asked.

"I have my sword."

"And no one waiting for you outside?"

"No."

"Then you had better come with me."

"Thank you, sir, but the way by the subterranean passage would take me too much time, and I have none to lose."

Cromwell placed his hand on a hidden handle, and opened a door so well concealed by the tapestry that the most practised eye could not have discovered it, and which closed after him with a spring. This door communicated with an underground passage, leading under the street to a grotto in the garden of a house about a hundred yards from that of the future Protector.

It was just before this that Grimaud had perceived the two men seated together.

D'Artagnan was the first to recover from his surprise.

"Mordaunt," he cried, "thank heaven!"

"Yes," said Porthos, "let us knock the door in, and fall upon him."

"No," replied d'Artagnan, "no noise. Now, Grimaud, you come here, climb up to the window again, and tell us if Mordaunt is alone, and whether he is preparing to go out or to go to bed. If he comes out, we shall catch him. If he stays in, we will break in the window. It is easier and less noisy than the door."

Grimaud started again.

"Keep guard at the other door, Athos and Aramis. Porthos and I will stay here."

The friends obeyed.

"He is alone," said Grimaud.

"We did not see his companion come out."

"He may have gone by the other door."

"What is he doing?"

"Putting on his cloak and gloves."

"He is ours," muttered d'Artagnan.

Porthos mechanically drew his dagger from the sheath.

"Put it up again, my friend," said d'Artagnan. "We must proceed in an orderly manner."

"Hush!" said Grimaud, "he is coming out. He has put out the lamp. I can't see anything now."

"Jump down then, jump down."

Grimaud leapt down, and the snow deadened the noise of his fall.

"Now, go and tell Athos and Aramis to stand on each side of their door, and clap their hands if they catch him. We will do the same."

The next moment the door opened, and Mordaunt appeared on the threshold, face to face with d'Artagnan. Porthos clapped his hands, and the other two came running round. Mordaunt was livid, but he made no cry nor called for assistance. D'Artagnan quietly pushed him in again, and by the light of a lamp on the staircase, made him ascend the steps backwards one by one, keeping his eyes all the time on Mordaunt's hands, who, however, knowing that it was useless, attempted no resistance. At last they stood face to face in the very room where ten minutes before Mordaunt had been talking to Cromwell.

Porthos came up behind, and taking down the lamp on the staircase re-lit that in the room. Athos and Aramis entered last and locked the door after them.

"Oblige me by taking a seat," said d'Artagnan, pushing a chair towards Mordaunt, who sat down, pale but calm. Aramis, Porthos, and d'Artagnan drew their chairs near him. Athos remained alone, and sat in the farthest corner of the room, as if determined to be merely a spectator of the proceedings. He seemed to be quite overcome. Porthos rubbed his hands in feverish impatience. Aramis bit his lips till the blood came.

D'Artagnan alone was calm, at least in appearance.

"Monsieur Mordaunt," he said to the young man, "since chance has at last brought us together after so many days lost in running after each other, let us have a little talk together."

70

A LITTLE TALK

MORDAUNT had been taken so completely by surprise, and had mounted the stairs in such a state of confusion, that his powers of reflection were not under his control. But when once seated, from the moment he saw a reprieve was accorded him, he concentrated all his ideas and rallied all his faculties. His eye wandered to a long stout sword on his flank, and he instinctively slipped it round within reach of his right hand.

D'Artagnan was waiting for a reply to his remark, and said nothing. Aramis muttered to himself, "We shall hear nothing but commonplace things."

Porthos bit his moustache, muttering, "A good deal of ceremony here about crushing an adder." Athos shrank into his corner, pale and motionless as a bas-relief.

The silence, however, could not last for ever. So d'Artagnan began:

"Sir," he said, with desperate politeness, "it seems to me that you change your costume almost as quickly as I have seen the Italian mummers do, whom Cardinal Mazarin brought over from Bergamo, and whom no doubt he took you to see during your travels in France."

Mordaunt did not reply.

"Just now," d'Artagnan continued, "you were disguised—I mean to say, attired—as a murderer, and now——"

"And now I look very much like a man who is going to be murdered."

"Oh! sir," answered d'Artagnan, "how can you say that when you are in the company of gentlemen, and have such an excellent sword at your side?"

"No sword is good enough to be of any use against four swords and four daggers."

"Well, that is scarcely the question. I had the honour of asking you why you altered your costume. Surely the mask and beard suited you very well, and as to the axe, I do not think it would be out of keeping even at this very minute."

"Because, remembering the scene at Armentières, I thought I should find four axes for one, as I was to meet four executioners."

"Sir," replied d'Artagnan, in the calmest manner possible, "you are very young; I shall therefore overlook your frivolous remarks. What occurred at Armentières has no connection whatever with the present occasion. We could scarcely have requested your mother to take a sword and fight with us."

"Aha! It's a duel, then?" cried Mordaunt, as if disposed to reply at once to the provocation.

Porthos rose, always ready for this kind of adventure.

"Pardon me," said d'Artagnan. "Do not let us be in a hurry. We will arrange the matter rather better. Confess, Monsieur Mordaunt, that you are anxious to kill some of us."

"All," replied Mordaunt.

"Then, my dear sir, I am convinced that these gentlemen return your kind wishes, and will be delighted to kill you also. Of course they will do so as honourable gentlemen, and the best proof I can furnish is this——"

So saying, he threw his hat on the ground, pushed back his chair to the wall, and bowed to Mordaunt with true French grace.

"At your service, sir," he continued. "My sword is shorter than yours, it's true, but bah! I hope the arm will make up for the sword."

"Halt!" cried Porthos, coming forward. "I begin, and that's logic."

"Allow me, Porthos," said Aramis.

Athos did not move. You might have taken him for a statue.

"Gentlemen," said d'Artagnan, "you shall have your turn. Monsieur Mordaunt dislikes you sufficiently not to refuse you afterwards. You can see it in his eye. So please keep your places.

like Athos, whose calmness is most laudable. Besides, we will not quarrel about it. I have a particular business to settle with this gentleman, and I shall and will begin."

Porthos and Aramis drew back disappointed; and, drawing his sword, d'Artagnan turned to his adversary.

"Sir, I am waiting for you."

"And for my part, gentlemen, I admire you. You are disputing which shall fight me first, and you do not consult me, who am most concerned in the matter. I detest you all, though not equally. I claim the right to choose my opponent. If you refuse this right, you may kill me, for I shall not fight."

"It is but fair," said Porthos and Aramis, hoping he would choose one of them.

"Well, then," said Mordaunt, "I shall choose for my adversary the man who, not thinking himself worthy to be called Comte de la Fère, calls himself Athos."

Athos sprang up, but after an instant of motionless silence he said, to the astonishment of his friends, "Monsieur Mordaunt, a duel between us is impossible. Give this honour to somebody else." And he then sat down.

"Ah!" said Mordaunt, with a sneer, "there's one who is afraid."

"Zounds!" cried d'Artagnan, bounding towards him, "who says that Athos is afraid?"

"Let him go on, d'Artagnan," said Athos, with a smile of sadness and contempt.

"It is your decision, Athos?" resumed the Gascon.

"Yes, irrevocably."

"You hear, sir," said d'Artagnan, turning to Mordaunt, "choose any one of us to replace the Comte de la Fère."

"As long as I don't fight with him, it is all the same to me with whom I fight. Put your names into a hat, and draw lots."

"At least that will conciliate us all," said Aramis.

"I should never have thought of that," said Porthos, "and yet it's a very simple plan."

Aramis went to Cromwell's table, and wrote the three names on slips of paper, which he threw into a hat.

Mordaunt drew one out and threw it on the table.

"Ah! serpent," muttered d'Artagnan; "I would give my chance of a captaincy in the '*Mousquetaires*' for that to be my name."

Aramis opened the paper, and in a voice trembling with hate and vengeance read, "D'Artagnan."

The Gascon uttered a cry of joy, and turning to Mordaunt—

"I hope, sir," said he, "you have no objection to make?"

"None whatever," replied the other, drawing his sword and resting the point on his foot.

The moment that d'Artagnan saw that his wish was accomplished, and his man would not escape him, he recovered his usual tranquillity.

He turned up his cuffs neatly, and rubbed the sole of his right boot on the floor, but did not fail, however, to remark that Mordaunt was looking about him in a singular manner.

"Are you ready, sir?" he said at last.

"I was waiting for you, sir," said Mordaunt, raising his head and casting at his opponent a look which it would be impossible to describe.

"Well, then," said the Gascon, "take care of yourself, for I am not a bad hand at the rapier."

"Nor I either," replied Mordaunt.

"So much the better. That sets my mind at rest. Defend yourself!"

"One minute," said the young man; "give me your word, gentlemen, that you will not attack me otherwise than one after the other."

"Is it to have the pleasure of insulting us that you say that, my serpentine friend?"

"No, but to set my mind at rest, as you said just now."

"It is for something else than that, I imagine," muttered d'Artagnan, shaking his head doubtfully.

"On the honour of gentlemen," said Aramis and Porthos.

"In that case, gentlemen, have the kindness to retire into the corners, and leave us room. We shall need it."

"Yes, gentlemen," said d'Artagnan, "we must not leave this person the slightest pretext for behaving badly, which, with all due respect, I fancy he is anxious to do."

This new attack made no impression on Mordaunt. The space was cleared, the two lamps placed on Cromwell's table, in order that the combatants might have as much light as possible, and the swords crossed.

D'Artagnan was too good a swordsman to trifle with his opponent. He made a rapid and brilliant feint, which Mordaunt parried.

"Aha!" he said, with a satisfactory smile.

And without losing a minute, thinking he saw an opening, he thrust right in, and forced Mordaunt to parry a counterquarte so fine that the point of the weapon might have turned within a wedding-ring.

This time it was Mordaunt who smiled.

"Ah, sir," said d'Artagnan, "you have a wicked smile. It must have been the devil who taught it you, was it not?"

Mordaunt replied by trying his opponent's weapon with an amount of strength which the Gascon was astonished to find in a form apparently so weak; but, thanks to a parry no less clever than that which Mordaunt had just achieved, he succeeded in meeting his sword, which slid along his own without touching his chest.

Mordaunt rapidly sprang back a step.

"Ah, you are losing ground, you are turning! Well, as you please. I even gain something by it, for I no longer see that sinister smile of yours. You have no idea what a false look you have, particularly when you are afraid. Look at my eyes, and you will see what your looking-glass never showed you—a frank and honourable countenance."

To this flow of words, not perhaps in the best taste, but characteristic of d'Artagnan, whose principal object was to distract his opponent's attention, Mordaunt made no reply, but, continuing to turn round, he succeeded in exchanging places with d'Artagnan.

He smiled more and more, and his smile began to make the Gascon anxious.

"Come, come," said d'Artagnan, "we must finish with this," and in his turn he pressed Mordaunt hard, who continued to lose ground, but evidently on purpose, and without letting his sword leave the line for a moment. However, as they were fighting in a room, and had not space to go on like that for ever, Mordaunt's foot at last touched the wall, against which he rested his left hand.

"Ah, now you cannot lose any more ground, my fine friend," exclaimed d'Artagnan. "Gentlemen, did you ever see a scorpion pinned to a wall? No. Well, then, you shall see it now."

In a second d'Artagnan had made three terrible thrusts at Mordaunt, all of which touched but only pricked him. The three friends looked on panting and astonished. At last d'Artagnan, having got up too close, stepped back to prepare a fourth thrust, but the moment when, after a fine quick feint, he was attacking as sharply as lightning, the wall seemed to give way, Mordaunt disappeared through the opening, and d'Artagnan's sword, caught between the panels, shivered like glass. D'Artagnan sprang back; the wall had closed again.

Mordaunt, in fact, while defending himself, had manœuvred so as to reach the secret door by which Cromwell had left, had felt for the handle with his left hand, turned it, and disappeared.

The Gascon uttered a furious imprecation, which was answered by a wild laugh on the other side of the iron panel.

"Help me, gentlemen," cried d'Artagnan. "We must break in this door."

"He escapes us," grumbled Porthos, ineffectually pushing his huge shoulder against the hinges. "'Sblood, he escapes us."

"So much the better," muttered Athos.

"I thought as much," said d'Artagnan, wasting his strength in useless efforts. "Zounds, I thought as much, when the wretch kept moving round the room. I thought he was up to something!"

"It's a misfortune which his friend, the devil, sends us," said Aramis.

"It's a piece of good fortune sent from heaven," said Athos, evidently pleased.

"Really!" said d'Artagnan, abandoning the attempt to burst open the panel after several vain attempts, "Athos, I cannot imagine how you can speak in that way. You cannot understand the position we are in. In this kind of game, not to kill, is to let oneself be killed. This wretched fellow will be sending us a hundred Iron-sided beasts who will pick us off like berries in this place. Come, come, we must be off. If we stay here five minutes more, there's an end of us."

"Yes, you are right."

"But where shall we go to?" asked Porthos.

"To the hotel, to be sure, to get our baggage and horses; and from there, if it please God, to France, where, at least, I understand the architecture of the houses."

So, suiting the action to the word, d'Artagnan thrust the sword pieces into its scabbard, picked up his hat, and ran down the stairs followed by the others.

At the door the fugitives found their lackeys and earnestly demanded intelligence of Mordaunt, but they had seen nobody pass.

71

THE "LIGHTNING"

AFTER having carefully closed the door behind him, Mordaunt, sheathing his sword, glided through the subterranean passage; but as he approached the neighbouring house, he stopped to examine himself.

"Good," said he, "a mere nothing. Scratches, that is all. Now to my work."

He walked on at a quick pace, till he reached a neighbouring cavalry-barrack, where he happened to be known. Here he borrowed a horse, the best in the stables, and in a short space of time was at Greenwich.

"Good," said he, as he came to the river bank. "I am half an hour before them. Now," he added, rising in the stirrup, and looking about him, "which, I wonder, is the *Lightning*?"

At this moment, as if to reply to his words, a man lying on a heap of cables rose and advanced a few steps towards him. Mordaunt drew a handkerchief from his pocket, and tying a knot at each corner—the signal agreed upon—waved it in the air, and the man came up to him. He was wrapped in a large rough cape, which concealed his form and partly his face.

"Do you wish to go on the water, sir?" said the sailor.

"Yes, just so. Along the Isle of Dogs."

"And perhaps you have a preference for one boat more than another. You would like one that sails as quick——"

"As lightning," interrupted Mordaunt.

"Then mine is the boat you want, sir. I'm your man."

"I begin to think so, particularly if you have not forgotten a certain signal."

"Here it is, sir;" and the sailor took from his coat a handkerchief tied at each corner.

"Good; quite right!" cried Mordaunt, springing off his horse. "There is no time to lose; now take my horse to the nearest inn, and conduct me to your vessel."

"But," asked the sailor, "where are your companions? I thought there were four of you."

"Listen to me, sir; I'm not the man you take me for; you are in Captain Richards' post, are you not? under orders from General Cromwell? Mine, also, are from him!"

"Indeed, sir, I recognise you; you are Captain Mordaunt.

Don't be afraid, you are with a friend. I am Captain Groslow. The general remembered that I had formerly been a naval officer, and he gave me the command of this expedition; has anything new happened?"

"Nothing."

"I thought, perhaps, that the king's death——"

"It has only hastened their flight; in ten minutes they will, perhaps, be here. I am going to embark with you. I wish to aid in the deed for vengeance. All is ready, I trust?"

"Yes."

"The cargo on board?"

"Yes; and we are sailing from Oporto to Antwerp, remember."

"'Tis well."

They then went down to the Thames. A boat was fastened to the shore by a chain fixed to a stake. Groslow jumped in, followed by Mordaunt, and in a few minutes they were quite away from that world of houses which then crowded the outskirts of London; and Mordaunt could discern the little vessel lying at anchor. When they reached the side of this felucca, Mordaunt, eager in his desire for vengeance, dexterously seized a rope, and climbed up the sides of the vessel with a coolness and agility very rare among landsmen. He went with Groslow to the captain's berth, a sort of temporary cabin of planks, for the chief apartment had been given up by Captain Richards to the passengers, who were to be accommodated at the other extremity of the boat.

"They will have nothing to do with this side of the ship, then," said Mordaunt.

"Nothing at all."

"That's a capital arrangement. Return to Greenwich, and bring them here. I shall hide myself in your cabin. You have a longboat?"

"That in which we came."

"It appeared light and well constructed."

"Quite a canoe."

"Fasten it to the poop with ropes, put the oars into it, so that it may follow in the track, and that there will be nothing to do except to cut the cord away. Put a good supply of rum and biscuits in it for the seamen; should the night happen to be a stormy one, they will not be sorry to find something to console themselves with."

"All shall be done. Do you wish to see the powder-room?"

"No; when you return, I will put the match myself; but be careful to conceal your face, so that you cannot be recognised by them."

"Never fear."

"There's ten o'clock striking at Greenwich."

Groslow, then, having given the sailor on duty an order to be on the watch with more than usual attention, went down into the longboat, and soon reached Greenwich. The wind was chilly, and the jetty was deserted as he approached it; but he had no sooner landed, than he heard a sound of horses galloping upon the paved road.

These horsemen were our friends, or rather a vanguard, composed of d'Artagnan and Athos. As soon as they arrived at the spot where Groslow stood, they stopped, as if guessing that he was the man they wanted. Athos alighted, and calmly opened the handkerchief tied at each corner, and unfolded it; whilst d'Artagnan, ever cautious, remained on horseback, one hand upon his arms, leaning anxiously forward.

On seeing the appointed signal, Groslow, who had, at first, crawled behind one of the cannons planted on that spot, walked straight up to the gentlemen. He was so well wrapt up in his cloak that it would have been impossible to have seen his face, even if the night had not been so dark as to render any precaution superfluous; nevertheless, the keen glance of Athos perceived that it was not Richards who stood before them.

"What do you want with us?" he asked of Groslow.

"I wish to inform you, my lord," replied Groslow, with an Irish accent, feigned of course, "that if you are looking for Captain Richards you will not find him. Unfortunately, he fell down this morning and broke his leg; but I'm his cousin; he told me everything, and desired me to look out for, and to conduct you to any place named by the four gentlemen who should bring me a handkerchief tied at each corner, like that one which you hold, and one which I have in my pocket."

And he drew out the handkerchief.

"Was that all he said?" inquired Athos.

"No, my lord; he said you had promised to pay seventy pounds if I landed you safe and sound at Boulogne, or any other port you chose, in France."

"What do you think of all this?" said Athos, in a low tone to d'Artagnan, after explaining to him in French what the sailor had said in English.

"It seems a curious story to me."

"And to me too."

"Besides, we can but blow out his brains if he deceives us," said the Gascon; "and you, Athos, you know something of everything, and can be our captain. I dare say you know how to navigate, should he fail us."

"My dear friend, you guess well; my father intended me for the navy, and I have some vague notions about navigation."

"You see!" said d'Artagnan.

They then summoned their friends, who, with Blaisois, Mousqueton, and Grimaud, promptly joined them—leaving behind them Parry, who was to take their horses back to London; and they all proceeded instantly to the shore, and placed themselves in the boat, which, rowed by Groslow, began rapidly to leave the coast.

"At last," exclaimed Porthos, "we are afloat."

"Alas!" said Athos, "we depart alone."

"Yes; but all four together, and without a scratch; which is a consolation."

"We have not yet arrived at our destination," observed the prudent d'Artagnan; "beware of *rencontres*."

"Ah! my friend!" cried Porthos; "like the crows, you always bring bad omens. Who could intercept us in such a night as this, pitch dark, when one does not see more than twenty yards before one?"

"Yes, but to-morrow morning——"

"To-morrow we shall be at Boulogne; however, I like to hear Monsieur d'Artagnan confess that he's afraid."

"I not only confess it, but am proud of it," returned the Gascon; "I'm not such a rhinoceros as you are. Oho! what's that?"

"The *Lightning*," answered the captain, "our felucca."

"We have arrived then?" said Athos.

They went on board, and the captain instantly conducted them to the berth destined for them—a cabin which was to serve for all purposes, and for the whole party; he then tried to slip away under pretext of giving orders to some one.

"Stop a moment," said d'Artagnan; "pray how many men have you on board, captain?"

"I don't understand," was the reply.

"Explain it, Athos."

Groslow, on the question being interpreted, answered:

"Three, without counting myself."

"Oh!" exclaimed d'Artagnan. "I begin to be more at my ease; however, whilst you settle yourselves, I shall make the round of the boat."

"As for me," said Porthos, "I will see to the supper."

"A very good deed, Porthos," said the Gascon. "Athos, lend me Grimaud, who in the society of his friend Parry has, perhaps, picked up a little English, and can act as my interpreter."

"Go, Grimaud," said Athos.

D'Artagnan, seeing a lanthorn on the deck, took it up, and with a pistol in his hand, he said to the captain, in English, "Come" (being, with the exception of an oath, the only English word he knew), and so saying he went below.

The lower deck was divided into three compartments: the first was covered by the floor of that room in which Athos, Porthos, and Aramis were to pass the night; the second was to serve as the sleeping-room for the servants; the third, under the prow of the ship, was underneath the temporary cabin in which Mordaunt was concealed.

"Oh!" cried d'Artagnan, as he went down the steps of the hatchway, carrying the lanthorn; "what a number of barrels! one would think one was in the cave of Ali Baba. What is there in them?" he added, placing his lanthorn on one of the bins.

The captain seemed inclined to go up on deck again, but, controlling himself, he answered:

"Port wine."

"Ah! port wine! 'tis good to know," said the Gascon, "that we shall not die of thirst; are they all full?"

Grimaud translated the question, and Groslow, who was wiping the perspiration from off his forehead, answered:

"Some full, others empty."

D'Artagnan struck the barrels with his hand, and having ascertained that he spoke the truth, pushed his lanthorn, greatly to the captain's alarm, into the interstices between the barrels, and finding that there was nothing concealed in them—

"Come along," he said; and he went towards the door of the second compartment.

"Stop!" said the Englishman, "I have the key of that door;" and he opened the door, with a trembling hand, into the second compartment, where Mousqueton and Blaisois were just preparing for supper.

Here there was evidently nothing to seek, and they passed rapidly to examine the third compartment.

This was the room appropriated to the sailors. Two or three hammocks hung up on the ceiling, a table, and two benches, composed all the furniture. D'Artagnan picked up two or three old sails hung on the walls, and seeing nothing suspicious, regained by the hatchway the deck of the vessel.

"And this room?" he asked, pointing to the captain's cabin.

"That's my room," answered Groslow.

"Open the door!"

The captain obeyed. D'Artagnan stretched out his arm, in which he held the lanthorn, put his head in at the half-opened

door, and seeing that the cabin was nothing better than a shed—
"Good!" he said. "If there is an army on board, it is not there
that it is hidden. Let us see what Porthos has found for supper."
And thanking the captain, he regained the state cabin, where his
friends were.

Porthos had found nothing; and fatigue had prevailed over
hunger. He had fallen asleep, and was in a deep slumber when
d'Artagnan returned. Athos and Aramis were beginning to close
their eyes, which they half opened when their companion came in
again.

"Well?" said Aramis.

"All goes well; we may sleep tranquilly."

On this assurance the two friends fell asleep; and d'Artagnan,
who was very tired, said good-night to Grimaud, and laid himself
down in his cloak, with a naked sword at his side, in such a manner
that his body barred the entrance, and no one could possibly come
into the cabin without walking against him.

72

A NEW KIND OF PORT WINE

At the expiration of ten minutes the masters were asleep; not so the
hungry and yet more thirsty servants.

"Grimaud," said Mousqueton to his companion, who had just
come in after his round with d'Artagnan, "art thou thirsty?"

"As thirsty as a Scotchman!" was Grimaud's laconic reply.

And he sat down and began to cast up the accounts of his party,
whose money he managed.

"Curse this rolling! I'm beginning to feel queer!" said Blaisois.

"If that is the case," said Mousqueton, "take some nourishment."

"Do you call that nourishment?" asked Blaisois, pointing to the
barley bread and the pot of beer.

"Blaisois," replied Mousqueton, "remember that bread is the
true nourishment of a Frenchman, who is not always able to get
bread: ask Grimaud."

"Yes, but beer?" asked Blaisois quickly; "is that their true
drink?"

"As to that," answered Mousqueton, puzzled how to get out of
the difficulty, "I must confess that to me beer is as disagreeable as
wine to the English."

"How? Monsieur Mousqueton! How—the English—do they dislike wine?"

"They hate it."

"But I have seen them drink it."

"As a punishment; for example, an English prince died one day because he was put into a butt of Malmsey. I heard the Chevalier d'Herblay say so."

"The fool!" cried Blaisois; "I wish I had been placed in his position."

"Thou canst be," said Grimaud, writing down his figures.

"How?" asked Blaisois; "I can? Explain yourself."

Grimaud proceeded with his sum, and cast up the whole.

"Port!" he said, extending his hand in the direction of the first compartment examined by d'Artagnan and himself.

"How—those barrels I saw through the door?"

"Port!" replied Grimaud, who began a fresh sum.

"I believe," said Blaisois, "that port is a very good wine."

"Excellent!" cried Mousqueton, smacking his lips. "Excellent!"

"Supposing these Englishmen would sell us a bottle," said the honest Blaisois.

"Sell!" cried Mousqueton, about whom there was a remnant of his old marauding character left. "One may well perceive, young man, that you are still inexperienced. Why buy when one can take?"

"To take?" answered Blaisois. "To covet one's neighbour's goods is forbidden, I believe."

"What a childish reason!" said Mousqueton condescendingly; "yes, childish; I repeat the word. Where did you learn, pray, to consider the English as your neighbours?"

"The saying's true, dear Mouston; but I don't remember where."

"Childish—still more childish," replied Mousqueton. "Hadst thou been ten years engaged in war, as Grimaud and I have been, my dear Blaisois, you would know the difference that there is between the goods of others and the goods of your enemies. Now the English are enemies; as this port wine belongs to them, therefore it belongs to us."

"And our masters," asked Blaisois, stupefied by this harangue, delivered with an air of profound sagacity, "will they be of your opinion?"

Mousqueton smiled as if in scorn.

"I suppose you think it necessary that I should disturb the repose of these illustrious lords to say, 'Gentlemen, your servant,

Mousqueton, is thirsty.' What does Monsieur de Bracieux care, think you, whether I am thirsty or not?"

"'Tis a very expensive wine," said Blaisois, shaking his head.

"Were it gold, Monsieur Blaisois, our masters would not deny themselves this wine. Know that Monsieur de Bracieux is rich enough to drink a tun of port wine, even if obliged to pay a pistole for every drop." His manner became more and more lofty every instant: then he arose, and after finishing off the beer at one draught, he advanced majestically to the door of the compartment where the wine was. "Ah! locked!" he exclaimed; "these devils of English, how suspicious they are!"

"Shut!" cried Blaisois; "ah, the deuce it is; unlucky, for I feel the sickness coming on more and more."

"Shut!" repeated Mousqueton.

"But," Blaisois went on to say, "I have heard you tell, Monsieur Mousqueton, that once on a time, at Chantilly, you fed your master and yourself with partridges, which were snared, carps caught by a line, and wine drawn with a corkscrew."

"Perfectly true; but there was an air-hole in the cellar, and the wine was in bottles. I cannot throw the loop through this partition, nor move with a pack-thread a cask of wine which may, perhaps, weight a couple of hogsheads."

"No, but you can remove two or three boards of the partition," answered Blaisois, "and make a hole in the cask with a gimlet."

Mousqueton opened his great round eyes to the utmost, astonished to find in Blaisois qualities for which he did not give him credit.

"'Tis true," he said, "but where can I get a chisel to take the planks out—a gimlet to pierce the cask?"

"The trousers!" said Grimaud, still busy with his accounts.

"Ah, yes!" said Mousqueton.

Grimaud, in fact, was not only the accountant, but the armourer of the party; and as he was a man full of forethought, these trousers, carefully rolled up in his valise, contained every sort of tool for immediate use.

Mousqueton, therefore, was soon provided with tools, and he started on his task. In a few minutes he had got out three pieces of board. He tried to pass his body through the aperture; but, not being like the frog in the fable, who thought he was larger than he really was, he found he would have to take out three or four more pieces of wood before he could get through.

He sighed, and began to work again.

Grimaud had now finished his accounts. He arose, and stood near Mousqueton.

"I——" he said.

"What?" said Mousqueton.

"I can pass——"

"True—you," answered Mousqueton, glancing at the long thin form of his friend—"you can pass, and easily—go in then."

"Rinse the glasses," said Grimaud.

"Now," said Mousqueton, addressing Blaisois, "now you will see how we old soldiers drink when we are thirsty."

"My cloak," said Grimaud, from the bottom of the cellar.

"What do you want?" asked Blaisois.

"My cloak—stop up the hole with it."

"Why?" asked Blaisois.

"Simpleton!" exclaimed Mousqueton; "suppose any one came into the room."

"Ah, true!" said Blaisois, with evident admiration; "but it will be dark in the cellar."

"Grimaud always sees, dark or light—night as well as day," answered Mousqueton.

"Silence!" cried Grimaud, "some one is coming."

In fact, the door of their cabin was opened. Two men, wrapped in their cloaks, came in.

"Oh, oh!" said they, "not in bed at a quarter-past eleven. That's against all rules. In a quarter of an hour let every one be in bed, and sleeping."

These two men then went towards the compartment in which Grimaud was secreted; opened the door, entered, and shut it after them.

"Ah!" cried Blaisois; "he's lost!"

"Grimaud's a cunning fox," murmured Mousqueton.

They waited for ten minutes, during which time nothing was heard which might indicate that Grimaud was discovered; and at the expiration of that anxious interval the two men returned, closed the door after them, and repeating their orders that the servants should go to bed, and extinguish their lights, disappeared.

At that very moment Grimaud drew back the cloak which hid the aperture, and came in with his face livid, his eyes staring wide open with terror, so that the pupil shrank almost to nothing, with a large circle of white around it. He held in his hand a tankard full of some substance or another; and approaching the gleam of light given by the lamp, he uttered this single monosyllable— "Oh!" with such an expression of extreme terror that Mousqueton started, alarmed, and Blaisois was near fainting from fright.

Both, however, cast an inquisitive glance into the tankard—it was full of gunpowder.

Convinced that the ship was full of gunpowder instead of having a cargo of wine, Grimaud hastened to awake d'Artagnan, who had no sooner beheld him than he perceived that something extra-ordinary had taken place. Imposing silence, Grimaud put out the little night-lamp, then knelt down, and poured into the lieutenant's ear a recital melodramatic enough not to require play of feature to give it force.

This was the pith of his story.

The first barrel that Grimaud had found on passing into the cellar, he struck—it was empty. He passed on to another—it was also empty; but the third which he tried was, from the dull sound that it gave out, evidently full. Here Grimaud stopped, and was preparing to make a hole with his gimlet, when he found a spigot: he therefore placed his tankard under it, and turned the spout; something, whatever it was that the cask contained, fell into the tankard.

Whilst he was thinking that he should first taste the liquor which was in the tankard, before taking it to his companions, the door of the cellar opened, and a man with a lanthorn in his hands, and enveloped in a cloak, came and stood just before the barrel, behind which Grimaud, on hearing him come in, instantly stopped. This was Groslow. He was accompanied by another man who carried in his hand something long and flexible, rolled up, resembling a washing-line.

"Have you the wick?" asked the one who carried the lanthorn.

"Here it is," answered the other.

At the voice of this last speaker Grimaud started, and felt a shudder creeping through his very bones. He rose gently, so that his head was just above the round of the barrel; and under the large hat he recognised the pale face of Mordaunt.

"How long will this match burn?" asked Mordaunt.

"Nearly five minutes," replied the captain.

"Then tell the men to be in readiness—you need not tell them why; when the clock strikes a quarter after midnight collect your men. Get down into the longboat."

"That is, when I have lighted the match?"

"I shall undertake that. I wish to be sure of my revenge—are the oars in the canoe?"

"Everything is ready."

"'Tis well."

Mordaunt knelt down and fastened one end of the train to the spigot, in order that he might have nothing to do but to set it on fire at the opposite end.

He then arose.

"You heard me; at a quarter-past midnight—in fact, in twenty minutes."

"I understand it all perfectly, sir," answered Groslow; "but allow me to say, there is great danger in what you undertake. I think it would be better to entrust one of the men to set fire to the train?"

"My dear Groslow," answered Mordaunt, "you know the English proverb, 'If you want a thing done well, do it yourself.' I shall abide by that rule."

Grimaud had overheard all this, had seen the two mortal enemies of the musketeers, had seen Mordaunt lay the train: then he felt, and felt again, the contents of the tankard that he held in his hand; and, instead of the liquid expected by Blaisois and Mousqueton, he found beneath his fingers the grains of some coarse powder.

Mordaunt went away with the captain. At the door he stopped to listen.

"Do you hear how they sleep?"

In fact, Porthos could be heard snoring through the partition.

"'Tis God who gives them into our hands," answered Groslow.

"This time the devil himself cannot save them," rejoined Mordaunt.

And they both went out.

73

IN THE OPEN BOAT

D'ARTAGNAN, as may be imagined, heard all these details with increasing interest. He awoke Aramis, Athos, and Porthos; and then, stretching out his arms, and closing them again, the Gascon collected in one small circle the three heads of his friends, so near as almost to touch each other.

He then explained to them under whose command the vessel was in which they were sailing that night; that they had Groslow their captain, and Mordaunt acting under him as his lieutenant. Something more deathlike than a shudder, at this moment, shook the brave musketeers. The name of Mordaunt seemed to exercise over them a mysterious and fatal influence to bring terror even at the very sound.

"What is to be done?" asked Athos.

"You have some plan?"

D'Artagnan replied by going towards a very small, low window, just large enough to let a man through. He turned it gently on its hinges.

"There," he said, "is our road."

"The deuce—'tis bitter cold, my dear friend," said Aramis.

"Stay here if you like, but I warn you, 'twill be rather too warm presently."

"But we cannot swim to the shore."

"The longboat is yonder, lashed to the lugger; we can take possession of it, and cut the cable. Come, my friends."

"A moment's delay," said Athos; "our servants?"

"Here we are," they cried.

Meantime the three friends were standing motionless before the awful sight which d'Artagnan, in raising the shutters, had disclosed to them through the narrow opening of the window.

Those who have gazed at such a spectacle know that there is nothing more solemn, more striking than the raging sea, rolling, with its deafening roar, its dark billows beneath the pale light of a wintry moon.

"Gracious heaven! we are hesitating," cried d'Artagnan; "if we hesitate, what will the servants do?"

"I do not hesitate, you know," said Grimaud.

"Sir," interposed Blaisois, "I warn you that I cannot swim except in rivers."

"And I not at all," said Mousqueton.

But d'Artagnan had slipped through the window.

"You have then decided, my friend?" said Athos.

"Yes," the Gascon answered; "Athos! you who are a perfect being, bid the spirit to triumph over the body."

"Do you, Aramis, order the servants—Porthos, kill every one who stands in your way."

And, after pressing the hand of Athos, d'Artagnan chose a moment when the ship rolled backwards, so that he had only to plunge into the water up to his waist.

Athos followed him before the lugger rose again on the waves: the cable which connected the boat to the vessel was then seen plainly rising out of the sea.

D'Artagnan swam to it, and held it, suspending himself by the rope, his head alone being out of the water.

In a second Athos joined him.

They then saw, as the lugger turned, two other heads peeping— those of Aramis and Grimaud.

"I am uneasy about Blaisois," said Athos; "he says he can only swim in rivers."

"When people can swim at all they can swim everywhere. To the barque! to the barque!"

"But Porthos, I do not see him."

"Porthos is coming—he swims like Leviathan."

Porthos, in fact, did not appear. Mousqueton and Blaisois had been appalled by the sight of the black gulf below them, and had shrunk back.

"Come along! I shall strangle you both if you don't get out," said Porthos, at last seizing Mousqueton by the throat.

"Forward! Blaisois."

A groan, stifled by the grasp of Porthos, was all the reply of poor Blaisois, for the giant, taking him by the neck and heels, plunged him into the water head foremost, throwing him out of the window as if he had been a plank.

"Now, Mouston," he said, "I hope you don't mean to desert your master?"

"Ah, sir," replied Mousqueton, his eyes moistening with tears, "why did you rejoin the army? We were so happy in the Château de Pierrefonds!"

And without any other complaint, passive and obedient, either from true devotion to his master, or from the example set by Blaisois, Mousqueton went into the sea head foremost,—a sublime action, at all events, for Mousqueton looked upon himself as dead. But Porthos was not a man to abandon an old servant; and when Mousqueton rose above the water, blinded, he found that he was supported by the large hand of Porthos, and that he could, without having occasion even to move, advance towards the cable with the dignity of a triton.

In a few minutes Porthos had rejoined his companions, who were already in the canoe; but when, after they had all got in, it came to his turn, there was great danger that, in putting his huge leg over the edge of the boat, he would have upset the little vessel. Athos was the last to enter.

"Are you all here?" he asked.

"Ah! have you your sword, Athos?" cried d'Artagnan.

"Yes."

"Cut the cable, then."

Athos drew a sharp poignard from his belt, and severed the cord. The lugger went on; the barque continued stationary, only moved by the waves.

"It was quite time," said the Gascon; "and you will now see something curious."

74

FATE

D'ARTAGNAN had scarcely finished speaking, when a shrill
whistle was heard on board the felucca, which was beginning to
fade away in the darkness.

"That, you may be sure," said the Gascon, "means something."

They then, at the same instant, perceived a large lanthorn carried on a pole appear on the deck, defining the forms of shadows
behind it.

And then a terrible cry, a cry of despair, was wafted through the
space, and, as if the shrieks of anguish had driven away the clouds,
the veil which hid the moon was cleared away, and the grey sails
and dark shrouds of the felucca were seen beneath the silvery night
of the skies.

Shadows ran, as if bewildered, to and fro on the vessel, and
pitiful cries accompanied these delirious walkers. In the midst of
these dreadful screams, they saw standing on the top of the poop,
Mordaunt, with a torch in his hand.

The figures, apparently excited with terror, were Groslow, who,
at the hour fixed by Mordaunt, had collected his men, and the
sailors. Groslow, after having listened at the door of the cabin to
hear if the musketeers were still asleep, had gone down into the
cellar, convinced by their silence that they were all in a deep
slumber. Then Mordaunt had opened the door, and run to the
train—impetuous as a man who is excited by revenge and full of
confidence, as are those whom God blinds, he had set fire to the
sulphur!

All this while Groslow and his men were assembled on deck.

"Haul up the cable, and draw the boat to us," said Groslow.

One of the sailors got down the side of the ship, seized the cable,
and drew it. It came without resistance.

"The cable is cut!" he cried, "but there is no canoe!"

"How! no canoe!" exclaimed Groslow; "'tis impossible."

"'Tis true, however," answered the sailor; "there's nothing in
the wake of the ship, besides, here's the end of the cable."

"What's the matter?" cried Mordaunt, who, coming up out of
the hatchway, rushed to the stern, his torch in his hand.

"Only that our enemies have escaped. They have severed the
cord, and gone off with the canoe."

Mordaunt bounded with one step to the cabin and kicked open the door.

"Empty!" he exclaimed; "the demons!"

"We must find them," said Groslow; "they can't be gone far, and we shall sink them by passing over them."

"Yes, but the fire," ejaculated Mordaunt; "I have lighted it."

"A thousand devils!" cried Groslow, rushing to the hatchway; "perhaps there is still time to save us."

Mordaunt answered only by a terrible laugh, threw his torch into the sea, and then plunged himself into it. The instant that Groslow put his foot upon the steps of the hatchway, the ship opened like the crater of a volcano,—a burst of flame arose towards the skies with an explosion like that of a thousand cannons; the air burned, ignited by embers in flames—then the frightful lightning disappeared, the embers sank down, one after another, into the abyss, where they were extinguished; and, except a slight vibration in the air, after a few minutes had elapsed, one would have thought that nothing had happened.

Only, the felucca had disappeared from the surface of the sea, and Groslow and his three sailors were consumed.

The four friends saw all this. Not a single detail of this fearful scene escaped their sight: at one moment, bathed as they were in a flood of brilliant light, which lit up the sea for the space of a league, they might each be seen, each in his own peculiar attitude and manner, expressing the awe which, even in their hearts of steel, they could not help feeling. Soon the torrent of flame fell all around them; then, at last, the volcano was extinguished. All was dark: the floating barque and the heaving ocean.

They were all silent and dejected.

"By heaven!" at last said Athos, the first to speak, "by this time, I think, all must be over."

"Here! my lords! save me! help!" cried a voice, whose mournful accents, reaching the four friends, seemed to proceed from some phantom of the sea.

All looked around—Athos himself started.

"'Tis he! 'tis his voice!" he said.

All still remained silent. The eyes of all were still turned in the direction where the vessel had disappeared—endeavouring in vain to penetrate the darkness. After a minute or two they were able to distinguish a man, who approached them, swimming vigorously.

Athos extended his arm towards him—"Yes, yes, I know him well," he said.

"He—again!" cried Porthos, who was breathing like a blacksmith's bellows, "why, he's made of iron."

"O my God!" muttered Athos.

Aramis and d'Artagnan whispered to each other.

Mordaunt made several strokes more, and raising his arm in sign of distress above the waves, "Pity, pity on me! gentlemen, in Heaven's name; I feel my strength failing me. I am drowning."

The voice that implored aid was so piteous, that it awakened pity in the heart of Athos.

"Miserable wretch!" he exclaimed.

"Indeed!" said d'Artagnan, "people only have to complain to you. I believe he's swimming towards us. Does he think we are going to take him in? Row, Porthos, row." And setting the example, he ploughed his oar into the sea—two strokes took the boat on twenty fathoms farther.

"Ah! ah!" said Porthos to Mordaunt, "I think we have you here, my hero!"

"Oh! Porthos!" murmured the Comte de la Fère.

"Oh, pray! for mercy's sake don't fly from me. For pity's sake!" cried the young man, whose agonised breathing at times, when his head was under the wave, made the icy waters bubble.

D'Artagnan, however, who had consulted with Aramis, spoke to the poor wretch. "Go away," he said, "your repentance is too recent to inspire confidence. See! the vessel in which you wished to destroy us is still burning; and the situation in which you are is a bed of roses compared to that in which you wished to place us, and in which you have placed Monsieur Groslow and his companions."

"Sir!" replied Mordaunt, in a tone of deep despair, "my penitence is sincere. Gentlemen, I am young, scarcely twenty-three years old. I was drawn on by a very natural resentment to avenge my mother. You would have done what I did."

Mordaunt wanted now only two or three fathoms to reach the boat—for the approach of death seemed to give him supernatural strength.

"Alas!" he said, "I am then to die! you are going to kill the son, as you killed the mother! Surely, if I am culpable, and if I ask for pardon, I ought to be forgiven."

Then, as if his strength forsook him, he seemed unable to sustain himself above the water, and a wave passed over his head, which drowned his voice.

"Oh! that agonises me!" cried Athos.

Mordaunt reappeared.

"For my part," said d'Artagnan, "I say, this must come to an end:—a murderer as you were of your uncle; executioner, as you were of King Charles! Incendiary! I recommend you to sink forthwith to the bottom of the sea; and if you come another fathom nearer, I'll break your skull with my oar."

"D'Artagnan! d'Artagnan!" cried Athos, "my son! I entreat you: the man is dying; and it is horrible to let even a wretch like him perish without extending a hand to save him. I cannot resist doing so—he must live."

"Zounds!" replied d'Artagnan, "why don't you give yourself up directly, feet and hands bound, to that wretch? Ah! Comte de la Fère, you wish to die by his hands? I, your son, as you call me; I will not!"

It was the first time that d'Artagnan had ever refused a request of Athos.

Aramis calmly drew his sword, which he had carried between his teeth as he swam.

"If he lays his hand on the boat's edge, I will cut it off—regicide as he is."

"And I," said Porthos. "Wait."

"What are you about to do?" asked Aramis.

"To throw myself in the water and strangle him."

"Oh, gentlemen!" cried Athos: "be men! be Christians! See! death is depicted on his face! Ah! do not bring on me the horrors of remorse. Grant me this poor wretch's life. I will bless you. I——"

"I am dying!" cried Mordaunt, "come to me! come to me!"

D'Artagnan began to be touched. The boat at this moment turned round, and the dying man was by that turn brought nearer to Athos.

"Monsieur the Comte de la Fère!" he cried; "I supplicate you! —pity me! I call on you! where are you? I see you no longer—I am dying—help me!—help me!"

"Here I am, sir!" said Athos, leaning, and stretching out his arm to Mordaunt with that air of dignity and nobleness of soul habitual to him; "here I am; take my hand, and get into our boat."

Mordaunt made one last effort—rose, seized the hand thus extended to him, and grasped it with the vehemence of despair.

"That's right," said Athos, "put your other hand here."

And he offered him his shoulders as another stay and support, so that his head almost touched that of Mordaunt; and these two mortal enemies were in as close an embrace as if they had been brothers.

"Now, sir," said the count, "you are safe—be calm!"

"Ah! my mother!" cried Mordaunt, with an eye of fire and a look of hatred impossible to describe, "I can only offer thee one

victim, but it shall, at any rate, be the one whom thou wouldst
have chosen!"

And whilst d'Artagnan uttered a cry, whilst Porthos raised the
oar, and Aramis sought a place to strike, a frightful shake given to
the boat precipitated Athos into the sea; whilst Mordaunt, with a
shout of triumph, grasped the neck of his victim, and, in order to
paralyse his movements, intertwined his legs with his—as a serpent
might have done around some object. In an instant, without
uttering an exclamation, without a cry for help, Athos tried to
sustain himself on the surface of the waters; but the weight dragged
him down: he disappeared by degrees; then everything disappeared, and the bubbling of the water, which, in its turn, was
effaced, alone indicated the spot where these two men had sunken
down.

Mute with horror, the three friends had remained open-
mouthed, their eyes dilated, their arms extended like statues, and
motionless as they were, the beating of their hearts was audible.
Porthos was the first who came to himself; he tore his hair.

"Oh!" he cried, "Athos! Athos! thou man of noble heart!
Woe to me! I have let thee perish!"

At this instant, in the midst of a vast circle, illumined by the
light of the moon, the same whirlpool which had been made by the
sinking men was again obvious; the first seen, rising above the
waves, were locks of hair—then a face, pale—with open eyes, yet,
nevertheless, those of death; then a body, which, after having
raised itself even to the waist above the sea, turned gently on its
back, according to the caprice of the waves, and floated.

In the bosom of this corpse was plunged a dagger, the gold hilt
of which shone in the moonbeams.

"Mordaunt! Mordaunt!" cried the three friends; "'tis
Mordaunt!"

"But Athos!" exclaimed d'Artagnan.

Suddenly the boat leaned on one side, beneath a new and unexpected weight, and Grimaud uttered a shout of joy; every one
turned round, and beheld Athos, livid, his eyes dim, and his
hands trembling, supporting himself on the edge of the boat.
Eight vigorous arms bore him up immediately, and laid him in the
boat, where, directly, Athos was warmed, reanimated, reviving
with the caresses and cares of his friends, who were overcome with
joy.

"You are not injured?" asked d'Artagnan.

"No," replied Athos, "and he——"

"Oh, he! Now we may say, thank God! he is really dead.
Look!" and d'Artagnan, obliging Athos to look in the direction

that he pointed, showed him the body of Mordaunt floating on its back, and which, sometimes submerged, sometimes rising, seemed still to pursue the four friends with a look full of insult and mortal hatred.

At last he sank. Athos had followed him with a look in which the deepest melancholy and pity were expressed.

"Bravo, Athos!" cried Aramis, with an emotion very rare in him.

"A splendid blow you gave!" cried Porthos.

"I have a son," said Athos; "I wished to live."

"In short," said d'Artagnan, "this has been the will of God."

"I did not kill him," added Athos, in a soft, low tone; "but Fate!"

75

AFTER BEING IN DANGER OF ROASTING, MOUSQUETON HAS A NARROW ESCAPE OF BEING EATEN

A PROFOUND silence prevailed in the boat for a long time after the terrible scene just described. The moon, which had shone for a short time, disappeared behind the clouds: every object was again plunged in that obscurity so awful in deserts, and still more so in that liquid desert, the sea, and nothing was heard, save the whistling of the west wind driving along the tops of the crested billow. Porthos was the first to speak.

"I have seen," he said, "many things, but nothing that ever agitated me so much as what I have just witnessed. Nevertheless, even in my present state of perturbation, I protest I feel happy. I have a hundred pounds' weight less upon my chest. I breathe more freely." In fact, Porthos breathed so loud as to do credit to the powerful play of his lungs.

"For my part," remarked Aramis, "I cannot say the same as you do, Porthos. I am still terrified to such a degree that I scarcely believe my eyes. I look around the boat, expecting every moment to see that poor wretch holding in his hands the dagger which was plunged into his heart."

"Oh, I am quite easy," replied Porthos. "the weapon was pointed at the sixth rib, and buried up to the hilt in his body. I do not reproach you, Athos, for what you have done; quite the contrary; when one aims a blow, that is the way to strike. So now, I breathe again, I am happy!"

"Don't be in haste to celebrate a victory, Porthos," interposed d'Artagnan; "never have we incurred a greater danger than we are now encountering. A man may subdue a man—he can't conquer an element. We are now on the sea, at night, without any pilot, in a frail barque; should a blast of wind upset our boat, we are lost."

Mousqueton heaved a deep sigh.

"You are ungrateful, d'Artagnan," said Athos; "yes, ungrateful to Providence—to whom we owe our safety in a miraculous manner. Let us sail before the wind, and, unless it changes, we shall be drifted either to Calais or Boulogne. Should the boat be upset, we are five of us good swimmers, and able enough to turn it over again; or, if not, to hold on by it. Now we are on the very course which all the vessels between Dover and Calais take, 'tis impossible but that we should meet with a trawler who will pick us up."

"But should we not find any trawler, and should the wind shift to the north?"

"Then," said Athos, "it would be quite another thing; and we should not see land again until we were on the other side of the Atlantic."

"Which implies that we may die of hunger," said Aramis.

"'Tis more than probable," answered the Comte de la Fère.

Mousqueton sighed again, more deeply than before.

"What is the matter? what ails you?" asked Porthos.

"I am cold, sir," said Mousqueton.

"Impossible! your body is covered with a coating of fat, which preserves it from the chilly air."

"Ah! sir, 'tis that very coating of fat which alarms me."

"How is that, Mousqueton?"

"Alas! your honour! in the library of the Château of Bracieux there's a number of books of travels."

"What then?"

"Amongst them the voyages of Jean Mocquet in the reign of Henry IV."

"Well?"

"In these books, your honour, 'tis told how hungry voyagers, drifted out to sea, have a bad habit of eating each other, and beginning by——"

"By the fattest among them!" cried d'Artagnan, unable, in spite of the gravity of the occasion, to help laughing.

"Yes, sir," answered Mousqueton; "but, permit me to say, I see nothing laughable in it. However," he added, turning to

Porthos, "I should not regret dying, sir, were I sure that by doing so I might still be useful to you."

"Mouston," replied Porthos, much affected, "should we ever see my castle of Pierrefonds again, you shall have as your own, and for your descendants, the vineyard which surrounds the farm."

"And you shall call it,—Mouston," added Aramis, "the vineyard of self-sacrifice, to transmit to latest ages the recollection of your devotion to your master."

One may readily conceive that during these jests, which were intended chiefly to divert Athos from the scene which had just taken place, the servants, with the exception of Grimaud, were not silent. Suddenly Mousqueton uttered a cry of joy, and held a bottle above his head.

"Oh!" said he, presenting the bottle to Porthos, "we are saved! the boat is victualled."

And feeling eagerly under the bench whence he had drawn the previous sample, he brought forth successively a dozen bottles of the same kind, some bread, and a piece of salt beef.

This intelligence restored every one, save Athos, to gaiety.

"Zounds!" exclaimed Porthos, "'tis astonishing how empty violent agitation makes the stomach."

And he drank off one bottle at a draught, and ate a good third of the bread and salted meat.

"Now," said Athos, "sleep, or try to sleep, my friends, I will watch."

In a few moments, notwithstanding their wet clothes, the icy blast that blew, and the previous scene, these hardy adventurers, with their iron frames, fitted for every hardship, threw themselves down, intending to profit by the advice of Athos, who sat at the helm, pensive and wakeful, guiding the little boat in the way it was to go, his eyes fixed on the heavens, as if he sought to discern, not only the road to France, but the benign aspect of protecting Providence. After some hours of repose, the sleepers were awakened by Athos.

Dawn had cast its light upon the blue ocean, and the distance of a musket's shot from them was seen a dark mass, above which was displayed a triangular sail; the masters and servants joined in a fervent cry to the crew of that vessel.

"A barque!" all cried together.

It was, in fact, a small craft from Dunkirk, which was bound for Boulogne.

The four masters, with Blaisois and Mousqueton, united their voices in one cry, which vibrated over the elastic surface of the waves, whilst Grimaud, without saying anything, placed his hat on the top of his oar, to attract the eyes of those whose ears might not be struck with the sound of the voices.

In a quarter of an hour they were taken in tow by the boat of this vessel, and soon after they found themselves on her deck. Grimaud, in his master's name, offered the captain twenty guineas; and the wind being favourable, our Frenchmen at nine in the morning were landed on their natal soil.

"*Morbleu!* how strong one feels here!" said Porthos, burying his big feet in the sand. "Let any one pick a quarrel with me now, —frown at me or tickle me,—and he shall see with whom he has to deal. I could now set a whole nation at defiance."

"I," said d'Artagnan, "advise you, Porthos, not to sound that challenge too loudly; for it seems to me the people here look at us with a little curiosity."

"Pooh, pooh!" said Porthos; "they are admiring us!"

"Hum!" replied d'Artagnan; "I cannot see anything to flatter my self-love in it, I swear. I only perceive men in black gowns; and, in our situation, men in black gowns terrify me, I must confess."

"They are the registrars of the merchandise of the port," said Aramis.

"Under the other cardinal, the great one," said Athos, "they might have paid more attention to us than to the merchandise; but under this one you need not be uneasy; they will pay more attention to the merchandise than to us."

"I won't trust them," said d'Artagnan, "I shall make for the dunes, and that quickly."

"And why not through the city?" said Porthos. "I should prefer a good inn to those frightful deserts of sand which Heaven made for rabbits only. Besides, I am hungry."

"Do as you please, Porthos!" said d'Artagnan! "but, for my part, I am convinced that the safest place for men situated as we are is in the open country."

And d'Artagnan, certain of the majority, started for the dunes, without waiting for Porthos's reply.

The little troop followed him, and they soon disappeared behind the sand-hills without having attracted public attention.

"Now," said Aramis, when they had gone about a quarter of a league, "let us talk."

"No," said d'Artagnan, "let us fly. We have escaped from Cromwell, from Mordaunt, and from the sea, three gulfs that wished to swallow us up; we shall not escape from Sieur Mazarin."

"You are right, d'Artagnan," said Aramis; "and my advice is that, for greater security, we should separate."

"Yes, yes, Aramis," replied d'Artagnan, "let us separate."

Porthos wished to combat this resolution; but d'Artagnan made him understand, by pressing his hand, that he ought to hold his tongue. Porthos was very obedient to those intimations of his companion, whose intellectual superiority he acknowledged with his usual good-nature. So he swallowed the words that were ready to issue from his mouth.

"But why should we separate?" asked Athos.

"Because," replied d'Artagnan, "we—that is, Porthos and myself—were sent to Cromwell by M. de Mazarin; and instead of serving Cromwell, we served Charles I.; that is not the same thing! By returning with the Comte de la Fère and the Chevalier d'Herblay, our crime is avowed; by returning alone, our crime remains doubtful; and in doubt men go a long way. Now, I wish to keep M. de Mazarin at arm's length!"

"That is right," said Porthos.

"You forget," said Athos, "that we are your prisoners—that we do not consider ourselves at all absolved from our parole to you—and that by taking us as prisoners to Paris——"

"Now really, Athos," broke in d'Artagnan, "I am sorry that a man of talent, like yourself, should be always uttering such puerilities as would make the scholars of the third class blush. Chevalier," continued d'Artagnan, addressing Aramis, who, leaning proudly on his sword, appeared at the first word to have come to his friend's views, although he had at first given a contrary opinion,—"Chevalier, understand that in this case, as in all others, my suspicious character somewhat exaggerates. Porthos and I run no danger, or next to none. But if, by chance, they were to attempt to arrest us in your presence—well, they could not arrest seven men as they arrest three; the swords would see daylight, and the affair, bad enough for all, would become a tragedy that would destroy all four of us. Besides, should any misfortune happen to two of our number, would it not be better that the other two should be at liberty to extricate them—to creep about, to mine and sap, in fine, to deliver them? And then, who knows whether we may not obtain separately—you from the queen, we from Mazarin—the pardon that would be refused to us united? Come, Athos and Aramis, do you take to the right; while you, Porthos, will come to the left with me. Let these gentlemen strike through Normandy, and let us get to Paris by the shortest route."

"But should we be arrested on the road, how shall we mutually inform one another of this catastrophe?" demanded Aramis.

"Nothing easier," replied d'Artagnan: "let us agree on a route from which we must not deviate. Go you to Saint Valéry, then to Dieppe, and then follow the direct road to Paris. We will proceed by Abbeville, Amiens, Péronne, Compiègne, and Senlis; and in every tavern, in every house where we stop, we will write on the wall with the point of a knife, or on the window with a diamond, a token that may guide the researches of those who are free."

"Ah, my friend," said Athos, "how I should admire the resources of your head, if I were not compelled to pay homage to those of your heart."

And he gave d'Artagnan his hand.

"And has the fox cleverness, Athos?" said the Gascon, with a shrug of his shoulders. "No; it knows how to gobble up poultry, to balk the hunters, and to find its way by night as well as by day —that is all. Well, is it settled?"

"Yes, it is."

"Then let us divide the money," said d'Artagnan; "there ought to be about two hundred pistoles remaining. How much is there left, Grimaud?"

"One hundred and eighty half-louis, sir."

"That is it. Ah, there is the sun. Good-morning, friend sun! Although you are not the same here as in Gascony, I know you again, or rather I pretend to do so. Good-morning to you! It is a long time since I have seen you."

"Come, come, d'Artagnan," said Athos, "do not assume too much mockery; the tears are in your eyes. Let us always be open and candid with one another; frankness brings out our good qualities."

"Do you think, Athos," cried d'Artagnan, "we can leave without anxiety, and at a moment full of danger, two such friends as you and Aramis?"

"No," said Athos, "so come to my arms, my son!"

"*Mordieu!*" said Porthos, sobbing; "I really believe I am crying. *Mordieu!* that is silly!"

And the four friends formed one group as they cast themselves into the arms of each other. These four men, united by a fraternal bond, had truly but one soul at that moment.

Blaisois and Grimaud were to follow Athos and Aramis; Mousqueton sufficed for d'Artagnan and Porthos.

They shared the money, as they always had done, with fraternal regularity; then, after having individually shaken hands, and mutually reiterated the assurance of an eternal friendship, the four gentlemen separated, each to take the road agreed upon, but not without frequently turning round, and sending back little kindly expressions which were repeated by the echoes of the dunes.

At length they lost sight of each other.

"D'Artagnan," said Porthos, "I must speak out at once; for I can never keep upon my heart anything against you—you have not appeared to me to be yourself in this affair."

"How so?" asked d'Artagnan, with his sly smile.

"Because if, as you say, Athos and Aramis run a real danger, it is not the time to abandon them. For my part, I confess I was quite disposed to follow them, and still am to rejoin them, in spite of all the Mazarins on earth."

"And you would be right, Porthos, if it were so," said d'Artagnan; "but learn one very little thing, which, little thing as it may be, will change the course of your ideas; that is, that it is not these gentlemen who are in the greatest danger, but it is we; it is not that we leave them to abandon them, but that we may not compromise them."

"Can that be so?" said Porthos.

"No doubt it is. If they should be arrested, the Bastille is the simple consequence; but if we are arrested, La Place de Grève is our lot."

"The devil!" said Porthos. "It is a long way from that to the baron's coronet you promised me."

"Bah! not so far as you imagine, perhaps, Porthos. You know the proverb—'Every road leads to Rome.'"

"But why do we incur greater danger than Athos and Aramis?" asked Porthos.

"Because they did no more than follow the orders they received from Queen Henrietta, while we have disobeyed those we received from Mazarin; because, having set out as messengers to Cromwell, we became partisans of King Charles; because, instead of helping to cut off the royal head condemned by those scoundrels, Mazarin, Cromwell, Joyce, Pride, Fairfax, and the rest, we were very near rescuing him."

"Faith, that is true," said Porthos. "But can you imagine, my dear friend, that, in the midst of his lofty occupations, General Cromwell would have time to think——"

"Cromwell thinks of everything—Cromwell has time for everything; and believe me, my dear friend, we must not lose ours, for it is precious. We shall not be safe till we have seen Mazarin; and more than that——"

"*Diable!*" exclaimed Porthos; "and what shall we say to Mazarin?"

"Let me alone for that; I have got my plan; he will laugh best who laughs last. Cromwell is very powerful, Mazarin is very crafty, but yet I prefer trying diplomacy against them, rather than against the late Mordaunt.''

"There now! How agreeable it is to say—*the late Mordaunt*!'' said Porthos.

"Faith, and so it is!'' replied d'Artagnan. "But forward!''

And both of them, without losing a moment, went across the country at a venture in the direction of Paris, followed by Mousqueton, who, after having been too cold all night, was, in a quarter of an hour, a great deal too hot.

76

THE RETURN

ATHOS and Aramis took the itinerary pointed out to them by d'Artagnan, and travelled as rapidly as possible. They thought, if they were to be arrested, it would be much better for it to take place near Paris than at a distance from that city. In proportion as they advanced towards Paris, the great events in which they had taken part, and which had changed the face of England, faded away from their minds like dreams; whilst, on the contrary, those which, during their absence, had agitated Paris and the provinces, presented themselves in an interesting manner before them.

During the six weeks that Athos and Aramis had been absent from France, the Parisians, finding themselves one morning without either a queen or a king, were greatly annoyed at being thus deserted, and the absence of Mazarin, so much desired, did not compensate for that of the two august fugitives.

The first feeling which pervaded Paris on hearing of the flight to Saint Germain, was that sort of affright which seizes children when they awake in the night, and find that they are alone. A deputation was therefore sent to the queen, to entreat her to return soon to Paris; but she not only declined to receive the deputies, but sent an intimation by Chancellor Sequier, implying that if the parliament did not humble itself before her majesty, by negativing all the questions that had been the cause of the quarrel, Paris would be besieged the next day.

This threatening answer, unfortunately for the court, produced quite a contrary effect to that which was intended. It wounded the pride of the parliament, which, supported by the citizens, replied by declaring that Cardinal Mazarin was the cause of all the discontents; denounced him as the enemy both to the king and the state; and decreed that he was to retire from the court that very day, and from France within a week afterwards; and enjoining, in case of refusal on his part, all the subjects of the king to pursue and take him.

Mazarin being thus placed beyond the protection of the law, preparations on both sides were commenced: the queen, to attack Paris—the citizens, to defend it. The latter were occupied in breaking up the pavement, and stretching chains across the street, when, headed by the Coadjutor, appeared the Prince de Conti (the brother of the Prince de Condé) and the Duc de Longueville, his brother-in-law. This unexpected band of auxiliaries arrived in Paris on the tenth of January, and the Prince of Conti was named, but not until after a stormy discussion, commander of the army of the king, out of Paris.

As for the Duc de Beaufort, he arrived from Vendôme, according to the annals of the day, bringing with him his high bearing, and his long and beautiful hair, qualifications which ensured him the sovereignty of the market-places and their occupants.

It was just at this time that the four friends had landed at Dunkirk, and begun their journey towards Paris. On reaching that capital, Athos and Aramis found it in arms. The sentinel at the gate declined even to let them pass, and called his sergeant.

The sergeant, with that air of importance which such people assume when they are robed with military dignity, said:

"Who are you, gentlemen?"

"Two chevaliers."

"And where do you come from?"

"From London."

"And what are you going to do in Paris?"

"We are going with a mission to her majesty the Queen of England."

"Where are you orders?"

"We have none; we left England, ignorant of the state of politics here, having left Paris before the departure of the king."

"Ah!" said the sergeant, with a cunning smile, "you are Mazarinists, who are sent as spies."

"My good friend," here Athos spoke, "rest assured, if we were Mazarinists, we should have all sorts of passports. In your situation, distrust those who are well provided with every formality."

"Enter into the guard-room," said the sergeant: "we will lay your case before the commandant of the post."

The guard-room was filled with citizens and peasants, some playing, some drinking, some talking. In a corner, almost hidden from view, were three gentlemen, who had preceded Athos and Aramis, and an officer was examining their passports. The first impulse of these three gentlemen, and of those who last entered, was to cast an inquiring glance at each other. Those first arrived wore long cloaks, in the drapery of which they were carefully enveloped; one of them, shorter than the rest, remained studiously in the background.

When the sergeant, on entering the room, announced that, in all probability, he was bringing in two Mazarinists, it appeared to be the unanimous opinion of the officers on guard that they ought not to pass.

"Be it so," said Athos; "yet it is more probable, on the contrary, that we shall enter, because we seem to have to do with sensible people. There seems to be only one thing to do, which is, to send our names to her majesty the Queen of England, and, if she engages to answer for us, I presume we shall be allowed to enter."

On hearing these words, the shortest of the other three men appeared more attentive than ever to what was going on, and he wrapped his cloak around him more carefully than before.

"Merciful goodness!" whispered Aramis to Athos, "did you see?"

"What?" asked Athos.

"The face of the shortest of those three gentlemen?"

"No."

"He seemed to me—but it can't be."

At this moment the sergeant, who had been for his orders, returned, and, pointing to the three gentlemen in cloaks, said:

"The passports are right; let these three gentlemen pass."

The three gentlemen bowed, and hastened to take advantage of this permission.

Aramis looked after them, and, as the least of them passed close to him, he pressed the hand of Athos.

"What is the matter with you, my friend?" asked the latter.

"I have—doubtless I am dreaming: tell me, sir," he said to the sergeant, "do you know those three gentlemen who have just gone out?"

"Only by their passports: they are three Frondists, who are gone to rejoin the Duc de Longueville."

"'Tis strange," said Aramis, almost involuntarily; "I fancied that I recognised Mazarin himself."

The sergeant burst out into a fit of laughter.

"He!" he cried; "he venture himself amongst us! Not so foolish as all that. It's more than his life is worth."

"Ah!" muttered Aramis, "I may be mistaken; I haven't the unerring eye of d'Artagnan."

"Who is speaking of d'Artagnan?" asked an officer, who appeared at that moment upon the threshold of the room.

"What!" cried Aramis and Athos, "what! Planchet!"

"Planchet," added Grimaud, "Planchet, and an officer, too!"

"Ah, gentlemen!" cried Planchet, "so you are back again in Paris. Oh, what happiness is ours; no doubt you are come to join the princes!"

"As thou seest, Planchet," said Aramis, whilst Athos smiled at the importance now assumed by the old comrade of Mousqueton in his new rank in the City Militia.

"Ah! so!" said Aramis; "allow me to congratulate you, Monsieur Planchet."

"Ah, the chevalier!" returned Planchet, bowing.

"Lieutenant?" asked Aramis.

"Lieutenant, with a promise of becoming captain."

"'Tis splendid; and pray how did you acquire all these honours?"

"In the first place, gentlemen, you know that I was the means of Monsieur de Rochefort's escape; well, I was very near being hung by Mazarin, and that made me more popular than ever."

"So, owing to your popularity——"

"No: thanks to something better. You know, gentlemen, that I served in Piedmont's regiment, and had the honour of being a sergeant?"

"Yes."

"Well, one day when no one could drill a crowd of citizens, who began to march, some with the right foot, others with the left, I succeeded in making them all begin with the same foot, and I was made a lieutenant on the spot."

"So I presume," said Athos, "that you have a large number of the nobles with you?"

"Certainly. There are the Prince de Conti, the Duc de Longueville, the Duc de Beaufort, the Duc de Bouillion, the Maréchal de la Mothe, the Marquis de Sevigné, and I don't know who, for my part."

"And the Vicomte Raoul de Bragelonne?" inquired Athos, in a quivering voice; "d'Artagnan told me that he had recommended him to your care, in parting."

"Yes, count; nor have I lost sight of him for an instant since."

"Then," said Athos, in a tone of delight, "he is well? no accident has happened to him?"

"None, sir."

"And he lives——?"

"Still—at the hotel of the Great Charlemagne."

"And passes his time——?"

"Sometimes with the Queen of England,—sometimes with Madame de Chevreuse. He and the Count de Guiche are never apart."

"Thanks,—Planchet—thanks," cried Athos, giving his hand to the lieutenant.

"Oh, sir!" Planchet only touched the tips of the count's fingers. "Oh, sir!—and now, gentlemen, what do you intend to do?"

"To re-enter Paris, if you will allow us, my good Planchet."

"Allow you, sir?—I am nothing but your servant!" Then, turning to his men,—

"Let these gentlemen pass," he said; "they are friends of the Duc de Beaufort."

"Long live the Duc de Beaufort!" cried the sentinels.

"Farewell till we meet again," said Aramis, as they took leave of Planchet; "if anything happens to us, we shall blame you for it."

"Sir," answered Planchet, "I am in all things yours to command."

"He is no fool," said Aramis, as he got on his horse.

"How should he be?" replied Athos, taking his seat in his saddle, "after having brushed d'Artagnan's hat so long?"

77

THE AMBASSADORS

THE two friends set off immediately, descending the steep declivity of the Faubourg, but on arriving at the bottom were surprised to find that the streets of Paris had become rivers, and the open places lakes; after the great rains which fell in the month of January, the Seine had overflowed its banks, and the river had inundated half the capital. The two gentlemen were obliged, therefore, to get off their horses and take a boat, and in that manner they approached the Louvre.

Night had closed in, and Paris, seen thus, by the light of some lanterns, flickering on the pools of water, with boats laden with patrols with glittering arms, the watchword passing from post to post, Paris presented such an aspect as to seize strongly on the senses of Aramis, a man most susceptible of warlike impressions.

They arrived at the queen's apartments, and were instantly admitted to the presence of Henrietta Maria, who uttered a cry of joy on hearing of their arrival.

"Let them come in! let them come in!" exclaimed the queen.

"Let them come in!" reiterated the young princess, who had never left her mother's side, but essayed in vain to make her forget, by her filial affection, the absence of her two sons and her other daughter.

"Come in, gentlemen," repeated the princess, opening the door herself.

The queen was seated on a chair, and before her were standing two or three gentlemen, and, among them, the Duc de Châtillon, the brother of the nobleman who was killed eight or nine years previously in a duel, on account of Madame de Longueville, on the Palais Royal. All these gentlemen had been noticed by Athos and Aramis in the guardhouse; and, when the two friends were announced, they started, and exchanged some words in a low tone.

"Well, sirs," cried the queen, on perceiving the two friends; "you are come, faithful friends!—but the royal couriers have been even more expeditious than you; and here are Monsieur de Flamareus and Monsieur de Châtillon, who bring me, from her majesty the Queen Anne of Austria, the most recent intelligence."

Aramis and Athos were amazed by the calmness, even the gaiety, of the queen's manner.

"Go on with your recital, sirs," said the queen, turning to the Duc de Châtillon. "You said that his majesty King Charles, my august consort, had been condemned to death by a majority of his subjects!"

"Yes, madame," Châtillon stammered out.

Athos and Aramis seemed more and more amazed.

"And that, being taken to the scaffold," resumed the queen,— "oh, my God! oh, my king!—and that, being led to the scaffold, he had been saved by an indignant people?"

"Exactly, madame," replied Châtillon, in so low a voice that, though the two friends were listening eagerly, they could scarcely hear this affirmation.

The queen clapped her hands in enthusiastic gratitude, whilst her daughter threw her arms round her mother's neck, and kissed her, her own eyes streaming with tears.

"Now, madame, nothing remains to me except to proffer my respectful homage," said Châtillon, who felt confused and shamed beneath the stern gaze of Athos.

"One moment, yes," answered the queen. "One moment, I beg, for here are the Chevalier d'Herblay and the Comte de la

Fère, just arrived from London, and they can give you, as eye-witnesses, such details as you can convey to the queen, my royal sister. Speak, gentlemen, speak; I am listening. Conceal nothing; gloss over nothing. Since his majesty still lives, since the honour of the throne is in safety, everything else is a matter of indifference to me."

Athos turned pale, and laid his hand on his heart.

"Well!" exclaimed the queen, who remarked this movement and this paleness. "Speak, sir!—I beg you to do so."

"I beg you to excuse me, madame,—I wish to add nothing to the recital of these gentlemen until they perceive themselves that they have, perhaps, been mistaken."

"Mistaken!" cried the queen, almost suffocated by emotion; "mistaken! What has happened, then?"

"Sir," interposed Monsieur de Flamareus to Athos, "if we are mistaken, the error has originated with the queen. I do not imagine you will have the presumption to set it to rights,—that would be to accuse her majesty, Queen Anne, of falsehood."

Athos sighed deeply.

"Or rather, sir," said Aramis, with his irritating politeness, "the error of that person who was with you when we met you in the guard-room, for if the Comte de la Fère and I are not mistaken, when we saw you there you had with you a third gentleman."

Châtillon and Flamareus started.

"Explain yourself, count!" cried the queen, whose anguish became greater every moment. "On your brow I read despair; your lips falter, ere you announce some terrible tidings; your hands tremble. Oh, my God! my God! what has happened!"

"Lord!" prayed the young princess, falling on her knees, "have mercy on us!"

A short altercation ensued in a low tone between the Duc de Châtillon and Aramis, during which Athos, his hands on his heart, his head bent low, approached the queen, and in a voice of deep sorrow, said:

"Madame! princes, who by circumstances are above other men, receive from heaven strength to support greater misfortunes than those of lower rank, for their hearts should be as elevated as their fortunes. We ought not, therefore, I think, to act towards a queen so illustrious as your majesty, as we should do towards a woman of our lowlier condition. Queen, destined as you are to endure every sorrow on this earth, hear the result of our mission."

Athos, kneeling down before the queen, trembling and very cold, drew from his bosom, enclosed in the same case, the order set in diamonds, which the queen had given to Lord de Winter, and the wedding-ring which Charles I. before his death had placed in the hands of Aramis. Since the moment that he had first received these two things, Athos had never parted with them.

He opened the case, and offered them to the queen, with silent and deep anguish.

The queen stretched out her hand, seized the ring, pressed it convulsively to her lips, and without being able to breathe a sigh, or to give vent to a sob, she extended her arms, became deadly pale, and fell senseless in the arms of her attendants and her daughter.

Athos kissed the hem of the robe of the widowed queen, and rising, with a dignity that made a deep impression on those around—

"I, the Comte de la Fère, a gentleman who has never deceived any human being, swear before God, and before this unhappy queen, that all that was possible to save the King of England was done whilst we were on English ground. Now, chevalier," he added, turning to Aramis, "let us go. Our task is finished."

"Not yet," said Aramis. "We have still a word to say to these gentlemen."

And turning to Châtillon, he said, "Sir, be so good as not to leave without hearing something that I cannot say before the queen."

Châtillon bowed in token of assent, and they all went out, stopping at the window of a gallery on the ground floor.

"Sir!" said Aramis, "you allowed yourself just now to treat us in a most extraordinary manner."

"Sir!" cried de Châtillon.

"What have you done with Monsieur de Bruy? Has he, perchance, gone to alter his visage, which was too like that of Monsieur de Mazarin? There are abundance of Italian masks at the Palais Royal: from harlequin even to pantaloon."

"Chevalier! chevalier!" said Athos.

"Leave me alone," replied Aramis impatiently. "I don't like things that stop half-way."

"Finish then, sir," answered de Châtillon, with as much hauteur as Aramis.

"Gentlemen," resumed Aramis, "any one but the Comte de la Fère and myself would have had you arrested, for we have friends in Paris, but we are contented with another course. Come and talk with us for five minutes, sword in hand, upon this deserted terrace."

"With pleasure," replied de Châtillon.

"Duke," said Flamareus, "you forget that to-morrow you are to command an expedition of the greatest importance, projected by the prince, assented to by the queen. Until to-morrow evening you are not at your own disposal."

"Let it be, then, the day after to-morrow," said Aramis.

"To-morrow, rather," said de Châtillon, "and if you will take the trouble of going so far as the gates of Charenton."

"Well, then, to-morrow. Pray, are you going to rejoin your Cardinal? Swear first, on your honour, not to inform him of our return."

De Châtillon looked at him. There was so much of sarcasm in his speech, that the duke had great difficulty in commanding his temper; but, at a word from Flamareus, he restrained himself, and contented himself with saying:

"You promise me, sir—that's agreed—that I shall find you to-morrow at Charenton?"

"Oh, sir, don't be afraid!" replied Aramis; and the two gentlemen shortly afterwards left the Louvre.

"For what reason is all this fume and fury?" asked Athos. "What have they done to you?"

"They did—did you not see them?"

"No."

"They laughed when we swore that we had done our duty in England. Now, if they believed us, they laughed in order to insult us; if they did not believe it, they insulted us still more. However, I'm glad not to fight them until to-morrow. I hope to have something better to do to-night than to draw my sword."

"What have you to do?"

"Egad! to take Mazarin."

Athos curled his lip disdainfully.

"These undertakings do not suit me, as you know, Aramis."

"Why?"

"Because they are taking people unawares."

"Faith, Athos, you would make a singular general. You would fight only by broad daylight; warn your foe before an attack; and never attempt anything by night, lest you should be accused of taking advantage of the darkness."

Athos smiled.

"Say, at once, you disapprove of my proposal."

"I think you ought to do nothing, since you exacted a promise from these gentlemen not to let Mazarin know that we were in France."

"I have entered into no engagement, and look upon myself as quite free. Come. come."

"Where?"

"Either to find the Duc de Beaufort, or the Duc de Bouillon, and to tell them about this."

"Yes, but on one condition—that we begin by the Coadjutor. He is a priest, experienced in cases of conscience, and we will tell him ours."

It was then agreed that they were to go first to Monsieur de Bouillon, as his house came first; but first of all Athos begged that he might go to the Hôtel du Grand Charlemagne, to see Raoul.

They re-entered the boat which had brought them to the Louvre, and went thence to the Halles; and finding there Grimaud and Blaisois, they proceeded to the Rue Guénégaud.

But Raoul was not at the Hôtel du Grand Charlemagne. He had received a message from the prince, to whom he had hastened with Olivain as soon as he had received it.

78

THE GENERALISSIMO'S THREE LIEUTENANTS

ACCORDING to arrangement, Athos and Aramis, on leaving the Hôtel du Grand Charlemagne, proceeded to the Duc de Bouillon's hotel.

The night was dark, and the town still resounded with all those noises which disclose a city in a state of siege. Athos and Aramis did not proceed a hundred steps without being stopped by sentinels placed before the barricades, who asked them the password; and on their saying that they were going to Monsieur de Bouillon on a mission of importance, a guide was given them under pretext of conducting them, but, in fact, as a watch over their movements.

On arriving at the Hôtel de Bouillon, they came across a little troop of three cavaliers, who seemed to know every possible watchword; for they walked without either guide or escort, and on arriving at the barricades had nothing to do but to speak to those who guarded them, and who let them pass with all the deference due probably to their birth.

On seeing them, Athos and Aramis stopped.

"Oh!" cried Aramis, "do you see, count?"

"Yes," said Athos.

"Who do these three cavaliers appear to you to be? These are our men."

"You are not mistaken; I recognise Monsieur de Flamareus."

"And Monsieur de Châtillon."

"As to the cavalier in the brown cloak——"

"It is Mazarin."

"How the devil do they venture so near the Hôtel de Bouillon?"

Athos smiled, but did not reply. Five minutes afterwards they knocked at the prince's door.

This door was guarded by a sentinel, and there was also a guard placed in the courtyard, ready to obey the orders of the lieutenant of the Prince de Conti.

Monsieur de Bouillon had the gout, and was in bed; but notwithstanding his illness, which had prevented his riding on horseback for the last month, that is, since Paris had been besieged, he was ready to receive the Comte de la Fère and the Chevalier d'Herblay.

He was in bed, but surrounded with all the equipments of warfare. Everywhere were swords, pistols, cuirasses, and arbuses, and it was plain that as soon as his gout was cured, Monsieur de Bouillon would give a pretty skein of silk to the enemies of the parliament to unravel. Meanwhile, to his great regret, as he said, he was compelled to keep his bed.

"Ah! gentlemen," he cried, as the two friends entered, "you are very happy! you can ride. You fight for the cause of the people. But I, as you see, am nailed to my bed—ah! this demon, the gout—this demon, the gout!"

"My lord," said Athos, "we are just arrived from England, and our first concern is to inquire after your health."

"Thanks, gentlemen! thanks! As you see, my health is bad, but you come from England. And King Charles is well, as I have just heard?"

"He is dead! my lord," said Aramis.

"Pooh!" said the duke, in astonishment.

"Dead on the scaffold; condemned by the parliament."

"Impossible!"

"And executed in our presence."

"What then has Monsieur de Flamareus been saying to me?"

"Monsieur de Flamareus?"

"Yes, he has just gone out. Deuce take it! this gout!" said the duke.

"My lord," said Athos, "we admire your devotion to the cause you have espoused, in remaining at the head of the army whilst so ill, in so much pain."

"One must," replied Monsieur de Bouillon, "sacrifice oneself to the public good; but, I confess to you, I am now almost exhausted.

My spirit is willing, my head is clear, but this demon, the gout, galls me! I confess, if the court would do justice to my claims, and give to the head of my house the title of prince, and if my brother de Turenne were reinstated in his command, I would return to my estates and leave the court and the parliament to settle things between themselves as best they could."

"You are quite right, my lord."

"You think so? At this very moment the court is making overtures to me; hitherto I repulsed them; but since such men as you assure me that I am wrong in doing so, I've a good mind to follow your advice, and to accept a proposition made to me by the Duc de Châtillon, just now."

"Accept it, my lord, accept," said Aramis.

He and Athos then took their leave.

"And what do you think of the Duc de Bouillon?" asked Aramis of his friend.

"I think," answered Athos, "that we have done wisely in not mentioning a word of the reason for our visit; and now let us proceed forthwith to the Hôtel de Vendôme." It was ten o'clock when they reached it, and they found it as closely guarded as that of the Duc de Bouillon. As they entered the courtyard, two cavaliers were coming out, and Athos and Aramis recognised the Duc de Châtillon and Monsieur de Flamareus, who had evidently been paying their respects to the Duc de Beaufort.

Scarcely had the two friends dismounted when a man approached them, and after looking at them for an instant by the doubtful light of the lanthorn, hung in the centre of the courtyard, he uttered an exclamation of joy, and ran to welcome them.

"Rochefort!" cried the two friends.

"Yes! We arrived four or five days ago from the Vendômois, as you know, and we are going to give Mazarin something to do. You are still with us, I presume?"

"More than ever. And the duke?"

"Furious against the Cardinal. You know his success—our dear duke? He's really the king of Paris; he can't go out without being almost stifled."

"Ah! so much the better! Can we have the honour of seeing his highness?"

"I shall be proud to present you;" and Rochefort walked on. Every door was opened to him. Monsieur de Beaufort was at supper, but he rose quickly on hearing the two friends announced.

"Ah!" he cried, "by Jove! you're welcome, sirs. You are coming to sup with me, are you not? Boisgoli, tell Noirmont that I have two guests. You know Noirmont, do you not? The

successor of Father Marteau, who makes the excellent pies you know
about. Boisgoli, let him send one of his best, but not such a one as
he made for La Ramée. Thank God! we don't want either ropes,
ladders, or pears of anguish."

"My lord," said Athos, "do not let us disturb you. We came
merely to inquire after your health and to take your commands."

"As to my health, since it has stood five years of prison, with
Monsieur de Chevigny to boot, 'tis excellent! As to orders, since
every one gives his own commands in our party, I shall end, if this
goes on, in giving none at all."

"In short, my lord," said Athos, glancing at Aramis, "your
highness is not satisfied with your party?"

"Not satisfied, sir; say that I am furious! To such a degree, I
assure you, though I would not say so to others, that if the queen,
acknowledging the injuries she has done me, would recall my
mother, and give me the reversion of the Admiralty, which
belonged to my father, and was promised to me at his death—
well! I should not be long before I could train dogs to say, 'that
there were greater traitors in France than the Cardinal Mazarin.'"

At this Athos and Aramis could not help exchanging not only a
look but a smile; and, had they not known it for a fact, they could
have been sure that de Châtillon and de Flamareus had been there
before them.

"My lord!" said Athos, "we are satisfied; we came here only to
express our loyalty, and to say that we are at your lordship's service, and your most faithful servants," and, bowing low, they went
out.

"My dear Athos," cried Aramis; "I think you consented to
accompany me only to give me a lesson—God forgive me!"

"Wait a little, Aramis; it will be time to perceive my motive
when we have paid our visit to the Coadjutor."

"Let us, then, go to the archiepiscopal palace," said Aramis.

They directed their horses to the city. On arriving at the cradle
from which Paris sprang, they found it inundated with water; and
it was again necessary to take a boat. The palace rose from the
bosom of the water, and, to see the number of boats around it, one
would have fancied oneself not in Paris, but in Venice. Some of
these boats were dark and mysterious, others noisy, and lighted up
with torches. The friends glided in between this confusion of
embarkations, and landed in their turn. All the palace was under
water, but a kind of staircase had been fixed to the lower walls;
and the only difference was that, instead of entering by the doors,
people entered by the windows.

Thus did Athos and Aramis make their appearance in the antechamber, where about a dozen noblemen were collected and waiting.

"Good heavens!" said Aramis to Athos; "does the Coadjutor intend to indulge himself in the pleasure of making us wait in his antechamber?"

"My dear friend, we must take people as we find them. The Coadjutor is at this moment one of the seven kings of Paris, and has a court. Let us send in our names, and if he does not send us a suitable message, we will leave him to his own affairs, or to those of France. Let us call that servant, with the wand in his hand. Exactly so—ah! if I'm not mistaken, here's Bazin. Come here, fellow!"

Bazin, who was crossing the antechamber majestically in his clerical dress, turned round to see who the impertinent gentleman was who thus addressed him; but seeing the friends, he went up to them quickly, and expressed great delight on seeing them.

"A truce to compliments," said Aramis; "we want to see the Coadjutor, and instantly, as we are in a hurry."

"Certainly, sir,—it is not such lords as you are who are allowed to wait in the antechamber, only just now he has a secret conference with Monsieur de Bruy."

"De Bruy!" cried the friends; "'tis then useless our seeing Monsieur the Coadjutor this evening," said Aramis, "so we give it up."

And they hastened to quit the palace, followed by Bazin, who was lavish of his bows and compliments.

At ten o'clock the friends met again.

There were still no tidings of d'Artagnan or Porthos, whom they had expected. Raoul was gone to Saint Cloud, in consequence of a message from the Prince de Condé, and had not returned; and Aramis had not been able to see Madame de Longueville, who was installed at the Hôtel de Ville, where she played the part of queen, not having quite courage enough, as Aramis remarked, to take up her abode at the Palais Royal or the Tuileries.

"Well, then," said Athos, "now, then, what shall we do this evening?"

"You forget, my friend, that we have work cut out for us in the direction of Charenton; I hope to see Monsieur de Châtillon, whom I've hated a long time, there."

"Why have you hated him!"

"Because he is the brother of Coligny."

"Ah, true! he who presumed to be a rival of yours, for which he was severely punished; that ought to satisfy you."

"Yes, but it does not; I am rancorous, the only point which

shows me to be a churchman. Do you understand? Let us go, then."

"If we go, there is no time to lose; the drum has beat; I saw cannon on the road; I saw the citizens in order of battle on the Place of the Hôtel de Ville; certainly the affray will be in the direction of Charenton, as the Duc de Châtillon said."

"Poor creatures!" said Athos, "who are going to be killed, in order that Monsieur de Bouillon should have his estate at Sedan restored to him, that the reversion of the Admiralty should be given to the Duc de Beaufort, and that the Coadjutor should be made a Cardinal."

"Come! come, dear Athos, you will not be so philosophical if our Raoul should happen to be in all this confusion."

"Perhaps you speak the truth, Aramis."

"Well, let us go, then, where the fighting is, for that is the most likely place to meet with d'Artagnan, Porthos, and Raoul. Stop, there are a fine body of citizens passing; quite attractive, by Jupiter! and their captain! see! in the true military style."

"What ho!" said Grimaud.

"What?" asked Athos.

"Planchet, sir."

"Lieutenant yesterday," said Aramis, "a captain to-day, a colonel, doubtless, to-morrow: in a week our late servant will be a field-marshal of France."

"Ask him some questions about the fight," said Athos.

Planchet, prouder than ever of his new duties, deigned to explain to the two gentlemen that he was ordered to take up his position on the Place Royale, where two hundred men formed the rear of the army of Paris, and to march towards Charenton, when required.

"The day will be warm," said Planchet, in a martial tone.

But the friends, not caring to mix themselves up with the citizens, set off towards Charenton, and passed the valley of Fecamp, darkened by the presence of armed troops.

79

THE FIGHT AT CHARENTON

As Athos and Aramis proceeded, and passed different companies on the road, they became aware that they were arriving near the field of battle.

"Ah! my friend!" cried Athos suddenly, "where have you brought us? I fancy I perceive around us faces of different officers in the royal army: is it not the Duc de Châtillon himself who is coming towards us with his brigadiers?"

"Good-day, sirs," said the duke, advancing; "you are puzzled by what you see here, but one word will explain everything. There is now a truce, and a conference. The prince, Monsieur de Retz, the Duc de Beaufort, the Duc de Bouillon, are talking over public affairs. Now, one of two things must happen; either matters will be arranged, or they will not be arranged, in which last case I shall be relieved of my command, and we shall still meet again."

"This conference has not then been preconcerted?"

"No; 'tis the result of certain propositions made yesterday by the Cardinal to the Parisians."

"Where, then, are the plenipotentiaries?" inquired Athos.

"At the house of Monsieur de Chauleu, who commands your troops at Charenton. I say your troops, for I presume that you gentlemen are Frondeurs?"

"Yes—almost," remarked Aramis.

"We are for the king, and the princes," said Athos.

"We must understand each other," said the duke; "the king is with us, and his generals are the Duke of Orléans and the Prince de Conti, although, I must add, 'tis almost impossible now to know to what party one is attached."

"Yes," answered Athos, "but his right place is in our ranks, with the Prince de Condé, de Beaufort, d'Elbeuf, and de Bouillon; but, my lord, supposing that the conferences are broken off, are you going to try and take Charenton?"

"Such are my orders."

"My lord, since you command the cavalry——"

"Pardon me, I am commander-in-chief."

"So much the better. There is a youth of fifteen years of age, the Vicomte de Bragelonne, attached to the Prince de Conti:—has he the honour of being known to you?" inquired Athos, diffident in allowing the sceptical Aramis to perceive how strong were his paternal feelings.

"Yes, surely, he came with the prince; a charming young man; he is one of your friends, then, Monsieur le Comte?"

"Yes, sir," answered Athos, slightly agitated; "so much so, that I wish to see him, if possible."

"Quite possible, sir; do me the favour to accompany me, and I will conduct you to headquarters."

"Hallo, there!" cried Aramis, turning round, "what a noise behind us."

"A stout cavalier coming towards us," said Châtillon; "I recognise the Coadjutor, by his Frondist hat."

"And I, the Duc de Beaufort, by his plume of white feathers."

"They are coming full gallop; the prince is with them: ah! he is leaving them."

"They are sounding an alarm!" cried Châtillon; "we must find out what's going on."

In fact, they saw the soldiers running to their arms; the trumpets sounded; the drum beat; the Duc de Beaufort drew his sword; and all the officers of the royalist army, mingled momentarily with the Parisian troops, ran to the prince.

"Gentlemen," cried Châtillon, "the truce is broken, that's evident; they are going to fight; go, then, into Charenton, for I shall begin in a short time—hark! there's a signal from the prince!"

The cornet of the troop had, in fact, just raised the standard of the prince. "Farewell, till the next time!" cried Châtillon, and he set off at full speed.

Aramis and Athos turned also, and went to salute the Coadjutor and the Duc de Beaufort. As to the Duc de Bouillon, he had such a fit of gout as obliged him to return to Paris in a litter; but his place was supplied by the Duc d'Elbeuf and his four sons, ranged around him like a staff. Meantime, between Charenton and the royal army, was left a long space, which seemed prepared to serve as a last resting-place for the dead.

"Gentlemen," cried the Coadjutor, tightening his sash, which he wore after the fashion of the ancient military prelates, over his archiepiscopal robe, "there's the enemy approaching us; we shall, I hope, save them the half of their journey."

And, without caring whether he were followed or not, he set off; his regiment, which bore the name of the regiment of Corinth, from the name of his archbishopric, darted after him, and began the fight. Monsieur de Beaufort sent his cavalry towards Etampes, and Monsieur de Chauleu, who defended the place, was ready to resist an assault, or, if the enemy were repulsed, to attempt a sortie.

The battle soon became general, and the Coadjutor performed many acts of valour. His proper vocation had always been the sword, and he was delighted whenever he could draw it from the scabbard, no matter for whom, or against whom.

Chauleu, whose fire at one time repulsed the royal regiment, thought that the moment was come to pursue it; but it was reformed, and led again to the charge, by the Duc de Châtillon, in person. This charge was so fierce, so skilfully conducted, that Chauleu was almost surrounded. He commanded a retreat, which began, step by step, foot by foot—unhappily, in an instant, he fell, mortally wounded. De Châtillon saw him fall, and announced it, in a loud voice, to his men, which raised their spirits, and completely disheartened their enemies, so that every man thought only of his personal safety, and tried to regain the trenches, where the Coadjutor was attempting to reform his disorganised regiment.

Suddenly a squadron of cavalry came to an encounter with the royal troops who were entering, pell-mell, into the entrenchments with the fugitives. Athos and Aramis charged at the head of their squadron; Aramis with his sword and pistol in his hands; Athos, with his sword in the scabbard, his pistol in his saddle-bags; calm and cool as if on the parade, except that his noble and beautiful countenance became sad as he saw slaughtered so many men who were sacrificed on the one side to the obstinacy of royalty, on the other to the rancorous party feeling of the princes; Aramis, on the contrary, struck right and left, and was almost delirious with excitement. His bright eyes kindled, and his mouth, so finely formed, assumed a dark smile; every blow he aimed was sure, and his pistol finished the deed—and annihilated the wounded wretch who tried to rise again.

On the opposite side, two cavaliers, one covered with a gilt cuirass, the other wearing simply a buff doublet, from which fell the sleeves of a vest of blue velvet, charged in front. The cavalier in the gilt cuirass fell upon Aramis and hit him a blow that Aramis parried with his wonted skill.

"Ah! 'tis you, Monsieur de Châtillon," cried the chevalier, "welcome to you—I await you."

"I hope you have not been waiting too long, sir," said the duke; "at all events, I am here."

"Monsieur de Châtillon," cried Aramis, taking from his saddle-bags a second pistol, "I think if your pistols have been discharged, you are a dead man."

"Thank God, sir, they are not!"

And the duke, pointing his pistol at Aramis, fired. But Aramis instantly bent his head, and the ball passed over him.

"Oh! you've missed me," cried Aramis; "but I swear to Heaven, I will not miss you."

"If I give you time!" cried the duke, spurring on his horse, and rushing upon him with his drawn sword.

Aramis awaited him with that terrible smile which was peculiar to him on such occasions; and Athos, who saw the duke advancing towards Aramis with the rapidity of lightning, was just going to cry out, "Fire! fire then!" when the shot was fired. De Châtillon opened his arms and fell back on the crupper of his horse.

The ball had penetrated into his chest through an opening in his cuirass.

"I am a dead man," he said, and he fell from his horse to the ground.

"I told you this; I am now grieved I have kept my word; can I be of any use to you?"

Châtillon made a sign with his hand, and Aramis was about to dismount, when he received a violent shock in the side. 'Twas a thrust from a sword, but his cuirass turned aside the blow.

He turned round and seized his new antagonist by the wrist, when he started back, exclaiming, "Raoul!"

"Raoul?" cried Athos.

The young man recognised at the same time the voice of his guardian and that of the Chevalier d'Herblay; several cavaliers in the Parisian forces rushed at that instant on Raoul, but Aramis protected him with his sword.

"My prisoner!" he cried.

At this crisis of the battle, the prince, who had seconded de Châtillon in the second line, appeared in the midst of the fight; his eagle eye made him known, and his blows proclaimed the hero.

On seeing him the regiment of Corinth, which the Coadjutor had not been able to reorganise in spite of his efforts, threw itself into the midst of the Parisian forces, put them into confusion, and re-entered Charenton flying. The Coadjutor, dragged along with his fugitive forces, passed near the group formed by Athos, Raoul, and Aramis. Aramis could not in his jealousy avoid being pleased at the Coadjutor's misfortune, and was about to make some jesting remark, more witty than correct, when Athos stopped him.

"On, on!" he cried, "this is no moment for compliments; or rather back, for the battle seems to be lost by the Frondeurs."

"That's a matter of indifference to me," said Aramis; "I came here only to meet de Châtillon; I have met him, I am contented; 'tis something to have met de Châtillon in a duel!"

The three cavaliers continued their road at a smart gallop.

"What were you doing in the battle, my friend?" inquired Athos of the youth; "'twas not your right place, I think, as you were not equipped for an engagement!"

"I had no intention of fighting to-day, sir; I was charged, indeed, with a mission for the Cardinal, and had set out for Rueil, when seeing Monsieur de Châtillon charge, a wish possessed me to charge at his side. Two cavaliers from the Parisian troops told me that you were there."

"What! you knew we were there, and yet wished to kill your friend and the chevalier?"

"I did not recognise the chevalier in his armour, sir!" said Raoul, blushing; "though I might have known him by his skill and coolness in danger."

"Thank you for the compliment, my young friend," replied Aramis, "we can see from whom you learnt lessons of courtesy: you were going, then, to Rueil?"

"Yes! I have a despatch from the prince to his Eminence."

"You must still deliver it," said Athos.

"No false generosity, count! the fate of our friends—to say nothing of our own—is, perhaps, contained in that very despatch."

"This young man must not, however, fail in his duty," said Athos.

"In the first place, count, he is our prisoner; you seem to forget that. What I propose to do is fair in war, and the conquered must not be dainty in the true choice of means."

"Give him the despatch, Raoul! you are the chevalier's prisoner."

Raoul gave it up reluctantly; Aramis instantly seized and hastily perused it.

"You," he said, "you, who are so trusting, read and reflect that there is something in this letter important for us to see."

Athos took the letter, frowning, but an idea that he should hear something in this letter about d'Artagnan conquered his unwillingness to finish it.

"My lord, I shall send this evening to your Eminence, in order to reinforce the troop of Monsieur de Comminges, the ten men whom you demand. They are good soldiers, fit to support the two violent adversaries whose address and resolution your Eminence is fearful of."

"Oh!" cried Athos.

"Well," said Aramis, "what think you about these two enemies, whom it requires, besides Comminges' troop, ten good soldiers to guard; are they not as like as two drops of water to d'Artagnan and Porthos?"

"We'll search Paris all to-day," said Athos, "and if we have no news this evening, we will return to the road to Picardy; and I feel no doubt that, thanks to d'Artagnan's ready invention, we shall then find some clue which shall solve our doubts."

It was, then, with a sentiment of uneasiness whether Planchet, who alone could give them information, was alive or not, that the friends returned to the Palais Royal; to their great surprise they found all the citizens still encamped there, drinking and making merry, although, doubtless, mourned by their families, who thought they were at Charenton, in the thick of the fight.

Athos and Aramis again questioned Planchet, but he had seen nothing of d'Artagnan; they wanted to take Planchet with them, but he could not leave his troop; who at five o'clock returned home, saying that they were returning from the battle, whereas they had never lost sight of the equestrian statue in bronze of Louis XIII.

80

THE ROAD TO PICARDY

ATHOS and Aramis, who were perfectly safe in Paris, did not hide from themselves that as soon as they got beyond it they would be in the midst of the greatest dangers. But one can imagine how such men look at a question of personal risk. Paris, however, itself was not tranquil; food began to be scarce; and wheresoever any of the Prince de Conti's generals wanted to succeed him in his command, some little commotion, which he always put a stop to instantly, took place.

In one of these risings, the Duc de Beaufort pillaged the house and library of Mazarin, in order to give the populace, as he said, something to gnaw at. Athos and Aramis left Paris after this event, which took place on the very evening of the day in which the Parisians had been beaten at Charenton.

They quitted Paris, beholding it abandoned to extreme want bordering on famine; agitated by fear, torn by faction. Parisians and Frondeurs as they were, the two friends expected to find the same misery, the same fears, the same intrigues in the enemy's camp; but what was their surprise, after passing St. Denis, to hear that, at St. Germain, people were singing and laughing, and leading a cheerful life. The two gentlemen travelled by by-ways, in order not to encounter Mazarinists, who were scattered about the Isle of France, and also to escape the Frondeurs, who were in possession of Normandy, and who would not have failed to conduct them to the Duc de Longueville, in order that he might know whether they were friends or enemies. Having escaped these dangers, they returned by the main road to Boulogne, at Abbeville, and followed it step by step, examining every track.

Nevertheless, they were still in a state of uncertainty. Several inns were visited by them, several innkeepers questioned, without a single clue being given to guide their inquiries. When at Montreuil Athos felt, upon the table, that something rough was touching his delicate fingers. He turned up the cloth, and found these hieroglyphics carved upon the wood with a knife:—

"Port . . . D'Art . . . 2nd February."

"This is capital," said Athos to Aramis; "we were to have slept here, but we cannot, we must push on." They rode forward, and reached Abbeville. There the great number of inns confused them; they could not go to all; how could they guess in which he whom they were seeking had stayed?

"Trust me," said Aramis; "do not expect to find anything in Abbeville. If we had only been looking for Porthos, Porthos would have fixed himself in one of the best of the hotels, and we could easily have traced him. But d'Artagnan is above such weakness. Porthos would have found it very difficult even to make him see that he was dying of hunger; he has gone on his road as inexorable as fate, and we must seek him somewhere else."

They kept to their route; it was now become a weary and seemingly hopeless task; and had it not been for the threefold motives of honour, friendship, and gratitude, implanted in their hearts, these two travellers would have given up, many a time, their rides over the sand, their interrogatories of the peasantry, and their close inspection of faces.

They proceeded to Compiègne.

Athos began to despair. His noble nature felt that their ignorance was a sort of reflection upon them. They had not looked well enough for their lost friends. They had not shown sufficient pertinacity in their inquiries. They were willing and ready to retrace their steps, when, in crossing the suburb which leads to the gates of the town, upon a white wall which was at the corner of a street turning round the rampart, Athos cast his eyes upon a drawing in black chalk, which represented, with the awkwardness of a first attempt, two mounted cavaliers, and carrying a roll of paper, on which were written these words: "They are following us."

"Oh!" exclaimed Athos; "here it is as clear as day. Pursued as he was, d'Artagnan would not have stayed here five minutes had he been pressed very closely, which gives us hopes that he may have succeeded in escaping."

Athos shook his head.

"Had he escaped we should either have seen him or have heard him spoken of."

"You are right, Aramis; let us go on."

To describe the impatience and uneasiness of these two gentlemen would be impossible. Anxiety took possession of the tender and constant heart of Athos; and impatience was the torment of the impulsive Aramis. They galloped on for two or three hours with the frenzy of two knights in pursuit. All at once, in a narrow pass, they perceived that the road was partially barricaded by an enormous stone. It had evidently been rolled across the path by some arm of gigantic power.

Aramis stopped.

"Oh!" he said, looking at the stone, "this is the work either of Ajax, or of Briareus, or of Porthos. Let us go down, count, and examine this rock."

They both alighted. The stone had been brought with the evident intention of barricading the road; but some one, having perceived the obstacle, had partially turned it aside.

With the assistance of Blaisois and Grimaud, the friends succeeded in turning the stone over. Upon the side next the ground was written:

"Eight of the Light Dragoons are after us. If we reach Compiègne, we shall stop at the Peacock. It is kept by a friend of ours."

"This is something positive," said Athos, "let us go to the Peacock."

"Yes," answered Aramis, "but if we are to get there, we must rest our horses, for they are almost wound up."

Aramis was right; they stopped at the first tavern, and made each horse swallow a double quantity of corn steeped in wine; they gave them three hours' rest, and then set off again. The men themselves were almost killed with fatigue, but hope supported them.

In six hours they reached Compiègne, and alighted at the Peacock. The host proved to be a worthy man, as bald as a Chinaman. They asked him if some time ago he had not received in his house two gentlemen who were pursued by dragoons: without answering he went out and brought in the blade of a rapier.

"Do you know that?" he asked.

Athos merely glanced at it.

"It is d'Artagnan's sword," he said.

"Does it belong to the smaller, or to the larger of the two?" asked the host.

"To the smaller."

"I see that you are the friends of these gentlemen."

"Well, what has happened to them?"

"They were pursued by eight of the Light Dragoons, who rode into the courtyard, before they had time to close the gate; but these men would not have succeeded in taking them prisoners, had they not been assisted by twenty soldiers of the regiment of Italians in the king's service, who are in garrison in this town—so that your friends were overpowered by numbers."

"Arrested, were they?" asked Athos; "is it known why?"

"No, sir, they were taken away directly, and had not time to tell me why; but as soon as they were gone, I found this broken blade of a sword—as I was assisting to raise two dead men, and five or six wounded ones."

"'Tis still a consolation that they were unharmed," said Aramis.

"Where are they taken?" asked Athos.

"Towards the town of Louvres," was the reply.

The two friends, having agreed to leave Blaisois and Grimaud at Compiègne with the horses, resolved to take post horses; and having snatched a hasty dinner, they continued their journey to Louvres. Here they saw only one inn, in which was made a liqueur which still preserves its reputation in our own time, and which is still produced in that town.

"Let us alight here," said Athos, "d'Artagnan will not have let slip an opportunity of drinking a glass of this liqueur, and at the same time, leaving some trace of himself."

They went into the inn, and asked for two glasses of liqueur at the counter—as their friends must have done before them. The counter was covered generally with a plate of pewter; upon this plate was written with the point of a large pin,—"Rueil. . . . D. . . ."

"They went to Rueil," cried Aramis.

"Let us go to Rueil," said Athos. "Had I been as great a friend of Jonah's as I am of d'Artagnan, I should have followed him even into the whale itself; and you would have done the same."

"Oh, yes—but you make me better than I am, dear count. Had I been alone, I should scarcely have gone to Rueil without great caution."

Next they went to Rueil. Here the deputies of the Parliament had just arrived, in order to enter upon those famous conferences which were to last three weeks, and produced eventually that shameful peace, at the end of which the prince was arrested. Rueil was crowded with advocates, presidents, and counsellors, who came from the Parisians; and, on the side of the court, with officers and guards; it was, therefore, easy, in the midst of this confusion, to remain as much unobserved as might be wished; besides the conferences implied a truce, and to arrest two gentlemen, even Frondeurs, at this time, would have been an attack on the rights of the people.

The two friends mixed with the crowd, and fancied that every one was occupied with the same thought that tormented them.

But every one was engrossed by articles of reforms. It was the advice of Athos to go straight to the ministers.

"My friend," said Aramis, "be careful; our safety proceeds from our obscurity. If we were to make ourselves known, we should be sent to rejoin our friends in some deep ditch, from which the devil himself cannot take us out. Let us try not to find them out by accident, but from our own notions. Arrested at Compiègne, they have been carried to Rueil; at Rueil they have been questioned by the Cardinal, who has either kept them near him, or sent them to Saint Germain. As to the Bastille, they are not there, though the Bastille is specially for the 'Frondeurs.' They are not dead, for the death of d'Artagnan would cause a sensation. Do not let us despond—but wait at Rueil, for my conviction is that they are at Rueil. But what ails you? you are pale."

"It is this," answered Athos, with a trembling voice, "I remember that, at the Castle of Rueil, the Cardinal Richelieu had some horrible 'oubliettes' constructed."

"Oh! never fear," said Aramis. "Richelieu was a gentleman, our equal in birth, our superior in position. He could, like the king, touch the greatest of us on the head, and in touching them, make the head shake on the shoulders. But Mazarin is a low-born rogue, who could only take us by the neck, like an archer. Be calm—for I am sure that d'Artagnan and Porthos are alive and well."

"Well," resumed Athos, "I recur to my first proposal. I know no better means than to act with candour. I shall seek not Mazarin, but the queen—and say to her, 'Madame, restore to us your two servants and our two friends.'"

Aramis shook his head.

"'Tis a last resource; but let us not employ it till it is imperatively necessary: let us rather continue our researches."

They continued their inquiries, and at last met with a Light

Dragoon, who had formed one of the guard which had escorted d'Artagnan to Rueil, by which they knew that they had entered that house.

Athos, therefore, perpetually recurred to his proposed interview with the queen.

"I shall go," he said, "to her majesty."

"Well, then," answered Aramis, "pray tell me a day or two beforehand, that I may take that opportunity of going to Paris."

"To whom?"

"Zounds! how do I know? perhaps to Madame de Longueville. She is all powerful yonder; she will help me. But send me tidings should you be arrested, for then I will return directly."

"Why do you not take the risk, and be arrested with me?"

"No, I thank you."

"Should we, by being arrested, be all four together again, we should not, I am sure, be twenty-four hours in prison without geting free."

"My friend, since I killed Châtillon, the adored of the ladies of St. Germain, I am too great a celebrity not to fear a prison doubly. The queen is likely to follow Mazarin's counsels, and to have me tried. Do you think that she loves this Italian so much as they say she does?"

"She loved an Englishman passionately."

"Well, my friend, she is a woman."

"No, no, you are in error; she is a queen."

"Dear friend, I shall sacrifice myself, and go and see Anne of Austria."

"*Adieu*, Athos, I am going to raise an army."

"For what purpose?"

"To come back and besiege Rueil."

"Where shall we meet again?"

"At the foot of the Cardinal's gallows."

The two friends parted—Aramis to return to Paris, Athos to take some measures preparatory to an interview with the queen.

81

THE GRATITUDE OF ANNE OF AUSTRIA

ATHOS found much less difficulty than he had expected in obtaining an audience of Anne of Austria; it was granted, and was to take place, after her morning's "*levée*," at which, in accordance with the rights he derived from his rank, he was entitled to be present. A vast crowd filled the apartments of Saint Germain; Anne had never, at the Louvre, had so large a court; but this crowd represented chiefly the second class of nobility, while the Prince de Conti, the Duc de Beaufort, and the Coadjutor assembled around them the first men in France.

The greatest possible gaiety prevailed at the court. The particular characteristic of this was, that more songs were made than cannon fired during its continuance. The court made songs on the Parisians, and the Parisians on the court; and the wounds, though not mortal, were painful, as they were made by the arms of ridicule.

In the midst of this seeming jocularity, nevertheless, people's minds were uneasy. Was Mazarin to remain the favourite and minister of the queen? was he to be carried back by the wind which had blown him there? Every one hoped so, so that the minister felt that all around him, beneath the obsequity of the courtiers, lay a fund of hatred, ill-disguised by fear and interest. He was ill at ease, and at a loss what to do.

Condé himself, while fighting for him, lost no opportunity of ridiculing or of humbling him. The queen, on whom he threw himself, as his sole support, seemed to him now very little to be relied upon.

When the hour appointed for the audience arrived, Athos was obliged to stay until the queen, who was waited upon by a new deputation from Paris, had consulted with her minister as to the propriety and manner of receiving them. All were fully engrossed with the affairs of the day, and there could be few opportunities less favourable to make an appeal upon; but Athos was a man of inflexible temper, and insisted on his right of being admitted into the queen's presence. Accordingly, at the close of the audience, she sent for him to her room.

The name of the Count de la Fère was then announced to Anne. Often must she have heard that name and felt that it had made her heart beat; nevertheless, she remained unmoved, and was contented to look fixedly at this gentleman, with that haughty gaze which can alone be permitted to a queen.

"Do you come, then, to offer me your services?" she asked, after some moments' silence.

"Yes, madame," replied Athos, shocked at her not recognising him. Athos had a noble heart, and made, therefore, but a poor courtier.

Anne frowned. Mazarin, who was sitting at a table, folding up papers, as if he had been merely a secretary of state, looked up.

"Speak," said the queen.

Mazarin turned again to his papers.

"Madame," resumed Athos, "two of my friends, named d'Artagnan and Porthos, sent to England by the Cardinal, have suddenly disappeared ever since they set foot on the shores of France; no one knows what has become of them."

"Well?" said the queen.

"I address myself, therefore, first to the benevolence of your majesty, that I may be informed as to the whereabouts of my friends, reserving to myself, if necessary, the right of appealing afterwards to your justice."

"Sir," replied Anne, with a degree of haughtiness, which, to certain persons, became impertinence, "this is the reason that you trouble me in the midst of so many absorbing concerns! An affair for the police! Well, sir, you ought to know that since we left Paris there no longer exists a police."

"I think that your majesty will have no need to apply to the police to know where my friends are, but that if you will deign to interrogate the Cardinal, he can reply without any further inquiry than into his own recollections."

"But, God forgive me!" cried Anne, with that disdainful curl of the lip peculiar to her, "I think you can inquire yourself."

"Yes, madame, here I have a right to do so, for it concerns Monsieur d'Artagnan—d'Artagnan," he repeated, in such a manner as to bow down the regal brow beneath the recollections of the weak and erring woman.

The Cardinal saw that it was now high time to come to the queen's assistance.

"Sir," he said, "I can tell what is at present unknown to her majesty. These individuals are under arrest; they disobeyed orders."

"I beg of your majesty, then," said Athos, calm, and not replying to Mazarin, "to take off these arrests from Messieurs d'Artagnan and du Valon."

"What you ask is an affair of discipline and police," said the queen.

"Monsieur d'Artagnan never made such an answer as that when the service of your majesty was concerned," said Athos, bowing with great dignity. He was going towards the door, when Mazarin stopped him.

"You have also been in England, sir?" he said, making a sign to the queen, who was evidently going to issue a severe order.

"I was present at the last hours of Charles I. Alas! Culpable, at the most, of weakness, how cruelly punished by his subjects! Thrones are at this time shaken, and it is to little purpose for devoted hearts to serve the interest of princes. This is the second time that Monsieur d'Artagnan has been in England. He went the first time to save the good name of a great queen; the second to prevent the death of a great king."

"Sir," said Anne to Mazarin, with an accent from which daily habits of dissimulation could not entirely chase the real expression, "see if we cannot do something for these gentlemen."

"I wish to do, madame, all your majesty pleases."

"Do what Monsieur de la Fère requests; that is your name, is it not, sir?"

"I have another name, madame—I am called Athos."

"Madame," said Mazarin, with a smile, "you may be easy—your wishes shall be carried out."

"You hear, sir?" said the queen.

"Yes, madame; I expected nothing less from the justice of your majesty. May I not, then, go and see my friends?"

"Yes, sir, you shall see them. But, apropos, you belong to the Fronde, do you not?"

"Madame, I serve the king."

"Yes, in your own way."

"My way is the way of all gentlemen; and I know only one way," answered Athos haughtily.

"Go, sir, then," said the queen; "you have obtained what you wish, and we know all we wish to know."

Scarcely, however, had the tapestry closed behind Athos than she said to Mazarin:

"Cardinal, desire them to arrest that insolent fellow before he leaves the court."

"Your majesty," answered Mazarin, "desires me to do only what I was going to ask you to allow me to do. These bravos, who bring back to our epoch the traditions of the other reign, are troublesome; since there are two of them already there, let us add a third."

Athos was not the queen's dupe entirely, but he was not a man to run away merely on suspicion—above all, when distinctly told that he should see his friends again. He waited, then, in the ante-chamber with patience, till he should be conducted to them.

He walked to the window and looked into the court. He saw the deputation from the Parisians enter it: they were coming to sign the definitive place for the conference, and to make their bow to the queen. A very imposing escort awaited them without the gates.

Athos was looking on attentively when some one touched him softly on the shoulder.

"Ah! Monsieur de Comminges," he said.

"Yes, count, and charged with a commission for which I beg of you to accept my excuses."

"What is it?"

"Be so good as to give me your sword, count."

Athos smiled and opened the window.

"Aramis!" he cried.

A gentleman turned round. (Athos fancied he had seen him among the crowd.) It was Aramis. He bowed with great friendship to the count.

"Aramis!" cried Athos; "I am arrested."

"Good," replied Aramis calmly.

"Sir," said Athos, turning to Comminges, and giving him politely his sword by the hilt—"there is my sword—have the kindness to keep it for me until I return from my prison. I prize it—it was given to my ancestors by King Francis I. In his time they armed gentlemen, they did not disarm them. Now, whither do you conduct me?"

"Into my room at first," replied Comminges, "the queen will ultimately decide on the place of your domicile."

Athos followed Comminges without adding a single word.

82

THE ROYALTY OF THE CARDINAL

THE arrest of Athos did not make the slightest commotion; and
the course of events was scarcely interrupted. To the deputation it
was formally announced that the queen would receive it. Accordingly it was admitted to the presence of Anne, who, silent and lofty
as ever, listened to the speeches and complaints of the deputies;
but when they had finished their harangues, not one of them could
say, so calm had been her face, whether she had heard them or not.
Whilst thus she was silent, Mazarin, who was present, and knew
what the deputies asked, answered in these terms:—

"Gentlemen," he said, "I shall join with you in supplicating the
queen to bring to a close the miseries of her subjects. I have done
all in my power to ameliorate them, and yet the belief of the
public, you say, is that they proceed from me, an unhappy
foreigner who has been unable to please the French. Alas! I have
never been understood, and no wonder. I succeeded a man of the
most sublime genius that ever upheld the sceptre of France. The
memory of Richelieu annihilates me. In vain, were I an ambitious
man, should I struggle against such a remembrance as he has left;
but that I am not ambitious I am going to prove to you. I own
myself vanquished. I shall obey the wishes of the people. If Paris
has injuries to complain of, who has not some wrongs to be re-
dressed? Paris has been sufficiently punished, enough blood has
flowed, enough misery has humbled a town deprived of its king,
and of its justice. 'Tis not for me, a private individual, to disunite
a queen from her kingdom. Since you require my resignation, I
shall retire."

"Then," said Aramis, in his neighbour's ear, "the conferences
are over. There is nothing to do but to send Monsieur Mazarin to
the most distant frontier, and to take care that he does not return
by that, nor any other entrance, into France."

"One instant, sir," said the man in a gown, whom he addressed;
"a plague on't! how fast you go! one may soon see that you're a
soldier. There's the article of remunerations and indemnifications
to be discussed and set to rights."

"Chancellor," said the queen, turning to this same man, "do
you, our old acquaintance, open the conferences. They can take
place at Rueil. The Cardinal has spoken of much which has

agitated me, therefore I cannot speak more fully now. As to his going or staying, I feel too much gratitude to the Cardinal not to leave him free in all his actions; he shall do what he wishes to do."

A transient pallor overspread the speaking countenance of the prime minister; he looked at the queen with anxiety. Her face was so passionless, that he was, as every one else was, incapable of reading her thoughts.

"But," added the queen, "in awaiting the Cardinal's decisions, let there be, if you please, a reference to the king only."

The deputies bowed, and went out of the room.

"What!" exclaimed the queen, when the last of them had left the apartment, "you would yield to these limbs of the law, those advocates?"

"To promote your majesty's welfare, madame," replied Mazarin, fixing his penetrating eyes on the queen, "there's no sacrifice that I would not make."

Anne dropped her head and fell into one of those reveries so habitual with her. Her recollection of Athos came into her mind. His fearless deportment—his words, so firm yet so dignified, the shades which by one word he had evoked, recalled her to the past in all its intoxication of poetry and romance, youth, beauty, the transports of love at twenty years of age, the bloody death of Buckingham, the only man whom she ever really loved, and the heroism of those obscure champions who had saved her from the double hatred of Richelieu and of the king.

Mazarin looked at her, and whilst she believed herself alone and freed from that world of enemies who sought to spy into her secret thoughts, he read her thoughts in her countenance, as one sees in a transparent lake clouds pass—reflections, like thoughts, of the heavens.

"Must we, then," asked Anne of Austria, "yield to the storm, purchase a peace, and await patiently and piously for better times?"

Mazarin smiled sarcastically at this speech, which showed that she had taken the minister's proposal seriously.

Anne's head was bent down, and she did not see this smile; but finding that her question elicited no reply, she looked up.

"Well, you do not answer, Cardinal; what do you think about it?"

"I am thinking, madame, of the allusion made by that insolent gentleman, whom you have caused to be arrested, to the Duke of Buckingham, to him whom you suffered to be assassinated, to the Duchesse de Chevreuse, whom you suffered to be exiled, to the Duc de Beaufort, whom you exiled; but he made no allusion to me, because he does not know the relation in which I stand to you."

Anne drew up, as she always did when anything touched her pride. She blushed, and that she might not answer, clasped her beautiful hands till her sharp nails almost pierced them.

"That man has sagacity, honour, and wit, not to mention likewise that he is a man of undoubted resolution. You know something about him, do you not, madame? I shall tell him, therefore, and in doing so I shall confer a personal favour on him, how he is mistaken in regard to me. What is proposed to me would be, in fact, almost an abdication, and an abdication requires reflection."

"An abdication?" repeated Anne; "I thought, sir, that it was only kings who abdicated?"

"Well," replied Mazarin, "and am I not almost a king—king, indeed, of France? Thrown over the foot of the royal couch, my robe, madame, is not dissimilar to the mantle worn by a king."

This was one of the humiliations which Mazarin made Anne undergo more frequently than any other, and which bowed her head with shame. Queen Elizabeth and Catharine II. of Russia are the only two female monarchs on record who were at once sovereigns and lovers. Anne of Austria looked with a sort of terror at the threatening aspect of the Cardinal. His physiognomy in such moments was not destitute of a certain grandeur.

"Sir," she replied, "did I not say, and did you not hear me say to those people, that you should do as you pleased?"

"In that case," said Mazarin, "I think it must please me best to remain: not only on account of my own interest, but for your safety."

"Remain, then, sir; nothing can be more agreeable to me; only do not allow me to be insulted."

"You are referring to the demands of the rebels, and to the tone in which they stated them? Patience! They have selected a field of battle on which I am an abler general than they are—that of a conference. No, we shall beat them by merely temporising. They want food already. They will be ten times worse off in a week."

"Ah, yes! Good heavens! I know it will end in that way; but it is not they who taunt me with the most wounding reproaches—but——"

"I understand; you mean to allude to the remembrances perpetually revived by these three gentlemen. However, we have them safe in prison: and they are just sufficiently culpable for us to keep them in prison as long as is convenient to us. One, only, is still beyond our power, and braves us. But, devil take him! we shall soon succeed in sending him to rejoin his companions. We have accomplished more difficult things than that. In the first place, I have, as a precaution, shut up, at Rueil, near me, under my own eyes, within reach of my hand, the two most turbulent ones. To-day, the third will be there also."

"As long as they remain in prison, all will be well," said Anne; "but one of these days they will get out."

"Yes; if your majesty releases them."

"Ah!" exclaimed Anne, following the train of her own thoughts; "on such occasions one regrets Paris!"

"Why so?"

"On account of the Bastille, sir; which is so strong and so secure."

"Madame, these conferences will bring us peace; when we have peace we shall regain Paris; with Paris, the Bastille, and our three bullies shall rot therein."

Anne frowned slightly, when Mazarin, in taking leave, kissed her hand.

Mazarin, after this half-humble, half-gallant attention, went away. Anne followed him with her eyes, and as he withdrew, at every step he took, a disdainful smile was seen playing, then gradually burst upon her lips.

"I once," she said, "despised the love of a Cardinal who never said 'I shall do,' but 'I have done.' That man knew of retreats more secure than Rueil—darker, and more silent even than the Bastille itself. Oh! the world degenerates."

83

PRECAUTIONS

AFTER having left Anne, Mazarin took the road to Rueil, where his mansion was; in those times of disturbance he went about with numerous followers, and often disguised himself. In the military dress he was indeed, as we have before stated, a very handsome man. In the court of the old château of Saint Germain, he entered his coach, and reached the Seine at Chalon. The prince had given him fifty light horse, not so much by way of a guard, as to show the deputies how readily the queen's generals dispersed their troops, and to prove that they might be scattered about at pleasure. Athos, on horseback, without his sword, and kept in sight by Comminges, followed the Cardinal in silence. Grimaud, finding that his master had been arrested, fell back into the ranks, near Aramis, without saying a word, and as if nothing had happened. Grimaud had, indeed, during twenty-two years of service, seen his master extricate himself from so many difficulties, that nothing disturbed him. At the branching off of the road towards Paris, Aramis, who had followed in the Cardinal's suite, turned back. Mazarin went to the right hand, and Aramis could see the prisoner disappear at the turning of the avenue. Athos, at the same moment, moved by a similar impulse, looked back also. The two friends exchanged a simple inclination of the head, and Aramis put his finger to his hat, as if to bow; Athos, alone, comprehending by that signal that he had some project in his head. Ten minutes afterwards, Mazarin entered the court of that château which his predecessor had built, at Rueil; as he alighted, Comminges approached him.

"My lord," he asked, "where does your Eminence wish Monsieur Comte de la Fère to be confined?"

"Certainly in the pavilion of the orangery; in front of the pavilion where the guard is. I wish every respect shown to the count, although he is the prisoner of her majesty the queen."

"My lord," answered Comminges, "he begs to be taken into the place where Monsieur d'Artagnan is confined—that is, in the hunting-lodge opposite the orangery."

Mazarin thought for an instant.

Comminges saw that he was undecided.

"'Tis a very strong post," he resumed; "and forty good men, tried soldiers, and consequently having nothing to do with Frondeurs, nor any interest in the Fronde."

"If we put these three men together, Monsieur Comminges," said Mazarin, "we must double the guard, and we are not rich enough in defenders to commit such acts of prodigality."

Comminges smiled; Mazarin read, and construed that smile.

"You do not know these men, Monsieur Comminges, but I know them—first, personally; also by hearsay. I sent them to carry aid to King Charles, and they accomplished prodigies to save him; had it not been for an adverse destiny, that beloved monarch would, this day, have been among us."

"But, since they served your Eminence so well, why are they, my lord Cardinal, in prison?"

"In prison?" asked Mazarin;" and since when has Rueil been a prison?"

"Ever since there were prisoners in it," replied Comminges.

"These gentlemen, Comminges, are not prisoners," returned Mazarin, with his ironical smile, "but guests; and guests so precious, that I have placed a grating before each of the windows, and bolts to their doors, that they may not be weary of being my

visitors. So much do I esteem them, that I am going to make the
Count de la Fère a visit, that I may converse with him con-
fidentially; and that we may not be disturbed at our interview,
you must conduct him, as I said before, into the pavilion of the
orangery; that, you know, is my daily promenade."

Comminges bowed, and returned to impart to Athos the result
of his request. Athos, who had been awaiting the Cardinal's
decision with outward composure but secret uneasiness, then entreated that Comminges would do him one favour, which was to
intimate to d'Artagnan that he was placed in the pavilion of the
orangery for the purpose of receiving a visit from the Cardinal,
and that he should gain by the opportunity, in order to ask for
some mitigation of their close imprisonment.

"Which cannot last," interrupted Comminges, "the Cardinal
said so; there is no prison here."

"But there are *oubliettes!*" replied Athos, smiling.

"Oh! that's a different thing; yes—I know there are legends of
that sort," said Comminges; "it was in the time of the other
Cardinal, who was a great nobleman; but our Mazarin—impossible! an Italian adventurer could not go to such lengths towards
such men as ourselves. *Oubliettes* are employed as a means of
kingly vengeance, and a low-born fellow such as he is dare not
have recourse to them. No, no, be easy on that score. I shall, however, inform Monsieur d'Artagnan of your arrival here."

Comminges then led the count to a room on the ground floor of
a pavilion, at the end of the orangery. They passed through a
courtyard, as they went, full of soldiers and courtiers. In the centre
of this court, in the form of a horse-shoe, were the buildings
occupied by Mazarin, and at each wing the pavilion (or smaller
building) where d'Artagnan was, and that, level with the
orangery, where Athos was to be. Behind each end of these two
wings extended the park.

Athos, when he reached his appointed room, looked through the
gratings of his window, walls, and roofs; and was told, on inquiry,
by Comminges, that he was gazing on the back of the pavilion
where d'Artagnan was confined.

"Yes, 'tis too true," said Comminges, "'tis almost a prison; but
what a singular fancy this is of yours, count—you, who are the
very flower of our nobility—to go and spend your valour and your
loyalty amongst these upstarts, the Frondists! Really and truly, if
ever I thought that I had a friend in the ranks of the royal army, it
was you. A Frondeur! you, the Comte de la Fère on the side of
Broussel, Blancmesnil, and Viole! For shame! you, a Frondeur!"

"On my word of honour," said Athos, "one must be either a

Mazarinist or a Frondeur. For a long time I had these words whispered in my ears, and I chose the last; at any rate, it is a French word. And now, I am a Frondeur, not of Broussel's party, nor of Blancmesnil's, nor am I with Viole, but with the Duc de Beaufort, the Ducs de Bouillon and d'Elbeuf; with princes, not with presidents, councillors, and low-born lawyers. Besides, what a charming thing it would have been to serve the Cardinal! Look at that wall, without a single window, which tells you fine things about Mazarin's gratitude!"

"Yes," replied de Comminges, "more especially if that could reveal how Monsieur d'Artagnan for this last week has been swearing at him."

"Poor d'Artagnan," said Athos, with that charming melancholy which was one of the external traits of his character, "so brave, so good, so terrible to the enemies of those whom he loves; you have two unruly prisoners there, sir."

"Unruly," Comminges smiled, "you wish to make me afraid I suppose. When he came here, Monsieur d'Artagnan provoked and braved all the soldiers and inferior officers, in order, I suppose, to have his sword back. That mood lasted some time; but now he's as gentle as a lamb, and sings Gascon songs which make one die with laughing."

"And du Valon?" asked Athos.

"Ah, he's quite of a different order; a formidable gentleman, though. The first day he broke all the doors in with a single push of his shoulder; and I expected to see him leave Rueil in the same way as Samson left Gaza. But his temper cooled down like his friend's—he not only gets used to his captivity, but jokes about it."

"So much the better," said Athos; and, on reflection, he felt convinced that this improvement in the spirits of the two captives proceeded from some plan formed by d'Artagnan for their escape. He did not wish, therefore, to injure them by exalting them too highly.

"Well," said he, "they are hot-headed fellows. Both take fire very quickly, but grow cool as speedily."

As this was also Comminges's own opinion, he retired somewhat more assured, and Athos remained alone in his vast room, where, according to the Cardinal's orders, he was treated with the consideration due to a gentleman.

84

CAGED

LET us now pass from the orangery to the hunting-pavilion. At the end of the courtyard, where, close to a portico formed of Tuscan columns, there were dog-kennels, rose an oblong building, the pavilion of the orangery, a half-circle, enclosing the court of honours. It was in this pavilion, on the ground floor, that d'Artagnan and Porthos were placed, suffering the hours of a long imprisonment in a manner suitable to each different temperament.

D'Artagnan was walking about like a tiger, his eye fixed, growling as he paced along by the bars of a window looking upon the servants' offices in the yard.

Porthos was ruminating over an excellent dinner which had been served up to him.

The one seemed to be deprived of reason, yet he was meditating. The other seemed to meditate, yet he was sleeping. But his sleep was a nightmare, which might be guessed by the incoherent manner in which he snored.

"Look," said d'Artagnan, "day is declining. It must be nearly four o'clock. We have been in this place nearly eighty-three hours."

"Hem!" muttered Porthos, with a kind of pretence of answering.

"Did you hear, eternal sleeper?" cried d'Artagnan, irritated that any one could doze during the day, when he had the greatest difficulty in sleeping during the night.

"What?" said Porthos.

"I say we have been here eighty-three hours."

"'Tis your fault," answered Porthos.

"How, my fault?"

"Yes, I offered to you to escape."

"By tearing down an iron bar and pushing in a door, Porthos. People like us cannot just go out as they like; besides, going out of this room is not everything."

"Well, then, let us kill the guard, and then we shall have arms."

"Yes; but before we can kill him—and he is hard to kill, that Swiss—he will shout out, and the whole picket will come, and we shall be taken like foxes—we, who are lions—and thrown into some dungeon, where we shall not even have the consolation of seeing this frightful grey sky of Rueil, which is no more like the sky of Tarbes than the moon is to the sun. Lack-a-day! if we only had some one to instruct us about the physical and moral topography of this castle. Ah! when one thinks that for twenty years—during which time I did not know what to do with myself—it never occurred to me to come to study Rueil. And, after all, 'tis impossible but that Aramis, that Athos, that wise gentleman, should not find out our retreat; then, faith, it will be time to act."

"Yes, more especially as it is not very disagreeable here, with one exception."

"What?"

"Did you observe, d'Artagnan, that three days running they have brought us mutton?"

"No; but if that occurs a fourth time I shall complain of it, so never mind."

"And then I feel the loss of my château; 'tis a long time since I visited my castles."

"Forget them for a time; we shall return to them, unless Mazarin razes them to the ground."

"Do you think that probable?"

"No—the other Cardinal would have done so: but this one is too low a fellow to risk it."

"You console me, d'Artagnan."

The two prisoners were at this point of their conversation when Comminges entered, preceded by a sergeant and two men, who brought supper in a basket with two handles, filled with basins and plates.

"What!" exclaimed Porthos, "mutton again?"

"My dear Monsieur Comminges," said d'Artagnan, "you will find my friend, du Valon, will go to the most fatal lengths if Monsieur Mazarin continues to provide us with this sort of meat; mutton every day."

"I declare," said Porthos, "I shall eat nothing if they do not take it away."

"Take away the mutton," said Comminges; "I wish Monsieur du Valon to eat well, more especially as I have news to give him which will improve his appetite."

"Is Mazarin put to death?" asked Porthos.

"No; I regret to inform you he is perfectly well."

"So much the worse," said Porthos.

"Should you be very glad to hear that the Count de la Fère was well?" asked Comminges.

D'Artagnan's small eyes were opened to the utmost extent.

"Glad!" he cried; "I should be more than glad! Happy!—beyond measure!"

"Well, I am desired by him to give you his compliments, and to say that he is in very good health."

"Then you have seen him?"

"Certainly, I have."

"Where? if it is not impertinent."

"Near here," said Comminges, smiling; "so near that if the windows that look on the orangery were not stopped up you might see the place where he is."

"He is wandering about the environs of the castle," thought d'Artagnan. Then he said aloud:

"You met him, I dare say, in the park—hunting, perhaps?"

"No; nearer, nearer still. Look behind this wall," said Comminges, knocking against the wall.

"Behind this wall? What is there, then, behind the wall? I was brought here by night, so devil take me if I know where I am. The count is then in the château!"

"Yes."

"For what purpose?"

"The same as yourself."

"Athos is, then, a prisoner?"

"You know well," replied Comminges, "that there are no prisoners at Rueil, because there is no prison."

"Don't let us play upon words, sir. Athos has been arrested?"

"Yesterday, at Saint Germain, as he came out from the presence of the queen."

The arms of d'Artagnan fell powerless by his side. One might have supposed him thunderstruck; a paleness ran like a cloud over his dark skin, but disappeared immediately.

"A prisoner?" he reiterated.

"A prisoner," repeated Porthos, quite dejected.

Suddenly d'Artagnan looked up, and in his eyes there was a gleam which scarcely even Porthos observed; but it died away, and he remained more sorrowful than before.

"Come, come," said Comminges, who, since d'Artagnan on the day of Broussel's arrest, had saved him from the hands of the Parisians, had felt a real affection for him; "don't be unhappy, I never thought of bringing you bad news. Laugh at the mischance which has befallen your friend and Monsieur du Valon, instead of being in the depths of despair about it."

But d'Artagnan was still in a desponding mood.

"And how did he look?" asked Porthos, who, perceiving that d'Artagnan had allowed the conversation to drop, profited by it to put in a word.

"Very well indeed, sir," replied Comminges; "at first, like you, he seemed distressed; but when he heard that the Cardinal had intended to pay him a visit this very evening——"

"Ah!" cried d'Artagnan; "the Cardinal going to visit the Comte de la Fère?"

"Yes; and the count desired me to tell you that he should take advantage of this visit to plead for you and for himself."

"Ah! the dear count!" said d'Artagnan.

"A fine thing, indeed!" grunted Porthos. "A great favour! Zounds! Monsieur the Comte de la Fère, whose family is allied to the Montmorency and the Rohan, is well worthy of Monsieur Mazarin's civilities."

"Never mind!" remarked d'Artagnan, in his calmest tone, and looking, but in vain, at Porthos, to see if he comprehended all the importance of this visit. "'Tis then Monsieur Mazarin's custom to walk in his orangery?" he added.

"He shuts himself up there every evening, and there, 'tis said, ponders over state affairs."

"Let the Cardinal take care of going alone to visit the Comte de la Fère," said d'Artagnan; "for the count must be furious."

Comminges began to laugh. "Really, to hear you talk, one would suppose you were cannibals. The count is an affable man; besides, he is unarmed; at the first word from his Eminence the two soldiers about him would run to him."

"Now," said d'Artagnan; "I've one last favour to ask of you, Monsieur de Comminges."

"At your service, sir."

"You will see the count again?"

"To-morrow morning."

"Will you remember us to him, and ask him to request one favour on my behalf—that his Eminence should do me the honour to give me a hearing: that is all I want."

"Oh!" muttered Porthos, shaking his head; "never should I have thought this of *him*! How misfortune humbles a man!"

"That shall be done," replied Comminges.

"Tell the count that I am well; that you found me sad, but resigned."

"I am pleased, sir, to hear that."

"And the same, also, for Monsieur du Valon——"

"Not for me!" cried Porthos; "I am not at all resigned."

"He will be so, monsieur; I know him better than he knows himself. Be silent, dear du Valon, and resign yourself."

"*Adieu*, gentlemen," said Comminges; "sleep well!"

"We will try."

Comminges went away, d'Artagnan remaining apparently

in the same attitude of humble resignation; but scarcely had he left than he turned, and clasped Porthos in his arms, with an expression not to be doubted.

"Oh!" cried Porthos; "what's the matter now? Are you mad, my dear friend?"

"What's the matter?" answered the Gascon, "we are saved!"

"I don't see that at all," answered Porthos. "I think we are all taken prisoners, except Aramis, and that our chances of going out are lessened since we were entangled in Mazarin's cunning."

"Which is far too strong for two of us, but not strong enough for three of us," returned d'Artagnan.

"I don't understand," said Porthos.

"Never mind; let's sit down to table, and take something to strengthen us for to-night."

"What are we to do, then, to-night?"

"To travel, perhaps."

"But——"

"Sit down, dear friend, at the table. Whilst we are eating, ideas flow easily. After supper, when they are perfected, I will communicate my plans to you."

So Porthos sat down to table without another word, and ate with an appetite that did honour to the confidence which d'Artagnan's imagination had inspired him with.

85

THE STRONG ARM

SUPPER was eaten in silence, but not in sadness; for from time to time one of those sweet smiles which were habitual to him in his moments of good-humour illumined the face of d'Artagnan. Not one of these smiles was lost on Porthos; and at every one he uttered an exclamation which betrayed to his friend that he had not lost sight of the idea which possessed his brain.

At dessert d'Artagnan reposed in a chair, crossed one leg over another, and lounged about like a man perfectly at his ease.

"Well?" he said at length.

"Well," repeated Porthos.

"You were saying, my dear friend——"

"No; I said nothing."

"Well, you were saying you wanted to leave this place."

"Ah, indeed!"

"To go away hence you would not mind, you added, knocking down a door or a wall."

"'Tis true, I said so, and I say it again."

"At what o'clock did you see, pray, the two Swiss guards walk last night?"

"An hour after sunset."

"If they go out to-day, as they did yesterday, we shall have the honour, then, of seeing them in half an hour?"

"In a quarter of an hour, at most."

"Your arm is still strong enough, is it not, Porthos?"

Porthos unbuttoned his sleeve, raised his shirt, and looked complacently on his strong arm, as large as the leg of any ordinary man.

"Yes, indeed," he said; "pretty fair."

"So that you could, without trouble, convert these tongs into a hoop, and the shovel into a corkscrew?"

"Certainly." And the giant took up these two articles, and, without any apparent effort, produced in them the metamorphosis requested by his friend.

"There!" he cried.

"Grand!" exclaimed the Gascon. "Really, Porthos, you are a gifted individual!"

"I have read," said Porthos, "of a certain Milo of Crete, who performed wonderful feats, such as binding his forehead with a cord and bursting it, of killing an ox with one blow of his fist, and carrying it home on his shoulders. I used to learn all these feats by heart yonder, down at Pierrefonds, and I have done all that he did except breaking a cord by the swelling of my temples."

"Because your strength is not in your head, Porthos," said his friend.

"No; it is in my arms and shoulders," answered Porthos, with naïveté.

"Well, my dear friend, let us go near the window and try your strength in severing an iron bar."

Porthos went to the window, took a bar in his hands, clung to it, and bent it like a bow; so that the two ends came out of the socket of stone in which for thirty years they had been fixed.

"Well, friend—the Cardinal, although such a genius, could never have done that."

"Shall I take out any more of them?"

"No; that is enough; a man can pass through that."

Porthos tried, and passed the trunk of his body through.

"Yes," he said.

"Now pass your arm through this opening."

"Why?"

"You will know presently. Pass it."

"I wish to know, however, that I may understand," said Porthos.

"You will know directly; see, the door of the guard-room opens. They are going to send into the court the two sentinels who accompany Monsieur Mazarin when he crosses into the orangery. See, they are coming out, and have closed the door of the guard-room after them."

In fact, the two soldiers advanced on the side where the window was, rubbing their hands, for it was cold, it being the month of February.

At this moment the door of the guard-house was opened, and one of the soldiers was summoned away.

"Now," said d'Artagnan, "I am going to call this soldier and talk to him. Don't lose a word of what I am going to say to you, Porthos. Everything lies in the execution."

"Good; the execution of a plot is my forte."

"I know it well. I rely on you. Look, I shall turn to the left; so that the soldier will be at your right, as soon as he mounts on the bench to talk to us."

"But supposing he doesn't mount?"

"He will; depend upon it. As soon as you see him get up, stretch out your arm and seize him by his neck. Then, raising him up as Tobit raised the fish by the gills, you must pull him into the room, taking care to squeeze so tight that he can't cry out."

"Oh!" said Porthos; "suppose I were to strangle him?"

"To be sure there would only be a Swiss the less in the world; but you will not do so, I hope. Lay him down here; we'll gag him, and tie him—no matter where—somewhere. So we shall get from him one uniform and a sword."

"Marvellous!" exclaimed Porthos, looking at the Gascon with the most profound admiration.

"Pooh!" replied d'Artagnan.

"Yes," said Porthos, recollecting himself, "but one uniform and one sword are not enough for two."

"Well; but there's his comrade?"

"True," said Porthos.

"Therefore, when I cough, stretch out your arm."

"All right!"

The two friends then placed themselves as they had agreed, Porthos being completely hidden in an angle of the window.

"Good-evening, comrade," said the Gascon, in his most fascinating voice and manner.

"Good-evening, sir," replied the soldier, in a strong provincial accent.

"'Tis not too warm to walk," resumed the Gascon.

"No, sir."

"And I think a glass of wine will not be disagreeable to you?"

"A glass of wine will be very welcome."

"The fish bites! the fish bites!" whispered the Gascon to Porthos.

"I understand," said Porthos.

"A bottle, perhaps?"

"A whole bottle? Yes, sir."

"A whole bottle, if you will drink to my health."

"Willingly," answered the soldier.

"Come then and take it, friend," said the Gascon.

"With all my heart. How convenient that there's a bench here. Egad! one would think it had been placed here on purpose."

"Get on it; that's it, friend."

And d'Artagnan coughed.

That instant the arm of Porthos fell. His hand of iron grasped, quick as lightning and firm as a vice, the soldier's throat. He raised him, almost stifling him as he drew him through the aperture at the risk of flaying him as he pulled him through. He then put him down on the floor, where d'Artagnan, after giving him just time enough to draw his breath, gagged him with his scarf; and the moment he had done so, began to undress him with the promptitude and dexterity of a man who had learned his business on the field of battle. Then the soldier, gagged and bound, was carried inside the hearth, the fire of which had been previously extinguished by the two friends.

"Here's a sword and a dress," said Porthos.

"I take them," said d'Artagnan, "for myself. If you desire another uniform and sword, you must play the same trick over again. Stop! I see the other soldier issue from the guard-room, and come towards us."

"I think," replied Porthos, "it would be imprudent to attempt the same manœuvre again; a failure would be ruinous. No: I will go down, seize the man unawares, and bring him to you ready gagged."

He did as he said. Porthos seized his opportunity—caught the next soldier by his neck, gagged him, and pushed him like a mummy through the bars into the room, and entered after him. Then they undressed him as they had done the first, laid him on their bed, and bound him with the straps which composed the bed, the bedstead being of oak. This operation proved as successful as the first.

"There," said d'Artagnan, "'tis splendid! Now let me try on the dress of yonder man. Porthos, I doubt if you can wear it; but should it be too tight, never mind, you can wear the breastplate, and the hat with the red feathers."

It happened, however, that the second soldier was a Swiss of gigantic proportions, so, except that some of the seams split, his dress fitted Porthos completely.

They then dressed themselves.

"'Tis done!" they both exclaimed at once. "As to you, comrades," they said to the men, "nothing will happen to you if you are discreet; but if you move, you are dead men."

The soldiers were complaisant; they had found the grasp of Porthos rather powerful, and that it was no joke to contend against it.

D'Artagnan then told Porthos of his plan of action, which Porthos then only partially comprehended.

"What is to happen?" he asked.

"Follow me," replied d'Artagnan. "The man who lives to see shall see."

And, slipping through the hole, he alighted in the court.

Scarcely had the two Frenchmen touched the ground than a door opened, and the voice of the *valet-de-chambre* called out, "Make ready!"

At the same moment the guard-house was opened, and a voice called out: "La Bruyère and du Barthois! March!"

"It seems that I am named la Bruyère," said d'Artagnan.

"And I, du Barthois," added Porthos.

"Where are you?" asked the *valet-de-chambre*, whose eyes, dazzled by the light, could not clearly distinguish our heroes in the gloom.

"Here we are," said the Gascon.

"What say you to that, Monsieur du Valon?" he added, in a low tone, to Porthos.

"If it lasts, it is capital," answered Porthos.

These two newly enlisted soldiers marched gravely after the *valet-de-chambre*, who opened the door of the vestibule; then another, which seemed to be that of a waiting-room, and showed them two stools—

"Your orders are very simple," he said; "don't allow anybody, except one person, to enter here. Do you hear—not a single creature! Obey that person completely. On your return you cannot make a mistake. You have only to wait here till I release you."

D'Artagnan was known to this *valet-de-chambre*, who was no other than Bernouin, and he had, during the last six or eight months, introduced the Gascon a dozen times to the Cardinal. The Gascon, therefore, instead of answering, growled out, "*Ja! Ja!*" in his very best German.

As to Porthos, with whom d'Artagnan had insisted on a perfect silence, and who did not even now begin to comprehend the scheme of his friend, which was to follow Mazarin in his visit to Athos, he was mute. All that he was allowed to say, in case of emergencies, was the proverbial and solemn *Der Tœffel!*

Bernouin went away and closed the door. When Porthos heard the key of the lock turn, he began to be alarmed, lest they should only have exchanged one prison for another.

"Porthos, my friend," said d'Artagnan, "don't distrust Providence! Let me meditate and consider."

"Meditate and consider as much as you wish," replied Porthos, who was now quite out of humour at seeing things take this turn.

"We have walked eight paces," whispered d'Artagnan, "and gone up six steps, so hereabouts is the pavilion, called the Pavilion of the Orangery. The Comte de la Fère cannot be far off, only the doors are locked."

"A great difficulty!" cried Porthos.

"Hush!" said d'Artagnan.

The sound of a step was heard in the vestibule. The hinges of the door creaked, and a man appeared in the dress of a cavalier, wrapped in a brown cloak, with a lantern in his hand, and a large beaver hat pulled down over his eyes.

Porthos stood with his face against the wall, but he could not render himself invisible; and the man in the cloak said to him, giving him his lantern:

"Light the lamp which hangs from the ceiling."

Then, addressing d'Artagnan—

"You know the watchword?" he said.

"*Ja!*" replied the Gascon, determined to confine himself to this specimen of the German tongue.

"*Tedesco!*" answered the cavalier; "*va bene.*"

And advancing towards the door opposite to that by which he came in, he opened it and disappeared behind it, shutting it as he went.

"Now," inquired Porthos, "what are we to do?"

"Now we shall make use of your shoulder, friend Porthos, if this door should be locked. Everything in its proper time, and all comes right to those who know how to wait patiently. But first barricade the outer door well, and then we will follow yonder cavalier."

The two friends set to work, and crowded the space before the door with all the furniture in the room, so as not only to make the passage impassable, but that the door could not open inwards.

"There!" said d'Artagnan, "we can't be overtaken. Come! forwards!"

86

MAZARIN'S OUBLIETTES

AT first, on arriving at the door through which Mazarin had passed, d'Artagnan tried in vain to open it; but on the powerful shoulder of Porthos being applied to one of the panels, which gave way, d'Artagnan introduced the point of his sword between the bolt and the staple of the lock. The bolt gave way and the door opened.

"As I told you, everything can be got, Porthos, by means of women and doors."

"You're a great moralist, and that's the fact," said Porthos.

They entered; behind a glass window, by the light of the Cardinal's lantern, which had been placed on the floor in the midst of the gallery, they saw the orange and pomegranate trees of the Castle of Rueil, in long lines, forming one great alley and two smaller side alleys.

"No Cardinal!" said d'Artagnan, "but only his man; where the devil is he then?"

Exploring, however, one of the side wings of the gallery, he saw all at once, at his left, a tub containing an orange tree, which had been pushed on one side, and in its place an open aperture. He also perceived in this hole the steps of a winding staircase.

He called Porthos to look at it.

"Had our object been money only," he said, "we should be rich directly."

"How's that?"

"Don't you understand, Porthos? At the bottom of that staircase is, probably, the Cardinal's treasury, of which every one speaks so much; and we should only have to descend, empty a chest, shut the Cardinal up in it, double-lock it, go away, carrying off as much gold as we could, put this orange-tree over the place, and no one would ever ask us where our fortune came from, not even the Cardinal."

"It would be a happy hit for clowns to make, but, as it seems to me, unworthy of two gentlemen," said Porthos.

"So I think; and we don't want gold—we want other things," replied the Gascon.

At the same moment, whilst d'Artagnan was leaning over the aperture to listen, a metallic sound, as if some one was moving a

bag of gold, struck on his ear; he started; instantly afterwards a
door opened, and a light played upon the staircase.

Mazarin had left his lamp in the gallery to make people believe
that he was walking about, but he had with him a wax-light to
explore with its aid his mysterious strong-box.

"'Faith!" he said, in Italian, as he was re-ascending the steps,
and looking at a bag of reals, "'faith, there's enough to pay five
councillors of the Parliament and two generals in Paris. I am a
great captain—that I am! but I make war in my own way."

The two friends were squatting down, each behind an orange-
tub, in a side alley.

Mazarin came within three steps of d'Artagnan, and pushing a
spring in the wall, the slab on which the orange-tree was, turned,
and the orange-tree resumed its place.

Then the Cardinal put out the wax-light, slipped it into his
pocket, and taking up the lantern, "Now," he said, "for Monsieur
de la Fère."

"Very good," thought d'Artagnan, "'tis our road likewise; we
can go together."

All three set off on their walk, Mazarin taking the middle alley
and the friends the side one.

The Cardinal reached a second door without noticing that he
was followed; the sand by which the alley was covered deadened
the sound of footsteps.

He then turned to the left, down a corridor which had escaped
the attention of the two friends; but as he opened the door, he
stopped, as if in doubt.

"Ah! *Diavolo!*" he exclaimed, "I forgot the recommendation
of de Comminges, who advised me to take a guard and place it at
this door, in order not to put myself at the mercy of that four-
headed devil." And, with a movement of impatience, he turned
to retrace his steps.

"Do not give yourself the trouble, my lord," said d'Artagnan,
with his right foot forward, his beaver in his hand, a smile on his face;
"we have followed your Eminence step by step, and here we are."

"Yes; here we are," said Porthos.

And he made the same friendly salute as d'Artagnan.

Mazarin gazed at each of them with an affrighted look, recognised them, and let drop his lantern, uttering a cry of terror.

D'Artagnan picked it up; by good luck it had not been extinguished by the fall.

"Oh! what imprudence, my lord," said d'Artagnan; "'tis not
good to go about here without a light. Your Eminence might
knock against something or fall into some hole."

"Monsieur d'Artagnan!" muttered Mazarin, unable to recover from his amazement.

"Yes, my lord, it is I—I've the honour of presenting you Monsieur du Valon, that excellent friend of mine, in whom recently your Eminence had the kindness to interest yourself."

And d'Artagnan held the lamp before the merry face of Porthos. who now began to comprehend the affair, and be very proud of the whole undertaking.

"You were about to visit Monsieur de la Fère?" said d'Artagnan. "Don't let us disarrange your Eminence. Be so kind as to show us the way, and we will follow you."

Mazarin was by degrees recovering his senses.

"Have you been long in the orangery?" he asked, in a trembling voice, remembering the visit he had been paying to his treasury.

"We have just arrived, my lord."

Mazarin breathed again. His fears were now no longer for his hoards, but for himself. A slight smile played on his lips.

"Come," he said, "you have taken me in a snare, gentlemen. I confess myself conquered. You wish to ask for your liberty, and I give it to you."

"Oh, my lord!" answered d'Artagnan, "you are very good; as to our liberty, we have that; it is something else we want to ask you."

"You have your liberty?" repeated Mazarin, in terror.

"Undoubtedly; and on the other hand, my lord, you have lost it; and now 'tis the law of war, sir, you must buy it back again."

Mazarin felt a shiver all over him, a chill even to his heart's core. His piercing look was fixed in vain on the satirical face of the Gascon and on the unchanging countenance of Porthos. Both were in shadow, and even a sybil could not have read them.

"To purchase back my liberty?" said the Cardinal.

"Yes, my lord."

"And what will that cost me, Monsieur d'Artagnan?"

"Zounds, my lord, I don't know yet. We must ask the Count de la Fère the question. Will your Eminence be pleased to open the door which leads to the count's room, and in ten minutes it will be settled."

Mazarin trembled.

"My lord," said d'Artagnan, "your Eminence sees that we wish to act with all due forms of respect; but I must warn you that we have no time to lose; open the door then, my lord, and be so good as to remember, once for all, that on the slightest attempt to escape or the least cry for help, our position being a very critical one, you must not be angry with us if we go to extremities."

"Be assured," answered Mazarin, "that I shall attempt nothing; I give you my word of honour."

D'Artagnan made a sign to Porthos to redouble his watchfulness; then turning to Mazarin—

"Now, my lord, let us go in, if you please."

87

CONFERENCES

MAZARIN unlocked a double door, on the threshold of which they found Athos ready to receive his illustrious guest; on seeing his friends he started with surprise.

"D'Artagnan! Porthos!" he exclaimed.

"My very self, dear friend."

"Me also," said Porthos.

"What means this?" asked the count.

"It means," replied Mazarin, trying to smile, and biting his lips in so doing, "that our parts are changed, and that instead of these gentlemen being my prisoners, I am theirs; but, gentlemen, I warn ye, unless you kill me, your victory will not be of long duration— people will come to the rescue."

"Ah! my lord," cried the Gascon, "don't threaten! 'tis a bad example. We are so good and gentle to your Eminence. Come, let us put aside all rancour and talk pleasantly."

"There's nothing I wish more," replied Mazarin. "But don't think yourselves in a better position than you are. In ensnaring me you have fallen into the trap yourselves. How are you to get away from here? remember the soldiers and sentinels who guard these doors. Now I am going to show you how sincere I am."

"Good," thought d'Artagnan, "we must look about us; he's going to play us a trick."

"I offered you your liberty," continued the minister; "will you take it? Before an hour will have passed you will be discovered, arrested, obliged to kill me, which would be a crime unworthy of loyal gentlemen like you."

"He is right," thought Athos.

And, like every other reflection passing in a mind that entertained none but noble thoughts, this feeling was expressed in his eyes.

"We shall not," answered d'Artagnan, "have recourse to violence, unless driven to it by necessity" (for he saw that Athos seemed to lean towards Mazarin).

"If, on the other hand," resumed Mazarin, "you accept your liberty——"

"Why, you, my lord, might take it away from us five minutes afterwards; and from my knowledge of you, I believe you will take it away from us."

"No—on the faith of a Cardinal. You do not trust me?"

"Circumstances enforce me to doubt your lordship's assurance."

"Well, on the faith of a minister."

"You are no longer a minister, my lord; you are a prisoner."

"Then, on the honour of a Mazarin, as I am, and ever shall be, I hope," said the Cardinal.

"Hem!" replied d'Artagnan. "I have heard speak of a Mazarin who had little religion when his oaths were in question. I fear he may have been an ancestor of your Eminence."

"Monsieur d'Artagnan, you are a great wit, and I'm quite sorry to be on bad terms with you."

"My lord, let us make it up; one resource always remains to us."

"What?"

"That of dying together."

Mazarin shuddered.

"Listen," he said; "at the end of yonder corridor is a door, of which I have the key; it leads into the park. Go, and take this key with you; you are active, vigorous, and you have arms. At a hundred steps to the left you will find the wall of the park; get over it, and in three jumps you will be on the road, and free."

"Ah! by Jove, my lord," said d'Artagnan, "you have well said; but these are only words. Where is the key you spoke of?"

"Here it is."

"Ah, my lord! You will conduct us yourself, then, to that door?"

"Most willingly, if it be necessary to reassure you," answered the minister; and Mazarin, who was delighted to get off so cheaply, led the way, in high spirits, to the corridor, and opened the door.

It led into the park, as the three fugitives perceived by the night breeze which rushed into the corridor, and blew the wind into their faces.

"The devil!" exclaimed the Gascon. "'Tis a dreadful night, my lord. We don't know the localities, and shall never find the wall. Since your Eminence has come so far, a few steps farther conduct us, my lord, to the wall."

"Be it so," replied the Cardinal; and walking at a straight line, he walked to the wall, at the foot of which they all arrived at the same moment.

"Are you satisfied, gentlemen?" asked Mazarin.

"I think so, indeed; we should be hard to please if we were not. Deuce take it! three poor gentlemen escorted by a prince of the Church! Ah! apropos, my lord! you remarked that we were all vigorous, active, and armed."

"Yes."

"You are mistaken. Monsieur du Valon and I are the only two who are armed. The count is not; and should we meet with any patrol, we must defend ourselves."

"'Tis true."

"Where can we find a sword?" asked Porthos.

"My lord," said d'Artagnan, "will lend his, which is no use to him, to the Comte de la Fère."

"Willingly," said the Cardinal; "I will even ask the count to accept it for my sake."

"I promise you, my lord, never to part with it," replied Athos.

"Well," remarked d'Artagnan, "this change of measures, how touching it is! have you not tears in your eyes, Porthos?"

"Yes," said Porthos; "but I do not know if it is that or the wind that makes me weep; I think it is the wind."

"Now climb up, Athos, quickly," said d'Artagnan. Athos, assisted by Porthos, who lifted him up like a feather, arrived at the top.

"Now jump down, Athos."

Athos jumped, and disappeared on the other side of the wall.

"Porthos, whilst I get up, watch the Cardinal. No, I don't want your help. Watch the Cardinal. Lend me your back—but don't let the Cardinal go."

Porthos bent his back, and d'Artagnan was soon on the summit of the wall, where he seated himself.

"Now, what?" asked Porthos.

"Now give me the Cardinal up here; if he makes any sound, stifle him."

Mazarin wished to cry out, but Porthos held him tight, and passed him to d'Artagnan, who secured him by the neck, and made him sit down by him: then, in a menacing tone, he said:

"Sir! jump directly down, close to Monsieur de la Fère, or, on the honour of a gentleman, I'll kill you!"

"Monsieur d'Artagnan," cried Mazarin, "you are breaking your word to me!"

"I—did I promise you anything, my lord?"

Mazarin groaned.

"You are free," he said, "through me; your liberty was my ransom."

"Agreed; but the ransom of that immense treasure buried under the gallery—must not one speak a little of that, my lord?"

"*Diavolo!*" cried Mazarin, almost choked, and clasping his hands; "I am a ruined man."

But, without listening to his grief, d'Artagnan slipped him gently down into the arms of Athos, who stood immovable at the bottom of the wall.

Porthos next made an effort, which shook the wall; and by the aid of his friend's hand, reached the summit.

"I did not understand at all," he said, "but I understand now; how droll it is!"

"You think so? so much the better; but, that it may be droll even to the end, let us not waste time." And he jumped off the wall.

Porthos did the same.

The Gascon then drew his sword, and marched as a vanguard.

"My lord, which way do we go? think well over your reply; for should your Eminence be mistaken, there might be very grave results for all of us."

"Along the wall, sir," said Mazarin, "there will be no danger of losing yourselves."

The three friends hurried on, but in a short time were obliged to slacken their pace. The Cardinal could not keep up with them, though with every wish to do so.

Suddenly d'Artagnan touched something warm, and which moved.

"Stop! A horse!" he cried; "I have found a horse!"

"And I likewise," said Athos.

"I too," said Porthos, who, faithful to the instructions, still held the Cardinal's arm.

"There's luck, my lord! just as you were complaining of being tired and obliged to walk."

But, as he spoke, a pistol-ball fell near his feet, and these words were pronounced:

"Touch it not!"

"Grimaud!" he cried, "Grimaud! what art thou about! wert thou sent by Heaven?"

"No, sir," said that personage; "it was Monsieur Aramis who told me to take charge of the horses."

"Is Aramis here?"

"Yes, sir; he has been here since yesterday."

"What are you doing?"

"On the watch——"

"What! Aramis here?" cried Athos.

"At the lesser gate of the castle; he's posted there."

"Are you a large party?"

"Sixty."

"Inform him."

"This moment, sir."

And, believing that no one could execute the commission better than he could, Grimaud set forth at full speed; whilst, enchanted at being all together again, the three friends awaited his return.

M. Mazarin was the only one in the group who was in a bad humour.

88

IN WHICH IT BECOMES CREDIBLE THAT PORTHOS WILL BE MADE A BARON, AND D'ARTAGNAN A CAPTAIN

At the end of ten minutes Aramis arrived, accompanied by Grimaud, and eight or ten followers. He was greatly delighted, and threw himself into his friends' arms.

"You are then free, friends! free without my aid!"

"Do not be unhappy, dear friend, on that account; if you have done nothing as yet, you will do something," replied Athos.

"I had well concerted my plans," pursued Aramis; "the Coadjutor gave me sixty men; twenty guard the walls of the park, twenty the road from Rueil to St. Germain, twenty are dispersed in the woods. I lay in ambuscade with my sixty men; I encircled the castle; the riding horses I entrusted to Grimaud, and I awaited your coming out, which I did not expect till to-morrow, and I hoped to free you without a skirmish. You are free to-night, without fighting: so much the better! how could you escape that scoundrel Mazarin?"

"'Tis thanks to him," said d'Artagnan, "that we are here now, and——"

"Impossible!"

"Yes, 'tis indeed due to him that we are at liberty."

"Well!" exclaimed Aramis, "this will reconcile me to him; but I wish he were here that I might tell him that I did not believe him to be capable of so noble an act."

"My lord," said d'Artagnan, no longer able to contain himself, "allow me to introduce to you the Chevalier d'Herblay, who wishes, as you may have heard, to offer his congratulations to your Eminence."

And he retired, discovering Mazarin—who was in great confusion—to the astonished gaze of Aramis.

"Ho! ho!" exclaimed the latter, "the Cardinal! a fine prize! halloo! halloo! friends! to horse! to horse!"

Several horsemen quickly approached.

"Zounds!" cried Aramis, "I may have done some good, then; my lord, deign to receive my most respectful homage! I will lay a wager that 'tis that Saint Christopher, Porthos, who performed this feat! Apropos! I forgot——" and he gave some orders in a low voice to one of the horsemen.

"I think it will be best to set off," said d'Artagnan.

"Yes; but I am expecting some one—a friend of Athos."

"A friend!" exclaimed the count.

"And here he is, galloping towards us."

"The count! the count!" cried a young voice, which made Athos start.

"Raoul! Raoul!" he ejaculated.

For the moment the young man forgot his habitual respect—he threw himself on his guardian's neck.

"Look, my lord Cardinal," said Aramis, "would it not have been a pity to have separated those who love each other so well? Gentlemen," he continued, addressing the cavaliers, who became more and more numerous every instant, "gentlemen, encircle his Eminence, that you may show him the greater honour. He will, indeed, give us the favour of his company; you will, I hope, be grateful for it. Porthos, do not lose sight of his Eminence."

Aramis then joined Athos and d'Artagnan, who were consulting together.

"Come," said d'Artagnan, after a conference of five minutes' duration, "let us start upon our journey."

"Where are we to go?" asked Porthos.

"To your house, dear Porthos, at Pierrefonds; your fine château is worthy of affording a princely hospitality to his Eminence; it is also well situated; neither too near Paris, nor too far from it. We can establish a communication between it and the capital with great facility. Come, my lord, you shall there be treated like a prince, as you are."

"A fallen prince!" exclaimed Mazarin piteously.

"The chances of war," said Athos, "are many; but be assured we shall not take an improper advantage of them."

"No; but we shall employ them," interposed d'Artagnan.

The rest of the night was employed by these cavaliers in travelling, with that wonderful rapidity of former days. Mazarin, continuing sombre and pensive, allowed himself to be dragged along in this way, which was like a race of spectres. At dawn twelve leagues had been passed, without stopping; half the escort were exhausted, and several horses fell down.

"Horses nowadays are not what they were formerly," observed Porthos; "everything degenerates."

In about ten minutes the escort stopped at Ermenonville, but the four friends went on with fresh ardour, guarding Mazarin carefully. At noon they rode into the avenue of Pierrefonds.

"We are four of us," said d'Artagnan; "we must relieve each other in mounting guard over my lord, and each of us must watch for three hours at a time. Athos is going to examine the castle, which it will be necessary to render sufficiently able to support a siege; Porthos will see to the provisions, and Aramis to the troops of the garrison. That is to say, Athos will be chief engineer, Porthos purveyor in general, and Aramis governor of the fortress."

Meanwhile they gave up to Mazarin the handsomest room in the château.

"Gentlemen," he said, when he was in his room, "you do not expect, I presume, to keep me here a long time incognito?"

"No, my lord," replied the Gascon; "on the contrary, we think of announcing very soon that we have you here."

"Then you will be besieged."

"We expect it."

"And what shall you do?"

"Defend ourselves. Were the late Cardinal Richelieu alive, he would tell you a certain story of the Bastion Saint Gervaise, which we four, with our four servants and twelve dead men, held out against a whole army."

"Such feats, sir, are done once, and are never repeated."

"However, nowadays there's not need of so much heroism. To-morrow the army of Paris will be summoned; the day after it will be here! The field of battle, instead, therefore, of being at St. Denis, or at Charenton, will be near Compiègne, or Villars-Cotterets."

"The prince will vanquish you, as he has always done."

"'Tis possible, my lord; but before an engagement we shall move away your Eminence to another castle belonging to our friend du Valon, who has three. We will not expose your Eminence to the chances of war."

"Come," answered Mazarin. "I see it will be necessary for you to capitulate."

"Before a siege?"

"Yes; the conditions will be better than afterwards."

"Ah, my lord! as to conditions, you would soon see how moderate and reasonable we are!"

"Come, now, pray what are your conditions? I wish to know whether I am among enemies or friends."

"Friends, my lord! friends!"

"Well, then, tell me at once what you require, that I may see if an arrangement be possible. Speak, Count de la Fère!"

"My lord," replied Athos, "for myself I have nothing to ask; for France, were I to specify, I should request too much. I beg you excuse me, and propose to the chevalier."

And Athos bowed, and remained leaning against the mantelpiece, merely as a spectator of the scene.

"Speak, then, chevalier!" said the Cardinal. "What do you want? Nothing ambiguous, if you please. Be clear, short, and precise."

"As for me," replied Aramis, "I have in my pocket that programme of the conditions which the deputation, of which I formed one, went yesterday to Saint Germain to impose on your lordship. Let us consider the debts and claims the first. The demands in that programme must be granted."

"We were almost agreed as to those," replied Mazarin; "let us pass on to private and personal stipulations."

"You suppose, then, that there will be some?" asked Aramis, smiling.

"I do not suppose that you will all be so disinterested as Monsieur de la Fère," replied the Cardinal, bowing to Athos.

"My lord! you are right! The count has a mind far above vulgar desires and human passions! He is a proud soul: he is a man by himself! You are right, he is worth us all, and we avow it to you!"

"Aramis!" said Athos, "are you serious?"

"Yes, yes, dear friend; I state only what we all know. You are right; it is not you alone this matter concerns, but my lord, and his unworthy servant, myself."

"Well, then, what do you want besides the general conditions before recited?"

"I desire, my lord, that Normandy should be given to Madame de Longueville, with five hundred thousand francs, and full absolution. I desire that his majesty should deign to be godfather to the child she has just borne; and that my lord, after having been present at the christening, should go to proffer his homage to our Holy Father the Pope."

"That is, that you wish me to lay aside my ministerial functions, to leave France, and be an exile."

"I wish his Eminence to become Pope on the first opportunity, allowing me then the right of demanding full indulgences for myself and my friends."

Mazarin made a grimace which was quite indescribable, and turning to d'Artagnan—

"And you, sir?" he said.

"I, my lord," answered the Gascon, "I differ from Monsieur d'Herblay totally in the last point, though I agree with him in the first. Far from wishing my lord to leave Paris, I hope he will stay there and continue to be Prime Minister, as he is a great statesman. I shall try, also, to assist him to put down the Fronde; but on one condition—that he sometimes remembers the king's faithful servants, and gives the first vacant company of musketeers to some one I can mention to him. And you, Monsieur du Valon——"

"Yes, you, sir! Speak, if you please," said Mazarin.

"As to me," answered Porthos, "I wish my lord Cardinal, to do honour to my house, which has given him an asylum, would, in remembrance of this adventure, erect my estate into a barony, with a promise to confer that order on one of my friends, whenever his majesty next creates peers."

Mazarin bit his lip.

"All that," he said, "appears to me to be ill connected, gentlemen; for if I satisfy some I shall displease others. If I stay in Paris, I cannot go to Rome; and if I become Pope I could not continue to be Prime Minister; and it is only by continuing Prime Minister that I can make Monsieur d'Artagnan a captain, and Monsieur du Valon a baron."

"True," said Aramis, "so, as I am in my minority, I give up my proposal."

"Well, then, gentlemen, take care of your own concerns, and let France settle matters as she will with me," resumed Mazarin.

"Ho! ho!" replied Aramis. "The Frondeurs will have a treaty, and your Eminence must sign it before us, promising, at the same time, to obtain the queen's consent to it—here is the treaty,—may it please your Eminence, read and sign it."

"I know it," answered Mazarin.

"Then sign it."

"But what if I refuse?"

"Then," said d'Artagnan, "your Eminence must expect the consequences of such refusal."

"Would you dare to touch a Cardinal?"

"You have dared, my lord, to imprison her majesty's musketeers."

"The queen will revenge me, gentlemen."

"I do not think so, although inclination might lead her to do so, but we shall take your Eminence to Paris—and the Parisians will defend us; therefore, sign this treaty, I beg of you."

"Suppose the queen should refuse to ratify it?"

"Ah! nonsense!" cried d'Artagnan, "I can manage so that her majesty will receive me well; I know one way."

"Well!"

"I shall take her majesty the letter in which you tell her that the finances are exhausted."

"And then?" asked Mazarin, turning pale.

"When I see her majesty embarrassed, I shall conduct her to Rueil, make her enter the orangery, and show her a certain spring which turns a box."

"Enough, sir," said the Cardinal, "you have said enough—where is the treaty?"

"Here it is," replied Aramis. "Sign, my lord," and he handed him a pen.

Mazarin arose—walked some moments, thoughtful, but not dejected.

"And after I have signed," he said, "what is to be my guarantee?"

"My word of honour, sir," said Athos.

Mazarin started, turned towards the Count de la Fère, and, looking for an instant at his noble and honest countenance, took the pen.

"It is sufficient, count," he said, and he signed the treaty.

"And now, Monsieur d'Artagnan," he said, "prepare to set off for Saint Germain, and to carry a letter from me to the queen."

89

THE PEN MIGHTIER THAN THE SWORD

D'ARTAGNAN knew his part well; he was aware that opportunity has a forelock only for him who will take it, and he was not a man to let it go by without seizing it. He soon arranged a prompt and certain manner of travelling, by sending relays of horses to Chantilly, so that he could be in Paris in five or six hours.

Nothing was known at Saint Germain about Mazarin's disappearance, except by the queen, who concealed, to her friends even, her uneasiness. She had heard all about the two soldiers who were found, bound and gagged. Bernouin, who knew more about the affair than anybody, had, in fact, gone to acquaint the queen of the circumstances which had occurred. Anne had enforced the utmost secrecy, and had disclosed the event to no one except the Prince de Condé, who had sent five or six horsemen into the environs of Saint Germain, with orders to bring any suspicious person who was going away from Rueil, in whatsoever direction it might be.

On entering the court of the palace, d'Artagnan encountered Bernouin, to whose instrumentality he owed a quick introduction to the queen's presence. He approached the sovereign with every mark of profound respect, and having fallen on his knee, presented to her the Cardinal's letter.

It was, however, merely a letter of introduction. The queen read it, recognised the writing, and, since there were no details in it of what had occurred, asked for particulars. D'Artagnan related everything, with that simple and ingenuous air which he knew how to assume on such occasions. The queen, as he went on, looked at him with increasing astonishment. She could not understand how a man could conceive such an enterprise, and still less how he could have the audacity to disclose it to her whose interest, and almost duty, it was to punish him.

"How, sir!" she cried, as d'Artagnan finished, "you dare to tell me the details of your crime—to give me an account of your treason!"

"Your majesty, on your side," said d'Artagnan, "is as much mistaken as to our intentions as the Cardinal Mazarin has always been."

"You are in error, sir," answered the queen. "I am so little mistaken, that in ten minutes you shall be arrested, and in an hour I shall set off to release my minister."

"I am sure your majesty will not commit such an act of imprudence; first, because it would be useless, and would produce the most serious results. Before he could be set free, the Cardinal would be dead; and, indeed, so convinced is he of this, that he entreated me, should I find your majesty disposed to act in this manner, to do all I could to induce you to change your intentions."

"Well, then! I shall be content with only arresting you!"

"Madame, the possibility of my arrest has been foreseen, and should I not have returned to-morrow at a certain hour, the next day the Cardinal will be brought to Paris, and delivered up to the Parliament."

"I think," returned Anne of Austria, fixing upon him a glance which, in any woman's face, would have expressed disdain, but in the queen's, spread terror to those she looked upon—"I perceive that you dare to threaten the mother of your king."

"Madame," replied d'Artagnan, "I threaten only because I am compelled to do so. Believe me, madame, as true a thing as it is that a heart beats in this bosom, a heart devoted to you, believe that you have been the idol of our lives; that we have, as you well know, good Heaven! risked our lives twenty times for your majesty. Have you then, madame, no compassion on your people, who love you, and yet who suffer, who love you, and who are yet famished, who have no other wish than to bless you, and who, nevertheless—no, I am wrong, your subjects, madame, will never curse you! Say one word to them! and all will be ended; peace succeeds to war, joy to tears, happiness to misfortune!"

Anne of Austria looked with bewilderment on the warlike countenance of d'Artagnan, which betrayed a singular expression of deep feeling.

"Why did you not say all this before you acted?" she said.

"Because, madame, it was necessary to prove to your majesty one thing of which you doubted, that is, that we still possess amongst us some valour, and are worthy of some consideration at your hands."

"Then, in case of my refusal, this valour, should a struggle occur, will go even to the length of carrying me off in the midst of my court, to deliver me into the hands of the Fronde, as you have done my minister?"

"We have not thought about it, madame," answered d'Artagnan, with that Gascon effrontery which had in him the appearance of naïveté; "but if we four had so settled it, we should certainly have accomplished it."

"I ought," muttered Anne to herself, "by this time to remember that these are men of iron mould."

"Alas! madame!" exclaimed d'Artagnan, "this proves to me that it is only since yesterday that your majesty has gained a true opinion of us. Your majesty will do us justice. In doing us justice you will no longer treat us as men of common stamp. You will see in me an ambassador worthy of the high interests which he is authorised to discuss with his sovereign."

"Where is the treaty?"

"Here it is."

Anne of Austria cast her eyes upon the treaty that d'Artagnan proffered her. "I do not see here," she said, "anything but general conditions; the interests of the Prince de Conti, or of the Ducs de Beaufort, de Bouillon, and d'Elbeuf, and of the Coadjutor, are herein consulted; but with regard to yours?"

"We do ourselves justice, madame, even in assuming the high position that we have. We do not think ourselves worthy to stand near such great names."

"But you, I presume, have decided to assert your pretensions, personally?"

"I believe you, madame, to be a great and powerful queen, and that it will be unworthy of your power and greatness if you do not recompense the arm which will bring back his Eminence to Saint Germain."

"It is my intention so to do; come—let us hear—speak."

"He who has negotiated the matters (forgive me if I begin by speaking of myself, but I must take that importance to myself which has been given to me, not assumed by me), he who has arranged matters for the return of the Cardinal, ought, it appears to me, in order that his reward may not be unworthy of your majesty, to be made commandant of the guards, an appointment something like that of captain of the musketeers."

"'Tis the appointment that Monsieur de Tréville had, that you seek of me."

"The place, madame, is vacant; and although 'tis a year since Monsieur de Tréville has left it, it is not yet filled up."

"But it is one of the principal military appointments in the king's household."

"Monsieur de Tréville was merely a younger son of a Gascon family, like myself, madame; he occupied that post for twenty years."

"You have an answer ready for everything," replied the queen, and she took a document from her bureau, which she filled up and signed.

"Undoubtedly, madame," said d'Artagnan, taking the document and bowing, "this is a noble reward; but everything in this world is liable to change; and any man who happened to fall into disgrace with your majesty would lose everything."

"What then do you want?" asked the queen, colouring, as she found that she had to deal with a mind as subtle as her own.

"A hundred thousand francs for this poor captain of musketeers, to be paid whenever his services should no longer be acceptable to your majesty."

Anne hesitated.

"To think of the Parisians," resumed d'Artagnan, "offering the other day, by an edict of the Parliament, six hundred thousand francs to any man soever who would deliver up the Cardinal to them, dead or alive—if alive, in order to hang him: if dead, to deny him the rights of Christian burial!——"

"Come," said Anne, "'tis not unreasonable,—since you only ask from a queen the sixth of what the parliament has proposed" —and she signed an order for a hundred thousand francs.

"Now then?" she said, "what next?"

"Madame, my friend du Valon is rich, and has therefore nothing in the way of fortune to desire; but I think I remember that there was a dispute between him and Monsieur Mazarin as to making his estate a barony or not. 'Twas even a promise."

"A provincial," said Anne of Austria; "people will smile."

"Let them!" answered d'Artagnan; "but I am sure of one thing, that those who smile at him in his presence will never smile a second time."

"Here is the barony," said the queen, and she signed a patent.

"Now there remains the chevalier, or the Abbé d'Herblay, as your majesty pleases."

"Does he wish to be a bishop?"

"No, madame, something easier to grant."

"What?"

"It is that the king should deign to stand godfather to the son of Madame de Longueville."

The queen smiled.

"Nothing more?" she asked.

"No, madame, for I presume that the king standing godfather to him, could do no less than present him with five hundred thousand francs, giving his father, also, the government of Normandy."

"As to the government of Normandy," replied the queen, "I think I can promise; but, with regard to the present, the Cardinal is always telling me there is little money in the royal coffers."

"We shall search for some, madame, and I think we can find some, and if your majesty permits, we will seek for some together."

"What next?"

"Madame, the Count de la Fère."

"What does he ask?"

"Nothing."

"There is in the world, then, one man who, having the power to ask, asks for nothing."

"The Count de la Fère is more than a man; he is a god."

"Are you satisfied, sir?"

"There is one thing which your majesty has omitted—the signature to the treaty."

"Of what use to-day? I will sign to-morrow."

"I can assure your majesty that if you do not sign to-day, there will not be time to sign to-morrow. Consent, then, I beg you, madame, to write at the bottom of this schedule, which has been drawn up by Mazarin, as you see."

"I consent to ratify the treaty proposed by the Parisians."

Anne was ensnared: she could not draw back—she signed; but scarcely had she done so, when pride burst forth in her like a tempest, and she began to weep.

D'Artagnan started on seeing these tears: since that time queens have shed tears like other women.

The Gascon shook his head: these tears from royalty melted his soul.

"Madame," he said, kneeling, "look upon the unhappy man at your feet. Behold, madame! here are the august signatures of your majesty's hand: if you think you are right in giving them to me, you shall do so; but from this very moment you are free from every obligation to keep them."

And d'Artagnan, full of honest pride and of manly intrepidity, placed in Anne's hands, in a bundle, the papers that he had, one by one, won from her with so much difficulty.

There are moments—for if everything is not good, everything in this world is not bad—in which the most frigid and the coldest hearts are softened by the tears of strong emotion, of a generous sentiment; one of these momentary impulses actuated Anne. D'Artagnan, when he gave way to his own feelings, which were in accordance with those of the queen, had accomplished all that the most skilful diplomacy could have effected. He was, therefore, instantly recompensed, either for his address, or for his sensibility, whichever it might be termed.

"You were right, sir," said Anne. "I misunderstood you. There are the acts signed: I deliver them to you without compulsion: go and bring me back the Cardinal as soon as possible."

"Madame," faltered d'Artagnan, "it is twenty years ago—I have a good memory—since I had the honour, behind a piece of tapestry in the Hôtel de Ville, to kiss one of those beautiful hands."

"There is the other," replied the queen; and that the left hand should not be less liberal than the right, she drew from her fingers a diamond—nearly similar to the one previously given to him— "take and keep this ring in remembrance of me."

"Madame," said d'Artagnan, rising, "I have only one thing more to wish, which is, that the next thing you ask from me should be my life."

And with this way of concluding—a way peculiar to himself— he arose and departed.

"I have never rightly understood these men," said the queen, as she watched him retiring from her presence; "and it is now too late, for in a year the king will be of age."

In twenty-four hours d'Artagnan and Porthos conducted Mazarin to the queen; and the one received his commission, the other his patent of nobility.

On the same day the Treaty of Paris was signed; and it was everywhere announced that the Cardinal had shut himself up for three days, in order to draw it out with the greatest care.

90

IT IS SOMETIMES MORE DIFFICULT FOR A KING TO RETURN TO THE CAPITAL OF HIS KINGDOM THAN TO LEAVE IT

WHILST d'Artagnan and Porthos were engaged in conducting the Cardinal to Saint Germain, Athos and Aramis returned to Paris.

Each had his own particular visit to make.

Aramis rushed to the Hôtel de Ville, where Madame de Longue-ville was staying. The duchess had loudly lamented the announce-ment of peace. War had made her a queen; peace brought her abdication. She declared that she had never expected the treaty, and that she wished for eternal war.

But Aramis consoled her, and pointed out the solid advantages that were the result of peace—the precarious tenure of all she had prized during war.

"Now," said Aramis to her, "detach your brother, the Prince de Condé, from the queen, whom he does not like—from Mazarin, whom he despises. The Fronde is a comedy, of which the first act only is played. Let us wait for the termination, for the day when the prince, thanks to you, shall have turned against the court."

Madame de Longueville was persuaded of the influence of her fine eyes, and was appeased; but Madame de Chevreuse frowned, and, in spite of all the logic of Athos to show her that a prolonged war would have been impracticable, contended in favour of hostilities.

"My dear lady," said Athos, "allow me to tell you that everybody is tired of war. You will get yourself exiled, as you did in the time of Louis XIII. Believe me, we have passed the time of success in intrigue, and your beautiful eyes are not destined to be blinded by regretting Paris, where there will always be two queens as long as you are there."

"Oh," cried the duchess, "I cannot make war alone, but I can avenge myself on that ungrateful queen and ambitious favourite— on the honour of a duchess, I will avenge myself."

"Madame," replied Athos, "do not injure the Vicomte de Bragelonne—do not ruin his prospects. Alas! excuse my weakness! There are moments when a man grows young again in his children."

The duchess smiled; half tenderly, half ironically.

"Count," she said, "you are, I fear, gained over to the court. I suppose you have a blue ribbon in your pocket?"

"Yes, madame; I have that of the Garter, which King Charles I. gave me a few days before he died."

"Come! one must grow into an old woman," said the duchess pensively.

Athos took her hand, and kissed it. She sighed as she looked at him.

"Count," she said, "Bragelonne must be a charming place. You are a man of taste. You have water—woods—flowers—there?"

She sighed again, and leaned her charming head, gracefully reclined, on her hand—still beautiful in form and colour.

"Madame!" exclaimed Athos, "what were you saying just now about growing old? Never have I seen you look so young—never more beautiful!"

The duchess shook her head.

"Does Monsieur de Bragelonne remain in Paris?" she inquired.

"What think you of it?" replied Athos.

"Leave it to me," replied the duchess; "really sir, you are delightful, and I should like to spend a month at Bragelonne."

"Are you not fearful of making people envious, duchess?" replied Athos.

"No, I shall go incognito, count, under the name of Marie Michou. But do not keep Raoul with you."

"Why not?"

"Because he is in love."

"He—he is quite a child."

"And it is a child whom he loves."

Athos became thoughtful.

"You are right, duchess. This singular passion for a child of seven years old may some day make him very unhappy. There is to be war in Flanders. He shall go thither."

"And at his return you will send him to me. I will arm him against love."

"Alas, madame!" exclaimed Athos, "to-day love is like war, and the breastplate is become useless."

Raoul came in at this moment; it was to announce that the solemn entrance of the king, the queen, and her ministers was to take place on the following day.

On the next day, in fact, at daybreak, the court made preparations to quit Saint Germain.

Meanwhile, the queen every hour had been sending for d'Artagnan.

"I hear," she said, "that Paris is not quiet. I am afraid for the king's safety; place yourself close to the coach-door on the right."

"Be assured, madame; I will answer for the king's safety."

As he left the queen's presence, Bernouin summoned him to the Cardinal.

"Sir," said Mazarin to him, "a disturbance is spoken of in Paris. I shall be on the king's left, and as I am the chief person threatened, remain at the coach-door to the left."

"Your Eminence may be perfectly easy," replied d'Artagnan; "they shall not touch a hair of your head."

"Deuce take it," he thought to himself, "how can I take care of both? Ah! plague on't, I shall guard the king, and Porthos the Cardinal."

This arrangement pleased all. The queen had confidence in the courage of d'Artagnan, and the Cardinal in the strength of Porthos.

The royal procession set out for Paris. Guitant and Comminges, at the head of the guards, marched first; then came the royal carriage, with d'Artagnan on one side, Porthos on the other; then the musketeers, for twenty-two years the old friends of d'Artagnan. During twenty years he had been their lieutenant, their captain since the night before.

The cortege proceeded to Notre Dame, where a *Te Deum* was chanted. All the people of Paris were in the streets. The Swiss were drawn up along the road, but as the road was long, they were placed at six or eight feet distance from each other, and one man deep only. This force was, therefore, wholly insufficient, and from time to time the line was broken through by the people, and was formed again with difficulty. Whenever this occurred, although it proceeded only from goodwill and a desire to see the king and queen, Anne looked at d'Artagnan anxiously.

Mazarin, who had dispensed a thousand louis to make the people cry "Long live Mazarin," and who had, therefore, no reliance upon acclamations bought at twenty pistoles each, looked also at Porthos; but the gigantic bodyguard replied to that look with his fine bass voice, "Be tranquil, my lord;" and Mazarin became more and more composed.

At the Palais Royal the crowd, which had forced in from the adjacent streets, was still greater; like a large impetuous crowd, a wave of human beings came to meet the carriage, and rolled tumultuously into the Rue St. Honoré.

When the procession reached the palace, loud cries of "Long live their majesties!" resounded. Mazarin leaned out of the window. One or two shouts of "Long live the Cardinal!" saluted him, but instantly hisses and yells stifled them remorselessly. Mazarin became white, and sank back in the coach.

"Low-born fellows!" ejaculated Porthos.

D'Artagnan said nothing, but twirled his moustache with a peculiar gesture, which showed that his fine Gascon humour was kindled.

Anne of Austria bent down and whispered in the young king's ear:

"Say something gracious to Monsieur d'Artagnan, Louis."

The young king leaned towards the door.

"I have not said good-morning to you, Monsieur d'Artagnan," he said; "nevertheless, I have remarked you. It was you who were behind my bed-curtains that night when the Parisians wished to see me asleep."

"And if the king permits me," returned the Gascon, "I shall be near him whenever there is danger to be encountered."

"Sir," said Mazarin to Porthos, "what would you do if the crowd fell upon us?"

"Kill as many as I could, my lord."

"Hem! Brave as you are, and strong as you are, you could not kill all."

"'Tis true," answered Porthos, rising in his saddle, in order that he might see the immense crowd—"there are many of them."

"I think I should like the other man better than this one,"

thought Mazarin, and he threw himself back on the cushions of the carriage.

The queen and her minister, more especially the latter, had reason to feel anxious. The crowd, whilst preserving an appearance of respect, and even of affection for the king and queen-regent, began to be tumultuous. Reports were whispered about, like certain sounds which announce, as they are echoed from wave to wave, the coming storm—and when they pass through a multitude presage a riot.

D'Artagnan turned towards the musketeers, and made a sign imperceptible to the crowd, but very easily understood by that chosen regiment, the flower of the army.

The ranks were closed, and a kind of shudder ran from man to man.

At the Barrière des Sergents the procession was obliged to stop. Comminges left the head of the escort, and went to the queen's carriage. Anne questioned d'Artagnan by a glance. He answered in the same language.

"Proceed," she said.

Comminges returned to his post. An effort was made, and the living barrier was violently broken through.

Some complaints proceeded from the crowd, and were addressed this time to the king, as well as the minister.

"Onwards!" cried d'Artagnan, with a loud voice.

"Onwards!" cried Porthos.

But, as if the multitude had waited only for this demonstration to burst out, all the sentiments of hostility that possessed it broke out at once. Cries of "Down with Mazarin!" "Death to the Cardinal!" resounded on all sides.

At the same time, through the streets of Grenelle, Saint Honoré, and Du Coq, a double stream of people broke the feeble hedge of Swiss Guards, and came, like a whirlwind, even to the very feet of Porthos' horse and that of d'Artagnan.

This new eruption was more dangerous than the others, being composed of armed men. It was plain that it was not the chance combination of those who had collected a number of the malcontents at the same spot, but the concerted attack organised by an hostile spirit.

Each of these two mobs was led on by a chief, one of whom appeared to belong, not to the people, but to the honourable corporation of mendicants, and the other, who, notwithstanding his affected coarseness, might easily be discovered to be a gentleman. Both were evidently actuated by the same impulse.

There was a shock which was perceived even in the royal

carriage. Then, millions of cries, forming one vast uproar, were heard, mingled with guns firing.

"The musketeers! here!" cried d'Artagnan.

The escort divided into two files. One of them passed round to the right of the carriage; the other to the left. One went to support d'Artagnan, the other Porthos. Then came a skirmish, the more terrible, because it had no definite object; the more melancholy, because those engaged in it knew not for whom they were fighting. Like all popular movements, the shock given by the rush of this mob was formidable. The musketeers, few in number, not being able, in the midst of this crowd, to make their horses wheel round, began to give way. D'Artagnan offered to lower the blinds of the royal carriage, but the young king stretched out his arm, saying:

"No, sir! I wish to see all."

"If your majesty wishes to look out—well, then, look!" replied d'Artagnan. And turning with that fury which made him so formidable, he rushed towards the chief of the insurgents, a man who, with a large sword in his hand, tried to clear out a passage to the coach door by a combat with two musketeers.

"Make room!" cried d'Artagnan. "Zounds! give way."

At these words, the man armed with a pistol and sword raised his head; but it was too late. The blow was sped by d'Artagnan; the rapier had pierced his bosom.

"Ah! confound it!" cried the Gascon, trying in vain to retract the thrust. "What the devil are you doing here, count?"

"Accomplishing my destiny," replied Rochefort, falling on one knee. "I have already got up again after three stabs from you; but I shall not rise after a fourth."

"Count!" said d'Artagnan, with some degree of emotion, "I struck without knowing that it was you. I am sorry, if you die, that you should die with feelings of bitterness towards me."

Rochefort extended his hand to d'Artagnan, who took it. The count wished to speak, but a gush of blood stifled him. He stiffened in the last convulsions of death, and expired!

"Back, people!" shouted d'Artagnan. "Your leader is dead; you have nothing more to do here."

In fact, as if the Comte de Rochefort had been the soul of the attack on that side of the king's carriage, the whole crowd which had followed and obeyed him took to flight on seeing him fall.

D'Artagnan followed up his charge with twenty musketeers into the Rue du Coq, and this part of the mob dispersed like smoke by spreading over the Place de Saint Germain-l'Auxerrois, and by directing their course towards the quays.

D'Artagnan returned, with the view of assisting Porthos if he should want it; but Porthos, on his side, had performed his work as conscientiously as d'Artagnan. The left of the carriage was not less set free than the right; and the blind, which Mazarin, less warlike than the king, had had the precaution to let down, was now raised. And yet Porthos looked very melancholy.

"What a devil of a face you are making, Porthos! You don't look much like a conqueror."

"Well," said Porthos, "you yourself seem a little agitated."

"I have reason, *mordieu!* I have just killed an old friend."

"Indeed!" said Porthos. "Who is that?"

"Poor Comte de Rochefort!"

"And I in the same manner have killed a man whose face was not unknown to me. Unfortunately, I struck him on the head, and in a moment his face was covered with blood."

"And did he say nothing as he fell?"

"Yes, he said 'Oh!'"

"I can understand," said d'Artagnan, unable to refrain from laughing, "that if he said nothing but that, that could not much enlighten you."

"Well, monsieur?" asked the queen.

"Madame," replied d'Artagnan, "the way is perfectly free; your majesty can continue your route."

In fact, the whole cortege arrived safely at the church of Notre Dame, under the portal of which all the clergy, with the Coadjutor at their head, awaited the king, the queen, and the minister, for the happy return of whom a *Te Deum* was sung. During the service, and as it was drawing towards a close, a *gamin*, apparently much agitated, entered the church, ran to the sacristy, dressed himself quickly as a chorister, and, thanks to the respectable uniform with which he had just covered himself, penetrating the crowd which filled the temple, went up to Bazin, who, clad in his blue robe, and with his silver-ornamented staff in his hand, stood gravely opposite to the beadle at the entrance to the choir. Bazin felt somebody pull him by the sleeve. He brought down his eyes to the earth, which were beatifically cast towards heaven, and recognised Friquet.

"Well, monkey, what is the matter, that makes you disturb me in the exercise of my functions?" demanded the beadle.

"The matter, Monsieur Bazin," said Friquet—"the matter is that Monsieur Maillard, you know who I mean, the giver of holy water at Saint-Eustache——"

"Yes; what next?"

"Well, he received in the row this morning a sword-cut on his head; it was that great giant you see yonder, with the lace all over his seams, that gave it."

"Yes, in that case," said Bazin, "he must be very ill."

"So ill that he is dying, and he wishes, before he does die, to confess to Monsieur le Coadjuteur, who has power, they say, to remit great sins."

"And he fancies that Monsieur le Coadjuteur will put himself out of the way for him?"

"Yes, certainly, for it appears that Monsieur le Coadjuteur has promised him."

"And who told you that?"

"Monsieur Maillard himself."

"You have seen him, then?"

"Certainly; I was there when he fell."

"And what did you do there?"

"Do! I cried 'Down with Mazarin! Death to the Cardinal! To the gibbet with the Italian!' Was it not it that you told me to cry?"

"Will you hold your tongue, you little monkey!" said Bazin, looking very uneasily around him.

"So that he said to me, did poor Monsieur Maillard, 'Go and look for the Coadjutor, Friquet, and if you bring him with you I will make you my heir.' Only think, Father Bazin! The heir of Monsieur Maillard, the giver of holy water at Saint Eustache— *hein!* I shall only have to sit with my arms across. That's all one. I should like to render him this service; what do you say to it?"

"I will go and inform the Coadjutor," said Bazin; and he went softly and respectfully up to the prelate, said some words into his ear, to which he answered by an affirmative; and then, returning as softly as he had gone, he said:

"Go and tell the dying man to wait patiently; his Excellence will be with him in an hour."

"Good!" said Friquet; "my fortune is made."

"By the way," said Bazin, "where did he have them carry him?"

"To the tower of Saint Jacques la Boucherie."

And, enchanted at the success of his embassy, Friquet, without taking off his chorister's dress, which, moreover, gave him a greater facility of getting about, hurried from the cathedral, and took the road to the tower of Saint Jacques la Boucherie as fast as he could.

As soon as the *Te Deum* was finished the Coadjutor, as he had promised, and without even putting off his priestly robes, proceeded towards the old tower that he knew so well.

He arrived in time. Although growing momentarily weaker and weaker, the wounded man was not yet dead.

The door was opened for him into the room where the mendicant was in the last agonies.

A minute after Friquet came out, holding a large leathern bag in his hand, which he opened the moment he was outside the room, and which, to his utter astonishment, he found to be full of gold.

The mendicant had kept his word and made him his heir.

"Ah, Mother Nannette!" screamed out Friquet, almost suffocated,—"ah, Mother Nannette!"

He could say no more; but the strength which failed him in speech left him the power of action. He began running desperately homeward; and, like the Greek of Marathon falling on the square at Athens with his laurel in his hand, Friquet reached the threshold of the Councillor Broussel, and on reaching it fell down, scattering on the carpet the louis-d'or which rolled out of the bag.

Mother Nannette first picked up the louis, and then she picked up Friquet.

In the meantime the grand procession was entering the Palais Royal.

"That M. d'Artagnan is a very valiant man, my mother," said the young king.

"Yes, my son, and he rendered very great services to your father. Encourage and take care of him for the future."

"Monsieur le Capitaine," said the young king, as he alighted from his carriage, "Madame the Queen has charged me to invite you to dinner to-day, you and your friend the Baron du Valon."

This was a great honour for d'Artagnan and Porthos; therefore Porthos was transported with it. And yet during the whole of the repast the worthy gentleman seemed preoccupied.

"What the devil is the matter with you?" asked d'Artagnan as they descended the great staircase of the Palais Royal; "you looked all the dinner-time as if the cares of the whole world were upon your back."

"I was endeavouring to remember where I had seen the mendicant I must have killed."

"And you cannot succeed?"

"No."

"Well, seek on, my friend, seek on; and when you have found out you will tell me, will you not?"

"That I will," said Porthos.

On gaining their lodging, the two friends found a letter from Athos, appointing a meeting at the Grand Charlemagne the next morning. They both went to bed early, but neither of them slept well. People don't arrive thus at the summit of their desires without that attained summit having the influence to drive away sleep—at least, the first night.

The next day, at the hour appointed, both repaired to Athos' lodgings. They found the comte and Aramis in travelling costumes.

"Well, then," said Porthos, "we are all going, seemingly? I have been making ready this morning."

"Oh, faith, yes," said Aramis; "there is nothing worth staying for in Paris now the Fronde is over. Madame de Longueville has invited me to spend a few days with her in Normandy, and has charged me, while they are baptizing her son, to go and prepare lodgings at Rouen for her. I will acquit myself of that commission, and then, if nothing new turns up, I will return and bury myself in my convent of Noisy le Sec."

"And I," said Athos, "am returning to Bragelonne. You know, my dear d'Artagnan, I am nothing but a plain country gentleman. Raoul has no other fortune but my fortune, poor boy, and I must watch over it, since I am, in some sort, a steward for him."

"And what do you mean to do with Raoul?"

"I shall leave him to you, my friend. War is going on in Flanders; you shall take him with you. I am afraid that a residence at Blois would be dangerous for his young head. Take him with you, and teach him to be as brave and as loyal as yourself."

"And as for me," said d'Artagnan, "I shall no longer have you with me, Athos; but I shall have this dear fair-haired boy; and although he is but a child, as your soul completely revives in him I shall always fancy that you are with me, accompanying and supporting me."

The four friends embraced, with tears in their eyes.

Then they separated, without knowing whether they should ever meet again.

D'Artagnan returned to the Rue Tiquetonne with Porthos, who was still meditating, and constantly trying to recollect who the man was whom he had killed. On coming opposite the Hôtel de la Chevrette, they saw the baron's equipage ready and Mousqueton in the saddle.

"Come, d'Artagnan," said Porthos, "leave the sword, and live with me at Pierrefonds, at Bracieux, or at le Vallon; we will grow old together in talking of our comrades."

"No," said d'Artagnan. "*Peste!* they are just going to open the campaign, and I must be there. I hope to gain something."

"And what, pray, do you hope to become?"

"A marshal of France, *pardieu!*"

"Aha!" said Porthos, looking at d'Artagnan, whose Gasconnades he could never thoroughly understand.

"Come with me, Porthos," said d'Artagnan; "I will make you a duke."

"No," answered Porthos, "Mouston has no desire to fight—besides, they have made a triumphal entrance for me into my barony, which will kill my neighbours with envy."

"To that I can say nothing," returned d'Artagnan, who knew the vanity of the new baron. "Here, then, to our next merry meeting."

"*Adieu*, dear captain," said Porthos, "I shall always be happy to welcome you to my barony."

"True—when the campaign is over," replied the Gascon.

"The equipage of his honour is waiting," said Mousqueton.

The two friends, after a hearty pressure of the hand, thereupon separated. D'Artagnan was standing at the door, looking after Porthos with a mournful gaze, when the baron, after walking scarcely more than twenty paces, returned, stood still, struck his forehead with his finger, and exclaimed:

"I recollect!"

"What?" inquired d'Artagnan.

"Who the beggar that I killed was."

"Ah! indeed! and who was he?"

"'Twas that fellow, Bonancieux."

And Porthos, enchanted at having relieved his mind, rejoined Mousqueton, and they disappeared round a corner of the street. The Gascon stood for an instant, mute, pensive, and motionless; then, as he went in, he saw the fair Madeleine, his hostess, who, uneasy at d'Artagnan's newly acquired honours, stood humbly on the threshold.

"Madeleine," said d'Artagnan, "I am obliged, now that I am captain of the musketeers, to make a better figure in the world. Let me have the apartments on the first floor. But, since no one knows what may happen, always keep for me my chamber on the fifth floor."

[The continuation of this story appears under the title of *The Vicomte de Bragelonne*]

BIBLIOGRAPHY

POETRY AND DRAMATIC WORKS

1825   *Élégie sur la Mort du Général Foy.*
       La Chasse et l'Amour (in collaboration).
1826   *Canaris* (Dithyramb).
       La Noce et l'Enterrement (in collaboration).
1828   *Christine* (or *Stockholm, Fontainebleau et Rome*).
1829   *Henri III. et sa Cour.*
1831   *Antony.*
       Napoléon Bonaparte, ou Trente Ans de l'Histoire de France.
       Charles VII. chez ses Grands Vassaux.
       Richard Darlington.
1832   *Térésa.*
       Le Mari de la Veuve (in collaboration).
       La Tour de Nesle.
1833   *Angèle* (in collaboration).
1834   *Catharine Howard.*
1836   *Don Juan de Marana, ou La Chute d'un Ange.*
       Kean.
1837   *Piquillo* (Comic opera. In collaboration).
       Caligula.
1838   *Paul Jones.*
1839   *Mademoiselle de Belle-Isle.*
       L'Alchimiste.
       Bathilde (in collaboration).
1841   *Un Mariage sous Louis XV.* (in collaboration).
1842   *Lorenzino* (in collaboration).
       Halifax.
1843   *Les Demoiselles de Saint-Cyr* (in collaboration).
       Louise Bernard (in collaboration).
       Le Laird de Dumbicky (in collaboration).
1845   *Le Garde Forestier* (in collaboration).
1856   *L'Oreste.*
       Le Verrou de la Reine.
1857   *Le Meneur des Loups.*

   NOTE.   Dumas also dramatised many of his novels.

NOVELS AND MISCELLANEOUS PROSE

1826 *Nouvelles Contemporaines.*
1833 *Impressions de Voyage.*
1835 *Souvenirs d'Antony* (Tales).
1838 *La Salle d'Armes* (Tales).
      Le Capitaine Paul.
1839 *Acté, Monseigneur Gaston de Phébus.*
      Quinze Jours au Sinaï.
1840 *Aventures de John Davy.*
      Le Capitaine Pamphile.
      Maître Adam le Calabrais.
      Othon l'Archer.
      Une Année à Florence.
1841 *Praxide, Don Martin de Freytas, Pierre le Cruel.*
      Excursions sur les Bords du Rhin.
      Nouvelles Impressions de Voyages.
1842 *Le Speronare* (Travels).
      Aventures de Lyderic.
1843 *Georges. Ascanio. Le Chevalier d'Harmental.*
      Le Corricolo. La Villa Palmieri.
1844 *Gabriel Lambert. Château d'Eppstein. Cécile.*
      Sylvandire. Les Trois Mousquetaires. Amaury. Fernande.
1844–45 *Le Comte de Monte Cristo.*
1845 *Vingt Ans Après.*
      Les Frères Corses. Une Fille du Régent. La Reine Margot.
1845–46 *La Guerre des Femmes.*
1846 *Le Chevalier de Maison-Rouge.*
      La Dame de Monsoreau.
      Le Bâtard de Mauléon.
1846–48 *Mémoires d'un Médecin.*
1848 *Les Quarante-cinq.*
1848–50 *Dix Ans plus tard, ou Le Vicomte de Bragelonne.*
1848 *De Paris à Cadix.*
      Tanger, Alger et Tunis.
1849 *Les Milles et un Fantômes.*
1850 *La Tulipe Noire.*
1851 *La Femme au Collier de Velours.*
1852 *Olympe de Clèves.*
      Un Gil Blas en Californie.
      Isaac Taquedem.
1853–55 *La Comtesse de Charny.*
1853 *Ange Pitou, le Pasteur d'Ashbourn. El Satéador.*
      Conscience l'Innocent.

1854   *Cathérine Blum; Ingénue.*
1854-58   *Les Mohicans de Paris* (in collaboration).
1855-59   *Salvator* (in collaboration).
1855   *L'Arabie Heureuse.*
1857   *Les Compagnons de Jéhu.*
1859   *Les Louves de Machecoul.*
          La Caucase.
1860   *De Paris à Astrakan.*

OTHER WORKS

Autobiographical

1854   *Souvenirs de 1830-42.*
1852-54   *Mémoires.*
1860   *Causeries.*
1861   *Bric-a-brac.*
1868   *Histoires de mes Bêtes.*

Children's Tales

Histoire d'un Casse-Noisette.
La Bouillie de la Comtesse Berthe.
Le Père Gigogne.

Also: Memoirs of Garibaldi. Reminiscences of various writers, historical writings, etc.

Théâtre.   1834-36   6 volumes.
               1863-74   3 volumes.

Dumas' Complete works were published by Michel Lévy Frères from 1860-84, 277 volumes in all.

BOOKS ABOUT DUMAS

Life by P. Fitzgerald   1873
Life by Blaize de Bury   1883
Life by Glinel   1885
Life by Parigot   1901
Life by H. A. Spurr   1902
Alexandre Dumas Père: his Life and Works by A. F. Davidson. (With Bibliography.)   1902.
Life by Lecomte.   1903.